GERALD A. BROWNE was raised in Litchfield
County, Connecticut. He attended the University of
New Mexico and Columbia University, where he
won several literary awards. His first novel, *It's All
Zoo*, was written while he was living in Paris and
working as a fashion photographer. His bestselling
novels, several of which have been made into
movies, include *11 Harrowhouse*, *Green Ice*, *19
Purchase Street*, *Stone 588*, and *Hot Siberian*. He
lives with his wife in Arizona.

ALSO BY GERALD A. BROWNE

Hot Siberian

*Stone 588**

*19 Purchase Street**

Green Ice

Slide

Hazard

*11 Harrowhouse**

The Arousers

The Ravishers

It's All Zoo

*18mm Blues**

*Published by
WARNER BOOKS

WEST 47th

GERALD A. BROWNE

Warner Books, Inc.
1271 Avenue of the Americas
New York, NY 10020

Visit our Web site at
http://pathfinder.com/twep

WARNER BOOKS

A Time Warner Company

This book is a work of fiction. Certain real locations, products, and public figures are mentioned, but all other characters and the events and dialogue described in the book are totally imaginary.

WARNER BOOKS EDITION

Cover design by Diane Luger
Cover photo of marble by Herman Estevez
Cover illustration of plaque by David Loew

Warner Books, Inc.
1271 Avenue of the Americas
New York, NY 10020

Visit our Web site at
http://pathfinder.com/twep

W A Time Warner Company

Printed in the United States of America

Originally published in hardcover by Warner Books.
First Paperback Printing: April, 1997

10 9 8 7 6 5 4 3 2 1

*For those who have 20/20
but are, unfortunately, blind*

Acknowledgments

The author wishes to express his gratitude to those who in one way or another helped generate this story. Such as Dr. Stephen M. Cohen, Dr. Jay Friedman, Dr. Robert Hambrick, Pam Bernstein, Joanna Tomkins, R. J. and Jill Wagner, Patricia and Robert Jesse Lovejoy, David the Wit and Jason the Clip, Robin Cumming, Norman Weisberg, Mark and Coleen McDowell and my dear cousin Joy Burkett.
Also, a special thanks to the swifts, fences, have-arounds and others of the underside who allowed me to know *the street* as it truly is.

CHAPTER 1

To look at him no straight person would think Charlie Gusano was anything more than a doorman.

He had the part down pat: the automatic off-and-on smile, the eagerness to serve, the anticipation and gratitude for tips. The whole convincing package.

Gusano, or Charlie Eyes as he was called by certain guys around who really knew him, had been at the game for twelve years. For seven he'd worked the curb of an upscale restaurant on 53rd Street. The place folded because the people who really owned it, those in the back, as they say, took too much out of it. Otherwise, Charlie would have still been there. For his purpose it was a prime spot.

Since then Charlie hadn't worked anywhere steady. That was his choice. Usually he'd do only a few nights here or there. Sometimes he didn't mind filling in for a couple of weeks or even a month. It depended on the place. It had to be upscale, a place that catered to the well-offs.

Apparently, Charlie was just being practical. People who had plenty could, without second thought or later discomfort, slip a ten or twenty into a palm merely for having a door opened or an umbrella held overhead.

But that wasn't it.

Charlie Eyes.

The sobriquet was appropriate and well-earned. At any reasonable distance Charlie had the ability to tell the precious from the fake. It was like he had natural, built-in loupes. For instance, say a well-to-do finger provided him with a glimpse of a ten-carat diamond ring. He didn't require a closer or even another look to know it was authentic. On the other hand, when even the finest grade, perfectly faceted, cubic-zirconium ten-carater flashed at him he saw it right off as the make-believe it was.

He wasn't infallible, of course, but right more often than not. About eight out of every ten times, on average, which was considered remarkable and appreciated by all concerned.

On that particular July Saturday night, Charlie, properly uniformed, capped and gloved, was tending to the comings and goings at the entrance of a way-overpriced restaurant on East 50th. It was his third consecutive night there. He'd worked the place in the past and it had never failed him. It wouldn't now. Already he had two sure things memorized. As good a night as he was having, in that regard, it didn't, however, make up for the rain.

At six, when he'd come in, there'd been a thunderstorm in progress and, since then, two more heavy downpours. A lot of rumbling and crackling above the city. During the letups the raindrops beaded like gems on the roofs and hoods of cars. The gutters were brooks.

Charlie's shoes were ruined. They were a pair of his newest best. Lightweight, thin-soled, Italian made. Three-hundred-dollar shoes. He'd bought four pair at the swag price of fifty a pair, but these were the only blacks. They'd never be the same.

Fucking weather, Charlie complained in the back of his throat. He flexed his toes and felt the squish of his socks. By two when he got off, his feet would be drowned-looking, shriveled. He'd hate them.

He glanced up at the space between the high-rise office buildings. The purgatorial glow of Manhattan. More clouds were roiling, ganging up, getting ready to let go. The city was washed but it didn't smell fresh. It smelled steamy, Charlie thought, like the Upper West Side cleaners where he usually waited while his suits and uniforms were being pressed.

His legs were hurting, the calves, the left one more. An ache and every once in a while a sharp spasm. They'd gone varicose from too much standing over the years. The doorman's ailment, the doctor called it. His advice was to move around more, and that was what Charlie was doing, pacing six or seven steps back and forth beneath the restaurant's canopy.

When the Lincoln arrived. A that year's white Lincoln stretched to the limit. It pulled up to the curb with insolent precision. At once the driver was out, scurrying around. He got to the handle of the rear door a reach before Charlie.

Charlie made the driver. A bully Hispanic in a gray, hard-finished suit that was tight on him. The piece underneath behind his right hip was obvious. It had become the thing for well-offs to hire ex-cons, formidable-looking guys such as this, to drive and be around. The meaner they looked the better, and, having done major time in some hard joint like Dannemora being the best kind of reference, it did wonders to ease paranoia.

The limo door was open.

Charlie was right there with the umbrella so the passengers wouldn't have to suffer a drop. He looked in and saw they were two. A man and a woman. The man was speaking on the car's cellular phone. A serious, important man having a serious, important conversation. He had dark, tight hair and a dark, neatly clipped mustache and beard. Arabic looking. The woman was seated on the far side, most of her out of Charlie's view.

Finally the man got out. He was slender, a head taller than Charlie. He proceeded across the wide sidewalk and on into the restaurant, leaving the woman to follow along.

She emerged from the limo with her head lowered, watching where she stepped. As she raised her head, her earrings came into sight. Diamonds, pear shapes and rounds of fine quality, arranged around oval-cut rubies. To the eyes of Charlie Eyes the rubies were fine Burma quality and would scale around four carats each. The woman straightened up. Charlie saw nine more such rubies and the numerous diamonds of her necklace.

Important jewelry, Charlie knew. No doubt among her best, and that was just it. This attractive Arab woman contending with her late forties with as much artifice as plenty of money allowed would have more goods just as good where these came from.

During his ten o'clock break Charlie went to the pay phone on the corner of Park. He dialed Ralph Lentini's New Rochelle number.

Ralph picked up on the second ring. Instead of a hello from him a grunt like some kind of disturbed animal. No goombah talk. As soon as Ralph heard it was Charlie Eyes, he asked: "What you got?"

"Three."

"Okay, let's have them."

"You still owe me for the last two."

"Fuck I do."

"Last week I gave you two."

"When last week?"

"Thursday I think it was."

"I was in Miami last Thursday."

"Then it was Wednesday."

"That could be," Ralph admitted, "but what I know for certain is the last two were shit. My crew came up empty."

"I heard different," Charlie bluffed.

"Anyway," Ralph bluffed back, "I paid you already."

"Like shit."

"I marked you paid. I'm looking at it right now, paid."

"You haven't been around all week, Ralphie. When you coming around?"

Ralph let the question hang.

Charlie was used to Ralph's routine. It was nearly the same every time. "Look, Ralphie, I'm standing out here in the fucking rain."

"So give me the three."

"Then you'll owe me for five."

A reluctant yeah from Ralph.

"Say it to me."

"Five."

"When will you be around?"

"Sometime during the week."

That was too vague to suit Charlie, however he told himself Ralph would eventually make good. Besides, at the moment Charlie didn't have anyone better to give his information to. Had he still been on good terms with Sal Crosetti he would have used him to make Ralph move. Okay, Ralphie, he would have said, I'm sure Sal will show me more respect. However, it was that sort of playing one against the other that had soured his arrangement with Sal.

From memory Charlie recited to Ralph the license plate numbers and letters of the three, including that of the white stretch, which happened to be a New Jersey. He ran them together and went too fast for Ralph and had to repeat them.

"Which would you say could be the bigger score?" Ralph asked.

"In my opinion?"

"No, in your ass." Ralph figured when he asked something it was asked.

"The Jersey," Charlie told him.

"What color is the Jersey?"

"Heavy red."

"No white?"

"A lot of white," Charlie replied. He could practically hear the churning of Ralph's greed.

"Sure they're not fugazis?" Fakes.

"Don't insult me."

No apology from Ralph, nor any thanks. This was business and he was laying out. He grunted goodbye and hung up.

Ralph had jotted down the information Charlie sold him on one of the telephone notepads he'd brought home from the Miami Hilton. He'd only stayed there two nights but that was more than enough time for him to load up on soap, shampoo, lotion, stationery, ballpoints and even some needle and thread mending kits. Also a couple of towels of better quality than he'd ever buy.

Ralph never stayed at a hotel that he didn't take such advantage. Whenever he came upon a maid's supply cart in a hallway he helped himself. Once at the Excelsior in Rome he'd gotten away with a solid brass hand shower, bracket and all.

As one of the more established and prospering fences in the metropolitan area, Ralph should have been above such pettiness. However it was in him, like a phobia. Just about any liftable or drivable thing that came before his eyes was automatically rated by him according to how easy it would be to steal.

What's more Ralph was cheap. Having to pay caused him psychological anguish, a sort of mental heartburn. Only rarely did he pay full civilian price for something and then only after he'd called around to find out if someone might be offering it at swag.

At the moment Ralph was seated at his kitchen table wearing nothing, not even his watch. The vinyl-covered seat of the kitchen chair was sticky to the cheeks of his bare ass. Charlie Eyes was also sticking him, Ralph thought, as he gave venal attention to the three plate numbers he'd just bought for two hundred each. Not long ago, Charlie's price per number had been a hundred. For doing nothing two hundred was taking advantage. Only way to deal with a guy who took advantage like that was to fuck him over. Next week when he straightened out with Charlie he'd give him only a hundred each and let him beef.

Ralph reached across the kitchen table and turned off the eight-inch Sony color television, reducing the ninth inning of a close Yankee at Cleveland game to a white dot. He hadn't been watching it anyway, even before Charlie's call. Rather, he'd been contemplating the open refrigerator across the way. It was something he often did. Sat there deliberating that vertical rectangle and its illuminated contents as though it was a rendered still-life.

Whenever his ex-wife, Carmella, had found him at it, she'd call him a *spuce* (crazy) and slam the refrigerator door shut.

He'd just grin his most intolerant grin, say fuck with a long f and claim he was only trying to decide what not to eat.

Ralph was constantly unfaithful to his diet as well as to Carmella. She was gone but that thirty pounds too many were still with him.

He got a stub of a pepperoni stick from the meat bin, closed the refrigerator and went up the back stairs.

Ralph's house was a nine-room, two-and-a-half-story Tudor situated in a residential area off upper North Avenue. Like most of the homes around there the twenties and thirties had been its better days. Ralph had lived in it nine years. During that time the side lawns had been mowed five times and the hedges trimmed twice. Upkeep, according to Ralph, was declogging a toilet with a plunger and throwing de-icer granules on the driveway a few times each winter.

It wasn't a house one could move about freely in, cluttered as it was with so much swag. A nine years' accumulation of things Ralph's crew of swifts had come in with. Jewelry was always their objective; however when a home didn't yield any jewelry, rather than waste the risk, they stole something. More often than not, even when they did score jewelry on their way out they'd throw something else into a pillowcase, some object they'd spotted and thought might possibly be of value

"Why you bringing me this shit," Ralph would complain. "You go out for goods, you come back with shit."

He would indulge them, peel off an additional fifty or two for the lamp or vase or little bronze statue that he had neither use nor room for. It didn't matter that among these *extras*, as he called them, shoved beneath a sofa along with some swag scuba gear and a couple of swag VCRs, were two pair of Empire ormolu four-light *bras de lumière* worth at least twenty thousand. Or that the glass figurine of a girl gathering dust along with a crowd of bric-a-brac on the top surface of a stack of swag television sets was signed by Argy-Rousseau and worth twenty-five thousand. Or that those two blue vases in the legion of vases and lamps on the steps of the stairway were exceptional blue ground Meissen circa 1740 worth thirty thousand each.

It didn't matter because such things were beyond Ralph's appreciation and knowledge. All he knew and cared about was they weren't jewelry. Even if he had known that the Chinese-looking thing lost and lonely in a corner of the upstairs hallway was a gilt-bronze figure of an extremely rare eleven-headed Kuan-Yin, where would he sell it?

For some reason the swifts stole a lot of clocks. They were all around the house, upstairs and down. About fifty of them, at least fifty. On the fireplace mantel in Ralph's bedroom were six. An English brass carriage clock that had run out of time and four Seth Thomases with misleading antique faces. The other was truly old. It was mounted in Sevres porcelain and Louis XV ormolu. Ralph had seen a clock exactly like it, or perhaps this very clock, in a 1990 Sotheby auction sales catalogue. Its estimated auction price was twenty-five thousand.

No one Ralph could think of, not even one of his wealthy swag-addicted private clients, would give him twenty-five for it. Or even five.

"Shit. Ralph, it's only a clock."

"Worth twenty-five large. Look." He'd show the auction catalogue.

"Probably isn't even running."

"It's been running for me. Besides I can have it fixed."

"Pass."

And he couldn't risk taking it to Sotheby's or Christie's hoping to have it auctioned. Their experts would most likely recognize it right off and never believe one of his highly original or ordinary lies.

So, there it sat in all its inconvertible spite, taunting him. Fucking clock, Ralph often said aloud at it. Someday it would get him so pissed he'd take it out somewhere and throw it in some dumpster.

Now he got dressed. No underwear. Sixty percent polyester slacks, the day-before-yesterday's shirt, Reeboks without socks and his Rolex Presidential. After patting his sparse hair into place he put to pocket a thousand in hundreds along with the slip of notepaper bearing the three plate numbers he'd gotten from Charlie.

Went out.

An unimpressive gray guy in a four-year-old Pontiac, that was Ralph.

He took North Avenue to where it offered exit 18 of the Hutchinson River Parkway. Two miles north on the Hutch he caught sight of the New York State Police patrol car. It was parked on the wide, inclined grassy shoulder with its lights off.

Ralph pulled off and stopped about twenty feet in front of the patrol car. He took a good look at it. The rain on its windshield prevented him from making out who was in it, whether or not it was Stempke. If it wasn't Stempke he'd simply ask some directions.

The rack on the patrol car came on, began rotating and strobing. Ralph walked back towards it. The grass of the shoulder had been recently mowed. Its slant was slippery beneath Ralph's Reeboks. He nearly went to a knee. The fresh-cut grass was fragrant in the damp, night air. Ralph took no notice of it. He had no side that appreciated such things.

The wet window of the patrol car descended into the door to reveal Officer Stempke. He was close to forty, had a round face with a nearly lipless slash of mouth and not enough space between his eyes. He held Ralph with his look for a long moment before doing a slight smile. "What say?" he greeted.

"I got three," Ralph told him. He read them off so Stempke could jot them down. Ralph thought Stempke would read them back to check that he had them right, but he didn't, he went right at entering them in the patrol car's computer.

Ralph turned away. He wasn't interested in how it was being done, just wanted it done. Headlights of passing cars caught him and let him go. Tires made ripping sounds on the parkway's wet surface. Ralph started thinking about elsewhere. The midtown bust-out bar he spent a lot of his late-night time at. Not tonight. Tonight was business. Tonight would have a big score in it.

He pictured the swag that would be piled up on his kitchen table. Imagined his first sight of it. Spectacular goods. The guys on West 47 would beg just to get a look. It would take him the better part of a morning to count the thousands they would pay. (He didn't trust their counting machines. Besides, those machines took some of the pleasure out of it.)

Stempke was done. "Got a pen?" he asked.

"No."

"You never have a pen. Get yourself some pens." Stempke handed his pen to Ralph. An ordinary sixty-cent ballpoint. He was wearing gloves, was always careful that his touch never shared anything with Ralph's. Except for the money. "Keep it," he told Ralph and in practically the same breath rapidly read aloud from his notes the names and addresses of the registered owners he'd gotten from accessing the Department of Motor Vehicles information terminal.

Ralph got only most of them. He asked Stempke to repeat them so he could fill in, and not until he was sure he had them right did he go into his pocket for Stempke's juice. He counted off six hundreds. "By now I ought to be eligible for a complimentary," Ralph remarked lightheartedly but with a degree of serious suggestion.

"Against my principles," Stempke told him.

Ralph drove home. He sat in his usual kitchen chair and phoned the Brooklyn number. He knew it so well that his finger almost performed it involuntarily.

A female voice answered, not one he recognized.

"Who's this?" he asked.

"Who's this wants to know who's this?"

She didn't sound black, Ralph thought. He disliked the idea of the swifts in his crew fucking around with white women. Not even street whites or pros. He didn't like the way he'd overheard the swifts talking about doing white women. He'd never said anything to them about it but that was how he felt.

"Floyd there?" he asked.

"Maybe."

"Put Floyd on."

"You haven't told me who's this."

"Fuck you, put Floyd on."

Next thing Ralph heard was dial tone. He redialed. This time Floyd picked up.

"Who's the cunt?" Ralph asked, irked.

"Nobody," Floyd told him.

"She hung up on me."

"Man, what do you give a shit?"

"You let a nobody cunt answer your phone on a Saturday night."

"She was just closest to it."

"Dumb thing," Ralph grumbled. He took a couple of deep, calming breaths. "Who you got there?"

"Tracy and me and her."

"Where's Ronnie?"

"He cut out."

"When'll he be back?"

"I don't know, man. From the way the brother went he's gone."

"It's Saturday night. His head must be up his ass. Did he take the car?"

"We don't want to work tonight," Floyd said, as though that was all he had to say.

"Oh?" It wasn't an unusual problem. "What you got to do that's more important?" Ralph asked patiently.

"Nothing. Just hang out."

Ralph handled it by going right through it. "Who can you get to drive?" The absent Ronnie was usually the driver.

Floyd didn't reply.

Ralph let the silence continue. It was now a matter of whichever spoke the next word. Finally, Floyd said: "I suppose I could get Dexter. He may be around."

"I know Dexter?"

"He worked a couple of times."

"When was that?"

"Two years ago."

"I don't remember any Dexter. What's he been doing since?"

"Time."

"Who else can you get?"

Floyd took a moment. "Corky maybe. He'll want a guarantee."

"How much?"

"Five."

"Corky's a fucking cowboy. Anyway, last time he worked he held out."

"What did he hold out?"

"Two nice blues, a four carat and a six. The next afternoon the cocksucker was moving around Forty-seventh with them. He ended up taking shit."

"How you know that?"

"I know Forty-seventh, Forty-seventh knows me." Something Ralph said to influence certain situations. He enjoyed the cryptic quality of it. He believed the pause in their conversation was those words sinking in.

"We don't want to work tonight," Floyd said.

Back to that. Ralph told him: "Just don't work Corky."

"Not unless I have to, okay?"

"Yeah."

"If I have to you'll come up with his guarantee?"

"Fuck no."

"I ain't taking it out of my end."

"Floyd, your end will be so big you won't even feel it."

CHAPTER 2

Later that same night the white stretch Lincoln was headed for home on Interstate 78. Doing an easy eighty-five and sometimes ninety. The driver kept to the left lane, bullied any car that got in the way by coming up too close behind and blinking the brights.

Sherman, which was what the people in the back had chosen to call him, enjoyed driving. It was one of the things he'd missed when he was inside. He'd done seven of a five to ten and it wasn't until he was out and behind a steering wheel that he realized what a longing he'd had for it. Now, after two years of doing plenty of it, he still didn't feel he'd gotten even.

These people in the back. He glanced in the rearview mirror. As usual the glass partition was up. The man always insisted that it be up. As though that permitted him to be breathing a better kind of air. Also, as usual, the man was way over on the right, the woman way over on the left. A lot of seat between them and no talk. Sherman wondered why they hadn't wanted to call him by his real name. What was wrong with Donnell? It sounded as good as Sherman. It couldn't have been that they knew when he'd been born in San Juan his mother had intended that his birth certificate read Donald but she hadn't known how to spell it.

These people knew practically nothing about him. During long waits at the airport or anywhere, with one or the other waiting with him, it seemed there should have been some personal exchange. But nothing, not even once. To pass that kind of time he usually read some magazine, while they, if they looked his way at all, were satisfied with the back of his size twenty-two neck.

Didn't matter. The same disinterest right back at them. About all he knew about them was what he'd surmised from overhearing. They had money, they were Iranian, they'd been in this country since the early eighties. Their last name was Kalali. Mr. Abbas and Mrs. Roudabeth. Kal and Rhoda to some.

They paid him seven-fifty a week off the books. No benefits, no medical coverage or Social Security credit or anything like that. It was made clear that he wasn't to expect any meals; however, the housekeeper slipped him a sandwich now and then.

For the seven-fifty he was to drive wherever they wanted whenever they wanted. And to get between them and any trouble. Up to now, he'd had to use only his heft a couple of times to discourage overly aggressive panhandlers.

Sherman had given thought to what he might do if someone made a serious move on them, tried to kidnap or hold them up. There was no question in his mind about how he'd react. Not for a second would he put himself on the line.

Not for these assholes.

The white stretch passed a sign that said Millburn. It told Sherman he had eighteen miles to go to his third-hand Honda Civic and the beginning of his day off. He had a place reserved on one of the fishing boats out of Elizabeth Port, scheduled to leave the pier at five-thirty. By the time he got to his apartment in Irvington and got his gear together it would be three. He'd stay up.

"Sherman."

Mr. Kalali on the intercom.

What you want dickhead? Sherman thought. What came out was "Yes, sir?"

"Lower the air conditioning. Mrs. Kalali is cold."

Actually Mrs. Kalali hadn't said a word since the restaurant. It was Mr. Kalali who'd been uncomfortable with the temperature. To admit that, he believed, would be to disclose a weakness in his endurance. No matter how minor and commonplace such admissions might be, they were like demerits. They added up to the man.

Mrs. Kalali did a derisive little scoff. She knew all too well how his male mind worked. She turned to the side window so none of him would be in her sight.

Still, he was in her mind, steadfast there like some tenacious decal that would require scraping off.

Him, Abbas, him and his insolent complacence. Now slouched and stretched out, his bony rump on the edge of the seat, ankles and arms crossed. Tie unknotted, shirt unbuttoned three down exposing a veritable tuft of black chest hair. To think she'd once admired his hair, each crop of it. His beard especially, the virility it had represented.

Could she ever have been so emotionally bound to him? That didn't say much for her, she thought, not unless he'd changed greatly for the worse and she didn't believe he had.

He had always been the man over there beyond reach. His breaths were bellowing this limited space, reeking it. Because of the courses of crab and lamb and garlic and chocolate and the espresso, wine and brandy he'd consumed. As well as the tuberose-based eau de toilette with which he'd doused himself, splashed his armpits. He kept a flacon of it in a compartment of the limousine.

To think.

To think of the years she'd followed along behind his dinner conversations, an accomplice to his opinions and desires. It was as though all that while she'd been in a spell, cast by his patriarchal presence. She'd been lucky to get a feeling in edgewise.

He'd always taken her passion for granted, had never con-

sidered it part of his responsibility. He assumed she was so li-
bidinal that it took very little for her to peak and finish. Was
that not so with all women? Didn't they need to be kept in
check from their erotic nature? If he ever gave thought to the
reason she often got up directly afterwards and went into her
private dressing room, ever suspected it was for the purpose
of some self-administered frictions, he attributed it to her female greediness for another orgasm.

He'd been a spigot and she nothing more than his receptacle. For all those years. More emphatically so for the last
three, although he hadn't demanded sex from her as frequently. Once a month on average. That was about the length
of time it took for his need to humiliate and fester. When he
skipped a month she presumed he'd taken it out on another
woman.

He would have her sit on the floor in a corner, trapped-like,
or on the toilet commode. No need for her to undress. He
would stand fully clothed before her and require that she take
his cock out, grope in eagerly and find it as though compulsed. He'd have her include the softness of it with her
mouth and remain perfectly still while it hardened. Then,
grasping her hair with both hands, he would hold her head in
place. Her head an object, a receptacle, that he'd jam himself
into thrust after thrust.

She was tempted to bite into it, through it. Each time she
vowed she would next time. He must have sensed that, for he
hadn't demanded it of her for the past several months.

Last Christmas season was when Roudabeth's self-worth
stopped draining. She remembered the exact day, in fact, the
very instant when it started being replenished.

She was gift-shopping in the city, had gone into Saks to buy
Kal some evening socks. The young male clerk who waited
on her showed her the best, black silk. He inserted his hand
into one of a pair to have her see the fine weave. To that point
he'd been nothing more than a helpful, informing voice. Her
attention went from the sock with his nice hand in it up to his

face, and for a long moment, a moment communicative because of its length, she remained eyes to eyes with him.

Young, fair-haired man who had lived at least two decades less than she. Clean-shaven young man with a straight, narrow nose and healthy, even teeth within what appeared to be a gentle mouth. Not a pretty young man but nearly. What must he think of her staring? she thought.

She found out later when he got off work for an hour.

His name was Roger Addison.

Next he told her, or perhaps not next but what had registered with early indelible impact, was how stunning he thought she was. How lovely, how aristocratic were her hands. How mellifluent her voice. That was the very word he used, mellifluent.

She believed him. She was empty, famished for such beliefs. She adored his fairness, his hair and complexion such a contrast to that which she'd been accustomed. His name sounded well-off, but he wasn't. He'd completed four semesters at Columbia, would go back when he'd saved up.

They usually met at his apartment, an everything room that fronted on Second Avenue above a fruit and vegetable market. Every so often she'd treat their lovemaking to an afternoon in a high room of the Plaza: vintage wine and delicious nibbles.

Now in the limousine being transported through the damp New Jersey night, she recalled the most recent afternoon she'd spent with Roger, certain joys of it: him kissing her thighs so lightly, his blue-green eyes glancing up to verify her pleasure.

On the opposite side of the limousine husband Kal stirred, as though disturbed by her thoughts. He now had his tasseled loafers off. He re-crossed his ankles. Eyes closed to remain within his self, he lowered his chin to his chest and rotated his head tensely to cause a little unctuous, realigning snap.

He had one of his many strings of prayer beads in hand, these of sapphire. Roudabeth watched his fingers work the beads and wondered if he was supplicating or hoping to pay off delinquent dues. He'd never catch up, she thought, and re-

turned her attention to outside. They had reached and taken
the Martinsville turn-off. Then came Liberty Corner and Far
Hills and the familiar winding way where large homes self-
consciously hid behind high walls or tall impenetrable
hedges.

A swing to the right.

A short distance to the steel gate.

The gate responded obediently, slid aside so the stretch
could continue up the paved drive. The appropriate door of
the four-car garage was equally obedient, completed its opening by the time the limousine got to it. Sherman drove in and
cut the engine.

Mrs. Kalali was quickly out and bound for the house via the
connecting breezeway.

Mr. Kalali waited for Sherman to open the limousine door
for him. He stepped out with his shoes in hand. For the last
mile or so he'd tried to put them on but his feet were swollen.

He had Sherman hold the shoes while he took out his billfold. It wasn't fat because it contained only brand-new hundreds. The bills stuck together. Mr. Kalali wet his thumb and
first finger and counted twice.

Eight of the hundreds onto the flat of Sherman's palm. Mr.
Kalali expected fifty change. Sherman didn't have it. Mr.
Kalali reclaimed one of his virgin hundreds and said he'd owe
Sherman the fifty until next payday.

Sherman wanted to say no way fucker. Instead he nodded
and ducked beneath the grinding descent of the garage door,
hurried to his car and was gone.

Mrs. Kalali, meanwhile, had entered the house and turned
off the security system. She found a note from the live-in
housekeeper on the kitchen counter. A lie about a family
emergency and a promise to return Monday morning.

By then, Mr. Kalali, carrying his shoes with his billfold in
one, was in the breezeway headed for the kitchen door that
had been left open for him.

Floyd timed his move perfectly, stepped out of the darkness

to be directly behind Mr. Kalali. Did so with such stealth that Mr. Kalali wasn't aware until he felt the pistol jab his spine.

Mr. Kalali started, bowed his back and turned enough to see Floyd's black face.

"Keep going," Floyd told him.

Mr. Kalali felt legless. It seemed he levitated into the kitchen.

Mrs. Kalali saw Floyd and his weapon and realized what was occurring. She stiffened. Her breath caught, and when she released it, an apprehensive female sound came from her. As though it was called for. She studied Floyd for a moment, then decided it would be best that she look away.

The others came in.

Tracy and the white girl.

They were also armed. The white girl had a Mach 10 machine pistol. It looked too heavy for her.

Floyd hadn't been able to reach out for Corky or anyone else who'd ever worked, and rather than phone Ralph to say it wasn't going to come off because they were shorthanded, it struck him that maybe the girl could drive, just drive. She was all for it at first, but when Floyd explained the work to her, she didn't want to. Not just drive. She wouldn't go along at all unless she could play a more important part.

The girl, whose most recent one name was Peaches, went back and forth about that with Floyd, but, finally, Floyd gave in and it was settled that the driving would be done by Dexter, who didn't care one way or the other. It was also agreed that having Peaches along was something they'd keep from Ralph.

On the drive they'd played a couple of Toni Braxtons, smoked some boo and Peaches had gotten some laughs out of them with stories about four years ago when she was a titless fourteen in Phoenix passing for a flat-chested twenty. Between stories she sucked on Floyd's second finger after alternately guiding it into a pint bottle of Southern Comfort and herself.

They'd had no problem finding the Far Hills area or the

Kalali house or which wall belonged to the rear of it. Dexter had left them off and would return to the spot frequently to see if they were there to be picked up.

The wall had been easy, not very high and no barbed wire, spikes or anything, and the rear grounds couldn't have been more accommodating: unlighted, wooded, overgrown with brush and landscaped with mature shrubs from the wall to two-thirds of the way to the house.

Now they were in the kitchen, the thieves and the Kalalis, weapons and edginess. Mr. Kalali was still carrying his shoes. Peaches noticed the wallet protruding from the one. She plucked the wallet out and was delighted with the nice new hundreds it contained. About twenty. She had on lightweight latex rubber gloves, as did Floyd and Tracy. There'd be no fingerprints.

"Who's here in the house?" Floyd asked.

Mrs. Kalali volunteered a bit eagerly that there wasn't anyone else. Floyd made sure, went from room to room. Throughout, the interior was white and sheer, minimally furnished. There was a lot of mirror, chrome and glass. All the floors were bird's-eye maple, fine-sanded slick and bleached pale. There were ten rooms in all, generous spaces with high ceilings. Off a wide entry hall was the living room and opposite that the library. One entire long wall there was bookcases with a sliding chrome ladder to help reach the volumes on the higher shelves. Every book was jacketed in identical white paper, its title and author noted in small lettering at the base of its spine.

The library also served as a music room. A piano, a Steinway baby grand, stood isolated in the deepest corner. Its black, curved form was a dominant contradiction.

Floyd didn't like the house. It lacked comfort and there wasn't a sign of joy anywhere. He thought if this was where he had to live he'd hang out elsewhere, hardly ever come home. Shit, he'd been in cozier bus stations.

He assembled everyone in the library.

Mr. Kalali plopped down onto the white leather couch.

Floyd told him to get up.

"Why?"

"I want you standing."

Mr. Kalali's legs still weren't with him. "I'd prefer to sit," he defied. But there were the guns. He felt his torso sort of float up off the couch.

Mrs. Kalali noticed how blanched her husband appeared. Anger normally caused his complexion to flush, so this, no doubt, was fear. She enjoyed telling him in Farsi to have courage.

"No talking in Hebrew!" Floyd snapped. It sounded like Hebrew to him, had that sometimes guttural, sometimes phlegmy, back-of-the-throat quality to it.

Mrs. Kalali apologized.

Floyd had to merely indicate her ruby and diamond necklace. She turned to allow him to get at its intricate clasp. He had trouble with it. She undid it for him.

Floyd examined the necklace briefly. His expression didn't change, no appreciation or approval. The necklace disappeared into one of the zippered pockets of his black, parachute fabric windbreaker. Mrs. Kalali, without being told, also removed her earrings.

Peaches had her eye on those. She stepped between Floyd and Mrs. Kalali, with her hand out and her fingers beckoning *give*.

Mrs. Kalali looked to Floyd.

He didn't object. He was amused by what an aggressive swift this little white girl was turning out to be. Like she'd been at it for years.

Mrs. Kalali gave the earrings to Peaches, who went with them to a nearby mirrored panel. Peaches held the Mach 10 pistol clamped between her thighs while she put the earrings on. She turned her head left and right, shook her head vigorously causing the earrings to articulate and throw red and white scintillations.

Floyd expected Peaches would remove the earrings and hand them over to him. Surely she would know they belonged in his pocket. However, Peaches kept them on, as though they were now hers. Floyd decided for the time being he wouldn't say anything about it.

"Now," Floyd said to the Kalalis, "your other jewelry?"

Mrs. Kalali looked away.

"This ain't all."

Nothing from Mr. Kalali.

"The stuff you got hidden someplace."

"We have a safety deposit box at the bank," Mr. Kalali said.

Floyd did a dubious face, looked away impatiently.

"You think we'd be foolish enough to keep such valuables here?"

"Fuck yes."

"You might as well take what you have and leave."

"We're the best at going through houses and finding what's supposed to be in some fucking bank." Floyd flicked his head in the direction of Tracy, who was standing off to the side holding a shotgun at the ready. "Right, brother?"

Tracy nodded and did a sneer.

"If I were you . . ." Floyd told Mr. Kalali, "I'd take a good look at that badass nigger." Tracy intensified his badass nigger attitude.

"Mess with him he'll smoke you. He don't put up with any white shit."

Mr. Kalali assessed Tracy: a young thick-built black with oily tendrils of hair hanging down and a fuzzy patch like a collection of black lint between his chin and prominent lower lip. He did, indeed, appear menacing but possibly that was only a purposeful demeanor he'd developed, something he'd practiced and perfected in front of a mirror.

This other black, the one apparently in charge, anyway, doing all the talking, might be even more of a pretender, Mr. Kalali thought. A cynical, dangerous, experienced black thief was the impression he was striving to make, and, admitted, he was convincing. However, it might very well be the only reality was the color of his skin. As for the girl, she was out of place. A juvenile, a skinny little show-off acting tough. That she was there validated his observations regarding the two others, Mr. Kalali thought.

He complimented himself for such insight. It had, he believed, always been one of his outstanding abilities.

The compliment acted like a restorative to his legs. He drew himself up, elevated his chin and told Floyd unequivocally: "You'll get nothing more from us."

Floyd blinked thoughtfully. "That's a motherfucking shame," he said with sardonic sympathy. He went to a niche that was built into the side wall. It had glass shelves and was lighted. Each shelf held artifacts of antique pottery and glass, evidently a collection.

He took up a small, lopsided, creamy-colored goblet. He nonchalantly tossed it into the air. It smashed to pieces on the hard floor.

Mr. Kalali grimaced.

Floyd had no idea that the goblet was a precious Persian piece that had miraculously survived six thousand years without a chip.

He enjoyed Mr. Kalali's reaction, so, next, he destroyed a pale blue faceted glass bowl that had been created in the holy city of Qom in the first century.

Mr. Kalali placed his hands over his eyes. If he'd had another pair they would have covered his ears.

Mrs. Kalali seemed somewhat amused.

Floyd swept shelves bare. He hurled tiny, two-thousand-year-old, museum-quality Sasanian bottles and urns at the far wall. Mr. Kalali had to duck.

He pleaded with Floyd to stop.

"Give it up."

Mr. Kalali still refused.

"Okay, let me tell you how this is going down. Two ways it can go. One, you give up where you got jewelry, we take it and go. Nobody gets hurt. The other way we have to look for it. It'll take time and trouble but, sure as shit, we'll find what you say ain't there. For putting us through the time and trouble . . . we kill you."

Mr. Kalali looked to his wife. He shook his head ever so slightly and hoped that she understood the message in his eyes, instructing her not to reveal anything. He wasn't going to melt down, especially not in front of her. For some reason she didn't appear to be the least bit frightened.

"What's it going to be?" Floyd asked.

"It's as I told you . . ."

"In the bank."

"In the bank."

"It's here in the house," Mrs. Kalali contradicted. "I'll show you."

Mr. Kalali spat at her.

She ignored him. She led Floyd and Peaches from the library and down a wide hall to the master bedroom area. In the adjacent dressing room she slid out one of the deep drawers of her vanity. It had a false bottom. She opened it for them.

The shallow compartment contained two sapphire rings, a cross-over diamond ring, a tanzanite pendant, a tourmaline bracelet, a diamond tennis bracelet, several gold chains, a pair of one-carat diamond studs, and a pair of pavé diamond ear clips. Nothing major but all of good quality.

"My everyday things," Mrs. Kalali explained, as Floyd transferred them from the compartment to his jacket pockets.

Peaches, meanwhile, was into the top drawer of Mr. Kalali's dresser. Confiscating cuff links and evening studs, and a ring set with a five-carat honey-colored cat's-eye chrysoberyl. The perfect, sharp, straight cat's-eye, what gemologists call chatoyancy, fascinated Peaches. She wished the ring wasn't so large. It was even too big for her thumb. Perhaps, she thought, she could wear it on her big toe, go bopping barefoot down some street with the cat's-eye winking at everyone. In that drawer she also found some gold wristwatches. It was like shoplifting without having to be sneaky.

They followed Mrs. Kalali into the bedroom. She kicked aside an antique silk Isfahan prayer rug. At first Floyd thought what he was seeing was just bare floor, but then, Mrs. Kalali pressed a certain place on the nearby baseboard and a small section of the floor sprung up. Lifting that aside disclosed a compartment. Protruding from the bottom of the compartment was the face of a safe. Floyd would never have found it. A highly rated safe. What's more, it was inset in the concrete foundation.

The sight of it evoked a little glee from Peaches. "You can get into that, can't you baby?" she said to Floyd.

As good and experienced a swift as Floyd was he'd never done safes. He knew swifts who did, had met a few who'd offered to impart the basics and finer points, but he just hadn't had the ambition.

So, understandably, he was grateful when Mrs. Kalali reached down in and performed the combination.

The guns and the badass nigger talk had gotten to her, Floyd thought. No other reason for her to be so cooperative.

The safe was open.

Its contents there for the taking.

First thing out, because it happened to be there on top of everything else, was a red Cartier ring box containing a six-carat cushion-cut diamond of superb quality.

Mrs. Kalali provided a blue Fendi valise for them to carry the jewelry away in.

They returned to the library.

Mr. Kalali was on the couch, groaning and holding his right foot up. His black silk sock was soaked red, dripping blood.

"I told the pussy motherfucker to stay where he was," Tracy said.

"I'm badly cut," Mr. Kalali said. In stocking feet he'd stepped on some shards of his antique Persian glass. Some of the same were now crunching noisily beneath the thick soles of Peaches' boots, aggressive black leather boots with shiny steel toeplates. She went so directly to Mr. Kalali that for a moment he thought she had taken pity and intended to administer to his foot.

She stopped in front of him.

She extended the Mach 10 pistol to within inches of his face.

His eyes fixed on the little opening of its muzzle. The miniature tunnel from which his death could come. He didn't dare move his head, just raised his eyes.

There was her blonde, frizzy hair, the slight upturn of her nose between the childish rounds of her cheeks, the inexperience of her mouth, lips slicked like they were coated with baby drool.

Having taken such close stock of her, Mr. Kalali believed he had determined her innocence. Never mind the gun, disregard it, he told himself. Children play. She was merely playing. Her innocence was definitely in his favor.

Peaches was sure she had this guy scared shitless. It was payback for all those times since she was thirteen, even before, when older guys had made her afraid. She didn't intend to pull the trigger. It was like her finger was on its own.

A five-round burst.

The last two rounds went wild. The first three tore off much of Mr. Kalali's head.

Mrs. Kalali screamed. Her composure left her, as did her compliance. She made a dash for the security alarm pad in the entry hall, for the panic button that would summon help.

Floyd had to shoot her.

CHAPTER 3

The flow from La Guardia was coagulated.

An eighteen-wheeler, like some behemoth suddenly intent on suicide, had swerved across the median, ended the lives of five and now lay there on the Grand Central Parkway with its exposed underside looking rigored.

Mitchell Laughton was the passenger in a much abused fleet taxi sixty-four lengths back from the collisions. In fatalistic measure, death had missed him by, at most, half a minute.

The taxi meter was ticking away voraciously. Each time it went *gu-luckit* to register a greater amount Mitch was made to think how this was another of those wastes of life time. A more equitable arrangement could have been created, he thought. For instance, when forced to wait like this, why shouldn't a person be allowed to call time-out or perhaps even receive a credit on the other end?

He'd certainly done more than a fair share of unfair waiting this day. The flight to Boston had been delayed a half hour because of air traffic; then his eleven o'clock appointment with Grayson at Fidelity Eastern Insurance had to be pushed ahead to one because Grayson was having a root canal emergency.

And now this tie-up.

Already it had cost Mitch nearly forty minutes.

For what must have been the hundredth time he told himself to relax, take it in stride, do what Maddie advised to cope with such unavoidable irritating instances. Turn mentally inside out was the way she put it. Think flowers, for example, not a mere bouquet but a whole skyful, or think of finding a downy bird-belly feather that could be kept mid-air by the slightest breath for miles and miles over an ideal endless meadow. Think of a happy home run, a bases-loaded, tenth-inning game winner. Whatever it took to transcend, Maddie prescribed.

At times Mitch had been able to perform her inside-out trick. Not often and not easily, but he had.

However, this afternoon it was impossible.

The taxi seat was one reason. The foam rubber within it had given up ten thousand passengers ago. What the rump got now was practically all inflicting springs. What's more, the seat refused to stay in place, kept shifting forward from its proper slot beneath the back cushion. The ashtrays stunk, were stuffed with stubs and used tissues. No air conditioning, the uncloseable windows were cross-ventilating exhaust fumes.

Then there was the driver of the next car over. Emaciated, brittle-looking woman with a mass of hair an impossible red. She had her dough-white, crepey arm out the window, hung down lifelessly except for her fingers doing nervous flicks at a cigarette. She brought the cigarette to her sparse lips, took a long, ugly drag, exhaled from her nostrils.

Mitch imagined she had tusks.

She noticed him noticing and shot him a scrinched-up, superior look that called him a creep.

Ordinarily Mitch would have chalked her up as one of those inconsequential frays in the fabric of life. However, right there as she was, hardly more than a spit away, he was stuck with her.

He got out of the cab. The concrete surface of the parkway

felt slippery underfoot. He stretched his back and limbs thoroughly, craned up, hoping to see movement ahead.

The taxi driver had gotten out earlier. He was on his haunches near the left front door, reading a tired copy of the *Daily News* that one of his morning passengers had left behind. The driver was a West Indian. His especially dark skin had a gloss to it. He stood, folded the newspaper and tossed it onto the front seat. Then he went back five or so lengths to a taxi that belonged to the same fleet, driven by someone he knew.

Mitch reached in and helped himself to the newspaper. He placed it on the left section of the taxi's hot, yellow hood, smoothed it out and stood over it.

During his wait in Boston he'd read most of that day's *Globe* and there'd been not a single line about what the *News* had chosen to front-page: the late-night frolic of an already notorious rock star who'd roller-bladed bare-ass around and around the Plaza Fountain so elusively it had taken six policemen to grab hold of her. The photo showed her looking stoned and gleeful, wrapped in a police jacket that had precisely slipped.

The Kalali murder.

It was on page seven. Just one of a dozen murders that had occurred in the tri-state area over the weekend. It did not involve anyone well-known, so page seven was generous positioning. Half a column bordering an ad for a Macy's sale of bras and girdles.

Mitch more or less read the Kalali item; anyway, got the gist of it:

A guy named Kalali had been slain night before last at his home out in Jersey. His wife was in a bad way. It looked to be robbery. They were Iranian people.

Mitch continued on through the paper several pages at a time, all the way to and past the sports section. A page just beyond sports offered a daily horoscope. Mitch put no stock in astrology, never had. He reasoned it was something thought up thousands of years ago when our solar system was considered the vast end-all. Now that we've had a look at Mars and Venus and so on and seen how arid, lifeless, hot or cold they were, and now that we know how huge the universe is and how this solar system is comparatively no more than a few motes in it, what basis was there for such beliefs?

Still, there on the page for contemporary consumption was the sign-characters of the Zodiac along with a bit of advice or prediction for each.

Purely for diversion Mitch read the horoscopes for Aries and Taurus and then skipped down the sign-by-sign listing for what might be said for Sagittarius.

It wasn't there. The list went from Scorpio to Capricorn. Why had they left out Sagittarius, his sign?

Mitch was amused at himself for feeling slighted.

He wouldn't mention the omission to Maddie, though. She'd make something of it.

The afternoon was practically shot by the time Mitch got into the city. The stingily filled egg salad, mostly chopped celery, sandwich he'd had at the Fidelity Eastern employees' lunch room and the packets of salted peanuts the airline had distributed weren't holding him. However, he'd persevere. In fact, it would be best if he did, because Maddie had said that morning, with a coating of promise, she'd be doing a cassoulet that night. He'd come close to telling her it was too warm for such a heavy meal.

Maddie had a fairly extensive kitchen repertoire, considering, but rarely was Mitch able to honestly compliment her on what she prepared. Cassoulet was her incessant nemesis. It never came out the same and never right. Too much thyme, or vermouth, or garlic, or cloves, one thing or another.

Anyway, tonight was supposed to be another cassoulet night and, maybe, if he stayed hungry and became even more so, hungry enough, he wouldn't have to fib to Maddie that it was delicious, wouldn't have to tell her he'd cleaned his plate when he'd hardly touched it, wouldn't have to perform appreciative sounds nor pretend he was helping himself to seconds.

He walked to the corner of Fifth Avenue, entered the Corvette Building and had one of the elevators all to himself up to the fourteenth floor to the corner office with his name on one of the two of its doors.

Shirley, his secretary, was at her desk not doing anything nor trying to appear that she was.

"You made it back," she said. "I was beginning to think you wouldn't."

"Any calls?"

"They're on your desk."

Mitch went into his inner office. Shirley following along, saying: "I lose the money I put down to layaway a pair of boots at Lord & Taylor if I don't pick them up today."

"Too hot for boots."

"It won't be soon enough."

"How much?"

"I put down twenty, I owe ninety."

"You're impossible."

"Otherwise I wouldn't be so ardently sought." Shirley arched as she accepted the hundred Mitch extended. Her smile thanked him. She had miraculous, rather large teeth, so white and even they looked a bit vicious. Her last name was Crowninshield. She was British but had been in America for half of her forty-two years. There was still considerable London in her manners and her manner of speaking and she could turn it on thick when she thought it advantageous, for herself or for Mitch. Guile she had, was smart as a skinned knee. She'd never been married, claimed she wouldn't be ever because why put an end to enjoyment.

One of Shirley's most apparent shortcomings was her weakness for layaways. At any given time she'd have small amounts of money deposited on things at Saks, Gallerie Lafayette, Bendel's, Bloomie's, wherever. All sorts of things that had spontaneously struck her fancy. She kept track of them on her calendar and nearly always waited until the final day before forfeiture to resort to having Mitch give her an advance.

After a number of such so-called advances she'd present Mitch with a detailed accounting, a printout showing she was a month or two behind in her salary. He'd keep it for a few days for effect then tear it up and drop it in her wastebasket where she was sure to discover it. Nothing said. She'd worked six years for Mitch. There'd been maybe a half dozen periods when she'd managed to resist layaways. Those times, Mitch noticed, coincided with hopeful love affairs.

Now, she'd already freshened her makeup, smoothed her pantyhose and was in the starting gate for Lord & Taylor's. "Anything you want done before I leave?"

"Nothing that won't keep."

"I'm all caught up with the Hyperion file."

"Good girl."

"Ta then," she said brightly to him and the whole place, grabbed up a soft leather tote that had, in its turn, once been a layaway at Bendel's and was gone.

Among the considerable number of pink *Called While You Were Out* slips on Mitch's desk were three from Maddie, the most recent only a half hour ago, two from Keith Ruder of Columbia Beneficial and one from Furio Visconti.

The latter caused Mitch to turn and look in the direction of the 580 Fifth Avenue building located diagonally across the intersection on the northwest corner of 47th. As coincidence would have it Visconti's place of business was also on the fourteenth floor.

Often, while gazing out merely to give his thinking more room, Mitch would catch on Visconti over there dealing away. Sometimes all he could see was the back of Visconti's head above his office chair. Other times, when Visconti had swiveled to face out, he and Mitch would peer across at one another, and once, Christmas week two years ago, Visconti had waved. Just a single, hand-up motion, and Mitch had responded rather automatically with the same.

That remote exchange across a city gorge was by no means the extent of what Mitch and Visconti saw of one another, although in Mitch's opinion both would have been better off had they let it go at that.

Seldom was Mitch on *the street* that he didn't run into Visconti. It wasn't altogether happenchance. In his particular way, Visconti was 47th. It was his allocated portion to chew on. Anyway, half his.

There he'd be, on the sidewalk outside an arcade or a jewelry merchant's window, talking to one of his minions or a fence. He'd stop talking or listening to make a point of saying hello to Mitch or sometimes more:

"How's it going?"

"Fine."

"Want to ask you something."

Mitch raises his chin, looks receptive.

"That a real Rothko I see over there on your office wall or just a print?"

"Real." A fib.

"That's funny. Thought I saw that one at the Museum of Modern Art a while back."

"I lend it out."

"You're a classy guy, Mitch."

Mitch agrees.

But this was the first time Visconti had ever phoned, wanted to be called back.

Mitch pressed the speaker button of his phone. He speed-dialed Maddie.

"Well, at last, there you are," she said.

"What's up?"

"No cassoulet tonight, darling. The inspiration deserted and left me lazy."

Mitch enjoyed the reprieve. "I'll pick up something on the way home."

"I'd rather go out," Maddie told him. "Maybe to Lespinasse or someplace."

She didn't mean the someplace. When she said Lespinasse Mitch knew she meant Lespinasse. His watch told him almost six. "Shall I come home first, or what?"

"Why don't you fiddle around there and I'll come by for you at seven."

"How did your day go?"

"Maybe I won't bother with putting on any makeup." She had this way of abruptly taking unrelated conversational side roads. Mitch had become used to it. "Would you mind terribly if I were bare-faced tonight?" she asked.

"I'll make reservations," he said.

"I already have. Are you okay? Your voice sounds a bit strange, sort of hollow."

She had hypersensitive hearing but he doubted she could pick up his empty, complaining stomach. "I've got you on speaker phone."

"I know, but that's not it. I did say seven, didn't I, precious?"

"If you want to make it sooner or later it's okay with me."

"No, just be out front. Billy already has the glove compartment crammed with parking violations and you know how he loathes having to circle the block."

She clicked off and was again up the avenue thirteen blocks away. But safe up there in the high apartment at the Sherry, way above the city's ordinary level and its dangers.

His Maddie.

Hung on the wall to his left were three framed, enlarged photographs of her. Ten years ago, five years ago, and last month. Any of the three were capable of causing him to lose his train of thought. Right now he was lost in the most recent, her pleasant, reassuring expression.

Mitch knew she ventured out more often than she admitted. He also knew she kept that from him to save him worry. Allowing her to take care of herself had from the start been part of their deal. For him it was the hardest part.

He dialed Keith Ruder, doubting that Ruder would still be in. The offices of Columbia Beneficial Insurance were located on Park in the twenties, in an imposing but spiritless building from which the drones of insurance stampeded out of each weekday at precisely five o'clock.

Ruder was there, said his last name instead of hello. He got right to it. "The file I had messengered to you, have you looked at it?"

"I was just going over it. I've been in Boston all day." Mitch reached for the oversize manila envelope bearing Columbia Beneficial's logo. He slit it open with the larger blade of a two-bladed Buck pocketknife that his father had given him because it had been his grandfather's.

As he removed the contents of the envelope he noticed the name Kalali but it took a moment for him to recall where he'd seen it before.

The files, besides Ruder's perfectly typed covering letter, consisted of a four-page itemized and numbered list of various pieces of jewelry, twenty pages of detailed descriptions and appraisals and a corresponding photograph of each insured item. Professionally taken photos. The appraisals were in order, done by Yavitz, a respectable upscale retail jeweler on Madison Avenue.

Mitch went to the bottom line. Replacement value for the entire lot came to six million one hundred thirty thousand. He purposely read the amount aloud, heard a disquieted grunt from Ruder.

"How long has the policy been in force?"

"Why do you ask?"

"Never know."

"Believe me, Mitch [usually it was Laughton], I've gone over and through every clause and all correspondence at least ten times today. It's tight."

"I'm sure if there's a way out you'll find it." Mitch was also sure Ruder would take that as a compliment.

"Our coverage began eight years ago," Ruder informed. "Before then Lloyds had it."

"Columbia is the sole underwriter?"

"Unfortunately."

"Smart bookies lay off heavy action," Mitch recited as though it was something from the Bible.

Ruder resented the bookie implication but let it pass.

"From the start our coverage of the Kalalis was a package. Dwelling, cars, liability, the works. They tacked on the personal property coverage, which, of course, was their option."

"All these jewelry items right off?"

"No. To begin with the jewelry rider was for three million something. As they acquired additional pieces they let us know, complied with our requirements and we covered."

"Who paid the premiums?" At thirteen dollars a thousand, about eighty thousand a year.

"For the first five years the husband paid. After that the wife."

"Wonder why. Why do you think?"

"I don't see that it matters. The fact is the beneficiary is the wife. Columbia has the usual ninety days to settle with her."

"Maybe she won't live that long."

"No matter, somebody will pop up demanding to be paid. Of course, if we were to recover . . ." The prospect of that drew a long, full sigh from Ruder. "God, would I ever be grateful if we recovered."

Grateful would be nice for a change, Mitch thought.

Columbia Beneficial was one of his regular clients. He was on retainer to Columbia and to several of the other major insurance companies. Any one of them would have preferred having him on staff. At one time or another each had approached him with an offer, attractive numbers and numerous perks. Possibly he gave one thought to their propositions but never a second. At any price being among the tight asses in the gray atmosphere and paper pile of insurance didn't appeal to him. He was heart and soul a freelancer.

For the insurance firms that was an innovation.

Prior to Mitch, whenever cases came up that involved West 47th—robberies, usually, but often a robbery with a distinctive diamond district twist—the companies had no choice but to draw from their staff of claims adjusters. These fellows, capable as they might be in handling claims in the everyday world, were out of their element on 47th.

They got blinded by the sparkle, left behind by the vernacular, spun by the milieu to the point of vertiginous confusion.

Mitch, on the other hand, could hardly have been more streetwise. For years, actually most of his life, without being conscious of it, really, he'd been stoking up on the workings of 47th. His was not merely a familiarity with the street, nor was he like someone-come-lately hoping to be accepted, needing to earn a place. The street had already conditioned him to its ways and confirmed him. It had even exposed for his awareness the cunning peristalsis of its underbelly.

He was not to be fooled. The street liked that about him. His expertise of gemstones was equal to nearly anyone's. He could take a bare-eyed look at a stone, an emerald, say, and not only tell in which part of the earth it had been taken from but, as well, which part of that part. In many instances, even which mine.

He was just as adept when it came to finished jewelry. After a brief examination of a piece that bore no hallmark or signature, something that would stymie most people, he more often than not was able to date it within a few years and, from its style and the quality of workmanship, say where it was made and by whom.

"It's a sweet little bracelet, quite nice. Done by someone in Carlo Giuliano's shop. I'd say in the early 1880s, but not by Carlo himself. It's not that sweet. Besides it wasn't in Carlo's Neapolitan nature to overlook signing."

Such was the extensive know-how, know-where and know-who Mitch offered the insurance companies when eight years ago at age thirty he decided to sell them his services. They didn't snap him right up. Typically they pretended to be mulling it over for a month or two, tried to negotiate with him, claimed he was too costly and not really needed.

Mitch stuck to his conditions, sure they would come around. Fidelity Eastern was the first to retain him. Within a week all the others fell into line.

He'd done well by them. Columbia Beneficial especially.

He'd worked ten of Columbia's major jewelry theft cases, made three total recoveries and two partials.

That wasn't to imply that his association with Columbia was close.

Anything but.

There was a bitterness towards Columbia in him, a personal thing that refused to be swallowed and digested by time. In Mitch's opinion all insurance companies were arctic-hearted, egregiously slick and one-way, but Columbia was the champion fine-printer of the bunch.

As for Keith Ruder, the person at Columbia he mainly dealt with, Mitch managed to keep him remote. He'd broken and parried so many luncheon invitations from Ruder that they'd finally stopped being extended, were reduced to the automatic and unmistakably insincere suggestion that they get together sometime soon.

At this moment there was Ruder on the other end of the line trying to sound buddy-buddy, forcing it, flavoring his tone with what he hoped was coming across as amiable conspiracy. It made Mitch think that this Kalali case, for some reason, was personally crucial for Ruder. Perhaps too many such large losses had piled up in Ruder's corner; maybe he was feeling the cold of an early, less compensating retirement hot on his neck.

"I assume you want me to get on this Kalali loss," Mitch said.

"I'd appreciate it."

"By now these pieces may have gone first-class carry-on to London or anywhere."

"Think so?"

Mitch really didn't but told Ruder: "Could be."

"Well . . ." A resigned sigh from Ruder. ". . . I suppose there's only so much to hope for. Can't expect a miracle."

"That's what it would take."

"Nevertheless you might as well sniff around a bit."

"What if I recover?"

"That would certainly be a blessing."

Blessings and miracles, Mitch thought. "I mean what would be in it for me?"

"Your usual percentage, of course. Three percent."

A hundred and eighty thousand. Fair enough, but out it came, pushed out by that old score that could probably never be settled by any amount: "I've raised my percentage to five."

"Since when?"

"I notified you. Surely you received my letter." There'd been no letter, but there would be.

Ruder reverted to type, got huffy. "Five is exorbitant."

"Not when you consider . . ."

"Five is out of the question!"

The money would be from Columbia's deep pocket, not Ruder's. Mitch figured that would come to Ruder in about ten seconds.

It took twelve.

CHAPTER 4

"Do you see him, Billy?"

"No, Mrs. Laughton. Wonder what color suit he put on this morning."

"It felt to me like one of his grays. Don't drive fast."

"I'm crawling."

"You are over on the left aren't you?"

"All the way."

"He should be there. What time is it?"

"I've got ten of. The car says twelve of."

"We're early. Go around."

"I could wait near the corner with the motor running."

"Do as you want but I'm not going to pay your damn tickets."

"They're as much yours as mine, Mrs. Laughton."

True enough, Maddie silently admitted. Billy got most of the tickets because he was so conscientious about waiting in no-standing zones for her.

They were now on Fifth Avenue in the black Lexus EL400. Only leftovers of the rush hour now. Lots of buses, though. One after another like elephants tusks to tails.

Despite the warm July night, Billy had on his uniform. Dove gray twill. Trousers and fitted, high-neck jacket, matching visored cap and gloves. His choice because he'd be doing some waiting out front of the St. Regis with other drivers. Otherwise he'd have worn regular slacks and shirt.

He committed the car to 46th Street and saw the way was clogged.

"Want some radio?" he asked.

She didn't want any radio.

He made conversation. "Which are you for, Mrs. Laughton, timber or owls?"

"Owls, of course."

"That's because you're not in need of any timber just now."

"Nor at the moment do I have occasion for an owl." Then, in the same breath: "Bet he was there and we missed him."

For her sake Billy held back saying he didn't think so. Billy knew when and when not to say things. He'd been Uncle Straw's driver for years.

Maddie made herself sit back. She measured her anticipation. Frequently at times like this she felt as though there was a sort of device in her, in her head or belly or pelvis, with which she was able to gauge how intensely she was looking forward to being with Mitch. It had been installed during their earliest time and now, after ten years of marriage, it was still there and she believed it always would be. Tonight it seemed to be on a cross circuit, arcing from her head to her pelvis, lingering at the latter.

Early. It would have pleased her if he'd been early, waiting on the corner of 47th and Fifth, his eagerness shifting him, making it impossible for him to stand still, his eyes searching up the avenue for her being brought to him. Him, her precious love, trying to hurry time, pacing, trying to bear the edge of his anticipation with pacing.

She adjusted her dark glasses. With a second finger reset them on the bridge of her nose. Gold wire-rimmed glasses with round magenta-tinted lenses. Chosen from her many pairs, an entire dresser-drawerful.

"Why are we stopped?" she asked.

"Garbage truck."

She pictured it and thought it wouldn't be difficult for her mind to go from a garbage truck to blank. But her mind wouldn't mind. It went from the garbage truck to the Manalo Blahnik navy satin pumps she had on, which still felt somewhat tight and made her wonder if her feet were getting fat, and from that to whether or not she'd remembered to close the door of her aviary, to wondering what Elise and Marian might be doing that moment in Spain where it was now midnight or later. The last she'd heard from Elise they'd wanted to move from Marbella back to Barcelona. Oddly that desire had arrived by letter rather than the usual phone call. To make sure Mitch was in on it, Maddie thought. "New stationery," Mitch had remarked before reading it aloud. Very fine, lined stationery from Armorial the Graveur on Fauborg St. Honoré. The letter said (its only purpose, really) that Marian had located a darling apartment in Barcelona's better district, expensive but darling, not all that large but sumptuous, more for intimacy than for entertaining. Why was it Elise couldn't communicate without using words or phrases that were certain to conjure up sexual images? Was it her intention to boast? It seemed so to Maddie.

"Phone him," she told Billy.

"I did, just now. No answer."

He's down on the street waiting, she told herself and then mentally told Mitch, *I didn't want you to have to wait tonight.* Fucking garbage truck.

As though her cursing was what had been needed to dispel the impediment the way was suddenly clear and Billy went ahead and left and left and left around the block and pulled over for Mitch.

Maddie felt the air disturbed by his climbing in. She inhaled the distinctive scent of him and leaned toward its source with her face up to receive his lips briefly on her cheek.

"You weren't early," she accused.

"Would have been but I needed to freshen up."

"You didn't reshave."

"Maybe later."

"Maybe," she arched.

"Look at you! Thought you said no makeup."

"Changed my mind." She removed her dark glasses to expose her eyes.

Mitch knew how long it had taken her to get them so right. Both eyes equally and perfectly outlined and shadowed, lashes thickened.

Care had also been taken in what she'd decided to wear. Mitch imagined her standing before their bedroom mirror imagining how she looked. Her dress was an Isaac Mizrahi she'd recently bought at Bergdorf and shown to him on a hanger, telling him what it was. Large white polka dots on navy blue ground. The bodice of silk crepe de chine, the short, ample skirt of filmy silk chiffon. At the time he'd said he liked it with just adequate heart. Now he set that straight, told her enthusiastically, "You look smashing!"

"Think so?" She soaked that up and hoped for another helping and he didn't disappoint, told her: "Being with you tonight is going to be dangerous."

Instead of thank you she paused and extended her lips for him to bring his to. She was feeling extremely feminine. Her arms like wings, her thighs full of blossoms. She re-crossed her legs and the chiffon obediently floated and lightly settled upon and around her. "Navy is a helpful color for me, don't you think, for my hair and all?"

Mitch thought so, said so. Her heavy healthy hair was naturally blonde, naturally variegated. Plenty of shine but no brass. She had it styled fairly short and in such a simple way it practically disciplined itself, required only a vigorous swish or two and a combing with her fingers here and there to look right.

Billy brought the Lexus to the curb.

Mitch got out, extended his hand back in to Maddie.

She expected it, got it, used it as she aimed her left foot and found the sidewalk, placed her weight on that foot, kept her head down and then she too was out and up.

Stumble, as always, was her enemy. At such times as this

her audacity challenged it. So far so good. She paused momentarily to gather her poise, glanced off as though to survey East 55th, then returned her attention to the direction that her highly honed senses told her was the entrance to the restaurant.

Mitch grasped her elbow firmly, started her.

She didn't shuffle or feel ahead with her feet. Took assured paces of a natural length, five to the held-open entrance door and twenty from it to where there were six steps up that she managed without so much as a toe bumping a riser. Mitch halted her while he dealt with the maître d'.

Mitch and Maddie had settled on this system years ago, his using her forearm like a tiller. By now they'd pretty much perfected it. She knew what each pressure of his hand meant, which signified to go left, which to right and to what degree each of those directions. Those for stop and start were easiest. Simply a restraining or slight forward shove. A little downward tug told her she'd reached the point where she could confidently sit. There were refinements, little squeezes of a certain number conveyed certain impending things. Stairs, for example.

Of course, their system wasn't infallible. Old enemy stumble often had its way and there'd been numerous collisions. One day, when attempting lunch at La Goulue, Maddie had misinterpreted a signal as the *sit* signal and taken an inelegant flop.

This night, however, no mishaps. She managed the zigzag course of tables and chairs and waiters without even a brush, and soon she was conspicuously seated on a banquette with the stem of a crystal wine goblet between her fingers, acclimating, actually sort of parsing, as she usually did, the sounds in the large, high-ceilinged room. The polyphony of conversations punctuated by trills of laughter and the effects of the waiters serving. She enjoyed Lespinasse, had been there numerous times for either lunch or dinner, and was acquainted well enough with the layout of the place to make a solo trip to the ladies' room.

"The stunning brunette two tables over," she said out of nowhere.

"Who?"

"The one who's hitting on you. Sneakily but nonetheless hitting."

"Two tables over?"

"Yeah."

"No brunette, just three paunchy businessmen at that table."

A waiter brought rolls and butter. Maddie told him: "That attractive lady, at the second table from here, the dark-haired one . . ."

"Yes, ma'am?"

"See the one I mean?"

"With a diamond clip in her hair, yes ma'am."

"Never mind," she said as though having a second thought. The waiter went about his business.

"You're tricky," Mitch said, wolfing a hunk of roll.

"You're a fibber," Maddie contended.

"Anyway, the brunette in question hasn't looked this way even once."

"Now how would you know that?"

Mitch retreated to the safety of silence.

Maddie went along with that for a short while, then let him off the hook by finding his hand and giving it three consoling pats. "Don't despair, precious," she said, "I was just guessing and happened to be right."

Again, Mitch came close to saying aloud.

Over the years there'd been numerous such instances, some so accurate it seemed she was able to recover her sight at will. She always claimed they were guesses; however they were too right and too frequent for Mitch to accept that. He thought a more likely explanation for these coincidental observations, as he called them, was she had developed an extraordinary ability that sometimes compensated for her blindness.

But wasn't that just as far-fetched as off-and-on seeing? Mitch's pragmatic side told him it was.

He'd gotten the first indication of this faculty of hers shortly after they'd met. He and Uncle Straw were out on the terrace of the Sherry Netherland apartment playing gin rummy for a penny a point. Maddie was sort of neutrally kibitzing, not commenting, just hovering around. Mitch drew the nine of diamonds. Discarded it. Maddie moaned, she moaned before Uncle Straw picked up the nine. How could Maddie have known the nine was Uncle Straw's gin card, Mitch wondered. Uncle Straw evidently thought nothing of it, just gave himself points and gathered up the deck to shuffle for the next hand.

Mitch didn't puzzle over the incident. But neither could he dismiss it. He tried to mentally re-create it, the sequence of it, and became less certain it had happened as he recalled.

Still, he found himself on the lookout for such occurrences.

For example, the three sapphires. Mitch had purchased them as part of an estate. Three oval cuts, each about six carats. Maddie's birthday was a couple of weeks off, her first birthday since they'd been married, and he wanted to have one of the sapphires repolished and mounted into a ring for her. He brought the three sapphires home, told her what he intended to do and explained the differences between the three.

One had a distinctive lavender cast, threw pink and cornflower blue scintillations.

Another was a typical Burma tone, dark blue, inky.

The other was a bright Ceylon that just missed because it was ever so slightly zoned, that is, it was a lighter blue in one area.

"Which do you think is most me?" Maddie asked, pleased by his thoughtfulness.

"The Burma is the more precious," he told her, "worth more and will always be, but the lavender is far prettier."

At that point the stones, enclosed by cotton in individual glassine bags, were on the sofa table where Mitch had placed them. Maddie considered for a moment, then her fingers went straight to the lavender and took it up, as though she knew surely which was which.

BARNES & NOBLE   STORE 2538 NEW YORK
, NY (212)727-1227

REG#16   BOOKSELLER#174
RECEIPT#   30855 03/05/97   1:14 PM

S 0446604135   WEST 47TH
                    1 @   6.99   6.99

SUBTOTAL   6.99
SALES TAX - 8.25%   .58
TOTAL   7.57
CASH PAYMENT   20.00
CHANGE   12.43

        BOOKSELLERS SINCE 1873

"Is that one the lavender?" Mitch asked.

"Well, isn't it?"

"How could you tell?"

"Just guessed."

He watched Maddie raise her wine glass precisely to her lips. She'd ordered the house red. She took a sip preclusive to a gulp.

"Elise was always such a wine snob," she said. "It never failed to irk me, the way she went on about a wine's staying power or well-structured flavor or roundness of character and all that. What shit."

"Maybe since she's been in Europe she's been shamed out of that."

"Let's hope. That and all things like that."

Elise was Maddie's mother. Biological mother was how Maddie qualified her, not bitterly, just to be truer about it.

"What do you think about Elise and Marian wanting to move to Barcelona?" Maddie asked.

An indifferent shrug from Mitch. He sometimes forgot Maddie couldn't see such body language.

She went on. "For some ridiculous reason they seem to feel your approval is required, or rather that I need it."

"Has there been any mention of how much it would set you back?"

"Not yet, but if it's anywhere near what it cost for their move from Paris to Marbella or their one before that, from Capri to Paris, it'll be a small fortune. Why do you suppose they all of a sudden believe you have the power to cinch my purse strings?"

"I've no idea."

"Maybe I should nurture the fear. If I wanted to be mean I would."

Mitch couldn't imagine her mean. She could be tough at times but never mean.

"Would that appeal to you?" she asked.

"What?"

"The power to cinch."

"You've asked that before."

"Numerous times but you might have changed your mind."

"We should order," Mitch said. A waiter was standing at the ready. Maddie went right through the suggestion. "Sunday afternoon," she said, "afterward, when you were snoozing, I was remembering when the only kisses Elise and Marian exchanged were hello-goodbye, left and right pecks on the cheeks. Uncle Straw contends that one night in parting they happened to put a lingering one smack in the middle and that was that."

Marian had been Uncle Straw's wife. Thus, Maddie's aunt by marriage. She and Elise bore such a resemblance they were often taken as sisters. They frequently fibbed about that, told people they were fraternal twins.

Mitch had met Elise and Marian only once. Not at the wedding. They didn't show for that. At the last minute Elise phoned to prove by sounding hoarse and sniffily that she had a terrible flu. Said she'd caught the bug while shopping in a chilly Paris rain for a wedding present, said it didn't matter, that nothing, not even her near death could keep her from attending, said they were merciful dears for not insisting she fly considering what a mess her sinuses were, said her heart would be with them.

The present, a pair of Christofle crystal candle holders, arrived miraculously intact two weeks later. Carelessly packed in a regular cardboard box rather than securely so in a Christofle carton. Reason enough for Mitch to suspect Elise had owned them for a while.

Two years after then Elise and Marian came over on the Concorde for a visit that actually was a combined inspection and refinancing, so to speak. They came dressed in Ungaro suits and matching matinee-length strands of ten-millimeter pearls.

From first sight, first cheek kisses, Mitch and Elise endured one another. She talked through her teeth at him and only barely tried to conceal her disdain. He, on the other hand, was tactfully polite and amiable while finding her little more dimensional than the photos he'd seen of her.

She was visually attractive, though. Mitch had to give her that. Slender and conscientiously kept up. No doubt she'd had tucks and redraping here and there. The sort of time-fighting, well-off woman whom Mitch had known practically all his young life as the typical client of the Laughton jewelry store up on Madison. Known without knowing them. Those who came in to sell away what they'd once cherished came in escorted by avarice and gossamer excuses for indulgence such as ennui, in need of a lift, deserving of reward. The kind who never twitched a lash when told the price of a piece, a diamond and platinum bracelet, say, that had struck their fancy, was a hundred thousand.

In Mitch's eyes Elise had that sort of cachet and whatever assets she presented were spoiled by both her smile and her laugh, which in his opinion couldn't have been more artificial. It was as though she had only a certain supply of sincerity and was afraid of running out.

Running out.

Elise and Marian were supposed to stay two weeks. After the third day it was apparent they wouldn't make it. On the sixth, having fulfilled the capital aspect of their mission (a six-figure wire transfer to their joint account at the main Champs-Elysées branch of the Credit Lyonnais), Elise and Aunt Marian each left three-minute messages of contrition on Maddie's answering machine, checked out of the Plaza and put to use what remained of their Concorde round-trip.

"Think they're happy?" Maddie asked.

"Sure, why not?" Mitch replied generously.

"The other day, to let them know for what must be the thousandth time that I don't give a rat's ass what they're up to, I had them sent a needlepoint pillow. You know those little pillows with sayings on them."

"What did it say, the one you sent?"

"Butch on the streets, femme in the sheets."

"That should do it," Mitch remarked wryly.

"I thought so."

"Let's order."

"Anyway," Maddie went on, "I'll bet anything that what Elise and Marian had, their sizzling, inconsiderate hots, have by now dampened down to a much less limiting arrangement, a mere sharing of preference. I picture them hitting on desperate young girls for one another." Maddie realized her spite, countered it by abruptly taking a bright side road. "Josie Jefferson was wonderful today!"

"I was wondering how it went."

"She arrived a quarter hour early, her lessons all practiced, a serious little artist eager to get tuned up and into Vivaldi."

"What piece?"

"Concerto in D Major, the Largo section. She virtually attacked it. For now she has more spirit than artistry but I heaped on the praise and asked her to solo next Sunday."

Maddie had been strumming and plucking at guitars since she could manage to hold one. She didn't become serious about it, however, until she lost her eyesight at age ten. Until the black, as she put it.

She'd taken instruction from an elderly Spanish man, a once highly recognized artist whose fingers had gone arthritic. Elise went along to his sixth-floor studio in the Carnegie Hall Building for the first few lessons, sat by the window in an ordinary folding chair counting minutes and turning pages of *Town and Country* and thinking why the hell didn't Maddie play something instead of doing those incessant exercises?

At fourteen she'd been accepted at Juilliard.

At eighteen she realized what a saving distraction the guitar had been.

She still played.

Various guitars and mandolins were propped around the apartment for her to take up whenever she was in that state of mind, and it pleased her whenever Mitch asked her to play for him. Some mornings, while he was shaving, she would sit on the edge of the tub and play pieces that she believed were sure

to ignite him for his day. "How's this for a starter?" she'd say
and go into a Stevie Ray Vaughan or a fandango by Rodrigo
and he'd have difficulty keeping his attention on the strokes
of his razor.

At other times, on Saturday afternoons or late after a night
out, he'd sit close and watch, entranced by her fingers so
deftly changing positions along the frets. How sure she was of
the music she made no matter how complicated. If she made
mistakes, which he doubted, his love prevented him from de-
tecting them. What could he say to convey his appreciation
for her performances? He, an audience of one, with thunder-
ous applause and countless bravos in his heart.

His favorite pieces were from the "Castles of Spain" by
Torróba, just about anything flamenco and the anonymously
composed old piece called "Spanish Romance" or "Forbidden
Games." He could only take infrequent doses of the latter as
the melody line of it would get into his head and intrude there
for a day or two.

To do her heart good Maddie gave guitar lessons twice or
three times weekly to certain underprivileged children. She
charged ten dollars a session and they often came pride in
hand hoping she'd allow them to owe for a week or two. At
one point Josie Jefferson had gotten two months in arrears.
Her grandmother, who worked for a midtown janitorial service, got her caught up with six installments.

The reason Maddie charged for the lessons was to increase
their importance and give them the strength of sacrifice. To
more than even things out her pupils were paid (by her,
though they didn't know who) to perform on every other Sunday afternoon at hospital wards and convalescent homes
around the city.

The waiter had brought more rolls and replenished the butter.

"Why don't we order," Maddie said a bit plaintively. "I'm
starved, practically skipped lunch, had only a roast beef and
cheese on rye." She was a big eater, ate mannerly but a lot,
and it was unreasonable that she was able to remain so ideally

slender. Mitch imagined within her a roaring metabolic furnace, knew she wasn't bulimic, as some suspected and rumored.

This night she started with the *mille-feuille* of crabmeat with spiced mint vinaigrette, went clean-plate through the grilled yellowtail, baby carrots, baby turnips and all, and ended up with a lime soufflé.

As though saving best for last, she waited until the decaf was brought and she was stirring it cool and contemplating the tray of little, fancy gratuitous cookies the waiter placed on the cleared-off table, to ask Mitch: "How did your day go, precious?"

He was certain she didn't want to hear about his command appearance in Boston and all the routine waiting he'd had to endure. His need to bitch about that to someone had already receded and taken its place in that remote region in him where all his similar low-level needs to bitch resided.

No. Such dry stuff wasn't what she was after. She wanted to know what new had occurred on and around 47th. For years Mitch had been bringing the street home to her and the darker side of her was definitely hooked.

To Maddie the vagaries of West 47th were more intriguing and often more extravagant than those of New York's upper social layer.

Like the prominent diamond broker whose embittered wife knew his combinations and, while he was in London on business but really in Barbados for side kicks with a pretty, nineteen-year-old hard body, went to his office on 47th and helped herself to twelve million worth from his safe.

Like those sanctimonious 47th big dealers who kept three or four sets of books and got peeled down to the bone of evasion by the IRS.

"Allenwood's okay. If you got a choice take Allenwood. They got a kosher line at Allenwood."

And like the recent but already legendary misunderstanding between two partners that grew so heated one threw a whole trayful of their best goods out the fourth-story office window. (It's hail! No, it's diamonds from outer space maybe.) Causing, on the 47th sidewalk and gutters below, such a free-for-all that ambulances and an aggregate 152 stitches were required.

Such 47th Street tribulations appealed to Maddie. They were indeed larger than life and she, so dependent on imagination, dilated them even more.

Mitch also let her know when the more spectacular deals went down. She found them interesting and would have felt shorted had he left them untold. However, more colorful than the big deals were the raw deals and the double deals, the scams and swindles, petty and large.

So it followed that, for her, the most fascinating of all were the robberies, and the bolder the better.

Like the one last year, which had been premeditated a year before when a couple of guys bought a restaurant on the north side of 46th Street between Fifth Avenue and Avenue of the Americas. A narrow, short-order sort of place with no booths, just ten stools at a counter and a small, trap-doored cellar for storing supplies. The rear of the restaurant coincided with the rear of a major jewelry arcade on the south side of 47th. What separated the two was an air shaft one hundred and fifty feet wide where sumac grew and the raw earth surface glinted like pavé with decades of pieces of broken glass.

It took the two fellows and two others eight months to mole their way underground across the air shaft to be directly beneath the strong room of the jewelry arcade. That was where all fifty of the concessions of the arcade kept their goods each night and weekend.

With professional patience the guys waited two weeks for the advantages of a holy holiday. Took their undisturbed, own good time burning through the floor of the strong room. Emptied it of six million worth. Left behind not even a 14k bale.

Maddie knew that robbery inside out. First from what Mitch told her about it, the generally exposed scenario, then from the privileged intricacies she extracted from Mitch's detective friend James Hurley.

Mitch hung out with Hurley quite a bit. Their affinity was West 47th. As a captain out of Midtown North Precinct, Hurley's domain included the street. It was both a trouble spot and a centerpiece for him and he made the most of it.

So there they'd be having a whiskey and talking Knicks or something and Maddie would sideroad in with: "You'll never catch those guys."

"Which guys?"

"The ones who pulled off the mole robbery." The tabloids had dubbed it that.

"We'll get them," Hurley said.

"Never," Maddie contended, "those guys won't blow it. For almost a whole year they took turns frying over-easies and tunneling. I'll bet on them."

Nothing from Hurley.

Maddie went on: "A greasy spoon like that, you'd think their prints would be all over the place."

"We'll get them," Hurley maintained. "Won't we Mitch?"

"I suppose," Mitch said neutrally, "but Maddie's intuition is usually dependable when it comes to such things."

"We got a new lead this afternoon," Hurley said.

"From one of your slimy snitches, no doubt." Maddie scrinched her face. She loathed snitches, pictured them rodent-like, sneaking about furtively, keeping close to walls and living off waste.

"A really promising lead," Hurley added.

"Tell me about it."

Maddie pumped and Hurley imparted.

That was how it usually went.

This night at Lespinasse Mitch didn't have anything even approaching sensational to put into Maddie's ears. He gazed over his coffee cup at her, sensed the extent of her expectation and was tempted to fabricate a street story. He reasoned, however, if he made something up she wouldn't let him be brief; she'd want details and he'd have to keep on inventing and the fibs would pile up and that wasn't how he wanted to spend the better part of the night.

He wanted to go home and lie with her, remain perfectly still while she traced him with fingers and mouth, as she loved to do and as he loved her to do, drawing the precise picture of him in her mind, drawing that part of him that would occupy her so nicely.

His memory suggested the Kalali robbery and murder.

There was that, and it suited the moment perfectly, Mitch thought. It had the components but wouldn't take up much time because he'd stick to what he knew about it.

Which, at this point, wasn't much.

CHAPTER 5

The following morning there was no guitar playing while Mitch shaved.

He'd awakened at five and, although the face of his bedside clock suggested that he doze off for another couple of hours, he knew when he got up for the bathroom he was up for the day.

He'd slept fewer hours than usual but it had been a deeper sleep. Perhaps he hadn't even once changed position; his pillow wasn't punished, was still plump and showed only a head-size impression.

Such a good sleep no doubt because of good, long lovemaking.

Last night had been one of those like-minded times for him and Maddie, when their sexual wants not only coincided but were, as well, simultaneously above the reach of restraint, up in that lover's stratosphere where lust also has its place.

"How does that feel?"

"Marvelous."

"Tell me."

"Soon as I get my breath."

"It doesn't hurt too much?"

"You can't hurt me now. Nothing you can do will hurt now."

He shaved with the bathroom door shut, ran the water from the tap only when needed and only with enough force to rinse his razor. He took a brief, gentle shower and dressed as quietly as possible. Everything not to disturb her, conscientious of how supersensitive her hearing was.

He went noiselessly to her side of the bed for a goodbye look at her. His love in the black within her black. Her usual sleeping attitude, legs knifed up to herself, chin to her chest, one hand beneath a cheek. As though she were contained within the invisible shell of an egg. His love, her system had been so swamped with the neurotransmitters of pleasure that she was still under their influence.

He watched and listened to her breathing. The shallow breaths of sleep. He wished he could leave her a note declaring his love in some unique, adequately expressive way.

He went down the thirty-four floors and through the Sherry Netherland's breccia marble lobby. The uniformed doorman gave the brass-framed revolving door a vigorous spin. Mitch hopped into a quarter section of it and came out on Fifth Avenue.

The flag of Japan next to the flag of Germany limp over there above the entrance to the Plaza.

The gold embellishments on the building down the way, the one that had been confiscated from Imelda Marcos, celebrating the sun.

A taxi swerved in, offered itself to Mitch. He waved it on, glanced up at the Sherry's landmark clock, saw twenty to six and headed downtown at a pace that conveyed important destination.

Twelve minutes later he was in his office.

As he usually first did, he stood at the window and sighted down 47th. He wasn't able to see the entire street from this vantage, only about half the north side and none of the south; however that was enough for him to take in the temperament of it. It was as though each day his imagination expected the street to change, to be upheaved or thronged in a panic or roiled from end to end with visible avarice.

At times, depending upon what mood he was viewing the street through, he thought possibly his regard for it didn't exceed by much what he felt about insurance companies.

At the moment 47th's disposition was tranquil, nearly deserted. The precious goods, diamonds and such, that determined its nature were locked away, waiting in the incompatible dark for their keepers to come liberate them and allow them to do their daily dazzle.

It would be two to three hours yet.

The windows of the upper stories of the 580 building across the way were reflecting early sun. There was no activity or lights on in the offices and workrooms over there that Mitch could see. Except, of course, for those of Visconti.

Visconti's private corner office was dark, but the adjacent spaces on each side that comprised his operation were lighted and possibly doing business. Visconti's people seemed to be continually at it, Mitch thought, even nights, weekends, holidays. Especially nights, weekends and holidays. How many millions did they do a year?

He sat at his desk.

Before him lay the case file Ruder had sent late yesterday, the eight-by-ten color photographs and the corresponding loss list.

The Kalali loss.

Mitch had gone over it cursorily, intended now to thoroughly familiarize himself with the pieces that had been stolen, the swag.

Last thing yesterday, before going down to meet Maddie for dinner, he'd been studying the photograph of a ruby and diamond necklace and matching pair of ear clips. In fact, he'd been admiring those items and thinking how attractively designed they were, the way the diamonds and rubies integrated to create a flow that carried attention to the larger center stones. The loss list didn't indicate who was the maker. They looked good enough to be Van Cleef & Arpels in Mitch's estimation; however that was a value-increasing attribute that certainly wouldn't have been omitted.

What occurred to Mitch now, and bothered him, was that the photo of those diamond and ruby pieces wasn't where it should be. He'd left it on top of the other Kalali photos, was quite sure of that. Now he found it several photos down.

Had he, in his eagerness to meet Maddie, just stuck that photo in among the others? Possibly, but he couldn't recall having done that, wasn't really convinced he had. He pushed the bother aside.

On top now for his consideration was a photograph of two emeralds. On the Kalali loss list these were described merely as two matching, unmounted emeralds of twenty carats each.

According to the photo they deserved more than that, Mitch thought, much more inasmuch as color was foremost when it came to emeralds. These appeared to be the ideal, deep, vibrant green that Mitch always compared to the green of crème de menthe.

Another thing. Their appraised value, indicated on the loss list, was one hundred fifty thousand.

Two stones at twenty carats each.

Forty carats in all.

That put them at only thirty-seven fifty a carat.

If they were as good as they looked to be in this photo they were worth several times that.

Strange.

Upon closer examination of the photo Mitch noticed what seemed to be scratches on the faces of the emeralds. Perhaps, although unlikely, unless they were deeper and more damaging than they looked, the scratches might be the depreciating factor. But then, they weren't scratches at all, Mitch realized. They were inscriptions, in what appeared to be Arabic.

He'd seen numerous carved emeralds, of course, but never any such as these. Usually the ones chosen to be carved were of lesser quality. These were fine. The only explanation for that would be they were old, Mitch thought.

The inscriptions.

It occurred to Mitch how they were going to cost some fence, how the buyer would contend that the emeralds, inscribed as they were and thus easily identifiable, were worth less than what the fence was asking. Mitch imagined the gist of the dialogue.

The buyer would make an offer slightly above the ridiculous level.

The fence would scoff and say the inscriptions could be polished away.

The buyer would say then go ahead and have them polished.

The fence, eager to have the incriminating swag out of his possession, would curse the inscriptions under his breath and take the buyer's offer.

So it would go.

Mitch looked up.

There stood Detective Hurley, a Styrofoam cup of coffee in each hand.

"Thought about calling but decided to come on up," he said, placing one of the coffees on a free spot of Mitch's desk. The pressure of his grip caused a puff of steam to come from the hole in the cup's lid. "You ought to keep your door locked," he advised.

"Thought it was."

"It wasn't," Hurley said. "What you working on?"

"Robbery over in Jersey, out of your jurisdiction."

"I got a call to help out on one over in Jersey." Hurley held his cup away from him as he snapped off its lid, so any spill would go on the carpet rather than him. He was wearing a tan summer suit fresh from the cleaners, a cotton and mostly polyester kind of suit. The jacket wasn't buttoned because Hurley had gained weight since the previous summer. He was thickly built to begin with and on him six gained pounds looked like a dozen. The tie he had on was an obviously old wide one, not a new wide one, and he hadn't tied it evenly. The narrow end was longer by a good four inches. He seldom got his tie even, and Mitch sometimes kidded him about that, told him: "Make a mark on the inside of your ties so you'll know where to start the knot. They have ties for teenagers like that."

"Who gives a fuck about a tie," was Hurley's attitude.

Now, as Mitch could have predicted, Hurley's attention went to the three framed photographs of Maddie hung on the far wall. He went up close to them, took in each for a long moment, seeming to draw from them, then nodded, evidently concurring with his private thoughts. "Some piece of work," he said. Nearly every time Hurley came to Mitch's office he paid the same homage and made such an observation. "You're a lucky bastard, Mitch," he said.

Mitch agreed.

Hurley grinned and took another lighthearted shot. "If Maddie could see how ugly you are she'd run." He blew on his coffee, gulped it and recoiled from the cup. "I apologize," he said, "not for insulting you but for bringing you this shit for coffee. To make it up to you I'm going to buy you breakfast."

Mitch gathered up the Kalali file, slipped it into a leather folio case and brought it along.

Hurley's city-provided Plymouth was parked at the curb with its engine idling, as though hoping to be stolen. With its black finish oxidized to gray and the numerous city scars on its body it looked like anything but a souped-up police car.

Hurley drove them up to Wolf's Deli on 57th. They took a table by the window. From there it was easy to imagine the outside was the inside confined by glass, and that they were outsiders, spectators of everything that passed. Sort of aquarium-like.

Hurley knew what he wanted for breakfast, quickly ordered a pastrami four-egg omelet and home fries. Mitch took longer, considered several such heavy entrees, but retreated to a bowl of oatmeal.

During the waiting period Hurley inquired: "How's your brother?"

"He's up in the Adirondacks somewhere with Doris. She

has a place up there. I think it's near Canoga Lake. Ever been up there?"

"No."

"Nice this time of year."

"A real jewelry junkie that Doris."

"Yeah."

"She really so loaded?"

"I guess."

"From what I hear she married well and divorced better."

"Something like that."

"She's known around as the holdout's best friend."

"I've heard," Mitch said, not wanting to hear it.

"Must be a sickness, not being able to look at a piece of pretty jewelry without wanting to own it. Think it's a sickness?"

"I think guys exaggerate, especially swifts and fences."

"That's a fact. Still, there's something to what's said about this Doris. Andy's been close with her how long now?"

"Going on a year."

"That long, really? I didn't think it was that long. So, okay, I'll give them another six months."

"Who are you, the general in charge of romantic rations?"

"I'm being generous with six."

"I like Doris," Mitch said solidly.

"She ought to lose twenty, thirty pounds. She'd be a stunner."

"I like her because she's as vulnerable as she is smart and because whatever she's bringing to Andy is making him happy. Furthermore . . ." Mitch paused and emphatically aimed his next words, ". . . when it comes down to it, I also happen to be a jewelry junkie."

The breakfast was brought.

Mitch's bowl of oatmeal looked typically sad. A sprinkle of sugar improved it some, made its surface glisten, and a pat of butter cheered it up considerably. However, then the butter was unwilling to melt and Mitch had to push it under with the round of his spoon. He wished he'd ordered eggs Benedict.

Hurley, meanwhile, was putting away his big omelet.

Mitch studied him some, forgave him for his cynical forecast of only six months for Andy and Doris.

Hurley had never been married but been as good as. To a girl he'd helped out of a jam and quickly gotten to know and love. About eight years ago. He was thirty then, she twenty. They'd hit it off from the start. He more than her, but it seemed that she'd catch up. They lived together, did all the usual things that people hoping to couple do together: painted kitchen cabinets, bought shoes, adopted cats, kissed votively.

The one consequential thing they didn't do together was her habit. Despite his being an experienced cop he didn't realize she had a habit until her habit had her, until in her head her habit came before him and she resorted to being cunning. Used his love for her to provide that which she had to have.

He took to shaking down cocaine dealers and bringing their packets home to her. On his time off he'd cruise Brooklyn streets, preying on dealers. They got to know his car, knew him for what those in the underbelly call a take-off guy. They disappeared when they saw him coming.

She often complained about the quality of the dope he brought her, demanded better. He'd never done the stuff, didn't know what better was.

One very late night he shook down a young dealer out in Bensonhurst. He should have known. It was too easy. The guy was obvious right out there on the corner of 20th Avenue and 78th Street, didn't run or resist, just whined protests and motherfucked him a lot. Gave up two fat packets that Hurley brought home to her. Eager to please. He should have known.

She freebased the stuff and it killed her.

Exactly as the young dealer, on behalf of the other dealers around there, intended it to.

These days Hurley lived alone on the West Side in a two-window, fourth-floor, rear apartment. Said he didn't need anyone, and when he couldn't live up to that he called certain numbers and got professionally serviced.

He could have done better, wasn't a bad-looking guy, had

all his dark brown Irish hair and agreeable green eyes that more often than not smiled when his mouth did.

He nudged Mitch. "Eat your porridge."

"Don't want it."

"Why'd you order it?"

"It appealed to me abstractly."

"Isn't that the way with so many things? Anyway, you should have had it with raisins. I knew you were going wrong when you didn't stipulate raisins. Does Maddie feed you oatmeal?"

"No."

"I wouldn't think so. She's not the oatmeal type."

"Shows how much you know."

"Tell me, what's this Jersey case you're working on?"

"A guy and his wife over in Far Hills took a major hit, over six million."

"And the guy got whacked."

"You read about it."

"Happens to be the case I'm on. The Jersey local and state people figure the swag might show up here. Which of your clients stands to lose?"

"Columbia Beneficial."

"That being that, maybe we shouldn't give it our best effort." Hurley was aware of Mitch's bad feelings towards Columbia and his reason for them. "On the other hand, if you recover you make a nice score, don't you?"

"Yeah."

"Count on me for help."

"I appreciate that."

"I'll throw leads your way, keep you up on any developments."

"Thanks."

"For a cut," Hurley added. "Say a fifth."

"A cut?"

"That way we'll be more in it together."

Hurley seemed serious, Mitch thought. He'd been helpful

on a couple of Mitch's cases but hadn't asked for anything in return and had declined when Mitch offered.

"I've already got something for you," Hurley said. "Could save you time, might even ultimately lead to recovery."

"Like what?"

"A fifth," Hurley pressed.

"Okay, a fifth."

"Make it Jack Daniel's," Hurley laughed. "In fact make it a case of fifths."

Mitch regretted. "Really," he told Hurley, "I'll cut you in."

"Forget it. I don't need it."

"Who doesn't need money?"

"True, but I think it would be bad for us to go commercial. Down the line it could cost what we've got."

Mitch thought Hurley was probably right.

Hurley waited a beat, stabbed up what remained of his home fries, waited another beat. "When I stopped by the preese this morning word was the Jersey people were holding somebody."

"Who?"

"Puerto Rican by the name of Donnell Costas. He was the Kalalis' driver. Maybe they knew or maybe they didn't that he had a rap sheet."

"Any robberies on the rap?"

"No, but two burglaries back in the early eighties when he was seventeen, eighteen. One was suspended, the other cost him a year and a half. More recently he did serious time in Auburn and various other joints."

"For what?"

"Driving a van of hairs [furs] that had lost its way between a warehouse on 35th and a retailer uptown. Claimed he didn't steal the load, was just driving it for some guy, wouldn't give up the guy or say where he was taking the hair, just stood up and did the time."

"Not many stand-up guys like that anymore. Have they got evidence to connect him to this thing?"

"Not that I know of. When they picked him up at his apartment in Irvington he was packing to run."

"Can't blame him for that. He had to know he was jammed up."

"He was also packing a snub thirty-eight, which is enough to put him back inside."

"What's your guess?"

"Who the fuck knows with these kind. They go from the lightweight to the heavyweight division in a night. Anyway, we'll have a better picture of the whole thing when Mrs. Kalali comes conscious. If and when."

"What hospital is she in?"

"Right now Elizabeth Mercy but her doctor wants her moved over here to New York University, his hospital."

"Whoever popped her must have left her for dead."

"You'd think they would have put four or five into her to make sure."

"That could be the break."

"Yeah, but for now Mrs. Kalali is flirting with the angels."

CHAPTER 6

At that moment in room 1118 of New York University Hospital Roudabeth Kalali was headed above in the direction of consciousness.

Below lay oblivion, a dark red, vacant realm of immeasurable depth where she'd been effortlessly suspended. A pleasant state, really, as quiet as an agreeable thought and void of responsibility. It had been as much Roudabeth's preference to remain there as it had been to leave; however she was compelled to ascend, as though she was lighter than this atmosphere, an etheric shape made up entirely of will. How long would it take, this strange rise? Time was without consistent character, meaningful one moment, inconsequential the next. Forever seemed as possible as never.

Above was the surface, a plane between somewhere and somewhere, between within and beyond. Ungeometric, illusory, and yet she now came to be pressed lightly against some sort of substantial inner underside, contained by it. It was like being trapped beneath the ice of a frozen-over pond, although she was having no problem breathing. Each breath promised there would surely be a next.

Was it only to pass the interim, or was it to pay off debts with explanations that her memory began having its way? Numerous gates of her memory sprung open, experiences rushed out, impressions competed for recollection.

A date came to her, clearly, like a title.

January 16, 1979.

Mehrabad Airport, Teheran.

It was the bright but cool afternoon of Shah Pahlavi's departure.

She, Roudabeth, was there, along with husband, Abbas. Among the Shah's entourage of fifty or so.

The Shah took off his homburg—he kneeled, bent and kissed the ground. The built-up heels of his black shoes were evident. The humility of his arched back. Did his lips actually touch the ground?

Queen Farah Diba could not entirely conceal her disapproval of this, the Shah's final gesture. She waited close by. Perhaps she sighed intolerantly. She looked away.

The Shah stood nimbly, gave no attention to where the kneel had soiled his trousers. He was in black, suit and topcoat, with a black and white diagonal striped tie.

Queen Farah had on a gray cashmere coat, belted snugly. She appeared more detached than solemn. Her plain pearl ear clips were an intentional understatement. There was no way of telling how much extravagant jewelry was contained in her oversize shoulder bag.

They, the Shah and Queen Farah, continued onto the jet, the Shah's private 707. Most of the entourage was only seeing off. Roudabeth and Abbas were included in those going along. The plane already had the belongings in its belly, the many packed trunks and all. Precious layers between layers. Precious stuffings in the toes of socks and the fingers of gloves. It was a getaway, a haul.

The boarding stairs were in place. Queen Farah was first to go up and in. Then the Shah. His black back was the last of him. He would pilot. He would fly himself away.

There were no questions regarding what or how much was taken. There hadn't been the indignity of a search. Thus, at thirty-thousand feet it had occurred to her, Roudabeth, that the jet was rigged to explode, that it might never reach Egypt.

Memory is documentary.

A personal newsreel of sorts that now cut to November 28, 1978.

Roudabeth and Abbas were at the house of the Shah's sister, Princess Shams. Forty-five kilometers west of Teheran. Shaharazad, the Princess's daughter, was also there. The four were seated munching apricots and pistachios, pomegranate seeds and strips of sugared ginger, drinking a vintage sauterne.

A phone call was expected from General Nassiri, head of Savak, the secret police. He had arranged for another sortie, as such undertakings had come to be called.

Princess Shams specified what she wanted taken for her. She laughed and said her age required embellishment. She was sixty-one. Shaharazad rattled off what should be gotten for her, as though placing an order. Abbas was feeling important, telling jokes he'd memorized from *Playboy* magazine. His phlegmy laugh, wide-open mouth. There was nutmeat impacted between his tea-stained teeth. Roudabeth recognized the opportunism in his eyes. She knew his eyes.

The telephone chirped.

General Nassiri would meet Roudabeth and Abbas at the Niavaran Palace. Princess Shams' limousine transported them. Crystal vials hung on the uprights of the car's passenger windows contained wilted springs of lavender freesia. Night was coming on. The limousine outsped it to Kheyabun-e-Sa-ad-Abad. They were shown to a remote room in the old Qajar section of the palace where they changed into suitable clothing. Roudabeth into a much worn, faded blue chador and veil, so she was only eyes and hands. A chador with extra deep pockets. Abbas, meanwhile, got into old, ill-fitting trousers, shirt, jacket and poor shoes. He had the appearance of one of those cheap labor sorts who, hoping to be hired to do anything, gathered each morning in Gamruk Square.

The General arrived. Roudabeth hadn't seen him since the

previous sortie three months ago. He seemed shorter and thinner, as though the imminence of deposal was depleting him.

Only three persons knew the most recent code and had a key: the Shah, the General, the Director of the Bank. Now the General handed over his key and revealed the code. Abbas repeated the code aloud several times to memorize it.

Within minutes Roudabeth and Abbas were under way in a poor, abused Peykan. Going south on Kheyabun-Vall-ye-Asr. That major street was deserted except for the military trucks that roared by. And the rebel factions that were bunched at corners. Black-hooded Shah-haters with automatic rifles and knives in their belts. Night was their accomplice. Overcome with fervor they charged across the street. All at once they were in the Peykan's headlights, hundreds pouring around and over it as though the little car was a boulder in a river. Roudabeth was terrified, grateful for disguise.

There were other similar incidents along the way into the center of the city. A left on Kheyabun-e-Takhit-e-Jamshid and a right on Villa brought them to Sevome-Isfand. Abbas parked the car behind the Officers' Club. If stopped they were to say they were janitors, lowly floor scrubbers.

They scurried through a maze of back alleys. From times before they knew the way to the rear of the Central Bank. It was a formidable, contemporary building, a fortress for wealth, normally impregnable but that night with a traitorous rear door.

The Director of the Bank was waiting just inside. He allowed them in. Not a word from him. His part done, he departed. As far as anyone was concerned, he'd never been there.

There were two vaults: one for money, the other for the hoard. The latter was subterranean, down a long, wide flight of hard-edged steps. There it was, with an electronic pad on the left: ten numerals and ten symbols.

Abbas entered the code. He got it right on his second try. The time lock deactivated, the bolts automatically retracted.

Abbas pulled the vault door open. It was massive, steel two feet thick, but it swung open easily. Immediately inside was the steel gate. The key opened it.

They were in.

The lights were on. No need to hurry. They couldn't be caught. They were one with the catchers.

First, there on a pedestal was the Pahlavi Crown of State with a white aigrette sprouted above a diamond the size of an apricot, and that above an elaborate diamond and pearl diadem.

Paired with it on the pedestal was Queen Farah's crown, created eleven years ago by Van Cleef & Arpels. Huge carved emeralds, thirty-four rubies, one hundred and five pearls, one thousand four-hundred sixty-nine diamonds for Farah Diba's head.

Roudabeth and Abbas disregarded the crowns, as well as the numerous tiaras. Even the tiara that displayed the world's largest rose pink diamond. The size of a peach pit.

Nor was the famous Peacock Throne given so much as a glance. Never mind that it was gleaming all-over gold studded with twenty-seven thousand precious gems. It might as well have been a commonplace chair the way Roudabeth and Abbas passed it by to be deeper in the vault.

The vault was large, about twenty feet wide and twice that long. It had built-in drawers all around and glass cases containing solid gold goblets and bowls, swords and daggers with gem-encrusted scabbards and hilts. One long island of shelves held trays of polished uncut emeralds. Emeralds piled haphazardly like so many ordinary river pebbles. Emeralds, emeralds, loose emeralds by the thousands. They'd been so long undisturbed a fine dust had coated them.

Roudabeth took one up, just any one from the top of a pile. She rubbed it on the sleeve of her chador before appraising it. A beauty! The most desirable emerald color, a vivid, eloquent green. She dropped that one in her pocket and went on from tray to tray, selecting a few emeralds here, more there, more and more. She was a finicky shopper. Only the finest would do

Next she put to pocket two strands of priceless ruby prayer beads. Fulfilling one of Princess Shams' and Shaharazad's stipulations. Then there were pearls in a large gold casket. Such an abundance of pearls they overflowed, cascaded and swagged over the casket's edge. Cream and white and pinkish strands of huge, incredible pearls. Roudabeth looped her neck with strand after strand. She was lost in the Persian plunder, the booty, the hoard. A thief with permission.

She slid open one of the large cabinet drawers. It was lined with black velour to softly accommodate a thick layer of faceted emeralds. So thick a layer that when Roudabeth scooped up a handful the remaining plenty filled in the loss.

From another such drawer she took a handful of rubies. Then came a heaping handful of sapphires, double handfuls of diamonds of two carats, three carats and larger. Now her every move caused clicks in her pockets and she could feel left and right the heft and bulge against her thighs.

Abbas had been similarly busy. He too was laden.

They went as they'd come, locked as they went, and soon enough were again under way in the Peykan, again having to run the gamut of the incited black-hooded packs on Kheyabun-Vall-ye-Asr. If they'd been stopped with their precious cargo they would have surely been killed.

At Princess Shams' house the contents of their pockets were emptied onto a sheet. The Princess and her daughter were delighted. They eagerly picked through the spread of gems, were entirely caught up in them until Princess Shams remembered to reward Roudabeth with a few pieces, casually tossed them to her.

A few also went to Abbas. He had to feign his gratitude, did so excessively. Because secreted within the sleeve of his poor jacket, between its outer material and its lining, was a veritable fortune.

Hospital room 1118.

The duty nurse entered. She checked the intravenous infusion Mrs. Kalali was receiving, its drip rate and connection. All was well. The unconscious Mrs. Kalali lay unchanged, absolutely still, and, as far as the nurse could tell, not having a thought.

CHAPTER 7

Mitch had Hurley leave him off on 50th Street at one of those *while you wait* places that did graphic reproductions. He ordered six copies of the Kalali photographs. The clerk there, a paper-faced young fellow whose lips looked as though they were shedding, told Mitch it would take an hour.

Mitch didn't see why inasmuch as he was the only customer, asked why.

The clerk did the New York thing, deliberately crumpled up and discarded Mitch's work order invoice.

Mitch handled it, did a smile from his New York repertoire, the one that begged pardon and asked for leniency.

The clerk filled out another work order.

While you wait is right, Mitch thought on the way out.

He went to the corner. Bought two pounds of big black grapes from a street vendor. Sat in the mid-morning sun on the bank of the stream of Avenue of the Americas, that is, on the raised ledge that bordered the pool and fountain of the IBC Building. Come noon, office people would be on this ledge, having their brought lunches. Tuna salad and marijuana would be in the air.

At the moment Mitch was alone there, digging rather automatically into the brown bag for grape after grape, storing their seeds in his cheek until they were many and then, careful of passersby, jettisoning them with maximum force.

It occurred to him that despite his well-dressed appearance, his loitering there at this hour might cause people to take him as one of the recently unemployed, a guy whose clothes hadn't yet gone shabby or out of style, a jobless guy who was still shaving every day.

Three hundred thousand and some.

That, Mitch reminded himself, was how much he stood to make if he recovered the Kalali jewelry. Possibly those goods had already been sucked up and taken apart by the street. Maybe not. Maybe the street wouldn't ever get a look at them because they had gone to Los Angeles and on to Hong Kong. No, that wasn't how it would go, his optimism predicted, he'd be lucky, the stuff would practically fall in his hands.

His pager beeped.

He went to the pay phone down the way and dialed his office.

Shirley was in her strictly business mode, recited his messages without gripe or comment. There'd been another *please return my call* from Visconti and Ruder had phoned twice suggesting lunch or, if not lunch, at least drinks later. Ruder hadn't believed when told Mitch wasn't in.

Mitch wondered why Ruder was reverting. He'd thought he had Ruder conditioned. As for Visconti, now that could prove to be timely.

He'd left the bag of grapes on the ledge. It was gone. He returned to the graphics place. His photos were ready, had been for half an hour. He'd specified that they be collated in sets and placed in individual gray envelopes, and that was how they were.

He walked down Avenue of the Americas to 47th. He felt suddenly changed, more assertive. It was as though the sight of the street and its prospects had injected him. He crossed over against the belligerent traffic and turned in at the entrance second from the corner.

The Capital Jewelry Exchange.

A deep, narrow place strongly lighted by spotlights on tracks. Typical of 47th. There were identical, contiguous counters with display cases that ran its entire length on the left and on the right. Each section of counter was a booth-like space occupied by a separate business.

No major dealers here. The seller of pearls on one side offered mainly *biwas*. Opposite, the merchandise was 14k gold chains sold by weight. Next, wristwatches, various makes of inexpensive digitals. Then came gold charms: French poodles, tennis racquets, names such as MaryLou and Rosalie.

Nothing better.

The counter-to-counter carpet of the center aisle wasn't living up to the claim that its geometric pattern wouldn't show dirt.

Mitch walked on it, went straight to the back, ignoring the verbal hooks that were cast at him. *Let me show you something. How about a nice pendant? I need the money. Take your pick at half price.* He resented that in their practiced eyes he was being taken as a chump.

A door in the back gave to a steep, narrow stairway up. Lighted by a bare hundred watts. The vinyl-covered steps of the stairs were gritty and edged with nailed-on metal stripping that in places had come loose enough to trip. Fifteen steps up was halfway up. At that point was a landing with a shallow alcove.

Snugged into the alcove was a daybed covered in red Naugahyde. The guy who got up from the daybed was one of Joe Riccio's have-around guys. He wasn't tall but he was big, with such a gut his trousers in profile were triangular.

Mitch took it all in: cigarettes grounded out on the floor, a bag of Cheetos on the daybed along with an overhandled porno magazine that had on its cover a hard-faced blonde grinning around her foreshortened buttocks. On the wall above the daybed an intercom. The have-around in a pink, short-sleeve shirt wasn't wearing a piece, although no doubt there was one within easy reach beneath the daybed.

The have-around blocked the way. "What do you want?"

"I'm here to see Riccio."

"Sure you are. Got an appointment?"

"Yeah, Mitch Laughton."

"For this morning?"

"Yeah."

"I think not. Riccio ain't seeing nobody this morning. He told me."

"Look on his agenda."

"Okay, asshole, down you go." The have-around crowded Mitch with his belly.

Mitch avoided it. "Don't contaminate me."

"I'll break your fucking face, that's what I'll contaminate."

Mitch did a take that stopped everything. He focused his interest on the guy's eyes, craned forward a bit, scrutinizing more closely.

"You wearing eye shadow?"

"Huh?"

"It's smudged. Your eye shadow. The left eye."

"You calling me a fagala?"

"You're also quick." Mitch indicated the intercom. "Call up and tell Riccio I'm here. You're bad for business. When I see Riccio I'm going to tell him you cost him."

"Fuck you. All I got to do is press that red buzzer and three cowboys will come down and rip your head off."

"And all you'd do is watch, right? What is it, you afraid you'll break a fingernail or something?"

The guy fisted his fat right hand and swung.

Mitch easily sidestepped it.

The momentum of the miss carried the guy forward in a sort of clumsy lunge, spun him on his fat legs so now his back was to the stairwell. While he was trying to recover his balance Mitch brought his foot up to the guy's gut and shoved.

The guy grabbed at the air as he went over backwards, pitched down the steep stairway, caromed from wall to wall with the sharp edges of each of the fifteen steps hurting grunts out of him all the way to the bottom. He lay there face up.

Mitch peered down at him, thought the fat of the guy

should have cushioned and prevented serious injury. Maybe not, though. The guy wasn't moving.

But then suddenly he was up and coming up, awkwardly clambering on all fours, gorilla-like.

Mitch had time to think how much he disliked this kind of guy, how this sort seemed to always bring out a mean part of him. It wasn't anything personal.

The guy's hands got to the landing. He tried to grab Mitch's leg.

Out of sympathy Mitch didn't kick him. A kick was in order and would have been easy, but, instead, Mitch merely gave the guy's face a push.

The fall the guy took this time was about the same, looked and sounded just as painful. He lay sprawled in a contorted position at the bottom of the stairs and, from the sounds of his moans, it was doubtful he'd attempt another climb.

Although the way was cleared now, Mitch had second thoughts about continuing on up to see Riccio. Before getting to Riccio there'd be more have-arounds to contend with and if he managed to get past those there would be Riccio's routine.

All Mitch had wanted was to exchange a few words with the man and leave with him a set of the Kalali photographs. But Riccio would never allow only that. He was an advocate of old-mob ways, slow, snaky, respect and all that. He'd insist on having espresso poured into merely rinsed cups and a couple of petrified anisette cookies placed on the saucers along with tiny stainless steel spoons.

Riccio would conversationally circle the reason for Mitch's unscheduled visit with irrelevant observations and opinions and throw in a mob anecdote here and there. As though he had all the time in the world and Mitch wasn't suffering the place with its cheap, tasteless furnishings. Black synthetic carpet with such a high pile it looked like a million writhing worms and no telling what might be hiding in it.

At times Mitch had given thought to that carpet and how many loose diamonds and other precious stones must have been carelessly dropped to it out of the many thousands of carats Riccio took in and dealt out. Mitch could imagine Riccio down on his knees searching the deep black for several D flawless caraters he'd accidentally sent flying from their unfolded briefke paper diamond containers when he put his feet up on his desk. An agitated, grumbling Riccio digging around in the tendrils, not finding, finally giving up and trying his best to put the loss out of mind. In that carpet a fortune lost.

Mitch looked up the stairs and knew what would be imminent. Riccio would sit there, backgrounded by a repaired wall enameled an avocado shade and punctuated by the faded prints of the Virgin and a De Beers magazine advertisement, and Mitch would have to endure Riccio's invitation of congeniality, his latter-day version of all the spaghetti suckers and mustache Petes he'd ever seen portrayed. Not for an instant admitting how anachronistic he was, he in his pointed, black, cap-toed shoes and white silk socks and overstarched shirt. A one-of-a-kind pinkie ring. Pavéd ruby, diamond, emerald version of the Italian flag.

Mitch had been up there in Riccio's lair maybe a half dozen times.

If he went up now he'd again have to stifle how amused he was by Riccio's voice. A voice too small, too thin, too high-pitched for any mobster, especially one who took such effort to come off as one. It was as though at age thirteen his pubes had refused to drop.

Riccio was well aware of this shortcoming, tried to overcome it by speaking breathily with as little throat as possible. So, Mitch, if he went up, would have to strain to hear him, would miss words and have a hard time keeping from laughing when Riccio's temper took over and he cocksuckered and scumbagged someone in his natural upper range.

Joseph Riccio.

He'd come quite a ways since back when he was an all-around, have-around guy for Nick Russo, when Russo was running the diamond district for the people who got answered to. For nineteen years Russo was the man those in the trade went to when the bank said no way. There was hardly a dealer on the street who at one time or another hadn't strung out what he owed the bank beyond the bank's tolerance. Many dealers were excommunicated for eternity by the bank's computer.

Such unfortunates were some of Russo's best customers.

Russo was also the man a dealer went to for fast money. When an opportunity came along that had to be jumped on right away or be lost. A packet of emeralds, for instance, nice Muzos that some coke mule from Columbia showed up with and was willing to let go at only slightly more than half what they were worth. Or a lot of nice-quality diamond rough that a black had carried in a white handkerchief all the way from Sierra Leone.

They came up, such chances, when going to the bank for a loan was out of the question. The bank would want to know all and require a week or so to process its forms.

Russo, on the other hand, wasn't interested in knowing anyone's reason for borrowing and there were never any papers. Ask for the money at eleven, it was there by noon, or sooner, politely delivered in a brown paper bag or a shoe box.

With the first week's interest of ten percent taken out in advance.

No matter, it was fast money, and also no matter that it was black money, the proceeds from pornography, extortion, numbers, bust-out bars, hijacking and the like. The important thing was it was there when needed, available with no more than a phone call. Forgive the usury. Whoever gave that illegal aspect much of a thought?

Thus Russo was a fixture on the street. In his criminal way a benefactor. Without him most of 47th wouldn't have been able to conduct business and many of those that could wouldn't have profited nearly as much.

That was especially true of the fences, guys on the first level of swag who worked teams of swifts. Russo was always there for them. He was the next level, a fence for the fences. He bought from established fences only, those that he knew, the dozen or so. He never bought from an unconnected swift or slick-looking jewelry crook.

"Someone told me you might be interested in something."

"Someone was wrong," Russo would say.

"Let me show you."

"Keep it in your pants."

However what the fences brought usually got bought. Russo was wise in the ways they did business and invariably he got the best of them. They were, he knew, like two-hundred-dollar whores who could be negotiated to lie down for fifty.

Swag.

Regarding it, Russo set some smart rules for himself. Like never keeping a piece of stolen jewelry intact for any unreasonable length of time, which to Russo meant no longer than an hour or two. Normally, a major piece that he'd acquired, say, a diamond necklace, would be broken up within minutes. It made no difference to him that the necklace was exceptional, made by Cartier or Van Cleef or whoever, he was merciless. Out came the stones, the gold and platinum tossed into the smelting crucible.

He had no appreciation for beauty.

And it was said of him that he could pop stones from their mountings by merely looking coldly at them.

Joseph Riccio was one of Russo's favorite have-arounds. One of.

Furio Visconti was just as much a favorite.

Russo played them against one another. Probably he figured that way he got more out of them. Eventually, when Riccio was made Russo's right hand, there was Visconti just as close on the left.

For years that's how it was. Russo telling Riccio he was number one in line and, practically in the same breath, telling Visconti the same. So, it followed that when Russo didn't have the heart to wake up one morning and forever, both Riccio and Visconti felt eligible to be allowed to take over the street.

It wasn't something they could settle amicably. They went at each other as early as during Russo's wake at the Scalise Funeral Home up on 188th Street, and again at the funeral. Scuffled and threatened around grave markers and consecrated ground and had to be restrained.

The suggestion was made that the way to settle the matter was the old way.

A sit-down.

On a sweltering Thursday afternoon in August Riccio and Visconti were transported in separate cars by guys they didn't know to the house of a man they'd only heard of. An unremarkable house on the Connecticut blacktop road between New Fairfield and New Milford. With a mailbox bearing the family name right on the road, as though that name didn't deserve to be self-conscious. House with aluminum siding and a screened-in rear porch overlooking a garden of zucchini and peppers.

They, Riccio and Visconti, sat on the porch in yellow canvas director chairs across from the old guy years past his days, who hooded his creamy eyes and did a great many nods and made a protruding lower lip so they would believe he was listening to their claims.

Riccio was in mob heaven. The only thing missing was an invisible orchestra playing *O Soave Fancinella*. Being in the presence of this fabled consigliere awed him, caused his little voice to go tremulous.

"I knew your uncle," the old guy said at Riccio, which made Riccio feel that he had an edge, until the old guy added: "Your uncle was a *spuce*.

"As for you," the old guy said at Visconti, "you probably think *bris-cola* is a soft drink."

Visconti knew it was a Sicilian card game but figured it best to let the old guy have his opinion.

The old guy announced that he had to take a leak. He went into the house, leaving Riccio and Visconti to ignore one another. Riccio craned up to get a better view of the garden. He would have stood but thought that might not be proper once one had sat at a sit-down. He considered complimenting the old guy on the garden and maybe make a point, but then he didn't know shit about gardens except that old guys like this one enjoyed fucking around in them and that was where he'd seen Don Corleone die six or seven times.

The old guy returned with the decision in his mouth. He'd had it in his head all along, even before they'd arrived, could have said it right off but knew some mob theater was expected of him.

He remained standing because to sit would probably give the impression that he intended to prolong this matter. He wanted to go down to Danbury and have the tires on his Lincoln rotated and get some fresh batteries for his flashlight so he could watch the raccoons try to beat the electrified fence he'd had put around his peppers and zucchinis.

He didn't say his say directly at either Riccio or Visconti. He aimed his words between and over their heads, focused on the screen where there was a blotch of bird shit. In a monotone that made it sound more like an indisputable decree he told them they were both good boys, they both deserved. Told them Russo had spoken equally well of them numerous times. (Actually, he'd only met Russo once about twelve years back when he needed a new stolen wristwatch.) Therefore, he concluded, it was fair that they both be promoted to caporegime and both have the territory.

Half each.

Riccio was to have everything from address number 39 to Avenue of the Americas and around that end of 47th.

Visconti would have everything the other way, from address number 38 to Fifth Avenue and around that end of 47th.

Shake hands.

Embrace left and right.

And the thing was done.

Except for the tribute, the cost of the sit-down, so to speak.

A hundred thousand was the figure mentioned, and to mention was like presenting an already overdue tab that would, if not promptly paid, be put into collection, so to speak.

Riccio and Visconti had to hustle around to come up with their parts of the hundred. The old consigliere got sixty of it. The two guys in the Bronx who'd arranged the thing split the rest.

Grazie.

Had Russo not died so soon this sit-down might never have taken place. The dispute between Riccio and Visconti over West 47th very likely would have fallen through the cracks of the old mob, because it was right about then that the old mob bosses— Persico, Salerno, Corallo, Rostelli and Castellano— as well as many of their minions, their underbosses, capos and soldiers, were being hit with federal grand jury indictments.

Unlike those times before when they'd been rounded up and brought in merely to rub them the wrong way or just for election headlines, this time what was at stake was serious time and there was a new thing called RICO, the Racketeer Influenced and Corrupt Organizations Act, to make the charges stick.

What a barrage of charges!

One hundred thirty-five counts against the top Genovese guys alone. One hundred twenty against the Lucchese leaders. Altogether, over five-hundred counts. Which, when translated into sentences, would mean consecutive lifetimes of time inside, would mean dying in the joint, getting out only after rigor mortis had set in.

Their mouths had brought them to this, their old-mob arrogance and their spillways mouths.

"How much he come up with?"

"Sixty-five, an extra five for being late."

"The piece of shit saying he was strapped."

"You smacked him pretty good. His fucking ear was bleeding. Fat Tony don't want him dead. He couldn't pay if he was dead."

"I hate poor-mouth late payers, that's all."

"Yeah. Listen, stop someplace when you see a place. I want to get a paper. You hear any more about Angelo?"

"Just that he's got to be done."

"*I mean when.*"

"*When Fat Tony says.*"

"*You give a shit what happens to Angie?*"

"*No.*"

"*You used to hang out with him a lot.*"

"*What happens, happens.*"

"*Makes no difference who it was that straightened him out. For what he did the cocksucker's got to get done, him and maybe his whole fucking family.*"

"*Whatever Fat Tony says.*"

Mouthing, while all around was infested with bugs. The government had them. The old mob on over a hundred hours of tape. (What should they have done, become mutes and taken up singing?) They shouldn't have trusted the dashboard of their cars or the water tanks of their toilets, not even the heels of their shoes.

Worse, they shouldn't have trusted one another.

Soldiers and have-arounds who'd been theirs and in on all sorts of moves for years shed their covers and revealed themselves as having been federal good guys all along. Not only that. Guys they should have been able to be positively sure of, properly initiated guys they'd known since childhood whose legacy from made fathers and made grandfathers was to uphold that old-mob honor, old-mob respect, old-mob everything, were turning out to have been turned sometime along the way, were, behind their *goombah* faces, informers.

Cacchio! Shit! What was this world of theirs coming to? The silence that had been the code and, in so many instances, been painfully, sacrificially kept, had given way to giving up. Giving up people, places, amounts, killings, anything to the federal District Attorneys in exchange for not having to do all their remaining years in joints where the brightest prospects of any tomorrow would be a game of boccie.

Even the underbosses, counted on to be the most stand-up of stand-ups, decided they'd rather kneel and offer to plea-bargain. It got to be a matter of who had the most on who.

Three of the older guys conveniently developed chest pains, were unable to get a deep breath.

Good riddance bad guys.

Arrivederci old mob.

Never to be the same.

Riccio and Visconti weren't among those held accountable. They got looked at and then were overlooked. None of their transgressions, terrible as they might have been, were mentioned on the taped conversations. They weren't notorious enough for anyone to use in plea bargaining and they hadn't been tight enough with the up-top mob guys for the government prosecutors to press out of them anything that might be helpful in those prominent cases.

Ironically, just as much a reason for the government not including Riccio and Visconti in the thick of it was the street.

The prosecutors regarded West 47 as a rather separate community with distinctive, shadowy ways. If they went digging and charging into it they'd be opening too complex a side issue, something, with its glittering appeal, that would surely distract from their main performances. They decided to leave 47th, including Riccio and Visconti, as it was and perhaps they'd take it on at some future time when their plate wasn't so full.

They never did.

Riccio loathed the transformation of the mob. The self-image he'd promoted all along refused to make room for any such change. He vowed that no matter what, even if he had to go it alone, he'd keep on keeping on, being loyal to the ways of his forebears. One day he suddenly claimed he was related on his mother's side to Albert Anastasia of Murder, Incorporated. He'd considered making it Meyer Lansky but that would have been contrary to the qualifying, pure Sicilian line and, besides, he favored Anastasia's legendary ruthlessness.

Riccio also enlisted only have-around guys with mentalities similar to his own.

Such as the fat one that Mitch had just moments ago shoved down the stairs twice. Mitch wasn't paying attention to him now, was hesitating there on the landing halfway up to Riccio, indecisive about those next fifteen steps. Thinking Riccio might want to again show off his new electronic money-counting machine, insist on demonstrating it, and Mitch would have to stand there and watch while in mere seconds the thing counted out a hundred thousand or two. "Just like they got in the big banks," Riccio would boast, which would cause Mitch to perhaps or perhaps not hold back cutting across Riccio's old-mob grain with a remark that the money counter was a *new* thing, a big improvement from the *old* days when it took all night for guys to count the take.

Mitch made up his mind.

Instead of going up he wrote on the face of one of the gray envelopes that contained a set of the Kalali photographs:

"Joe—take a look at these and call me."

He included his business card, tossed the envelope onto the daybed, gave the summoning button of the intercom a sure, long press. Went down where the fat have-around was expecting a kick, so sure of it he had his hands over his groin like a cup-jock.

Just stepped over him.

CHAPTER 8

Coming out of the Capital Jewelry Exchange, Mitch told himself that his passing on a personal visit with Riccio hadn't been a shirk.

The purpose of the visit had been to determine whether or not the Kalali swag had already found its way to and through Riccio. Not that Riccio would have admitted right out that he'd bought it; however, chances were, in keeping with his style, Riccio would have allowed Mitch to read him by replying with his eyes and doing an appropriate, lopsided, mob guy grin.

Mitch believed that the way he'd handled it, leaving the series of photos and a vague note, would accomplish the same determination. That is, if he didn't hear from Riccio he would assume the swag was gone, was no longer in its Kalali form and it would be a waste of him if he went chasing around hoping to recover.

On the other hand, if Riccio bothered to phone and wanted to know about the photos, it would indicate, at least as far as Riccio was concerned, the case was still alive.

Mitch headed east on the north side of 47.

It was busy now, normally so, its various elements into their usual concerns.

Carriers were out, dispatched by dealers whose offices were in the buildings above street level. Unexceptional-looking types, better for that reason, hurriedly threading through the crowd with gems on their person worth perhaps a hundred thousand or more, bound for the eyes of someone in the trade, another dealer who had a call for such goods, or a cutter or a maker.

Hasids stood out uniformed in their black long coats and trousers. Gone shiny in the seats and elbows. Home-laundered white shirts buttoned at the collar, no jaunt to the way they wore their wide-brimmed black hats, as though jaunt would be sinful. Black and white men shunning color and haggling in Yiddish. Their inventories in their pockets, their offices the curbs.

Swifts with residual stealth in their walks, given away too by their expensive running shoes, designer jeans, T-shirts printed with the name of exclusive resorts they'd never spend a night at or a university that wouldn't admit them. In pairs or threes they conspired, tried to agree upon which dealer might pay most fairly for the piece of swag they'd held out from last night's thievery. A two-carat diamond perhaps, freed from the prongs of an engagement ring that had been held dear for years and rarely taken off. A formerly meaningful diamond reduced now to impersonality, a mere stone.

East Indian dealers. Emerald and ruby melee their specialty, calibrated green and red nearly as tiny as Christmas glitter. On the sunstruck south side of the street their burnished complexions seemed to have a somewhat aubergine cast and, at a distance, they appeared well-dressed. However, at closer range it was apparent their suits were cheap, pressed while soiled, their cuffs frayed and the tight knots of their ties grimed. They were not well-liked in the trade because of their distrustful dispositions.

Sephardics, genuinely congenial but shrewd, and good-hearted but underhanded Armenians, and compulsively aggressive Israelis. More Israelis than ever, leaning insouciantly against the doorjambs of their shops, their dark eyes sharp to spot likely passersby that they tried to spiel in.

Wives from the suburbs. Dressed in smart numbers from Ann Taylor, clipping along on hardly worn heels. On their way with elevated heart rates to a recommended 47th gem dealer, a friend of a friend who they naively believe will show them the best and charge them the least.

Ex-wives past the point of keepsakes or sacrifice, merely wanting to divest themselves of the accumulations of ten to twenty anniversaries and other futile occasions.

Then, of course, there were the sightseers. How easy it was to pick those out, as they scalloped along from window to window, vainly trying to appear blasé to what seemed to them to be exhibited treasure troves. Everything placed just so under the most helpful lights. Numerous black or gray or white velour-covered shallow boxes propped up diagonally for advantageous display, symmetrically slotted to accommodate rings, twenty slots to a box, four rows, five across, every slot occupied by a diamond ring. Some of the rings had small hand-printed placards in their proximity, saying: *"radiant cut"* or *"one day low price"* or *"5 carats"* or *"visibly flawless"* or any of an assortment of exemptible 47th fibs. *"Not quality enhanced,"* was one the sightseers didn't comprehend. They whispered to one another: *"Can't be real, look at the huge one in the top row, I'd be afraid to wear it, do you think they're real?"* The precious stones sizzled their eyes, seemed to enjoy belittling the jewelry they had on.

Mitch, with his appearance and attitude, could hardly be mistaken for a sightseer. However, the way he usually walked that block was to some extent similar, the way he was seldom able to resist looking into a few windows.

This day was no exception.

About three-quarters of the way to Fifth his legs insisted he stop before a shop that he knew featured estate jewelry. Quite a few attractive pieces were displayed. Mitch appreciated a pair of chalcedony, black onyx and coral ear pendants, and a pair of ear clips of pavé set yellow diamonds, and a diamond and rock crystal jabot pin.

Then he spotted it, off to the right, recognized it immediately. The cushion-shaped blue sapphire. It greeted him with a flare of its eternal bright blue, and he mentally replied:

Hello, old friend. Where've you been? Haven't seen you around in quite a while. Remember when we first met? Must have been ten, maybe twelve years ago. You didn't have that calibré-cut diamond border then, but I know you. I must say you're looking sharp, none the worse for all you've been through. Bought, stolen, reset, sold at auction, stolen, bought, stolen, and so on. And now, here you are again, back on the street again, being offered again. Nice to see you. Maybe you enjoy being repeatedly bought and being owned and being stolen and coming back here, but it seems to me you'd be better off occupying one lovely finger for a lifetime. It's not your duty, of course, and, anyway, you're not alone in your transientness. Half the goods on the street keep making the cycle. See you around.

Mitch continued on to Fifth and entered the 580 building. He passed through the security checkpoint in the lobby and took an elevator up to the fourteenth floor.

At the far end of the corridor on fourteen was the substantial paneled door to Visconti's office. PARAGON GEMS, INC. gold-leafed on it. The door opened before Mitch was halfway to it.

A man stepped out.

A distinguished-looking man conscientiously dressed in a light gray gabardine vested suit and black and white wing-tipped oxfords.

Mitch was at a range that permitted a complete look at the man. The swarthy, foreign complexion, the bushy black brows and the dark hair tight to the skull arranged straight back. He was in his mid-fifties or possibly in good shape in his sixties. He had a black-banded creamy panama hat in hand. He paused to put it on, was adjusting it just so as Mitch approached.

The man acknowledged Mitch with a single stranger-to-stranger nod. Mitch returned it. After going a short ways in their opposite directions they caught one another glancing back.

A foreign dealer, Mitch thought, or perhaps one of Visconti's wealthy Italian privates. Not anyone he'd ever seen around the district but certainly someone he'd remember if he ever saw him again.

Mitch entered Visconti's.

The offices had been redone since Mitch was last there about a year ago. The modest-sized reception area impressed. A pair of Louis XVI beechwood armchairs offered as seating on the left were upholstered in pale blue silk damask and were matched identically by another pair on the right. On the wall directly ahead hung a seascape so large and realistic that Mitch's imagination smelled ocean. Situated below the painting was a mahogany bureau plat inset with a blue leather writing surface and bordered by ormolu. Lighting was indirect and kind. The unobtrusive music was Stravinsky.

The surface of the desk was clear except for a dark blue intercom phone, a notepad contained in dark blue leather and a dark blue lacquer and gold DuPont fountain pen. The .44 caliber semiautomatic pistol in the right-hand drawer would probably also be blued, Mitch thought.

Behind the desk sat a young man in his late twenties. Another about the same age was sentried beside the closed door that evidently gave to where business was conducted. They had such mannerly ease and were so comfortably well-dressed they looked as though they were ready to pose for a *GQ* ad. Mitch knew them as two of Visconti's have-arounds and, as such, they typified the polarity of style between Visconti and Riccio.

New mob and old.

Mitch's intention was to elicit Visconti's cooperation at arm's length as he had Riccio's, by leaving a set of the Kalali photographs and a similar cryptic note. However, when he handed over his business card the young man behind the desk immediately got on the phone and announced him, and, before Mitch could say much else, the inner door was opened for him and he felt obliged to go on in.

Visconti's private office was buffered by an interior hallway. The door to it was closed and Mitch was left to open it on his own, a privilege of sorts.

Visconti came around from behind the desk, bringing a handshake and doing a smile that, even after the preliminaries, he didn't turn completely off.

"Nice of you to drop in," he said. "I called you a couple of times."

"I happened to be in the building."

"Great. I was about to have some tea. Have some with me?"

"Thanks."

"There's coffee too if you prefer."

"Tea's fine."

"Earl Grey?"

"Fine."

"I never used to drink the stuff but an English actress I spent some time with down on Mustique got me hooked on it. Maybe you know her." Visconti said her name.

Mitch knew of her, of course. A well-known. He wasn't surprised that she and Visconti had been socially or otherwise close.

"Ever been down there to Mustique?" Visconti asked.

"No."

"Lovely island, very exclusive. I wanted to buy a place down there but the fucks wouldn't sell to me. How do you like that?"

"Their loss," Mitch said liberally.

Visconti didn't resume behind his desk. He sat with Mitch on the visitor's side.

"My reason for phoning," he said, "was to invite you and your wife to my house in Watermill this coming weekend. I'm having a few people to dinner Saturday." He named a fashion designer, and a motion picture director who was in town to promote a major summer film that wasn't doing as well as expected. "You could come out Saturday and stay over."

"I'll have to consult Maddie. Seems to me she had something planned." Mitch's evasion wasn't meant to sound as obvious as the way it came out. He was a little embarrassed. He detected resignation in Visconti's expression.

Visconti eased the moment by calling attention to a painting on the wall to the left, a Jasper Johns flag. "Woman had it," he said. "Actually it was her husband's. When he died recently I traded her something for it."

Which meant to Mitch that Visconti had gotten it for next to nothing, just some swag material he'd paid little for.

The Jasper Johns was slightly awry. Visconti got up to straighten it, giving Mitch an opportunity to update the man.

He was slight-framed and of average height. About the same age as Mitch but looked older because of his high forehead and a hairline that was beginning to recede. He was wearing a white, amply cut silk shirt, triple-pleated cotton slacks tapered at the ankle and a pair of Superga tennis shoes. No socks. No jewelry.

It occurred to Mitch that he didn't really know Visconti as well as he thought. He'd never spent much time with him; there'd never been any discussions over drinks, or for that matter, any lengthy business dealings, just professional brushings every so often. Over the years it was actually their reputations that had mingled and thus, acquaintance was a sort of illusory effect.

On the whole, unless one was able to look close and long, Visconti didn't appear to be what he was. He had the demeanor of a successful, legitimate entrepreneur, someone smartly on top of his game, comfortable in his skin, nervousness never apparent. That was the impression he hoped to achieve. He promoted it, campaigned, ever trying to have the exposed side of him accepted as a sensitive human being with utmost regard for life's higher aspects.

For example, the poster he had hung in his office, better

positioned than the Jasper Johns. Anyone entering would
have to notice it right off. A large framed poster for a retro-
spective showing of films by the director Luchino Visconti.

The Leopard, The Damned, Death in Venice.

Furio Visconti claimed the director was an ancestor.

He backed up that claim convincingly with dates and
places, fond memories and proved opinions gleaned from the
extensive research he'd done. Luchino Visconti, the films
and the man, was a topic Furio Visconti would cleverly bring
a conversation around to and not allow to be quickly
dropped.

Only once or twice was he questioned about the Visconti
line that preceded *Uncle Luchino*. Each time he managed to
parry and sidestep. He'd read and knew quite a bit about the
Viscontis and how prominent they were in Northern Europe
during the fourteenth and fifteenth centuries. Were, through
the female side, related to such dynasties as the Valois of
France, the Hapsburgs of Austria and Spain and the Tudors
of England. No, he didn't want to get into all that. It was too
much of a better thing, too rich for his blood. And, regarding
blood, while the Viscontis were a Milanese family, his own
was Sicilian. Necessarily so for him to have been at such a
young age conferred with the mob's coveted *made* status. His
true legal name was Vescotini. His grandparents, like so
many others who entered the country around the turn of the
century, had lost the proper spelling to the impatient processing on Ellis Island.

From the various efforts Furio Visconti put out and kept
up, it might have been thought he was trying to polish away
his capo self. Quite the contrary, he was new mob. He wanted
the duality. But if ever he were to be confronted with having
to make a choice between sensibility and menace he'd have,
without a second thought, opted for the latter. Because he enjoyed it. Just as much as did his old-mob-style counterpart at
the other end of the street.

"Tell you what, call your wife now and find out about the

weekend. That way, if it's okay with her, I'll be able to look forward to it."

Mitch did a glance at his watch. "She'll be in the middle of a lesson."

"What's she taking?"

"Giving. Guitar lessons." Actually this wasn't one of Maddie's lesson days. At that moment, Mitch thought, she was probably putting fresh water in the aviary and feeding her lady finches. He had no intention of mentioning Visconti's invitation to her, knew that if he did she'd want to accept, insist on accepting. Not because of the social amusement or the possibility of an after-dark beach stroll, for some extemporary al fresco loving in the lap of a dune. Rather, the allure for her would be the prospect of sitting on a terrace until long after dinner with Visconti and a couple of his have-arounds, drawing from them recollection of mob escapades, smart moves, big scores, justifiable paybacks, graphic tall tales and short from genuine mob mouths, underscored by wafts of alyssum and the concussion of crickets. She'd love it.

Visconti stepped back to see if he'd corrected the hang of the Jasper Johns. It looked straight to Mitch but Visconti gave the lower right hand corner of its frame a slight tap before he was satisfied. He returned to sit, asking: "Ever play the big casino?" Meaning, of course, the stock market.

"Used to some, not recently."

"Who's your broker?"

"The Bear."

"I get a good thing now and then, a can't-miss thing. Next one I get I'll give to you, as long as you promise it won't go any further. Most guys, when they get something sure can't wait to let others in on it. Like they've got a fucking list of people they want to have owe them. You're not that way though."

"How can you tell?"

"I got a sense about people. You, I want to get to know better. We'd get along."

Mitch thought actually Maddie might not be seeing to her birds at that moment. She'd be making the bed, stretching, tucking, smoothing the sheets and plumping the pillows by spanking them as though they'd been naughty. Before Maddie he'd been a one-pillow sort and more often than not that one ended up tossed to the floor during the night. She'd turned him into a steadfast, multi-pillow man. The head of their bed was piled with as many as eight European squares filled with finest goose down and cased in high-count shams. Each night he and Maddie sunk together. He sometimes wondered how it felt to her in her black, that soft, sinking escape. He'd closed his eyes to help him imagine but he was sure it wasn't the same.

"I've something I want to show you," Mitch told Visconti. He reached for his folio to take out a set of the Kalali photographs.

But just then the tea came.

It wasn't just tea, not just in mugs as Mitch had expected. One of Visconti's young have-arounds wearing a fresh white waiter's jacket brought it. On a huge silver tray, ivory handles. The matching silver service was of art deco design, unusually refined with hardly any surface decoration.

Mitch recognized the pieces as creations of Jean Puiforcat, believed by many to be the foremost French silversmith of the twenties and thirties. Worth plenty, Mitch thought, and wasn't it miraculous that the swift who'd stolen the tray and tea set hadn't banged them up? Usually such things were carelessly thrown into a knotted sheet where, in the lugging and all, they traded dents.

Also on the tray were several doileyed dishes precisely arranged with Sarah Bernhardts and cat's tongues and madeleinettes and a variety of crustless half-slice sandwiches. Altogether quite a load that the have-around, as physically well-conditioned as he appeared, was relieved to place down on the low table between Visconti and Mitch.

"I'll take it from here," Visconti said, dismissing the have-around. He lifted the lid from the tea pot, peeked in, sniffed, before pouring into the two elaborately hand-painted bone china cups. "Sugar?" he asked.

Mitch didn't have time to reply.

"You shouldn't, you know. Sugar is bad for the prostate, and . . ." he grinned conspiratorially, ". . . the last thing we want to go is the prostate."

"I prefer honey."

"There isn't any."

"Plain is fine."

They slurped. Mitch felt the rim of the cup click against his lower front teeth. Visconti seemed pleased to have company. Did he go to such elegant ritual when alone? Mitch wondered. It was certainly a far cry from Riccio's dirty espresso cups and stainless steel spoons.

"What was it you were about to show me?" Visconti asked.

Mitch handed him the gray envelope.

Visconti slid the photographs from it. He looked through them, giving each a moment but coming back for a second, longer look at the two inscribed emeralds. "So?" he said.

Mitch told him what the photographs were, how these pieces of jewelry had been stolen three nights ago, that one of the owners had been killed during the robbery. It seemed to Mitch that Visconti only half listened.

"What do you want me to say?" Visconti asked.

"Nothing if these pieces have already found their way to you."

"There's blood on the fucking stuff. I wouldn't touch it."

Mitch doubted that was a line Visconti had ever drawn. He got Visconti eyes to eyes for a long moment. The man wasn't easy to read. He was adept at hiding whatever he chose behind whatever he chose to reveal in his eyes and facial expression. Only when he allowed were his eyes and mouth in accord, so a person seldom knew which to go by.

Mitch decided to believe him in this Kalali matter. "All I ask is if these pieces come in or get offered you let me know."

"Why?"

"Only so I don't waste time trying to recover."

"That's it?"

"That's it."

"I got no problem with that. I'm not saying I'll call you up and tell you straight out but I'll let you know some way."

"However."

Mitch went for a couple of the madeleinettes. They were dusted with powdered sugar. He was sure his prostate could handle it.

"One condition, though," Visconti said.

"What?"

"If and when *you* recover the stuff you let *me* know." Visconti didn't give Mitch a chance to ask why. He stood abruptly. "Now I've got something to show you," he said and left the room.

Mitch poured more tea and had one of the Sarah Bernhardts and then two more by the time Visconti returned. Bringing a protective black flannel pouch drawn and tied by a scarlet grosgrain ribbon.

Visconti handed the pouch to Mitch, who gathered that he was expected to open it and that it contained something valuable.

Which turned out to be a *bonbonnière* or what was called a *boîte à bonbon* back in the 1700s. This particular one was circular, about three inches in diameter and an inch deep. It was finished in translucent pink mounted in borders of finely chased gold. The circumference of its lid was embellished with a row of old-cut diamonds. Such little boxes were used to hold dragées for sweetening the breath back then when most breaths were so badly in need of sweetening.

Mitch appreciated it, ran a finger delicately over the diamonds and pressed the one located at six o'clock. The hinged lid sprung open. Nothing inside.

"Lovely," Mitch managed to say, hearing his voice as though it originated outside himself.

Visconti waited for more. When he realized that was all

the reaction he was going to get, he told Mitch: "Don't ask me. It's natural you'd want to know but don't ask. All I can tell you is it came in week before last and evidently the same guy, anyway the guy's daughter, has had it all the while."

Mitch did a shrug.

He clicked the *bonbonnière* shut and put it back into the pouch. Placed the pouch on the table. "I've got to get going," he said. "Can I assume we have an understanding on the Kalali material?"

"Yeah, sure. What's Kalali anyway? Sounds East Indian."

"Iranian."

"They've got a hard-on for us, the Iranians."

"Some do."

"Let me know about the weekend." Visconti did a goodbye smile. No handshake. They'd already done that and once a day was sufficient.

Mitch saw himself out, through the reception area with the eyes of the have-arounds on his back. He was about ten strides down the corridor when Visconti hurried out to catch up with him.

"I suppose you're aware of what your brother's into," Visconti said.

An immediate, purely reflex nod from Mitch. "Andy and I never keep anything from one another."

"I thought that's how it was but I wasn't sure so I didn't mention it."

"I wondered if you'd bring it up," Mitch said, fishing.

"But why Riccio," Visconti exaggerated slightly. "If he was going to run an errand, why not for me? Riccio's no friend."

"Andy's decision," Mitch said while thinking the long-shot wish that it wasn't true, that it was only something Visconti had heard.

The street was like that.

Along with its held tongue there was always a lot of bad-mouthing.

CHAPTER 9

The first pay phone Mitch tried digested his quarter but didn't give him a dial tone. On the next he and secretary Shirley could hardly hear one another.

"Where are you?" she asked.

He told her. He'd made it as far as the lobby of his building and almost into an elevator.

"You don't sound like you," she said, "not at all well."

"I'm okay."

"Perhaps, but you don't sound it."

"What's happening?"

"Just Ruder."

"So, close up."

"I've some filing and a couple of letters you think I've already done."

"Take off. Go somewhere and lay away something."

"I might. You've probably got a touch of the summer flu. Do your bones ache?"

"I'm going home," he told her, and within the minute he was outside heading up Fifth, dragging. He would, he thought, go straight home, get way up there in the Sherry with Maddie and forget there was a down here.

However, when he got to 50th and St. Patrick's he went in,

and it seemed that radical change of atmosphere would be a palliative for his condition with its meek light, votive candles jigging, serious prayers barraging the altar with supplications.

He sat in the very last pew, distant enough from everyone and practically hidden by a fat pillar.

To take it on.

All at once rather than have it eat at him a bite at a time.

He gazed down at his hands. They were empty, relaxed on his thighs, but felt as though they were still holding the past.

That *bonbonnière*.

Twenty years ago it was among the estate pieces his father, Kenneth Laughton, brought back from a buying trip to London. At first sight Mitch had been attracted to the box and, when his father tagged it and placed it along with other merchandise in one of the store's display cases, he'd boyishly put a hex on it that he hoped would prevent it from being sold. At the same time he created a romantic story for the box, caring to believe it had early on belonged to a woman of nobility, a woman whose beauty and exceptional taste excused her numerous carnal caprices.

Mitch's attachment to the *bonbonnière* was not unnoticed by his father. Hardly a day passed that Mitch didn't wipe possible finger smudges and motes of dust from its pink and gold exterior, and press the six o'clock diamond on its lid to have it spring open, as though providing it with the exercise it required to keep agile.

His father understood.

Hadn't he at one time or another experienced the same sort of fondness for a thing so pretty?

Mitch expected any day the *bonbonnière* would be sold. He was prepared to accept that event, but weeks went by and it didn't sell and he noticed its coded price tag had been removed and he overheard his father inform a customer that it wasn't for sale.

Thereafter the *bonbonnière* was spoken of as Mitch's box. It hadn't ever been formally presented to him, was only possession understood, but it was his. He kept Läkerol lemon mint pastilles in it. Right up to the last.

It was about that time that Kenneth Laughton made the move of his dreams. From on Lexington in the fifties to on Madison in the sixties. A corner location. What's more, the oblong shape of the space and the relatively intimate size of it, only four hundred square feet, lent itself nicely to being made elegant.

K. Laughton and Sons.

Within a few months the business had established its cachet. No ordinary run-of-the-mill manufactured merchandise; it carried only estate jewelry and only the finer level of that.

Nearly every piece Laughton's offered came with an interesting or colorful or notorious past. Much more appealing was a one-of-a-kind diamond choker that had known the neck of a one-of-a-kind demimonde, pieces of another age in their original fitted cases that had been the conciliatory gifts to the wives of caught-straying robber barons, pieces from the not so long ago when the daughters of scions were marrying for titles and diamond tiaras and crotch-length strands of pearls were *de rigueur*.

The precious bijouterie of snooty English ladies and stars of the silent screen and Ziegfield show-offs who'd worn little or nothing else—could be found at Laughton's.

There was, of course, only a limited supply of such finer jewelry. Kenneth Laughton had to seek it out. He went on what he called hunting trips, sometimes accompanied by Mitch or Andy or both, to Geneva, St. Moritz, Milan, Monaco and other likely places. He and his sons were also prominent at the Sotheby and the Christie auctions. They'd be pointed out and when a particular piece was knocked down to them that usually verified its value. "Laughton got it," people would whisper and make that notation in their sales catalogues.

Often lovely pieces came to the store, brought by misfortunates embarrassed by the need to sell but rightly under the impression Laughton's would not take advantage of their plight.

A pair of Winston ear clips for instance.

"Why certainly Mrs. Whoever, we'll clean them for you."

"That's most kind of you."

"No bother, no bother at all. It will take only a few minutes."

"While we're at it, I was wondering, could you give me an idea of what they're worth? To you, I mean."

Others, whose fortunes had ascended, brought in pieces wanting to trade or leave on consignment. In fact, much of the Laughton stock was left by owners to be sold.

"Why in the world would you want to part with such a lovely bracelet. It's Van Cleef you know."

"I never wear it. It's a hand-me-down from my bitch-from-hell aunt. Anyway, I'm bored with it."

Many of those were frail, spindly-looking, overdieted women with scalpeled features, addicted to self-indulgence.

Mitch had learned to recognize their requirements. He knew how to wait on them. For one thing they didn't want him to be too well-mannered. Nor did they ever want to be called ma'am. At times he found them amusing, forgivable, and more often than not, his good nature was sincere.

All in all, Laughton and Sons was doing well, and there seemed to be no reason why it wouldn't continue to do so.

Came then the bitter cold morning, a Monday in February. The events of that day had had such a long run on the stage of Mitch's memory that he knew their every word and nuance.

To begin with, at about nine-thirty, a half hour before opening, Harvey Miner phones, to say his wife has fallen on the icy sidewalk. She has fractured her hip and he's at the hospital with her and won't be in until noon or one. Sorry.

Miner sounds unlike his usual laconic self, stressed, but considering his circumstances that's understandable.

Miner is the armed security man for the store, has been for several years. A retired cop of formidable height and bulk, intimidating even when he smiles. Normally, during business hours, Miner stands inside the entrance, from where he can watch over what's going on in the store and, as well, scrutinize and pass on those who wish to come in.

The entrance is arranged to prevent anyone from just walking in off the street. There's an outer and an inner door, both of thick glass heavily framed: and between the two is a vestibule that will accommodate no more than three persons at a time. The bolt of the inner door is electrically controlled. A button to activate the bolt and click it open is located inside within easy reach of where Miner stands. A second such button is located on the underside of the main display counter.

So, Miner won't be in until later and that's not important because its doubtful there'll be anyone out spending on this kind of day. It's punishingly cold. No sun and twenty degrees below freezing. The sidewalks and buildings along Madison appear brittle and depressed. There's no fast traffic to speak of and the cars and buses stopping and continuing along are coated dull with winter chemicals, their undded with frozen muddy slush.

Still, like most other shops along the avenue, Laughton's is making ready. It is routine, the transferring of merchandise from the vault to the display cases and windows. Mitch and Andy and Kenneth pitch in and by regular opening time at ten the task is done.

At ten-thirty it's a welcome surprise when a customer comes from the street into the vestibule. A woman. Her impatience is apparent. It's as though she fears that if she's not immediately allowed in, the cold, like a monster, will catch up with her and consume her. And it is that impression, along with her qualifying well-off appearance, that prompts Andy to hastily click open the inner door.

Then she is in, standing there in calf-length sable, hunkered down, her head surrounded, nearly buried by the collar of the abundant fur.

"Damn cold!" are her first words.

She does a shiver, then sits and removes her expensive shoes. She rubs her feet vigorously to warm them. In front of strangers a self-confident, assertive act. She owns the world.

Through her sheer stockings Mitch sees the snug, enforced arrangement of her toes. Her toenails. Its seems too intimate. Her reddened nose and cheeks look as though they've been sharply pinched.

She's quite beautiful, Mitch thinks, anyway, a lot more attractive than most. Her hair and ears are contained by a black, wrapped turban which is pinned by an art deco period diamond, ruby and onyx jabot. A nice piece that Mitch's expertise makes out to be an authentic La Cloche Frères.

Also, she has on dark brown kid skin gloves. Outside the gloves on the second finger of her right hand is a large ring studded with various colored sapphires. Mitch appreciates that show of independent style.

A gasp from her, and another shiver. "I only walked over from Park," she says plaintively, "and I'm frozen to the marrow. One has to be mad to be about on such a day."

It's difficult to feel sorry for her, Mitch thinks, this lovely, privileged woman, temporarily uncomfortable. Her manner of speech is throaty, contains broad vowels with diphthongs here and there. An affectation that has probably become a habit. Mitch would never forget her voice. Later on, in one public place or another, he would hear a similar voice and be disappointed when he saw it wasn't her.

Kenneth asks her would she care for some coffee.

No thank you.

Kenneth suggests a glass of port.

She tells him archly that it depends on the port.

A twenty-year-old vintage finest reserve W. & J. Graham is presented, approved with an *mmmm* and poured into two finely etched claret glasses. Two because Kenneth won't allow her to drink alone.

In three uninterrupted swallows the port is down inside her and she is saying "Ah, that'll do the trick. May I have another?"

Kenneth obliges and that second portion limbers her. She ceases hugging herself. She slips back into her shoes and allows the sable to fall open enough to reveal a good, ample

sling bag. The dress she has on is expensive but rather over-
stated, inappropriate for a winter Monday morning. Mitch
thinks she should know better and must have her reason.

A paragraphic moment.

"What can we do for you?" Kenneth inquires.

"For one thing," she replies lightheartedly, "let my husband
in. After all, he'll be paying the bill."

There's a man in the vestibule. Dressed in black. Well-
tailored double-breasted topcoat, leather gloves, small-fig-
ured silk scarf.

Kenneth clicks the inner door open.

The woman calls the man Charles. He looks to be somewhere in his fifties. He gives her a brief hug and apologizes
for being late. "Have you been waiting long?"

"Yes," she lies.

"I would have been on time but there was a call from
Rome."

She forgives him with a smile and a slight shrug.

Mitch notices the man has a powdered face, aftershave
powder that is a bit light for his complexion. Also, his shoes
aren't up to the rest of his attire. They're round-toed, thick-
soled, made to last ten or even twenty years with visits to a
cobbler. Policeman shoes or those of a train conductor. Perhaps he has a foot problem, Mitch thinks.

Kenneth offers the man coffee or port.

The man declines with a gesture and asks the woman:
"Have you chosen anything?"

She tells him she hasn't and he removes a pair of gold wire-
rimmed eyeglasses from an inside pocket, puts them on and
begins considering the pieces on display in the wall cases.

The woman, meanwhile, gives her attention to the main
counter. She peers down through the glass surface to the items
arranged just so. So many beautiful pieces. A diamond and
ruby *sautoir* catches her eye and refuses to let go.

Kenneth is quick to realize her interest. He removes the
necklace from the case and places it upon a cushiony square

of black velour on the counter. "Exquisite, isn't it?" he says almost objectively.

She takes up the necklace, holds it up, enjoys examining it.

Kenneth pitches gently, informs that it once belonged to an heiress who, in her time, had been—how shall he put it?—a very free-spirited debutante.

A knowing grin from the woman. "I must have it," she exclaims.

It happens swiftly.

She drops the necklace into her sling bag. Her hand follows it in and comes out with the pistol. It has a silencer on it.

At once the man admits two other men. They go at it, methodically emptying the windows and the display cases, throwing piece after piece into Bergdorf Goodman shopping bags.

Mitch has never seen valuable jewels treated so harshly. He wants to tell the men to be more respectful.

The woman has moved to the open end of the main counter where she has a sure view of Kenneth, Andy and Mitch. The pistol she holds on them is barely visible, only the lethal tip of the silencer protrudes from the wide sleeve of her sable coat. Her expression has changed little. She's not apparently nervous and, although that's reassuring, better than having her jittery and overheated, Mitch believes it's best not to move.

There's an alarm button inset in the floor beneath the counter. Kenneth is making a try for it, inching his foot toward it. The woman seems unaware. The alarm is the silent sort, connected directly to the Nineteenth Precinct.

No warning from the woman.

She shoots Kenneth in the foot, the instep. It's almost as though the pistol has done it robotically, altered its aim, fired with absolute accuracy.

Pain clogs Kenneth's breath. What comes from him is a short guttural bleat. He slumps to the floor.

Mitch is surging with fury. There's an automatic pistol in the drawer to his left but his better judgment tells him he'd never get to it, his better judgment reminds him that he has always believed it would be best to not resist an armed robbery, that no amount of jewels would be worth dying for.

He and Andy and Kenneth are ordered into the vault, made to lie on the floor among the emptied vault drawers and trays and cartons. They're bound with their neckties and belts. Positioned as they are, right there before Mitch's eyes is the blood oozing from the tongue of his father's shoe.

He hears the robbers going. They are gone. Everything is gone.

The loss comes to twelve million. It seems an inordinate amount but the Laughton books prove it. About seven of the twelve is the value of goods that were Laughton-owned. The remaining five is the value of pieces that had been left on consignment.

There's insurance. A policy that all along promised complete coverage. For all its years Laughton's has paid the pricey premiums to Columbia Beneficial. However, now that there's been a loss, and such a large one, Columbia Beneficial says there are considerations.

A term in the fine print, not ambiguous or vague; it's right there, clearly a stipulation of the policy.

Keith Ruder, the Columbia Beneficial representative who handles the claim, is insincerely sorry to point it out.

In so many words what the term says is that security measures must include an armed guard inside the store during all business hours.

Which, of course, had not been the case.

No matter that Harvey Miner, the Laughton guard, had been under mortal pressure—a pistol held to the back of his head—that morning when he called in and recited the lie of his wife's injury.

Ruder seems to take personal pleasure in having found the loophole for Columbia Beneficial. Smugly, he says the extenuating circumstances make no difference. He refuses to budge from that stand, doesn't until Kenneth Laughton's lawyers get into it. Then Ruder budges only some.

The settlement.

Columbia Beneficial agrees to pay out six million. Kenneth must absorb the rest of the loss.

Five of the six million that comes from Columbia goes at once to make good on the jewelry Laughton's had on consignment. From what remains of the six Kenneth buys out of his long-term lease and pays his legal bills.

There's relatively little left. Not enough for Kenneth to start over. Besides, he's as empty as the store, can't stop grieving over all those precious pieces of jewelry, lovely tasteful pieces that he'd so carefully acquired, being put to death, so to speak, their gems extracted, their fine mountings sacrificed to some smelter's crucible.

He retreats, moves to the west coast of Florida, lives in a modest condo, sits in the sun, watches the sea, walks with a limp. He has a collection of canes, most of which Mitch and Maddie or Andy send him. His favorite and one most used is a nineteenth-century blackthorn from the West of Ireland. Another that he treasures once belonged to Lord Byron.

A tinny clunk imposed on Mitch's self-communion. Then several more of the same.

Coins were being dropped through the slot of the brass poor box situated a short distance from where Mitch sat in the most rear pew of St. Patrick's.

He felt much better, in a way exorcised. The aftereffect of the *bonbonnière* was gone from his hands and the performance for his past that it produced on the stage of his memory was over, at least for the time being, without so much as a curtain call.

Perhaps Visconti would sell him the *bonbonnière,* he thought, but then maybe it wouldn't be good to have around. No. Leave bad enough alone.

Off to his right where the pew ended at the main aisle Mitch noticed the comers and goers doing genuflects that were actually only slight bobs in the direction of the distant altar.

Ask for the moon but don't bruise a knee.

CHAPTER 10

The elevator attendant wasn't fazed by what he'd been hearing from the thirtieth floor on up. He was a New York serving sort with acquired terminal apathy, and if Mrs. Laughton was playing music so loud it went through the Sherry's thick interior structures like a sonic ray, he didn't care to know why.

Mitch, on the other hand, tried to imagine what Maddie might be up to this time. He recognized the music but didn't know the name of the piece ("Pena Penita"). It was a fast one by the Gipsy Kings.

Maddie played the Gipsy Kings frequently, but not like this, not at such a decibel that it caused Mitch's latchkey to veritably vibrate when he inserted it to let himself into the foyer of the apartment. Where the Gipsy Kings and their seven guitars were louder yet.

Usually, when Mitch arrived home, along with his first step inside he'd call out to Maddie, her name. Often she beat him to it, would call out to him to let him know which of the apartment's five rooms she happened to be in.

Mitch liked when that happened. It was evidence that her waiting for him hadn't been an ordinary wait but more a yearning honed and dilated with impatience.

There'd be none of that today, though. Not even a full-out scream would do. He went down the connecting hallway, glanced into the kitchen on the chance that Maddie might be using the music for frame of mind while having a try at some complicated, loudly spiced Spanish recipe.

But no, nothing cooking.

On to the living room, the Persian carpets there were rolled up and the chairs and tables were moved aside, creating an expanse of hardwood floor. The same in the adjoining study.

Maddie was in the study, standing between the stereo speakers. At point-blank range of their blast. She had one foot up on the seat of a side chair. The most she was wearing was her favorite Spanish guitar, slung by a woven strap around her neck. Otherwise only sunglasses with mirrored lenses and a pair of black patent pumps with klutzy heels.

The double French doors that gave to the terrace were wide open. The white skin and the windows of the upper reaches of the General Motors Building were like a backdrop closer than across 59th Street. A rhomboidal shape of sunlight was striking the floor, barely missing Maddie's bareness.

Her aviary, situated against the wall opposite the balcony, was also open. All her beloved finches were out and around. Some were making passes at her, attention-seeking swoops and dives, fluttering her forehead and shoulders. Bishop Weaver finches from Sudan, orange and black and brown. Twinspot finches from southern Ethiopia, brilliant green and polka-dotted. Several exact look-alikes were in a row on the top edge of the draperies, an audience in the cheap seats.

Mitch was certain Maddie had no idea that he was there across the room from her. She was completely caught up in keeping up with the Gipsy Kings, the fingers of her left hand scurrying up and down the neck of the guitar, working the frets, the fingers of her right raking the strings with such swift force it seemed she was inflicting punishment.

This afternoon interval was obviously meant to be Maddie's alone. Mitch felt the intruder; however, he rationalized, wouldn't it be wrong to interrupt, make his presence known?

Either he should leave, return to street level and perhaps go to a Central Park bench, buy one of those bags of overpriced peanuts and shell away some time or, the other option, remain undisclosed where he was, play the peeper, the adoring thief.

Watching her. From the start of them it had been a pleasant diversion for him. By now it had become a need. The extent that he indulged in it was, of course, made possible by her sightlessness.

He thought of it as stealing, but had long ago exonerated himself. How privileged he was to be able to steal like that, to witness so much of her physical privacy, unlike most others to never be deprived by self-consciousness or shame. The thing about it that bothered him, though, was its one-sidedness. Many times he thought the wish that he and Maddie could exchange circumstances for a while, let her have the advantage of seeing him without being seen. To have her steal and steal, learn his most intimate and private self and still want and love him, would, he thought, even them up perfectly.

He removed his suit jacket, tossed it and his folio onto the nearest displaced chair. He admitted to himself that not for a moment had he really considered Central Park over this. He slipped his tie loose, unbuttoned his collar and cuffs. Arms crossed, nonchalantly leaning against the jamb of the connecting wide archway, he gave in totally to being the compulsive spectator.

Look at her, just look at her, he thought, what a remarkable love she was. He wouldn't have her be any less unpredictable. He fed, thrived on her eccentricities.

The music didn't seem so loud now. With her as she was in his eyes the complaint of his ears was being ignored. The rhomboid of sunlight was creeping up on her, had overtaken a lower leg. She stopped playing, raised the guitar in order to get at a place to the left of her navel. Three scratches there and she went on playing, picked right up with the tempo and chords.

A pair of lady finches, evidently overcome by the need to be more involved, flitted from somewhere in the room to light upon the upper end of the guitar. They weighed next to nothing, so they weren't a bother. They improved their grasp, settled and hung on through the various bobbing and dipping motions caused by Maddie's playing. Just as they would had they been perched precariously on a bough in an erratic breeze. Tiny participants, they weren't startled enough to fly off even when in Gypsy flamenco style she thumped and drummed on the guitar's soundboard. They took the ride all the way to the vocal.

One of the Gipsy Kings sang it. He got a head start and Maddie had a devil of a time catching up. The lyrics were too rapid and run together for her just passable Spanish. No matter, in this kind of singing the meanings of the words weren't as important as the wail with which they were supposed to be coated. An effect accomplished by creating a stricture at the outlet of the throat in order to more emphatically convey the excruciating possibilities of love: love cruel or prohibited, misunderstood or, for any of the countless reasons, tortured.

The requirement of flamenco singing to be somewhere off the notes and seldom on them suited Maddie. She had a dreadful singing voice, couldn't even carry "White Christmas." It was as though she couldn't hear herself. When she went around attempting Broadway numbers for example, such as something from *Phantom of the Opera* or *Evita*, Mitch would wince and look sick. "Don't cry for me Argentina . . ." Ughh. He was thankful that no words had been set to Ravel's "Daphnis and Chloé," although there was Maddie's humming, which also had the disease.

Now well into her flamenco duet, faking it, keeping a partial beat behind so she could imitate, she got reckless, missed one of the higher notes so badly that she kept veering with it and was unable to recover.

She segued into a laugh.

Broke herself up.

She took off the guitar and set it aside. Mitch thought that next she'd switch off the stereo.

She stepped forward onto the bare floor. The bright rhomboid was like an inaccurately aimed spotlight catching the lower half of her. She raised her arms above her head, straight up and stiffly like a gesture of surrender, then relaxed them a bit and formed them into an arch, the wrists gracefully rounded, the fingers close to touching. She tensed her buttocks, tucked them, causing a thrust to her pelvis. Raised her chin, put stretch into her neck, turned her head a quarter turn so her point of view was away, over that elevated shoulder. All her weight was on her left foot.

What sort of posturing was this? Mitch asked the situation. Did she have in mind some sort of yoga exercise?

She snapped her fingers like castanets and began.

First, a single stomp with her free foot, the substantial heel of her shoe brought down with such force it was like the report of a shot.

It was now obvious why the carpets were rolled out of the way.

Maddie tattooed the bare, hardwood floor with her heels, did a rapid-fire series of flamenco stomping with both feet.

What came to Mitch's mind was the demonstrative protests of a spoiled child who hadn't gotten her way; however the incongruity of that association was at once made apparent by Maddie's mature figure, the way her movements were causing her fully formed breasts to respond, the triangular forest of fair floss at her intersection.

Now she went into long, dipping strides, an exaggerated, haughty prance and some swirls. Punctuated with exclamation points of stomping.

Where and when had she learned this? Mitch wondered. She was no María Benítez but obviously this wasn't her first go at it. The people who lived in the apartment below had never complained. As far as he knew.

Fists on hips, elbows out, she flamencoed past him and on into the living room. Typically, her attitude shifted from aloof to defiant to sensually promising. She knew the apartment by steps, its dimensions, so there were no collisions (another of her enemies, collision), only near misses. Even though Mitch doubted she was entirely there. With make-believe overlaid upon her blackness, something that was ordinarily easy for her, made easy by the blackness, she was probably somewhere in Spain. Seville perhaps. Being a Carmen.

On her way back from the living room she paused to flamenco in place a short ways from him. Facing him, she came closer, and even closer and did five sharp stomps that seemed to Mitch to be expressions of reprimand. He saw himself in her mirrored lenses. Their convexity distorted him, gave him a big, lopsided nose.

Maddie snapped her head back dismissively and spun away, holding the imaginary hems of imaginary flouncing petticoats.

The music ended.

The Gipsy Kings were gone.

The apartment had been so full of sound it now felt vacant.

Mitch, the spectator, was stuck in place by the sudden quiet. It wouldn't take Maddie long to detect him, he knew. She had collapsed over the fat arm of a sofa chair down into its lap. Was breathing hard. Should he speak up, pretend he'd arrived that moment, hadn't witnessed any of her performance? He'd merely inquire about the furniture being out of place, the carpets, and accept any fib she offered.

He'd do better than that.

He silently removed his shoes and stocking-footed it out to the foyer. There he put his shoes back on and, imitating his usual arrival, opened the entrance door noisily. Called out to Maddie. Slammed the door shut.

"In here!" he heard her shout, which reassured him that his ruse had worked. On the way to her he exaggerated the sound of his walk on the bare floor, his own flamenco. For some reason he felt a flush of well-being and realized it probably should be attributed to the stealing he'd done, his brain having processed it and triggered some neurotransmitters. Overanxious endorphins, no doubt. He'd gotten about a two-thirds erection while stealing Maddie, which, he had to admit, was rather gluttonous considering how erotically sated he'd been with her little more than a dozen hours ago.

She was still in the sofa chair, knifed cross-wise, legs over one of its arms, head resting upon its other. She was perspiring. Her hair was damp and stringy. Her mouth let it be known that it expected a hello kiss.

Mitch delivered it. An upside-down kiss, noses to chins, brief, not so brief that she didn't get in a single dart of her tongue.

What a rascal she is, Mitch thought. He was such a fortunate lover.

"Home early," she said.

"Rearranging the furniture?" he asked.

She didn't reply.

"Felicia's been helping you, I hope." The live-out housekeeper.

Mitch still didn't get the fib.

"Warm in here," he said after watching a rivulet of perspiration run from her collarbone to an aureole.

"The air conditioning is on," she said.

"Won't do any good with the terrace doors open. Besides, aren't you afraid your finches might fly out?"

"They wouldn't. They'd never betray me." The birds had returned to the aviary, were chattering, sounded as though they might be commenting on the merits of the Maddie performance and having an after-show bite.

Mitch went to close the terrace doors. He caught a glimpse of office workers gathered at some of the windows of the fluorescent-lighted spaces across the way. Gapers, voyeurs. What were they expecting, an encore? He was tempted to flip them off. Instead, he decided what had been had been and just closed up.

Maddie was gone into the bedroom.

Mitch put together a vodka and tonic and took a couple of gulps before attending to the carpets and furniture. He got everything back in position by the time Maddie returned.

She'd showered. Was now in a long, pale silk kimono tied

by a sash fringed on its ends. Mules of a matching shade with a pouf of Maribou on their insteps. She went directly to the sofa, as though knowing it was back in its familiar place. Sat and crossed her legs. The silk poured expensively around her.

"I'm having a drink," Mitch said, "want one?"

"Just a Perrier, thanks, and, as Mother Elise would put it, *avec glace.*"

While Mitch decapped the Perrier and poured he thought the wish that there was some way of obliterating Elise from Maddie's mind, cauterize her, at least stick her in some way out of the way sepulchral niche.

Maddie chug-a-lugged the Perrier and chewed on the ice. "I'm too fair-haired for a convincing flamenco," she said.

"Huh?"

"A black wig might help but I'd still otherwise be blonde. Unless, of course, I wore a merkin and that would be a mess and a bother. Anyway, you didn't seem to think much of my dancing."

Mitch tried to choose what he should say. Her teeth crunching ice didn't help.

"You didn't applaud or anything, not even a bravo," she said.

"How did you know I was watching?"

"I sensed you were."

"Don't give me that."

"I always know."

"Come on."

"Okay, I usually know."

A dubious grunt from Mitch.

"Sometimes I know," she admitted in a tone that implied rock bottom.

"Okay, where was I standing?"

She told him precisely. "I got a whiff of you when I went by and on the way back I zeroed in."

"You have an uncanny sniffer."

"At times it can be less than a blessing," she said. "Like this morning in the reception at Ronald's office. As you know it's

not all that large, and a man waiting there smelled as though he hadn't been able to wait ... more than once. Phew."
Ronald Albertson was her attorney, an earnest fellow, who looked after the interests of the Strawbridge family.

"So you went out this morning."

"Had to sign things."

"Couldn't they have been messengered to you?"

"I wanted to go out."

Mitch assumed her business with Ronald involved contributions she was making to her causes such as the United Nations Children's Fund and the World Wildlife Fund and AIDS research. She gave on a regular basis to these, and to numerous others when they appealed to her. It then occurred to Mitch that the Elise fund had made a pitch for a new apartment in Barcelona and decided that had probably been Maddie's business at Ronald's. What would happen, Mitch wondered, if she turned Elise down and instead gave to preserving the population of the Louisiana black bear?

"What was it with all that sneaking?" Maddie asked.

"Sneaking?"

"The way you snuck out to the foyer and slammed the door and all that?"

He was cornered.

"What a loony way to act."

"You should talk."

"Me? I'm unceasingly sane."

"I left my folio out on the landing," he fibbed.

She crunched more ice rather menacingly and then let him get away with it, did about a seventy-five percent version of her best smile; anyway enough of it to cause nice commas at the corners of her mouth. "I love you, precious," she declared unequivocally.

"Love you too," he said on the way over to her. They kissed a fairly lengthy one and held on after it. She told his ear: "I bought something for you today."

From her kimono pocket she brought out a small, leather-covered jeweler's box, gold-embossed and worn at its edges.

Fitted within the box's creamy velour interior was a pair of cuff links. They were Edwardian, guilloche green enamel and gold centered with rubies and diamonds. Even before taking them up Mitch believed they were Fabergé. And yes, there was the hallmark in Cyrillic on the underside of each line: ФАБЕРЖЕ along with Я.А., the initials of the work master Hjalmar Armfelt. "The man at the shop said they're the real thing."

"They are."

"He said people used to make Fabergé imitations and some still do."

"Yeah."

"He also said these had once belonged to Cary Grant, that they were a gift from Barbara Hutton when Grant married her in 1943. Believe that?"

Colorful provenance. Shades of the days of Laughton and Sons, Mitch thought. The cuff links must have set Maddie back at least twenty-five thousand. He took another admiring look at them before placing them back in their velour bed. "You shouldn't have," he said.

"Well, I have."

"Whoever you bought them from will take them back."

"No returns. He made a point of it. I'll bet it even says so on the sales receipt."

"How did you pay for them?"

"By check."

"Just stop it."

"No, you stop it. I know you like the cuff links. I heard your breath do a little catch right after I heard the box snap open."

"Not true."

"I listened for it."

"Whether I like them or not doesn't matter. The fact is you're way over your quota."

"It's a silly arrangement."

"It's what we agreed on."

"You bullied me into agreeing."

"I've never bullied you. Frankly I doubt anyone ever could."

"Okay, I'll put it another way; you suckered me into it. I was led to believe you'd eventually come around to seeing it differently."

Setting a quota had seemed to Mitch to be a solution. Until then Maddie had squandered money on him. Hardly a week passed that she didn't buy him something extravagant, something he himself couldn't so easily afford:

A thirty-four-thousand Gerald Genta perpetual calendar watch, a six-piece set of Hermès luggage (the overnight bag alone cost four thousand), ten suits in a range of fine worsteds and gabardines by the leading tailor in Milan (she sent his favorite-fitting one as a model and, for the while it was away, fibbed that it was misplaced at the dry cleaners), a Watteau sketch of a nude adolescent girl done in black and sienna charcoal which she hung to the left of his side of the bathroom vanity. For morning and evening inspiration, she said.

That was not to mention the less-costly things she splurged on, that she shrugged off as mere fripperies. Solid-gold Bulgari comb, Bucellati letter opener, Cartier lacquered fountain pens (everyone should have a spare) and so on. Necessary unnecessaries: antique English paperweight from Shrubsole, box of silver dominoes from Asprey, lots of things from Asprey.

Mitch enjoyed being the recipient of such largesse. Who wouldn't? However, for the sake of his male stuff, the health of that gender-conscious part of him that couldn't be merely a stand-in for the role of provider, he had to put a stop to it.

Maddie reasoned: What difference did it make whose money was spent? Why not just blend his lesser amount with her greater and let it be theirs? Sure, have Ronald put hers and his into a sort of financial blender and press the frappé button. Besides, giving to the one she loved as well as those who needed was a major pleasure for her. Would he deprive her of it?

Her contention was sensible. And comfortable for her. Her

nature was to be generous. After the robbery of the Laughton store she'd offered Kenneth whatever it would take to restock and restart. Kenneth appreciated her willingness to help but couldn't see any direction other than out.

At various other times she'd also proposed putting up the money for an upscale store for Mitch. They'd be strolling upper Madison and come upon frontage space for lease and she'd ask his opinion on whether or not it would be a good location.

She'd slip in the topic during their pillow talks. Her insight told her that having such a store was his latent ambition. He never said it was something he craved. However he did contribute to visualizing a store with her, enjoyed doing so, often got carried away with that and allowed his enthusiasm to turn him inside out.

It had happened recently. Realizing how exposed he was at that moment she'd taken a shot. "We should stop talking about it and do it," she said.

Nothing from him.

"You deserve to be well-known for your taste in jewelry and all you know about it."

"Yeah." His enthusiasm having retreated.

She'd gotten exasperated. "What is it with you? Are you afraid people will point you out as a bounder who lives off his wife?"

"Bounder?" A new old one. Where did she dig that up?

"Bounder," she maintained.

"Maybe that's it."

"Another sample of double standard. A kept woman is entirely acceptable, even fascinating, but a kept man . . ."

"All men are kept in some way," Mitch asserted philosophically.

"As are women." Maddie shrugged.

They laughed at the truth.

So, a quota was the compromise. It put a cap on the amount she could spend on him each month. She abided by it diligently for a while but subsequently only once in a while, maybe half the time.

Mitch never made it a combustible issue. Actually, as time went on he became more reasonable about it, several times came close to admitting that he was macho stubborn and she was right. He shouldn't squelch her generosity.

But not in this instance with the Cary Grant–Fabergé cuff links.

He calmly insisted Maddie return them to the store.

She calmly told him before she'd do that she'd give them to just anyone. "You don't understand," he told her. "I seldom wear cuff links and I already own three pair. Only a couple of my evening shirts have cuffs that require them."

"That never occurred to me. So, we'll have to have some shirts like that made for you."

"I prefer regular cuffs."

"Oh," she acquiesced.

"But these links are exquisite, Maddie, and thank you anyway."

"No harm done," she said blithely. "I'll take them back and get you something else." And then, without a pause: "What'll we do for dinner?"

"Want to go out?"

"Not really. Did you have a proper lunch?"

"No."

"That's not smart. It's essential to us that you take care of yourself, precious. Can't have your energy level getting diminuendo, can we?"

Mitch tried to think of another way he should take that. He'd known men who were the last to know they weren't keeping pace. Just recently he'd read an article that dealt with the inequitable allotment of sexual potential to the genders. Maddie certainly had a wealth of passion, a swiftly replenishing fortune. Was free to spend all she wanted on him.

"I could whip up a tuna and something casserole," she said. "We haven't had one in weeks."

Mercy, Mitch thought. He resourcefully reasoned: "Felicia

left the kitchen all tidy. Be a shame to mess it up. I'll go out and get something."

"Suits me," Maddie said, settling the matter with a loud, languid sigh.

Mitch changed into a pair of cotton tans and a sweatshirt worn once but not sweated in. When he returned to the study he saw Maddie was having a silent conversation with herself. He sat across from her in his usual chair and read much of that day's *Times* and a little here and there of last week's *New Yorker.*

Around six he put a bit of cash and credit cards into pocket and went down to find dinner. He had in mind some take-out from Barney's, a variety of delicacies, goose paté plentifully truffled, some kind of cold pasta maybe, certainly a loaf of well-done, crisp-crusted peasant bread. He'd munch on the heel of it on the way home. They'd eat on trays, find a movie on television, a Robert De Niro gangster or the like, one that on some previous similar night he'd narrated much of the action for Maddie so now she knew what was happening from the dialogue and sound effects.

Ruder was in the lobby. That was so unexpected that he didn't register on Mitch right off, but it was unmistakably Ruder standing to one side of the way out.

Ruder was wearing a white cap, the sort most proper for golfing. Perhaps that morning, when choosing how to present himself to the day and those who'd be in it, he'd decided the cap was called for by his blue and white seersucker suit, bought off the rack, of course, at Tripler's, of course, six summers ago. Add on white, kilted loafers. He'd lost sight of what he looked best in because he didn't look good in much. There was slightly more than a hint of simian about him. Short in the legs, long in the arms, a large head.

All in all he didn't appear to be what one might visualize as a best-school person, which was what he was: Hotchkiss, Yale, Skull and Bones and so on. He lived up in Rye in a handed-down house, enjoyed a handed-down membership at

Wykygyl, had been married only once but been left numerous times.

Ruder did a pleasant surprise. "I was having a drink here at Harry's with a friend in from Philadelphia," he said. "He just now left and I myself was about to."

Mitch thought Ruder deserved a fairly high rating as a makeup man but then decided he'd probably had that line in his mouth all the way uptown.

"I'd forgotten you live here at the Sherry," Ruder added on.

"I'd invite you up but my wife isn't feeling well," Mitch told him. "I'm on my way to pick up a prescription for her."

"Nothing serious, I hope."

"Never know."

"Right. Friend of mine's wife went to bed spry that other night, was dead at dawn."

"Your friend from Philadelphia?"

"No, another."

"You have a lot of friends."

"Who can have too many?"

He'll blow his nose any moment now, Mitch thought. Whenever they'd been together Ruder had blown his nose repeatedly, although he apparently didn't have a cold or allergy. It was like he was vainly trying to expel something from his brain. His way of thinking, perhaps.

"Well," Mitch said, "I've got to hurry. Nice seeing you."

"I'll tag along if you don't mind. Give us a chance to talk. I've been trying to reach you all day. Didn't you get my messages?"

"Yeah," Mitch said, preferring not to waste a fib. He made for the revolving door, didn't wait for the doorman's assist, gave the door such a vigorous shove that Ruder had to let two compartments go by before he could confidently jump in and come out on Fifth. By then Mitch was a half dozen strides up the avenue.

Ruder jogged to catch up and then it wasn't easy for him to keep up because Mitch had about six inches of leg on him and was purposely using all of it.

"You're a strange one, Mitch. Really, I mean you have a twisted perception of how to deal with a client."

"An attitude."

"If I didn't like you so much I wouldn't put up with it."

What was this, like Mitch day? First Visconti, now Ruder, Mitch thought. "You wanted to talk?"

"Maybe we could stop in some place and have an iced tea. How about in here?" They were on 60th with the north entrance of the Pierre just ahead.

"I've got to get back to Maddie with the antibiotic. Can't what you want to discuss hold until tomorrow?"

"Certainly, but tomorrow it might have to keep until Thursday and Thursday it might have to . . . well, you know. My better judgment tells me while I've got you I'd better take advantage." Ruder did a smile that ended beseechingly. Both the smile and the beseeching were contrary to his nature and, knowing that, Mitch figured whatever Ruder had on his mind was of unusual importance.

"Okay," Mitch said, stopping on the corner, "but make it fast."

Ruder took out a bunched white handkerchief, found an unused section of it and blew his nose productively. He briefly examined what had been jettisoned from him before stuffing the cloth back into his rear trousers pocket.

It occurred to Mitch that some unfortunate had the task of laundering Ruder's daily hankies.

"I'd feel more at ease seated inside someplace," Ruder said. "I really would."

Mitch looked past those words to the drugstore located mid-block on the other side of the street. He hoped he didn't have to carry his pretense that far.

"I need you to save my ass," Ruder blurted.

"Huh?"

"My standing in Columbia is in jeopardy."

"I thought they loved you."

"They should. No one at Columbia has written more business with less risk. Hell, I've sold coverage with exclusions others have never been able to slip in." Ruder paused, blinked to show he was reflecting, swallowed to show he was distraught. Mitch let him go on. "We've had changes above my level. People have come aboard who don't know me. All they're seeing is where I've overstepped, those instances when I've had to put not only my toe but my whole foot over the line in order to write business. It makes no difference that I've often had to sacrifice my own ethics. No appreciation for that. The hard-hearted pricks. Losses are all that matter. Can't have losses, especially when they're sizable. One is too fucking many and I've had one right after another lately."

Ruder sagged, hung his head, like a man looking over the edge of an imminent long fall.

Mitch couldn't bring himself to do a sympathetic comment.

"The Kalali claim," Ruder said. "As it turns out the Kalali claim is the maker or breaker for me."

That brought back to Mitch the phone conversation he'd had yesterday with Ruder regarding the Kalali claim. He'd been right about Ruder being under critical pressure.

"You can save me," Ruder said.

"I don't see how."

"I've sorted through my chances and you come out as my most likely hope. You're going to recover the Kalali goods."

An amused scoff from Mitch.

"It's not just a hunch, more like a premonition, a foregone thing. You're going to make a total recovery, you're going to let no one, absolutely no one know that you have, you're going to hand the goods over to me and . . . I'm going to be off the hook."

"And grateful."

"Extremely."

"To what extent would extremely be?" Mitch asked less amused.

"Yesterday I quibbled with you over a five percent bonus. That was just a reflex, my spontaneous inclination to look after Columbia's interest. I should have been putting myself first. Now I am. Now I'm willing to agree for a ten percent bonus. That would make your end about six hundred thousand."

"Columbia won't go for that. Five would have been pressing them."

"They've paid five."

"Not to me."

"But they've paid it, believe me. You needn't worry. Anyway, whatever part they won't pay I'll personally come up with. It'll be worth it to me."

Mitch acted as though he was considering the proposal. He did a covered gaze, aimed it at the traffic contest out on Madison, particularly noticing the black messengers on bicycles, admiring how creatively they won out over the crams and pincering between bumpers and side panels. What was it that compelled those guys to give such flair to the menial?

Really there wasn't much for Mitch to think over. The extra that Ruder was offering him was pure windfall, inasmuch as he'd already decided to give the Kalali claim no less than his best effort. The only difference seemed to be Ruder's stipulation that if recovery was made he not mention it to anyone, hand the goods over and let Ruder take the bows.

That struck Mitch as a bit odd but not unreasonable. Ruder probably wanted to put a little extra drama into his vindication, perhaps wanted to choose the perfect moment to scatter the Kalali recovery across the desk of whoever it was at Columbia who was kneeing his neck. Shit, for three hundred thousand on top of three hundred thousand Ruder could bow until it got to be aerobic, and curtsy too.

"Can I count on you Mitch?"

"Yeah, start counting."

Chapter 11

For the rest of the week Mitch worked the district. Not just 47th but, as well, where the concentration had spilled the gem trade over onto 46th and 48th.

He didn't give away his purpose. He never did. There was no discernible eagerness or degree of prowl to him. He kept in apparent neutral, circulated casually in and out of places, as though he had time on his hands.

Of course there were those of the street who knew him so well they knew better. At the very least they could guess he was around with some interest. That was especially so in the major exchanges where many of the more established dealers had concessions.

"Simon."

"Mitch."

A meaningful handshake.

"What's new with you?"

"Nothing to sing about."

"You're looking well."

"I've got trouble with my eyes. A cataract or something the doctor says. Don't tell anybody."

"I won't."

"What would I do if I lost my eyes, even a little."

"You won't."

"One can't feel how good or bad a stone is. You ever know a half-blind gem dealer? My bones will be picked." A moan.

"Simon, my good friend, you'll be finding flaws bare-eyed when you're ninety."

"I should have such luck."

Thus, person to person, Mitch worked the labyrinths of the major exchanges in both Visconti's and Riccio's territories. He made his way from booth to booth, not expecting to come across the Kalali goods, or even a part of them. It hadn't ever been that easy, wouldn't be this time.

The most he hoped for was a shred of a lead, some little thing that might start an unraveling. It could be as subtle as a divulging quality in the eyes of someone who wouldn't inform outright but wanted to let him know there was currently an important swag deal going down.

He had at least that much coming from Miriam Birkus, who did business out of booth 32 in the Manhattan Exchange. Five years ago Miriam and her husband, Sid, were stuck in a losing streak. It got so bad they were forced to sell many of the special, better pieces of jewelry they'd put aside over the years to fall back on later on.

As so often happens, what Miriam and Sid's plight eventually came to was a week with a turnaround deal in it. Not a totally rectifying deal but one that might start things going the other way for them. A prosperous acquaintance of Sid's was opening a retail store in a large mall outside Chicago. He needed stock, particularly engagement and wedding ring sets in the three to five thousand dollar wholesale range. A New York manufacturer that Sid knew specialized in such a line. He allowed Sid to have thirty-five sets on memo. That is, Sid signed for them, assuming responsibility for their value.

What could go wrong? It was a sweet, quick deal. All Sid had to do was fly the goods to Chicago. His end would be eighteen thousand.

He took an early morning flight. At O'Hare he needed to use a men's room, found one and had his pick of vacant stalls.

He covered the seat with a tissue and sat with his briefcase between his bare knees.

He was in the middle of defecating when they came over the top from the adjacent stalls, struck him once behind the ear with something hard and grabbed up the briefcase.

Later, Sid said dolefully that he must have looked too much the gem dealer. He didn't think there was such a look but what else would explain his having been spotted? Fingered by someone at the manufacturer's? Whoever, whatever, suspicions weren't going to change that he had to come up with $122,500 to cover the memo.

Visconti knew enough to not lend.

Sid considered suicide.

Mitch heard of the situation.

He went to the exchange and stopped by booth 32. Just Miriam was there. He was commiserating with her when a young swift came up beside him wanting to sell a swag ring he'd held out from a recent night's work. He was obviously an inexperienced swift, didn't know what he had or the value of it or any better than to bring it out and place it on the counter in plain sight.

An oval-cut fancy pink diamond weighing 4.58 carats flanked by tapered baguettes in a platinum mount. Appraised value: two hundred eighty thousand.

That was the description as it appeared on the Empire Mutual Insurance Company's loss list that Mitch had been going over just that morning.

No mistaking it.

The ring lay there on the counter. To Miriam it was salvation. To the swift some fast money. To Mitch a pat on the back from a client for the partial recovery and a few thousand bonus.

Three times the swift asked too loudly how much Miriam would give him for it. To his knowledge all diamonds were white.

A figure low enough to not contradict that impression was in Miriam's mouth; however she deferred to Mitch.

It was up to him.

He weighed the circumstances for a long moment and then turned his back on the transaction. He heard Miriam say two thousand in a typical 47th take it or leave it tone. He thought what a steal and, after allowing ample time, he turned back around to the counter. The swift was gone, the ring was out of sight. He resumed with a nervous but unburdened Miriam as though the interruption had been imaginary.

Thus, on this day, had the Kalali swag or, for that matter, any other heavy, hot material been on the move within the exchange, Miriam would have informed Mitch with a telling look. However, he didn't discern even a hint of that flavor in her eyes.

Nor was Mitch able to glean anything helpful from Saul Heimel, the cutter whose workshop was located fourth-floor rear of a building on 46th. Heimel, normally a wag who delighted in fertilizing any rumor, was too preoccupied with parrying an insult to his expertise. With the painful-sounding screech of faceting under way on a nearby scaif, a horizontal wheel charged with oil and diamond powder spinning at about twenty-five hundred revolutions per minute, Heimel wanted corroboration:

"Here, you tell me the girdle is thick." He handed Mitch a ten-power loupe and a four-carat brilliant-cut diamond locked in a pair of tweezers.

Mitch examined the diamond's widest part, that which divided its upper section from its base. "I wouldn't say so," he said, which didn't necessarily mean it wasn't.

"The son of a bitch claims I've ruined his stone. No thanks for the inclusion I've managed to hide with the bezel facets."

"Who?"

"Brings me an old miner piece of shit and expects me to recut it into the Star of India or something." Heimel was close to frothing. "I know his trick. He wants to pay me not so much. Fuck him. He pays or I keep his goods."

Mitch tried rerouting the topic but to no avail.

And that was how it went for him Wednesday and Thursday. For all his tactical nosing around, nothing. The less optimistic side of him suggested that what he had purely out of the torment suggested to Ruder was quite possibly the case. The Kalali goods were gone, out of the country perhaps, already sold off. He countered that thought with reminding himself how early it was, less than a week since the robbery.

Still, he knew from experience how brief was the expectancy of a recovery. Normally a couple of weeks at most. After that, kiss the goods goodbye.

CHAPTER 12

Friday morning.

Mitch first went to his office. He dictated a couple of letters, composing patiently to accommodate Shirley's sort-of-shorthand. He signed the checks she put before him and complimented her on the new silk blouse she'd recently liberated from layaway. He also called Visconti regarding the Watermill invitation.

"We have to go up to Maddie's uncle's place," was his true excuse. "It's his birthday and he hasn't been too well lately." Both fibs that when they'd been said Mitch knew they were overkill.

"Some other time then."

"For sure."

"You heard from Riccio?"

"As a matter of fact, yeah."

"I heard you'd heard."

Who was Visconti's wire at Riccio's? Mitch wondered. It had to be someone close in. What would be any have-around's good enough reason to take such a risk? If found out Riccio would tear him apart.

Riccio had phoned Mitch on Wednesday, wanting to know about the Kalali photos Mitch had cryptically left at his place.

"Good-looking material," was Riccio's opinion. "I take it somebody lost it."

"Yeah."

"Well, I ain't found it," Riccio said unhappily.

Mitch believed him. He asked of Riccio the same courtesy he'd asked of Visconti, which was to be told if the Kalali goods got fenced and became a dead issue. Riccio said he'd go along with that and, in the next breath, asked Mitch to let him know if the goods got recovered. That struck Mitch as odd. Visconti had also wanted to be notified.

"Why would you want to know?" Mitch asked Riccio, just curious.

Riccio's reply wasn't to be believed. "No big reason. I like to be on top of what's happening around, that's all."

Now it was Visconti on the phone, saying: "Look over."

Mitch swiveled his desk chair, looked out the window and across the chasm of Fifth to Visconti's office. Visconti was at his desk but turned to meet Mitch's view. He was holding something up to his face.

"You're a sharp dresser, Mitch," Visconti said. "Who picks out your ties?"

"My wife."

That stopped Visconti. His amiability had caused a blunder. He regained with "You make a great knot, small but not too tight, like today. I especially like the tie you've got on today. What is it, a Hermès?"

"I don't know. She cuts out the labels." Mitch now realized Visconti was on him with a pair of miniature binoculars. "You've got me at a disadvantage," he said.

"Not for long. I'm sending you over a pair identical with these. Zeiss ten by twenty-fives. They'll put you right in here."

Mitch nearly forgot how close-up Visconti was seeing him, almost allowed his true sentiments to show.

"By the way," Visconti asked as though just making talk. "Did you come onto those goods yet?"

"Which goods?" Mitch pretended.

"The Kalali goods."

Mitch couldn't recall having told Visconti whose goods they were, not by name. "No, but I'm getting there."

"When you do don't forget to let me know."

"Why?"

Visconti was faster and better with a reply than Riccio. "So I can help you celebrate," he said, "what else?"

Immediately after hanging up Mitch got up and drew the blinds. After a short while he went down and out to continue angling for a lead. That the Kalali goods apparently hadn't hit the district as of yesterday didn't mean they wouldn't today. He had to keep circulating and hope his going over the same tracks didn't give away how purposeful he was.

He put in two hours of moving around. Was, at that point, on the south side of 47th a couple of numbers over from Fifth Avenue, having a few words with an older 47th Streeter whose fingertip skin was stained black and eaten away by years and years of acid-testing things, stolen things usually, to determine their gold content. From his overconditioned point of view life was degrees of purity: 22k, 18, 14, 10, less. His eyes were zero k, gone creamy dull, tarnished, resigned to never being worth more. He had nothing for Mitch.

Across the way was the major West 47th building designated number 1. Mitch looked up the face of it to a certain set of windows. He'd looked up to them numerous times over the past few days. They'd always been dark. Now, however, there were lights on.

He crossed over, entered the building and went up to six.

His brother Andy's place of business was a short ways down the corridor. The LAUGHTON logo was gold-leafed on the door along with ESTATE JEWELRY in smaller letters. It was two adjoined rooms of modest size fixed up to give the impression that Andy could, if he needed, afford twice again as much space.

Mitch went in.

Doris, Andy's love and lover, was standing there with a smile already on, as though having foreseen Mitch's arrival.

Perhaps she'd noticed him from the window, seen him cross the street, had positioned herself and waited. She greeted him with left and right cheek kisses, real contact ones, said his name fondly instead of a hello. "We got back only a few minutes ago," she told him.

The dress she had on looked long-journeyed in, Mitch noticed. Her makeup was fresh but her eyes seemed sleepy. She wasn't wearing any jewelry, which was rare for her. Usually she decorated herself with better pieces. Like several rings, as though the large selection she owned had all vied for her fingers and she'd given in to as many as possible. The same with bracelets. But now, for whatever reason, she didn't have on even simple gold ear loops.

Jewelry was Doris' addiction. She admitted it. She didn't really need it. Harry Winston had once told her that. Her beauty was enough, it accessorized her, Winston had fibbed for whatever reason.

"How was the trip?" Mitch asked. Standing aside were four pieces of luggage with first-class JFK destination tags attached to their handles.

"Andy will tell you," she said evasively, "when he gets off the phone."

The door to the inner office was not quite closed. Mitch's view of Andy was a slit and he couldn't hear what was being said. Probably he had Riccio on, Mitch thought. He could have gone in, crowded Andy, but he decided to wait, be easier.

"How about something to drink, a Coke or something?" Doris offered.

"A root beer, got a root beer?"

"You and Andy," she remarked and got a Hire's from the small fridge. Mitch watched her pop the tab. He hoped she didn't break a nail.

Andy came hurrying out, glad to see Mitch, demonstrating that with a strong hug. He was a six-year-younger and slightly shorter version of Mitch. Nearly the same smile, and eyes. A lot of his gestures and body language was imitative of Mitch's, picked up early.

"You didn't get any sun," Mitch said.

"No."

"Do any fishing? I had you in a stream making a perfect presentation to a big one."

Andy looked away, as though a second self was standing nearby to advise him whether or not he should continue the pretense. He came back to Mitch to be eyes to eyes with him for a long moment, during which he told the truth without saying it. "How did you find out?" he asked.

"Visconti. One half of the street always knows what the other half is up to. You should know that by now."

"Since when have you and Visconti been buddies?"

"It was a stupid move, Andy."

"Went off without a hitch," Andy said.

"This was your first errand?"

"Second."

Mitch exhaled a disgusted breath with an expletive on the end of it.

Andy needed to lift the situation to his own high. "Let me show you something," he said brightly.

They went into the inner office.

"I haven't delivered yet," Andy said as he opened his briefcase and from it removed an oblong black leather box with a snap closure. The box contained ten or so briefkes, those double papers folded eight times a certain special way, which gem dealers use to inescapably hold their precious stones. Andy chose one of the briefkes, unfolded it.

They lay in a crease like an accumulated ridge of the clearest frost. Forty pieces of D-flawless one-carat diamonds.

"Russian goods," Andy said, "electronically faceted, perfect makes."

Mitch took the briefke, rocked it slightly and ran the tip of his finger through the lot of diamonds, disturbing them, causing them to scintillate as though they'd been provoked and were resorting to that, their weapon.

"Stunning, aren't they?" Doris said rather covetously.

"Riccio should be pleased," Mitch remarked, holding back expressing his admiration. "How did you manage to get them?"

"Through a broker in Antwerp named Hamner. An older guy Dad used to deal with occasionally."

"You were lucky."

"It really didn't take much doing."

"You were lucky."

"We were careful," Andy contended.

"Very," Doris confirmed.

They'd flown to Buffalo, rented a car there and crossed over into Canada as though they were just part of the traffic bound for a Blue Jays night game in Toronto.

Three million was in the trunk, snugly packed in one of the pieces of luggage. Sixty-two pounds of used, untraceable hundreds.

The crucial banking part of it had been prearranged for by Andy on a previous trip to Toronto. The private bank on the fringe of the financial district was glad to handle such a sizable deposit. It specialized in such temporary transactions at a fee of one percent.

Next they'd flown to Brussels where they opened an account at another private bank. Then went on to Antwerp where the diamond broker, Hamner, and the goods were waiting. Andy hadn't specified Russian goods. That had been an unexpected plus. Russian diamonds, because of their ideal color and consistently perfect makes, had up to lately demanded a premium price; however Russia's needful economic situation had brought the price down into the more competitive range.

Andy had examined and chosen four lots of caraters: eighty pieces of D-flawless, sixty-four pieces of D-color VVSIs, thirty pieces of E-color VVSIs and twenty-five pieces of F-color VVSIs. An even two hundred pieces in all.

Prices had been discussed and after sufficient, rather ritualistic haggling, agreed upon.

The bank in Toronto was instructed to wire transfer $2,970,000 (the $3,000,000 less its fee) to the bank in Brussels, which immediately disbursed $2,479,021 to Hamner, the broker (that included his 8 percent fee). The remaining $490,979 (less the Brussels' bank charges) was Andy's margin. He had it wire-transferred to a bank in the Caymans.

Thus, Riccio's dirty three million cash, that unwieldy, incriminating bulk, had been transformed into the most lasting and dazzling of commodities. Negotiable anywhere, transportable in a shirt pocket, diamonds were a mob guy's best friend.

"Have to go some to make an easier, faster four hundred." Andy grinned.

A cynical grunt from Mitch. He folded the briefke to escape the influence of Riccio's diamonds. "Have you thought how it could have gone?"

"Sure, there was a downside."

"A way downside."

"You're going to piss on my score."

Maybe not, Mitch thought. Maybe, considering Andy's elation at the moment, he should back off, wait until a more neutral time. That was hard for Mitch to do because of the worry that had steamed up in him. "I'm glad it went okay," he said.

Andy read him. "You don't have to pretend you approve. I know you don't, I knew you wouldn't. That's why you had to hear about it the hard way."

"Let's drop it."

"No, you're primed. Go ahead."

"All right. Let's say it all went like it was computerized: the money across the border, the banks in Toronto and Brussels, the broker in Antwerp, the smear. Let's say you've got the diamonds and you're headed back to Riccio with them, but let's also say a take-off guy gets to you and you have to hand over the goods. You tell that to Riccio. He seems to buy it at first, but then he doesn't, he decides the take-off guy never was, that you're lying three million worth. He's insulted. He cocksuckers you twice in every sentence, tells you in otherwise-you'll-be-found-full-of-holes-off-Wards Island terms that you'd better come up with the three. What he doesn't tell you . . ."

"You surprise me."

"How?"

"The way you're not seeing me. You know what, you think you're the shaman of the street. While you've been going around dispensing cures and curses, where is it you think I've been, in a fucking trance?"

"Let me finish."

"I resent it."

"What Riccio doesn't tell you is the take-off guy is one of his crew, if not one of his have-arounds then a zip out to prove. You were set up. You owe Riccio three million and so much vig you'll never get to the nut. You're his. Do or die, his."

"I wouldn't let it get to that," Doris vowed. Unlike Andy, she'd been hanging on Mitch's every word. "I'd raise the three million," she said.

Andy went to the window and gazed down at 47th. At that moment to his eyes it had never looked greedier or grimier. Probably it would regain its more acceptable impression later on, he thought. It always had. The scenario Mitch had just depicted was by no means a revelation to him. He'd watched his back, been wary all the way. Several guys he noticed during the trip home he'd suspected of being take-offs.

He remained at the window. "I figure I could do a couple of errands before Riccio pulled anything like that. He probably had it in mind for next time."

Mitch took that to mean Andy didn't intend there to be a next time. He was relieved, told himself Andy hadn't really resented his concern.

They'd always looked out after one another. As youngsters they'd even gone so far as to play at doing that. For instance, at the cottage in Connecticut where the family spent summers, they'd be out in the lake, a long ways from shore.

"It's your turn to not be able to swim."

"You saved the last time."

"Like hell, but okay. Then I get two saves in a row."

Desperate thrashing of the water and credible cries for help. It alarmed their father at first but after he caught on to what they were doing he understood and enjoyed watching them.

In winter they'd create avalanches and take turns at digging one another out.

"Don't stop breathing. I'm almost to you!"

Realistic gasps for air. "Hurry!"

There was no mother to alarm. She'd died while giving birth to Andy. Thus he didn't own any memories of her, had to be satisfied with those he borrowed from those that were related to him and whatever he imagined by making photographs of her come to life.

Mitch didn't remember much about her, actually. Not her voice or her touch or her scent or any of the important things like that. However, early on, whenever Andy wanted to know about her, asked, Mitch passed on things Kenneth had told him at one time or another. A verbal legacy. For Andy's sake, and just as much his own he realized later, he elaborated creatively, invented various incidents to exemplify her caring. Mitch still believed that helped Andy cope with the presence of her absence. Perhaps even saved him.

Now Andy turned his back to the street, told Mitch: "I've over a million in the Caymans. Doris will match that and you and Maddie can kick in whatever you think would be fair."

"For what?"

"The only reason I ran Riccio's errands was so I'd have a large enough hunk to throw into the pot."

"I'm also throwing in my jewelry," Doris said. "Not all of it but a lot. I've got too much, just stashed away, pieces I was temporarily in love with but have been ignoring for ages. It's a crime. I bet I've at least enough to fill a whole showcase."

"There's a location on Madison in the seventies that's coming available," Andy said. "I've talked to the real estate agent about it."

He and Doris went on about what the new Laughton establishment on Madison would be like, how successful it would be. They jumped right over asking Mitch if he was for it or not. Their enthusiasm assumed he was.

What was it with everyone trying to get him back into a store on Madison? Mitch thought. Did it ever occur to them— Andy, Doris, Maddie—that he didn't want to be a goddamn shopkeeper, that he hadn't been cut out for it in the first place, that it had been something he'd fit himself into but not without having to squeeze and force the shape of his true nature? In fact, since there'd not been a family store, not had to kissy-kissy ass all those spoiled, well-off women every day he'd felt better about himself.

That wasn't to say he liked what he was now doing for a living. It was, as he secretly thought of it, something that kept him from doing what he didn't want to do, which was shop-keep. Put the goods on display every morning, put the goods back in the vault every night. Set the alarm. Pay the insurance company on time and hope switchers and lifters didn't pick you clean or some lady looking as though she could buy the place out didn't have a .380 automatic up her sable sleeve. Fuck no. Maybe he didn't know what he wanted to do and maybe it was a little late to be undecided about that, but for sure he wasn't going to be a shopkeeper.

He did a smile along with some nods that made him appear interested. "You're way ahead of me," he said. "Let me think about it some and catch up."

To change direction he took a set of the Kalali photos from his folio. Tossed it on Andy's desk. "Some things I'm hoping to recover for a client," he explained. "Take a look when you have a moment."

His pager beeped.

Hurley wanted to be called.

Mitch reached him at the precinct.

"What you up to?" Hurley asked.

"Just shagging around."

"And?"

"Nothing."

"I got an okay from the Jersey guys to take a look at the Kalali house. Who knows? Want to go along?"

"I'm having lunch with Maddie and afterwards I promised her the museum."

"Which museum?"

"The Met." She preferred the Met over the Museum of Modern Art and the Whitney. Whenever she'd sat aimed at the abstract paintings of either of the latter, she'd gotten low to medium grade anxiety attacks, sometimes even a bit nauseous; however the Fantin-Latours, Whistlers, Cassatts and Boudins at the Met had a mollifying effect.

"Bring Maddie along," Hurley suggested. "We'll stop and have lunch at a place I know in Jersey City where the top mob guys used to go and there's still a lot of what they once were in the atmosphere. It's very Maddie."

CHAPTER 13

Having had lunch they were again under way in the Lexus with Billy driving and Mitch up front with him, Maddie and Hurley in the back.

Billy sort of remembered the way they'd come. All through there was typical New Jersey waterfront and most of the ways weren't streets as much as cobbled or unpaved accesses from one unremarkable section to another. So Billy was to be forgiven for choosing a couple of turns that led to only the loading platforms of warehouses. He finally came onto Avenue E and a ramp that put them on the Turnpike Extension.

Bound for Far Hills.

"Anybody against some music?" Billy asked.

No one replied so he assumed, clicked the radio on and began scanning. He passed up some gloomy Mahler and a newscast that managed to get out the word *killed*. Some mellow jazz was what he hoped to find, some Oscar Peterson or John Coltrane. He went up and down the megacycles twice. The air was congested with the agony of heavy metal and the high school poetry and scratches of rap.

Shit, was what Billy thought of it and nearly said aloud. He gave up on the radio.

His patience this day was thin, stretched. He saw it as a sort of membrane with abnormal elasticity that ran sheet-like. Horizontally within his skull from his brow line to the stem of his brain. Impervious up to now.

He'd never allowed the tension of his patience to show. Wouldn't today. He'd be as expected, in the part of amenable Billy the driver, wait-here guy, on call and carry guy, a kind of satellite person the way his time revolved around that of others.

Before, when he'd driven Mr. Strawbridge, he'd done whatever was required to make himself indispensable, and there'd been no letup in that endeavor since he'd been driving Mitch and Maddie. Not once had there been a mention, not even a veiled hint of his being let go, nor had he implied that he might quit. By now the indispensability was mutual he believed. Wasn't he bound to them?

Admitted, he had himself a steady, soft spot. The salary was generous and the treatment liberal.

Those, however, weren't his reason for staying on. Not his way down inside reasons.

Years ago, over a series of lengthy waits for Mr. Strawbridge, particularly one of six hours at Kennedy because Mr. Strawbridge had missed his return flight from London, Billy had done what he considered to be some deep introspection. Opened himself up beyond his layers of ordinary motives and came up with why, despite the frequent urge to make a change, he should remain where he was.

The need to resent.

That was it. His need to resent.

Not devotion nor security, but the advantage of being able to resent with ease, confident that his resentment wasn't about to spill over (desert the Lexus and Maddie mid-traffic on 50th) or gather into a temperamental tornado and havoc everything in his vicinity to such an extent he'd have no recourse other than to hang head and remove himself to another vicinity.

It was a matter of counterpoise.

Mr. Strawbridge's genuine good nature and other personal

merits, the various likabilities of Mitch and Maddie. Attributes that adequately outweighed (but not by much) his resentments, that kept the umbrageous side of him contained.

Where, he often asked himself remindfully, would he ever again find such suitability, such an accommodating ratio—never less than fifty-one percent honest-to-goodness consideration to offset his rarely more than forty-nine percent grudge?

He imagined having to endure employers who behaved less agreeably. He wouldn't put up with it. It wasn't in him to put up with it. He'd be forever deserting, escaping, quitting and being let go. There'd be too many trial periods, the begging for letters of reference.

Couldn't have that.

Couldn't risk having to have that, Billy thought.

So, what about this four-way pull on his patience today? What had brought it on?

Had to be the proposition.

Made to him Wednesday night when he was having his usual slice of pound cake at the narrow coffee shop around the corner on Columbus Avenue, when that guy came in and helped himself to the same booth. No introduction, no preamble, just the proposition straight out.

The guy was well-dressed. In gray. Had on a hundred-dollar tie. Seemed real enough, serious eyes, serious mouth. Talked like he had sense until the number came out of him. Twenty-five million.

From that point on Billy was sure what he had was another city crazy.

Still, as the guy had stipulated, he'd kept the proposition to himself, hadn't spoken about it to Mitch.

"What was it called, what I had to eat?" Maddie asked.

"Orecchio d' Elefante," Hurley told her.

"Which is what?"

"The literal translation is ear of elephant. Actually a loin veal chop pounded so thin it's floppy."

"The clams were delicious," she said. For a starter she'd ordered a dozen littlenecks on the half shell. Slurped them down without the disguise of Tabasco, Worcestershire or lemon. Mitch, a bit impressed, had visualized her stomach a pink resting place, albeit temporary, for all those homeless clams.

"Most women can't even stomach the idea of eating raw clams," he said now.

"It's a carnal thing," Maddie said and allowed that to hang in the air. "With me, of course, it's purely tactile, and I can accept the resemblance but why be so nasty nice? You know, Elise adores raw clams, oysters as well, always has. She fed me my first when I was three or so." Then, without a half beat or breath: "Did you happen to overhear those three men at the next table, I thought they were mob guys planning arson and a hit but it soon became apparent that two of them were trying to sell the third some fire and life insurance. Most disappointing."

"Used to be a guy couldn't get a waiter's job there unless he'd done a hitch in some joint."

"I'd have appreciated it more then," Maddie said.

"That's for sure," Mitch commented to the windshield.

At that moment they were passing over Newark Bay. It occurred to Mitch that once its water had been clean enough to drink. Black-hulled freighters were tied up like animals on short leash. The beaks of cranes picking their bellies empty. Then came Newark Airport on the left. A 747 on its glide path. Mitch imagined the collective quickening of the passengers' heartbeats.

He wished Billy would hurry the Lexus, get them to Far Hills sooner. He opened the glove compartment. It was stuffed with traffic citations, crumpled up malevolently and shoved in there. So many that some, as though relieved, flew out. A couple of years ago Mitch had paid off just as much of an accumulation, hoping a clean slate would inspire Billy to be more conscientious. All it did was set a precedent.

"I'm not going to put out for your goddamn tickets again," Mitch said. "You expect me to but I won't." He retrieved those that were on the floor.

Billy did a shrug.

"You'll get your license taken away."

Billy agreed with some nods that unmistakably conveyed it would be Mitch's loss.

Mitch noticed the black butt of a revolver in the compartment, no holster, just the weapon in among the cram of traffic tickets. He took it out. A Smith & Wesson .357 Magnum. A hefty piece.

"I recall you having a thirty-two automatic," Mitch said.

"A plinker. I traded it."

"This loaded?"

"Of course."

"You ought to keep it on safety."

"No one ever gets in there but me."

"I'm in there now."

"So you are," Billy said intractably.

Mitch put the revolver on safety and placed it back in among the tickets. He closed the glove sharply, closing the subject.

Maddie was back on the clams. "I'll bet I don't get hepatitis from them," she was saying. "Not in that restaurant. It's probably the safest place north of Miami to eat clams."

"Why?"

"If a mob boss ever got hepatitis the place would get bombed. Don't you think?"

They were on 78 now, headed west. New Jersey was sliding by, nothing pleasant. The city of Newark, off on the right, was aided by distance.

A wave of depression invaded Mitch. Not the deep sort, just a minor concavity, enough to be felt. It wasn't because of Billy's shaded insubordination or because Maddie was in the back with Hurley, Mitch told himself. Sure, Hurley had it for Maddie. That had been obvious for a long while but it was a long way from being active.

She used Hurley. Like right now, she was pumping the Kalali case out of him. Maybe Hurley thought it was conversation, but listening to it Mitch recognized it as pure Maddie, one-sided pump. By the time they got to Far Hills she'd know more about the Kalali case than he did.

He read, as though interested, what was displayed on the rear and side of an eighteen-wheeler that Billy passed doing a good twenty over the limit. He thought the wish they'd get stopped for speeding. By a hard-mouthed state cop. That would change the climate.

A green highway sign announced Irvington importantly.

Named after some guy Irving, Mitch thought. Never forget Irving what's-his-name. Irving Toplitz, that was it. A 47th guy who used to sell piqué goods out of his pocket. Dirty little diamonds in dirty overhandled briefkes. Got hold of an eighty-pointer (four-fifths of a carat) that was loupe clean, first quality. A held-back piece of swag popped out of an engagement ring. Irving showed the stone up and down the street. Turned down better than fair offers for it because once he sold it all he'd have to show was money. In his own way in love with that eighty-pointer, like an unfortunate-looking guy who'd come by a beautiful girl. One afternoon at curbside he was showing his prize possession to someone when he was accidentally jostled by a tourist. The eighty-pointer was flipped out of its open briefke. It bounced twice and found the sewer drain. Irv Toplitz felt victimized. He gave up on the street, was never seen upon it again.

Mitch thought a plaque should have been installed marking the spot, saying, for one and all to see forever, *here is where Irv Toplitz lost his spirit*. But then, if that was the criterion there'd be plaques all over the place.

"What time you want to get started tomorrow?" Billy asked.

"Early," Mitch told him.

"Not too early."

"Say seven, seven-thirty."

"Let's make it nine or ten."

"I want to be up there by then."

Billy didn't promise seven, seven-thirty.

Hurley now had out a set of the Kalali photos, was describing them to Maddie piece by piece.

Mitch adjusted his seat for more recline, closed his eyes and overheard: "A belle époque period diamond and pearl head ornament."

"What exactly is a head ornament?" Maddie asked.

"A comb."

"Why didn't they say a comb?"

They, Mitch thought cynically.

Hurley told her: "This one's made of real tortoiseshell mounted with a band of diamonds and bordered with natural pearls. Signed by Cartier."

"Sounds sweet. This Kalali lady had some lovely jewelry."

Had, Mitch thought.

"Wonder where she got it all. Maybe she bought swag."

Hurley went on to the photo of the two twenty-carat emeralds fitted in their ivory box. As he was describing them in detail to Maddie, Mitch visualized them, their Arabic-looking inscriptions and all.

"What do the inscriptions say?" Maddie asked.

"How should I know?"

"I'd think you'd want to," Maddie said. "It's probably important."

Mitch wondered why Hurley didn't tell her what the inscriptions said was irrelevant, that all that mattered was they'd been stolen and whoever stole them had killed one Kalali going on two.

Hurley went on describing other pieces.

Mitch wished he had earplugs.

But then Maddie reached forward and found his head, gave it a couple of loving strokes and mussed his hair some. That easily he was brought up to the brighter surface and the miles to the scene of the crime were made to seem not so many.

The gate of the Kalali house was open but the police crime scene tape was still up.

Mitch told Maddie he wouldn't be long, she was to wait in the car with Billy.

She did a brief, obedient smile.

Mitch and Hurley walked up the drive. It was lined with an abundance of blue hydrangeas at their peak. An oriole was enjoying ablutions in a cantilevered bath. Altogether a summer contentment about the place, not robbery and homicide.

They entered the house and immediately had to step around the outlined indication of where Mrs. Kalali had been shot down. The dried pool of her week-old blood dimensional on the slick, hardwood floor of the reception hall.

They proceeded to the study where shards of Persian glass crunched beneath their steps and books were heaped helter-skelter. Their attention was immediately drawn to the white sofa upon which was the dark red stain of Mr. Kalali's bleeding, a grisly Rorschach.

Now it was a place of robbery and homicide.

They went throughout the expansive house, absorbing the stark, cold, contemporary character of it. The master bedroom had been left as found, except for a lot of messy dusting for fingerprints.

Mitch and Hurley agreed that the condition of the dressing room was unusual, didn't look as though swifts had been there. Why hadn't it been ransacked, the dresser drawers yanked out, their contents dumped on the floor?

And the gaping, empty floor safe in the bedroom. A high-rated safe that would have taken considerable time and experience and special equipment to force open. What else could be assumed except that one of the Kalalis had opened it under duress?

"For all the good it did them," Mitch remarked.

"Getting any ideas?" Hurley asked.

"Could have been anyone's crew," Mitch said.

They went out to the rear terrace and further out on the grounds. The Jersey guys had already gone over the area but there was the chance that they might have missed something, something that had been dropped or whatever.

"Couldn't have asked for a more ideal setup with the easy wall, the overgrown grounds and all," Mitch commented.

"Here's where they came over. It was soggy so they left good, deep shoe prints. The Jersey police took impressions. According to them two of the guys weigh about one seventy-five, both had on Nikes. The other guy was a real lightweight, a hundred ten or so. Maybe not even that. Had on boots with pointed toes. Tiny narrow feet. Know a crew that has a swift like that?"

"Not offhand."

"At least it's something to look for. And the fact that they were a hard crew."

"That narrows it down some."

"Not much these days though. Would have ten years ago."

A hard crew was one that carried guns. Most swifts didn't used to and some still didn't because if caught the charge would be armed robbery rather than just burglary. Armed robbery carried a five-year-longer sentence.

Piano music.

Contradicting the moment with bits and passages of romantic Tchaikovsky. It seemed to be coming from somewhere neighboring but then Mitch and Hurley realized it was coming from the Kalali house.

They hurried in.

Maddie was seated at the black baby grand in the study. Her left hand struck three ominous-sounding chords, sort of Mozart. "This place is like a mausoleum," she complained.

"You were supposed to wait in the car," Mitch told her somewhat reproachfully.

"I needed to go to the bathroom." She did a lively, double upscale run all the way to the last ivory key, along with a Ray Charles chin up, head back. "I had no problem finding it."

CHAPTER 14

Such a summer Saturday!

Why, the very air was different from yesterday's. Not nearly so ladened nor polluted with responsibility. There'd be no Ruder, no Visconti, no Riccio, not a mote of 47th in this air, Mitch thought.

He lay on his left side on his side of the bed, curled enough so the base of his spine was pressed to the base of Maddie's. At times when they got into this position Mitch played with the illusion that they were permanently attached, like Siamese twins. The romantic fantasy was always spoiled by the inconveniences and impossibilities that would come with it. At other times he imagined their touching spines formed an erotic circuit for a current that would recharge them, in a sort of tantric way.

He'd been awake since five-thirty. It was now close to six.

If he got up now, didn't continue to lie there letting thoughts pass through his head like neutrinos, he'd be able to leisurely do whatever he had to do before Billy picked them up at seven-thirty.

He put his feet to the carpet.

Noise didn't matter. Maddie should get up. He said her name for the first time that day, softly. She didn't respond. He nudged her with it, twice, louder.

She did a torporous protesting *mmm* and reached with her legs to where he'd vacated. "Come back," she murmured.

"Billy will be here in an hour or so."

She burrowed in under her pile of pillows, pulled one of Mitch's to her, hugged it and was again taking the downward passage to sleep.

She'd be having to rush around later furious at herself, Mitch thought on his way to the kitchen.

Fresh-brewed Kona.

Well-buttered cinnamon toast.

He brought them into the bedroom. Placed the tray on the bed. The aromas would get to her. He compounded the enticement by pouring himself some of the rich, steaming black and crunching a bite of toast.

Maddie huffed and complained: "It's too fucking early."

"Maybe you'd rather not go to the country today."

"At a decent hour."

"You and Billy," Mitch remarked.

She sat up amidst the plump. "Coffee me please."

Mitch obliged and her first finger found the handle of the mug.

Mitch was used to her blind precision.

She helped herself to a slice of toast. Mitch didn't care for it all that much but he knew it was one of her every-so-often morning favorites.

"Are you dressed?" she asked.

"No."

"What do you intend to wear?"

"I don't know, why?"

"Wear jeans, a tight pair."

"It'll be too warm for jeans."

"And boots. You do have a pair of high-tops, don't you?"

She was up to something, Mitch thought.

"The Doc Martens I bought you. Did you leave them in the country?"

"Yeah," Mitch fibbed and thought he'd wear lightweight khakis, a T-shirt without a name or place on it and pair of sneakers. No matter what she was specifying or why, he was going to be comfortable.

She got up for the bathroom with a whole slice of toast clenched between her teeth. Mitch heard simultaneously the diametric sounds of the toast being crunched and the stream of her striking the water in the commode.

"I love you, precious," she called out from in there.

"Love you too," Mitch said, and with that exchange it seemed what had ensued up to then in his day had been merely overture.

Maddie was in the shower.

"We've about a half hour," he told her. Apparently she was being diligent about the time. However, when she was out and had dried herself she set about waxing her legs.

"You can do that up at Straw's," Mitch said.

She went on pressing the sheets of wax around her shins and calves. As she ripped them off it sounded and appeared painful to Mitch.

"Don't dawdle," he told her.

"Is that what I'm doing? I thought I was doing something that might please you later on."

Cheeks and thighs, he thought.

"Did you take in the paper?" she asked.

"No."

"Why don't you?"

He got that morning's *Times* from the landing. It was already quarter after seven and he wasn't yet dressed. Nor was Maddie. She was now before the mirror, leaning to it, fussing with her hair, picking at a tendril here, another there, as though she was seeing her image.

"I'll read to you on the way up," Mitch said.

"What are the headlines? Never mind, go to the fourth page. What's juicy on the fourth page?"

"Only a lot of wars."

"How about the Living Arts section?"

"That doesn't come on Saturdays."

"At least there must be some editorials."

There were two. She agreed with one, and the other having to do with the overfishing and the plights of Columbia River salmon made her temporarily irate.

Reading the *Times* aloud to her wasn't a daily must but something Mitch did fairly regularly. He enjoyed it. He often omitted or inserted words to make the articles more controversial or slanted more toward his views.

As he got into today's business section Maddie remarked *same old shit* and squirmed into a pair of black jeans. She sucked in, zipped up and ran an approving hand over her snugly contained buttocks. "What do you think?"

"You'll swelter."

Seven-thirty, quarter to eight.

"Where the hell is Billy?"

"He'll be along," Maddie assured.

"Think I should call Straw and let him know we're coming?"

"He'd rather we just showed up."

They spent one or two weekends each month up at Straw's. And nearly all holidays. A room designated as theirs was kept ready for them, plenty of changes for each season in its closet, a stock of personal needs in the adjoining bath.

Ready to go, they sat in the study.

More wait, more waste, Mitch thought.

There wasn't much of consequence one could do while doing wait, it was too distracting an activity in itself.

Maddie felt the hands of her special, exposed wristwatch. "Nine o'clock," she said.

Mitch's *Where the hell is Billy?* intensified to *Where the fuck is Billy?*

At nine-thirty Billy called up from the lobby. "I'm here," was all he said.

Maddie told Mitch to go on down. "I've a thing or two I want to take along."

"Like what?"

"Just a thing or two," she replied vaguely.

Now that Billy had arrived Mitch found his aggravation was

anti-climactic. What, really, did a couple of hours matter? It wasn't imperative that they get to the country early, just a notion he'd fixed on. Still, he was going to have to do some reproach. He wasn't good at it, but Billy's attitude towards him, the client, had to be set straight.

Double standard, Mitch, double standard, he realized as he reached the lobby level. Nevertheless, he stepped out of the elevator, did an annoyed face and put some bite in his stride.

Billy, the Sherry doorman and their smiles were out front. A small flatbed trailer was hitched to the Lexus.

Mitch instantly revised his act.

On the flatbed was the reason Billy had been so insistent on nine-nine-thirty. Why Maddie had been taking her own sweet time.

At once, a gate of Mitch's memory sprung open and out for front and center came a certain night last winter during an afterwards among the pillows. He and Maddie had taken turns revealing things they'd at one time or another wanted and might again, material things.

He'd begun with the obligatory assertion that as long as he had her he wanted nothing more.

"As long as?" she'd arched.

"Okay, inasmuch as."

"Do I have to go first?"

"No," he said. "Let me think. I always wanted a hog."

"Really, a hog?"

"Uh huh."

"Are you sure, precious? You'd have to slop it. That's what they do, don't they, slop hogs?"

And now, there in front of the Sherry was the hog. Held upright on the flatbed by guy cables. Saturday New York walkers were pausing to admire it because it was up there on the flatbed looking exhibited.

What Maddie had gotten him in place of the Fabergé cuff links.

A Harley-Davidson no less.

A new Heritage Softail Classic in serious black with

chrome-laced wheels, chrome fishtail mufflers, a shotgun style exhaust, fat boy tank, everything. Even black cowhide fringes with chrome beads dangling from the hand grips and chrome studs and conchos that played up the black, harness-leather saddlebags.

Mitch and Billy were wheeling it down the ramp of the flatbed when Maddie came out.

"How's that for a cycle?" she said brightly.

"Where's yours?" Mitch said.

"Don't I wish," she laughed. "Man, you're just going to have to pack your bitch." Evidently while buying the bike she'd made them throw in some vernacular. "You're not going to insist I take it back, are you?"

That hadn't entered Mitch's mind. It would be his next two Christmases and birthdays. "You're much too good to me," he said.

"Just trying to keep even," was her nice comeback.

Mitch rolled the Harley to parallel with the curb and leaned in on its kickstand.

Billy got two visored helmets from the Lexus, full-face, mean-looking black Arai Quantum/s helmets. Identical his and hers. They'd been custom-fitted with two-way intercoms that allowed helmet-to-helmet conversation. Billy also distributed pairs of black cowhide gloves.

The helmet and gloves suited Maddie's black jeans and short black jean jacket with a genuine club insignia on the back. STAMFORD STEALTHS, speed-lined skull and all, stitched in acid green. Her box-toed construction worker's boots were also right. The jacket was far from new, had been bought by phone from a far downtown military surplus and second-hand clothing outlet. Maddie had called a half dozen such places. The store man had thought she was another New York nut when she wanted the jacket delivered to the Sherry. He'd hung up on her twice but right off on her third call she blurted that she'd pay double what he was asking and that made it worth the chance.

All in all Maddie looked every bit the biker.

Mitch, on the other hand, in his T-shirt, khakis and bare feet in sneaks came nowhere near the image. His bare neck, forearms and ankles were going to be graveyards for airborne insects.

"There's an owner's manual somewhere," Maddie told him. "But you don't need instructions now, do you precious?" She was anxious to get on and get going.

"I really ought to go back up and put on some jeans and a different shirt," Mitch said.

"You'll swelter," Maddie mimicked.

Mitch went up to change.

Billy drove the Lexus and flatbed away.

Maddie removed two pistols from the waistband of her jeans. She put them in one of the Harley's saddlebags. Also four spare clips and a couple of boxes of cartridges.

She wasn't furtive about it. They were, after all, legally her husband's guns, and to hell with any passersby who were made apprehensive by the sight of them or, even more, by the sight of her, the bad-looking biker, with them.

On her own she found her way onto the Harley's rear seat, so when Mitch came down he had only to show her where to place her feet. He kneeled and positioned them for her.

He legged over and got settled in the saddle. Paused a minute to enjoy the initial feel of having the Harley under him.

He started it up and allowed it to idle.

Potato, potato, potato.

The unmistakable Harley sound.

"C'mon man," Maddie urged, "put the pedal to the metal."

Mitch waited for a break in the Fifth Avenue traffic to cut across and get on Central Park South. He decided not to go up through the park because there'd be so much roller-blading and other kinds of rolling in there. He continued on to Columbus Circle, went up to the west side of the park to 72nd and then made all the lights to the Henry Hudson Parkway.

It was jammed with headed-out traffic, but, in this instance, Mitch wouldn't have to wait in it. He put the Harley in the narrow between lanes and, defying exhaust and the possibility of abrupt lane changers, ran the gauntlet doing fifty.

He heard Maddie's breath catching. Maybe she was sensing the risk. "How is it back there?" he asked.

"I've never been so carried away!" she exclaimed.

Actually, Maddie wasn't certain how she was faring. Part of her was exhilarated by the open speed and tenuousness, while nearly as much of her wished she'd stipulated a back support for the seat she was on. Her black heightened the sensation that any moment she might go flying off to oblivion. The Harley salesman had suggested a back support; however, he'd referred to it in the vernacular as a *sissy bar* and that had settled it for her.

It took about twenty miles of wind and Harley growl to chase most of her trepidation. Her normal existential attitude took over. "Swerve some," she told Mitch.

"Huh?"

"Do some swerves. I like it when I'm made to lean."

"There'll be lots of corners."

"Don't deprive me."

He waited until there was a clear stretch. He covered all two miles of it with back-and-forth full-width swerving.

Maddie's squeals of delight and fright were appropriately diphthonged.

He went back to going straight.

"Why?" she asked.

"There's a car just ahead."

"Cop car?"

"No."

"What kind of car?"

He anticipated her, told her it was a Porsche.

"Which model?"

"Looks to be a nine-eleven."

"Blow it away."

"We're already doing eighty." Actually sixty-five.

"What the fuck, crank it!"

Mitch added just enough throttle to snap Maddie's head and roar past the four-year-old, laboring Toyota Tercel.

And so it went as they proceeded up the Saw Mill and got on the Taconic, headed for upstate. Maddie did about ten miles of humming and then got to singing a Mary-Chapin Carpenter and Mitch was relieved when instead of a third chorus she asked how much further.

"About fifty miles, a little less. You okay?"

"Yeah, but you know what this thing is?"

"What thing?"

"This hog of yours. It's a seven-hundred-pound vibrator."

"It's having its way with you?"

"I may get off before I get off," she laughed. "It's almost as relentless as you are."

"Oh?"

"At times," she added, tempering the compliment.

"Everything you say is true."

"But you're a big fibber."

Don't admit, don't deny, he told himself.

"I've caught you in more fibs than there are beans in a jar," she said. "It's part of your charm. Did I mention that when Straw phoned the other day he said he had a surprise for us?"

"Big or little surprise?"

"He tried to make it sound little but my hunch is it's big-time."

Maddie leaned forward, pressed against Mitch's back, put her arms around and invaded his jeans. It was a tight squeeze for her hands but he helped by sucking in his abdomen.

CHAPTER 15

Claverack, Austerlitz, Kinderhook.

And there, at noon, the private drive of Uncle Straw's place was beneath the Harley's wheels.

An unpaved drive.

Numerous times there'd been inclinations to have it black-topped and once, two Strawbridges back, that so-called improvement had come as close as a bid from a local paving company. The morning the workmen arrived with their graders, rollers and macadam cookers, it was decided paving would be too costly a change, too costly to the eyes.

The alternative was a gravel of a compatible shade.

A mile-long drive, it serpentined through an apple orchard. Sixty of the orchards' eighty-five trees were still encountering seasons. Many of the sixty were old survivors with major amputations. They'd seen the trunks of neighbors topple over from interior rot. They resolutely continued to bear.

In return for their loyalty they were tended, pruned severely for their own good each spring and sprayed at the first sign of blight or rust or leaf hopper.

Further in on the drive the apples gave way to pines. A prevenient comfort zone, thick above, refreshing below. Carpeted with needle drop.

After the pines came openness, lawn, a gently sloped expanse of it. Cared for but by no means manicured or formal. Lawn like a wide green skirt arranged around the sit of the house.

The Strawbridge house.

It had never been otherwise known. Unlike so many of the residences up there along the Hudson, manor houses and such, it hadn't once belonged to the Stuyvesants or the Rensselaers or any other of those early New Amsterdam families with a Van between their names.

Nor was there any Dutch in its architectural personality.

It was a Georgian revival, almost a replica of a house Nelson Strawbridge, Maddie's great-grandfather, had admired in 1910, while spending a weekend in Surrey. Nelson was so taken by that Surrey house that he filed it in his ready memory and, fourteen years later, when he decided to build on what he called his patch of four hundred acres up in Kinderhook, he sent his architect to England to sketch the lines of it.

The architect did him one better. Made acquaintance with the owner, who happened to be in a financial squeeze and therefore considered it a blessing that he was able to realize ten thousand for anything so dispensable as a set of the original plans.

The Strawbridge rendition was a large house by ordinary standards but much less than what was considered a mansion by those who owned mansions.

Sixteen rooms.

The majority of which were situated in the three-story main section. The exterior was of clean, aged brick with a sharply pitched, blue-slate roof. Crisp white trim at every opportunity. Nine over nine sash windows eared by black shutters. A house of elegant proportions and details while escaping pretension.

There it was now, coming into Mitch's view and Maddie's mind. The pines had notified her. Being family, they ignored the front entrance and went around the side to the apron of the four-car garage.

It was good to have the helmets off.

Maddie thought that might be what it was like for a chick to come out of incubation. Stop thinking weirdly, she chided herself. Her thighs and pelvis were tingling.

Mitch stretched his back and shoulders and came close to complaining on behalf of his rump. Such a long ride first time out had been asking too much of it.

Where was Straw? Usually he heard them arrive and came out right away to greet them. Not today for some reason.

They entered through a side gate which gave to a herring-bone-patterned brick wall along the rear of the house. The service and kitchen areas were located in the wing opposite, about a hundred feet away. They'd gone only a few steps when someone came out from the kitchen, causing a hitch in Mitch's stride.

"What is it, precious?" Maddie asked.

"I believe it might be Straw's surprise," Mitch told her.

"What's she like?"

"How do you know it's a she?"

"Straw told me."

"I thought it was to be a surprise."

"I mean what he said with words didn't tell me, his voice had some gratified mischief in it. There's no mistaking gratified mischief. Describe her to me."

Where to start, with what words? "She's tall," Mitch said.

"How tall?"

"Quite tall?"

"Nose to nose with you?"

"Possibly."

"Why am I having to drag this out of you? Is she attractive? How old would you say? Say, for Christ's sake."

"I didn't get that much of a look at her." Which was true. He'd only gotten the merest glimpse of the woman's face, and apparently, she hadn't noticed them at all. She'd come out intent on a destination in the opposite direction. Was now on her way.

The fingers of her right hand had two bottles of Heineken

by their throats. The way she was swinging those beers spoke her frame of mind.

Mitch guessed she was about six-one, maybe two. Her slenderness made her appear even taller, and, give and take as physiques often do, her height made her look all the more slender.

Hers was indeed a remarkable and fortunate body.

At the moment she had it adorned by only three things, two of which were green mucking boots, Wellingtons. The other was the bottom of a thong bikini, the merest triangle of silvery material. The boots were too large for her. She had to scuff along, hardly raising her feet. Straw's boots, Mitch surmised. There was something candidly intimate about her being in Straw's boots, undressed as she was.

Wherever this woman was headed, no doubt there would be Straw. Mitch steered Maddie's elbow and followed along. It wasn't lost to him that again he was observing someone unaware.

He maintained an accommodating distance, not so far behind the woman that he couldn't make out the quality of her skin. Ivory pale, too pale to risk exposure on such a sunny day. Her hair was black as crow feathers, and as shiny. Styled close to her skull, somewhat like a bathing cap.

There was something unique about her bearing, Mitch noticed. For one thing her head was taking a level ride on her neck, as though it was attached by some motion-absorbing device. And her buttocks with that silver string out of sight between them, materializing above. Tight, ideally sufficient buttocks, they too seemed like passengers left and right not required to be affected by her walk.

With Mitch and Maddie in her wake, the woman went along a brick wall that served as backdrop for a crowd of craning double hollyhocks. Through the allée formed by eight paired seventy-year-old maples. Close by and past the thousand panes of greenhouse. Out to where Straw had his vegetable garden, and into it.

The woman stopped there. Where was Straw? Her eyes

sought him. She called out. His name on the undulate of the mid-day, mid-summer air. It seemed a cue he'd been awaiting. Certain leafy stalks in a row of corn were like a curtain that Straw parted and stepped through.

The woman handed him one of the beers. Was paid for it with a peck of a kiss on her mouth.

As Straw swigged he spotted the approach of Mitch and Maddie. He stood his ground, allowed them to come to him, so he could feed on the full-length sight of them together.

He gave a hug to each, hugs with their names said fondly in them. Mitch's also contained two comradely pats on the back.

"I came out to cut some Bibb for lunch and got challenged by some weeds," Straw said. He introduced the woman.

Wallis Wentworth.

Assumed or not, Mitch thought, both the Wallis and the Wentworth suited her. Cindy, Amy, Chrissie or whatever would have been unfortunate. Straw called her Wally. He put his arm around her, drew her to his side possessively. "I sent Wally in for beers," he said. He extended his. "Have a swig."

Maddie's reach went right to the bottle. She took three swallows and pressed the cold sweating green glass to her hot sweating forehead before handing it on to Mitch.

Wally apparently thought nothing of standing there so nearly nude. She had her arms crossed, which partially covered her breasts; however that was a natural aspect of her stance, not self-consciousness. Her breasts were small but not meager. Firm, almost adolescent-looking with pink nipples like the tips of a baby's finger. A slight, nice pooch to her abdomen.

Mitch guessed Wally was beyond her thirties by maybe four or five years. A time-fighter. Well-boned features that wouldn't give up easily. She reminded him somewhat of the late actress Kay Kendall. He appreciated the way her smile annihilated her aloofness. How could he describe it to Maddie? An explosive smile, he might say, and probably Maddie would quip that she hadn't heard it.

Straw and Wally.

A good physical match, and perhaps not only that, was Mitch's early impression. Straw had the size and substance such a woman would play against best. Her black cap of hair counterpoint to his straight, thinning gray and white. Her lengthy leanness, Straw's above average height and bulky build. Her forties, his sixties. And yes, his wealth and her urgency to be underwritten.

Need for need, they were a pair of providers who had evidently opened up supply lines.

Gratified mischief, Mitch thought.

"I've yet to cut the lettuce," Straw said. He was effortlessly aristocratic-looking. It was incongruous that his hands and forearms should now be so caked with dirt, that soil was impacted beneath his fingernails. A transfer of lipstick was discernible on his nearly white brush mustache. He had on frayed cutoff jeans and ruined moccasins.

"Why don't you all go inside," he said, "and I'll be along shortly."

Chapter 16

Lunch on the upper terrace.

Everyone freshly bathed and changed into whites. Pleated linen shorts, sheer shirts hardly buttoned, oversize tank tops with loose ventilating armholes.

Straw had on a creamy Ecuadorian hat, its brim shaped just so for maximum jauntiness. It was new.

"Coveting my hat, are you? Here!" He put it on Wally before she could dodge. Like his boots it was too large for her, slipped down over her forehead to her brows, caught on her ears.

She laughed gorgeously, went along with it as though the hat was now hers and she intended to wear it. Then, suddenly, as though it was her right, she flung it anywhere. Her hair had gotten mussed. She didn't bother with it.

Above the table, well above them, a stretch of bleached muslin tamed blaze into shadowless flattery. The scents that had been atomized on wrists, throats and ankles competed with the fragrance of the sweet williams in the close-by Versailles planters. The food appeared too beautiful to disturb.

Everything cool.

Green beans, red peppers, white Argenteuil asparagus, magenta beets. Poached salmon sprinkled with dill, a legion of identical and equally decapitated Brisling sardines, tomatoes, cornichons, a paté. And that wasn't all.

The wine was a vintage Gewürztraminer.

Aside on a serving table, to be anticipated throughout, was a *tarte aux poires* and something else layered that was extremely chocolate and a silver platter of fresh green figs so perfectly ripe they required a bed of cotton.

Straw tore at a crusty loaf of French peasant bread. He used the hunk to sop up some olive oil, then dabbed it into a saucer of grated parmesan. He'd be a vigorous eater this day. In keeping with his state of mind.

Mitch had noticed the change in Straw. Not that Straw had been so evidently heavy-hearted before now but it seemed as though an encumbering skin had been shed. Straw's eyes and hands were quicker, his posture higher, his voice rounder and coming from deeper in him.

Mitch had mentioned it to Maddie.

"Told you," she'd said, "but no need to be concerned about Straw."

"Who's concerned?"

"He could never be an old fool," and after scarcely a half beat: "but we'll keep on the lookout for symptoms, won't we?"

The conversation at lunch, which was really the main course, skipped and skimmed along randomly and landed on Wally.

"I was once married to a golf hustler," she said. "He was terribly good at it, would purposely slice and hook his drives, thrash around in the rough and miss easy putts to sucker whoever happened to be his opponent into betting really big on the last couple of holes. Then, of course, he'd play up to his game and make the killing."

"When was that?"

"Oh." Wally smiled. "Too many years ago to divulge. I was practically a child."

"Do you golf?" That from Maddie.

Wally didn't miss the implication. "Never have," she replied.

She went on to tell of her days as a runway fashion model in New York and in Europe. She'd been a regular for Geoffrey Beene, Cardin and Valentino. When that silly business had had enough of her, she'd certainly had her fill of it. She got into something similar, became a Las Vegas showgirl, one of those detached walking displays, costumed in a few sequins, a feather or two and an enormous headpiece. Eyelashes out to here, she laughed, a self-penalizing laugh.

Mitch stole from her left breast by way of the armhole of her tank top. Earlier he'd seen her a mere triangle short of naked, he thought, and now here he was stealing. What a thief he was. He ought to be caught and convicted. That Wally had been a runway fashion model and a Vegas exhibitionist explained her haughty head, ass control and physical audacity. He liked her.

"That's where Wally and I met," Straw said, "in Vegas. About a month ago when I was out there. She won at baccarat, for me."

"Nine hands in a row," Wally said.

"Ten," Straw corrected. "Then one thing led to another."

Mitch imagined the another.

Hooray for Straw, Maddie nearly blurted. She augured that this Wally would prove to be more forthright and beneficial than all the *mal mariées* that had been circling Straw for years.

Maddie popped nine tiny Niçoise olives into her mouth, stored them in her left jaw. Her tongue conveyed them consecutively to her chew and helped collect the pits in her right jaw. She had an urge to eject the pits forcefully, machine-gun them out. She spat them into her hand and deposited them on her butter dish. She did an interested-in-all-things face and kept it on until there was an adequate break in the conversation. "Mitch is going to teach me to shoot," she announced.

"Splendid idea!" Straw said.

As though his niece's vision was twenty-twenty.

"Good thing for a woman to know," Wally contributed.

"You are going to teach me, aren't you precious?" Maddie said.

"One of these days," Mitch replied.

"Tomorrow," Maddie scheduled.

"With what? Straw doesn't have a pistol, do you Straw?" Mitch signaled Straw should say no.

Straw fibbed reluctantly. "A shotgun or two is all."

Maddie vetoed shotguns. "But say we had a pistol for tomorrow, you'd teach me wouldn't you?"

"Sure," Mitch told her, believing he was on safe ground.

"Marian was an excellent shot," Straw said. "Really, a veritable sharpshooter. She owned a forty-four magnum. Whenever we had a squabble she'd go out and shoot at something. As you can imagine, it unnerved me." He grinned and shook his head as though remembering a close call. "By the way," he told Maddie, "I received another request for foreign aid this past week."

"So did I," Maddie said.

"There's a house in Aix-en-Provence that Marian says she must have."

"To me it was in Barcelona. How much did she hit you up for?"

"Three hundred. What about Elise?"

"The same. I've had it sent."

"So have I."

Better they had given the money to an elephant or rhino cause than to that pair of girl-eating piranhas, Mitch thought. He imagined Elise and Marian with six hundred thousand to blow, and blow it they would.

The same amount Ruder had promised him if he recovered the Kalali goods. Don't think about that, Mitch told himself. It hadn't been on his mind all day. Anyway, not featured.

He backed his chair away from the table some and turned it to better his view. A pair of sparrows were on the terrace railing nervously considering the tray of figs. If the birds got up enough courage to make a go at the figs, how long, Mitch wondered, would he pretend to not notice?

Fig, he thought, and associated *figa,* which was an Italian gutter term he'd often heard Riccio use. Why didn't Riccio just say *cunt?*

Strawbridge land.

Mitch gazed over the railing at it. To his left, south of the house, was about two hundred level acres of pastures. A scattered herd of Holstein-Friesian cows in it. Black and white all-day munchers. The cows didn't belong to Straw but to the dairy farmer whose complex of barns, silos and such were miniaturized in the distance. Straw just allowed the cows.

Mitch had walked over to the dairy farm a few times. He learned from the farmer that Holsteins gave more milk than other breeds. On the average a butterfat content of 3.7 percent. But the milk from Guernseys was higher in protein.

In the opposite direction, north of the house, the terrain was uneven and mainly wooded. Oaks, elms, maples and pines vied for sunlight with their heights. A few hickories. Numerous inexplicable clearings and patches of wild blackberries. Also several energetic springs with runoffs that insisted their ways to lower terrain and spread into a marsh, mysterious, inviolable.

Straight west was the river, the Hudson. A Strawbridge mile and a half between the house and it. That distance made easier by traditional paths. It was something always there to go to, the river, to spend a while on the three-hundred-foot-high granite bluff that overlooked it. Admiring the river's perpetualness, expending some worship on it in a way as probably the native Americans once had, the Mohicans for instance.

Those bluffs high above the river had become a favorite place for Mitch. He'd explored them up and down, gotten to know their obscure traversing ledges, their deceiving crevices and dead ends. They were a long ways from West 47.

Gazing out from the upper terrace, Mitch thought how at

one time this land had been an incidental part of a vast Dutch land grant and how smart of great-grandfather Nelson Strawbridge to have acquired it. It was said he won the parcel in a one-on-one croquet match while spending a Fourth of July in Newport.

Grandfather Gordon Strawbridge had also demonstrated his judiciousness by passing the house and land on to his son, Martin (Straw), rather than to his daughter, Elise.

Elise hadn't been entirely omitted from her father's will, but she had good reason to feel slighted. She was left two million, an erotic sketch by Mihaly Zichy that she never knew Gordon owned (why not one of his Fantin-Latours?). And two balls, baseballs autographed by Babe Ruth and Bill Dickey.

The remainder of the estate, estimated to be in the five hundred million range, was divided equally between Straw and Elise's fatherless thirteen-year-old daughter, Madeline (Maddie), whom Gordon had always doted on. Maddie's portion would be looked after by the family lawyers, Albertson and Albertson, otherwise there were no restricting conditions.

Elise was more irate than hurt. She'd never gotten along well with her father. The most that could be said was they'd been fairly compatible for brief periods now and then.

Elise had always taken perverse pleasure in disappointing him. She'd promote herself in his eyes to the point where he'd begin to count on her, then let him down. He often told her she was selfish. She never denied it.

A psychiatrist suggested she was using her negative behavior to test the extent of her father's love for her, to determine how much he would put up with.

She parried the suggestion. "What shit. I'm not that scheming."

She seemed to believe that candor was the fee for indemnity. "It's just not in me," she'd say. "I don't have what it takes to endure even the merest self-deprivation."

No wonder, then, that inheriting only two million was

tragic for her. She'd counted on so much more. As sure as she was of her own blood she'd believed it would be coming to her.

She spent close to a hundred thousand on legal fees, trying to invalidate the will. On the basis that her father had been mentally disturbed, a bigot, unbalanced by his extreme intolerance. She claimed the sole reason he'd shorted her was she'd been honest in disclosing her sexual preference for women.

A lady lawyer with whom Elise happened one night to be sharing a three A.M. afterwards ceiling forthrightly advised her to drop her legal action. No court would find in her favor. Even if she won sympathy, which was unlikely, hadn't her father's will been drawn up eleven years *prior* to her *coming out?*

Elise withdrew but not for a moment would she be resigned. She went on a bitter fling. Ran through the two million and was left with no bearable option other than to go on Maddie's dole.

It was difficult for her but she managed to feign affection for Maddie. Brushed her hair, took her to Bergdorf for new shoes, tucked her bedcovers. To her way of thinking it was a sort of self-deprivation. She couldn't sustain it and was greatly relieved when she found she didn't need to, that Maddie would never refuse her.

If Elise had any redeeming qualities she kept them obscured. Was it possible that she was completely without parental conscience? It seemed so. For her, conceiving Maddie had been unpleasant, carrying her had been disfiguring, delivering her had been painful, and having to care for her was over the top.

She didn't keep these justifications to herself, sardonically articulated them for the amusement of her cohorts, most of whom could not feel sorry for her because they needed their full supply of pity for themselves.

About then Maddie had gone blind.

It wasn't really a going. That is, it wasn't gradual.

She awakened one morning believing she hadn't awakened, that the black she was experiencing was still the black
of sleep. She often had very realistic dreams, so she lay there
awaiting where this one might take her.

She touched her eyelids, caused them to blink. She felt
them slipping up and down over her eyes. It was weird. How
many million times before had she blinked and never felt that.
The tip of her finger felt the flickings of her lashes.

As swift as her realization a volt of panic shot through her.
She sat up. She cried out, an unrestrained bawl. When no one
came she fell back on her pillows.

Black.

There was no reason for it. She hadn't gotten anything
harmful in her eyes.

It was temporary, she assured herself, would go away in a
while. Calm down, calm down.

She regretted having cried out, hoped no one had heard her.
She wouldn't again no matter what. If this inability to see didn't
go away, she'd stay in bed, say she felt achy, had caught a
virus, was feverish. Perhaps she'd be brought some water and
antihistamine capsules and a thermometer but other than that
there'd be no concern.

She would be alone in the black.

It frightened her but, at the same time, its possible advantages occurred to her. What if she plunged into it, floated on
it. What if this black was something she could bring on at
will. How useful that could be. If it went away, as it surely
would, she hoped she'd be able to get it back.

She lay there listening to herself. Her breathing was a private wind, her heartbeat a friendly, signaling drum. She
scratched an itch from her cheek, clicked her teeth, sniffled,
swallowed. Her insularity was amplified. With a little more
concentration she might be able to hear the coursing of her
blood.

Look! Weren't those angels? Angels outlined by trails of
glittering effervescence, moving about against the black? If
not for the black she wouldn't have been able to see them.

Her black.

She claimed it and felt suddenly serene, as though she'd been granted a wish.

On the third such day when Elise looked in on her, Maddie was up and dressed.

"How are you today?" Elise inquired dutifully.

"I'm blind," Maddie replied matter of fact.

"What nonsense."

The initial examination of Maddie was conducted by an elderly ophthalmologist at his office on East 72nd. He found nothing wrong with her eyes and said in Maddie's presence it was his opinion that she was malingering, faking it.

Uncle Straw took Maddie to see specialists at Johns Hopkins and Mayo and the Hermann Eye Center at Texas Medical. Many of the country's most reputable ophthalmologists, neurologists and neurobiologists had their go at her.

Her head was scanned repeatedly. Each doctor didn't seem to want to rely upon the diagnostic procedures done by the doctor who'd preceded him. Time and again Maddie was placed on a stainless steel tray and, like a torpedo, slid into a tube. Sandbags on each side of her head to keep her from moving, while not only her visual system but her entire brain could be looked at dimensionally and in slices.

Computerized axial tomography, positron-emission tomography, nuclear magnetic resonance, biomagnetic imaging. Scanning laser ophthalmoscopes mapped her retinas in three-tenths of a second.

All diseases that cause blindness were detectable, but the reason for Maddie's loss of sight eluded the specialists.

Had she ever had meningitis?

Meningoencephalitis? Birds carry it.

Cat scratch fever?

No, no and no. Of course, she'd owned a few parakeets and fed pigeons in the park countless times. She adored cats, had had several over the years. There might very well have been scratches, but fever?

Each doctor who beamed into Maddie's eyes and viewed as

deep in as he could saw normal, healthy-looking retinas. Nothing wrong with those vital slivers of neural tissue located at the back of the eyeball. No degeneration or even inflammation.

Where the optic nerves stemmed from the retinas also appeared normal. Beyond that point couldn't be seen with an ophthalmoscope. The cause had to be in there, somewhere beyond.

At the optic chasm, perhaps, where the optic nerves split and ran to the left and right like an intersection of a four-lane highway. Or possibly further on in the thalamus, where the optic nerves fed into the switchboard-like geniculate bodies.

The search for a diagnosis proceeded into the visual cortex and on into the cerebral cortex, a region of the brain that still baffled medical science when it came to the part it played in seeing and processing what was seen. All sorts of astounding things could be going on in there that the scans weren't picking up.

Despite their sizable fees the doctors were at a loss.

Maddie's visual system had just shut down, turned off, closed shop.

And Lord knows why.

Maddie vowed to kick the shins of anyone who proposed another scan.

Early on, at one of the most prestigious eye clinics, a young female neurobiologist, relegated to a third-team silent observer, had dared to speak out of turn with the suggestion that Maddie's blindness might be psychologically caused.

Her words were lost to everyone but Maddie, and she only recalled them when the rummage for a pathological reason ran out of steam.

Could the psyche block a person's ability to see? It wasn't a common occurrence but neither was it unheard of. In fact, over the past fifty years, the number of reported cases of *hysterical blindness,* as it was called, had increased considerably.

According to psychiatry, the condition was brought about

by chronic emotional stress. The unconscious, overloaded with such stress and tired of putting up with it, converted it into a physical disorder, such as blindness.

It fit. The more Maddie thought about it the more comfortable she felt with it, although the *hysterical* label bothered her some. She'd never been in a state of hysteria, there'd never been any tantrums or uncontrollable anxieties. Of course, those things could have been going on in her unconscious, couldn't they?

Possibly.

Anyway, no more doctors, no more scans. She was tutored in Braille. She also learned to tap about with one of those long white canes and to trust the guidance of a specially trained dog.

It wasn't so terrible, being blind, she tried to convince herself. Consider all the ugliness she wouldn't be visually subjected to. Still, blind was blind, and she hadn't seen enough beauty to satisfy her.

Normally, a person who couldn't see couldn't do much, wasn't expected to. There were traditional limitations.

Maddie was determined to surpass those limits, stretch them as far as her black would permit, and then some, if she could. It was, she believed, much a matter of spirit. Her spirit was her ally, just as stumble and fumble were her enemies.

She exercised her functioning senses, her hearing, smell, touch. They became increasingly enhanced. Eventually she found, as she'd hoped, that she was able to consolidate them into a sort of superperception.

See, her spirit said, *told you so.*

The white cane stayed propped in a corner next to her dresser. The guiding dog was contributed to someone who needed it.

Elise was seldom around. Maddie's blindness would have deprived her even more.

Maddie lived with Uncle Straw.

And now, this remarkable, valiant, spirit-charged woman

lives with me, Mitch thought, as there on the upper terrace of
Straw's Kinderhook house, he turned and gave his attention to
what she was into at the moment.

She was putting on a little show.

She had Wally blindfolded with one of Straw's neckties.
The luncheon plates, glasses and all had been moved to one
side so about half of the tabletop was clear. On the cleared
part lay a black and white hundred-dollar baccarat chip, a
keepsake from the night Straw and Wally had met at the
Golden Nugget.

"Find the chip," Maddie told Wally. "Go ahead, find it."

Wally reached out with her right hand. She changed her
mind three times before deciding where she believed the chip
was located. She was way off.

"I don't think it's possible," Wally said, "not for me, anyway."

"You weren't seeing with your fingers," Maddie said. "As
I told you, you have to see with your fingers. Try again."

Wally missed again. She laughed and pulled off the blindfold.

Maddie would show her it could be done. Of course, no
blindfold was needed. "Place the chip anywhere," she said.

Wally kept the chip in her fist. She winked at Straw.
"Okay," she challenged Maddie, "now, you find it."

It was something both Straw and Mitch had seen Maddie
do numerous times. *Spatial reckoning* was her label for it.

At first it had been a notion inspired from having heard all
those neurologists and neurobiologists speak about the vagaries of the human brain, how one special process of it
could override another special process, how it was frequently
forced to be cross-worked, how impulses and signals from
banks of hundreds of millions of rods and cones circuited information back and forth at the rate of a quadrillionth of a
second.

Thus, Maddie visualized her brain as a tremendous tangle
that might not always function as perfectly as it was supposed

to. Trade-offs of responsibilities could be going on in there, especially between the sensory cells.

For instance, occasionally, hearing cells might smell and smelling cells might hear.

Touching cells might see.

And, maybe, rather than mutually agreeable switching like that, certain more aggressive cells took over doing things they were not supposed to do on their own.

Whenever they felt the urge or were asked to emphatically enough by the landlady.

Spatial reckoning.

Seeing with the fingers.

A way for Maddie to know things were where they were.

She couldn't do it at will. It wasn't something she could absolutely depend on, as she wished it would be. Nor did she believe that her fingers could literally see. However, from all her practice at it and the many times she'd been right, she felt there was something to it. The neurobiologists would scoff at her notion, but by their own admission, they didn't know everything.

Maddie held her hand above the tabletop and concentrated. After about a minute she gave up. "No fair," she said.

Wally was impressed that Maddie had perceived that the chip wasn't on the table. She was further impressed when she suddenly flipped the chip into the air heads or tails fashion and Maddie somehow knew she had and made a mid-air stab at it.

The sparrows were pecking at the figs.

Mitch shooed them away. Less than a minute later they were back on the railing getting set to make another foray. Like me and 47th, Mitch thought.

Maddie pinched his earlobe, as she often did when she wanted his entire attention to what she was about to say. "Be a love," she said, "and fetch the things from the saddlebags of the Harley."

Mitch realized almost immediately what the things would be. He knew her, what a tricker she was, the beautiful, all-time, undefeated champion rascal of the world. He did some exasperation and shook his head incredulously because it was unbelievable that he could love her so much.

"And while you're at it," Maddie told him, "why don't you show Straw your new hog."

Mitch and Straw went down to the Harley. Straw admired it all around, ran his hand over it in places. "Great-looking machine. I've never been on one."

"Never too late."

"For many things. What do you think of my Wally?"

"I think you're almost as lucky as she is."

Straw appreciated that nice way of putting it. They traded smiles, were eyes to eyes for a suspended moment.

Mitch took a bank check from his shirt pocket, handed it to Straw.

"What's this?" Straw asked as he always did.

"The mortgage payment."

"Don't you think it's time we did away with this nonsense?"

The apartment of the Sherry had been Straw's. He'd wanted Mitch and Maddie to have it as a wedding gift. Straw insisted, reasoned that the apartment was territory familiar to Maddie, from the go she'd be at home in it. Mitch compromised. Straw could give half the apartment to Maddie, he'd buy the other half. Thus, the monthly mortgage payments. They were sizable and with interest included.

"Really . . ." Straw protested.

"June and July are also in there," Mitch told him. He'd gotten that much in arrears.

Straw didn't look at the check.

Mitch felt three months lighter.

He unbuckled the saddlebags and took out the two pistols. One was a Glock M-22, a real stopper, the pistol preferred by Secret Service and Drug Enforcement guys. The other was a Beretta 92F Centurion, a backup weapon but also one that had good take-down power.

As a jeweler Mitch had been licensed to carry. Still was but hadn't for years.

He did a little scoffing grunt. "Next," he grumbled, "she'll be wanting to take up knife throwing."

CHAPTER 17

The following morning, while Maddie helped with the breakfast dishes, Mitch went out to find a place to shoot. He wanted to be done with it so he and Maddie could devote the rest of the day to sloth and passion.

He had in mind the old barn out in the middle of what the Strawbridges had always called the West Meadow.

The undisturbed meadow made it appear as though it would be an easy half mile; however, it turned out to be more of a wade than a walk with the perennial rye grass as it was, thick and crotch high.

Good for the legs, Mitch told himself as he pushed ahead, noticing the contradictions of Queen Anne's lace, less romantically known as wild carrot, and huge hydra-headed purple clover.

He, the intruder, was the cause of countless grasshoppers to bound about, for red-winged blackbirds to be flushed up. Garter snakes were running ahead of him.

The sun hadn't yet gotten to the dew deep down. He was soaked to the knees. He paused mid-meadow to look skyward. The moon was a leftover piece of tissue.

The barn was large and lonely. No one visited it anymore. The elements were having their way with it, peeling its coats, bleaching it, promoting rot and rust in places. A dying barn. Its roof looked healthy, though, Mitch noticed. That would help prolong its stand.

He'd intended to use one of the exterior sides for the shooting, but now it occurred to him that considering Maddie's handicap it would be more prudent to do it inside where there were walls all around.

He went in. He saw right away the roof actually wasn't all that good. Sunlight was shafting through it in numerous places. No loft. It wasn't that kind of barn. It had high rafters. An owl was asleep in one. Bats were hung from others.

On the left was some farm machinery past use. A hay rake with its big, curved intimidating prongs. Next to it, a hay baler that looked as though it resented obsolescence and would like nothing better than to compact something or someone.

There were other abandoned items. A lot of rat droppings. Mitch heard the scuttling of mice claws on the wooden floor, hornets whizzing.

He returned to the house for Maddie. She had the weapons and everything in a plastic shopping bag that she refused to give up. She slung it over her shoulder and followed Mitch across the meadow.

She'd been in the barn many times when she was sighted but not since. She had a vague recollection of it. Outstanding was the time Uncle Straw had come as close as a trouser leg of being bitten by a copperhead there. The snake had sprung and gotten its fangs snagged in the woolen fabric.

Mitch tried to move the old potbelly cast iron stove that was in one corner. It was too heavy but he outwitted it, disassembled it and put its manageable components back together where he wanted it, out in the open before the rear well.

He counted off ten paces from the stove and placed at that spot the enamel-topped kitchen table with one leg missing and another wobbly. He covered the grimy surface of the table with some newspaper he'd brought along. Laid out the pistols, clips and cartridges.

"You're too good to me," Maddie remarked.

"Just trying to stay even," Mitch said, which made the next turn with those words hers. "Hold out your open hand."

She did.

He slapped the Beretta into it.

"Is it ready to shoot?" she asked.

"No."

"So why are you giving it to me?"

"So you can load it. A shooter should know how."

"Give me a clip."

"They're on the table."

She found one. "It's empty."

"Load it."

She fumbled around before she found the carton of nine-millimeter cartridges. She sure hated fumble. She removed a round from the carton and felt it for shape and size.

Like a tiny, hard penis, she thought, and then, upon second thought, like a not so tiny clitoris. She often thanked the power in charge of handing out such equipment that she hadn't been given a shy, find-me-if-you-can sort.

Mitch told her how to load the clip. A couple of times he was tempted to guide her fingers but knew she'd be miffed if he did.

Finally, she had in all the clip would hold. Fifteen rounds. "Now I put it into the handle, right?"

"The butt."

"Okay, the butt."

She inserted the clip partway.

"Ram it in," Mitch told her.

"That's what the actress said to the bishop," she quipped. She rammed the clip into place.

Mitch showed her how to break open the barrel of the Beretta so a sixteenth round could be put into the chamber. She did it the second time without his help. "Now?" she asked.

"You ready?"

"In which direction do you suggest I shoot?"

"Wherever except at me." Letting her shoot the first load

on her own would teach her a lot, Mitch figured. She might even want to quit after a taste of it.

She held the Beretta slack-armed, didn't have much of a grip on it. She pointed it at anything and pulled the trigger. Kept it pulled as though that was her only option.

The pistol nearly jolted itself out of her hand. As the sixteen rounds fired in rapid succession her aim was snapped further upwards. The last couple of rounds splintered boards at the peak of the roof.

The owl fluffed itself and turned its back on the disturbance below.

The bats tightened their talons.

The mice scurried to the fields.

Maddie was astonished. She hadn't expected such ferocity. It was as though the Beretta was a lethal infuriated creature on the end of her arm, one that would do her bidding. She liked the smell of the exploded gunpowder, the way the concussion caused her ears to ring.

Now Mitch taught her. The importance of a solid stance, rigid arm, a tight two-hand grip. The advantage of holding her breath and squeezing the Beretta's trigger rather than jerking it.

She improved with each load. The cast iron stove became her target, her adversary. Her sense of direction was uncanny. Mitch spun her around several times to try to confuse her, but she brought her aim to the stove and fired at it.

Her hits rang and ricocheted. Eventually, almost as many hits as misses.

The smoke from so many explosions layered in the air in the barn. The carton of ammunition for the Beretta was depleted. Mitch told her it was.

Again, she'd astounded him, he thought, and again he'd enjoyed it. His blind love, on her way to being a sharpshooter. However, enough was enough. They should go out to the bluff, its mossy spot, do anything to one another. The proposal didn't get out of his mouth because . . .

"Now," she said, extending her arm, "hand me the Glock."

CHAPTER 18

"The patient's name."

"Kalali." He spelled it for her.

"First name?"

How many Kalalis could there be in this hospital, Mitch thought. "Roudabeth," he replied.

"Are you a relative?"

"Brother-in-law."

"Her condition is improved."

"How much improved? Is she conscious?"

"All I'm allowed to tell you is her condition is improved and that she's no longer in intensive care. For anything else you'll have to speak to her doctor."

"What room is she in now?"

The middle-aged woman with the teenage hairstyle and nearly no chin had already caused her computer to escape from Kalali. She took a persevering New York breath and punched it up again. "Room eleven eighteen east," she informed Mitch in a tone that conveyed that was the last he'd get from her.

He gave her a New York ambiguous thanks and went from patient information to the last-minute gift and other stuff shop off the lobby. Not especially to buy anything, only to sort of hyphenate what might be his next move.

He hadn't intended on being there at New York University Hospital this morning. On his way downtown he'd admitted how much he wasn't looking forward to another day of poking around 47th. At practically that same instant someone vacated a taxi right there and Mitch climbed in. He'd allowed his intuition to tell the driver where to go.

All along he'd been hoping for a conscious Mrs. Kalali. She'd seen the swifts, might be able to make them from the police photo files. At least she could describe them. Mitch had kept up on her condition, phoned the hospital to inquire twice each day, even during the weekend from Straw's. Each time he'd been told there was no change.

But now on Monday morning apparently there'd been a change. Mrs. Kalali was improved. That might mean she was no longer unconscious, perhaps well enough to talk.

He put back the butterscotch Life Savers he was about to buy and went out to the elevator. The up one he chose made a lot of stops. By the time he got off on eleven he was disguised in an attitude of belonging where he was and knowing where he was going.

Everyone at the nursing station of 11 East was busy. Mitch didn't stop and wasn't stopped. Room 1118 was at the far end of the corner. A private room with its door closed.

Maybe, Mitch thought, Mrs. Kalali was being given a sponge bath or was using a bedpan. He prepared himself for any such encounter, would do a medically blasé face, say he was Dr. Laughton, beg pardon and retreat.

He went in.

Mrs. Kalali was face up, eyes closed, head bandaged like a turban. Oxygen leaders were clipped to her nostrils. The only animated thing was the registering of her vital signs on the monitor above her bed.

She might be only sleeping, Mitch thought, might respond if he called out her name. He went close to the side of the bed, stood over her. She appeared insubstantial, still in the throes of trauma. Would it be dangerous to startle her? He'd arouse her gently with a whisper, was about to when the toilet was flushed in the room's private bath.

A young man came out. Preoccupied with himself, the hang of his suit jacket, buttoning it, correcting his shirtsleeves. He was fair-haired and somewhat on the pretty side. When he became aware of Mitch his composure deserted him.

Mitch was experienced with awkward moments. "Has she come to?" he asked with impersonal interest.

"Not yet."

"But anytime now, so the doctor told me."

The young man acted like someone being cornered. He evaded Mitch's eyes and left without another word.

Mitch wasn't about to lose him, whoever he was. He followed him down the corridor and into the same elevator. They didn't speak during the descent. Mitch allowed the young man to exit first, then tagged along behind him to the hospital cafeteria there on the ground floor. At this morning hour all but a few tables were vacant.

The young man took a carton of chocolate milk and a plastic-wrapped egg salad sandwich to a table next to the window. Mitch got an iced tea and closed in, chose the table next over.

Outside on practically the same level was the East River Drive. The hurrying traffic on it was distracting, a lot of taxi yellow. The river beyond contaminated-looking.

Continuing to avoid with his eyes, the young man said: "You're the police, aren't you?"

Mitch did a shrug that could have been taken for a yes.

"I knew you'd be showing up about now."

"Why didn't you run?" A good prompt, Mitch figured.

"Why should I? I didn't do anything."

"Depends."

"What do you mean depends?"

"Eat your sandwich."

"I intend to."

"Tell me about you and Mrs. Kalali."

"Nothing to tell."

"Why were you up there with her?"

"Just looking in on her."

"A concerned visit."

"That's all."

"Your first time here probably. You been here before?"

"Could I see some police identification? I refuse to say anything more until you show me identification."

Mitch complied, went into his jacket pocket, but, as though diverted by a sudden realization, he brought nothing out. "I just now made you," he said. "You work girls at a bust-out bar on 43rd."

"Not me."

"I'm sure of it."

"That's ridiculous."

"What name do you go by?"

"Roger Addison."

A dubious grunt. "That's not a real name."

"It most certainly is." Roger presented his driver's license.

Mitch pretended to examine it suspiciously front and back. "Guess you only resemble the guy who works that bust-out," he conceded.

"It so happens I work at Saks."

Mitch let him suck up some of the chocolate milk before telling him: "You're in deep shit Roger."

"I didn't do anything."

"Tell me about you and Mrs. Kalali."

"Like I said, there's nothing to tell."

"If she comes out of the coma there'll be plenty to tell, won't there?"

An indifferent shrug from Roger. His flushed complexion didn't go along with it.

"Maybe what you're hoping is she doesn't come out of it," Mitch said.

"That's not true."

"Then why are you hanging around here claiming you're family so you can sit bedside at all hours?"

An accurate assumption.

"I've been keeping a sort of vigil," Roger admitted. "I want to be the first person she sees when she comes conscious."

Mitch could relate to that.

"Besides," Roger went on, "one of the doctors told me it's possible that things said to her may be registering."

"So you've been having one-sided conversations."

"It's frustrating."

"I'll bet. What is it you say to her?"

"Mainly I want her to understand that what happened wasn't my fault. There wasn't supposed to be any violence." Roger dropped his head and remained downcast for a long moment. He came up with: "I should have a lawyer, shouldn't I?"

"Can you afford a good one?"

"Not really."

"You claim you didn't do anything."

"I didn't."

"Tell me what you did do and I'll tell you if it's anything."

"I have to be at work at noon," Roger stalled.

"That gives us a couple of hours. Is your story longer than that?" Mitch threw in a smile because it was so evident Roger could use it.

Roger began on the sandwich. Took small bites and chewed slowly. Each swallow brought him closer to disclosure. He had such a need to vent that once he opened up it came pouring out.

He told how he'd met Mrs. Kalali at Saks. He hadn't taken up with her for what he could get out of her. At least that wasn't his only reason and, after a while, as they became more involved, he hardly gave a thought to what he might gain. She was dreadfully unhappy. Her husband was vilely abusing her. There was such satisfaction in being meaningful to her, Roger said. Besides, he had always been physically attracted to mature women.

She would leave her husband. They would go somewhere,

anywhere kinder, and be together. No longer would they have to sneak afternoons.

They would. If they had the money.

Mrs. Kalali had little of her own. A few thousand was all. There was, however, the jewelry.

She proposed they sell it. It was worth far more than they'd get for it. That was the way with jewelry. Buy dear, sell cheap. The dealers on 47th, for example. They feasted on misfortune. They seemed able to smell one's need to sell and, once they got the scent, they started grubbing.

New music, old words, Mitch thought.

Anyway, Roger continued, there was the jewelry. And there was the insurance on the jewelry. He wished now she'd never mentioned the insurance.

She brought the policy to one of their afternoons at the Plaza. It was like a catechism. Questions and answers. Clearly, if the jewelry was stolen the insurance company had to pay Mrs. Kalali the appraised value within ninety days. The future contained a check for six million.

"So, you arranged for a gimmie," Mitch said.

"A what?"

"You made a deal with someone to steal it."

"What did you call it?"

"A gimmie. It's a street term."

"Oh."

"Did you or Mrs. Kalali make those arrangements?"

It was like Roger hadn't heard the question.

Mitch asked again.

Still nothing from Roger. He got up. It seemed he was going to leave; however he went to the cafeteria counter. He returned to the table with a plastic container of bread pudding and, evidently, a decision. Between the second and third spoonfuls of the pudding he mumbled something.

"What?"

"I took care of it," Roger repeated.

"The gimmie?"

"Whatever you call it."

"You know those kind of people?"

"I didn't. I happened to know someone who knew someone of that sort."

"Who?"

"I'd rather not say."

"I mean who did this acquaintance of yours hook you up with?"

"I met the man. I met with him twice."

"Where?"

"The Four Seasons."

"Really, the Four Seasons?"

"He bought lunch. With a platinum American Express."

"What was the man's name?" The key question.

"He introduced himself as Frank Melton."

Frank Melton didn't ring a bell with Mitch.

"But," Roger said, "I got a glance at the name on his platinum card. It was Crosetti. I didn't get the first name."

Crosetti? That rang all kinds of bells. Sal Crosetti.

Roger continued: "He wasn't very receptive until I told him the jewelry was valued at six million. I gave him the layout of the Kalali house, the alarm system and everything. He told me more or less how it would go, assured me there wouldn't be any violence. Just a nice, quiet robbery were his words. I believed him. I'm in trouble aren't I?"

"You're in trouble."

"But I didn't do anything."

Mitch sat back and took a moment to study this Roger Addison. His hair was well-cut. His ears had an almost translucent quality to them. Mitch still hadn't gotten a direct look at his eyes. There was a small birthmark, purplish, like a berry stain on the back of his neck just above the collar of what was probably this Monday's version of his daily fresh shirt. In a better world this Roger would never have stepped into the stream of 47th and been carried in over his head.

"I didn't do anything," he was again insisting.

Mitch wondered if he should level with him, tell him he was an accessory to murder for one thing and would probably do ten to fifteen on that count alone, tell him he wasn't the sort who'd do well in the joint, that he'd get fucked to death.

No use spoiling his day, Mitch decided.

CHAPTER 19

Salvatore Crosetti had been an outside-insider of 47th for going on twelve years. At one time he'd been just a have-around guy for an underboss in Providence, which was his hometown. Back then, when he wasn't just being around, he was out collecting from or paying off people who bet on sports. Mostly collecting from. He got paid a fixed amount weekly for doing that.

He saved a few thousand. Chances for scores came along and he'd had the money to take advantage. Like a certain race on the Saturday card at Narragansett that he knew the winner of the Thursday before. He also handled a little side action from suckers on football and baskets. No telling to what extent his boss wouldn't have appreciated that.

The big break for Crosetti came when a friend of his Uncle Mario developed emphysema and was advised by the doctors to go live as long as he could someplace where the air was easier to breathe and he wouldn't have to move around much. This friend was an established New York City fence with a crew of swifts and numerous 47th Street contacts. He sold out to Crosetti for fifty thousand. Twenty-five on the handshake, twenty-five on the come.

Crosetti was a fence to be dealt with from his first week at it. It was as though he was spontaneously transformed, the way he assumed the image. Probably it was the way he'd had himself in mind for years. No more acrylic in his suits. No more once-a-month haircuts. He dressed tastefully conservative, bought his suits and accessories at Dunhill. His knowledge of gems and jewelry was limited, but he bluffed convincingly while he picked up on them quickly.

He had an instinctive sense of how to handle his swifts, when to be hard or lenient on them. His crew consisted of three blacks and two whites. They all lived in Mount Vernon.

Early on, Crosetti caught one of the whites holding back and got rid of him. Refused to take him on again. Another was apprehended in the closet of a house and was sentenced to three years. For the year and a half the swift was inside Crosetti kept true to the code, provided for the guy's wife and kids. An envelope containing cash every month.

Crosetti wasn't married. He always had a juggle of women friends, both straights and hooks. He preferred hooks who looked straight and straights with a hooker semblance to them. He had a physical reputation that, according to persistent firsthand testimony, must have been deserved.

During his first few years on 47th Crosetti did business with both Riccio and Visconti. Then he had a falling out with Riccio over a piece of swag Riccio had bought from him. A ring with a fair-sized stone in it that looked for all the world to be a good ruby. Refractive tests proved it was a spinel, and, as such, wasn't worth a tenth of what Riccio had paid.

Typically, Riccio old-mobbed. Didn't merely ask for his money back but demanded and insulted, claimed for all the street to hear that Crosetti had intentionally cheated him.

Crosetti took exception. His reputation was at stake. Out of resentment rather than deceit he counterclaimed he'd sold Riccio a ruby that was a ruby and that Riccio was trying to fuck him out of both the ruby and the money.

The bitterness between the two men reached its apogee one noontime when Riccio was out on the street and happened to spot Crosetti across the way. "Piece of shit!" Riccio shouted.

"Dirty prick!" Crosetti fired back.

What ensued was a name-calling battle that continued for the length of the block. Riccio on one side of the street. Crosetti on the opposite side. A crowd followed each along as they *scumbagged* and *cocksuckered* at one another. Spit sprayed the air, fists were raised. Every so often Riccio did a meaner face and feinted a charge across. Crosetti sneered defiantly, extended his arms and beckoned Riccio to come ahead.

How many times and ways could they shout *asshole?* When they'd exhausted such everyday defilements, they found fresh ammunition in calling down venereal diseases on one another.

At various times in the past there'd been other al fresco arguments on 47th, but never one to compare with Riccio versus Crosetti. It was an event still being recalled. People who'd been nowhere near 47th that day claimed to have witnessed it.

Mitch was one of those who missed it; however both Riccio and Crosetti told him their conflicting versions of it— what brought it about and who got the best of it.

He preferred to believe Crosetti.

Because he enjoyed disbelieving Riccio.

In Mitch's opinion, of all the fences, Crosetti was the least slippery. That was not to say Crosetti was entirely lacking in that unctuous quality. He had a reserve of it in him that he could apply to help him squeeze out of a tight spot; however, slippery wasn't his everyday way.

As yet, Crosetti and Mitch hadn't needed to confront one another head-on. They'd only sideswiped a few times.

Like five years ago when Mitch was out to recover a pair of Van Cleef & Arpels diamond bracelets that were the major pieces taken in a robbery up in Larchmont. Mitch was on the corner of 46th and Fifth having a hot dog and a Hire's at a street vendor's wagon. Crosetti came up. He had an unlighted seven-inch Cohiba Robusto protruding from the left corner of his mouth. An element of his cachet. Mitch had never seen him light up. He literally conducted conversations with it, held it between his first finger and thumb and wielded it like a baton.

The color of the cigar was a perfect match for the beaded-stripe, double-breasted suit he had on that day. A blue paisley silk square puffed stylishly from his breast pocket.

"I'll have what he's having," Crosetti told the vendor, "except for the kraut, no kraut."

He removed the cigar from his mouth so he could put in a third of the dog and roll. He hardly chewed before swallowing.

"How's it going, Mitch?"

"Okay, Sal, how about you."

"Good and bad, you know. A little of each and not too much of either. That's what keeps things interesting, right?" Another bite and then, as though the exchange had been going on for a while, "By the way, the two similar Van Cleef pieces you been looking for."

"What about them?"

"They ain't anymore."

"You know that for sure."

"Why should I shit you? They went three days ago. I personally saw them go. Personally."

Crosetti was letting Mitch know that the diamonds of the Van Cleef bracelets had been plucked from their platinum settings and the settings had been melted down. It wasn't good news but being told was a sort of favor.

Mitch thanked Crosetti for it.

Now was another time. Now was the Monday when Roger Addison had revealed Crosetti's involvement in the Kalali robbery and it looked as though a head-on between Mitch and Crosetti was inevitable.

Mitch went directly from New York University Hospital to 47th. He worked the street, on the lookout for Crosetti, inquiring here and there in an offhand manner.

"Crosetti."

"He was around."

"When?"

"Last week. Tuesday I think it was. He hasn't been around since."

"I understand he hasn't been offering much lately." A leading remark from Mitch.

"Not to me anyway."

"He usually throws you a little something, doesn't he?"

"Very little and not usually."

Crosetti hung out, when he hung out, in the Monarch, a large exchange located mid-block on the north side of the street. His spot was the concession of a somewhat hooked-up guy who was seldom there. A narrow spot in the left front corner of the exchange. No display cases, no merchandise. Business was done pocket to pocket. Crosetti would sit in there at the window and watch the street, as though it was an all-day movie.

But he wasn't there today.

He wasn't around.

Mitch pay-phoned Visconti, who immediately came on. His excuse for the call was to thank him for the binoculars.

"How was it up in Kinderhook?" Visconti inquired.

"Fine."

"Nice country, especially this time of year."

How, Mitch wondered, did Visconti know Straw's place was in Kinderhook, not just upstate somewhere, but specifically Kinderhook? Just as puzzling, why did he know?

"You missed out on a great weekend Mitch. Besides the people I told you would be there, there were some others you know."

"Such as?"

"The dealer, Ben Ziegler, for one. He dropped by. You know Ben, and Sy Plansky, the colored stone guy from L.A."

Mitch knew Plansky from the Laughton and Sons days. A business acquaintance of his father's who, when a better piece was missing one of its colored stones, could be depended upon to come up with a close enough match.

"Sal Crosetti was also out," Visconti said. "You know Sal, of course, but I bet you didn't know he could do magic."

"He's never done any time. I guess that's magic." Mitch did a little laugh.

So did Visconti. "Sal dazzled us with his sleight of hand. The only thing he didn't make disappear was his hard-on. You should have seen the quality bimbo he had with him."

"What else did he have with him?"

"Like what?"

"Like anything?"

"We didn't do any business if that's what you mean. Shit, Mitch, you want to know you should ask. I'm not saying I'd tell you true, but, you and me, we're close enough for you to ask straight out."

Such bullshit, Mitch thought.

"What is it," Visconti wanted to know. "Does Sal have something you're after?"

"No."

"Like the Kalali goods?"

"If he did you'd know it," Mitch said. "You'd be the first to know, wouldn't you?"

"Fucking right. If he didn't bring it to me I'd shove his tongue up his ass."

Silence in reverence for that image.

"Come to think of it," Visconti went on, "the Kalali thing isn't Sal's style. There's never been blood on any of his goods. His crew never carries."

"You're making too much of this. I just inquired and you stretched it."

"You're right, Mitch. Yeah. Hey, you play squash or handball?"

"Used to."

"How about one of these afternoons going with me to my club? Later this week maybe."

"It's possible."

"Pick a day, I'm yours."

"I'll let you know."

"If you don't happen to be in the mood for a match we can just take some steam and a plunge. They got a special pool they keep at around forty degrees. Turns any size dick into an acorn."

Mitch nearly winced. He struck the pay phone's push button panel with the heel of his hand, clicked down the cradle a couple of times and hung up. It would sound as though electronic trouble had disconnected him. He'd heard enough. Evidently Crosetti hadn't moved the goods in Visconti's direction. Not yet, anyway.

He went to the intersection and was crossing when Hurley's police Plymouth turned the corner and intercepted him in the crosswalk.

"Where you headed?" Hurley asked.

"The office."

"Fuck that."

Crossers were having to go around Hurley's car, were grumbling about it being in the way. Some pounded on the trunk.

"Get in before I get lynched," Hurley told Mitch.

He hung a left on 46th and went north on Park. While stopped at a light, he glanced out at a talker. A young guy who looked three times his age, wearing clothes he probably hadn't had off in a year. Matted hair and a long-ignored beard. He was striding along hard, ranting hatefully to someone in his head.

"Sal Crosetti . . . " Mitch began.

"A loonybin," Hurley said. "That's what we got, a fucking open zoo for crazies, know what I mean? Someday I'm going to get uncommitted."

"Sure," Mitch said indulgently.

"What I could go for is a place down on the Maryland-Chesapeake shore. Plenty of land with a keep-out sign every five feet. Have some horses. Ever been down there, around Prince Frederick, that part?"

"No. You ever owned a horse?"

"A piece of a claimer once. Wiseguy bookie talked me into it, the fuck. I owned a tenth or something like that. The horse never won, never. Dropped in class and ran out three times."

Mitch tried to imagine Hurley on a Maryland horse farm. It was most unlikely. "Take a lot of money to own a place like that. If you had that much you probably wouldn't want to."

"Probably not," Hurley said dourly. "I'd go live in Monaco or some such place. Lay around and get waited on."

Hurley was about as down as Mitch had ever seen him. Maybe, Mitch thought, hearing about Addison and Sal Crosetti would lift him. Those would have been Mitch's next words, however . . .

"How about this?" Hurley said. "A lady, a well-off type, shops at Bergdorf. Buys a few things, walks over to the park and up to her apartment house in the sixties. Goes into the lobby, gets into the elevator. A guy gets in with her. Another guy is covering the lobby attendant. These two cowboys had spotted her in Bergdorf, and the ring she's wearing—a six-carat diamond, emerald-cut, a Tiffany stone. The guy in the elevator orders her to hand over the ring. She refuses. He doesn't tell her a second time. He takes out a pair of pruning shears and lops off her finger."

"This happened?"

"Saturday."

"Christ!"

"Yeah, Him, Mary, Joseph and the rest."

"Promise me something."

"Sure, what?"

"Don't tell this New York true romance to Maddie."

"I won't."

"Promise."

"I said I won't."

Mitch did a grin and kept it on, challenging Hurley to decipher it.

"What did you do, find the Kalali swag in your Rice Krispie box this morning?" Hurley said.

"Not quite."

Mitch related the question-and-answer session he'd had with Roger Addison that morning, how Addison, on behalf of Mrs. Kalali, had arranged a gimmie with Sal Crosetti.

"Crosetti?" Hurley considered that dubiously for a long moment. "I guess there's always the possibility that one of his swifts lost it and began whacking out people."

"Going to have him picked up?"

"How do you want to play it?"

"You know. I'd like the chance to shake him down before you start shaking him up." Mitch was concerned with making the recovery. According to the terms of his agreement with Columbia if the police recovered he got nothing. Hurley knew that. "Do what you have to," Mitch said resignedly.

"You want a first shot at Crosetti, you got it," Hurley told him. "Just don't take all week."

"A couple of days."

"Maybe not even that. I have an idea where Crosetti might be later tonight, around eleven or so."

"Where?"

"I'll come by for you."

Those were possibly six-hundred-thousand-dollar words, Mitch thought. Things were falling into place. "Want to go have a coffee?"

"Can't. Got another case and paperwork up to my ass at the preese."

Hurley dropped Mitch off outside his office and continued on crosstown. He didn't know by memory where Crosetti now lived, had to look it up in the directory he kept on such people, a small, simulated-leather-covered address book badly in need of a refill. Soiled pages, smeared and crossed-out entries, alphabet tabs missing.

He drove uptown on Tenth Avenue. Tenth became Amsterdam. At 71st he took Broadway for two blocks and parked on 73rd. He entered the Ansonia.

Crosetti's suite was on the fifteenth floor of the old, face-lifted, renovated hotel. Hurley called up on a house phone, allowed a full minute of rings. To make double sure he also dialed Crosetti's number on one of the pay phones and let it ring twenty times.

He took the self-service elevator up to fifteen, located

Crosetti's suite and went right to work on the three locks. Two old, one new, all three relatively easy for Hurley to tumble.

The suite was two rooms, a bedroom and a sitting room. A bathroom but no kitchen, just a small refrigerator in a closet.

Searching wasn't difficult. There weren't many hiding places and Hurley was familiar with all the usual ones: the flip-top trash pail, the air conditioner, the ice trays, the toilet tank, toes of shoes. He went through each room swiftly and methodically, not being overly careful because no matter how careful he might be Crosetti would know someone had been there.

On a table in the sitting room positioned close to one of the windows was a millimeter gauge, a Mettler PC 400C electronic scale, some tweezers, a triplet ten-power loupe, a jar of diamond-washing alcohol, a bottle of sulfuric acid and its companion piece of slate for determining gold content. A fence's usual essentials.

A brown paper bag contained a handful of gold and platinum ring and bracelet mountings. Bereft of their stones, they appeared merely metallic, forsaken.

No sign of what Hurley was hoping for.

He took a last look around and went out.

CHAPTER 20

At twenty after eleven that night Mitch was waiting outside the Sherry. He'd been there for over a half hour, talking bygone baseball and recent violence with the doorman.

Hurley's police Plymouth pulled to the curb.

"I was about to give up on you," Mitch told Hurley.

"I said around eleven. Twenty after is around."

Wait had again chafed Mitch. "Where we going?"

"Hopefully to get you your six hundred large. Does Maddie know you're with me?"

"Sure."

"You tell her everything?"

"No, you do."

They took 59th over to Third and went uptown. To a high-rise apartment house on 70th. Thirty-six stories trying for the impression of upscale. Its oversize lobby contained a lot of overstuffed furniture, mirrors and several hanging light fixtures comprised of clear plastic unsuccessfully imitating crystal.

Both of the lobby attendants on duty knew Hurley by name. They also assumed to know what he was there for. The elevator was self-service. Hurley punched in the button numbered 22. The coalesced smell of diverse food preferences was pronounced. Even more so in the corridor of the twenty-second floor. Various sounds leaked through the many closed doors.

All the way down the corridor and around another to the last possible apartment. Hurley pressed the square chime button in the face of the door. They were looked out at through a peephole.

The woman who admitted them acted a bit too glad to see Hurley, gave him a quick hug. She was a one-name person that Hurley introduced as Gloria. Chunky and plain-faced. The cotton print dress she had on concealed her shape. Her shoes were black flats.

There was a narrow table in the entryway. Business cards on it. Mitch picked up one of the cards on the way in. It had the word INTERIORS and a phone number.

No doubt about the place. A typical, twenty-five-hundred-a-month unfurnished. Three bedrooms, living room, dining alcove, narrow New York kitchen. Effortlessly decorated in black and beige and chrome. Two eight-foot sofas were separated by a low glass table. An artificial ficus with lima bean–shaped pebbles around the base of its trunk. Framed $19.98 prints of tropical scenes: a black native's head eternally burdened by a stalk of bananas.

Mitch was on the sofa that was vacant. The sofa opposite was occupied by two working girls. One was blonder but the hair of both was a mass of split ends and done to death by repetitive chemical warfare.

The two were neither pretty nor ugly. One way or the other would depend on the light, the angle and the degree of arousal that had been attained. They were overdressed, as though there was to be a party. Their long fingernails were rectangular-shaped and enameled white.

Interiors, Mitch thought. Evidently this was one of the places Hurley came to get serviced or called for a delivery. At the moment he was off somewhere having a few private words with Gloria.

The girls did smiles at Mitch. It was Monday night slow. Any action would be a godsend.

"What's your name?" the less blonde asked.

Mitch told her his first.

"What do you do Mitch?"

"I have a business on 47th Street."

"You a diamond dealer?"

"Yeah," Mitch fibbed for the hell of it.

"Can you get me a diamond?"

The predictable question. Mitch shrugged.

"Actually, what I want is studs. Two-carat studs, although I'd settle for one-carat."

Said as though her wanting was enough. Mitch doubted she was really that spoiled. "What's wrong with those you have on?" he asked.

"These? These are fakes. You can tell can't you?"

"They look okay," Mitch told her.

"No shit, can you get me some studs?"

"He's a stud," the more blonde put in.

"Keep out of this," the less blonde snapped.

The more blonde didn't. "A guy I saw a few weeks ago told me he was a diamond dealer," she said. "He promised me a ring but didn't come through." She did a pout.

"You gave it a try but he gave it a lie," the less blonde smirked competitively.

"Mitch wouldn't do that, would you Mitch?"

"Never know," Mitch replied.

"I'd like to find out what you're made of, so to speak," the less blonde said.

As though it was an unpremeditated, brand-new, marvelous idea, the more blonde proposed that they go into the bedroom for a triple.

"Not tonight," Mitch said.

From that point on, as far as the girls were concerned, he wasn't there.

Hurley came and sat, told Mitch: "He's here. Getting his oil changed."

"We're not going to confront him here, are we?"

"No. I promised Gloria we wouldn't."

They waited nearly a half hour. To Mitch it seemed much longer. Crosetti came from one of the bedrooms, tie and jacket off. He looked as though he'd just gotten well-laid. There was a sort of loose, slow float to his head.

He was surprised but not taken aback to see Hurley and Mitch there. He greeted them amiably. Hurley suggested they go someplace for a talk.

They went down to the lobby and settled in armchairs in the far corner.

Crosetti took out one of his Cohiba Robustos. It fit perfectly into the hole he shaped with his lips. He worked it in and out a few times, rotated it, licked it, went through the entire ritual except for lighting up. He looked to Mitch, looked to Hurley, asked, by raising his chin, what this was about.

"Saturday before last," Hurley began, "there was a robbery over in Jersey."

"Where in Jersey?" Crosetti asked.

"Far Hills."

"Where's that?"

"Don't shit us."

"I'm strictly Westchester," Crosetti said. "You both know I'm strictly Westchester. Yeah I might reach up into Greenwich or someplace once in a while but as a rule I don't cross state lines."

"Far Hills," Mitch insisted.

"Believe me, Mitch, I wouldn't go all the way over to Far Hills for the fucking crown jewels in a bureau drawer."

"That's not what we're getting, Sal."

"From who are you getting?"

"How about a young civilian named Roger Addison?"

"The name means nothing," Crosetti replied too quickly. "Some snitch is playing with your heads. When did you say this Far Hills job was?"

"A week ago last Saturday."

"I was in A.C."

"But where was your crew?"

"I gave them the weekend off."

"Sure you did."

"They didn't do Far Hills," Sal said unequivocally.

"I want to believe you, Sal, but I don't," Hurley said.

"How much swag is involved?"

"Six million."

"So I heard," Sal admitted.

"With blood on it."

"That I also heard."

"Sal . . . "

"Jimmy, honest to Christ, me and my crew had nothing to do with Far Hills."

"Let me bring you up to speed," Mitch told Sal. Told him point by point the information he'd extracted that morning from Roger Addison. The two lunches at the Four Seasons, the gimmie that was arranged, all of it.

Sal listened level-eyed and expressionless. Then came a moment of decision, a silent, paragraphic moment during which he cocked his head and looked off to his left as though a prompt would be forthcoming from that direction.

He held his cigar upright. "Okay," he said, "there was a gimmie. At least there was supposed to be. Why the fuck not? Gimmies are good for the economy. The people make out; I get, my swifts get, whoever buys gets, the street gets. The only one out is the insurance company and they already got so fucking much they don't deserve. Know what I mean? Circulation, good for the economy."

Mitch had to admit to himself there was some validity to Crosetti's reasoning. Long ago he'd arrived at a similar philosophy. Of course, that the insurance companies lost appealed to him.

Crosetti continued:

"This kid what's-his-name and me made an arrangement. I had it scheduled in my head for Friday night. That was the Friday before last. But my best swift's wife is having a baby, the Lamaze way, you know, and he's got to be there, and another got punched out pretty bad Thursday afternoon and he's a mess. I'm shorthanded. So, I reschedule it in my head for sometime the following week and with nothing happening take off for A.C. I'm back on Monday and I drive over to Far Hills to take a look at the job. The place is all tied up with crime scene ribbon and there's all kinds of law all over it. Needless to say, I don't even stop."

Mitch looked at Hurley to see if he was buying it. Hurley did a *could be* shrug.

"You're saying the thing never came off, somebody got to the place ahead of you?"

"That's it," Crosetti said. "You're blaming me for something I would have done but it got done before I could do it. *Capish?*"

Mitch and Hurley didn't let it go at that. Crosetti glanced from one to the other for reaction, but they gamed him, just sat there silent and blank. Which pulled the story out of Crosetti again.

He repeated it in part or entirely three times more. Each time he omitted something or added another detail, but, basically, he stuck to the same version and each time both Mitch and Hurley found the gimmie that never happened more acceptable.

"Sure, Sal, but let me ask, personally, in your professional opinion, who do you think did the Kalali thing?"

"I got no fucking idea. Honest. Nobody has put even initials in my ear. I do know the street wants the goods bad. I know that for sure because of the way I've been pressed. This past weekend I got pressed hard by certain people and they got pissed at me, but what the fuck, I can't come up with goods I ain't got."

All the while Crosetti kept time and jabbed for emphasis with his unlighted cigar. As though he was in front of the New York Philharmonic.

"Anyway," he went on, "why is everybody making such a big fucking deal out of these particular goods? They show up, they show up. They don't, they don't. It ain't like there's never going to be more."

Mitch watched Crosetti go.

He felt somewhat drained. That made him realize to what measure he'd been counting on the recovery, actually the six hundred thousand. Unconsciously maybe but nonetheless counting. Having big money of his own wasn't really all that important, he fibbed to himself.

A resigned sigh. "Well," he said, "back to the starting blocks."

"Yeah, false start," Hurley said.

They stood up to leave.

"By the way," Hurley said, "I forgot to mention, I have to go out of town for a few days."

"When?"

"Tomorrow morning. I'm going to Maryland."

"To look over some properties, I suppose," Mitch said wryly.

"Don't I wish. I have to testify on a case in Baltimore. I gave a deposition but they want me on the stand."

"How long will you be gone?"

"I'll be back Thursday. Friday, the latest. Anything turns up give me a call at the Chesapeake Motel."

CHAPTER 21

Lois Mae Dayton, more frequently known as Peaches, had dire needs again.

Like a place to go back to. She had been sharing a fourth-floor, one-and-a-half-room walk-up on Cebra Avenue in the Stapleton section of Staten Island. With a girl about her own age named Debbie something. During the past week, while Peaches was hanging out with Floyd and others in Brooklyn, Debbie had taken off, and that same day the walk-up had been rented to someone else.

Debbie had taken everything with her. Along with her own stuff every stitch and shoe and possession of Peaches.

Considering what little Peaches was left with—the dress she had on and whatever happened to be in her shoulder bag—she took the loss fairly well. She'd asked for it, she believed, as she had more or less times before. It was her fault for having trusted a size-seven roommate. No use wasting anger on Debbie. She was gone to somewhere.

Peaches was now on the Staten Island Ferry, returning to Manhattan. Out on the upper deck on the portside seated on one of the fixed benches. The ferry trip was a time-out. The next phase of her life and having to cope with it wouldn't begin until the ferry pulled in. In the meantime the vessel was growling and shuddering under her and she didn't have sunglasses to offset the late morning glare on the water.

She closed her eyes.

To sort of celebrate the beginning that lay ahead, she restricted her thoughts to things she would like. Foremost, a place of her own. Entirely hers, no roommate or guy staying over longer than a night or two and then moving in. A place on the Upper West Side not far from the park, or, even better, a loft in the TriBeCa area. She'd furnish it with truly new furniture, not a single broken thing retrieved from the street or lugged out of some second-, third-, fourth-hand store.

It wasn't unthinkable that she'd have a car. Sure, a convertible she'd go like hell and look outstanding in. A driver's license with her photo on it, a genuine Social Security number rather than just nine numbers she made up. A checking account? A credit card? There'd be lots of dinners out. She'd know all the best eating places.

As for clothes, she might go DKNY. At the very least Calvin. The shoes she'd have!

She opened her eyes. Yawned. Her teeth needed brushing. The ferry still had quite a ways to go. The water didn't look like anything she'd care to swim in. Once she'd almost learned to swim.

She got up and went inside to the restroom. It smelled like what it was mainly for. She pulled off her panties and threw them into the trash basket. Tore open the packet of three she'd bought for a dollar off an outside table of a store on Orchard Street that morning. Put a fresh pair on and felt that much improved.

Her makeup needed repair.

She brushed her hair, and used her fingers to give it the desirable muss.

She dug into the very bottom of her bag for the loose change she'd thrown in at various times. Made sure she got every penny. Three dollars forty-three cents. She put the change into her small, inside purse, which then contained altogether sixteen dollars and some.

Also in that inside purse were the earrings.

She decided to put them on.

The light in that enclosed space was yellow and dim. It cost the diamonds nearly all their glitter. The rubies looked more black than red.

Peaches had had a falling out with Floyd over the earrings. After the robbery she wouldn't take them off, contended they were hers, her part of the swag.

That wasn't how Floyd saw it. He tried to sweet-talk and fondle them off her. Offered her a hundred for them. Finally he lost patience and set about to rip them off. They were made with locking French backs and held fast to her ears.

She managed to struggle free of Floyd, made a dash down to the street. He wasn't about to chase after her and cause a public fuss. Little kicking, honky ass bitch with bleeding earlobes: swag earrings with much more serious blood on them.

The ferry was bumping pilings, lining up with its slip.

Peaches returned the earrings to her inside purse and hurried out to the unloading ramp to be among the first off. Next was the subway. She believed it a significant positive sign that she was exactly on time to catch the Lexington Avenue express, and, after long stretches of unsteady, noisy speed and seven screeching stops, she came up out of the ground at 59th Street.

There were numerous jewelry stores in the area, including Tiffany and Winston and Van Cleef & Arpels. She decided against those imposing establishments, settled on a small shop on 60th because it felt comfortable to her.

She went in with one of the earrings in her fist and what she believed was her most winning expression. She made it immediately understood that she was a seller not a buyer.

The jeweler was an ordinary-looking man named Eli Phelps. He had pale, pampered hands. He examined the earring with a ten-power loupe and concealed his interest.

"Where's the other?" he asked.

"I lost it."

"How unfortunate."

"One ought to be worth something."

"Not nearly as much as a pair."

"So, what's one worth?"

Phelps counted the diamonds and rubies, realized their superb quality, estimated their size within a point or so. At the same time he took stock of Peaches, gauged her knowledge and concluded that she was too young to know the true value.

"Five thousand," he told her.

"Is that all?" Peaches scrinched her face. Actually, five thousand was more than she'd expected.

"I might be able to do six," Phelps conceded, "but that would be cutting it painfully close. Painfully," he repeated because he enjoyed using the word for such circumstances.

Peaches pretended to rummage around in her bag. She did a gasp of surprise. "What do you know, I found it." She brought out the other earring, placed it next to its match on the black velour square on the counter. "Now how much?" she asked straight at Phelps.

He was both impressed and rubbed the wrong way by her artifice. No matter, he was going to make out. "Twenty thousand," he replied.

Peaches was sure her eyes were dancing. See how good fate can be if you just slap it on the ass, she thought. "Cash," she specified.

"I'm afraid that's impossible."

"Why?"

"It just is, impossible."

"I won't take a check," Peaches stated unequivocally. At least two out of every five checks she'd ever accepted had been the no account or insufficient kind. She wasn't about to get stiffed this time.

"Okay," Phelps said, "here's what you do. Take the earrings to this person." He wrote the name and address on the reverse side of one of his business cards. "I'll phone him and tell him to expect you. He'll pay you cash."

"Twenty thousand."

"Without a quibble. I guarantee it."

It was what Phelps had in mind all along. The way he preferred to handle such matters, not lay out any money, just refer. In return he'd get a ten percent cut of the difference between the twenty thousand this girl would be paid and the hundred thousand or so the earrings would bring at auction or wholesale.

Peaches' walk to twenty thousand down Fifth Avenue seemed to take hardly any time. She was in a state of extreme personalization. Just about everything in sight, especially handbags, shoes, compact disc players and such, had a new attainable significance for her.

Twenty thousand.

Two hundred hundreds. One thousand twenties.

Her imagination exaggerated what a stack it would be. A far cry from the paltry amount she'd earned from nearly bare-ass dancing. Those dollar bills and rare fives slipped in under the elastic of her G-string by male fingers in appreciation of the convincing way she squirmed and snapped her crotch and performed make-believe fucks with an upright pole.

When she reached 47th Peaches turned right and entered the first major building, designated number 1. The name that had been given to her by Phelps was on the directory in the lobby. And on the sixth floor she also found it on one of the doors.

She went in.

There was Andrew Laughton.

At the desk in the outer office going over invoices. It took a moment for his expectation to adjust to the sight of Peaches. Eli Phelps had said a *young lady* would be along momentarily wanting to sell some fine earrings that she didn't understand. Meaning she had no idea of their value.

Young lady.

Not an apt description of this person in a flimsy halter dress of pink that barely reached down to her crotch, this gangly-limbed, not yet entirely developed creature whose eyes were way overexaggerated by makeup, whose lower lip appeared swollen and incapable of meeting her upper, a mouth that looked ready to suck on whatever might be offered.

Andrew stood and introduced himself.

Peaches said she was Miranda Turner, a name she'd used before. She gave Phelps' business card to Andrew. "This guy told me you'd give me cash for my earrings."

Andrew offered her a chair.

As she sat, the crotch of her white panties was exposed and remained in sight. She got the earrings from her inner purse, handed them to Andrew.

He took a quick look at them. "They're quite lovely," he said. "And they'll be ever more so once they've been cleaned. May I do that for you?"

"Just give me the money and you can do whatever the fuck you want with them later."

"How much are you hoping to get?"

Peaches thought that had been settled. She didn't want to go through it again. She did a persevering sigh. "Twenty thousand," she said firmly.

The amount seemed incongruous coming from that mouth, Andrew thought. "They certainly appear to be worth that much," he said, "but I'll need to take a closer look."

He placed the earrings on the desk and went into the inner office, ostensibly to get a loupe. Doris was there. He quickly looked through the photographs of the Kalali swag that Mitch had left with him the previous Friday. His experienced eyes had almost immediately recognized the earrings and he was now checking to be certain. And, yes, there, without question, was the photo of them. Was it possible the earrings the girl had were coincidentally the same design? Exactly? No they had too much quality for that to be the case: one-of-a-kind quality.

Andrew whispered swift instructions to Doris. She accompanied him to the outer office. Peaches accepted a Pepsi and Doris complimented her on her fingernails, which had kitten faces enameled on them. "They were nicer," Peaches said, "but now some are chipping off. I had them done by a Korean woman two weeks ago. She also does great palm trees and flags."

Andrew, meanwhile, was examining the earrings under ten-times magnification, noticing the insurance registry code number scratched on the backs near the base of the posts, so tiny it was hardly visible. "How much?" he asked again.

"Twenty thousand," Peaches replied again.

"And you want cash you say?"

Will he ever get it? Peaches thought. She nodded.

"At the moment," Andrew told her, "I don't have that much in the safe . . . "

"Shit," from Peaches with a lot of *sh*.

" . . . but Doris will go to the bank for it."

Peaches brightened. "Where's the bank?"

"I won't be ten minutes," Doris assured and hurried out.

She was true to her word. She returned in eight.

Mitch was with her.

Peaches took a quick look at him and then tried to not look at him. Her instinct told her he could be a problem: he could be a cop. Or perhaps he was only a guy who naturally had that don't-fuck-with-me look. She also noticed Doris had come back empty-handed. "Hey, how about my money?" she demanded.

Andrew introduced Mitch as Investigator Laughton. Mitch went right at it. "Where did you get these earrings?"

"I found them," Peaches said.

"Where?"

"In a taxi. I got in and there they were. Lucky for me, huh?"

Mitch pretended he was believing her, then shifted. "Who gave them to you?"

"I told you I found them in a taxi."

"I know, but someone gave them to you."

"Actually, yeah, someone."

"Who?"

"My aunt. She left them to me when she died."

"On her deathbed."

"How did you know?"

"She took them off and tossed them to you."

"Something like that."

Mitch did an amused laugh. "Where else did you get them?"

Peaches thought for a while before saying smugly: "I blew a guy for them." She enjoyed that explanation because there was a degree of truth to it.

"Generous guy."

"Great blow job." Peaches grinned.

"Who was the guy?"

The truth again. She saw no harm in it. "A guy named Floyd."

"Floyd what?"

"A lot of people don't have last names anymore."

"Is he from around here?"

"Brooklyn." Once more she told herself no harm. There had to be ten thousand Floyds in Brooklyn. What fun it was telling truths this cop was taking to be lies.

Mitch had noticed the boots Peaches was wearing, their pointed steel-capped toes. He'd also guessed her weight to be around a hundred five or ten. He mentally placed her in the footprints he'd seen on the rear grounds of the Kalali house. She fit. She was the lightweight swift.

"You're full of stories," he told her.

"Is that a nice way of saying I'm full of shit?"

"Yeah, now let me tell one. Saturday night, week before last, around midnight, you went with some guys out to Far Hills, New Jersey, to do a robbery. You got left off on the road that runs along the rear grounds of the house. You climbed over the wall and made for the house. Big, white contemporary house. Remember it?"

Don't say anything, Peaches told herself.

Mitch kept on. "The owners of the house had just gotten home from dinner. A man and his wife. They were the only ones at home. They were held at gunpoint while the jewelry was gathered up. The wife was cooperative. The husband wasn't. He got out of line and was killed. The wife panicked and was also shot." Mitch paused. He could almost see his words sinking in. "How am I doing?"

Peaches tried to conceal her astonishment. This fucker knew everything, she thought. It was as though he'd been there when it happened.

She glanced at the way out. Should she try to make a run for it? She could outrun these people. She looked at Mitch and knew she'd never make it.

Keep on lying, her instincts advised.

She glanced at the earrings on the desk. Fucking earrings. She wished now she'd never seen them, that she'd let Floyd have them. She wished now that the only problem she had was having only sixteen dollars to her real name and no place to live.

Keep on lying, her instincts insisted.

She reached down into that place in her where her lies seemed to originate. She chose one but didn't believe it would get her out of this. She was jammed up, seriously jammed this time. Not like before. Those minor offenses such as shoplifting when she was juvenile. If she was still juvenile she'd tell this cop to kiss it.

What to do?

Her instincts told her to twist the truth.

She did a lengthy frown and bit her lower lip crookedly before giving in with a smaller, fragile voice. "It was supposed to be just a joy ride," she said. "Floyd talked me into going along. I had no idea they were out to rob a house."

Andy went into his inner office and phoned the police.

By the time they arrived Mitch had drawn it out of Peaches, the identity of Floyd. Mitch knew that particular Floyd, knew the crew. What's more he knew the fence that crew belonged to.

CHAPTER 22

"I'll wait up."

"No," Mitch told her, "go on to bed."

"You won't be long."

"I may be a while." He was in the Lexus talking to her on the no-hands cellular. It was like she was a mid-air spirit.

"No matter, I'll wait up. I'll listen to something. One of those Dashiell Hammetts you got me."

"I thought you'd already heard those."

"Why are you still in the car?"

"I'm just sitting here."

"I don't like tonight," she said.

"Got the jeebies?" One of her resurrected words. She had others such as *nifty* and *hunky-dory*.

"Some," she said vaguely, and then, more pointedly: "I felt around in your bottom drawer."

"Oh?"

"You took the Beretta. You should have taken the Glock. And you didn't take a spare clip. Why did you take the Beretta?" Rapid firing at him.

"No particular reason. Just in case."

"Nine to five should be enough. I want you home nights."

"I usually am."

"This is the second night out of four that you've been out. We should find you a nice, safe nine-to-fiver. Even better, how about a sleep-til-nooner?"

"Sure."

"Sex and sloth. Doesn't that appeal to you?"

"I have to make a living Maddie."

"Same old same old. When should I expect you?"

"Go to sleep."

"Can't. I'm wired. You should have taken a spare clip. You should have taken the Glock. Where are you?"

"New Rochelle."

"Hurley called a while ago."

"What did he say?"

"He'll be back in town tomorrow."

Mitch had spoken to Hurley on the phone around dinnertime. He'd told him about Peaches, the Kalali earrings and all, and Hurley had agreed with him on which crew and which fence was involved. Hurley had made him promise to put himself on hold, to wait, not make a move until he got back. Hurley had been adamant about that, so much so he'd drawn that promise out of Mitch three times during the course of their phone conversation.

For naught. Mitch couldn't possibly wait, knew he couldn't, gave it a halfhearted try and was still trying when he changed into some jeans and sneakers, and strapped on the holster rig for the Beretta next to his bare skin so the weapon would be out of sight beneath a lightweight chambray shirt. "Where did you tell Hurley I was?"

"Out. Just out. What else could I tell him? I didn't know where you were and now all I know is New Rochelle, which you've got to admit isn't very specific. Are you hungry?"

"No." She'd made fresh gaspacho for dinner and had unintentionally inundated it with cayenne. "I had two helpings," he fibbed. They'd gone down the disposal.

"Did you now?" she said skeptically.

"I could have gone for three."

"Still, anytime you're out adventuring, you ought to carry

along a snack. So you don't get low blood sugar. Low blood sugar could be a fatal handicap."

Fatal, he thought, indicated where her mind was. "You have to give some lessons tomorrow, don't you?"

"One. I did have two but Georgie Watson had to cancel."

"Which is he?"

"The three-card monte kid who works on that cardboard box outside Winston's. He showed me how he does it. It's just a way of lying with your hands. Know the difference between lying and fibbing?"

"Yeah, but what?"

"Mercy."

"I would have said consideration."

"Same thing, sort of. Do you ever lie to me with your hands?"

"Never."

"I love you, come on home."

"I will in a while."

"Whatever it is you're doing it's not worth it."

"Not to you maybe."

"Worth was the wrong word," she said a bit apologetically. "What I meant to say was it's not essential."

No comment from Mitch.

"Seriously, have you given any thought lately to not doing what you do?"

"And becoming a shopkeeper?"

"No, I agree you're not the shopkeeping sort. We could travel. We could go lots of lovely places and you could describe them to me. You know, like you did when we went to Florence."

"Think so?"

"You weren't reading from a guidebook when we were in Florence, were you?"

"You asked me that at the time and I believe I told you I wasn't."

"I know, but sometimes, not often, but sometimes when I ask you the same thing twice you give me different answers."

"Can't put anything over on you."

"Except yourself."

Mitch tried to imagine what that would be like, just traveling around, going anywhere first-class with first-class her. Maybe he'd do it if he had the money, that much.

"You ought to see what I have on," she said.

"Nothing?"

"Uh uh. A little silk something and four-inch heels. A little silk something is more effective than nothing. Especially with four-inch heels, wouldn't you say?"

Effective, he thought.

"It wouldn't take you long to get home. I could be doing sensational things to you only a half hour from now."

"Stop worrying."

"I'm not. I know you can take care of yourself, no matter what."

"Keep thinking that."

"I'll try. You're on the Kalali case, aren't you?"

"Yeah."

"I wish you were just out playing poker. I'd even settle for out playing around," she said and clicked off without a goodbye because, as usual, when it came to them, she disliked the word.

Mitch was parked off the corner of Paine Avenue where it intersected with Lyncroft. Ralph Lentini's house was diagonally across the way. There were no streetlights; however Mitch was able to see the house well enough.

Two stories topped by a shorter third and a wood-shingled roof that looked as though wind, with the help of rot, had made off with more than a few. Around the base of the structure scraggly, slighted rhododendrons were expressing their discontent, and along the property lines on each side were wild-looking twelve-foot-high boxwood hedges. On the right was a double-width concrete driveway.

Mitch had been parked there for nearly an hour and nothing about the house had changed. On the first floor there was still only one paltry light on, which Mitch guessed was a hall light, and there was still the variegated flickering of a television screen reflected upon a wall of the second-floor front room that Mitch believed was most likely a bedroom.

He'd decided not to make a move until there was a change, something that would tell him more definitely what the situation was. He had to contend with his impatience, told it to hang on, that this wasn't ordinary, wasteful wait, the difference being it had a high degree of anticipation in it, as well as imminent reward.

He punched in the CD player. Of the eight-disc load the most compatible with the moment was a rendition of composer Carl Maria von Weber's romantic concerto *Konzertstück* for piano and orchestra. Mitch was well-acquainted with the piece and its four movements: a lady's longing for her absent love, her fears for his safety, the excitement of his impending return and the passion of reunion.

A car went by, and, five minutes later, another, then a huffing, overdoing, middle-aged jogger and a woman walking a brace of pugs to all their pissing places.

Mitch fast-forwarded the Weber to the last movement. Wait was getting to him. He felt to see that he had his all-purpose knife, and his tiny waterproof Mag Lite. He made sure his sneaker laces were tied. He checked that he had a round in the firing chamber of the Beretta.

He took the Beretta off safety, snugged it back into its holster. It felt reassuring.

He got out of the car. It was good to stand. He walked to the corner and down Paine at a strolling pace, hands in the back jean pockets. There were no sidewalks. He crossed over and after a short ways was directly in front of Lentini's house. From that vantage the television was reflecting on the ceiling in that upper room. Maybe Ralph was up there asleep with the television on. Maybe he'd gone out and left it on, Mitch thought. There were various maybes.

He went up the drive. The grass at the rear of the house was high, dry and gone to seed. There was a swimming pool enclosed by a five-foot-high steel wire fence and a shed that

Mitch surmised contained the pool heater, filter and mainte-
nance equipment. The pool looked like a rectangular swamp.
Its surface was coated with green scum. Algae upon algae.
The smell of organic decay reached out beyond its bound-
aries.

Mitch surveyed the back of the house. Ground floor left to
right: two-car garage, rear entrance, cellar door, window, window, two bay windows, glass-enclosed porch. Second floor
right to left: balcony above the porch, window, window, six
more windows, balcony over the garage.

He was looking at the house for a way in, as would a swift.
He was a swift. A stealer. Out to steal from the stealers. Wasn't
this the reason he enjoyed what he did, moments such as
now? Wasn't this why he was reluctant to give it up, this more
fitting and fulfilling payback for the lady with the automatic
up her sable sleeve? His secret heart fed on it, was eating it up
now at a hundred and twenty a minute.

He tried the rear door, the windows, the cellar door and the
door to the porch. He didn't expect it to be that easy but sometimes people were careless and forgetful.

Not Ralph, though.

How about the second-story windows? People rarely
locked their second-story windows. As though that much
height was protective. Considering Ralph's profession he
probably had his double-bolted and nailed shut, Mitch
thought. Then again, maybe not. The only way to find out was
to go up and try them. There was a rain gutter that would give
him access. He'd be able to sidle along on it once he got up.
There was a wisteria vine gone crazy at the corner of the
garage. It would be an easy climb for a second-story man. He
was a second-story man.

He'd chosen his first grip and made his first foot placement
on the vine when the garage door started opening. An elon-
gated rectangle of light struck the concrete turnaround section
of the drive. It became wider, brighter as the electric door
opener performed its noisy function.

Ralph started the Pontiac. As he backed it out, its headlights raked the foliage of the wisteria at the corner of the garage.

Mitch remained perfectly still. Ralph shifted out of reverse, reached up to the sun visor and pressed the garage door's remote-control switch.

The door commenced its descent.

Ralph took it for granted, didn't wait for the door to be entirely closed before he got under way down the drive.

Mitch realized the chance. He dove for it, rolled in under the descending door, just made it.

He lay there on the garage floor for a moment. The boast he'd heard over the years from so many swifts was true, he thought. There wasn't a house, old or new, that couldn't somehow be gotten into.

The first part of the house Mitch entered was a narrow utility area. Determined to be thorough and systematic, he reached down into the top-load clothes washer and felt around in the clothes dryer. Nothing. Nor in a dirty laundry bag was there anything but offensive socks and underwear and such. Across from the washer and dryer was an upright freezer. It contained numerous wrapped, labeled and frozen veal and pork roasts and an assortment of the cheapest sort of frozen complete dinners. Mitch examined a few of the roasts. They were all about equal size and felt about the same.

Possibly a certain two or three of them were layers of meat around a stuffing of jewels. Was that too much cleverness to expect? Mitch chose at random a couple of the frozen roasts, took them into the adjacent kitchen and placed them in the microwave on high.

He swiftly searched in the kitchen, the obvious places: cabinets, refrigerator, canisters, and the not so obvious, such as down in the belly of the waste disposal unit.

In the adjoining room, which was meant to serve as a dining room, he was made to realize what he was up against.

Ralph's cumulate of swag . . .

Swag upon swag in front of swag beneath swag. The only

way to get from room to room was to stay within the narrow aisles that cut through it.

It would be impossible for Mitch to search the many hiding places it presented. How could he determine which of the fifty or more television sets in sight contained the Kalali jewels in place of electronic guts? Which among the legion of vases and lamps and statues should he suspect?

Considerably disheartened he proceeded up the main stairs to the second floor. There was less of an amassment of swag up there but still far too much. Only what was evidently Ralph's bedroom, the room in which earlier Mitch had seen television reflections, was reasonably furnished. Two cartons of VCR porno tapes at the foot of the bed. Precarious stacks of the same on top of two side-by-side giant-screen television sets. Could Ralph's concentration handle two at a time? Under the bed only a pair of wayward panties, another pair shoved between the mattress and box spring. In the top dresser drawer about twenty wristwatches in a neat row, good gold ones, well-known makes, several with diamond bezels and numerals. On the bare floor of the next room a waist-high pile of fur coats with their labels and monograms cut out.

Mitch went up a short flight of lesser stairs to what evidently had once been servants' quarters. Small rooms, low ceilings, one long-abandoned bath. Empty rooms except one, which contained a haphazard heap of luggage. An assortment of overnight bags, suitcases, valises, satchels. No street vendor rip-offs. These were the real expensive things. Vuitton, Hermès, Morabito, Bottega Veneta, Mark Cross and the like. Ralph's swifts had, week after week, brought swag in them and he'd just thrown them in this room.

The many burglaries they represented, Mitch thought, the amount of jewelry and other precious things they had helped carry away. He happened to look down. There, practically at his feet, was a blue Fendi satchel stamped with the initials RK.

Roudabeth Kalali.

Mitch took up the satchel. Its emptiness taunted him. What

had been brought in it was most likely still somewhere in this house, hidden among the overwhelming stolen. He hated the house. Ralph and it had beaten him.

A wipe of light, headlights.

Ralph had returned.

Mitch could hear the grind of the garage door, the car pulling in. What should he do? Try for the first floor and a door out? Go down a flight and out one of the windows? Now he heard Ralph in the main part of the house, Ralph and someone, their voices. They came up to the second floor and down the hall and into Ralph's bedroom.

Ralph and a woman.

They were directly below.

Why, Mitch wondered, should he be overhearing them so clearly?

He spotted the register inset in the hardwood floor. Such registers were commonplace in older houses. Made of cast iron with a grille-like arrangement of adjustable louvers, their purpose was to allow heated air to rise from one level to another. An unadvertised convenience was they allowed a person in the upper room to view what might be taking place in the room below.

Mitch kneeled to the register. He saw it was located above Ralph's unmade bed. By getting down closer to it he widened and improved his vantage.

They were undressing.

Ralph quickly, the woman just as much so. She had a face that appeared twice as old as her body, and considerably harder. Not a genuine blonde by any means. Her lower hair was dark and plentiful. Every sound she and Ralph made seemed to rise amplified: the unzipping, the slipping down and out of, the tumbling discard of shoes. It was apparent to Mitch that Ralph was anxious to get to it and the woman was anxious to get it done.

"You didn't happen to find a barrette, did you?" she asked.

"A what?"

"A barrette. You know, to hold my hair in place. I think I lost it here last time."

"I ain't seen nothing like that."

"It was gold."

"I would have noticed."

"A nice one."

An amused grunt from Ralph. "Next you'll be telling me it was eighteen K."

"Maybe it was," she arched.

"You want I should put on a couple of helpers?"

"Whatever puffs your panties."

Ralph inserted a porno film into each of the two VCRs at the foot of the bed.

The audio preceded the picture by several seconds, long enough for some moaning and a few *yeses*. Ralph turned off the sound. He got settled on the bed, adjusted a pillow, laced his fingers and placed his hands behind his head.

Ready to receive.

From Mitch's point of view Ralph's flaccid penis looked like a butchered chicken neck lying in a nest of steel wool. In another moment it was obscured by the woman's head, which immediately started pistoning.

Ralph's eyes began to glaze.

Mitch stopped watching, kneeled up, ignored the register. Now was a good time to leave, he thought. Any incidental noise he might make on his way out, such as a creak on the steps or whatever, wouldn't be heard. No use staying here while some passé suburban hooker serviced a fat fence. He might as well forget tonight, go on home empty-handed.

Another, less pragmatic part of him insisted on having its say. It told him not yet, told him there was still a chance that he might overhear or see something that would aid his cause. This woman wasn't about to stay all night. Ralph would be alone later. Maybe then, inadvertently or otherwise, he'd give away the hiding place. Stay there, Mitch, keep an eye on him.

Mitch returned his attention to the register and what was happening below.

The woman was still at it. And doing a lot of obligatory *humming* along with it to fake enjoyment.

Ralph's eyes were shifting from porno to porno.

The woman stopped abruptly. She got up and lighted a cigarette. As though she had no intention of continuing, had gone on strike.

"What're you doing?" Ralph asked, perturbed.

"Nothing."

"Why'd you stop? I was right there, for Christ's sake. Didn't you know I was right there?"

"Yeah."

"So why?"

"You don't treat me right," she complained matter of fact.

"How don't I?"

"You never give me a little something extra."

"I give you a hundred. I can remember when you were fifty."

"I'm not talking about money."

"What are you talking?"

"You gave Maxine a nice bracelet. You haven't given me shit."

"That was over a year ago with Maxine. I don't even see her anymore."

"All the more reason."

"You want a bracelet?"

"Sure."

"I'll give you a fucking bracelet," Ralph voiced gruffly. He got up. His erection was half lost. From a drawer of his dresser he got a pair of heavyweight leather work gloves. He put them on and went across the room to a Japanese ceramic planter that contained, of all things, a cactus. A variety generally known as a barrel cactus due to its stumpy, symmetrical shape. It was about fifteen inches in diameter at its girth and had countless needle-sharp prickers protruding from its skin. Not at all a friendly plant.

The leather gloves permitted Ralph to painlessly lift the cactus out. He placed it on the floor while he rummaged around in the bottom of the planter. Finally, he replaced the cactus. It looked none the worse from having been disturbed.

"Here's your bracelet," he said begrudgingly, tossing it to the woman.

It was a man's ID bracelet.

With SHORTY engraved on it.

The woman hardly looked at it before tossing it back to Ralph. "Keep it, Ralph," she said derogatorily, "it describes you."

"Don't be such a smart-ass cunt."

Silence was the extent of her apology. She reached for her panties, determined the back from the front.

"Okay," Ralph said, "you really don't want a bracelet. What is it you really want?"

"A Rolex. An eighteen K blue face, oyster with diamonds around the dial."

"I ain't got a Rollie right now, but I will, sooner or later. First one that comes in is yours."

"Yeah."

"I'll save it for you."

"Yeah."

"You don't believe me what the fuck can I do?"

"I'll settle for a hair," the woman said.

"How about a mink jacket?"

"How about a full-length chinchilla?"

"Let's take a look."

They went out of the room, out of Mitch's view. When they returned the woman had on a full-length silver fox coat.

She didn't know furs. While going through the pile she'd passed over a Russian sable and a Russian belly lynx. If she'd latched on to either of those Ralph would have had to throw her out and neither of them would have gotten satisfied. As it was the fox was worth about thirty-five hundred off the rack new, which it was about six years from being, and Ralph figured he'd be lucky to get five hundred for it come cold weather. As swag, it had cost him a hundred.

She didn't take off the coat.

Ralph got back in position on the bed and she went about getting him a second hard-on. When she'd accomplished that she swung a leg up over him, found herself with him and settled on him. "Full length," she uttered and did some blandishing gasps and exhales.

It wasn't going to be that easy for her. Her extortionate intermission had cost Ralph much of his mental momentum. At about the fifteen-minute mark she was still in a straddle, sliding back and forth and performing her best pelvic ovals.

Both Ralph and the woman were so caught up in trying they were unaware that three guys had entered the room.

Three of Riccio's have-arounds.

They appeared so all at once it was as though they had materialized, Mitch thought, as he observed from overhead. He knew these three from their having been around with Riccio on 47th.

The tall, extremely round-shouldered one was Bechetti. The equally tall heavyweight with boxer's ears was Caselli. The shorter Fratino was slick and nervous. Like all Riccio's minions they came off as old-mob sorts with old-mob ways. They wore wide trousers with overly roomy seats, sleeveless knit shirts and sports jackets too one thing or another: tight, long, loud.

"Get rid of the bimbo," Bechetti said. Evidently he'd been given charge of this business.

The woman had already dismounted Ralph. She'd instantly taken the temperature of the situation and knew it was too cold for her. She thought about asking Ralph for her hundred. Only thought about it, as she gathered up her things and was hurried off, barefoot in her fur.

Ralph remained face up on the bed. He reasoned he'd be less liable to be knocked down if he was already down. He felt exposed and more vulnerable however because he was naked. His cock had rapidly retracted. What little could still be seen of it was glistening wet.

Bechetti stood on one side of the bed, Caselli on the other side. Like they were visiting a hospital patient. They just stood there without saying anything for a while letting Ralph's imagination get up speed.

Bechetti did a smile. "Where you been, Ralph?"

"I been here. What do you mean where have I been?"

"You ain't been on 47th lately."

"I been nowhere. I got food poisoning or something."

"People wonder why you ain't been around."

"I was going to be down on 47th tomorrow." Ralph managed some indignation. "What is this, you come busting into my house?"

"People figure you're stiffing."

Ralph knew who *people* was. "I didn't promise anything to Riccio," he said.

"Who said anything about a promise? Promises don't mean shit," Caselli said.

"Riccio expects," Bechetti recited.

"Tomorrow," Ralph said, "I'll be on 47th tomorrow."

"That's a promise," Bechetti pointed out.

"Tomorrow is late, Ralph."

"That's why we're here tonight."

"For what?"

"For what you haven't been to see Riccio with."

It occurred to Ralph that these guys might be there on their own. That they were just cowboying, shaking him down. Possibly Riccio didn't know anything about this move. Not that that improved the situation. Anyway, he wasn't about to give up swag that would bring him a million and a half or two. "I ain't got much," he said, "just a few things, nothing big."

Bechetti reached quickly and took a clamping hold on Ralph's upper lip with his thumb and first finger. He pulled sharply upward. Ralph went with the pain rather than resist and cause more of it. He came up like he was on springs. It hurt so much he skipped two or three breaths. Now they had him standing.

Bechetti hardened about a thousand percent. "Listen you piece of shit. We know what you got. What we want is where you got it."

"How can I show you where I got something when I ain't got it," Ralph contended. "What am I, a fucking magician, I can make things right out of the air?" The inside tissue of Ralph's upper lip was ripped from where it joined his gums. Blood was filming his teeth. "Look around all you want. Take what you find," he told them.

Mitch, meanwhile, peering down, hoped Ralph would stick to the lie. How was it, he thought, Riccio knew Ralph had the Kalali swag? That was easy: Peaches was now in police custody, the police had taken her statement, and that information, quick as a phone call, had found its way into Riccio's ear.

A more puzzling question was why should Riccio be so eager to get hold of that particular swag? Sure, he'd enjoy having the goods, but it wasn't like him to use so much lean. Normally, he tried to keep on good terms with fences such as Ralph and, although the fences didn't consider Riccio *good people*, they brought to him peacefully and he paid peacefully. What was happening in the bedroom below was definitely out of order and definitely for some important reason, Mitch decided.

Fratino returned to the bedroom from having seen to the woman. "He tell yet?"

"No."

"He's a fucking *spuce*. I'll make him tell."

"I ain't got nothing big," Ralph insisted. "I don't know who said otherwise but I ain't got nothing big."

"He's a lying scumbag."

"What is it you want Ralph, you want Frat to give you a fifteen-minute fist fuck?"

"Bend him over," Fratino said.

"You want him to ram his fist up your ass?"

"See if there's some cold cream or something in the bathroom," Fratino said, as he took off his jacket. He also took off his wristwatch. "Bend him over."

Nothing from Ralph. He'd heard about Fratino. He never thought it would happen to him.

Caselli grabbed Ralph by the back of the neck, needed only

one of his huge, broken-knuckle hands to shove Ralph's
upper half face down on the bed. Ralph's knees buckled and
went to the floor.

"That's good," Fratino said. "Just like that is good. And
never mind the cold cream. I'm going to fuck him dry all the
way up to my elbow."

Bechetti was amused. "Maybe that's where he's got the
stuff, up his ass. That where you got it Ralph?"

Ralph was out of struggle. "Please," he pleaded.

"Where you got it?"

"I'll show you."

Goodbye recovery, Mitch thought. So long six hundred
thousand. Once the Kalali swag was in Riccio's hands it
would be reduced to mere precious stones and disappear into
that abyssal aspect of 47th dedicated to refashioning.

Mitch hated to see it. Ralph was going to go over to that
planter and remove that fat cactus.

However, Ralph didn't. He didn't give that hiding place as
much as a glance. He asked could he put on his trousers and
Bechetti said no and he asked why and Bechetti told him forget it and called him a piece of shit again and Ralph went obediently from the bedroom and Bechetti and the others
followed along.

It occurred to Mitch that they might be coming up. He was
relieved when he heard their steps on the main stairs as they
went down to the first floor.

Ralph was stalling them, Mitch thought. Playing them for
time, probably hoping for a chance to bolt. If Ralph could just
keep them on the first floor long enough . . .

Mitch went swiftly but stealthily down to Ralph's bedroom. The leather work gloves were right there. As he put
them on he realized how charged he was, now so close to
stealing the swag. No matter that he was stealing it back, it
was stealing.

The cactus was heavier than it appeared. It almost slipped
from his hands. He placed it on the floor and looked into the
planter, Ralph's secret repository.

Apparently it wasn't Ralph's only secret repository. On the inner bottom of the planter were a few modest pieces of gold jewelry, manufactured stuff with a touch of diamond pavé, and a couple of rings set with semiprecious stones. Altogether not worth more than three thousand.

So, *where was* the Kalali swag?

Ralph really was leading them to it, Mitch thought. He might as well find the safe way out and head for home while everyone was distracted.

He pulled off the gloves and threw them across the room. He felt like kicking the cactus. He went from the bedroom and down the second-floor hall. He didn't feel like being sneaky. He had to repress the urge to stomp. He could hear them downstairs. Ralph doing a lapse of memory, saying he was trying to remember where he put the swag, then a commotion as they smacked him. There was the smell of meat cooking. The roasts in the microwave. What if he'd been right about the swag being inside that meat? Jewelry roulade. To hell with it.

At the end of the hall he unbolted the door that gave to the balcony above the enclosed porch. The porch railing was weathered rotten and a section of it broke away when he leaned over it to see what he'd have for help. No vines, nothing, and no shrubbery below.

It was about a sixteen-foot drop. He hung on to the edge to make it a nine-foot drop. At the very moment he let go he heard them come out. Perhaps that's what caused him to land wrong.

He got up quickly. In a moment they'd be rounding the corner of the porch. He had only one way to go. He made a dash for the swimming pool area. It was possible they'd seen him. He crouched behind the small shed that housed the pool equipment. What a night, he thought, he'd be glad to get home. What a way to make a living.

They were headed for the pool area, coming straight at him. The naked Ralph leading, complaining when he happened to step on something sharp. What were they doing out here?

They kept coming. All the way to the shed. They were on the other side of it, no more than six feet from Mitch for a moment, when Ralph threw a switch that turned on the pool light.

The scummy green surface of the water, now illuminated from underneath, looked deceivingly attractive. Like an emerald of impossible size. There was no clear opening. The bottom of the pool wasn't visible. The scum covered from side to side and end to end. It had such a putrid odor in its calm that surely it would smell a lot worse if it was ever churned up.

Ralph gazed down at the water and walked back and forth along one side of the pool. The have-arounds waited. Ralph walked around the pool. Four times.

"How about it, Ralph?" Bechetti pressed.

"Give me time," Ralph said.

"I'll give you maybe another breath."

"He's fucking with our heads," Fratino said. "There ain't nothing out here. Why are we out here? What a stink. In a minute I'm going to throw up."

"This is all just shit," Caselli said. He'd had enough. As Ralph passed by him on the fifth time around the edge of the pool, Caselli grabbed him by the throat, got him with one of his huge, broken-knuckled hands.

Ralph didn't resist, knew better, just suffered it, stiffened and went up on his toes.

Bechetti interceded. "Let him go. Don't kill him yet. Let him go."

"Maybe the fuck wants to go for a swim," Caselli said. He released his grip with a shove.

Ralph went into the deep end of the pool backwards.

Into the green scum.

There was no splash. The scum was like an instantaneous healing membrane the way it came together to mend the place where Ralph's weight had torn through it.

Surely he was drowned.

Trapped beneath a surface as unified as ice.

But then, he broke up through it, flailing at it, fighting it, coughing and spewing. "I can't swim," he managed to shout.

The have-arounds laughed.

Ralph only knew how to float. In desperation, he brought his legs up and kicked little kicks, extended his arms and worked his hands. His thirty pounds of overweight helped his buoyancy. He wasn't however going anywhere. The thick blanket of scum had him locked in place.

"Okay, Ralph, tell us where," Bechetti said.

"I was trying to show you," Ralph told him.

"You don't have to show, just say."

"Get me out," Ralph begged.

"We will, after you say."

Ralph knew better. Perhaps he suddenly accepted his doom. "Fuck you," he shouted with bite.

"What kind of attitude is that? I always took you for smart. All you got to do is say."

"Fuck you," Ralph said again more emphatically, as though he enjoyed the words.

Fratino took out his pistol. So did Caselli. They hurriedly threaded on silencers.

Fratino got off the first shot. It caused a sharp sucking sound as it struck the scummy surface close by Ralph.

"Don't pop him yet," Bechetti said behind his hand.

Fratino nodded. "I'll just put a little lead in his pencil."

They aimed for Ralph's genitals. They fired rapidly, as though competing for hits. Each used up an entire clip.

Ralph realized their target. He shielded his genitals with his hands. His upper body sank. He used his hands to keep afloat. His genitals were exposed. It was either-or like that for him until the slugs slammed into his upper thighs, groin and lower abdomen.

He went under, started breathing water.

The bright red of blood bubbled up amidst the green. Ruby and emerald.

"I told you not to pop him," Bechetti reprimanded.

"I was trying not to," Fratino said.

That was also Caselli's excuse.

"Now we got to find the stuff on our own."

"No sweat. It's in the house some fucking place. We'll find it."

Bechetti turned off the pool light. They headed for the house.

When they were surely inside Mitch came out from around the shed. He'd had some difficulty not feeling sorry for Ralph. He'd even considered doing the heroic, stepping out with Beretta leveled, confronting the three, rescuing Ralph. His better judgment asked if he disliked living that much. Ralph wasn't the kind he should put himself on the line for.

So, it had been a perverse, one-act play that he'd experienced from the wings. His view had been the back of the performances, the mistakes.

Something peculiar he'd noticed about Ralph: the way Ralph had walked around and around the pool and each time around when he came to a particular spot there'd been a slight hitch in his walk, the merest hesitation, as though he was ambivalent about whether to stop there or continue on.

If there was one thing Mitch knew about fences such as Ralph it was how they loathed losing swag once they had it in their possession. Sell it, yes. That was their reason for being, but to have it taken from them or having to give it up was unthinkable. Attesting to that attitude was Ralph dead beneath the scum.

Those hesitations of Ralph's had been very subtle, but now Mitch's recollection expanded them, made them obvious, definite. And possibly, meaningful.

He went around to the other side of the pool to where he believed the hesitations had occurred. He kneeled and ran his hand along the tiles just above the scum line.

He found it.

A cleat cemented to the tile, the sort of small cleat to which normally a drop line and thermometer would be attached to ascertain water temperature. A length of twine was tied to the cleat. It was ordinary, hemp packing twine. Mitch tried pulling at it. It wouldn't just come up. There was something much more substantial than a thermometer attached to its submerged end.

Mitch got a good grip on the twine and began hoisting slowly hand over hand. He couldn't see because of the scum but something was coming up.

But then it wasn't.

The twine had broken and whatever had been on the end of it was now on the bottom of the pool.

Mitch cursed the cheap twine and cheap Ralph. At the least the twine could have put off breaking until he'd determined what was tied to it. For all he knew his hope had him pursuing an old bucket.

He tried to see what it was, pushed aside some green scum to make a patch that was only water. He shined his Mag Lite down. Even when he extended it below the surface its beam was defeated by the murk.

There was no doubt about him going in. Reluctance, but no doubt. The only question at the moment was whether he should go in clothed or naked.

He chose naked, undressed quickly and placed his clothing and the Beretta out of sight behind the shed. In case they returned to the pool for some reason. He could hear them inside, rummaging around roughly, breaking vases and such. They were searching in vain, he told himself, the house might be full of swag but the swag wasn't in there. Maybe.

He tried to bring himself to dive. It would be a swift slice down through the layer of scum. He stood on the edge, poised to spring, even went up on his toes a couple of times. But he couldn't bring himself to do it.

He turned and slipped in feet first, lowered himself slowly, told himself the scum was imaginary, that his bare skin wasn't feeling the slime of it, he was going for a dip in a pristine pool, sparkling, clean water. Mind over scummy, green matter.

He couldn't, however, shut out the stench. The malodor of organic decay invaded his nostrils and lungs and got to his brain. It made him retch. He was in up to his chin. To escape the air he took a deep breath of it and went under.

He was about midway between the deep end and the shallow. At the point where the bottom began to slope. He felt with his feet along the coving. His feet came in contact with something. He maneuvered down to beam his Mag Lite on it.

The woman.

The body of her. Her arms caught in the sleeves of the fox coat. The ampleness of the coat spread out wing-like on each side of her. She had the appearance of some lazy, hairy water creature, unwilling to exert itself unless stirred.

The mere touch of Mitch's foot had impelled her. She coasted along the bottom, bound gradually for the deepest part.

Ralph's body was also in there somewhere, Mitch thought. He was bathing with the dead.

He shined his light around in various directions. No sign of whatever had been tied to the twine. It should have been right here. He reasoned that it, like the dead woman, must have slid down the slope of the bottom.

He needed a breath, had to go up for some of that awful air. He'd need a big deep breath of it. He expected to go up where he'd gone in; however, the top of his head met the resistance of scum. It was gelatinous, tight layers upon layers of decomposition and algae, several inches thick. It gave way, and as Mitch's head emerged, it seemed to slip down over his face like he was putting on a heavy turtleneck sweater, but putrid.

He gasped. Took the breath as quickly as possible and went back under.

He swam for the deepest part. Felt the pressure increase. He came to the body of the woman. His bare thigh brushed the fur as he passed by, and a moment later he saw he was headed for the body of Ralph.

It was at the drain on the bottom, appeared to be hovering over the drain, trying to escape by way of it. Ralph's legs were crouched, his back bent forward, his arms encircling.

Mitch swam closer.

He could have easily missed the twine. Merely the frayed end of it protruded from beneath Ralph's body. He shoved the body away and saw attached to the other end of the twine, tied securely, closed by it, a white plastic kitchen trash bag.

He grabbed it by its neck and sprang for the surface.

CHAPTER 23

It was a little after three when Mitch arrived home.

There were no lights on. Lights were of no use to Maddie, of course, and often, when she was home alone at night, she simply neglected to turn them on.

Mitch went directly to the bedroom. The bed was only ready to be occupied, the top sheet folded down as precise as an envelope, the goose-down-filled pillows plumped and piled in place, but no Maddie. Mitch's eyes needed her . . .

. . . found her in the living room.

She was on the sofa in an awkward position, as though sleep had suddenly won out over her and toppled her. Her eyes were closed. Sometimes, contrary to normal reflex, she fell asleep with her eyes open and Mitch would gently lower her lids like shades. But her eyes were closed now, and, according to the rate and sounds of her breaths, she was surely sleeping.

Mitch stood there, taking her in, replenishing, replacing the make-do image of her with the actual her. Why hadn't she minded him, gone to bed as he'd told her? She'd tried to wait up.

She had on headphones. A Walkman was somewhere on the sofa with her. Cassettes were scattered about on the floor.

Mitch gathered them up to not step on them. He carefully removed the headphones and believed he'd done so without waking her. He'd leave her as she was for the time being, would carry her in to bed.

"How about a kiss?" she murmured.

"In a minute," he said and went into the bathroom. He undressed, threw everything into the laundry hamper, then turned to the familiar mirror.

Look at me looking at me, he thought. What a mess. There were remnants of the green scum caked here and there on him. A lot of it in his hair. His nostrils were green. So were his eyelashes and ear holes.

He grinned. For what may have been the fiftieth time since he'd pulled over beneath a New Rochelle streetlight. Before then, actually as soon as he'd gotten out of the pool, he'd squeezed and shaken the white plastic trash bag and believed what it contained felt right, had the right weight. It wasn't until he was well away from Ralph's house, and all, however, that he cut the twine from the neck of the bag and took a look.

No trash in that trash bag.

The Kalali swag.

He deserved to grin. He deserved to tell himself *nice going* along with telling himself that it had been twenty, maybe thirty percent his resourcefulness and seventy percent luck, but it was also okay if he transposed those figures. Wait until Hurley heard how it had come off. He'd love it. There'd be no need to exaggerate. It had been bizarre enough. For instance, Ralph's typical fence paranoia, his using the scummy swimming pool as a hiding place. And the way Ralph, even after death, had seemed to be trying to hold on to the bag of swag.

Mitch relaxed the corners of his mouth so he could watch them form another grin.

"What's with this 'in a minute' stuff?" Maddie demanded to know as she padded somnolently into the bathroom leading with her lips. "I've been deprived all night and now . . . " She stopped short of reaching within range and cringed. "You smell awful," she said, "worse than a grave robber."

"You've known grave robbers?" Mitch jested.

"Don't you dare come near me."

Maddie backed off four steps. Mitch got into the shower stall. It took three all-over lathers and rinses for him to feel free of scum and death. Maddie had two big towels waiting. He dried his upper half while she kneeled and tended to the rest, not slighting any part or crease. She even had him lift his feet so she could dry between his toes. There was a degree of ritual to it but nothing of dominance-submission. It was simply something she sometimes did and always enjoyed doing. At first, years ago, he'd resisted, felt awkward and rather embarrassed by having her toweling him dry as though he was a child, but then he tried turnabout and understood and accepted the adoring, caring quality of it.

Now she was done. She remained down, pressed her cheek to the socket of his groin and said: "You must be hungry."

He was, but wouldn't her suggestion be a helping of that gaspacho from hell? "I'll just get a glass of milk," he said.

She insisted on getting it for him, brought it and several ginger snaps to him in the bedroom, and, while he stood and drank and munched, she got into bed so she'd be there when he got in, would be sort of receiving him.

She'd made the bed fresh and allowed it to remain fresh so that he would experience that pleasure now: the chaste sensuality of fine, imported sheets. He sighed luxuriously when he'd inserted himself between them. She let him acclimate before claiming her kiss, a brief, sweet one.

They lay face up, side in touch with side, silent for a while. Finally she said what he expected: "Tell me."

He didn't want to. He was being shared by exhilaration and fatigue and he favored giving in to the latter. "Tomorrow," he told her.

"Promise?"

"Yeah."

"You'll remember everything? You won't leave anything out?"

"Promise," he fibbed, knowing he'd omit telling her what

Fratino had wanted to do to Ralph and that he probably wouldn't reveal the extent he'd been repulsed by that putrid pool and having to swim with those bodies. She'd most likely detect his omissions, however, and pump them out of him, he thought. "What time is it?" he asked.

"I don't know. You've got the sight. What time do you have to get up?"

"Eight or so," he replied. His bedside clock told him it was now quarter to four. He set its alarm for eight. When he clicked off the light it was as though he also clicked himself off.

Maddie let an estimated ten minutes go by before she got up and went around to his side to mercifully un-set his alarm.

CHAPTER 24

Pickings on a mandolin.

The accompaniment to Mitch's ascent to consciousness that brought him face to face with his bedside clock, its arms indicating frantically, mutely, five to eleven. What happened to eight o'clock? Mitch complained, feeling betrayed.

He got up quickly. This was supposed to have been one of those rare days of days, he thought, a full course of glorious victorious hours, a six-hundred-thousand day. He'd wanted to enjoy every minute of it and now, here it was, nearly half over. No matter about the alarm, Maddie should have awakened him. He'd told her eight.

He rushed through his ablutions. Put on a suitable suit and a tie of celebratory color and pattern. As somewhat of a payback he merely peeked in on Maddie in the study giving the mandolin lesson. She'd have to discover him gone.

With the throat of the white plastic trash bag inescapably in his grasp, Mitch taxied down to 47th to his brother Andy's place of business. Andy was delighted when Mitch emptied the Kalali swag onto the work bench in the inner office. The bracelets, necklaces, rings, brooches, strands, pins and all. A six-million-dollar array. Andy congratulated and gave Mitch a prideful, well-done slap on the back.

"Fine goods," Mitch admired, holding up an intricately worked diamond and calibré-cut sapphire art deco bracelet.

"It looks Boucheron. Is it signed?"

Mitch louped the bracelet, saw that it did indeed bear the Boucheron hallmark.

"You still have the good, fast eye," he said.

"You don't?" Andy smiled. He nudged certain of the Kalali pieces, urging them to show more life. "A shame to see these beauties not looking their best," he said. Precious stones, particularly diamonds, have an affinity for grease. The swifts and Ralph had handled this jewelry so much that it was considerably dulled by their body oils.

"I thought I'd clean it up," Mitch said, "if that's okay with you." Andy had the needed professional equipment there on the work bench.

It wasn't merely okay with Andy; he was glad to help.

Piece by piece the jewelry was placed in a wire basket and immersed in a Bransonic 521 ultrasound cleaning tank filled with a degreasing solution. It was rather like deep frying but with sonic vibrations instead of heat and degreaser instead of oil.

Next, each piece was held by tweezers while it was exposed to pressurized steam from the nozzle of a box-like appliance called a Steamaster HPJ-25. That to get rid of any stubborn residue that might be lodged in the mountings. Time and again, the mundane steam seemed to hiss spitefully at the special beauty it was being forced to enhance.

Andy and Mitch worked in tandem, as they once had when there'd been a Laughton store. They were done in less than an hour. Now the Kalali swag lay there in its utmost brilliance, its numerous facets barraging the air sharply with scintillations.

The pieces were put into individual clear plastic, self-sealing envelopes. There was just barely enough room for the lot in Mitch's attaché case.

It was still lunchtime when Mitch arrived at his office. Shirley was eating in at her desk.

"There you are!" she said with a chiding tone countered immediately by a smile. "I've been beeping you."

"I haven't been beepable."

"You lost your beeper?"

"Either that or Maddie hid it."

"You've never been a loser," was Shirley's opinion. "Have you had lunch? You don't look as though you've had lunch."

"No, what are you having?"

"My more or less usual. I'd be glad to share."

Shirley more frequently than not brought her lunch from home. Her more or less usual was a cream cheese and watercress on raisin wheat, London tea room style, the bread sliced extremely thin and its crust amputated. Mitch didn't think it qualified as a sandwich. Shirley often said she'd rather starve than subject herself to one of those feeding troughs New Yorkers line up at.

"Order me a roast beef on rye, fries and a Mountain Dew," Mitch told her. "Has Ruder called?"

"No, but George Bickford has, twice."

Bickford was a client, Ruder's counterpart at Northland Providential, a Philadelphia insurance company from which Mitch had been receiving a retainer every month for six years.

"And Hurley stopped by about an hour ago," Shirley went on, "said he'd be back. And," she added pointedly, "*I* need to talk to you."

"About a layaway?"

"No. Anyway, my need can keep until you have a free moment."

Mitch did a fast read of Shirley and believed what he saw was either she was getting married, needed money for an abortion or wanted a raise.

"You want a raise," he said.

"A rise," she corrected.

"A raise," he corrected back. "In this country a rise is something else altogether and I'm sure you've caused a great many but what you want in this case is a raise."

"Whatever."

"Please order my sandwich."

Mitch went into his office. He cleared his desk and moved the two visitors' chairs aside to make enough room on the carpet. He wanted to do this alone, indulge in the doing.

He placed the Kalali file on his desk. The four-page numerically itemized loss list, the twenty pages of corresponding descriptions and appraisals and the eight-by-ten color photographs of each of the forty-eight stolen, now restolen, items.

He arranged the photographs on the carpet. According to their loss list numbers in four orderly rows, twelve to a row with space in between to move about from row to row.

He paused to consider and appreciate what he was doing. No need to hurry, make it last, he thought, although at the finish there'd be the phone call to Ruder, the six-hundred-thousand phone call. He thought the wish that he'd made the recovery for someone, anyone, other than Ruder.

Shirley came in with his lunch. She laid it out nicely on the ledge behind his desk and he sat upon the ledge while he ate. He invited her to join him and she got her thermos of tea and sat with him.

"About the raise . . . " he started.

"It's nothing that has to be decided right off," she told him. "I mean, it's not critical."

"Oh?"

"If you say no then no it is and none the worse."

"You won't quit on me?"

"Lord no. I have the best job in the district. Working elsewhere would be bloody painful. It's just that I'm so far behind on my layaways that it seems I'll never catch up. Saturday last I went overboard, put twenty down on a silk blouse at Saks and forty more on a jacket that hooked me with its reduced sign at Bergdorf." She did a sag. "I'm incorrigible."

Mitch had the urge to give her an encouraging hug as well as a raise. A mere, platonic hug couldn't be misconstrued as sexual harassment, could it? "Would a hundred more a week help?" he asked.

Shirley's sun came on. "It would just about free me!"

"Then make it a hundred and fifty."

"That's too much."

"Today it isn't."

Shirley kissed him. On the cheek but close to the mouth. He noticed she was wearing an expensive scent. She immediately gathered up the remnants of his lunch and went out to her desk. Mitch hadn't thought it possible that he could feel any better but he did. Not hugely, but he did. Generosity is therapeutic, he thought, especially when it's affordable.

He returned his attention to the Kalali swag. He removed it all from the attaché case, and referring to the loss list, used a black magic marker to note the designated number of each piece on the outside of the transparent envelope that contained it.

That done, he set about to place each piece on its corresponding photograph. He was busy at it when Hurley showed up.

A gesture was Hurley's hello. No smile.

Mitch would let Hurley have the first word, sure it would be congratulatory, something such as *hey, nice going*. But Hurley just stood there taking in the rows of photos on the carpet and the swag. His expression had some glower in it, as though he resented what he was seeing.

"What's your problem?" Mitch asked.

"You didn't wait."

"I couldn't."

"Yeah, it was right there and so easy you had to make the move, couldn't help yourself, had to."

"You know me and having to wait." Mitch shrugged nonchalantly, trying to lighten the moment.

"I practically perjured myself down in Baltimore in order to make it back here today. You should have waited."

"What's the difference?"

"None," Hurley replied too quickly.

Mitch was disappointed by Hurley's reaction, but then Hurley made it right, grinned as though he'd been kidding. "You did good," he said exuberantly.

"I got lucky," Mitch said modestly. He related some of his previous night's adventure. The high points and a little of the in-between. He'd gradually dole out the details. "You'll probably want to let the New Rochelle police know about the bodies in the pool."

"Maybe," Hurley said, "or maybe somebody should just find them sooner or later."

Mitch didn't understand that but let it go. He was about half done with correlating the pieces of jewelry and the photographs. Hurley showed mild interest as Mitch returned to that task. "What's with this piece?" Hurley asked, indicating a yet vacant photo of a diamond-encrusted bangle bracelet.

"That one? It's here. I saw it. I just haven't gotten to it."

Hurley continued perusing the rows of photographs. "And these?" he asked offhand. "Did you happen to notice these?" The two enscribed emeralds.

Mitch was distracted, barely glanced to see which photo Hurley was referring to. "Probably," he replied.

A grunt from Hurley, a sort of deep subversive sound that seemed to emanate from a Hurley within Hurley. He walked to the window and looked down at 47th. "You'll be turning over everything to Ruder."

"Yeah."

"He know you've made the recovery?"

"Not yet."

"I guess you can't wait to tell him."

"Six hundred thousand."

"Anybody know you've got this stuff, other than you and me? Maddie, I suppose she knows."

"Not even Maddie."

Hurley unbuckled his belt and retucked his shirt, to offset with preoccupation the directness of what he was about to suggest. "How about fuck Ruder," he said as though it was an impetuous notion that shouldn't be taken seriously. Unless, of course, Mitch chose to jump on it.

"Sure," Mitch played along.

"How about you were never in New Rochelle last night. You were anywhere other than New Rochelle. We pop the stones from all this shit, melt down and Ruder gets fucked."

That last part appealed to Mitch.

Hurley knew that. "How much do you think we'd be looking at?" he asked.

"Two, maybe three million."

"So, I get my horse farm in Maryland, you can have an all-paid-for place on Martha's Vineyard or somewhere."

In the various recoveries Mitch had made over the years there'd never been an opportunity such as this. Everything about it was right for doing wrong. No one except Hurley knew he'd made the recovery; Mrs. Kalali and Roger Addison would get their six million from Columbia Beneficial; Ruder would be out on his ass.

"Could you handle it?" Hurley pressed.

"Nearly."

"I don't think so," Hurley challenged, "you're too fucking straight. How anyone in this twisted business could stay so straight is beyond me."

"You're right," Mitch said, his tone letting Hurley know as far as he was concerned the subject had ended. He continued correlating the swag and was soon done. When he went down the loss list he saw every piece was accounted for.

Except one.

Number 32.

The two enscribed emeralds.

He mentioned that to Hurley.

"Are they actually *missing?*" Hurley asked.

"What do you mean *actually?*"

"Just that maybe they appealed to you."

"You must be kidding."

"I wouldn't blame you."

"Hurley, go out and come in again."

"Nothing sinful about helping yourself to a little hold-out."

"Make up your mind. One minute I'm too straight, the next I'm holding out. Shit, if I was going to hold out something from these goods it wouldn't be those two scratched-up emeralds."

"I guess."

"No guess to it."

"Then maybe the emeralds got accidentally dropped someplace. In your car or at home. That possible?"

Mitch considered it. Car? No. Home? No. Andy's during the clean-up? He didn't think so, no. But it was strange that only one item should be missing and that it should be this one. Might Ralph have taken a fancy to them and put them aside? He could have, but would he? Why would he? They weren't the sort of things an experienced fence such as Ralph would keep. They were too identifiable.

"Anyway," Mitch brightened, "forty-seven out of forty-eight isn't bad."

Hurley agreed. "Want to go have a beer?"

"I've too much work to do."

Hurley almost let it go at that. He looked off thoughtfully, as though weighing what had ensued during the last quarter hour. When he brought his look back he did an amending face. "Sorry about the attitude," he said. "I'm on the rag. My room at the motel in Baltimore was right next to the ice machine."

"Forget it."

"Sure about the beer?"

"Maybe later."

"Later's not good for me. See you tomorrow."

With Hurley gone, Mitch decided on a time-out. He left the photographs and the swag on the floor, switched off the light and shut himself in. Seated at his desk, he tried to blank his mind. It had been overaccelerating since yesterday and Peaches.

He wished his was the sort of mind that *could* be turned off

and on. Some people claimed they could do that. The medi-
tators. He'd never been good at meditating. Once, years ago,
he'd attended a transcendental meditation class and given it
an open-minded month. At least once each day, sometimes
twice, he'd sat quietly with eyes closed and chanted the nonsense syllable that was his mantra. But always some aspect
of 47th Street came jabbing in, as though the mantra had
usurped its place.

Now he drew in deep breaths, relaxed his shoulders and
defeated the urge to turn and peek through the slats of the
drawn blinds at Visconti's office across the way and 47th
below in its Wednesday summer afternoon mode. Instead of
the peek, Mitch imagined it, which was, really, as compulsive as a peek.

The back of Visconti's head above the back of his expensive leather chair. The Luchino Visconti movie poster on the
wall beyond. A silver salver of fruit on the side table? On the
street below two-thirds of the people would be tourists. Obvious because of the way they were dressed and their stop-
and-go walks from window to window, diamonds to
diamonds. Tomorrow, Mitch told himself, he'd walk the
street, down one side and back up the other. By tomorrow the
street would have heard of the recovery. He wouldn't, however, be taking any bows. The street didn't like being deprived. Swag was grist for its mill.

The telephone.

Were his eyes caught on it or was it staring at him? Why
hadn't Maddie called? He regretted now not having given her
a departing hug. Maybe she was out shopping, defying curbs
and bumpers, or maybe at that moment she was seated on a
hard bench in the Grecian wing of the Metropolitan absorbing vibrations from ancient marble nudes. He should have
hugged her, put some love in her ear. There should never be
any should haves.

Why hadn't Ruder called? It would be better if Ruder
called him rather than . . .

It was as though he'd launched the wish and it had been immediately granted. Shirley came on the intercom with:

"Ruder on one."

Mitch didn't get on the line for nearly a minute, then opened with a busy: "Yes, Keith." He rarely called Ruder by first name, never thought of him that way.

"How are you, Mitch?"

"Depends on who you ask. What's up?"

"Having not heard from you I was wondering how things were going."

"You sound as though you've got something," Mitch told him.

"What do you mean?"

"Could be it's your sinuses. I seem to recall your telling me you had a problem with allergies. A lot of ragweed in the air this time of year. And pollen." Actually, Ruder sounded the same as ever, stuffy and dry.

"It's probably the connection," Ruder said a bit exasperated. "Anyway, do you have good news for me? The situation here is getting rather squeezy to say the least."

"Hang on a second." Mitch held the receiver at arm's length and covered the mouthpiece lightly while he pretended to be giving instructions to Shirley regarding a letter that had to go out today. The figure two million eight hundred thousand was nonchalantly mentioned. "Now," he got back to Ruder, "where were we?"

"I was asking if you had any news for me."

"Oh, yes. I guess you mean regarding the Kalali case."

"Of course."

"Didn't you get my message?"

"Message?"

"Yesterday afternoon. Come on now, Keith, you're toying with me."

"I don't toy!" Ruder snapped, his true disposition coming through. He controlled. "You left a message with my secretary?"

"No."

"Then with whom?"

"Your secretary must have been out. The electronic answering system was on. You know, that press one if, press two if thing."

"I didn't get the message."

"Goes to show that system isn't infallible. Really Keith, you sound raspy. It could be your throat. You ought to have it looked into. I had an acquaintance who sounded similar. He ended up in Sloan-Kettering."

"What was the goddamn message?" Ruder was only a few nerve ends from losing it.

God, how much he disliked this man, Mitch thought. Why not do what Hurley had suggested: not mention the goods, pop the stones and let Ruder take his fall?

Moment of truth.

"I've recovered the Kalali swag," Mitch said so rapidly and run together it sounded like nonsense.

"What? What was that?"

"What you wanted to hear."

"I didn't get it."

Mitch did an impatient exhale and said again what he'd said, but this time disconnecting and drawing out each syllable.

Ruder was overwhelmed, overjoyed, couldn't hold in a short length of laugh. "You're remarkable," he said. "I knew you'd come through for me, Mitch. You're remarkable."

"Yeah."

"So, where's the jewelry?"

"I have it."

"Bring it down."

"You'll cut me a check."

"First of the month."

"Okay, first of the month I'll bring it down. That's only ten days."

"Be reasonable Laughton [now it was Laughton]. This is a large, structured organization. A check of that size takes some doing. Certain people have to approve, certain signatures are required. You understand."

"Certainly."

"Bring it down."

"Cut a check."

In the silence Mitch could hear capitulation. "I'll do my best," Ruder told him.

Mitch hastily gathered up the pieces of jewelry from the floor.

Shirley helped.

She also supplied an Henri Bendel shopping bag with another of the same inside it for Mitch to carry the jewelry in. It would be safer than his attaché case. There had been a rash of snatch-and-run robberies lately involving 47th Street dealers. Thieves waited around the district, spotted a likely-looking dealer with his case in hand, followed him and, at his least wary moment, sideswiped him full speed.

Just another variation in the perpetual foray between West 47 dealers and stealers.

No one, however, went about with six million worth of jewels in a shopping bag. Shirley topped the jewelry with layers of tissue paper, tucked the paper in well around the edges.

Mitch was in high spirit during the taxi ride downtown. The shopping bag on his lap. He forgave the cramped, cage-like back seat and the suicidal Israeli driver. He forgave the buses for their bullying and sooty exhausts. A happy hello to that mix of marvelous New Yorkers crossing at 39th. The same for the well-off obscured by the dark-tinted windows of the chauffeured Rolls-Royce equivalently stopped for the light.

He gave the taxi driver an undeserved two-dollar tip and entered the thirty-two-story gray fortress that was the Columbia Beneficial building.

The elevator was like a pneumatic box with its soft, long stops. The reception area had nothing on its gray walls except the company name. The receptionist, a prototypical older aunt, once married forever divorced, didn't have even a New York smile for Mitch, told him it would be only a minute. He believed her and remained standing.

At the five-minute mark he opted for one of the gray leather sofas. It wheezed as he sat. The magazines on the low table were only *Sports Afield, Reader's Digest* and *Life.*

At the seven-minute mark Mitch realized this qualified as a wait and at twenty minutes his needle was nearing the red.

Ruder's secretary saved the moment, came out to lead Mitch in. She was professionally pleasant. Mitch didn't know her by name, just by sight. She had a wide, humpy ass, and, to make it worse, it was in a tight, white flannel skirt.

Mitch followed it down the corridor past executive offices to the one that was Ruder's.

"Mr. Ruder has been called into an emergency meeting," the secretary said. "You're to leave what you've brought with me." She extended her hand to receive the shopping bag.

"Nothing doing," Mitch told her. "I need to see Ruder."

"That's impossible."

"Call him out of the meeting."

"It's not being held here. It's an outside meeting."

"When will he be back?"

"Not this afternoon."

The dickhead knew about this when I spoke to him, Mitch thought. Or else Miss all-ass here is fibbing for him while he hides in the executive toilet.

"My instructions are to put what you've brought into Mr. Ruder's safe, to give you a receipt and an appointment for ten tomorrow morning."

She said it straight, it sounded straight.

Mitch glanced at the safe inset in the wall to the left. It was open, empty. He didn't relish the prospect of having this six million in a shopping bag on the end of his arm any longer. Besides, rush hour was about to occur and he'd have a problem getting a taxi uptown. He pictured himself on the subway with the shopping bag.

"What kind of receipt?" he asked.

"The loss list."

Mitch's reluctance had its say: "I don't think so. Are you absolutely sure Ruder isn't coming back? Is he where I might reach him by phone?"

"I've already revised Mr. Ruder's schedule to accommodate you at ten tomorrow morning."

Mitch's compliance had its say: "May I please see that loss list?" The secretary handed it to him. He saw it was identical with the one he had, in fact, the original. That each page was separately signed and dated as received by Ruder was reassuring. Ten tomorrow morning wasn't unreasonable.

"Who knows the combination to that safe?" Mitch asked. "Do you?"

"No, only Mr. Ruder knows the combination. He had it changed only a few weeks ago."

Mitch's trust was not total. He wouldn't permit the secretary to put the jewelry into the safe. Saw to it himself, inserted the shopping bag and all into that steel hole. It was a tight fit. He closed the safe door, twisted the handle which slid the bolts into place and locked it by rotating the combination dial four times around.

For a while that night was a sensational night for Mitch. Despite his less-than-satisfactory trip to Ruder's office, he climbed back up to the altitude of his high of that day and stayed up throughout dinner and afterwards.

Maddie soared with him.

In keeping she chose to wear a next-to-nothing, a red silk satin number by Alberta Ferretti that was bare on top and bottomed out mid-thigh.

"It calls for a strong mouth, don't you think?" she said while getting ready.

"By all means a strong mouth," Mitch insinuated.

"Oh, you," she admonished archly.

The center drawer of her dressing table was fitted with a slotted rack for her tubes of lipstick. About a dozen tubes arranged according to shade left to right from nearly naive to saturnalism. This night she went straightaway to the extreme right for Yves St. Laurent's *Mischievous Rose,* spun it up and began applying.

She paused from that effort to ask: "Do you think it's absolutely essential that I wear panties?"

"Yeah."

"Were I eighteen and going out to a rock club I wouldn't. It's okay, though, isn't it, that my titties are on their own?"

"Yeah."

"This fabric shows off my nips."

"You're treacherous. I don't think you realize how treacherous you are. Want a refill?"

They were having some blanc de blanc as an overture. The bottle was only about two drinks from empty. Mitch poured and Maddie started on her lips again. She paused again. "Did I mention that Straw phoned today? From Kennedy. He and Wally are off to London to give the Cleremont a try. Something tells me they'll come back married. That would really scorch Marian."

"How long will they be gone, did he say?"

"I suppose as long as it takes."

"It," Mitch thought aloud.

Maddie stared at the mirror, intensely, as though she could see her image. "Tell me true, precious," she said, "am I beginning to look as though I've been around the garden a few times. All I have to go on is what you tell me. Do I? And don't fib."

Mitch leaned and delivered a mere touch of a kiss to the round of her bare shoulder. "You look like you've just found the path and are still amazed by the blossoms."

"What a sweetie you are."

They were slightly sloshed by the time Billy dropped them off at Le Cirque. Everything was pleasant to amusing. Even things that ordinarily weren't so pleasant or amusing. The dinner was superb. They shared some *moules.* Couldn't decide on dessert so they ordered six of the offerings and took only nibbles of each.

During coffee and calvados doubles Maddie brought up the Kalali recovery. She'd been saving it, the real dessert.

Mitch started by relating the Peaches episode. Then proceeded to his adventure at Ralph's house. His intention was to omit certain gruesome things; however it was all linked and he got going and it all came out. From his first impression of Ralph's swag-laden rooms to his repulsive but rewarding dip in what had to be the world's scummiest swimming pool.

The part that especially amused Maddie was Mitch on the uppermost floor peering down through the register at the give and take routines of Ralph and the woman. Mitch performed all their dialogue in a Cary Grant manner. Then, of course, there'd been the cactus.

After dinner, feeling the calvados, they went to the cabaret at the Russian Tea Room for an hour of Liliane Montevecchi singing about the varieties and vagaries of love.

Then they went home and made a few of their own versions.

Normally, following such late night lovemaking, Mitch slept like he was in hibernation. This night, however, his consciousness gave him a jolt after only an hour. His eyelids refused to remain shut. He lay there fixed on the blade of light on the ceiling from the night bulb in the bathroom.

A plentiful dose of endorphins were yet at work in his bloodstream, doing their best to make him feel well-being. Sleep should have been easy.

Finally he gave up trying for it, got up and went quietly into the study.

He would read, make use of the wakefulness by catching up on the last few issues of *Gem and Geology*, the quarterly journal of the Gemological Institute of America.

The first article of interest to him was entitled "Update of Mining Rubies and Fancy Sapphires in Northern Vietnam."

One of Mitch's secret someday things was to spend time at a gem source such as that mentioned in the article: the mining areas around the town of Luc Yen located in the Bac Bo mountains two hundred kilometers northwest of Hanoi. Mitch read sections of the article twice so his fantasy was well-nourished.

He would be there. He would traipse around the small, likely valleys with head down, eyes scanning the gravelly ground. It would be tropical, sweltering. He would have on suitable boots, fang-proof leather fortresses. His shirt would be ten times its weight with sweat. Rivulets of sweat would roll down his torso and pool at his beltline. He'd have on his Glock in a holster rig. And an old, good-enough hat.

How sure-eyed he'd be! Any ruby or sapphire in his path would end up in his pouch. Here and there as he ambled along he would suddenly stop and squat and poke at the alluvial gravel where the merest bit of red or pink had peeked up at him. It would turn out to be much more than a hint when it was in his fingers and he spat on it and held it up to the sun.

The next article he got into was entitled "Gem Wealth of Tanzania" and off he went to a diamond-bearing stream bed a few miles south of Mwadui. Africa! Natural pink diamonds! Worth a fortune.

Dawn intruded.

Mitch went into the bedroom and lay next to Maddie, drew her to him.

A complaining moan from her. She shucked off his arm and wiggled away. She was having her own pleasant mind trip, wasn't ready for realities. "Go to work," she grumbled sleepily.

Might as well, Mitch thought. He got up and dressed and left a loving note Scotch-taped to the flushing lever of the toilet commode where she would surely find it. He'd read the note to her when he got home.

He arrived at Columbia Beneficial at twenty to ten. Self-imposed wait was a lot more bearable. The thirty-first floor reception area was unchanged, same gray atmosphere, same auntie receptionist, same magazines.

Mitch yawned.

He felt like stretching out on the sofa. He could say he was having a dizzy spell. His right foot was keeping time to some internal composition.

At precisely ten Ruder's secretary came out to fetch him. Today her prodigious rump was worse off in black and white plaid. She escorted him into Ruder's office. Ruder wasn't there. "Mr. Ruder will be with you shortly," she assured and, before going out to her desk, suggested that Mitch sit.

He remained standing. Sitting might imply that this was a meeting. He was there only to pick up his check. Ruder, being Ruder, wouldn't let it go at that, Mitch thought. There'd be small talk, cordial bullshit.

He glanced around the office. The wall safe was closed. The Kalali jewelry was in the dark, unable to scintillate, impotent. One of the framed photos on the cabinet behind Ruder's desk was of ex-president Gerald Ford. It bore Ford's hurried signature, just the signature, no best wishes. Possibly Ruder had forged the signature, Mitch thought. He decided that was what he'd believe.

The brass nautical-looking clock next to Ford's photo said it was ten after ten.

This was the most inflicting kind of wait, Ruder-caused.

At quarter after Ruder showed up. He closed the door, went directly to his tufted leather desk chair. He acknowledged Mitch with a curt good morning, the *good* barely audible. He put on his reading glasses. They were strong, made his eyes appear hyperthyroidic. He gave routine attention to some papers on his desk.

Mitch had expected Ruder would be all grin and gratitude. Not that it mattered.

Finally, Ruder removed his glasses and focused on Mitch. A hard, contemplative stare. "You're a slick son of a bitch, Laughton," he said.

"What's the problem?"

"I expected more of you."

"You shouldn't have," Mitch quipped just to keep up. He guessed perhaps the recovery of the Kalali jewels hadn't been enough to save Ruder's ass. What else could account for his being so sour-tempered?

"As of now, neither I nor this company want anything more to do with you," Ruder said. "I dictated our notice first thing this morning. You'll receive it in the mail."

"What the hell did I do?"

"You're not to be trusted."

"Evidently there's some misunderstanding."

"No misunderstanding. You've defined yourself quite clearly. Underhanded greed is something we won't put up with."

Mitch wasn't about to beg for an explanation. If Ruder had a bug up his ass he hoped it stung him. "Okay," Mitch said, "just give me my check and I'll be out of here."

"You'll get your check on the first of the month. According to our agreement with you we're required to give you thirty days' notice of termination. Our retainer check on the first will more than cover that thirty days. However, we're through with you as of now, is that understood?"

"I'll be getting my retainer fee on the first as usual."

"Yes."

"And a check for ten percent of the appraised value of the Kalali recovery."

"Five percent," Ruder corrected.

"We agreed on ten."

"Ten if you made a full recovery, five if you made only a partial."

"There was no such stipulation."

"Perhaps you failed to hear it. Your mind is usually elsewhere."

"Not when it comes to a six-hundred-thousand deal."

"I distinctly recall the condition," Ruder insisted, "you would receive an extra five percent for making a full recovery." He took up a copy of the Kalali loss list. He didn't need to refer to it, did so only for effect. "Item thirty-two was not included in the goods you left here yesterday."

The two enscribed emeralds.

Mitch realized now what Ruder was up to. He intended to pull the old insurance trick: invent a loophole and squirm out of paying by way of it.

"Evidently you've taken quite a liking to item thirty-two," Ruder remarked snidely.

"Those emeralds are not in the recovery because they weren't in the recovery. I've never seen them." It was the second time he'd been accused of holding back. Hurley yesterday, today Ruder.

"What gets me is here you are quibbling over a paltry three hundred thousand," Ruder said.

Why had three hundred thousand suddenly become paltry? Mitch wondered. He told Ruder straight across and unequivocally: "I want what I've got coming, what you know fucking well we agreed to. Ten percent, ten. The loss list total is six million one hundred thirty thousand. The appraised value of the two emeralds according to the loss list was one hundred fifty thousand. Deduct that one fifty from the six million one thirty and the recovery total comes to five million nine eighty. At ten percent Columbia Beneficial owes me five hundred ninety-eight thousand. Now, why don't you cut the insurance bullshit and go to whoever you need to in this penitentiary and cut me a check for five ninety eight."

Ruder just sat there with upper-hand complacency.

"I'll wait," Mitch said.

"I've a good mind to not pay you a damn cent."

"I'd sue."

"Sure you would. You'd run the gauntlet of our lawyers and end up bloodied and broke." Even before those words were out Ruder was giving his attention to the paperwork of some other matter. As far as he was concerned Mitch was no longer there.

"You're a prick," Mitch said.

"You're a thief," Ruder retaliated without so much as a glance up.

Mitch turned to leave. He took three steps in the direction of the way out. The fuse in him, already lighted, reached its detonation point. With an explosion of rage he spun around and went for Ruder. Dove across the desk.

Ruder might have evaded if he'd seen it coming a second sooner or if Mitch hadn't been so quick. Mitch didn't get him with his hands as he intended. His shoulder caught Ruder beneath the chin.

The desk chair toppled over, sending the two men sprawling behind the desk.

Ruder landed on top. He tried to get off and get up.

Mitch grabbed Ruder's shirt front with his left hand. Such a furious, twisting grab that the placket of the shirt ripped and the buttons were torn off. Keeping that hold, Mitch punched with his right.

One, two, three, straight jabbing punches.

The first two were glancing, but the third landed solid on Ruder's nose, and Mitch's fist felt both the give of the fleshy part and the more resistant cartilage and bone.

He let go.

Ruder rolled off and scrambled to the nearby corner, where he remained down, his hand cupping his nose. Blood seeped from between his fingers. Most likely his nose was broken. "I'll have you arrested," he muttered and made a move to reach the telephone. Mitch feinted a lunge.

Ruder flinched and drew back.

Mitch wouldn't hit him again. He didn't need to. That one perfect punch on the nose was enough. He stood, took his time, straightened his jacket and tie and shot his cuffs. He felt great. His heart was zapping. There was a laugh in his chest. It was as though some sort of elation-causing body chemical had been released into his bloodstream.

It had been in him for years, that punch in the nose.

It had cost a fortune.

Three hundred thousand.

But it was worth it.

CHAPTER 25

It seemed to Mitch that the order of his life was immutable.

Each moment called for a decision, and whenever he decided to act contrary to what appeared to be the expected, the unavoidable, that contrariness became what had really been inevitable.

Fate was convenient to itself.

Why not just boat the oars and ride the rapids?

Thus, Mitch told himself he was only doing what had been predetermined, when, right after breaking Ruder's nose, he phoned his office and told Shirley to close up, take what remained of that day off. And while she was at it, she might as well also take tomorrow, Friday, off. And Monday. He'd see her Tuesday morning.

"You're off center," she said. "Did someone smack you on the head and make off with the shopping bag?"

"No."

"You left it in a taxi?"

"No."

"Then why are you hyperventilating so? You ought to hear how hard you're breathing. Like you've run a mile. I'll wager your heart rate is up. Place the mouthpiece to your chest so I can have a listen. Better come back to the office and I'll make tea. You're in no condition to be out there in the wilds. Bring some shortbread cookies. You know the kind."

"Go layaway."

A four-and-a-half-day hiatus.

He wouldn't set foot on 47th, wouldn't give it so much as a thought. To hell with it. He wasn't addicted to the street. It didn't have him psychologically tethered. He could take it or leave it. After all, do away with its glitter and what was it? A hive swarming with traffickers who were constantly trying to out-hondle one another.

"To you, my friend, twenty-two a carat. I paid twenty."

"You have a receipt?"

"Am I not entitled to make? Let me make two a carat."

"I'm short at the moment."

"Who isn't? I should be asking twenty-four and getting it, even twenty-five. Look at the goods."

"I have already."

"Another look."

"I know the goods."

"Tell me they're not worth twenty-five."

"They're nice goods. Not for twenty-five but nice goods."

"All I'm asking is twenty-two."

"Why?"

"I'm ashamed to tell."

"So don't tell."

"Truthfully, I went in on something that went bad. I need cash to cover. You know how it is. My reputation is at stake, everything."

"I told you, I'm short right now. I'd help maybe if I could but . . . "

"Tomorrow maybe. I have been given until tomorrow."

"I offer twenty-one today."

"Twenty-two."

"Twenty-one."

"You're taking advantage."

For instance.

Mitch was reasonably true to his pledge. He stayed away from 47th, and each time it threatened to enter his mind he barricaded as best he could with distraction.

Friday night he and Maddie were on their way down to Chinatown to alleviate her craving for *dim sum*. Billy was driving them. Mitch was seated in back on the left. They were at 50th. Mitch felt 47th coming up. He would demonstrate his irreverence by closing his eyes.

However, when they were stopped by a light at that intersection, Mitch leaned forward in order to look past Maddie and out the window.

Forty-seventh was in its dormancy. The city streetlights along that chasm illuminated its inactivity. Every upper window of its outdated, shoulder-to-shoulder buildings was dark, every street-level window was barren. The sidewalks were vacant. Only a few cars were using the way for passage to the theater district. Forty-seventh had the appearance of a street stricken, commercially forsaken.

Perhaps a day would come when it would be, Mitch thought. As for now its impoverishment was an illusion. Within its numerous safes, vaults and strong rooms lay a collective hoard of gems worth millions upon millions. Precious stones that begged for light, required it. In the darkness now but not sleeping. They never slept. They with their facets, their tables and pavilions, girdles and cutlets. It was as though they were being punished for their brilliance.

"What is it precious?" Maddie was asking.

"Hmmm?"

"You're being awfully quiet."

"Just thinking."

When they were first married Mitch believed, because Maddie couldn't see his eyes or his facial expression, the only way she could discern his disposition was by the tone of his voice. In time he learned that silence didn't always conceal, that she was often able to sense what was brewing in him.

"Just thinking ahead to some sweet and sour soup," he told her.

"It's the three hundred thousand, isn't it?"

"Not really."

"I must say you're being courageous about it. Any number of men have leaped from very high floors after losing a lot less."

"Not me."

"Just checking."

Saturday they went to the park and sat on a rock. Listened to Borodin's Symphony No. 1 in E Flat Major and some old Fleetwood Mac.

Sunday he read her most of the *Times* and they then took a growling ride around town on the Harley.

Monday he met Hurley for a drink at Harry Cipriani's, the intimate restaurant situated off the lobby of the Sherry. Their table next to the window was about the size of a Frisbee. By craning up Mitch had a clear view of the passersby out on Fifth. When he sat relaxed the sheer café-type curtains transformed those into transitory ghosts.

Harry's was crowded as it usually was from four on. Show people, cheaters, wives in pairs putting off having to go home from shopping, business sorts who'd given only an hour to the office since the last drink at lunch.

Mitch had a scotch and water.

He was down to the cubes before Hurley told him too coincidentally, just dropped it on him: "Ruder is missing."

"What do you mean missing?"

"Just that. He hasn't been seen or heard from since last Thursday."

"You know what happened Thursday?"

"Yeah, you gave him a nose job. You heard from him?"

"No."

"Around noon last Thursday he got an emergency appointment with his doctor on 65th to have his nose set. According to the doctor Ruder said he was going to sue you. After the doctor's he disappeared."

"I need an alibi?"

"He fucked you out of how much?"

"Three hundred for sure, maybe six."

"You need an alibi." Hurley did a serious expression, then nullified it with a grin. "Ruder had a slight concussion. He was advised to go home and rest. He didn't. Anyway, he didn't get there."

"Maybe he went blank, you know, got amnesia."

"Yeah, at this moment he could be shuffling in and out of the men's toilet at Grand Central."

"What a break for him not knowing himself."

They ordered another and drank to that.

When Hurley was gone, Mitch went out onto Fifth. He decided against a walk over to Lex. Instead he just stood out of the way to the left of the Sherry's canopied entrance. The late afternoon sun was yellowing the city. Soon it would go to orange. The air was thick and unsettled, redolent with hurry. Across the way, runners were funneling into the park by way of its southeast corner. They seemed to be people with less-complicated lives.

Really, where was Ruder? Mitch asked.

Wandering mindlessly, a blank among the scribble, a someone whose identity had sprung a leak and drained?

More to it than that, Mitch suspected.

A dog came along, a black and white of an oriental breed with a pushed-in face. Its walk had some proud prance in it, not at all a lost walk. It stopped at the water main that protruded from the exterior wall of the Sherry just above street level. Gleaming brass, double-headed pipe, diligently kept polished. The dog appraised it with several discriminating sniffs, then lifted his right hind leg to it.

No piss.

He was out of piss from having dispensed on the many corners, posts and such he'd encountered along his way.

He glanced in under at his genitals, as though to say he was doing his part, they should cooperate. He sidled into perfect position, lifted. Failed again. Sniffed at the brass to make sure he had or hadn't and continued on up the east side of Fifth.

Mitch watched the dog go. When it reached the intersection

of 61st it was lost to the legs of pedestrians and cars making the turn. Mitch regained sight of it mid-block to 62nd. By then, the rear-end view of it at that distance was no longer a dog shape.

Smart little guy, Mitch thought, the way he accepted being on empty and headed nonstop for his bowl and probably the lap of a Scalamandre covered sofa chair.

Within a split second of his having made that opinion, Mitch saw the receding creature break from its straight course and revert to a dog shape in profile as it veered to the left, to the curb, to the hubcap of a Bentley.

Mitch went inside. He stopped at the lobby newsstand for a magazine and just did catch an elevator that was closing to go up. There were two other passengers: a man and a woman. That was the extent of what Mitch made of them, no special regard, no reason to take particular notice, just that swift impression: a man and woman. The upward ride began. Mitch minded his elevator manners, faced forward and kept his eyes fixed ahead on the grain of the walnut paneling. To stare or even to briefly glance aside at a stranger in the confines of such a cubicle might be considered, according to unwritten New York law, an invasion of person, a potential nosiness.

The woman got off on twelve.

During the minor commotion of her exit Mitch happened to glance down at the shoes of the man.

Black and white wing-tipped oxfords.

It registered immediately, when and where Mitch had recently noticed someone wearing black and white wing-tips. They weren't shoes one saw every day, not even twice in two weeks. He was ambivalent about turning and taking an obvious look at the man, and by the time he'd decided he would, the elevator reached the thirty-second floor, leveled and opened.

Mitch stepped out onto the landing.

So did the man.

There was no doubt about it now. The black-banded panama hat, the impeccably groomed appearance. Not a gray-vested gabardine suit today, a vested black one of equally fine quality and cut. Bushy brows. It was definitely the man Mitch had practically collided with entering Visconti's office the week before last. The man Mitch had then thought from appearance was one of Visconti's wealthy foreign clients.

"I believe you must be Mr. Laughton," the man was amiably saying now. "Mr. Mitchell Laughton?"

"Yes?" Wary as usual.

"Might I have a word with you?"

"Depends on the word."

The man produced a calling card from out of a black alligator leather card case.

Mitch expected it would be a business card; however it had only the man's name tastefully engraved on it. Centered in small letters.

Manonchehr Djam.

What kind of name is that? Mitch thought.

The man pronounced it for him. He was always having to pronounce it. "I've been trying to reach you at your office since last Thursday afternoon," he said. "I was beginning to fear that you might be away on vacation."

"How did you find out where I live?"

"I inquired," Djam said as though that was plausible and sufficient. "I apologize for the intrusion but the matter I wish to discuss with you is most pressing."

"Couldn't it hold until tomorrow?"

"Yes, of course . . . "

Mitch had his key out, was finding the cylinder hole with it. What he'd had in mind was an old movie night. A certain channel he and Maddie often turned to had a triple feature of *Thin Man*'s scheduled and such a dose of Loy and Powell solving crimes between martinis would be just the palliative he needed. He and Maddie would get naked and hunker down among the pillows with an exorbitant bottle of vintage Graves and, as usual, he'd narrate the action for her between the lines of dialogue.

He had the apartment door unlatched and open a crack. His

curiosity hadn't really been oblivious. Now, at the last moment, it jumped up to ask: "What's it about, this matter of yours that's so important?"

"It concerns the Kalali jewels," Djam replied.

"Come on in."

Mitch took Djam's panama and showed him to the study. The aviary door was open but all the birds were perched inside. One, a lady finch, came winging out as though dispatched by the others. It circled three times around Djam like it was on a reconnaissance mission. Djam didn't know quite what to make of it. He finally decided he should be amused, stopped ducking and broke out into a wide grin that exposed large, tea-stained teeth.

The lady finch's return to the aviary caused a lot of bird chatter.

Djam accepted a chair. He crossed his legs somewhat gracefully. A waste because he immediately stood up as Maddie entered the study.

She was fresh out of a shower, had washed her hair. The blonde of it was darker wet. She hadn't yet toweled it, so it was a mass of short tendrils.

Nor had she belted the full-length white terry cloth robe she had on. It hung open.

Djam respectfully averted his eyes. Maddie sensed there was someone other than Mitch in the room. She insouciantly sashed the robe, exercising her contention that one of the advantages of being blind was it forgave most immodesties.

Mitch introduced Djam, mispronounced his name three different ways.

Would Djam care for something to drink?

"I'd thoroughly appreciate a glass of tea," he said.

That was more bother than tossing some ice cubes into a glass and sloshing in vodka or whatever; however Mitch managed to be hospitable. "Any preference to the kind of tea?"

"Black tea, thank you. Any good kind of black tea."

"I don't think, in fact, I know we're all out of black," Maddie said. A fib because they never drank it. "But I believe we have some jasmine."

"That will do fine," Djam told her. Actually, he deplored such fragrant teas, considered them too feminine for his taste.

"And I should warn you," Maddie added, "we do our tea with bags. We used to ritualize. You know, preheat the pot, measure exactly and steep and all that but lately it's been merely bags."

What bullshit, Mitch thought. There'd never been any steeping.

"Any way you fix it will be fine," Djam assured.

"Did I understand that you wanted a glass of tea?"

"Yes."

"Iced tea?"

"No, hot, thank you . . . " Djam regretted that he hadn't declined. Now he was going to have to suffer a glass of dreadful, prissy jasmine that was not even correctly prepared. Oh well.

Mitch excused himself, left Djam seated there and went into the kitchen to help Maddie make the tea. He looked into the cupboard while she put water on to boil. "I don't see any jasmine," he said.

"We don't have any. I only said we did in the hope that he wouldn't want it and settle for an easier scotch on the rocks. Who the hell is he, anyway?"

"I don't know."

"What do you mean you don't know?"

"I just met him."

"That's not like you, bringing home a total stranger."

"Here's some tea bags."

"What's got into you? He's not British you know."

"Not with that name."

"Nor that accent."

"He doesn't have an accent, other than British I mean."

"Hell he doesn't. Most of it's been schooled out of him but it's there. Cambridge probably."

She was always hearing things most people missed.

"Anyway, he said he wanted to have a word with me," Mitch said.

"What about?"

"The Kalali jewelry."

"Oh?" Maddie had an instantaneous rise in interest. In place of the ordinary glass for the tea she got out a Waterford goblet, Celia pattern, and wrapped one of her best linen napkins around it so Mr. Djam wouldn't burn his fingers.

Mitch carried in the tray.

Maddie announced: "No jasmine I'm afraid but some scrumptious lemon zinger."

Djam was on his haunches examining the underside of a corner of the room's main carpet. "A very pleasing Tabriz" was his opinion of it. "I assume you realize that other carpet over there, though much smaller, is the better of the two." He was referring to the prayer-size carpet near the bookcase.

"You must mean Killer," Maddie said. She'd named the carpet that because of the numerous times it had tripped her. She'd often verbally admonished it for its behavior and even threatened to throw it down the trash chute.

"A fairly fine nineteenth century silk Heriz," Djam said. "It deserves to be hung rather than trampled on." He had resumed sitting with legs crossed, the glass of tea resting on his knee. Lemon zinger. He glanced down at it. It appeared insipid, attenuated. Perhaps he could get away with a single sip and then place it aside and forget about it.

"Is that your metier, carpets?" Maddie asked.

"In part," Djam replied. "My responsibilities require it. During the two or three years that preceded the revolution, especially when the revolution became imminent, a great number of our finest carpets were shipped to the West. Planeloads went by way of Syria, others were sent overland by truck to Germany and Switzerland. I regret we shall never recover the greater part of those national treasures; however we continue to do what we can. Only last October I spotted a pedigreed sixteenth century carpet in the exhibition prior to sale at a major auction house in London. The reserve on it was ninety thousand pounds. You can imagine how delighted I was that it had come out of hiding, so to speak. I proved provenance and the carpet is now back where it belongs."

It sounded to Maddie that Djam expected applause. "And where's that?" she asked.

"In the Bastan Museum. Of course."

"Did you say Boston?"

"No, Bastan," he said, his long A's making it sound as much like Boston as it had before. "In Teheran," he added.

The lemon zinger was on its way to his lips when suddenly something occurred to him. He placed the glass on the side table next to his chair. "How remiss of me," he uttered sharply, "I haven't yet introduced my professional self." From that same elegant black case he slipped out another card, identical in quality to the first but bearing, along with his name:

Committee of Cultural Reclamation
Islamic Republic of Iran

Mitch read the card aloud for Maddie's benefit. Now they realized with certainty which revolution Djam was talking about.

"So you see," Djam said. "You and I, Mr. Laughton, are involved in the same sort of business. We are both bent on recovering precious things. You for your reasons, myself for quite another."

Mitch saw the comparison but what was the point? Whatever it was, if this Djam got to it quickly enough, there might still be time to catch the *Thin Man* triple feature. Anyway, two-thirds of it. "You mentioned the Kalali jewelry," Mitch prompted.

"Yes."

"What's your interest in it?"

"Substantial," Djam replied. "What are your chances of making a recovery?"

A shrug from Mitch. Evidently Djam was unaware that the recovery had already been made. Rather than inform him of that, Mitch decided he'd take this a little further. Not far, just enough to get some of the intrigue out of it. He told Djam: "I guess you feel the same towards the Kalali jewels as you do about those contraband carpets you spoke of."

"Even more strongly."

"They once belonged to your government and it wants them back."

"Exactly."

Mitch had known about the Iranian hoard for many years. At various times he'd read about it in trade articles and books on gems. There had been photographs illustrating the extent of this treasure. Tray after tray on shelf after shelf piled with precious stones. Chests filled to the point of overflow with emeralds, sapphires, rubies, diamonds. It infected the mind with fantasy. It was the stuff of impossible fables, and yet, there it was, as real as could be, causing more than mere fascination, an ache to get one's hands into it, to fill one's pockets, a lusting that just about anyone, but especially a dealer in gemstones, would be susceptible to.

Djam relaxed his gaunt face and did a slight smile to help the impression that he was a pleasant-natured Iranian. While inwardly he was annoyed by having just noticed a scuff mark on the white area of his right oxford. It was tantamount to a bruise. He looked to Maddie, who was comfortably situated in the corner of the deep sofa across from him. Her legs doubled up so the soles of her bare feet were directed right at him. He'd been informed that Mitchell Laughton's wife was blind and, thus, he'd expected that would be apparent in all the ordinary ways. Up to now, however, Mrs. Laughton seemed able to get about as well as any sighted person. No uncertainty in her walk, no hesitancy in her hands. Nor did her eyes have a fixed functionless quality. Her eyes appeared to be involved with whatever was taking place, reacting reflexively as normal eyes do to what was being said and who was saying it, and, somehow, incredibly, to what was being done and who was doing it. Djam believed it was probably an affect she'd perfected. It and the affront of the bottom of her feet caused him to be uneasy.

He redirected his attention to Mitch. "Imagine, if you will, what a temptation the Iranian treasury must have been to a certain privileged few in nineteen seventy-eight. By then it was inevitable that the Shah would be ousted. Various members of the Shah's family had already fled, were residing in France, Switzerland, this country and elsewhere. Many prominent government officials had done likewise. Not to feel sorry for them. Hundreds of millions in currency had preceded their departures.

"For those of the elite who remained in Iran but knew they would soon take flight, the national treasure was impossible to ignore. It couldn't be merely left behind. At least not all of it. Such a trove of precious stones. Worth billions, was the guess. How accommodating that it had never been properly inventoried and appraised. The task would have taken five, maybe ten years, and then been obsolete. The attitude had always been no need to know more about it other than that it was there.

"During those final months of the Shah his relatives and close associates discreetly pilfered the treasure. They were allowed to get to it and take nibbles and bites of it every now and then. A handful of diamonds wouldn't be missed, nor would a pocketful of rubies, sapphires or emeralds. Abundance covered up each little ransacking.

"Abbas Kalali and his wife, Roudabeth, were among those who paid such visits to the vault in the Central Bank where the treasure was kept. Not that the Kalalis were high in favor with the Shah or within the coterie of the elite. Kalali was never more than a mid-level official assigned to one bureau or another. His well-being was dependent on a remote and tenuous connection: the wife of one of his uncles happened to be the cousin of General Nassiri, the head of Savak, the Shah's secret police.

"Perhaps the most accurate measure of Abbas Kalali's standing was his bribery price of only a million dollars. Only? you say. Remember, this was at a time when the going rate for influence by a member of the Shah's family was a hundred million. Prime ministers were slipped fifty million, generals went for thirty.

"You might wonder, then, how it was that Abbas Kalali got to dip into the treasure, what was it about him that gave him access? Why him? Well, Abbas Kalali was the apotheosis of sycophancy. He knew when to laugh and when to commiserate, when to take a side, which side to take, when to lose, when to appear or disappear. Thus, it was often agreeable for the coterie of the privileged to have him around. You know the sort."

Yeah, Mitch thought, he knew have-arounds.

"Kalali was obviously willing to be used and use him they did. Especially during the final months of the Shah when it was dangerous to be making trips to the vault at odd hours. They enlisted Kalali to go for them. He was their designated thief and carrier."

Nothing so unusual about that, Mitch thought.

"No doubt," Djam went on, "they expected that while Kalali was at it he would help himself to a helping. That didn't matter to them as long as it wasn't too much and he didn't embarrass by letting them know about it. And, as long as he brought from the vault whatever it took to satisfy them."

Djam paused. Evidently he had more to say. He shifted his position in the chair and transposed the cross of his legs.

"Your tea must be cold," Maddie said.

Djam wondered how she could know he hadn't drunk it.

"I can heat it up for you."

"No, please, don't bother," Djam said. "I prefer it luke-warm."

A nearly inaudible grunt of disbelief from Maddie.

"So," Mitch said, "according to what you say, I gather you believe the Kalali jewels are made up from gems that were taken from the Iranian treasury."

"Mainly they are, yes," Djam replied. "Of course there was more, much more, loose cut stones and quite a bit of rough. Diamonds and rubies mostly. Kalali sold those in various lots over the years. He must have realized plenty for them, plenty."

"How come you're just now laying claim?"

"As reluctant as I am to admit it, we were never able to catch up with him. He was like a damn cricket. You know, one of those elusive bugs. Pounce to capture it, think you have, open your hands only to find you haven't. When he first came to the United States, which was in August of 1980 after the death of the Shah, he lived in northern California under an assumed name, always under a document-supported assumed name. Then it was Arizona and South Dakota of all places. We never gave up on him altogether but after a half dozen years we more or less left it to God's will that he would somehow, someday turn up. Which he did most recently, turned up dead."

"Not under an assumed name."

"No. Apparently time caused him to believe he was forgotten."

"And all was forgiven. You still want them back, those gems, what's left of them?"

"We do."

"The Iranian treasure must be getting pretty paltry."

"I assure you the Iranian treasure would still make you momentarily forget to take a breath."

Mitch was thinking of a lady in a coma and her vigilant lover, their hopes. "Strikes me as greedy," he told Djam. "Those piles of gems you have and here you are eager to recover these relative few. Greedy, wouldn't you say, Maddie?"

"How about hoggish?" Maddie enjoyed replying.

If Djam was either embarrassed or insulted it didn't show. He did another pleasant Iranian smile and several thoughtful blinks and said: "Actually, I would be satisfied with the recovery of just one piece of the Kalali jewels."

"You would?"

"Yes."

"Any piece?"

"One particular piece."

"Name it."

"It appears on the insurance company loss list as item number thirty-two."

The loss list. When, where, Mitch wondered, had Djam become so familiar with the loss list? As for item number thirty-two, what a bane it had been.

Those two enscribed emeralds.

"Instead," Mitch suggested, "how about a pair of diamond and ruby ear pendants, an exquisite pair, Burma rubies, clean E-color diamonds. They might even be D's." Selling.

"Only the emeralds will do," Djam told him.

"Why?"

"Must I tell you?"

Mitch sensed a long wind coming up. He almost got to say his *no* before Maddie's *yes*. She, with her usual penchant for accounts that might smack of thievery or any sort of sharp practice, was all ears.

"Very few people in this country are knowledgeable when it comes to Iranian history," Djam said. "I don't suppose you're the exception."

Oh Christ, Mitch thought, how far back will he go?

As though answering Mitch's mind, Djam began with: "Seventeen thirty-six was the year that Nadar Shah took over the throne of Iran from the Safavids, who had ruled for more than two hundred and thirty years. He was an Afsharid Turkman from northern Khorasan. At the time, Iran was by no means a wealthy country. Its primary source of revenue was the silk trade, and carpet weaving. What's more, being remote from Europe, literally cut off from Europe by Ottoman territory, any trade in that direction was sporadic at most.

"Nadar Shah was not the sort to remain content with such marginal solvency. His was an aggressive nature. He was also obsessed with treasure and jewels. Thus, in seventeen thirty-eight, only two years after taking rule, Nadar and his army went plundering."

Now, this is getting good, Maddie thought.

Djam went on: "He didn't go charging around grabbing up

whatever he just happened upon. He knew where the real riches were and went straight for them. The Moghul emperors of India were then the wealthiest of the world's wealthy. No one had more. They hoarded nearly all the fine diamonds from their prolific mines at Panama and Cuddapah. They merely had to reach out to neighboring Burma and Ceylon for whatever rubies and sapphires they desired. With the same ease they acquired the choicest pearls from the Andaman Sea located immediately to the east.

"The Moghuls were especially fond of emeralds. The finest came from the mines of distant Colombia, those that the Spanish conquistadors discovered north of Bogotá in the region of Muzo. Spain had the emeralds, the Moghuls had the money. Spain preferred money, the Moghuls preferred emeralds. It couldn't have been a more agreeable arrangement. Spanish ships carried the emerald rough from Colombia to the Philippines where it was cut and polished before being delivered to Delhi.

"So, thus were the riches Nadar Shah was set upon. The Moghul armies fought but were no match. Nadar's forces overran all of Delhi. They appropriated the treasure and headed home.

"Picture if you will that victorious homeward-bound trek. I have, numerous times. What a sight it must have been! What jubilance must have occupied Nadar's heart as he led that caravan laden with booty! Literally hundreds of thousands of precious stones! Layer after layer rolled up in leopard and tiger skins, caskets of pearls, a dozen pack horses needed to convey the emeralds!"

Djam realized he was getting carried away. He checked his exuberance, sort of shook it off and elevated his torso to recapture his previous dignity. "The Iranian treasure that we spoke of before, that which the Kalalis and others dipped into, is, of course, comprised mainly of the spoils of Nadar Shah's Delhi campaign."

"You hardly touched on the best part, the robbery," Maddie complained.

"Robbery?"

"Nadar Shah might have appropriated, as you put it; however it was robbery."

"It wasn't thought of as such in those days," Djam told her.

"I suppose not; however he was a swift, big-time but no less and swift, and the stuff he stole was swag."

Mitch assumed the two enscribed emeralds that were on the Kalali loss list had been part of Nadar Shah's Moghul booty. But so what? If that was their only significance it was trivial, considering the enormous amounts of emeralds in the Iranian treasury. What made those two that, from what Mitch could see weren't special, so special? He asked Djam.

"That is the most salient part of what I'm telling you," Djam said.

"There's more?"

"Yes, what I've just related is only background. I thought you would enjoy it."

Mitch was now about eighty percent restive, twenty percent curious. He looked to Maddie, thinking she might have had enough and would do an excuse such as having to get ready for a dinner party out; however she was distracted, vigorously roughing up her hair with her fingers to help it dry.

"Husayn al-Qasim Muhammad ibn Hashid," Djam said with an ethnic, gargling-like quality that, because of its change, sounded exaggerated, "was a poet who lived in a province of Esfahan. An admirably devout man. He was a descendant of Iran's most revered mystical poet, Jahal Ad-Din-Ar Rumi."

"When was this?" Maddie interrupted.

"The precise year is a matter of controversy," Djam replied. "Some accounts have it as eighteen ten, others at eighteen eight. It surely was around that time, the early eighteen hundreds. Anyway, Husayn al-Qasim, as I said, was a religious person. Pious would be a more accurate description. He placed his own contentment and even his meager requirements second to his worship. His most joyful pursuit was in composing verses of devotion to God, and praying, of course.

"Esfahan is for the most part an arid province. Except for the provincial capital it is sparsely inhabited. The small village where Husayn lived was far from any other settlement. Such remoteness suited him. He had no desire or need to associate or experience what lay beyond his view.

"The radiance of such a pious man transcends distance. He was known of, spoken of. That was how Ali-Bin al-Nizami, who at the time was the Imam of the most important mosque in Teheran, learned of Husayn's ailment. Husayn was going blind.

"There were those who said that Husayn's swiftly progressive blindness was a result of his having seen the heart of the sun while staring directly into it. Probably the less mythic cause was a condition we now know as macular degeneration, wherein the macula part of the retina leaks fluid which destroys the retinal nerve tissue. It is untreatable.

"As a gesture of sympathy and hoping to ease, the Imam selected two large emeralds from the treasury and sent them to Husayn along with the suggestions that Husayn hold them up to his eyes and gaze through them whenever he felt inclined. According to the Koran green is the color of heavenly bliss, the color of paradise."

Djam paused.

Mitch believed he could save words and time. "So," he said, "those enscribed emeralds are the two you now want to recover."

"Please, you're getting ahead of me," Djam said and went on: "Husayn was grateful for the Imam's concern and followed his suggestion. For forty days, at intervals throughout each day, he brought the two emeralds to his eyes, and through them, as well as he was able, saw the colorless aridity of the Esfahan countryside transformed into a blessed verdancy.

"That he did so for forty days was not just arbitrary. In our Koran as in your Bible the number forty is given mystical significance. It is the stipulated length of time for a period of mourning or repentance, for example, or steadfastness.

"Husayn spent the fortieth morning of those forty days composing verses in praise of the Khider, the figure spoken of in sura twenty of the Koran as the unnamed companion of Moses. The Khider is the patron saint most frequently related to the green color of paradise. Husayn was especially inspired that morning and his verses flowed so freely from him it seemed as though he was a mere conduit, a go-between. To this day they are considered to be his best.

"Came noon Husayn performed his ablutions, and, after saying his mid-day prayers, he had a little to eat. Almonds, pomegranate seeds and goat cheese. There, seated on the bare ground on the shady side of his modest house, he treated himself to the enjoyment of gazing through the two emeralds. Within a short while he became drowsy and could not resist falling into a deep sleep.

"When he awakened it was late afternoon. The sun had come around to him and there were independent fluffs of clouds in the sky. He could see those clouds clearly. He was able to make out their edges, layers and forms. He saw that the line of the horizon was distinct, and everything, all the way to it, each shape and each variety of hue, was no longer obscure, but sharply visible to him. The eyesight he'd lost had been returned.

"Husayn looked down at his clenched hands and opened them. Each contained one of the emeralds. Just as he had undergone a change so had those green stones. The flat surface of their faces had been plainly polished. Now, however, each bore a finely engraved inscription in old Farsi, the original Persian language. The inscriptions pertained to what we call *yagin*, the light of intuitive certainty by which the heart sees God."

"Oh, what a fascinating story," Maddie said.

"And true," Djam assured.

"Could be," Mitch compromised.

"I'm sure you can now understand why we are so anxious to have those emeralds returned," Djam said. "They are sacred to us, an affirmation of our beliefs. It's as if you had in your possession one of the commandment tablets of Moses and someone made off with it."

Mitch thought that was stretching it. Maybe it was true that Husayn what's-his-name's eyesight had improved to some extent for some more earthly reason and maybe it was also true that someone had realized the advantage of the circumstances and had the inscriptions done. The shroud of Turin came to mind, that contrivance.

Mitch's thoughts in that direction halted and went another way. Why was he such a doubter? he asked himself. Nearly every time, right off, a doubter. Why couldn't he be more often spontaneously receptive, at least a potential believer? It wasn't a new question. The answer, the excuse, the explanation or whatever had always been that it was something West 47 had done to him, as ambiguous and abstract as that. Also, more specifically, some of the blame belonged to the woman with the pistol up her sable sleeve. "Kalali probably took them unknowingly," Mitch reasoned. "He probably thought they were just ordinary emeralds."

"No," Djam told him. "Kalali was well-aware of what he was taking. Those emeralds were kept in a special glass case in the vault. He knew their religious history, how much they were valued. That was what he was counting on, how much we would be willing to pay to have them back."

"How was it you knew Kalali had them?"

"We didn't at first. It could have been any one of the Shah's entourage who had swiped from the vault. There were dozens. It could even have been the Shah himself, considering it was such an audacious act. We learned that it was Kalali when he made an overture in a roundabout way to negotiate a price. That was early on during his California days. His trepidations must have gotten the best of him. He broke off contact and disappeared."

"One would think with your resources . . ."

"This large country is inhabited by diverse people. It's much less difficult for someone to get lost than it is for someone to be found."

True enough, Mitch thought. His curiosity asked Djam: "How much would you have paid Kalali for the emeralds?"

"Kalali was a condemned man."

"Say he wasn't, how much?"

"The same amount we're now offering."

Had Mitch heard right? "What do you mean offering?"

"I am authorized by the Committee of Cultural Reclamation to reward whoever recovers the emeralds for us with twenty-five million dollars."

Wishful hearing, Mitch told himself, the guy hadn't really said twenty-five million. "How much did you say?"

"Twenty-five million."

"American dollars."

"Naturally."

Oh how that would fit, Mitch thought. If true, his pessimism reminded. "To whom have you made this offer?" he asked.

"I would rather not say. To several people." Djam did that smile again. Unfortunate teeth. "And now you," he said.

Riccio, Mitch thought. It explained why Riccio had resorted to such extreme, old-mob violence with Ralph. Rather than wait for the Kalali swag to possibly come his way he'd gone after it. It also explained why Ruder had done such a quick change when he realized the emeralds weren't in the recovery. Item thirty-two, missing. Sure, Ruder was looking at a nice, fat twenty-five-million score. Out of which he was going to give Mitch, for doing all the work, a skinny extra three hundred thousand. Big-hearted Ruder, the prick. And since Mitch had seen Djam coming out of Visconti's office, no doubt Visconti was in on it. "Why didn't you come to me first?" Mitch asked.

"You were on my agenda," Djam replied. "However, I was told you wouldn't be amenable to such a proposition."

"Who told you that?"

"You were described as . . . I believe the way they put it was . . . too straight. Also, it was said you wouldn't be motivated, you didn't need the money because your wife was wealthy."

A chuckle from Maddie. "Mitch was your best shot," she told Djam. "He probably would have recovered your precious emeralds for nothing. Isn't that right, Mitch darling?"

Mitch turned partially away as though to deflect Maddie's words. The numbers got into him, took over and ran across the front of his mind like a repetitive electronic sign, starting with a two, then a five, then a comma and all those zeros.

He could handle that.

CHAPTER 26

He was in his office on the phone with Hurley.

"Is the guy real?" Hurley asked.

Mitch had just told him about Djam, the emeralds and the twenty-five million offer. "Hard to tell. It looks it, sounds it." In the cooler light of Tuesday morning Mitch had allowed his skepticism to snap back into place like a filter.

"Could be he's a throwback," Hurley said.

"What do you mean throwback?"

"The Arabs had their day. Was a time when any prototype Arab who could afford a good suit, impressive luggage and a suite for a week at the Pierre was someone who got his ass kissed. Remember? A lot of them were into it only for that reason."

"Yeah."

"Then came the Japs. Same thing. Next maybe the Chinks coming out of Hong Kong. So, could be your guy . . . what did he call himself?"

"Manonchehr Djam." Mitch still had trouble with the name.

"Could be he's a throwback."

"You're probably right. I'd prefer that you weren't but probably you are." If so, Mitch thought, the Iranian was also

fucking with Riccio's head, and Visconti's. Djam hadn't
struck him as that foolish but who knows how far someone
doing such an ego scam might dare to take it. "This morning,"
he told Hurley, "just for the hell of it I was going over the
chain of possession of the Kalali goods. The link that's missing is the swift, Floyd."

"We picked him up."

"What's his version?"

"We picked him up in a body bag. He had a mouth-first
hole in his head. Now, I ask you, when you want a guy to give
up something how can he say what you want to hear when
he's got a throat full of pistol?" A short inured laugh from
Hurley.

"How about the other swifts?"

"We got the one called Tracy. He's about as stand-up as a
paraplegic. We only sort of promised a plea and he laid the
whole thing out for us. Says the girl Peaches popped Mr.
Kalali."

"Believe him?"

"Yeah."

"He mention the emeralds?"

"Come to think of it I did ask him about them. He never
saw them. Everything except Peaches' earrings went to
Ralph."

"How's Peaches getting along?" Mitch inquired.

"I should be such a lie artist. So far she's changed the scenario eight times. You heard from Ruder?"

"Why should I?"

"No reason. He just might get it in his head to call you . . .
from the spot on the floor where he sleeps in the West Side
bus terminal. How's Maddie?"

"The same, perfect."

"Give her my best. No, give her *your* best."

"I try."

While Mitch was on line one with Hurley line two had
started blinking, and Shirley had picked it up. She'd brought
in a message slip. Mitch read it now. Originally her precise

handwriting had said: *Riccio wants to talk with you.* She'd crossed out the *talk with* and replaced it with *see* and an exclamation point.

Twenty minutes later Mitch was climbing Riccio's gritty, vinyl-covered stairs. The same fat have-around was on duty on the landing halfway up. He wanted no part of Mitch this time. He backed aside awkwardly and sat on the edge of the daybed. "You got an appointment?" he asked.

Mitch ignored him, went on up to Riccio's rooms. He had to go through Bechetti to get in to Riccio but there was no problem: he was expected. Riccio was at a Formica-topped table against the wall, going over some swag that had come in from the preceding weekend. In a small adjacent room off to the right a couple of have-arounds were watching a television talk show.

Riccio didn't usually get up to greet someone but now he did. He came at Mitch with a big smile, a two-handed shake and flattery. "Nice to see you, Mitch. What is this with you? How come you're looking so good. You just get a haircut or something? Come on, sit. I was just going to have some coffee."

"None for me, thanks," Mitch said, mindful of the billions of bacteria there would be on the rim of one of Riccio's dirty cups.

"How come no coffee?"

"Doctor's orders."

"What is it, the belly?"

"Nerves."

"Nerves can lead to an early death," Riccio recited as though it was sky-writing.

They were seated at the Formica-topped table, diagonally across from one another. Folding metal chairs that didn't match. Eight skinny black twists of cigars bound by a rubber band. The swag. Three separate lots. Mitch assumed one lot was that which would be broken up. Another was what would be kept, the third awaited Riccio's decision. Mitch tried to disregard it.

"What do you think of this?" Riccio asked, tossing Mitch a piece from the unsorted lot.

Mitch thought, for one thing, that it didn't deserve such rough handling, especially when he held it up and realized how fine it was. A *sautoir* consisting of natural seed pearls and tiny diamond rondelles suspending a frosted rock crystal hoop that was delicately bordered with bagettes of calibré onyx and tasseled with ruby heads. Mitch's appreciation was obvious.

"Like it?" Riccio asked.

"It's nice," Mitch understated. Not to waste his expertise, he held back telling Riccio it was Mauboussin circa 1910.

"It's yours," Riccio said.

Mitch placed the *sautoir* on the table. It didn't belong here, he thought, not in this ugly, smelly place being mishandled by coarse hands. It deserved to be around the neck of a lovely, high-fashioned lady, to give her fingers something to fuss with, during the public phase of a rendezvous at the bar of the Ritz in Paris.

"What's the matter?" Riccio asked.

"It's not my taste," Mitch told him.

"That's not right. You don't like it you should still accept. If it was anybody but you I'd consider it an insult." Riccio gathered up the *sautoir* and relegated it to the break-up lot.

To Mitch that was a kind of murder.

"Let's be more comfortable," Riccio said.

They moved to a nearby couch. It was new but cheap, the sort that would soon go lumpy. "I take a nap now and then," Riccio explained. A regular foam rubber bed pillow had a pink and yellow floral case. A crucifix over the bed. "I hear you had some good luck," he said.

"How's that?"

"The stuff you brought me the pictures of a couple of weeks back. You found it."

"Who told you?"

"That insurance guy. What's his name?"

"Ruder."

"That's it, Ruder. He said you found the whole package and made a nice score. I'm happy for you. You deserve."

"When did you talk to Ruder?"

"Last week sometime. I think it was Wednesday. Yeah, Wednesday." Riccio called out to Bechetti who immediately showed himself in the doorway of the television room. "Wasn't it Wednesday we talked with that insurance guy?"

"Yeah, Wednesday," Bechetti corroborated.

If Riccio and Ruder knew each other it was news to Mitch. One thing for certain: if they had talked and Ruder had mentioned the recovery it couldn't have been Wednesday. Ruder didn't know about it until Thursday. "I heard that Ruder is missing," Mitch said offhand.

"No shit. You mean he ain't been around anywhere?"

"Since Thursday afternoon."

"So, who gives a fuck? Guy like that gets missed for a while, month or two it's like he fucking never was." Riccio inserted a finger behind the top button of his shirt. He stretched his neck. The shirt was overstarched, the collar like a blade at his throat. "Tell the truth, I didn't like the guy. He was a piece of shit."

Mitch noticed the past tense.

"Know what happens to a guy like that?" Riccio went on. "He fucks with the wrong people. They take exception. He keeps on fucking with them and they have to hurt him. They could pop a cap into him but that ain't satisfying enough, they don't want to just do that. Know what they do? They hold his mouth open and pour diamonds into him. Then they give him four or five shots in the belly, hard right hands right in there. He's an asshole. He's coughing blood but he's still fucking with these wrong people. What can they do? Throw him in the river? Not yet. First, to make sure he sinks, you know, that he doesn't gas up and bloat and come to the top someplace, they slit him up the front and rip his guts and everything out like he was a fish. That way they also get back the diamonds. Happens to a guy like that who fucks with the wrong people."

Mitch had never disliked Ruder to the extent that he'd wish

him such a fate. He knew, however, as sure as he'd just heard Riccio's horror story, it had probably happened. A shiver climbed the ladder of his spine. His facial expression remained unchanged.

"Anyway," Riccio said, "Ruder told us when you handed over that swag to him you held out."

"I turned in all there was."

"Except a pair of emeralds."

"I never had them."

"Look, I don't blame you for putting those emeralds aside, not when there's this sand nigger moving around saying he'll give twenty-five extra large for them."

Riccio's phone rang. He went over to his desk and answered it. A grunt instead of a hello. It wasn't a conversation, at least not from Riccio's end. Just a series of flat *yeahs* and *nos*. Mitch looked past him and saw Fratino in the television room, the doorway framing him. Like a tableau, Mitch thought. Have-around in a short-sleeve wrinkle-proof shirt with pistol rig on. Hyper reality. He should be exactly done in acrylic and exhibited at the Whitney.

Riccio returned to the couch. "I'll make you a deal for the two emeralds," he said.

"I told you, I don't have them."

"Sure you do."

"What can I say?"

"You can say what kind of a deal like the sensible, straight guy I think you are and I'll tell you I'm willing to give you one extra large for them and you can think about it for five or ten seconds in order to look smart before you say okay, Riccio, that's what you can say."

While those were Riccio's words, Mitch was asking himself why was he there? Breathing the same air as this man and the others. He wasn't one of them. He would never be one of them. No matter how the street shaped him. They happened to be inhabitants, an ingredient of the mix. They tolerated him. He tolerated them. The bubbling coo of pigeons in the eaves. Transmitted television voices. Precious stones lost in the high-pile weave of the wall-to-wall rug. Riccio farted without apology. What am I? Mitch asked himself, a social chameleon?

"I don't get it," he told Riccio.

"What don't you get?"

"If I had the emeralds why should I give them to you for a million when I could get twenty-five million for them?"

"Because you're not greedy. Because the million I'd pay you wouldn't come with any bad feelings along with it, no hurt, nothing like that. Because you don't need the money. You got a rich wife, who, by the way, you should worry about when she goes out shopping and places. Even in the daytime, on any street, you should worry about the wrong people fucking with her."

Riccio's brain was rotten, Mitch thought. There were calluses on his eyes. He was eaten with pathology, putrefied by habit, perhaps by birth. The air that had the misfortune of being sucked into him came out contaminated. He had a wife and children he kissed, a priest he confessed to, holy water went to his head, the chamber of his rottenness, each week.

"How about it?" Riccio pressed.

"No deal," Mitch replied unequivocally. He was surprised how much pleasure he got out of telling Riccio that, how angry and yet calm he was. "And, as for my wife," he said, "I'll look out for her. Anyway, no need for me to worry about her for a while." He paused and did a smug punishing smile, "She's leaving tonight to spend some time in France . . . with her mother."

CHAPTER 27

Shortly before nine that night she came out of the Sherry. Her luggage had preceded her and Billy and the doorman had loaded it into the trunk of the Lexus.

She was wearing an outfit suitable for traveling: slacks and a pullover and an amply cut, lightweight, long coat. Her hair was contained in a latter-day cloche.

When she reached the curb she hesitated in order to adjust her dark glasses. The open, rear door of the Lexus awaited her. Her right hand searched and found the upper part of the car's frame along the roofline before she ducked down and got in.

Caselli and Fratino, Riccio's two have-arounds, were parked across the avenue. When the Lexus pulled out they followed along behind. Crosstown to the FDR Drive and up to and over the Triborough and all the way to Kennedy to the TWA terminal.

"Maybe she really ain't going," Fratino said.

Caselli agreed.

They watched Billy help get her luggage checked at the curb. A TWA courtesy attendant showed up with a wheelchair. She refused it. The attendant guided her. Through the automatic doors and on into the terminal.

Caselli stayed with the car.

Fratino got out and followed her. That she had checked some luggage didn't prove anything. The luggage could make the trip without her.

Fratino followed her to the security pass-through and on to the gate. The attendant remained with her. She was traveling first-class, could board then or later. She waited to be last, then she and the attendant entered the boarding ramp and were out of sight.

Within a short while the attendant emerged and the doors to the boarding ramp were closed.

Fratino was beginning to believe. He watched from a window as the 747 disconnected and pulled away. As it taxied out to the runway he thought he caught a glimpse of her in a window seat of the first-class section.

Still, he waited, allowed more than enough time for a takeoff before going to the nearby bank of telephones to call Riccio.

"The cunt's gone," he said.

"What did you do to her?"

"I didn't do nothing to her. I'm at Kennedy. She got on a plane and it took off."

"You sure?"

"Positive."

CHAPTER 28

At that moment Mitch and Maddie were going seventy-five through the heavy night air, northbound on the Taconic State Parkway. The unrelenting growl of the Harley beneath them seemed strong and reassuring, as though declaring *make way, I'm carrying my owners to safety*.

They arrived at Kinderhook and Uncle Straw's house at half past eleven. The house was summer stuffy from having been shut up for several days, so, first thing, they went about opening windows to allow the slight breezes from the west across the Hudson to flow through.

Maddie turned down the bedcovers in their usual room, second floor rear. Mitch, meanwhile, made some toasted cheese sandwiches and brought them up on a tray. Oven-warmed potato chips, two sweating bottles of St. Pauli Girl.

"Want some music?" he asked.

"Got some," she replied, meaning the chorus of the pastoral night being performed by the tiny creatures moving about enormously brave deep among the grasses and perched higher upon the platforms of leaves.

Mitch placed the tray upon the table by the window. He lighted an old glass oil lamp and switched off the electric ones, thinking it would lend to the mood. He was immediately reminded that lighting did not matter to Maddie. It had been a while since he'd made such an oversight.

"I smell an oil lamp," she said.

"Yeah."

"That's one of the countless things I love about you," she smiled, "you have a sense for the appropriate."

Somehow she knows when I need to be saved, Mitch thought. The oil lamp was smoking, blackening its glass chimney. He reduced the wick.

They ate in silence. Mitch observed her. Actually, it was more an examination the way he employed his sighted advantage, took lengthy notices of her various features, appreciating them so much and focusing so intensely upon them that at times they seemed magnified. The left corner of her mouth, the perfect crease of it that made a faultless transition to her cheek. It alone momentarily occupied his entire visual field. As did the textures of her various parts. The space between her eyelid and brow. Her instrumental hands.

He rode her finger up to her teeth. Caught a glimpse of the slick pink pillow of her tongue. His thought came with an ache. I won't let anyone harm her, he vowed. They'll have to go through me, over me.

He loathed being reminded by his practical side they would probably do just that.

He left the oil lamp burning when they went to bed. Its captive flame projected a shadowy ring upon the ceiling. Maddie snuggled into the cave of his arm and fell asleep quickly. He was left awake with his worry. Shirley was thirty-five thousand feet over the Atlantic. Riccio's have-arounds had bought the impersonation. They wouldn't be coming this night. This night was a stay; he could rest easy.

Still, when he finally gave in to sleep he remained in the shallows.

The birds woke him at dawn with their chirping. He got up, dressed quietly and went down to grind some coffee and set it to brewing. He stood there at the kitchen counter as though caught in a spell by the explosive hisses and drips of the automatic coffee maker. His mind felt dull and vulnerable, a heavy head. The glass pot seemed to be purposely slow to fill. He couldn't wait for it, went out onto the covered rear porch, intending to go back inside shortly and pour himself a cup.

His legs, however, as though they were independent and, at that moment, in charge, took him down the porch steps and across the wide rear lawn to a gated opening in the neatly masoned brick wall on the south. That gave to a buffer of mowed meadow and a piled rock wall beyond which lay the expansive area where the neighbor's cows were permitted to pasture.

The cows.

The sight of them caused both his mind and body to brighten and snap into alignment for this day. They were mere black and whites in the distance, being let out; however there was no mistaking they might be other than cows.

He had patience for them, could have stood and waited for all the time it would take for them to make their slow amble to him. A large herd. How many? Fifty at least, more.

He strode right at them and soon was among them. They with only slight or no acknowledgment of him, the most meager curiosity. Their huge dark eyes. Their barreled girths and bony rumps. Tails switching out of habit.

Mitch was lost in them, their simple worthiness. They were so removed from diamonds, emeralds and such, and above all, threatless.

He circled back to the piled rock wall and walked along beside it for quite a ways. He climbed up onto it and sighted across the West Meadow, that large gently undulating open area of crotch-high grass that he'd waded the weekend before last. No trace of his trek through it now. The grasses and the Queen Anne's lace that his weight and motion had injured had fully recovered.

He traversed the meadow by the old equipment barn where he'd taught Maddie to shoot, and entered the woods. The sun was not yet high enough to cause dapple. Patches where the branches did not umbrella still had some night wet on them.

Offsprings of maples and oaks were submissive whips. The chatter of a squirrel. The metallic cry of a jay. The leaves of last year, superficially dry, damp a layer down, especially slippery on the inclines. And, underneath, the accumulated drop and rich decay of countless autumns, spongy.

About a quarter of a mile in ledges broke the regularity of the woods. Blocks of nearly black granite, more massive than high. A modular series of those individualized by their varying heights and defining faults. Water, from what seemed their secret source, seeped from them, ran down their faces, preferred the grooves of their fractures. Mitch's mouth was dry. He stood at the base of a ledge, leaned to it for his tongue to catch some of the trickle. He pressed his forehead against the rough wet. Closed his eyes and imagined his brain being bathed.

With his face dripping and shirt-front soaked, he followed one of the runoff gullies down to the lower land. The marsh there was at its summer low, having receded and left all the clumps of skunk cabbage standing on their roots like columns. The water of the marsh was no more than a foot or two deep out in its middle. It appeared blacker because of that, its surface closer to the black silt of the bottom.

Mitch found a fallen branch and used it to poke at the bottom. The branch went down into the silt easily, penetrated nearly a foot before it met resistance, and that was just there at the edge.

The bass croaks of frogs. Their frantic leaps for underwater. Mitch knew, of course, that he was not out on some empty-stomach, early morning hike. It was reconnaissance, looking at the lay of the land in a way that he had never perceived it. A battleground. If Riccio's have-arounds came, and chances were they eventually would, they'd outnumber him. He was desperately in need of allies. Possibly, he was finding some.

He crossed several clearings. One was particularly wide, had blackberries growing in a thorny patch. He picked as many as his hand could contain and ate them on the way out to the bluff overlooking the Hudson. The wide river, two hundred feet below, was silvery green. It seemed to be at a standstill. The deceptive river, hiding its currents. It was too formidable to be friendly, Mitch thought. He climbed down the bluff by way of the unapparent, back-and-forth trail that he was certain had once been used by the Mohicans. There was a more accessible, roundabout way down to the Strawbridge boathouse but Mitch had seldom used it.

The boathouse was a well-preserved wooden structure situated on a float that allowed it to adjust to the rise or fall of the river. It consisted of three slips below a room used for storing boating equipment, life jackets, oars, seat cushions, pennants and the like. Its interior smelled of oil and gasoline and baked wood. There were three boats:

Two were Chris-Craft speedboats: a relatively new one and a sixty-year-old classic. The other boat was far more ordinary: an outboard with a fiberglass hull. Mitch had been out in the Chris-Craft several times with Uncle Straw, but the outboard was the one they used to go upstream to fish the mouths of the tributaries for trout.

Mitch took a comprehensive look around the boathouse. Then climbed the bluff and went straight home. Maddie was in the kitchen, barefoot and half dressed. Her hair was spiking every which way. She was about to scramble a half dozen eggs. The butter in the pan was scorched. She poured the bowl of disturbed eggs into the pan and overdosed them with Worcestershire.

"Great coffee!" she said, raising her mug to the level of her smile.

Mitch poured some. It was a little too strong, on the bitter side. He was hungry, tempted to settle for a bowl of cereal and raisins; however he waited for her eggs, endured them with large bites and quick swallows. "Good eggs," he fibbed.

She knew better. "You're nice," she told him.

"What would you like to do today?" he asked.

"You," she replied wickedly, "but later."

There were three phone calls that morning. The first was

from Shirley to say she was staying at a charming hotel off Boulevard St. Germain and that if she wasn't so worried about them she'd be having a marvelous time. When would this crisis be over? She'd met an extremely attractive businessman on the plane. Please let her know as soon as all was well so she could breathe easy and take full advantage of him.

The second call, not a half hour later, was from Uncle Straw and Wally, both on the line at the same time, so it was a four-way conversation. They'd done well at the casino in London, although actually, they hadn't spent all that much time at the tables. Now they were in Monaco, staying at the Hôtel de Paris, had been there two days and hardly been out of the suite. They had some surprising news, Straw said, and Maddie tried to drag it out of him, but he remained cryptic, would only say it was happy news, which caused Wally to confirm that it couldn't be happier. Maddie had all she could do to keep from guessing aloud that they were either married or had agreed to be. She was sure that was it, that Straw wanted to wait until he got home to more intimately share it. When were they coming home? They weren't sure, thought they might go on to Baden-Baden or somewhere or anywhere. They sounded so up. *Pick the tomatoes* were Straw's words before disconnecting.

The third call came an hour later. Mitch picked it up. His several hellos got no response. He heard background sounds and what he took to be breathing and then only dial tone.

"Who was that?" Maddie asked.

"A wrong number," he told her.

While Maddie went out to the garden to pick some tomatoes, Mitch went into Straw's study. A cabinet there was where Straw kept his guns. Three shotguns, a rifle and four pistols. Mitch settled on a shotgun. The one he liked the weight and feel of was a Mossberg 500 pump-action 12-gauge with a short eighteen-and-a-half-inch barrel. It wasn't loaded and there didn't seem to be any ammunition in the drawers of the cabinet.

He took the shotgun up to his bedroom and placed it on the

bed. Also his own two weapons, the Beretta and the Glock. He examined each in turn, saw that they were clean and in surely reliable working order. He cocked and dry-fired the automatics, released and inserted clips.

Then the shotgun. He'd never fired a pump-action, never even had one in his hands, but how complicated could it be? The forward hand operated the action by pulling back to eject the fired shell and pushing forward to position the next round into the firing chamber. He snugged the butt of the gun to his shoulder, pumped and dry-fired it until he was comfortable with the required rhythm. Did the same from the hip, got really good at it from the hip.

Maddie walked in on him. "What on earth are you doing?" she asked.

"Nothing," he told her, "just . . . just trying to get this door latch to work properly. It seems to be sticking."

"Sounded to me like you were pumping a shotgun," she said wryly.

"Any tomatoes?" he veered.

"Plenty."

He wondered how she could tell the ripe ones, asked her.

"Squeeze," she told him. He held back telling her that two of those she'd picked were green.

"I have to do some errands, get a few things. Want to stay here?"

"No, I'm with you." Exactly what she'd said yesterday, when he'd tried to get her to fly to Paris to stay with friends, out of harm's way until this Riccio thing simmered down. No words, not even his adamant, angry ones, could sway her. "I'm with you," was how she wanted it no matter what.

They were in Straw's blue Chevy pickup. Into town and then north on Route 9, the highway to Albany. First stop was at a building supply place for the planking. Mitch found that the widest they had in ready stock was fourteen inches. If he wanted wider it would be a special order. They'd have to mill it. That would take two days, maybe three. Mitch couldn't count on having two days, maybe three. So, in place of planking he got four sheets of four-by-eight half-inch plywood and had the mill hand-rip them lengthwise down the middle to make eight pieces two feet wide, eight feet long.

In the hardware and paint section Mitch bought a battery-charged professional stapler and a supply of one-inch staples, three gallons of latex enamel, two black and a green and a couple of rollers and roller pans.

A mile or so further up Route 9 was a strip mall dominated by a nervous red neon that declared RICK'S GUNS AND AMMO. While Mitch went in Maddie waited in the pickup, scrunched down with her bare feet up on the dash and a Clint Black playing.

Rick's offered just about everything imaginable for ordinary and fancy killing. Assault rifles on the left, power bows on the right. Ostensibly for animal hunting and benign target competitions. Rick was the man behind a locked glass counter crowded with handguns. He had a shaved head five days in need of a shave.

Mitch ordered up two cartons of double-ought buckshot shells and a carton of 12-gauge slugs. A couple of cartons of 9mm 115-grain Starfire balloon points and an equal number of 180-grain .40 calibers. "Want those forties in hollow point too?" Rick asked.

"Yeah."

"A lot of shooting," Rick commented passively while figuring the tab.

"Just stocking up."

"Smart. Season will be here before we know it."

Was there ever not a season for the Riccios? Mitch thought.

"Got a special on throwing knives in case you're interested," Rick said. "Ever throw a knife?"

"No." But Hofritz steak knives taken from a dining room drawer to the backyard and, inspired by James Coburn in *The Magnificent Seven*, thrown from ten feet end over end at the tough trunk of an oak. Set of eight knives in a fitted case. Four for himself, four for Andy for alternate tries. Not enough force to make them stick. Only one out of every twenty or more throws hitting point first. Kenneth rightfully giving them hell for having broken the tips off two.

"Not as hard to do as you think, throwing a knife," Rick said. "Guy used to part-time here got about as good as anybody could at it. Word got around and nobody would mess with him."

Mitch realized Rick wasn't selling as much as he was merely telling.

"Another advantage with having a throwing knife for a weapon is you're not required to be licensed to carry it," Rick said.

Mitch had noticed camouflaged combat fatigues stacked on a table in the rear. He went to them and held up a pair. They were the leaf-mottled type with a great many different pockets. Evidently they weren't marked for size. He grabbed up any two pair and a couple of matching beaked caps.

On Mitch's mental shopping list next was an audio cassette player-recorder. A store on Elm Street in Kinderhook had one that would do. It was about the size of an average hardcover book, could be battery-powered and had outlets to accommodate two auxiliary speakers. Not that Mitch would need two. The speakers he bought were the miniature, cube-shaped sort about four by four by four. He also bought a fifty-foot length of speaker wire that had the appropriate male adapters on each end, a half dozen size C Duracell batteries and a Maxell XLII ninety-minute high-resonance audiotape cassette.

He had thought he was leaving the most surely available thing until last. Red poster paint. The stationery and art supply store there in Kinderhook had poster paint in quite a few colors but was all out of bright red. Mitch had to drive the ten miles to Chatham to get it. It came in four- and six-ounce jars. He bought three of the sixes.

They arrived home mid-afternoon. Mitch went right to work, carried the plywood sections and the latex enamel to the large shed situated on the back side of the four-car garage. He transferred the enamel into a five-gallon plastic pail. One part green stirred into two parts black created what Mitch be-

lieved was a close enough murky shade. He leaned the eight
plywood sections separately against the side of the shed and
was about to start on them when Maddie came humming and
da-da-tee-da-ing off key, bringing tomatoes in a basket and a
shaker of imported LaBaleine sea salt. She made him stop and
sit with her. The basket in her lap. The base of their backs
against the shed's warm boards.

She handed him one of the tomatoes and took one for herself. He hesitated. He watched. He suspected she knew he was
watching, as she, not altogether subtly, ritualized, commencing with the twist and painful-looking plucking out of the star-
like stem, followed by a long efficient lick up one area of the
red skin to leave it wet. So the sprinkle of salt would adhere.

Mitch's vision again seemed capable of magnification.

The intricacies of each motion he observed seemed slowed.

Her mouth opened, exposing her teeth, perfect and sharp,
white unrelenting blades. The taut red skin no match for their
incredible erotic precision. Juice tried to escape, was captured. The red pulp and seeds were at her mercy, chewed and
sucked out.

Mitch forced himself to look away. How much he loved
her, he thought against the blank sky. So much that everything
about her had become extraordinary. Madly in love. That
seemed to fit. Did all extreme lovers experience such close
encounters with this special, pleasureful insanity or was he an
anomaly, cursed and blessed? No doubt, he decided the imminence of danger, the possibility of losing all, was having its
effect.

Two tomatoes eaten, Maddie dabbed at the corners of her
mouth with the sleeve of her T-shirt.

"I'm ready to paint," she said.

He'd promised she could help. He poured some of the
enamel into one of the roller pans while she located the plywood sections and determined how he'd leaned them in a predictable row. She was anxious to begin, went at it
enthusiastically.

"No need to do both sides, right?" she said.

"No."

"But we have to do the edges, don't we?"

"And the ends."

"We mustn't overlook the ends. Am I putting it on too thick?"

"No, you're doing fine."

"Why don't you do something else? I can handle this."

He went into the shed. It was where Straw kept his tools, gardening implements and other odds and ends. It wasn't very orderly. Each spring Straw put it neat and from then on allowed it to become cluttered. For the past several years Mitch had helped with the annual straightening, so the place wasn't unfamiliar to him.

He immediately spotted the lopping shears and the gasoline-powered hedge trimmers. He'd need those.

He might also put to use one of those sash window weights that Straw kept for old time's sake. Shaped like a summer sausage with an eye on one end where a line could be tied. Mitch had to climb up onto the work bench to get one down and it was while he was up there that he noticed the trap. Heavily rusted old thing hanging on a nail by its anchor chain. He took it down and saw it was a leg trap, the common sort, that would, when sprung, clamp together two sets of steel teeth. At one time it must have had six, perhaps ten feet of anchor chain which would be secured around a tree or whatever to keep the caught varmint from making off with the trap. Now, for some reason there was only about four feet of chain. Along the base, barely readable because of the layers of rust, was ARMSTEAD WOLF TRAP and a patent number.

Mitch tried to work the trap. Its parts were frozen in place. He searched around and finally found an aerosol can of a substance that was especially meant to penetrate and dissolve rust. He sprayed the trap thoroughly with it and waited a couple of minutes. The trap's parts still wouldn't give. No matter, he thought, it wasn't, after all, something he'd counted on but rather an added innovation. He gave the trap another spraying and left it for now.

Maddie was finishing up on the last section of plywood. She gave it a couple of final rolls. "How did I do?" she asked. "Did I miss a lot of places?"

"No," Mitch fibbed. Later, when he had the chance, he'd touch up the areas where raw board was visible. Actually, considering, Maddie had done well.

She put down the roller and roller pan. Her white sneakers were splattered, her hand coated to the wrist. "What's next?" she asked, ready for anything.

They went into the house. After washing up in the kitchen sink they sat at the table there and saw to the guns. Mitch was undecided about which shells he should load into the pump shotgun, the buckshot or the slugs. Both had advantages, depending on circumstances. The slugs had more range and penetration, made one big hole. On the other hand, closer in with the buckshot it was almost impossible to miss. The shotgun could hold eight rounds. Mitch loaded in some of each in no particular order.

Meanwhile, Maddie was loading the clips for the pistols. Four for the Glock and the same number for the Beretta. She inserted a full clip into the butt of each pistol and rammed them home.

"We'll each have three extra clips," she said. "Think that'll be enough?"

Mitch didn't reply.

Maddie knew why. "The Glock is yours but the Beretta is mine," she said.

That wasn't how Mitch intended it. She wouldn't be doing any shooting and no one would be shooting at her.

"The Beretta is mine," she repeated, unequivocally.

"Yeah," Mitch said as though that had been his understanding all along. There'd be clashes enough he figured.

The day was making its slow exit.

They went out and sat on the front steps. There were deer down in the apple orchard. Mitch counted eight. Two with antlers, four does and a pair of fawns. Foraging for windfalls, intent on that, but yet, alert, untrusting, bringing their heads up high, sniffing, glancing around frequently.

Mitch described the deer to Maddie. He couldn't make out their eyes at that distance, and no doubt she realized that; however she allowed him to make much of their huge black pupils, dilated by possible danger, the way they didn't dare blink.

"I could live on your descriptions," she said gratefully.

What he didn't describe to her was what he was foreseeing as he gazed down at the winding gravel drive. That was how they would come. They wouldn't be stealthy, wouldn't come sneaking from various directions. Their arrogance wouldn't allow that. They would drive in and park just about there, he thought, settling on a spot about a hundred yards away. They would be so sure of themselves, the killings they'd been sent to do. They would get out of the car, nonchalantly re-tuck their shirts and straighten their suit jackets, and probably talk about something extraneous, perhaps about a meal they'd eaten or planned to eat, as they proceeded up the rest of the drive to the house. Mitch despised how sure of themselves they would be. Sure of his death, of Maddie's.

The emeralds were no longer Riccio's first issue, Mitch believed. The emeralds had been superseded by the call for old-mob satisfaction. That Mitch had had no choice but to refuse Riccio didn't matter. Riccio hadn't believed it and turning Riccio down was like wounding him, like throwing pepper in his eyes. It prevented him from seeing reasonableness. To put up with it, to just let it pass, would, according to Riccio's code, shrink him. He'd be smaller inside himself for it. If he allowed it once he might allow it again and he'd become small enough inside himself to be stepped over, if not on.

The emeralds? If they came with the thing all the better. Twenty-five extra large was twenty-five extra large. However, in Riccio's world the void left by lost money had a way of being surely and swiftly filled by other money. Riccio would consider himself ahead when his have-arounds returned and told him the thing had been done.

"That twenty-five million . . . " Maddie said.

"Which twenty-five million?" Mitch quipped.

"If you'd had those emeralds and if the Iranian had come across with the twenty-five for them as he said he would, what difference would it have made?"

"Who knows?"

"For you, I mean."

"No use speculating."

"Oh? I say speculation is next best to a sure thing."

"I've never heard you say that."

"You probably weren't listening. Quite often speculations *are* sure things; they're just not apparent."

Mitch was amused. He kissed her a short, adoring one high on her cheek.

"With that twenty-five you'd no longer have to endure West 47th."

"I don't endure it," he contended and immediately realized that was only partially true. "Not all the time," he added.

"Naturally, you'd miss it for a while."

"I'd miss it," he admitted.

"But only for a while, and it would go on and on missing you."

He scoffed.

"We'd be miles away, wouldn't we?"

"Like where?"

She didn't have to give it even a moment's thought. "You'd be picking up big tabs at lots of extravagant places. Maybe we'd have a sort of permanent place on the lake to convenience your going to the Geneva auctions. You'd have clients in Milan and Paris. Maybe a small, flawless office in Zurich with a secretary who'd know the perfect way to say you weren't in, in ten languages. You'd only dabble in fine jewelry. You'd temperamentally dole out your expertise to the huge spenders. We'd motor the Loire and you'd describe. You'd keep me from dancing off edges into canals in Venice and St. Petersburg. You'd walk me into the rose fields of Grasse." She paused a digestive beat. "What do you think?"

"Sounds good," Mitch replied as brightly as he could manage, and, rather than allow futility to further blunt his edge, he asked, "How would you like me to read to you tonight? Some Carlos Fuentes perhaps."

"Uh uh," she said emphatically, "this morning I told you what I wanted to do but later, and later is now."

CHAPTER 29

The summer night embraced the house, pressed it with fragrances and every so often sent a scuff of wind to the open bedroom windows to play spectrally with the sheer curtains. All was dark. The nearest prevailing light was a moon distant, and that but only the merest sliver, unproviding.

Thus, even when Mitch was open-eyed he was equally blind.

Her hands were vessels, nearly weightless. They skimmed along him, his sea of flesh. She knew his courses and currents, where she was most likely to encounter maelstroms. Her hands drifted, here and there and here, persistently under way but avoiding destination, just barely, tacking at the last moment.

He lay still, as he knew she wanted. Already his cock did not seem to have enough skin to contain itself. It would burst from sensation when her mouth enclosed it, when her tongue lashed and her teeth made brief, inflicting visits.

She was such a greedy lover, greedy taker and greedy giver. Or, wasn't it generous giver and generous taker?

Frequently she removed her mouth, all at once, and breathed upon the warmth and wet she'd caused. Cooled his cock before resuming. Her hands never stopped. Burrowing, gliding, fingernails threatening.

Having her way with him.

She was sopping, puffed apart by the time she legged over and found herself with him. She did not ride him. She did not move at all immediately. The slick, tight channel of her held him surrounded. Oppositely, she had impaled herself all the way to her belly. The sop ran from her.

She did not ride him. Did not need to. She leaned forward up over him, just so, to become more parted below, just so, and helped herself to as much sensitivity as she wanted.

Her want. She took it in portions, marveled at his restraint, shared the sixth time she came.

With him.

CHAPTER 30

Nudged by all he had to do, Mitch came awake at first light. He got up immediately, dressed and went downstairs and out to the shed. Temporary diamonds on the grass. Much of the sky a funereal mauve. Sparrows frightened to fly from under the eaves.

He applied paint to the places on the plywood sections that Maddie had missed, and then went into the shed to check on the wolf trap. The trap appeared unchanged but, when he picked it up, flakes and clumps of rust fell from it. The solvent had lived up to its claims. The parts that made the trap a trap, its hinges, spring and release, now worked freely, easily. Mitch set the trap and sprung it with an old hardwood broom handle. He sharpened the trap's double set of triangular teeth. First with a metal file and then more with a whetstone. He set the trap again, sprung it again. The razor-sharp teeth crunched clear through the broom handle.

The plywood sections weren't yet thoroughly dry but he didn't want to wait. They were heavy and unwieldy. Once he got squatted beneath them and got them balanced he could manage three at a time layered on the bend of his back.

He had to pass through the woods to get them to the marsh, through the underbrush, the crazy vines and young trees. The young trees seemed capricious the way they hung on to his legs and the edges and corners of the plywood. He felt like telling them this wasn't a game.

Three round-trips with plywood sections. He placed them down at the edge of the marsh. He'd get back to them when he was done with the blackberry brambles.

The width of the bramble patch varied from twenty to fifty feet. It was wider across and thicker as well where the growth was new. Those greener, more vigorous canes were five to six feet high, thousands in the collective competing for the sun with familial strangle. Thorns on them like the spurs of a fighting cock.

Mitch put on the tough, leather gloves and began with the hedge trimmers. Before long he had cut a short ways into the patch, creating what appeared to be a shallow lair. It wasn't easy going. He was on his knees, having to crawl along hunched, being snagged and scratched at every turn. The canes seemed to resent his intrusion. Even the thorns dropped by those long dead stabbed through the fabric of his jeans.

What had appeared to be a lair became the tunnel that Mitch intended. He shaped it with the loppers, leaving the overhead canes as they were, intricately meshed.

Forty feet of bramble tunnel. He would add the final elements to it later.

He returned to the marsh, to the plywood sections. He sighted across and estimated that from where he stood the distance to the opposite bank was too great for his purpose. He moved along the edge where the summer had receded the water, leaving the silt dry and black like gunpowder. The huge green leaves of the skunk cabbage and the tufts of swamp grass were chest high. After a short ways he came upon a place where the temporary shore was somewhat elevated and jutted out. He went back for the plywood sections and got busy on them.

He laid two of the sections end to end, painted sides up and overlapped about six inches. He joined the two sections by driving two rows of one-inch staples into the overlap. He stapled the coiled length of quarter-inch nylon line to the first section and tied the free end of the line to the six-pound window sash weight. He twirled the weighted line until it was singing with momentum. Let it go. The weight, with the nylon line trailing after it, sailed high over the marsh and landed on the opposite shore some fifty feet away.

He went around the far end of the marsh to that spot, took up the line and gathered in its slack. He pulled the first plywood section into the water and most of the second. He went back around and stapled together the ends of two more sections and added those to the length of the first two. On the opposite shore again, he tugged all but the very end of those into the water.

It took all eight sections of plywood to complete the span, and even then it didn't quite reach, was a couple of feet short. He had to use rocks, some seventy-pounders, to weigh down each end and keep the span in place, and that, as it turned out, was for the better, because it concealed the ends nicely, caused them to be buried in the silt at the shoreline.

Now the span of plywood sections was below the water line, but barely, an inch or so at most. Just enough to not cause a break on the surface. The ugly green-black that the sections were painted was a good, close match to the murky color of the water.

Mitch, aware that the span was there, could make it out; however it wasn't obvious, would take some study for anyone to detect it.

He tested the span. Walked out a short ways onto its two-foot width. His weight caused it to go under another couple of inches. As he went on he found the coating of vinyl enamel was slippery when wet. He sloshed across to the other side, unsure of his footing. After a few back-and-forth crossings he got used to the feel of it and was able to hurry across. He ended up taking several round-trips running.

He was on his way to the pasture when he heard the first shot coming from the direction of the house. When he heard the next three he was already sprinting full out. The have-arounds had come, he thought. He'd underestimated Riccio.

Several more shots.

The sadistic bastards were peppering Maddie. He pictured her all shot up, bleeding, already dead, and, for their amusement, being disfigured by their bullets.

She wasn't.

When she came into sight he slowed to a walk, a casual walk the rest of the way, allowing him to catch his breath. He wouldn't tell her what he'd feared, how grisly and graphic it had been.

She was in the high grass off to one side of the old equipment barn. At that moment jamming another full clip into the Beretta. For a target she had nailed one of his best shirts to the side of the barn and was positioned about twenty paces from it.

Mitch paused, he noticed how indecisive her aim was before she fired a few rounds. He let her know he was there in case she completely lost her sense of direction.

"Getting in a little practice," she said.

"Who is it you're shooting at?"

"Them," she said toughly. "Be a love and go see how many I hit."

He went to the shirt. The only holes in it were its button holes. He examined the barn siding around it and didn't find where any bullets had struck.

"Four hits," he reported.

"Really?"

"Four right where the heart would be and a couple of just misses."

Maddie didn't react as Mitch expected. No self-delight, no smartass grin. "You're fibbing me," she said calmly. "I know you are, so don't bother to deny it."

Best not to say anything, Mitch thought.

"I'm not blaming you. It's me," she said. "I'm just so damn easy to fib to, aren't I? I'm always letting you get away with it because you have sweet intentions and it helps avoid a lot of the silly little bumps and potholes that would otherwise be in our way . . . "

"Maddie . . . "

" . . . but this time there's too much at stake." She scoffed, a self-berating scoff. "Christ, I'm such a mess."

"What happened?"

"I got the shirt nailed up without any trouble and was walking off ten paces when, on about the fifth pace, I stubbed my toe on something, a tuft of grass or an uneven spot or whatever, and I got all turned around. For some reason I just couldn't get my bearings." She disliked admitting that. "I tried to sense where the barn and the shirt were but each time I thought I had doubt got to me and made me less and less certain and I didn't want to shoot in any old direction. Who knows what or who I might have hit."

Mitch discerned the increasing change in her voice, a tightening. She was coming closer to crying with every syllable. As a rule she wasn't a crier. Anyway, not the usual sort. Plights and misfortunes, the hardest-luck and unfairest-unfair stories seldom brought forth a tear. Little patience for those. However, she was very susceptible to all forms of happiness. Merely hearing about happiness happening and various beautiful accomplishments coming about could cause her throat to lump up.

"I'm not going to be any help at all," she said. "Without you, without your helping me to get aimed in the right direction I can't hit the broad side of a fucking barn."

Mitch took her into his arms, held her. He felt her sag and let go. Her tears on his neck. The butt of the Beretta pressing his shoulder blade. "It'll be all right," he told her.

"No fibbing?"

"We'll come out the other side of this and look back on it for shivers and laughs," he said. His actual thought was she should have flown away. He should have insisted on it. There was still time. He could phone Billy and have him come get her, take her to Kennedy and the Concorde to Paris.

He suggested it.

She let it go right around her.

"Is my nose running?" she asked.

"No."

"Feels like it is. What about my eyes?"

"A little red around the edges."

"I'm famished."

"Just do what I tell you and everything will be all right," he reassured.

"How about some pancakes? I'll let you make them."

After pancakes, Maddie sat on the rear porch steps and cleaned her Beretta while listening to an Elmore Leonard. Mitch drove into town with a grocery shopping list.

He was at the supermarket, had nearly everything in his cart and was waiting to be waited on at the deli counter when he spotted the have-around. The fat guy who was usually stationed on the landing halfway up to Riccio's offices; the one Mitch had twice pushed down the stairs. Their eyes caught upon one another simultaneously, caught and held. The have-around had a paper bag in one hand and a glazed donut, like a helpless victim, in the other. Mitch did a contemptible up and down and decided he might as well go over to him.

"What's your name?" he asked aggressively.

"Angelo," the have-around replied.

"What do they call you around?"

"Fat Angelo."

"I never would have guessed."

"My real name is Anthony."

"Fat Tony was taken."

"Yeah."

"A hundred times."

"This is Little Mike. You know Little Mike?"

Little Mike stepped out from behind Fat Angelo. He was appropriately named. About five feet tall at most, a muscle-layered chunk with a bilious complexion. He looked like he'd have no trouble getting in under the axle of a car and holding it up while someone changed a tire. "I seen you around," he said to Mitch. "On the street."

"What are you doing up here?" Mitch asked Fat Angelo.

"Nothing. Just looking around."

"Sightseeing," Mitch said.

"Yeah, that's it. We already saw the sights, didn't we?"

"Enough," Little Mike replied.

"So now you're headed back to the city," Mitch said.

"They got good donuts here but the coffee tastes like shit," Fat Angelo said.

"You should know," Mitch said but Fat Angelo wasn't fazed, maybe didn't get it.

Little Mike was eating potato salad out of a half-pound plastic container. He appeared as conspicuously out of place as Fat Angelo. A pair of midtown lowlifes in white short-sleeve polo shirts that displayed their respective fat and muscles. Unbuttoned to exhibit swag gold chains and crosses that were nearly lost among their chest hairs.

"How about me and you having a private word?" Fat Angelo said.

Mitch moved with him beyond the hearing range of Little Mike, who understood and paid more attention to the potato salad.

"We can do a little business," Fat Angelo said confidentially. "You interested?"

"Maybe."

"You got those two emeralds?"

"Another maybe."

"What we do is you give them to me and I go back to Riccio and tell him you weren't up here like he figured."

"You'd do that?"

"Sure, what the fuck."

Mitch did a considering expression, some blinks. "What if I was to let Riccio know you tried to get between on him?"

"No problem. I just tell him I saw you but nothing else, just saw. Who's he going to believe, me or some guy he wants taken out?"

Mitch turned and pushed his cart towards the checkout.

Fat Angelo flung six Sicilian obscenities at his back.

That he had run into two of Riccio's have-arounds at the supermarket was yet another thing Mitch decided was best left unmentioned to Maddie. No use making her edgier. He imagined how unstrung he would be if he was in the black, dependent upon someone else's eyes under such threatening circumstances.

All along he had believed Riccio would catch on and show up. Now that was not only imminent but soon. Perhaps tomorrow, possibly before, Mitch thought. He couldn't put anything off.

On the way home there was a short section of road where construction was under way. Marked off by striped orange and white barriers, battery-powered blinking amber lights on them. Mitch didn't care who saw him stop and toss a couple of the barriers into the back of the pickup.

It was early dusk when he went to the bramble patch. After completing things there he went all the way out to the bluff. The river motionless as a deserted road. The hills to the west black and humped like resting beasts. The going sun skulking behind them.

CHAPTER 31

Wait.

Never had Mitch disliked it more, having to sit there in the recess of a dormer, watching for them. Too much time to think, to not be able to put out of mind that everything had come down to this, all he'd ever done or been, hoped to do or be, compacted to grim wait in this niche above the roof line of Straw's three-story house.

A few hours ago, when there'd still been daylight, this high vantage had provided Mitch with a fairly clear view far down the gravel drive, beyond its twists, nearly to the point where the orchard began. What he'd kept watch for then was any interruption their car would cause on the pale, motionless drive. However, now that night had taken over, the first sign of their arrival would be headlights.

Might they park outside the grounds and approach unseen and quietly? No, that wasn't them. Probably it wouldn't even be suggested. Why should they be unnecessarily inconvenienced? They'd drive in like expected guests, turn off the loud car radio at the last moment, slam the car doors shut.

Maddie had tried to make the dormer niche comfortable. She'd layered it with two down comforters and piles of pillows. Plump European squares and tiny silk-covered rounds.

She had also laundered the camouflaged combat fatigues Mitch had bought. To remove the scratchy stiffness from them. She'd washed hers separately in hottest water, given them a long hot cycle and double hot rinse, hoping to accomplish a three- or four-size shrink. But they hadn't shrunk an inch and she was having to make the best of what she thought of as their monstrous fighting man size. She turned the legs and sleeves up several folds.

"Does nothing for me," she complained.

"Put on something else, some jeans or something."

She pretended not to hear. She was wearing the Beretta in its shoulder rig. Extra clips in her most reachable upper pockets. Mitch had on the Glock. The shotgun was propped close at hand. Mitch had discovered a sling for it in the back of a drawer of Straw's gun cabinet.

So, there they sat. Low light coming from the third-floor hallway. The dormer window entirely open. Mitch close to the sill of it, Maddie across from him.

To vary and temper and help pass the wait, she played the guitar. Started out with some Wes Montgomery and without missing a pick or strum, went to the third movement, *Recitativo*, of Mompou's *Compostelana Suite*, and, from that, some vigorous Van Halen. Then on to Mitch's favorite favorite, *Spanish Romances*. She gave him a lengthy dose of the latter, repeated its melodic theme numerous times.

Normally the piece evoked within Mitch a sort of sensuous sway, but this time it hollowed his upper chest and lumped his throat and Maddie, with her finely honed sentience, stopped playing abruptly, laid the guitar aside and told him: "Look at it this way, precious, not everyone gets a chance to accumulate such exciting recollections for their recliner chair years."

She went down to the kitchen and returned with a silver tablespoon and a pint carton of ice cream. Ben and Jerry's Chunky Monkey. She resumed her place opposite Mitch on the comforter and dug into it. She extended the first generous spoonful. Mitch brought his mouth to it. The rich, frivolous treat hitched him up a couple of minor notches.

"Two for you, one for me," she said, as though it should apply to all things, then thought to add: "Except, of course, when it comes to comes." She held out another helping. Within ten minutes she was noisily scraping the sides and bottom of the cardboard carton, licking the spoon.

She saw to Mitch's pillows. Plumped and re-situated them behind his back and shoulders. That done, she stretched out face up, perpendicular to him with her head resting on his thigh. The house a silent container of possessions. Squirrel claws scuttling the rain gutter. The night laying siege beyond the sill.

"Tell me one," Maddie said.

"You've heard them all."

"Surely not all."

"I'd have to make one up."

"Have you ever?"

"No."

"Probably have, a fibber like you."

"I could rehash an old one, if you'd settle for that," he told her. "A real old one that you may have forgotten by now."

"Save me."

"Okay then, you'll just have to accept that as of now I'm all out."

"Don't give me that, you with your extravagant repertoire. Are you going to deprive me of your riches?"

My riches, Mitch thought. Well, yes, perhaps that was what they were, all those mainly nefarious West 47 incidents and special little melodramas accumulated firsthand over the years, along with the headful of others of the same ilk he'd acquired second- or third-hand or more. She was demanding a fresh one and he doubted he could come up with it, his frame of mind being what it was. Her motive was obviously well-intentioned. She was trying to normalize things. He should co-operate. However, he felt in need of some good quiet, to just be, be there with her, to observe her and, again, as he had so often, marvel that she existed. And that she loved him. And he loved her. And they were attached. Not attached in the ordinary sense, not merely together for convenience or distraction or to bodyfill the chasm of human separateness, but somehow, miraculously, spiritually overlapped, Mitch felt.

The trouble was if he reflected upon such romantic assets they would soon remind him that they were what he stood to lose, and, as immediate as a shift of thought he would be overcome by gloomy prospect, his and Maddie's slim to no chance against the onslaught of Riccio's heartless have-arounds.

Maddie wasn't going to have any such negative wallowing if she could help it. She did a decisive little grunt. "If you put your mind to it you could," she said.

"Could what?"

"Find them. As resourceful as you are. It's one of the zillion things I adore about you, your resourcefulness. Granted it's not foremost. There are any number of more pleasurable aspects ahead of it, but it's right up there."

Mitch did some silence.

Maddie answered it. "Those emeralds."

"Which emeralds?" Mitch joked, going along with her but thinking *those fucking emeralds*. They were entirely to blame. Had it not been for those fucking emeralds he'd now have little more to cope with than his usual problems, like making ends meet and deciding each night how to get out of having dinner at home. As for recovering those emeralds and being the recipient of twenty-five extra large, forget it. Nothing mattered but survival.

"How much do you buy that story the Iranian what's-his-name Djam told us?" Maddie asked.

"What part?"

"The pious poet who gazed through the emeralds and got back his eyesight."

"Things like that are usually bullshit."

"Usually?"

"Maybe not always," Mitch conceded.

"Anyway, if you did recover those emeralds I probably wouldn't give them a try."

Which Mitch knowingly interpreted to mean she might. He

imagined her bringing the emeralds up to her eyes. Holding them there. The verdancy of paradise. When she took them away, instantaneous vision! And he would be the very first thing she would see. That old notion.

"Of course," she went on, "I might if you insisted on it. Would you insist?"

Test question, Mitch thought. How not to fail it? It really asked had her handicap become a burden on him? Had he wearied of her dependence?

At times, not frequently, just every now and then, she had brought up the possibility of regaining her sight. What it would mean to them. It always started out as something she desired and ended up as something she'd just as soon would never happen. She was, she declared, quite comfortable with her condition, in fact, she probably preferred it. While it made her vulnerable it also provided protection of a sort, kept her from having to directly witness sleaze and suffering, the apathy and deliberate madnesses of these times.

Would he insist that, given the opportunity, she have a go with those wonder-working emeralds? He decided against a yes or no, told her: "I wouldn't push it."

She yawned genuinely. The yawn turned into an exaggerated grimace. She sat up and drooped her head. "I've a crook in my neck," she said with only slight complaint. She rotated her head twice counterclockwise and twice the other way and that seemed to do the trick. She raised her left shoulder and, as though she had perfect articulate vision, vamped at Mitch over it. "Jimmy Comforti," she said.

"What about him?"

"Tell me one of those."

"You're weird, know that?"

"Not any more so than you."

"You've got a crook in your head."

"Always," she admitted. "You don't I suppose. Come on precious, stop being stingy, give a girl a fix."

"What if I refuse?"

"You won't."

Mitch was hooked and being pulled up to her lighter level. He did a skeptical grunt.

"Refusal," she warned, "would call for retribution. I'd have to get back at you some suitable punitive way."

"Such as?"

She hardly gave it a thought. "Like never again giving you a massage and so forth while wearing a pair of my antelope skin gloves."

"I don't believe never."

"You'd go begging," she vowed, "believe me."

"You really are weird."

"Everything you say is true," she arched.

How fortunate he'd been, he thought. He had other riches. All the sensational, shame-free-loving times he'd shared with her. Maybe, in a way, it was beyond reasonableness to expect a whole, long life span of it. They'd already had far more than most.

Maddie lay back, returned her head to his thigh and waited while Mitch sorted through his mental Comforti file for one he possibly hadn't told her. From the numerous Comforti exploits both Mitch and Hurley had fed her over the years she more or less enjoyed the illusion that, though she'd never met Comforti, he was a personal acquaintance.

Actually, not even those few upscale West 47 dealers who were the favored buyers of Comforti's pricey swag knew the man well. He was seldom seen on the street, never walked it just to walk it, never socialized along it. When, for some unavoidable reason, he showed up on West 47 it was like the sighting of some colorful rare bird and like such a bird he was quickly gone. As a rule, to do business with him a dealer had to venture out of the district to wherever Comforti stipulated, which might be anywhere from the rear seat of a hired limo to a suite at the Ritz-Carlton.

A swift he was, however no one's swift but his own. Early on, some twenty years ago, he had belonged to a crew, but before he was nineteen he'd outclassed it and defected. He didn't need any such protection or direction. He didn't have anyone who'd need caring for while he did time. He also didn't get enough kick out of doing houses. They were too hit or miss. The city, on the other hand, was a surer thing, a veritable treasure trove. All one had to do was learn how to get to it.

Comforti hung around the entrances and lobbies of the better hotels. Watching the high-grade goods come and go on the necks, ears, wrists and fingers of the visiting well-offs. He took particular notice of how many failed to deposit their valuables into the hotel's vault when they came in late at night all high and happy or tired or anxious to get up to their rooms for some improved, away-from-home sex.

Hotels became Comforti's specialty. Within a year he possessed the master passkey of every major hotel in Manhattan. It was so easy. Before long he progressed from hotel rooms to hotel vaults. The first vault he did encouraged such focus. A hotel on upper Park at three in the morning. Comforti and another guy went in, frightened the resistance out of the night clerks and other staff. Got to the strongboxes with a prybar. It was so easy. The first box they forced open contained two hundred thousand in hundreds. The second and third yielded five hundred thousand in jewels. It went like that, so easy. They gathered up ten minutes' worth, the contents of fourteen strongboxes. Went out the front in no hurry.

Got away with it.

He didn't always, of course. He served some three to fives but the way he accounted life and its pleasures his scores had him way ahead. Glamorous scores, headline scores, seemingly impossible, audacious scores. So many that eventually the police had him come in and, as a favor to them, clear away the unsolved jewelry theft cases from their books. In return one hundred percent immunity. While he was at it, as a gesture of professional largesse, he admitted responsibility for a few sizeable scores he'd had nothing to do with, thus absolving some other swifts he probably didn't even know.

The Jimmy Comforti episode Mitch chose to tell Maddie now was one that had taken place about four years back. It began when Comforti was released from Attica state prison.

A Thursday. He arrived in the city and went directly to the Hotel Carlyle.

He had paid a porter of that hotel two hundred a month, half in advance, to hold three pieces of very presentable luggage down in the guest's storage room. The luggage was sent up to the suite Comforti had reserved from Attica using his platinum American Express. One of the Carlyle's high-priced, high-up suites with an ascendant southerly view. Bouquet of Casablanca lilies. Huge black grapes swagged from a silver salver of fresh fruit. Fax machine, five telephones including one on the wall next to the commode.

The liberated Comforti immediately set about to liberate his belongings. He summoned the valet on duty to have some pressing done and within a half hour was approving of his appearance in a full-length mirror. He hadn't gained or lost a pound or inch while in the joint all those months, so his suits and shirts were still perfect fits. Nothing about him gave him away as an ex-convict, nor would anyone guess that his tasteful guise and easy countenance concealed a first-class criminal mind. For all the world he looked like a respectable civilian, in town for a few days to take care of some little legitimate matter, and perhaps to visit his tailor.

He sat slouched in one of the sofa chairs and brought the nearest telephone to rest on his crotch. His first call was to a certain West 47th dealer named Wattenberg who middled upscale swag behind a straight reputation. Wattenberg was more than pleased to hear from Comforti again. He agreed to the meeting Comforti arbitrarily set much later that night.

Comforti's second call was to a certain young woman he'd never been with. He'd met her just before he'd gone inside and had held her in mind all the while, so she'd become somewhat essential. The given name she'd given herself was Laura. The two family names she'd chosen to go with it were hyphenated.

The thing about this young woman Laura that appealed to Comforti was her well-bred looks and mien, and the fact that she had enough imagination to carry off that impression most of the time.

When it came to women Comforti's preference was unusually limited. No bimbos or go-go's for him. To qualify for his ardent attention a woman had to at least convincingly seem as though she might have had some years at Smith, Wellesley or the like, possess a desperate sort of wildness to compensate for being quickly bored with everything, and whose family could possibly have an engraved brass nameplate on a reserved pew at St. James's Episcopal.

Comforti had never bedded the genuine article. However, there was a type of young woman scattered in the social mélange of Manhattan who looked pretty much the part, who had the requisite features, figure and bones, acquired taste and such, as well as the appropriate range of high-strung attitude. Usually these young women were aware of their assets, relied on them, placed hope in them. Believing that because of them there'd come a day, a just reckoning, when they'd no longer need to receptionist or sales clerk.

This was the wellspring from which Comforti drew. What made this young woman Laura so vital to him. There'd be others like her when he got back into circulation; however, at the moment, she was it.

Maddie interrupted with a scoff. "How could you possibly know what went on inside Comforti's head? You're embroidering, aren't you?"

"I'm telling it the way it was told to me," Mitch said.

"You're not embroidering it for my sake?"

"Not much."

"How much is not much?"

"Shall I go on?"

Maddie re-settled. "Please do."

After the Laura phone call Comforti went out and down Madison a short ways to a branch of a major bank where he kept a safety deposit box. He had four boxes at four different branches in which he stored what he called his "sleeping beauties." These were swag goods that he'd chosen to not sell. A reserve of some of the finer pieces. He awakened two, so to speak, put them to pocket and returned to the Carlyle.

Wattenberg showed up at the appointed hour. Three in the morning. Normally he was in bed by eleven but the prospect of huge gain had him high. A stocky sort with a weak, nearly indistinguishable chin and a pate that looked as though it had been buffed. He said the routine opening lines. No mention of prison. Nice to see, looking good, all that. It was like Comforti had been away on a long trip. Wattenberg declined a drink and accepted one of the chairs opposite the sofa but didn't sit back in it.

Comforti took the sofa. He wasn't merely relaxed. His limbs felt softly, delicately attached to his torso, his edges blunted. He was wearing a suit but nothing else. Bare chest, bare feet.

The door to the bedroom was partially open. A bright light on in there. A section of the used bed was visible, a bare part of woman upon it. Wattenberg couldn't help but notice. He got momentarily caught on that view, then self-consciously looked anywhere else. He tried to sit back but couldn't remain back, seemed to not know what to do with his hands.

Comforti noticed Wattenberg's abruptly increased unease, a giveaway of erotic envy. That amused him, caused him to put off for a moment his bringing the bracelet out from his jacket pocket. He placed it on the low sofa table.

Wattenberg took up the bracelet and sighted it with his loupe. First, a cursory all-over look, then a longer, thorough examination of its individual stones.

Eight sugarloaf-shaped cabochon sapphires spaced by eight emerald-cut diamonds, mounted in platinum. It was signed *Cartier*.

Wattenberg asked what was the aggregate weight of the sapphires and Comforti told him without hesitation it was seventy-four carats. Comforti anticipated what Wattenberg's next question would be, and said the total carat weight of the diamonds was a few points less than twenty-six.

Wattenberg remarked that the bracelet was a pleasant piece. An obvious understatement. He hopefully complimented the sapphires by saying they were nice number-one Burmas.

Comforti knew the game, stated that the sapphires were Kashmir. Which made them much rarer and five or six times more precious.

Wattenberg took another lengthy look and pretended only now to recognize the sapphires' Kashmir characteristics.

It was at that point the young woman Laura came from the bedroom. In a full-length bias-cut nightgown of gray silk charmeuse. Bare on top. The thinnest possible straps. She was possibly over twenty-five but not thirty, a fine-boned, slender brunette with every good reason to be confident of her body. There was an attractive disorder about her. Without acknowledging Wattenberg or even Comforti she went directly to the room service cart that was off to one side. Helped herself to a leftover toastpoint.

Wattenberg noticed a tiny price tag discreetly attached to the rear hem of her nightgown by a tiny gold safety pin. He had a momentary battle with distraction, particularly the way the silk charmeuse fabric declared her gorgeous buttocks.

Maddie interrupted again. "Now I'd call that overembroidering."

"Would you rather have it plain, a less colorful, more abridged version?"

"Not really," Maddie decided, "just go a little lighter on the gorgeous buttocks stuff, hmmm?"

Amused by that, Mitch went on.

Telling how this lovely pseudo-highbrow Laura came over and occupied the other sofa chair across from Comforti. True to her affectation, she managed to be blasé about the Cartier bracelet. It couldn't dazzle her. Even when Wattenberg laid it back onto the table where it was right before her eyes, the diamonds shooting scintillations, the sapphires glowing their vivid blue, she disregarded it. As though such a thing was commonplace to her. She also appeared completely disinterested in whatever transaction Comforti and Wattenberg were involved in. It meant nothing to her.

Wattenberg was into his own act, containing his enthusiasm for the swag bracelet, concealing his eagerness to buy it. He waited a long beat, scratched his temple and did an ambivalent mouth before asking Comforti how much.

Comforti had the figure ready. Four hundred and fifty thousand.

The amount hung in the air.

Wattenberg wasn't fazed. He had a lady client in Milan who would consider eight hundred thousand a bargain. He nearly agreed to four hundred fifty; however, his West 47 nature caused him to ask if four hundred fifty was the asking price.

Comforti just looked at him.

Wattenberg offered four hundred.

Comforti didn't make a big thing of it. Calmly, he picked up the bracelet, held it up at eye level, dangled it for a moment as though bidding it goodbye.

Wattenberg felt certain it was about to become his.

Comforti tossed the bracelet to Laura. Gave it to her, just like that. No big deal.

Within the next minute Wattenberg was out in the hotel corridor awaiting the elevator. Unable to not hate himself. He realized the gaffe he'd committed. How could he have been so stupid? How could he have forgotten that Comforti always considered his stated price for a piece of swag to be more than fair, a price that allowed everyone to make. Comforti's cardinal rule, as proverbial as the man: no haggling, ever.

Perhaps, Wattenberg thought, all wasn't lost. He hung around the lobby of the Carlyle believing sooner or later he'd catch this Laura on her way out. She'd want the money more than the piece.

Came noon he gave up on that.

The following day, just by chance, he spotted her as she came out of the 580 Fifth Avenue building. Bound for a limo at the curb.

She pretended to not recognize Wattenberg at first, which was understandable, considering prior circumstances.

He didn't waste words, offered her three hundred seventy-five for the bracelet.

Her face went weary, but then she managed to modulate her regret. She did a resigned shrug and informed Wattenberg that just minutes ago she'd sold the bracelet to Visconti . . .

. . . for two fifty.

Maddie chuckled. "You tell one hell of a bedtime story," she said, "but, you know, I seem to recall Hurley telling me that one sometime back."

"When?"

"Four, maybe five years ago."

"Why didn't you say so?"

"You were really into it."

"I suppose it was better the first time you heard it."

"To the contrary," she said turning onto her side and snuggling his thigh. "I'll bet years and years down the road from now you'll forget you told it and tell it again and I'll probably enjoy it even more."

Years and years from now, Mitch thought. He'd discerned a degree of sleepiness in Maddie's voice and it was even thicker as she smiled a mainly inward smile and said: "I love you, precious."

She began to sleep. It always amazed Mitch how quickly she could drop off. He believed it might have something to do with her black. Perhaps her black made it less of a fall for her. He heard her breathing change and although her eyelids were partly open he knew she was a goner. He waited, allowed time for her to get surely, really deep, then, disturbing as little as possible, he got up and lifted her. Carried her down to the second floor to their bedroom and gently laid her on the bed.

Placed a pillow close next to her, his surrogate for her hugging.

He hurried back up to the dormer, settled down. For some reason, now that Maddie was asleep and he her lone guardian, he was instilled with even greater resolve. They wouldn't get to her. He wouldn't let them get to her. He gazed out at the night. It seemed changed, as though the dark had solidified everything out there into one piece.

He leaned out the dormer window and gazed upwards. Overcast, no stars, no sky. He told himself that didn't mean no heaven. He settled down again.

He couldn't prevent Ralph Lentini from coming to mind. Ralph and the fur-coated hooker. Their bodies shriveled white and bloated with the gas of decay, risen by now, trying to break through that layer of green scum.

Ruder was another matter. Probably the harbor current and undertows had scuttled him along the bottom, and the fish, all sorts and sizes, the blues and snappers and such, had fed on him. For sure the sharks down off Sandy Hook.

Poor Ruder.

CHAPTER 32

Riccio's have-arounds didn't come that night, nor the next morning.

Since daybreak a fine rain had been falling, so misty a rain that it seemed to be atomizing the land. Every exterior surface looked slick and darker, as though it had been varnished, especially the trunks and leaves of the apple trees down in the orchard.

The rain contributed to the complacency that was now sharing Mitch's outlook. He had begun to think that inasmuch as the have-arounds hadn't come by now they might not come. Possibly Riccio only intended to intimidate. Wasn't it, after all, a ridiculous vengeance, senseless, way out of proportion? At that very moment Riccio was probably in his West 47th lair operating his money-counting machine or popping caraters out of their mountings, while his have-arounds, all of them, were in that room off to the side eating heros and watching reruns. The killing of Mitch Laughton and wife the furthest thing from their minds, or, if they gave that any thought, it was to laugh at the way they had Mitch shitting in his pants.

On the other hand, quite possibly Riccio had dilated this situation and couldn't bring himself to return it to its appropriate size. Riccio's old-mob mentality. What he said he was going to do he had to do. Such an ugly face to save.

Anyway, Mitch felt that Riccio's one-sided assault was somewhat less inevitable than it had been yesterday. Less enough to leave the dormer at mid-afternoon, go down and make a fresh pot of coffee and a tuna salad sandwich. Less enough so that when Maddie remarked she felt cruddy and was going to take a bath, he told her, only after brief reservation and no second thought, to go ahead.

He heard the tub filling and went to the bathroom to observe her. She was already in. On the floor lay her combat fatigues and sneakers, shoulder rig and Beretta. A container of bath oil was on the edge of the tub; the air redolent with the scent of lilies. Maddie often had difficulty determining measures and evidently she'd given this bathwater a huge overdose. The oil coated Maddie's skin as she shifted about. She scrunched down, submerged all save her head and, a moment later, when she sat up, the oil caused water to scurry into beads on her shoulders, arms and breasts.

Mitch had to escape from the overly fragrant air. He went back up to the dormer to resume his vigil.

He looked out and saw the rain had let up. He looked further out and caught sight of the chrome grille of a Lincoln Town Car, a black Lincoln followed close behind by another identical. They were coming in on the drive, slowly, as though they were part of a funeral procession. They stopped short of the spot Mitch had figured, a good hundred yards from the house. No one got out. For some reason they just sat there with the engines off. For several minutes not a move.

Mitch waited to see how many he would be up against. He'd expected one car.

They got out then. All at once. Fat Angelo, and Little Mike from the lead car. Bechetti and Fratino from the other. They were regularly dressed, in suits and sports jackets. A city entourage.

Car door slams. A hundred blackbirds frightened out of the pines like applause. From the trunk of the lead car weapons taken out and distributed. There was a brief dispute over who would get a machine pistol. Bechetti claimed it and a spare magazine.

One of the rear doors of the second car had been left open. Another person got out.

Riccio.

Mitch thought it a bad sign that Riccio had chosen to be personally involved. But really what difference would it make? He'd probably given in to his craving for firsthand violence. The old-mob maniac in one of his ill-fitting suits, the collar turned up and the lapels folded across. He paced a couple of circles to get the ride from his back and legs. He looked up at the sky as though ordering it to cooperate. He used the stub of the twisted Sicilian cigar he'd been smoking to light another, puffed up a cloud that, in the damp, heavy air, hung around him and instead of rising descended onto his shoulders. He stood apart from his have-arounds. They, waiting in a group with the pistols on the ends of their arms. Riccio called Fratino over, said something to him and then with a disdainful gesture signaled the other have-arounds to get on with it.

They started for the house. Mitch slung on the shotgun and rushed down the stairs shouting to Maddie. She was quickly out of the bath and, without toweling dry, into her combat fatigues. No time for her sneakers. She grabbed up the shoulder rig and the Beretta and, along with Mitch, using him to lead, dashed down to the first floor and out the back way.

On the run across the maintained rear grounds, past the greenhouse, through Straw's vegetable garden. All the way to the edge of the West Meadow.

They paused there. Mitch glanced back to the house. As yet no sign of have-arounds. He looked at Maddie, beheld her intensely, desperately, feeling perhaps this might be his last sight of her. At least in this world.

"Do exactly as we discussed," he told her.

"I will."

"Don't take any chances."

"I won't."

He thought to head her in the direction of the old equipment barn located far out in the meadow; however she had already set out for it.

It was crucial that she reach the barn before the have-
arounds could spot her. Mitch stood there and looked back
and forth, from the house to her. If they came out and spotted
her in the meadow he would change his plan, follow her to the
barn and make a stand there, a stand that he'd have no chance
of winning.

He mentally hurried her. She was doing as best she could,
unable to run, barely able to stride in that thick, unmowed,
thigh-high grass. To make matters worse, the grass was wet
and heavier for that. No doubt the legs of her fatigues were
sopped by now. Tough going, Mitch thought.

The have-arounds surely must have reached the house by
now, were somewhere within it.

Maddie still had a ways to go.

Just grant me this, Mitch pleaded to whatever power determined such crises.

He looked back to the house.

He looked ahead to Maddie.

She reached the barn, entered it, was no longer visible.

Not a moment too soon. The have-arounds came out onto
the second-floor rear terrace, from where they had an easy
view of the meadow.

Mitch made sure they spotted him. Though way out of
range, he fired an attention-getting shot and immediately
made a dash for the high piled-rock wall about a hundred
yards away, the wall that served as a separating boundary between the West Meadow and the adjacent expanse of pasture-
land.

He stood on the crest of the wall, and took stock of the
have-arounds, who by now had come from the house and
were hurrying in his direction. Little Mike, Fat Angelo and
Bechetti. All intent on him with no interest in the equipment
barn. Good.

Mitch took off across the pasture. The herd of cows was still out. About fifty or so. They weren't a tight herd this day, not gathered at one particular area of the pasture, but spread far and wide as though in an antisocial mood. Soon, out of habit of schedule or using cow sense, they would start for the distant dairy farm. Many were already grazing their way towards it. Others appeared to be through for the day, were at rest on the damp, chewed-up, hooved-up ground. They lay motionless, like ideal depictions of their kind, front and rear legs folded just so beneath them to avoid placing too much weight on their distended utters.

Mitch had thought the cows would play in his plan. He would scurry among the herd, use them in a darting now-you-see-me-now-you-don't manner, while he took a roundabout course back to the rock wall. However the herd was too widespread for that, and he was already about a hundred or so yards into the pasture, committed to it, would have to improvise.

He decided on some resting cows off to his right. A loose group of a half dozen. They were only mildly disturbed by his sudden presence, not enough to rise and move off. He used the nearest cow for temporary cover, kneeled out of sight on the far side of it. Cautiously, he peeked over the bony ridge of the cow's back.

Bechetti and Fat Angelo were standing on the piled-rock wall, like spectators. Little Mike was into the pasture and coming on. It appeared that he was the designated hitter. Either that or he was just much faster and more eager than the others, had gotten to the wall and up and over it ahead of them. Malingering and amused in their typical have-around way, they were letting him do the job, waiting to see how he made out.

Little Mike was some kind of runner. Seen at a distance, with his stubby legs scooting him along, he resembled a wind-up mechanical toy, but, as he drew closer Mitch could see his legs working like pistons. He was closing fast.

Mitch changed cows, made a dash to another of those at

rest about twenty feet away. There was the chance that this tactic hadn't been noticed and, if so, Little Mike, coming on so fast and headlong, might overrun him.

Mitch hunkered down behind the cow. A big old bossie, intolerant but too comfortable to move. She whipped her switch at him a couple of times and indicted him with a look. Pink lips, yellowed, cracked horns, a runny nose that she licked with her long tongue. The earlier rain had soaked her down to her hide.

Mitch snugged against her. He heard the thumps of her tremendous heart, which at first he thought was the pounding of his own. He heard the digesting gurgle of her stomachs as she reswallowed her cud.

Would Little Mike overrun on the left or right? Mitch had the Glock in hand, ready for either direction. Little Mike would run past. His back would be the target. It didn't matter that Little Mike would be so disadvantaged, Mitch told himself. He'd never shot a living thing. Don't give it a thought, don't think of the Glock being arbitrary death, make it absolute, stopping death. Just aim, shoot and kill the little fucker. Kill him in the back, side, head, chest, didn't matter.

Three rapidly fired bullets struck the old cow. Easily penetrated her tough hide and tore into her. She threw her head up and bellowed and bucked and almost managed to stand for a moment before her front legs gave way. Her hind half, still useful, wanted to run. It struggled with the wounded rest of her, tugged and staggered.

Little Mike fired again. Two more point-blank shots from fifteen feet. That brought all of the innocent animal down, but not out of the way. Rather sacrificially, her bulk still concealed Mitch.

He was spontaneously filled with shame for his kind, the inhumanity, a shame that converted into rage, a rage that overrode his trepidations. Thus, it was not altogether courage that brought him suddenly upright, exposed him to the next two shots Little Mike got off.

Mitch wasn't sure he hadn't been hit. He only knew there

was no pain and he wasn't prevented from pointing the Glock in Little Mike's direction. No time but also no need to take careful aim. It was impossible for him to miss simply because Little Mike so deserved to be shot.

He fired twice.

The first .40 caliber hollow point smacked into Little Mike's chest about an inch or two above the sternum, spread upon impact and was close to twice its diameter when it tore through the right atrium of his heart. The slug that followed a split second later was so equally accurate that it had a ready-made entry, didn't spread until it struck and shattered the spine.

Little Mike knew what hit him. He was jolted back and literally lifted off his feet. Like an awkward, unaccomplished tumbler he went heels over head, and failed to complete a somersault. He lay there, a crumpled extinguished thing in a beige suit, having lifeless twitches.

Now look what you've done, Mitch thought, but immediately revised that to look what you had no choice but to do. There were fourteen rounds left in the Glock, including the one in the chamber ready to be spent. His adrenals had given him another spurt. He felt somewhat beyond control but capable of anything. He glanced at the cow. It was belly-up, flailing with all fours as though kicks could stave off death. Mitch had to look away.

The other two have-arounds were coming into it now, scrambling down the distant rock wall to the pasture. They set out for Mitch at a fast walk. No need to go running after him. Little Mike, the stupid runt, had run and look what it had gotten him. As they saw it Mitch was way out there in plain view with nowhere to hide. Not even a rock or tree, just cows. All they had to do was keep him in sight and keep after him to eventually get to him.

What they didn't take into account was how deceptive a vast open space such as this two-hundred-acre cow pasture could be. These city guys hadn't ever had any experience with pastures. It seemed to them their every step was on a straight course. They didn't realize the illusion until they saw that the piled-rock wall which had been behind them at the start was now up ahead and Mitch was approaching it. He, their only reckoning, had been purposely misleading them, taking a wide gradual circling course.

Now the have-arounds ran after him.

He climbed over the rock wall and crossed the West Meadow, keeping well away from the rear side of the equipment barn. When he reached where the meadow bordered the woodlands to the north he paused in plain sight, looked back and saw that the have-arounds were following the swath he had caused in the thick, high meadow grass. He disappeared into the woods.

Moments later the have-arounds entered the woods on the run.

After going only a hundred feet it was as though they were a hundred miles deep into its world, suckered into a domain that was rife with unfamiliar defiance and contraries. Flagellating saplings, loops of exposed roots that tripped, undergrowth that grabbed at their confining suits.

They couldn't have been more out of their element.

Their hard city heels sunk into the spongy rot of the woodland floor. In some places they went in over their ankles and dirt got into their shoes, their two-hundred-dollar, made-in-Italy, fifty-dollar swag shoes.

Bechetti, as usual, was in charge, and it was he who first spotted the pulsating amber light. They hurried ahead to it, approached it warily, weapons ready. It appeared to be only an ordinary orange and white highway construction site barricade. The single upright sort about three feet tall counting the enclosed battery and light on top.

"What do you think?"

"I don't know."

"What the fuck's this thing doing way out here?"

"Some kind of trick, got to be."

"The cocksucker is trying to throw us off, that's all," Bechetti decided.

"Maybe."

"Kick it over," Bechetti told Fat Angelo.

"You want the fucking thing kicked over, you kick it."

Bechetti went to the barrier, kicked it over. It lay there mocking with its amber blink, amber blink, amber blink. Fat Angelo stomped on it to make it stop. "Okay," Bechetti said, "let's find the piece of shit and do him so we can get out of here." The pursuit had become a search.

They tried to stick together, to proceed in a sort of phalanx, two across. But the woods combed them apart the way unpathed woods can. When they encountered a tight stand of hemlocks, for instance, Bechetti chose to go round the right side of it while Fat Angelo avoided by going left. Dense clumps of undergrowth and outcroppings of sizeable boulders called for the same circuitous left or right decisions. Thus, the distance that separated them increased. Eventually they lost sight and sound of one another, and each was on his own; a rare circumstance for any have-around.

Fat Angelo hated how this thing was going down. From the moment he'd come into the woods there'd been a squadron of gnats attacking him. So tiny he could hardly see them. He needed to keep swatting and shooing them or else they landed and fed on him. Why the fuck were they picking on him and not Bechetti? It didn't seem like this place was making Bechetti half as miserable as it was him. The only other time he'd been in a woods something like this was the day about five years back when he'd had to make a trip to Danbury for Riccio. Driving up 684 he had pulled over and gone into the woods a short ways to take an emergency shit. This was like then.

He was sorry now that he'd come along on this thing. He could have said his hemorrhoids were bothering him, or his ulcer. The reason he came was the other have-arounds wanted to and Riccio had made it sound like it was going to be easy, enjoyable work. Riccio had promised a ten large bonus to whoever whacked the guy and the bimbo. Another twenty to anyone who came up with the goods, those two emeralds.

Sometimes Riccio kept his word on things like that. Another reason he'd come along was the guy who was going to get whacked was the one who'd shoved him down the stairs twice and also called him a *fagala*, so this thing would be a chance for payback, Fat Angelo had figured.

Now, however, he figured where he'd much rather and ought to be was back on West 47th in his regular spot halfway up the stairs at Riccio's. He could be relaxing on the daybed looking at pussy magazines. He was thirsty. He was pissed. He decided what he'd do is sit someplace and let Bechetti, wherever he was, do the guy. Just wait to hear the shots.

He was trying to find a place to sit that wasn't wet or rotten when the amber light blinked at him from down the incline. Another of those highway barricades. It was, he guessed, about a hundred yards away, blinking at him through the branches. He decided to ignore it. He found that if he moved a little to the right or left the light was obscured and he could pretend it wasn't there; however, curiosity edged with apprehension compelled his eyes to locate it.

Amber blink, amber blink, amber blink.

Fuck it, Fat Angelo thought.

His legs seemed to think otherwise. They took him down the incline in the direction of the light, with difficulty across a couple of mushy runoffs and through a tangle of wild grape. By then he was inspired by the possibility that maybe the light was on his side, leading him to the guy so he could do him and be the one who did him and Riccio would count him off ten large, which would make him a five hundred across-the-board player when he went to Aqueduct come Friday. Or, he might even get luckier. It wasn't too much to ask that after he'd done the guy he'd find those two emeralds on him. In that case Riccio could keep his measly twenty large. Fat Angelo knew the whole lot more he could get for those emeralds. He'd have to hide them somewhere better than a pocket, though. He'd stick them up his ass. Hemorrhoids or no hemorrhoids, up they'd go.

He paused a moment to check his weapons. He had two. A

.45 automatic that he'd killed twice with, but not recently, and a snubby .38 caliber backup revolver he'd never had to use. The latter was holstered to his belt behind his left ham, concealed by his suit jacket.

He was surprised to come upon the marsh, nearly tromped right into its southern end where it was thick with cattails and reeds. The blinking amber light was in the clear at the water's edge about a hundred feet away. Same as the first, mounted on an orange and white stupid highway construction barrier. No reason for it to be there.

Then he saw the guy. About a hundred feet beyond the blinking light. Standing at the edge of the water with his back turned, just standing there, the asshole. Be perfect if he'd just stay like he was, Fat Angelo thought.

Mitch had seen Fat Angelo come down the incline, and, although he was turned away, he knew to the moment when Fat Angelo got to the marsh. From the frogs Fat Angelo had startled, their noisy leaps from the bank into the water.

And now, from those same blurping sounds in succession he knew Fat Angelo was sneaking along the bank in order to get into range. He waited until the frogs told him Fat Angelo had covered about halfway. Then he stepped out onto the precisely submerged span of painted plywood.

Fat Angelo froze. From his point of view it appeared as though Mitch was walking on water. He brought his pistol up to take a shot but he was awestruck. How could he shoot a guy who could walk on water? Besides, both of his previous killings had been close in, practically muzzle against the back of the head.

Mitch reached the opposite bank. Fat Angelo was directly across the way, apparently unaware of the submerged span that was right there below him. Perhaps reflections on the surface of the water prevented him from noticing it. Mitch acknowledged him with the universal *fuck you* gesture.

Fat Angelo emphatically returned two of the same. What to do? He set out for the opposite bank by going around the end of the marsh. A stumbling, sloshing trek.

Mitch jogged easily back across the span, so again they were on opposite sides.

In all his inciteful and frustrated life Fat Angelo had never been more incited and frustrated. He glared across at the inaccessible Mitch, who was now taunting him with open arms and beckoning fingers. Come on, come on over.

Fat Angelo couldn't take much of that. He averted his eyes downward.

He saw the trick. His pointed-toe shoes were pointing right at it: the two-foot width of painted plywood weighted down on that end by several large rocks, the way it extended across the marsh.

No way was he going to go across on that board, Fat Angelo told himself. Not even if he was one hundred percent sure the guy had those emeralds on him. He imagined himself doing the guy and finding the emeralds in one of the guy's pockets. He imagined the ride back to West 47th, him sitting on a fortune, knowing they were his secret, tucked up into him. Some wish.

Compelling enough to cause him to take a testing step out onto the plywood span. It was sort of slippery but it hardly gave. He took another cautious step and another slightly less cautious and, after the next, he was thoroughly encouraged.

However, as he went along he had to split his attention between where he was stepping and the guy on the bank ahead. No telling when the guy would make a move. So far all the fuck had done was stand there, like maybe he was waiting for the Lexington Avenue local.

Fat Angelo was nearly halfway across. About forty feet to go. He thought about chancing a shot from there but, being far from a good shooter, he decided to give himself the advantage of another step closer, and still another.

The closer he got the more he had to keep an eye on the guy, which meant he couldn't pay real careful attention to where he placed his feet.

It took only one misstep.

By his right foot, which happened to be more off than on

the span. He went into the water front first, a sort of low-level belly flop. There was some thrashing and spewing before, with considerable difficulty, he managed to get himself upright.

The water was up to his waist. Actually only about half that depth was water. The other half was silt. His legs were mired deep in the mucky decomposed stuff of the bottom. He tried to lift his feet but it was as though he was cemented in place. Bubbles like underwater farts rose to the surface around him and silently exploded dreadful-smelling methane gas. He still had his pistol in hand. He used it as an instrument of surrender, held it harmlessly up and out to the side and let it drop into the water.

Because he was no match for the shotgun Mitch now had pointed at him.

"What you going to do?"

Mitch didn't say.

Fat Angelo asked again.

"I'm deciding," Mitch told him.

"Why don't you get a branch or something and help pull me out?"

"I'm deciding whether to shoot you or leave you there to starve and rot."

An unnerved smile from Fat Angelo. "You're just trying to sweat me."

"Yeah," Mitch lied and lowered the shotgun some.

Fat Angelo figured that was a cue for his plea. He went into a self-deprecating rant. About what a low-life, lowest kind of greaseball he was. A nothing, a *babbo*, a *shmuck*. Everybody treated him like the scumbag he was, including Riccio. Riccio especially. He'd been a garbage collector before. Had been better off. He was no have-around. Only reason he was up there on this thing today was Caselli got sick. He had to take Caselli's place. Caselli got the shits and pukes and couldn't make it.

Throughout this babbling appeal Fat Angelo underscored

and punctuated with his hands. Typical of his nationality, a lot of intricate and wide gesticulating.

Mitch appeared to be listening attentively to Fat Angelo. Actually, he was only half hearing him. He was thinking about what West 47th would be like if the likes of Fat Angelo weren't working it. Not a tender-conscienced, guileless, untainted West 47th, to be sure, but enormously improved.

Inside of one of Fat Angelo's gesticulations his right hand went to his belt behind his hip for the snubby .38.

Mitch's mind wasn't that much elsewhere. He fired from the hip. A round of buckshot. In bringing the gun up he had overcompensated slightly so the hit was a little high. The tight pattern of 12-gauge steel pellets struck Fat Angelo in the collarbone, throat and face. Didn't merely damage, and probably would have been enough; however Mitch rapidly pumped another shell into the chamber and fired. The 12-gauge slug blasted into the center of Fat Angelo's chest, and that was more than enough.

Due to his obesity and because his lower legs were mired Fat Angelo went down strangely. A fast flop that settled into a contorted sort of backbend.

Uncomfortable to say the least, Mitch thought. It seemed to be true that a second killing was easier. He wasn't feeling a single pang of remorse. It was as though his conscience was having an outage and he was on his own, telling himself no harm, that this guy he'd wasted had been a waste. He raised his eyes a fraction and vowed to the sky and whatever overseer might be in it that if he got through this day he would never kill again. Wouldn't even swat a fly or step on an ant.

After today.

CHAPTER 33

Bechetti would come, Mitch knew, surely he'd heard those two shots. He couldn't be far off. He'd come.

Mitch placed the shotgun aside. It might be of further use; however he'd found that it restricted his movements in the woods, especially where there was dense brush and branches. He had the Glock. It would do.

There still wasn't any sun. Everything damp. Drops from tips of leaves. A primeval impression influenced by the marsh. A massive reptile might rise from it. Not Fat Angelo.

Bechetti was coming down the incline at the far end of the marsh. Yet out of sight, but the saplings were being disturbed. Mitch waited, watched for the tan suit, the inverted white triangle of shirt front, the contradicting oblong of human head. There would also be the black of the Tech 19 machine pistol.

Bechetti broke into view and paused at the edge of the marsh, warily taking it in.

Mitch couldn't be missed, little more than two hundred feet away. To make sure he was seen he raised and waved his arms.

What was it with this guy? Bechetti wondered. It looked as though he was signaling, wanting to give up. Like he figured then this thing would end in a push or something. Civilians didn't know, they just didn't fucking get it.

Mitch kept on waving.

Bechetti rushed ahead and was close to being close enough to pull off some shots when Mitch bolted into the woods. Bechetti followed and within thirty paces found himself again surrounded by contraries, the branches, roots and vines. Fallen trunks. Sticky webs on his face, nothing substantial underfoot. It would seem that way out here would be a good place to do a guy, but it wasn't, Bechetti thought. There was too much life here. Be different if this was some stairwell, warehouse, any kind of room. He had whacked fourteen guys up to now, eight of those had been in bed.

So, where was this guy? It occurred to Bechetti that maybe the guy had cut back and was coming at him from behind. He stopped, crouched, scanned slowly all the way around. Everything was different and yet the same, green-leaved and damp. No movement. A dangerous silence. Bechetti convinced himself the guy was somewhere ahead. He hurried on.

Past a gang of boulders, across the trickle of a habitual runoff. To the upper edge of a shallow swale. Directly opposite was a stand of pines. And there on its perimeter between two close, competing trunks, stood the guy. Arms folded, as though simply waiting.

He was close enough. Bechetti opened fire, a couple of bursts.

The guy scampered into the pines.

Bechetti went after him and was immediately in the maze of straight trunks, a darker atmosphere. The ground, carpeted with slippery needles, handicapped him because of his leather-soled shoes.

There was, however, an advantage being among the pines. No undergrowth. Only the tree trunks for concealment.

Bechetti caught a glimpse of the guy. Scurrying from behind one trunk to behind the next further on. The camouflaged fatigues didn't help the guy much here. He'd been clearly visible, but only for an instant, not long enough for Bechetti to get off a shot.

Within a minute the guy again darted from trunk to trunk,

but again all Bechetti got was the merest glimpse. He figured the guy now realized what a wrong move he'd made in getting into these pines and was now trying to work his way out of them.

Too fucking bad.

Bechetti focused his attention and aim on the space between two of the tree trunks. Just a guess as to where the guy might next show himself. He held on it for what seemed a long while and was about to give up on it when the guy darted into view, was right there.

Bechetti fired two bursts from the Tech 19. A spray of ten or so rounds. Bullets splatted into bark and ground and, as well, into the guy, according to what Bechetti heard—a loud painful gasp.

Bechetti cautioned himself that even a sound so truly agonizing could be a trick. Shouldn't the guy's legs or some other part of him be in view? Bechetti gave it some time and then advanced stealthily. He would finish the guy off if he wasn't already done. There'd been no other sounds so he was probably done.

The guy wasn't there. Just a lot of his blood. Bright, wet red on the base of the tree and on the layer of brown pine needles.

The fuck was hit bad, Bechetti thought. He wouldn't be able to go far.

There was an obvious trail of blood. Drops of various sizes and smears in places. Bechetti had no difficulty following them, anticipating that at any moment he would come upon the guy unconscious or dead or perhaps just weakened and unable to go on. Bechetti hoped for the latter because of the inconvenience this guy and these woods had caused him. A slow finish would be a payback.

The blood led him on. All the way through the stand of pines and out to a clearing where the terrain was more congruent. No sign of the guy or his blood. Bechetti had lost the trail of blood. He didn't, however, have to search much to pick it up. Bright red on the tufts of wild grasses. Even more apparent on the white, wild daisies that were closed for the day due to lack of sun.

Faint groans.

Also gasps and entreaties to God. They seemed to be coming from across the way where there were a lot of bushes of some sort. Now Bechetti had the blood and the suffering of the guy to go by.

As he approached the bushes he saw what they were. Brambles, a large tight patch of them. The situation wasn't hard to figure, Bechetti thought. The guy, seeking any possible refuge, had taken cover somewhere in this bramble patch, had somehow crawled into it, and maybe that was smart and he might even have gotten away with it except he was bleeding too much and had so much pain he couldn't keep it to himself.

Bechetti stood at the edge of the patch listening to the groans and blubbering supplications. They were alternately louder and indistinct. He watched the top of the brambles for any sign of movement but they were perfectly still. A catbird glided in to light upon one of the high arching canes, had hardly perched before it realized there were humans about and flew off.

Bechetti decided precisely where the guy was. Only about twenty-five feet in. He raised the machine pistol and strafed the spot with a couple of bursts. The 9mm bullets tore through the canes and leaves but it didn't stop the guy's groaning. Nor did another couple of bursts. It didn't make sense, Bechetti thought, the guy had to be there, at least some of those bullets had to have hit him.

He noticed then there were drops of blood off to his right. They led to where, along the edge, the guy had crawled into the patch. It was almost like a tunnel, probably made by some animal, was Bechetti's guess. The guy just happened to find it. Bechetti hunched down for a cautious look in. He couldn't see in very far. It didn't go straight in. He fired several shots in but the groaning continued along with some cursing.

Leave the fuck there, Bechetti suggested to himself. The guy was hit bad so just leave him to die in there.

Bechetti's exasperation vetoed that. He took off his suit jacket, folded it just so and placed it down where he wouldn't miss it later. He removed his tie and unbuttoned his shirt collar. Rolled his shirtsleeves up to his elbows. Like there was work to do, to do this guy.

He got down on all fours and crawled into the tunnel. He found it not as large as it had appeared and denser. Even when he kept low the thorns on the brambles got to his back and shoulders, snagged at the hips of his trousers. As he crawled along his trousers were being ruined, especially at the knees, by the soft earth and fallen blackberries. He swore he'd finish this guy slower than any guy he'd ever finished. When he got to him.

And he was about to get to him. The groans and delirious swearing were louder now, real close, coming from around the slight bend in the tunnel that was just ahead. Bechetti crawled on, more cautiously. He didn't want to get whacked by an almost dead guy.

The guy wasn't there. A big spill of blood but no guy. The guy's voice but no guy.

Bechetti dabbed up some of the blood, felt its slick but slightly gritty texture. He smelled it. A distinctive smell that his memory recognized and connected to the innocent paint of a second grade class thirty years ago.

The voice? There in plain view was the tiny speaker attached to the battery-powered audio cassette player. Still groaning and uttering.

But the guy *had* been there, Bechetti reasoned. No other way could he have spilled the paint along the tunnel and here at this dead end. He must have done it in a hurry and backed out. There was no room to turn around. It seemed to Bechetti there hadn't been enough time for the guy to do all that, but he couldn't see any other explanation, which meant he too would have to make his exit in reverse.

That, as it turned out, was more difficult than Bechetti expected. The tunnel seemed narrower and with less headroom now that he was going ass first. He kept backing into brambles on one side or the other, giving the thorns plenty of chances at him. They were like organized, malicious adversaries, the thorns. Some would snag his trousers as though delaying him, so others might stab and lacerate his thighs and buttocks.

Fuck doing this guy, Bechetti thought. It was a piece of shit, not the piece of cake Riccio had said it would be. Fuck this place, fuck Riccio, fuck everything!

At that moment Mitch was also in the brambles. Crawling out by way of the getaway tunnel that ran from the apparent dead end that Bechetti had encountered. Mitch had created the impression that it was a dead end, had concealed the getaway tunnel by stuffing a large tight tangle of blackberry canes and foliage into place. Bechetti had nearly caught him at it.

The getaway tunnel allowed access all the way out to the far side of the patch. It was straight enough but now as Mitch crawled along it he was sorry he hadn't made it larger. The thorns were impartial, meting out as many or even more inflictions on Mitch as on Bechetti. There were places in the getaway tunnel where hugely thorned canes had fallen and crisscrossed, as though resenting and thus intent on prohibiting passage. There were places where Mitch was so thoroughly snagged, front, back and sides, that he could barely move. He still had a ways to go.

Bechetti, meanwhile, unaware that he wasn't alone in the brambles, was struggling along.

On the way in he hadn't noticed the wolf trap. It was situated at about the midway point a little off to the right covered with leaves. On the way in Bechetti had missed springing the trap by a mere inch or two and now, as he was backing out, his right foot and leg avoided it by about that same margin. So did his right forearm and hand.

It was the machine pistol that sprang the trap.

The steel jaws snapped shut.

The teeth that Mitch had honed so sharp chomped together with tremendous force.

They clamped onto the trigger guard of the pistol and, in so doing, impaled Bechetti's trigger finger, sliced deep into the knuckle of its second joint, nearly to the point of amputation.

Bechetti's howl had some tremolo in it. He knew nothing of traps, hadn't ever seen one. His spontaneous reaction was that some animal had him in its bite, but then, through his pain, he realized the thing was made of metal and had a chain attached to it.

He tried to extricate his mutilated finger from the trigger guard. The teeth of the trap had it, flesh and bone, skewered against the trigger, pressed so tightly that all the slack of the trigger was taken up and the merest additional pressure would cause the pistol to fire. With his free hand he tried to pry open the trap. It couldn't be done one-handed. The effort intensified his pain.

How could he deal with this? Why was he being made to suffer? That guy. Was he ever going to do that fuck. Once he got out of these bushes.

He resumed his backwards crawl. It was even more difficult now. Not only was he having to contend with the thorns but, as well, his every move aggravated the torment of his finger.

He couldn't bear either.

His impatience exploded.

Without giving a second thought to the consequences, he got his feet under him and heaved upward. Full force against the weave of thorn-studded brambles overhead. Some gave, more defied, refused to relent unless Bechetti accepted their punishment.

His fury was anesthetic.

Head first, he burst up out of the green tangle, then tore his shoulders and arms free. Like a grotesque throwback suddenly risen from its breached domain bearing countless wounds. Blood streamed from his scalp and neck, ears and cheeks. Even from his eyelids. A deep slash on his nose ran from bridge to tip and it must have been particularly vicious thorns that had clawed his mouth.

Just seconds earlier Mitch had emerged from the getaway tunnel. He stood at the rear edge of the patch surveying his advantage. It had gone as he'd hoped. Bechetti was in the thick of the brambles where he couldn't see out but could be easily picked off. Mitch would just stand there or anywhere around the patch and blast away at him. In fact, certain uppermost brambles were being disturbed, betraying where Bechetti was at that very moment.

It was then that the bloodied Bechetti heaved up through the top of the brambles little more than twenty feet away, chest and head exposed.

An easy shot for Mitch. He went for his Glock.

His holster was empty.

At some point in the getaway tunnel it must have gotten snagged out.

Bechetti spotted him, leveled the machine pistol and let go with a burst.

Mitch dove for cover, crawled swiftly along the edge of the patch to put some distance between himself and Bechetti.

Bechetti was resolutely forging his way out of the chest-high patch.

Mitch had to make a run for it. The clearing wasn't entirely level. A zigzagging dash and another desperate dive got him safely to a shallow depression and gave him a moment to consider his options:

He would be exposed to Bechetti's fire when he crossed the clearing and got back into the pines. He would rush through the pine grove and over the boulders and runoffs and down the wooded incline to the edge of the marsh, to where he'd left the shotgun.

The shotgun wouldn't be there. It would be in the marsh where Bechetti must have surely thrown it. Maybe not but most likely.

Mitch craned up and saw Bechetti was now pulling free from the last of the brambles, would be coming on. Mitch was quickly up and out of the depression and into a sprint. Down the clearing in the direction of the river. When he reached where the clearing made a transition to woodland he glanced back at Bechetti and saw he'd gained considerable distance.

Bechetti was limited to less than a full-out run but more than a jog. Because of the wolf trap, the clamp its teeth had on the machine pistol and his trigger finger. He was using his left hand to hold and steady his right, pistol, trap and all. Otherwise it felt as though his finger was being ripped off. His having to do that prevented his arms from moving normally in opposing sync. Then, too, there was the trap's anchor chain. Its heavy four-foot length dangled and kept hitting his crotch.

Still, he pressed on, found a path through the woods that made the going easier. All the way to the granite bluff overlooking the Hudson. He hadn't expected a river, didn't know what river it was. He went close as he dared to the edge of the bluff and peered down. It was like looking from the roof of a thirty-story building.

He disliked heights, avoided them. They always caused his insides, from his balls to his throat, to cringe and go hollow, as though giving him a taste of what it would feel like to be falling a long fall.

After that one look down he backed off from the edge, kept well clear of it as he proceeded along the hard granite shoulder of the bluff. Looking for the guy. Where was he? He couldn't have gone any further unless he could fly, Bechetti thought. He wouldn't put anything past this tricky fuck.

Actually, Mitch *had* gone over the edge. He was now crouched on a narrow mantel-like formation that jutted out just below the bluff's rounded shoulder. He was able to estimate Bechetti's whereabouts by listening to the sound of his steps on the granite surface, the clips and grates being caused by the leather soles and heels of Bechetti's shoes. Shoes surely not meant for such terrain, suffering it. To make mat-

ters even worse, or for Mitch, better, Bechetti had metal insets
in the heels to save sidewalk wear, an old-mob thing.

Bechetti's footsteps receded. He had gone further on along
the bluff. He'd be able to go only so far before coming to a
vertical sheer rise of granite, like an insurmountable wall.
He'd have to return.

Mitch waited, listened for him. What he heard was distant
gunfire. The distinct sharp cracks of pistol shots being fired in
rapid succession. Coming from the direction of the house,
which also meant the equipment barn. The shots ceased but
after ten seconds or so resumed, about a dozen shots again
rapidly fired.

Mitch thought the worse, just as he had when he'd heard
similar shots from there the day before. Now, however, they
certainly wouldn't be Maddie target-practicing. They could
only mean . . .

Bechetti was coming back along the bluff. His footsteps on
the uneven granite surface became more and more distinct.

To hell with taking a peek, Mitch decided. He loomed up
suddenly, leaped up over the rounded edge of the bluff and
charged at Bechetti.

Bechetti was turned away. Mitch went at him bull-like,
head down, and, before Bechetti had a chance to react,
rammed into the small of his back.

Bechetti went front down hard upon the hard granite. Momentum carried Mitch down with him. Bechetti recovered
quickly, managed to stand.

The machine pistol was firing skyward, as though it could
do so at will. Bechetti brought its muzzle down to Mitch's
level.

The burst of 9mm bullets and Mitch were headed in con-
vergent directions as Mitch again charged Bechetti, bulled
past the extended machine pistol and into Bechetti's midsec-
tion.

Bechetti was driven back but managed to keep his feet.

Mitch held on, kept close in, clutched Bechetti with his left

fist while his right delivered three hard blows below
Bechetti's rib cage.

The machine pistol quit, its magazine spent. Bechetti used
it and the trap as a club. They slammed down between
Mitch's shoulder and neck. Twice more.

Mitch hung on, kept the struggle in close. He made a de-
fensive grab for the pistol, didn't get it. However, the trap's
dangling anchor chain was whipping about and his hands
found it. Before its links could run through his grasp he got a
grip on it.

Now he backed off. He pulled on the four-foot-long chain
and heard and saw the pain that caused Bechetti. The chain
was like a tether connected to the trap and its teeth that were
connected to the pistol and Bechetti's deeply incised finger.

Mitch yanked the chain sharply.

Bechetti cried out in pain and, needing slack for relief,
came with it.

Mitch yanked the chain again spitefully and then, not allowing slack, he began circling Bechetti.

Bechetti circled with him, alternately pleading for mercy
and calling Mitch a *stronzolo*, which Mitch didn't know
meant *piece of shit*.

Mitch circled faster.

Bechetti was being whirled, round and round. He wanted to
let go, would have, but the trap had his trigger finger.

The fibrous ligaments and connective membranes of that
finger were nearly severed. It was a wonder they'd held together until now, couldn't any longer. The lacerated soft tissue also gave way.

The finger tore off, second knuckle to tip.

With it came the pistol and the trap.

For Bechetti it was like being thrown from a speeding
carousel. The sudden release from the centrifugal force sent
him reeling across the width of the bluff. He tried for balance,
fought the momentum, and he might have been able to stop
himself had he been wearing appropriate shoes rather than the
typical have-around city sort with leather soles and heels that

slipped on the granite and couldn't for the life of him put on the brakes.

He was reaching wildly, as though the air might offer him anything to grab on to, when he hurtled over the edge.

CHAPTER 34

Riccio felt the bathwater. It was on the hot side. She couldn't be long out of it. The tile floor was wet where she'd dripped.

The smell in the bathroom made him not want to breathe. It brought to mind embalmed guys laid out and surrounded like they always were with lilies. A couple of months ago up in the Bronx he'd paid respects to an old, onetime capo, and, although he'd only stayed a polite half hour, he'd come away so stunk up by lilies he'd had to hang his best black suit out to air.

This place was worse than four funerals. So bad it had his eyes watering. He pinched his nose shut and jerked open the door that was at one end of the bathroom. She wasn't in there. Just a toilet bowl with blue water, and a bidet. Only rich people have such special little rooms where they piss and shoot water up their cunts, Riccio thought.

He and Fratino went on with their search of the house. They were sure she was hiding somewhere in it. Probably, because she was blind, it would be an obvious place such as beneath one of the beds or in the back corner of a closet, wishing she was invisible.

Riccio had Fratino believing there'd be something extra in

it for him if they found her and got what they wanted out of her. Intentional emphasis on the word *extra* so Fratino would take it to imply it meant one of the twenty-five extra large the two emeralds would bring. Riccio had said all along and too often that to him this thing was first and foremost a matter of saving face. If the emeralds came it would just be a nice plus, he didn't expect them, they probably wouldn't come but if they did it would be as he put it, *nice*.

The have-arounds knew Riccio well enough to see through that old-mob shit. The emeralds were what Riccio had first in his head. Not to say that doing the guy and his wife wasn't also there.

The wife, the rich wife, she'd know where the emeralds were, Riccio reasoned. Mitch wouldn't have kept that from her. Civilians usually made the mistake of letting their women in on such things. She'd know, and when Fratino had her bound and bent over and greased and it became evident what he intended to do to her she'd give them up.

Her give-up, however, wouldn't make a difference to Fratino. He'd keep on with it, and there'd be no reason for Riccio to stop him. Fratino had never had his way with a blind man or woman, someone unable to see how repulsive he was. He'd remarked to Riccio that just the idea of it caused him to have half a hard-on.

They gave the house a thorough going over from cellar to roof. For Riccio, not finding her was an insult. He couldn't accept it. About twice a minute he grunted like he was being poked with a stick.

He went from room to room looking for things to take that might appease his disappointment. Nothing he saw was going to make up for twenty-five extra large. What's more he didn't have the understanding or appreciation for the valuables that were there. None of the paintings. He passed up a Jackson Pollock and a Willem de Kooning and an Egon Schiele nude that he believed must have been painted by some whacko with the shakes.

Grudgingly he settled on a Georgian silver service. Placed

it near the front door for one of his have-arounds to carry to the car on the way out.

Fratino uncorked a couple of bottles of vintage red. He and Riccio went out onto the second-floor rear terrace. They sat close to the rail. Riccio lighted another of his Sicilian twists. He grunted between swigs and puffs.

"Did you look on the roof?" he asked.

"Yeah."

"Maybe she's up on the roof."

"I tell you I looked."

"How could you see the roof?"

"I went outside and looked up. It's slanted."

An increase in grunts.

"This fucking place," Riccio grumbled. "How'd you like to live up here?"

"Not me, no fucking way."

"I'd go crazy up here. Think how it must be in winter."

Some shots were heard from deep in the woods off to the right.

"They're doing the guy," Fratino commented flatly, as though reading from a program.

"Be perfect if we could only find the fucking wife. Wrap this thing up. I got to be back in town by seven, no later than eight."

"What can I say?"

"Nothing. Keep quiet," Riccio snapped. His bad cigar was spoiling the taste of Straw's good wine, not that he realized that.

His attention was drawn to a mid-air skirmish almost directly above the terrace. A pair of starlings trying to peck and outmaneuver one another like enemy aces. The two birds were really going at it and neither seemed to be getting the best of it until one took flight out to a field beyond where the grounds were kept.

Distance transformed the bird into a black, indefinite creature that dropped from sight out there in the tall, untended grass.

Riccio, with nothing better to distract his aggravated mind, had followed the bird's retreat. In doing so he happened to notice that the uniform texture of that grass was interrupted by a contrasting line that ran straight all the way to a large white structure. It was worth a look, he decided. He and Fratino went down and out to the unmowed meadow.

It was obvious to them that someone had recently cut through the grass, and they had no difficulty following the same trampled course. To the large double doors of the barn. Fratino slid those apart and they went in.

Riccio knew in a breath she was in there. The predominant old barn odor of the interior was laced with the scent of lilies. Now, exactly where in here was she?

He looked around, then walked around clockwise. An insouciant, old-mob smugness about him as he took in the disparate contents of the place: cardboard boxes of canning jars, storm windows, a stack of mildewed and rusted steamer trunks, various pieces of unfortunate furniture, a dresser minus two drawers, chairs without seats.

He paused every few steps to sniff and gauge the strength of the giveaway scent. At the far end of the barn stood the stove, the potbelly that Maddie and Mitch had pocked up with shots from the Beretta. The scent was not entirely undetectable there but much fainter.

He moved on, down the barn's other long side. Past a pileup of tubular outdoor loungers and numerous sections of cast iron grillwork.

The lily scent was more pronounced.

And even more so when he came to the lineup of forsaken farm equipment. Two tractors, a backhoe with all tires flat, a rake and a hay baler.

Only the hay baler offered a hiding place.

Riccio centered his attention upon it. He raised his chin a fraction to indicate it and gestured to have Fratino come over to him. Riccio was positive that she was hidden in the baler. He savored the moment, relighted his cigar, chewed it from the left corner of his mouth to the right. He rotated his pavéd diamond, ruby and emerald Italian flag ring.

The pressing chamber, the oblong, lidded compartment where the hay was compressed and bound, was just barely large enough to contain Maddie. She was doubled up tight and hunched in a kneel and, for the first time in her life, experiencing claustrophobia. She felt crammed, crunched, as though her flesh and bones were now literally the shape of a bale of hay. And what a relief it would be when, if ever again, she was able to take a deep breath.

Her heart was galloping, the roof of her mouth had gone dry. She had the Beretta in her right hand. Off safety.

Riccio was about to order Fratino to open the lid on the baling compartment and pull her out. No need to be concerned about her being armed. She was blind. At most she'd put up a clawing, kicking struggle.

The lid flew open.

Maddie sprung up like a released jack-in-the-box and began firing the Beretta. She relied entirely on her sense of direction, altering her point of aim slightly every couple of rounds. She fired the clip empty, released it, rammed in a full and rapid-fired another fifteen rounds in the same hopeful left to right manner.

The smell of lilies and gunpowder and Sicilian cigar.

It had been over for fifteen minutes by the time Mitch got there.

Riccio and Fratino were down, sprawled in surely dead positions. Blood was pooling beneath and around their heads. There was an entrance wound in each of their temples. Neat little holes in almost precisely the same spot.

A shaft of sunlight permitted through the barn's old roof was striking upon Riccio's hand, causing scintillations from his Italian flag ring.

Maddie was seated off to the side on the edge of a rusted-out cast iron love seat. She looked bedraggled. The Beretta was still in her hand.

Mitch spoke up to keep her from possibly taking a shot at

him. He went to her, held her. To have her in his arms again was an unexpected pleasure. She, however, wasn't able to give entirely to the embrace. Some of her body's usual compliance had been appropriated by rigidity.

"Are you all right?" she asked.

"Yeah."

"No wounds or anything?"

"Some scrapes and scratches is all."

"Tell me, if I could what would I be seeing?"

He told her, but didn't elaborate. It was evident to him that she wasn't too happy with herself at the moment.

She did an on and off small smile, trying to demonstrate her pluck.

"Let's go in," she said. "Maybe a little later on I'll feel up to fixing you something special for supper."

CHAPTER 35

The bodies of five mob guys.

What to do with them had Mitch sitting in the dark on the side of the bed. Waiting for daylight as though it might bring the answer.

Five dead mob guys strewn all over Strawbridge land. What a feeding frenzy the police and the media would have with that, Mitch thought. He could hear himself attempting to explain it: "There were these two emeralds, see . . . "

A mass grave was the most expedient solution he'd been able to come up with. He'd get that forsaken, old backhoe running somehow, fix its flats and all and use it to dig a hole so deep that hungry dogs would walk right past it. Somewhere remote on the land, in the woods maybe where the disturbed ground would cover over quickly with leaves and brush.

It would take a lot of doing, at least all day.

It would also mar the pleasure of this land for him. He'd never be able to see it the same, knowing its grisly, buried secret.

He dressed, went down, microwaved a mug of yesterday's coffee and at first light, went out to the West Meadow. Along the way he reminded himself that he knew nothing about operating a backhoe. He also wondered by what means he'd be able to extract Fat Angelo from the muck of the marsh. That would take a goddamn derrick.

When he arrived at the equipment barn he didn't believe what he saw, or, rather, he disbelieved what he didn't see.

The bodies of Riccio and Fratino weren't there.

Coagulated blood but no bodies.

Was it possible that his wishful thinking was so intense that he'd manufactured an illusion? Had something supernatural occurred? When he'd last seen Riccio and Fratino they'd been dead as dead could be dead and he didn't believe in resurrections, anyway certainly not when it came to mob guys.

No bodies in the barn.

Nor was the body of Little Mike or the carcass of the cow out in the pasture.

Nor was the corpse of Fat Angelo mired in the marsh.

Mitch hurried to the bluff. At the base of it not a sign of Bechetti, who'd plunged the equivalent of thirty stories.

There was, however, a clue on the exterior ramp of the Strawbridge boathouse. Along the length of it, soaked into its dry, weathered wood were numerous streaks of blood. As would be caused by bleeding bodies being dragged.

Within the boathouse Mitch noticed the boat with the outboard motor was tied up in its slip bow first. It had previously been tied up bow out. The motor was cold. Blood had been wiped from the gunwales, seats and floorboards. Dried, remnant smears of it were visible to a close look.

Mitch gazed down the wide Hudson. Like many major rivers, especially in summer, its placid appearance belied its swiftness and currents. The water he was now looking at would be flowing past Manhattan, including West 47th, in practically no time.

CHAPTER 36

It was the second day that Mitch and Maddie had been back in the city. Four o'clock in the afternoon.

Since early yesterday Mitch had been putting off going to see Visconti and, now, standing on the corner of West 47th outside 580 Fifth he was still procrastinating.

It seemed to Mitch that Visconti was the final person he'd have to contend with regarding this Iranian emerald matter. He'd expressed to Maddie that it was about seventy-five percent his opinion that he shouldn't wait for Visconti to make a move but face up to him with the truth and hope he believed it. Visconti was new mob, Visconti was not as irrational as Riccio had been, Visconti had enough understanding of the abstract to accept unapparent circumstances. Thus were the sort of persuasions Mitch had been offering his judgment. His better judgment insisted on having its say, to remind him that new-mob Visconti and his type of have-arounds were far more efficiently lethal.

Maddie convinced Mitch's other twenty-five percent that it would be best if he took the initiative. Besides, she said, she had important things to tend to in town. Her birds were, no doubt, in need of fresh water and would stop loving her unless she provided some soon, and Casimiro Ramírez was scheduled for a lesson.

Casimiro Ramírez was a ringing name Mitch would have remembered had he heard it.

"He's an eight-year-old who wants to be a great jazz guitarist," Maddie had told him.

"Another prodigy."

"He plays like he has webbed fingers. If anything he should take up cymbals."

"So why the lesson?"

"That'll *be* the lesson," she'd said.

So, now, while she was high up in the Sherry gently dashing the dreams of Casimiro Ramírez, there was Mitch doing some last-ditch vacillating. He thought he was thirsty enough to have an iced tea somewhere; he thought he'd go to Barnes & Noble and see what new books on tape they had in for Maddie; he thought he'd stroll down five blocks, like it was some other day, and sit on the New York Public Library steps.

Not because he was intimidated to the point of weak-knee by Visconti. He'd just undergone such an ordeal with Riccio that he felt, in all fairness, life ought to give him a breather. When had any straight good guy such as himself had to go up against two crooked bad guys so consecutively?

Not fair but fuck it, he decided.

He entered the 580 building and went up to Visconti's offices. In the tastefully done reception were the same pair of youthful have-arounds as the time before. Dressed to kill in Calvin and looking as though they swam two hundred butterfly laps every day before breakfast and did Shorin-Ryn Karate during lunch breaks.

They remembered Mitch by name. It was like he was expected. His arrival was phoned in and without wait he was shown down the narrow interior hall to Visconti's private office.

Visconti was in shirtsleeves seated at his desk. On the phone. He raised his chin abruptly as though throwing his smile to Mitch. He placed his hand over the mouthpiece. "Be right with you," he said and continued with his phone conversation.

Mitch couldn't help but overhear some of it. Large sums of money being stipulated and, cryptically, a hundred pieces of white, two hundred of blue, which Mitch knew meant diamonds and sapphires.

The phone call in progress gave Mitch time to fit into the situation with more ease. Most of his misgivings were being chased. Coming there had definitely been the right decision.

The phone call also allowed him to appraise this day's Visconti: lively blue custom-tailored shirt with long closely separated collar points and monogrammed cuff, dyed blue ostrich skin suspenders, Hermès two-hundred-dollar silk tie. No casual shirt and canvas tennis shoes this day. For some special reason, Mitch presumed.

Finally, Visconti hung up, stood up and came from around his desk for a handshake. A firm grip with his right, four pumps instead of the usual two, while his left clasped Mitch's upper arm. "I was getting concerned about you Mitch."

"No reason to be."

"For days now whenever I happened to look across your office was dark."

"I've been out of town."

"I thought as much." Visconti squinted, examined. "Hey," he frowned, "that's a nasty scratch." Referring to the perforated-looking scratch that ran from the outer corner of Mitch's left eye to below his earlobe. He also had numerous scratches on the back of his hands. Those on him elsewhere were concealed. "Where did you get that?" Visconti asked.

Mitch evaded the inquiry with admiration for Visconti's necktie.

Visconti let him evade and for a moment Mitch thought he was about to take off the tie and give it to him. Be a shame to undo the perfect, tiny knot.

As before they sat in the visitors' chairs.

"How's your uncle-in-law?" Visconti asked.

"Better," Mitch replied, and because Wally came to mind, added: "greatly improved."

"And Maddie?"

"She's fine."

"I bought a town house," Visconti said.

"Where?"

"In the seventies. East, of course. Actually, I bought it about eight months ago and had it renovated to suit. Practically gutted the place."

Mitch thought of Ruder.

"This coming Saturday I'm having people in for the first time. Not a large crowd. Just a few special people like yourself. You'll recognize some of the faces. And some of the figures too." Visconti did a slightly salacious smirk. "Movie people."

"This Saturday."

"Hope you can make it."

"Depends on Maddie."

"She'll want to come. Anyway, come solo if it gets to that. I'm sure Maddie doesn't keep you on too short a leash."

She doesn't *keep me* at all was what Mitch wanted to say. He was becoming increasingly resentful of Maddie being called Maddie by Visconti, who had never met her, and never would if Mitch had his way. How, under the circumstances, could he turn Visconti down on this Saturday night thing?

"Along with my new town house I have a new lady friend," Visconti said. "I want to impress her with you and Maddie. She thinks my only close acquaintances are emaciated models and way overweight gem dealers. How about a drink?"

Mitch nearly automatically declined but decided he could use one. "Any scotch," he said, "straight or on the rocks, doesn't matter."

Visconti ordered the drinks through the intercom on his desk and returned to his chair. "I'm planning on showing a film Saturday night," he said, "one that hasn't yet been released. Not coincidentally I have a sizeable chunk invested in it." Visconti named a couple of stars who were the leads. "Film-making must be in my blood, the way I'm drawn to it." He directed a glance intended to direct Mitch's attention to the Luchino Visconti poster on the wall to the left.

Mitch pretended to be unaware that was expected of him.

Which irked Visconti but only slightly and he was able to smooth it over. "Something you ought to get into, financing films," he said. "That it's such high-risk is only greedy bull-shit spread by those making plenty from doing it. Perhaps you and I could do a film venture together. I'd enjoy that. Wouldn't you?"

Mitch did a very small smile and a single, almost imper-ceptible nod, meanwhile thinking Visconti's surmise that he was so financially well off came from the impression that he could dip into the Strawbridge money pot anytime for any amount. Or else . . .

He got Visconti eyes to eyes and got to the point. "I don't have those Iranian emeralds."

"Of course you do."

"No."

"Perhaps what you mean is you no longer have them."

"I've never had them."

"You either still have them or you've already cashed them in."

"Neither."

Visconti didn't appear upset; however Mitch couldn't trust that.

"You made a nice score. Why deny it?"

Visconti will turn any moment, Mitch predicted.

"Is it because you think it's so fucking important to me, that I'll press you for a piece of your score, or even all of it?"

Don't say, Mitch thought.

"You insult me, Mitch. That was Riccio, not me."

Mitch noted the past tense.

"Think I got no feelings, I don't mean sympathy, I mean feelings, for what a guy with such a rich wife has to put up with, the constant stretch it is for him to keep his *cogliones?*"

When Mitch didn't comment, Visconti did a little conced-ing shrug and went on. "Sure, twenty-five extra large isn't chicken fat by anybody's count, and if this particular twenty-five had come my way I would have gladly stuffed it away down in the Caymans or put it out to the street. But the way it went down it didn't come to me, it found you, and I'm not going to begrudge you a dime of it. *Capish?*"

Mitch didn't *capish*. There had to be a catch. Say yeah, he told himself. "Yeah."

"That didn't sound like thanks," Visconti said coolly.

A thanks won't kill you, Mitch thought. "Thanks."

Visconti warmed up as instantly as he'd cooled. "Anyway, it's not entirely magnanimity on my part. I owe you."

"For what?"

"For clipping Riccio, what else?"

How it was that Visconti knew of Riccio's death was only momentarily a question, for just then the answer entered carrying the drinks on a silver tray. Mitch recognized him right off, despite his changed appearance, the immaculate white serving jacket, fresh white shirt and neatly executed black bow tie; despite the polished, mannerly way he acquitted himself as he underlaid the drinks with coasters before placing them just so on the marble-topped table and arranged appropriate, small linen napkins folded just so and, before making his exit, inquired just so with a *sir* if anything more was wanted.

Caselli.

Riccio's oversize, old-mob sort of have-around, the one who according to what Fat Angelo related to Mitch, had not gone along on the Kinderhook move ostensibly because he had the shits and pukes. Caselli wasn't Riccio's have-around but Visconti's on the inside. He knew when the move was made and how it turned out.

As though drinking to that, Visconti gestured with his glass. It was superb scotch. The best Mitch had ever tasted. It went down his throat like molten gold. His belly was a crucible.

"We all know what Riccio was," Visconti said, "a crude, outdated psychopath."

As opposed to a slick, contemporary one, Mitch thought.

"Not only me but the whole street owes you for doing him."

What would be Visconti's reaction, Mitch wondered, if he told him that actually his blind wife had done Riccio. "You could have taken Riccio out whenever you wanted," Mitch said.

"So it might seem to a civilian such as yourself. Sure, Riccio could have suffered what would appear to be a fatal accident. That was always in the back of my mind and frequently in the front. I could have arranged it."

"Why didn't you?"

"Such things have a way of getting fucked up. No matter how far I was removed from it I'd ultimately have to answer and then it would get complicated."

"Like how?"

"The guy who did it for me would have to be done, then the guy who did the guy who did it would have to be done. A lot of words get piled up inside people and eventually come spilling out."

A percipient shrug by Mitch.

"A hooked-up guy like Riccio never gets clipped without permission," Visconti recited as though he'd memorized it from a rule book. He paragraphically downed a gulp of scotch and, when the afterscringe of his face subsided, went on:

"Consider," he said, "how much it pissed me to have to share the street with that thieving piece of shit, the humiliation of having to sit here and accept that he was entitled to half."

Mitch did some empathy. Behind it he wondered if there would be any payback forthcoming for his having been responsible for Riccio's death. He asked Visconti.

"No," Visconti assured, "you've got no worries. The people Riccio was answering to know what went down. The way they see it he got whacked in the line of duty. Matter of fact, I'll be with them later today. They're going to take down the no-trespassing sign, if you know what I mean."

Mitch understood. Those people who got answered to were

going to decree that all of West 47 from Fifth Avenue to Avenue of the Americas, as well as the spillovers that comprised the district, would henceforth be the franchise of Visconti. His alone.

"The sit will be only a little sit, a formality," Visconti said. "Already some of my crew are over at Riccio's place with an industrial vacuum. What's your guess how much goods they suck up out of Riccio's wall-to-wall shag carpet?"

"Maybe a million worth."

"I say five, at least five. According to Caselli, who witnessed a great many drops and scatters, there's even a first-quality six-carat Burma ruby lost somewhere in that jungle." Visconti chuckled, shook his head. "What an asshole Riccio was. Be a pleasure to forget him."

"Yeah."

"Understand now why I owe you? Why I'm not going to press you for even a cut of that Iranian twenty-five extra large?"

Mitch's pager beeped. Maddie wanted to be called.

"Use my phone," Visconti offered.

Mitch went to Visconti's desk and dialed home. Maddie picked up on the first ring. She sounded hurried.

"Where are you?" she asked.

Mitch told her.

"How's it going?"

"Okay."

"We're not to have another gang war?"

"Evidently."

"Make any excuse and get your ass out of there."

"I was just winding things up."

"We'll pick you up. We're leaving this minute. Be down in front."

"Ask her about Saturday night," Visconti suggested. However she'd already clicked off.

It was at that moment, while still standing close by Visconti's desk, that Mitch noticed it. Lopped over the gold and ebony pen of Visconti's DuPont desk set.

Pavéd rubies, diamonds, emeralds.

Riccio's one-of-a-kind Italian flag ring.

Mitch had last seen it in the equipment barn on dead Riccio's finger. Seeing it here now triggered off a series of realities for Mitch. What had actually occurred three days ago up in Kinderhook.

Starting with the informer, Caselli. He had let Visconti know in advance what Riccio intended to do and when.

Visconti recognized the opportunity.

He dispatched some of his crew.

They followed along, hung back, kept from sight while they observed every move made by Riccio and his have-arounds. They got their chance when Riccio and Fratino went out to the equipment barn in search of Maddie.

It wasn't Maddie who shot Riccio and Fratino. She thought she had. It seemed she had.

Those precisely placed head shots were the work of Visconti's shooters. Fired simultaneously with Maddie's rapid barrage so they hadn't been distinguished.

How accommodating for Visconti. Slick, the way he'd used the circumstances, used Mitch and Maddie.

Then, there was the overnight cleanup.

Visconti's have-arounds had seen to that, gathered up all five bodies and given them to the river. It was essential that the bodies not be found because of the kind of bodies they were. Too much would have been made of it. By all means avoid that. The people who got answered to wouldn't have wanted that.

Mitch was tempted to let Visconti know he wasn't so clever by telling him how clever he was. He could color that single remark with slight implication, not elaborate on it, just let it hang while his eyes said it all.

Visconti would then suspect that Mitch had undone the twist. It would worry Visconti, build up in him. The satisfaction would be short-lived but the apprehension would persist, Mitch warned himself. It wasn't worth it.

Visconti put on his suit jacket, made sure of his tie, shot his cuffs.

Mitch assumed he was getting ready to depart for the sit. He should hurry his own departure or Visconti would be going down with him. Maddie would be waiting at the curb in the Lexus. It would be difficult to avoid an introduction. Saturday night would be mentioned and Maddie, aware of what Visconti was, would likely accept.

Deliverance. A phone call for Visconti. Important business that required his immediate attention. He got right into it, entirely into it. He was finished with Mitch, merely bade him goodbye with a perfunctory gesture.

Out on Fifth Mitch found Maddie and the Lexus weren't waiting as he'd expected. At that hour both the avenue and its sidewalks were all rush and clog. Maddie was probably up the avenue somewhere caught in it. Mitch disregarded the New York exasperations he caused as he cut across the pedestrian flow to reach the curb.

While waiting there, protected against jostle by a perilously piled city waste receptacle, he thought how fortunate it was that he'd spotted Riccio's ring. Otherwise he might have remained fooled forever. Anyway, he'd come out ahead. There'd be no violent confrontation with Visconti. That was the main thing. And it would hardly hurt to have people thinking he was now batting twenty-five extra large in the independent league.

Mitch was right about the Kinderhook episode. Except for one thing.

Riccio's body hadn't been sent downstream with the others. Rather, it had been dumped into the trunk of one of the black Lincoln Town Cars and transported to the Scalise Funeral Home on 188th Street in the Bronx.

Even before the body arrived at Scalise's the death certificate had been filled out and officially signed. The stated cause of death was cerebral hemorrhage. Sort of true.

And right away a couple of guys showed up on behalf of

the people who got answered to. They checked out the hole in Riccio's head, stuck their little fingers into it, heard how it had gotten there and concluded that yes, Riccio had brought it on himself.

Within an hour Riccio was embalmed. The hole in his head was plugged with putty and cosmetically concealed, and he was in other ways made to look better than he had alive.

Visconti's generosity was admired. He insisted on choosing and paying for the casket. It was bronze but not waterproof.

This very night for respects Riccio would be on display from the waist up.

Surrounded by several hundred white lilies.

Chapter 37

They were in the Holland Tunnel. Possibly halfway through. Perseverant white tiles machine-gunning by. Light after light after light and the dirty ass end of an eighteen-wheel monster directly ahead.

"We're in the tunnel," Maddie said.

"Yeah," Mitch told her, noticing that her fingers were laced, and she couldn't keep from biting the left side of her lower lip. Since her confinement in the hay baler she'd been susceptible to the *clausties*, as she called them.

Fucking tunnel was enough to undo anyone, Mitch thought. He himself was being made to feel uneasy. He couldn't put out of mind that there was all that water of the Hudson above and perhaps Riccio and his have-arounds, their downstream journey delayed for some reason, were at that moment scuttling along the river bottom overhead.

"We should have taken the bridge," Maddie remarked.

"The bridge would have been out of the way, Mrs. Laughton," Billy told her. He was driving, of course. Hurley was up front with him.

"But not so oppressive," she said.

It would seem that only a sighted person could have claustrophobia, Mitch thought. He chalked it up to Maddie's so-called *spatial reckoning,* her sense of where things were, close or far and all that. "Want to get into my hug?" he offered.

"No, I'm okay," she said with a modicum of courage. "How far to go?"

"Pretend you're elsewhere."

"For instance where?"

"Anywhere you like."

"Help me."

"How about somewhere in France?"

"Be more specific."

Several possibilities trekked across his imagination. The one he chose was where he might also like to be, from what he'd read and photographs he'd seen. "On the soft, grassy bank of a canal in Chantilly, north of Paris," he said as though it was a title.

"It's a sunny day," Maddie contributed.

"We're being dappled."

"There are dragonflies."

"Iridescent."

"I've my feet in the water. So do you. Is there anyone else around?"

"Just us."

"You're sure no one is peeking through the bushes."

"No one within a mile."

"So we could be wicked if we wanted."

"Or we could take a nap."

"After being wicked," Maddie preferred.

Hurley laughed. He'd been occasionally privy and amused before by their fanciful exchanges. At times, without their knowing it, he made their flights with them. Almost to the point of getting a hard-on.

Finally, no more tunnel. Billy paid the toll and got onto the New Jersey Turnpike Extension. It was the same route they'd taken the time before, past Newark Airport on 78.

By then Maddie was entirely recovered. Her mood bright

and swollen with anticipation. "A little more foot, Billy," she said.

"I'm doing eighty-five Mrs. Laughton."

"Feels like we're snailing. Give it another ten."

"They're your tickets," was Billy's proviso.

"Hurley will fix them," Maddie promised.

"Which reminds me," Hurley said. "While you were away I got greased with box seats at the Stadium. It was a great game, went twelve innings and ended with a bases-loaded strikeout."

Mitch knew of the invitation. It had been one of the messages on the answering machine. He hadn't told Hurley about what had ensued up in Kinderhook. He might someday but for now he was trying to forget it. And as for revealing things, tonight he'd let Maddie know she hadn't killed Riccio and Fratino. Lift that load from her. She hadn't admitted being affected by it but Mitch was sure she was. No matter that they were bad guys and it had been self-defense. As for his own killings, he'd have to live with the change they'd made in him. A facet hardened.

"Dragonflies," Maddie whispered sibilantly, extending it to early a whistle.

She was still on that, Mitch thought. He took her in. She had on a white cotton waffle-knit sweatshirt with HARLEY-DAVIDSON lettered large in black on the right sleeve from cuff to shoulder. A very short white wraparound skirt and white suede sandals. He surmised that she'd put on her makeup hurriedly. Her left brow didn't quite match her right and her lipstick had created a slightly lopsided mouth. But beautiful, oh so beautiful, Mitch thought.

After a few silent miles he asked: "You say it just came to you out of the blue?"

"Black," she corrected. "I was at the kitchen table sorting through beans for a cassoulet. You know, culling out the dry, hard ones, when it was suddenly very obvious."

"An angel whispered in your ear."

"Don't poke fun at me."

"I wasn't. I'm serious."

"You don't put credence in anything supernatural and you know it."

"Don't be so sure." He leaned over and blew a tiny dark hair from high on her cheek. No doubt from one of her fluffy sable makeup brushes.

"Anyway," she said, "it occurred to me that the reason no one has been able to come up with those pair of stolen Iranian emeralds was simply because they were never stolen. Had you ever thought that?"

"No," Mitch fibbed to allow her glory.

"Neither had Hurley," she said. "Isn't that right, Hurley?"

"Right," Hurley also fibbed.

"So," she said, "I immediately stopped fucking with the beans and went into the den to dwell on it, and then I was lying on the floor with my feet elevated, gathering my senses, I mean literally bringing them all together and latching them on to my memory and letting my memory tell me what it knew."

"And it came to you out of the black."

"Did it ever! Exactly where those emeralds have been, were, still are."

An indulgent self-exonerating shrug from Hurley. "I just happened to phone at that moment," he explained to Mitch. "Maddie told me about it and I invited myself along. I figured at the very least we could have dinner, maybe at some fish place, on the way back."

Billy raised his eyes a fraction to have Mitch in the rearview mirror. Mitch assumed by now Billy was used to such far-fetches. "You're serious," Mitch said to Maddie.

"Never been more so."

"You're claiming you know where the emeralds are?"

"Sure."

"Well, where are they?"

"I'm not telling."

"Why not?"

"In case they're not there," she said straight-faced.

Billy asked the Lexus for another five and put it on cruise control.

They arrived at the Kalali house in Far Hills shortly before sundown. No police tape now. The house was no longer designated a crime scene. The electronic gate to the drive was closed. It couldn't be opened manually.

Billy drove around the area and located the road that ran parallel with the rear wall of the Kalali grounds. At about the same spot where the swifts and Peaches had gone over, Billy angled the car off the road and brought it close up to the wall.

By standing on the hood the top of the wall was easily within reach. Maddie, short skirt no matter, was first to climb up and over. Mitch and Hurley followed. Billy would wait.

They paused for a moment to get their bearings. It wasn't yet dark. Dusk had another half hour or so. The large, white, contemporary house was clearly visible a hundred yards from there.

A light went on in one of the rooms of its north wing. And another. Was someone inside? Certainly not Mrs. Kalali. She was still unconscious in the hospital. Hurley had been checking on her condition daily.

"Some of the interior lights are probably on automatic timers," Hurley said. That seemed plausible.

They headed for the house.

"I know," Mitch remarked facetiously, "the emeralds are buried somewhere out here in a mayonnaise jar."

Maddie didn't let that faze her. "You just wait and see," she told him smugly.

The landscaped area of the rear grounds had been neglected and so had the swimming pool. The water in the pool appeared somewhat gelatinous and well on its way to a chartreuse shade. The sight of it pulled a grunt out of Mitch. "I sure as hell hope they're not in the pool," he said.

They went to the door that led in from the garage. It was locked but Hurley quickly picked it open. The alarm pad mounted on the interior wall indicated that the security system wasn't on.

Mitch and Hurley stood aside in the kitchen while Maddie opened and felt around in drawers and cupboards, the microwave and the dishwasher. From what she'd said, from her certainty, they'd expected she would go directly to where she believed the emeralds might be. But now here she was, evidently searching for them. It verified their skepticism; however they wouldn't be inconsiderate, remained silent and let her go at it.

From the kitchen to the living room, the reception hall, the library. Maddie appeared to be at a loss.

Actually, she knew exactly what she was doing. Toying with them and, as well, putting off the chance that she was wrong; that she in her black had gotten carried away and this undertaking would prove to be nothing more than an intuitive error.

She, for her own reasons, needed that not to be so. If she was right about the emeralds it would be a confirmation of her sentiency, a measure of how real and reliable it was. Or, were those extra-ordinary senses only what she believed she had, and it was the strength of her belief that helped her expand, stretch the limits of her functioning? A mere illusory aid; could that be all there was to it?

The library.

It had been left much the same since the night of the robbery. The shards of ancient Persian glass, large and small, had been swept into a pile so they wouldn't be constantly underfoot; however that considerable pile remained in the middle of the slick maplewood floor. The two cushions stained by Mr. Kalali's blood were missing from the white couch, taken for evidence. The long, floor-to-ceiling bookshelves were yet vacant, their hundreds of volumes still where they'd been tumbled in an ugly heap, looking seriously injured.

Maddie moved about the library in the same rather aimless manner. She ended up seated at the baby grand piano. She performed a glissando, slid two fingers along the entire length of the keyboard from left to right, low A to high C. And another upscale on all fifty-two of the white keys, this time ending with several playful plinks of the top-most key.

Mitch and Hurley thought she was playfully giving up, using the piano to convey that her notion regarding the whereabouts of the emeralds was no longer to be taken seriously. Surely that was the case when she insistently plinked that highest key and then worked into a sprightly, Erroll Garner—like version of "I Only Have Eyes for You."

Mitch and Hurley were across the spacious room discussing where on the way home they might have dinner.

Maddie stopped playing and concentrated her attention on the key to the far right. She tried to wiggle it. No wiggle. She depressed it and applied downward pressure. No give. She told herself not to be so careful with it. She placed her knuckle under the small protrusion on the forward edge of the key and pried upward. It seemed to yield slightly but so slightly that it could have been her imagination.

She gave the key a sharp upward snap.

That did it.

The entire key seemed to come up and out. But then, it wasn't the entire key, only the exterior ivory facing of it.

When Maddie had previously played this piano her sense of touch had noticed, upon striking that upper key, that it was slow in coming back up into position. It also felt a fraction heavier than the other keys. All in all it seemed in need of some sort of repair. Perhaps there was something wrong with its balance rail, jack spring or whatever.

She'd thought no more than that about it until today when she'd mobilized her senses and dwelled upon where the emeralds might be. Unstolen in the Kalali house, but precisely where?

Her black had chosen to present her with the possibility of the piano and then, like a camera moving in for a close-up to make a point, it had suggested that particular piano key.

The ordinary reasoning that followed provided support. That highest key was the one least likely to be worn or damaged. Because it was the one played the least. At its best it contributed an almost inaudible note. Rarely was it included in compositions for that reason. Shostakovich, for example, had done so only out of caprice.

Now, having removed the ivory covering from the key, Maddie explored what she had exposed. The wood body of the key, which should have been solid, was partially routed out to create a rectangular recess. Within the recess, snugly cushioned by cotton so it would not rattle and in that way be detected, was a small ivory case.

Maddie plucked the case from its hiding place. It measured about two inches by an inch, a half-inch deep. Delicate hinges. Its lid sprang open with slight pressure.

She ran a finger over its contents. A pair of gems nestled in silk velour. She felt their inscriptions.

No doubt about it.

Mitch was going to be in raptures, she thought. How should she break it to him—him over there with Hurley, the two of them running low on patience, their interest on empty? It was one of those very seldom, absolutely justifiable opportunities for comeuppance. It called for a double dose of the good, old superior female what-for.

Instead, for a show of class, she said nothing, walked over to Mitch with her hand extended, the little ivory case on the flat of her upturned palm.

"What's this?" Mitch asked, hoping, of course, what it might be.

"It's some little something, I suppose," she understated. She wished she could see his happiness.

He opened the case.

Even in the waning light the pair of emeralds gave off a rich, green glow. Mitch switched on the overhead lights and held the open case directly beneath a downward beam.

It was as though the emeralds had been dozing and now, suddenly awakened, were demonstrating how bright and lively they were. In fact, it seemed to him that every stone he'd ever touched had been sullied at some time in one way or another. But this emerald . . .

He held it up to the light, brought it to his eye. Paradise, he thought. Had that blind Persian poet really been God-sent twenty-twenty?

At that moment Mitch tended to be a believer. Possibly the prospect of twenty-five extra large had some influence.

He returned the emerald to the case.

"May I?" Hurley asked, wanting to see. His interest seemed natural.

Mitch handed him the open case.

Hurley took a good long look at the emeralds, called upon his many years of experience on West 47th to determine whether or not they were genuine. No need to sacrifice a friend over a couple of fakes, he reasoned.

He closed the case.

He dropped it into his jacket pocket and in practically the same motion drew his pistol from his hip holster.

Everything that had been going Mitch's way stopped. "You're kidding," he said.

Hurley's eyes were cold now. They spoke for him, as did the pistol when he raised it to Mitch's heart level.

Mitch didn't think Hurley would go so far as to shoot him; however like anyone under gunpoint he couldn't be entirely sure of that. "The Iranian got to you too," Mitch said.

"Why not? He had half the street scuffling around for his big numbers."

"What's happening?" Maddie wanted to know.

"I suppose it never occurred to you that I was in the race," Hurley said.

"Never," Mitch said bitterly. "You were my helper. Remember?"

"Will someone for Christ's sake tell me what's going on," Maddie demanded.

Mitch told her how Hurley had a gun on them and the emeralds in his pocket.

"That stinks, Hurley," she said. "That really stinks."

"What doesn't?" was his attitude.

"Mitch, tell him to fuck off," Maddie said, "tell him he can have the emeralds. We don't need the money, right?"

Mitch was trying to decide which of the many voices in him he should heed. He managed to do some nonchalance. "You know, Hurley, this is a chance for you to come out way ahead."

Hurley agreed.

"What I mean is this is a chance for you to do the decent thing."

"Which would be?"

"We split the Iranian's number and forget about now. You come to my place on the Vineyard when the weather's right; I learn to ride down in Maryland."

Rather than quickly reject that idea Hurley did a considering face. "I turned such an arrangement over a few times along the way," he said. "As a matter of fact during the drive over here today I told myself if it came to it be decent, but now . . . " He patted his jacket pocket. " . . . I'm all out of decency."

"You're tiresome," Maddie said. "I don't know why I haven't realized until now how dreadfully tiresome you are. I should have seen right through you. Go away." She dismissed Hurley and the emeralds with a flaccid, backhanded gesture.

Mitch, at that moment, was looking beyond Hurley, taking care not to fix his attention there and give away . . .

. . . Billy.

Hurley was unaware that Billy was noiselessly approaching from behind, the .357 Magnum revolver in hand.

Reliable, loyal Billy, Mitch thought. Billy was going to save everything. He took back every criticism or disapproval of Billy he'd ever expressed or kept to himself. Billy was a gem, a devoted, single-hearted, first-class, stand-up guy. Billy was going to poke the muzzle of the .357 into Hurley's back and order Hurley to drop his pistol and that would be that, Mitch thought. Billy was now close enough.

He brought the revolver down upon Hurley's head. A vicious, cracking blow.

Hurley dropped, was that suddenly transformed into an unconscious heap.

Dead cop, Mitch thought. Nothing would explain a dead cop. Billy shouldn't have hit him, certainly not so hard. Mitch stepped forward to see to Hurley.

Billy pointed the revolver at Mitch and gave notice with a threatful thrust. "Back off," he snarled.

Mitch obeyed. Was there anyone in this world the Iranian hadn't propositioned? It was hard to imagine Billy with twenty-five million. What a waste.

"Now what's going on?" Maddie asked.

"Just stay where you are Mrs. Laughton," Billy told her.

"Why should I? What's gotten into you, Billy?"

Mitch told her.

She did a loud, intolerant sigh. "Let's just leave," she told Mitch.

Billy leaned over the unconscious Hurley, who was sprawled front down. Hurley's suit jacket was twisted beneath him, so it wasn't a matter of Billy simply reaching down into Hurley's pocket for the emeralds. He'd have to dig in under Hurley.

He transferred the revolver to his left hand and worked his right beneath Hurley's deadweight. He felt for the pocket, squeezed into it and got the case containing the emeralds.

He was so intent on that he relaxed his grip and his point of the revolver, and much of his attention was diverted from Mitch.

Mitch noticed.

No time for thinking twice.

He charged at Billy, aimed a kick at Billy's left hand, missed the hand but caught the wrist.

The revolver was jolted free.

Billy dodged Mitch's grab, darted out of its range. Mitch stalked him. Billy evaded, skipped and paced semicircles. He had the case containing the emeralds clutched in his right hand. Had them. Now it was only a matter of getting away. Millions when he got away, Billy thought. However, Mitch stood between him and the way out. He might be able to out-run Mitch but first he had to get around him.

He feinted to the left, then bolted right.

Mitch lunged and just did get enough of Billy's lower legs to stumble him in the direction of the bookcases.

Billy went down among the books. Hundreds upon hundreds of them strewn every which way in irregular layers as many as ten deep. Slippery dust jackets, jutting spines, the sharp hard corners of covers.

He got to his feet and it seemed he'd be able to easily scramble over and out of the books; however they slid and collapsed under his first step, causing him to fall backwards.

Mitch dove on him, intending to pin and subdue him and wrest the ivory case from his hand.

Billy squirmed and bucked. Mitch raised up in order to get off a punch. Billy rolled aside. Mitch held on and rolled with him and they ended up on the fringe of the book pile with the advantage Billy's. Him on top, straddling Mitch and throwing lefts and rights.

Billy wasn't much of a puncher. Mitch fended off most of the blows.

It must have been the counterforce of Mitch's forearm blocking one of those blows that jarred the ivory case out of Billy's fist.

Mitch saw it fly out. From his low-level point of view he saw it land and skitter across the slick, bare hardwood floor. In a fraction of a second it was all the way to the piano, missing the caster of the piano's forward leg by only an inch or so.

It was like the case knew its destination and was hell-bent for it. It didn't stop until it reached the far side of the piano, where it gently collided with the heel-to-heel angle formed by the shoes, the black and white wing-tipped oxfords.

Djam, the Iranian, had also come to the conclusion that perhaps the emeralds were never part of the Kalali swag. So, for the past several days he'd been spending time here at the house, searching through it. He was giving the master bedroom another going over when he heard the arrival of Mr. and Mrs. Laughton and the others.

Now, calmly, as though experiencing an inevitability, he reached down and picked up the case. He verified its contents and then, by way of the nearby sliding glass door, he slipped out into the early darkness and away.

Getting the emeralds back hadn't cost him a penny.

CHAPTER 38

Ten days went by.

Mid-morning of the eleventh Mitch was at David Baum-feld's place of business on the sixth floor of one of the better-kept-up buildings of West 47th.

There to choose a diamond for Straw.

Straw had phoned from Monaco to say that he and Wally might be returning home in about a week. *Might* and *about,* told Mitch that Straw and Wally were still caught up in romantic vagabonding. He wouldn't be at all surprised if they didn't show up for another two or three weeks, maybe a month. Lucky them, Mitch thought with a smidge of envy.

Straw said they'd gone to an auction of important jewels in Geneva. He'd wanted to bid on several items for Wally but she wouldn't have it. Each time he'd raised his hand to make a bid she'd yanked it down, maintaining that they were *just looking.*

Would Mitch do him the favor of locating a diamond? Straw asked. One suitable for an engagement ring. Surely Wally couldn't, wouldn't deny him that pleasure.

Mitch was happy to do it. He needed to know the particulars: what size, how much?

We can handle a little overstatement, Straw had said.

So now there was Mitch considering the four stones that lay in a shallow velour-lined tray on Baumfeld's desk. Baumfeld's assistant, a dark-haired young woman with an obvious nose job and an unfortunate overbite, had just brought them from the vault.

Baumfeld had his suit jacket on. A minor show of respect for Mitch. He was a third-generation dealer living up to the excellent reputation handed down by his father and grandfather. Shrewd but fair. Mitch had known him for going on twenty years.

The four diamonds Baumfeld had chosen to show to Mitch ranged in size from three to eight carats. He sort of tickled each in turn with his tweezers, causing them to perform glints.

"Some of the best of my inventory," he said, merely stating. "From what you said I gathered you wouldn't be interested in anything less."

Two of the stones were round cuts. They appeared to be identical. Each exactly three carats.

Mitch thought the wish that he could afford those two for Maddie. Extravagant studs. He'd come close to being able to, so close.

He put that out of mind, tweezed up and louped the largest of the lot. An emerald-cut of eight carats, ten points. "Russian goods," he thought aloud.

Baumfeld confirmed that.

Mitch had never seen a better diamond. Just as good but not better. He appreciated its make, the definite, sharp edges of its facets and girdle, its perfect proportions. Not a flaw to be found. The stone was colorless, clear as water. He sighted into it longer than he needed to. Its purity was beneficial. After what he'd been through recently, he could use a measure of purity.

He asked the price.

"Forty thousand," Baumfeld told him.

Forty thousand a carat. Which made it three hundred twenty-four thousand.

Mitch waited for that number to settle. It didn't. It stayed way up there. "Can you do better?" Mitch asked, knowing it was expected.

"Is it intended for family?"

"My wife's uncle."

"In that case . . . " Baumfeld's pupils nearly disappeared up in under his eyelids, as though he was consulting the deity of profit. " . . . I could do thirty-seven without pain."

Mitch allowed some silence for Baumfeld to possibly do thirty-five.

"Less would hurt," Baumfeld told him.

A barely perceptible nod from Mitch to acknowledge rock bottom. He pictured the lovely Wally wearing the diamond, her left hand doing aerial acrobatics for emphasis during a dinner party conversation. Eyes following the glints of the stone as though it was a prompter. Sure, she could carry it off.

"Let me give it some thought," he told Baumfeld in a tone that couldn't be construed as a turndown.

"I'll put it aside for you," Baumfeld assured.

Mitch went down and out onto West 47th. It was one of those bright days that put a sharp edge on every shadow. The street was well into its usual commerce, tourists gawking, sellers of gold chains by weight hawking from the doorways of their shops. Mitch wasn't in the mood to hurry. He went along the street, taking it in, stopping at certain windows to contemplate the goods being offered.

He believed he recognized two or three old friends. Particularly an authentic art deco period necklace comprised of various-colored sapphires. He wondered where it had been lately, and what had brought it back to this sordid temple.

He wasn't seeing the street through the same eyes. It was like something in him, his enthusiasm certainly, had been quenched. What had been colorful was now revealed as blighted. Most of the upper windows of the old buildings hadn't been opened or washed for perhaps a decade or two. Pigeon droppings caked thick on the sills and eaves. The curbs fractured, the gutters grimed. How tacky, really, the legions of diamond rings in the store windows, the way they were stuck into slotted squares of cardboard. And so falsely spotlighted.

West 47th should live up to itself, Mitch thought. Its every window should sparkle immaculately. All its edges, curbs, sills, steps and fronts should be crisp and sharp as the most conscientiously executed facet. And clean, above all, clean rather than sleazy.

Hurley.

Mitch noticed Hurley headed west in his beat-up but souped-up official Plymouth. He'd suffered only a concussion as a result of Billy's blow to the head and had spent two days in the hospital on restricted fluids and Tylenol. Now Mitch looked the other way. So did Hurley. They might not ever speak again. Might not.

As for Billy, he'd been let go, was begging for a reference.

Mitch came to Fifth Avenue, crossed over and went up to his office. Shirley was slitting the mail open. She'd been back from Paris for a week. New hairstyle, revised makeup, recharged with self-worth.

"I was beginning to wonder about you," she said.

"Yeah, I'm to be wondered about," Mitch said dourly.

"You're still in a funk."

He went into his office.

Shirley shouted in to him. "It's not like quicksand, you know. You can jump right out of it any old time."

A bearish grunt from Mitch.

Shirley came to the doorway. "No calls," she told him. "Did you have breakfast? You don't look as though you had breakfast."

"I could use a fried egg sandwich."

"On what?"

"Rye," he growled decisively.

Before sitting at his desk he glanced out the window to Visconti's office across the intersection. Visconti had people there. Two or three guys. He was pacing around, ranting, gesticulating broadly. He appeared upset. Evidently in the midst of some sort of serious crisis. Mitch hoped so. He closed the blinds.

Today was his day for going over the books. Same as yesterday, but he didn't blame himself for putting it off. He knew what he'd be facing. The retainer from Columbia Beneficial would no longer be coming in, and Northland Providential, his Philadelphia client, had decided to cut back and given notice that his services were included in that slice. What with Shirley's salary and the rent along with other operating expenses and his personal living costs the water of merely breaking even was practically up to his nose.

Such thoughts brought to mind that Andy and Doris had gone ahead and leased the store on upper Madison. They were commencing renovations next week. They were still urging him to come in with them.

Andy, as a favor to Mitch, was making sure Roudabeth Kalali got a fair price for her jewelry. It wouldn't go to 47th Street. At least not yet. Some of it had already been purchased by one of Andy's dealer friends in Beverly Hills. The pieces that remained would be consigned to the new Laughton store where it would be displayed and sold to best advantage. Roudabeth had come conscious and been discharged from the hospital three days ago. She and her Roger Addison had gone off to Vermont. Roger behind the wheel of a new Infiniti Q45.

Phone call from Maddie.

"Can you come home right now?" she asked.

"Why?"

"I need you to read something."

"Like what?"

"An instant pregnancy test. I just gave myself one and have no way of knowing if the red strip came up."

"Oh."

"I doubt you'd want me to have the elevator operator read it."

"What makes you think you're pregnant?"

"The way we carried on in the country, the intensity and all that. I felt very vulnerable."

"When are you due?"

"Don't you keep track?"

"No," he fibbed.

"Next week," she told him.

"You're jumping the gun."

"I suppose," she relented. "How's your day going?"

"Fine," he fibbed again.

"Same old kind of day? Nothing extraordinary happening?"

"No."

"I was speaking with Elise earlier."

"And?"

"She started off with a lot of sobbing because . . . guess what?"

"She's overdrawn."

"Marian left her high and dry, went back into the closet."

"Really?" Mitch tried to sound concerned more than amused.

"Marian ran off with someone connected to the Paris Ballet. I believe Elise said he's a rehearsal pianist. Imagine. I stoked Elise with consolation and positive thinking. By the time she rang off she was looking forward to some solo cruising in St. Tropez."

"I'll be home early," Mitch promised.

Shirley brought the sandwich, laid it out for him, little packet of ketchup, pickle and all. The bread was sogged and the fries limp.

"This just came," she said.

A registered letter.

No return address on the envelope.

Probably another client bailing out, Mitch thought, and, that being the prospect, it could sure as hell wait. He placed the letter aside.

After he'd eaten he reluctantly opened it.

And it opened his eyes.

It was from a private bank located in Zurich on Bahnhofstrasse. A very courteous letter informing him that a sum of twenty-five million dollars had been placed in deposit on his behalf by a party who expressly wished to remain unmentioned.

A second page contained instructions regarding the formalities necessary for him to activate the numbered account. Along with details of bank terms, charges, minimums, policies and so on.

Mitch read the letter three times, the last two times slowly and aloud, before allowing reaction.

He made a fist and gave fate a short, victorious jab in the belly. "Yes!"

He felt like doing a time step . . . right up the wall and across the ceiling.

He speed-dialed Maddie.

He read the letter to her.

"Are you sure it's not someone playing a sick joke?" she asked.

"Doesn't appear to be. No," he said definitely, "it isn't."

"The Iranian came through!" she exclaimed happily.

That, of course, was also what Mitch had surmised. But now, all at once, he and realization hit head-on. "So it would seem," he said.

"Think so?"

"Who else but Mononchehr Djam?" Mitch pronounced the name correctly for the first time.

"Has to be," Maddie concluded.

Contrivance and motive peeked out from behind her reaction. And, after a bit more back-and-forth praise for Djam, his being a man of his word and all that, after Maddie had clicked off, Mitch sat there for a long while . . .

. . . asking himself whether or not he should let her get away with it.

Diana T Sweeney

THE JUDAS TREE

The Judas Tree

A. J. Cronin

NEW ENGLISH LIBRARY

TIMES MIRROR

First published in Great Britain in 1961 by Victor Gollancz Ltd.
© by A. J. Cronin 1961

*

FIRST NEL PAPERBACK EDITION MARCH 1973

*

NEL Books are published by
New English Library Limited from Barnard's Inn, Holborn, London, E.C.1.
Made and printed in Great Britain by Hunt Barnard Printing Ltd., Aylesbury, Bucks.

45001393 6

PART ONE

CHAPTER 1

THE AUTUMN MORNING was so brilliant that Moray, judiciously consulting the rheostat thermometer outside his window, decided to breakfast on the balcony of his bedroom. He had slept well: for an ex-insomniac six hours was a reassuring performance: the sun shone warm through his Grieder silk robe, and Arturo had, as usual, prepared his tray to perfection. He poured his Toscanini coffee – kept hot in a silver Thermos – anointed a fresh croissant with mountain honey, and let his eye wander, with all the rich, possessive pleasure of a discoverer. God, what beauty! On the one hand, the Riesenberg, rising to the blue sky with heaven-designed symmetry above green, green grasslands lightly peppered with little ancient red-roofed peasant chalets; on the other, the gentle slopes of Eschenbrück, orchards of pear, apricot and cherry; in front, to the south, a distant ridge of snowy Alp and beneath, ah yes, beneath the plateau of his property lay the Schwansee, beloved lake of so many, many moods, sudden, wild and wonderful, but now glimmering in peace, veiled by the faintest skein of mist, through which a little white boat stole silently, like . . . well, like a swan, he decided poetically.

How fortunate after long searching to find this restful, lovely spot, unpolluted by tourists, yet near enough the town of Melsburg to afford all the advantages of an efficient and civilised community. And the house, too, built with precision for a famous Swiss architect, it was all he could have wished. Solid rather than striking perhaps, yet stuffed with comfort. Think of finding chauffage à mazout, built-in cupboards, tiled kitchen, a fine long salon for his pictures, even the modern bathrooms demanded by his long sojourn in America! Drinking his orange juice, which he always reserved for a final bonne bouche, a sigh of satisfaction exhaled from Moray, so blandly euphoric was his mood, so sublimely unconscious was he of impending disaster.

How should he spend his day? – as he got up and began to dress he reviewed the possibilities. Should he telephone Madame von Altishofer and go walking on the Teufenthal? – on such a morning she would surely want to exercise her weird and wonderful pack of Weimaraners. But no, he was to have the pleasure of taking her to the Festival party at five o'clock – one must not press too hard. What then? Run into Melsburg for golf? Or take out the boat and join the fishermen who were already hoping for a run of felchen in the lake? Yet somehow his inclination lay towards gentler diversions and finally he decided to look into the question of his roses which, suffering from a late frost, had not fully flowered this summer.

He went downstairs to the covered terrace. Laid out beside the chaise longue he found his mail and the local news sheet – the English papers and the Paris *Herald Tribune* did not arrive until the afternoon. There was nothing to disturb him in his letters, each of which he opened with a curious hesitation, a reluctant movement of his thumb – strange how that ridiculous phobia persisted. In the kitchen Arturo was singing:

> 'La donna è mobile . . .
> Sempre un' amabile . . .
> La donna è mobile . . .
> E di pensier!'

Moray smiled; his butler had irrepressible operatic tendencies – it was he who had chosen the blend of coffee once favoured by the maestro on a visit to Melsburg – but he was a cheerful, willing, devoted fellow and Elena, his wife, though stupendous in bulk, had proved a marvellous if temperamental cook. Even in his servants he was decidedly lucky . . . or was it merely luck, he asked himself mildly, moving out upon the lawn with pride. In Connecticut, with its stony soil and unconquerable crab grass, he had never had a proper lawn, at least nothing such as this close-cropped velvet stretch. He had made it, determinedly, uprooting a score of aged willow stumps, when he took over the property. . Flanking this luscious turf, a gay herbaceous border ran, following a paved path that led to the lily pond, where golden carp lay motionless beneath the great sappy pads. A copper beech shaded the pond, and beyond was the Japanese garden, a rocky mount, vivid with quince, dwarf maples, and scores of little plants and shrubs with Latin names defying the memory.

The further verge of the lawn was marked by a line of flowering

8

bushes, lilac, forsythia, viburnum, and the rest, which screened the vegetable garden from the house. Then came his orchard, laden with ripe fruits: apple, pear, plum, damson, greengage – in an idle moment he had counted seventeen different varieties, but he owned to having cheated slightly, including the medlars, walnuts, and large filberts which grew in great abundance at the top of the slope, surrounding the dependence, a pretty little chalet, which he had converted to a guest house.

Nor must he forget his greatest botanical treasure: the great gorgeous Judas tree that rose high, high above the backdrop of mountain, lake and cloud. It was indeed a handsome specimen with a noble spreading head, covered in spring with heavy purplish flowers that appeared before the foliage. All his visitors admired it and when he gave a garden party it pleased him to display his knowledge to the ladies, omitting to reveal that he had looked it all up in the *Encyclopaedia Britannica*. 'Yes,' he would say, 'it's the *Cercis siliquastrium* . . . the family of *Leguminosae* . . . the leaves have an agreeable taste, and in the East are often mixed with salad. You know, of course, the ridiculous popular tradition. In fact Arturo, my good Italian, who is amusingly superstitious, swears it's unlucky and calls it *l'albero dei dannati*' – here he would smile, translating gracefully, 'the tree of lost souls.'

But now he discovered Wilhelm, his gardener, who admitted seventy years and was seventy-nine at least, nipping buds by the cucumber frame. The old man had the face of the aged Saint Peter and the obduracy of a cavalry sergeant. It took tact even to agree with him, but he had proved his worth in knowledge and labour, his one drawback an embarrassing, if useful, propensity for making water on the compost heap. Straightening his green baize apron, he removed his hat and greeted Moray with a grimly impassive:

'Grüss Gott.'

'Die Rosen, Herr Wilhelm,' said Moray diplomatically. 'Wollen wir diese ansehen?'

Together they went to the rose garden where, once the old man had scattered blame in all directions, the number of new varieties required was discussed and determined. As Wilhelm departed, a delightful diversion occurred. Two diminutive figures, the children of the village piermaster, aged seven and five, were observed breasting the steep path with that breathless speed and

9

importance which denoted the delivery of an invoice; Suzy, the senior, clutched the yellow envelope, while Hans, her brother, carried book and pencil for the receipt. They were the most attractive, bright-eyed children, already smiling, glowing actually, in anticipation of the ritual he had established. So, after glancing at the invoice – it was, as expected, from Frankfurt, confirming the arrival of two cases of the special 1955 Johannisberger – he shook his head forbiddingly.

'You must be punished for being such good children.'

They were giggling as he led them to their favourite tree, a noble Reine Claude loaded with yellow plums. He shook a branch and when a rain of juicy fruit descended they burst into shrieks of laughter, scrambling down the slope, pouncing on the ripe rolling plums.

'Danke, danke vielmals, Herr Moray.'

Only when they had filled their pockets did he let them go. Then he looked at his watch and decided to be off.

In the garage, adjacent to the chalet, he chose to take the sports Jaguar. For one who had attained the age of fifty-five and had from choice retired to a life of leisure and repose, such a vehicle might possibly have been judged too racy, the more so since hs other two cars, the Humber estate wagon and a new Rolls Silver Cloud – obviously, he favoured the British marque – were notably conservative. Yet he felt, and looked, he had often been told, far far younger than his years: his figure was slim, his teeth sound and even, he had kept his hair without a thread of grey, and in his smile, which was charming, he had retained an extraordinarily attractive quality, spontaneous, almost boyish.

At first his road ran through the pasture land, where soft-eyed, brown cows moved cumbrously, clanging the great bells strapped about their necks, bells which had descended through many generations. In the lower fields men, and women too, were busy with the eternal cycle of the grass. Some paused in their scything to lift a hand in greeting, for he was known, and liked, no doubt because of his kindness to the children, or perhaps because he had taken pains to interest himself in all the local junketings. Indeed, the rustic weddings, made dolorous by the final sounding of the Alpenhorn, the traditional processions, both religious and civil, even the brassy discords of the village band, which had come to serenade him on his birthday . . . all these amused and entertained him.

Presently he came to the outer suburbs: streets which seemed to have been scrubbed, green-shuttered white houses, with their front plots of asters and begonias, their window-boxes filled with blooming geraniums and petunias. Such flowers – he had never seen the like! And over all such a clean quiet air of neatness and efficiency, as if everything were ordered and would never break down – and indeed nothing did; as if honesty, civility and politeness were the watchwords of the people.

How wise in his special circumstances to settle here, away from the vulgarity of the present age: the hipsters and the beatniks, the striptease, the rock-and-roll, the ridiculous mouthings of angry young men, the lunatic abstractions of modern art, and all the other horrors and obscenities of a world gone mad.

To friends in America who had protested against his decision, and in particular to Holbrook, his partner in the Stamford company, who had gone so far as to ridicule the country and its inhabitants, he had reasoned calmly, logically. Hadn't Wagner spent seven happy and fruitful years in this same canton, composing *Die Meistersinger* and even – this with a smile – a brilliant march for the local fire brigade? The house, now a museum, still stood as evidence. Did not Shelley, Keats and Byron spend long periods of romantic leisure in the vicinity? As for the lake, Turner had painted it, Rousseau had rowed upon it, Ruskin had raved about it.

Nor was he burying himself in a soulless vacuum. He had his books, his collection of beautiful things. Besides, if the native Swiss were not – how should he put it nicely? – not intellectually stimulating, there existed in Melsburg an expatriate society, a number of delightful people, of whom Madame von Altishofer was one, who had accepted him as a member of their coterie. And if this were not enough, the airport at Zurich lay within a forty-minute drive, and thereafter in two hours, or less, he was in Paris . . . Milan . . . Vienna . . . studying the rich textures of Titian's *Entombment;* hearing Callas in *Tosca*; savouring the marvellous *Schafsragout mit Weisskraut* in Sacher's Bar.

By this time he had reached the Lauerbach nursery. Here he made his selection of roses, resolutely adding several varieties of his own choice to the list Wilhelm had given him, although wryly aware that his would probably perish mysteriously while the

11

others would survive and flourish. When he left the nursery it was still quite early, only eleven o'clock. He decided to return by Melsburg and do some errands.

The town was pleasantly empty, most of the visitors gone, the lakeside promenade, where crisp leaves from the pollard chestnuts were already rustling, half deserted. This was the season Moray enjoyed, which he viewed as an act of repossession. The twin spires of the cathedral seemed to pierce the sky more sharply, the ring of ancient forts, no longer floodlit, grew old and grey again, the ancient Mels Brücke, free of gaping sightseers, calmly resumed its true identity.

He parked in the square by the fountain and, without even thinking of locking the car, strolled into the town. First he visited his tobacconist's, bought a box of two hundred of his special Sobranie cigarettes, then at the apothecary's a large flask of Pineau's Eau de Quinine, the particular hair tonic he always used. In the next street was Maier's, the famous confectioner's. Here, after a chat with Herr Maier, he sent off a great package of milk chocolate to Holbrook's children in Connecticut – they'd never get chocolate of *that* quality in Stamford. As an afterthought – he had a sweet tooth – he took away a demi-kilo of the new season's *marrons glacés* for himself. Shopping here really was a joy, he told himself, one met smiles and politeness on every side.

He was now in the Stadplatz where, answering a subconscious prompting, his legs had borne him. He could not refrain from smiling, though with a slight sense of guilt. Immediately opposite stood the Galerie Leuschner. He hesitated, humorously aware that he was yielding to temptation. But the thought of the Vuillard pastel drove him on. He crossed the street, pushed open the door of the gallery, and went in.

Leuschner was in his office looking over a folio of pen-and-ink sketches. The dealer, a plump, smooth, smiling little man, whose morning coat, striped trousers and pearl tie-pin were notably *de rigueur*, greeted Moray with cordial deference, yet with an uncommercial air which assumed his presence in the gallery to be purely casual. They discussed the weather.

'These are quite nice,' Leuschner presently remarked, indicating the folio, when they had finished with the weather. 'And reasonable. Kandinsky is a very underrated man.'

Moray had no interest in Kandinsky's gaunt figures and simian faces, and he suspected that the dealer knew this, yet both spent the next fifteen minutes examining the drawings and praising them. Then Moray took up his hat.

'By the way,' he said offhandedly, 'I suppose you still have the little Vuillard we glanced at last week.'

'Only just.' The dealer suddenly looked grave. 'An American collector is most interested.'

'Rubbish,' Moray said lightly. 'There are no Americans left in Melsburg.'

'This American is in Philadelphia – the Curator of the Art Museum. Shall I show you his telegram?'

Moray, inwardly alarmed, shook his head in a manner implying amused dubiety.

'Are you still asking that ridiculous price? After all, it's only a pastel.'

'Pastel is Vuillard's medium,' Leuschner replied, with calm authority. 'And I assure you, sir, this one is worth every centime of the price. Why, when you consider the other day in London a few rough brush strokes by Renoir, some half-dozen wretched-looking strawberries, a pitiful thing, really, of which the master must have been heartily ashamed, brought twenty thousand pounds. . . . But this, this is a gem, worthy of your fine collection, and you know how rare *good* Post-Impressionists have become, yet I ask only nineteen thousand dollars. If you buy it, and I do not press you, for practically it is almost sold, you will never regret it.'

There was a silence. For the first time they both looked at the pastel which hung alone, against the neutral cartridge paper of the wall. Moray knew it well, it was recorded in the book and it was indeed a lovely thing – an interior, full of light and colour, pinks, greys and greens. The subject too, was exactly to his taste: a conversation piece, Madame Melo and her little daughter in the salon of the actress's house.

A surge of possessive craving tightened his throat. He must have it, he must, to hang opposite his Sisley. It was a shocking price, of course, but he could well afford it, he was rich, far richer even than the good Leuschner had computed, having of course no access to that little black book, locked in the safe, with its fascinating rows of ciphers. And why, after all those years of sterile work and marital strife, should he not have everything he wanted? That snug profit he had recently made in Royal Dutch could not be put to better use. He wrote the cheque, shook hands

13

with Leuschner and went off in triumph, with the pastel carefully tucked beneath his arm. Back at his villa, before Arturo announced lunch, he had time to hang it. Perfect . . . perfect . . . he exulted, standing back. He hoped Frida von Altishofer would admire it.

CHAPTER II

HE HAD INVITED her for five o'clock and, as punctuality was to her an expression of good manners, at that hour precisely she arrived – not however as was customary, in her battered little cream-coloured Dauphine, but on foot. Actually her barracks of a house, the Schloss Seeburg, stood on the opposite shore of the lake, two kilometres across, and as she came into the drawing-room he reproached her for taking the boat, holding both her hands. It was a warm afternoon and the hill path to his villa was steep; he could have sent Arturo to fetch her.

'I don't mind the little ferry.' She smiled. 'As you were so kindly driving me I thought not to bother with my car.'

Her English, though stylised, was perfectly good, with just a faint, and indeed attractive, over-accentuation of certain syllables.

'Well, now you shall have tea. I have ordered it.' He pressed the bell. 'We'll get nothing but watery vermouth at the party.'

'You are most thoughtful.' She sat down gracefully, removing her gloves; she had strong supple fingers, the nails polished but unvarnished. 'I hope you won't be too bored at the Kunsthaus.'

While Arturo wheeled in the trolley and, with bows that were almost genuflections, served the tea, Moray studied her. In her youth she must have been very beautiful. The structure of her facial bones was perfect. Even now at forty-five, or six . . . well, perhaps even forty-seven, although her hair was greying and her skin beginning to show the faint crenellations and brownish stigmata of her years, she remained an attractive woman, with the upright striding figure of a believer in fresh air and exercise. Her eyes were her most remarkable feature, the pupils of a dark tawny yellowish green shot with black specks. 'They are cat's eyes.' She had smiled once when he ventured a compliment. 'But I do not scratch . . . or seldom only.'

Yes, he reflected sympathetically, she had been through a lot, yet never spoke of it. She was horribly hard up and had not many clothes but those she possessed were good and she wore them

15

with style. When they went walking together she usually appeared in a faded costume of russet brown, a rakish *bersagliere* hat, white knitted stockings and strong handsewn brogues of faded brown. Today she had on a simple but well cut fawn suit, shoes of the same shade, as were her gloves, and she was bareheaded. Taste, distinction, and perfect breeding were evident in every look and gesture – no need to tell himself again, she was a cultured woman of the highest class.

'Always what delicious tea you give me.'

'It's Twining's,' he explained. 'I had it specially blended for the hard Schwansee water.'

She shook her head, half reproachfully.

'Really . . . you think of everything.' She paused. 'Yet how wonderful to be able to give effect to all one's wishes.'

A considerable silence followed while they savoured the hardwater tea, then suddenly, an upward glance arrested, she exclaimed:

'My dear friend . . . you have bought it!'

She had seen the Vuillard at last and rising, excitedly, though still skilfully, retaining cup and saucer, she moved across the room to inspect it.

'It is lovely . . . lovely! And looks so much better here than in the gallery. Oh, that so delightful child, on the little stool. I only hope Leuschner did not rob you.'

He stood beside her and together, in silence, they admired the pastel. She had the good taste not to over-praise, but as they turned away, looking around her at the mellow eighteenth-century furniture, the soft grey carpet and the Louis XVI tapestry chairs, at his paintings, his *Pont Aven* Gauguin, signed and dated, above the T'ang figures on the Georgian mantel, the wonderful Degas nude on the opposite wall, the early Utrillo and the Sisley landscape, his richly subdued Bonnard, the deliciously maternal Mary Cassat, and now the Vuillard, she murmured:

'I adore your room. Here you can spend your life in the celebration of beautiful things. And better still when you have earned them.'

'I think I am entitled to them.' He spoke modestly. 'As a young man, in Scotland, I had little enough. Indeed, then I was miserably poor.'

It was a mistake. Once he had spoken the words he regretted

16

them. Had he not been warned never to look back, only forward, forward, forward. Hastily he said:

'But you . . . until the war, you always lived . . .' he fumbled slightly, '. . . in state.'

'Yes, we had nice things,' she answered mildly.

Again there was silence. The half-smiling reserve she had given to the remark was truly heroic. She was the widow of the Baron von Altishofer, who came of an old Jewish family that had acquired immense wealth from state tobacco concessions in the previous century, with possessions ranging from a vast estate in Bavaria to a hunting lodge in Slovakia. He had been shot during the first six months of the war and, although she was not of his faith, she had spent the next three years in a concentration camp at Lensbach. On her eventual release, she had crossed the Swiss border. All that remained to her was the lakeside house, the Seeburg, and there, though practically penniless, she had striven courageously to rebuild her life. She began by breeding rare Weimaraner dogs. Then, while the ignominy of an ordinary pensionnat was naturally unthinkable, friends – and she had many – came to stay and to enjoy, as paying guests, the spaciousness of the big Germanic schloss and the huge overgrown garden. Indeed, a very exclusive little society had now developed round the Seeburg, of which she herself was the centre. What fun to restore the fine old place, fill it with furniture of the period, replant the garden, recondition the statuary. Had she hinted? Never, never . . . it was his own thought, a flight of fancy. Selfconsciously, rather abruptly, he looked at his watch.

'I think we should be going, if you are ready.'

He had decided to take her to the party in full fig: Arturo wore his best blue uniform, a lighter shade than navy, and they went in the big car. Since this was the only Rolls in Melsburg its appearance always made something of a spectacle.

Seated beside her, as they glided off, his sleeve touching hers on the cushioned armrest, he was in an expansive mood. Although his marriage had been a catastrophic failure he had, since his retirement, seriously considered the prospect of – in Wilenski's vulgar phrase – *having another go*. During the eighteen months they had been neighbours their friendship had developed to such an extent as to induce gradually the idea of a closer companionship. Yet his mind had hitherto dwelt on young and tender images. Frida von Altishofer was not young, in bed she

17

would not prove so succulent as he might wish, and as a man in whom the intensive demands of his late wife had induced a prostatic hypertrophy, he now had needs that should, if only for reasons of health, be satisfied. Nevertheless, Frida was a strong and vital woman with deep though concealed feelings, who might be capable of unsuspected passion. Such, he knew from his medical training, was often the case with women who had passed the menopause. Certainly, in all other respects she would make the most admirable aristocratic wife.

But now they were in the town and sweeping round the public garden with its high central fountain. Arturo drew up, was out in a flash to remove his uniform cap and open the car door. They mounted the steps towards the Kunsthaus.

'Some of my friends in the diplomatic corps may have come up from Bern for this affair. If it wouldn't bore you, you might care to meet them.'

He was deeply pleased. Although not a snob – good heavens, no! – he liked meeting 'the right people'.

'You are charming, Frida,' he murmured, with a sudden quick intimate glance.

CHAPTER III

THE PARTY HAD been in progress for some time: the long hall was filled with noise and crushed human forms. Most of the notables of the canton were there, with many worthy burghers of Melsburg and those of the Festival artistes who had performed during the final week. These, alas, were mainly of the old brigade since, unlike the larger resorts of Montreux and Lucerne, Melsburg was not rich, and between sentiment and lack of funds, the committee fell back year after year upon familiar names and faces. Through the haze of cigarette smoke Moray made out the aged and decrepit figure of Flackmeister, who could barely totter to the podium, held together by his tight dress coat, green with the sweat of years beneath the arm holes. And over there stood Tuberose, the 'cellist, thin, tall as a beanpole, and, through long clasping of his instrument, very gone about the knees. He was talking to the superbly bosomed English contralto, Amy Rivers Fox-Finden. Well, it made no odds, Moray reflected, gaily edging his way into the crush with his companion, the applause at the concerts was always rapturous and prolonged, reminding him, much as he loved his neighbours, of row upon row of happy sheep flapping their front legs together.

They were served with a beverage of no known species, tepid, and swimming with fragments of melting ice. She did not drink hers, merely met his eye in a humorous communicative side glance which plainly said, 'How wise you were, and how glad I am of your delicious tea' – almost, indeed, 'and of you!' Then, with a gentle pressure of the elbow, she steered him across the room, introduced him first to the German, then to the Austrian minister. He did not fail to observe the affectionate respect with which each greeted her, nor her poise in turning away their compliments. As they moved off Moray was hailed exuberantly across the press by a sporty British type, all amiable plastic dentures and alcoholic eyeballs, dressed in a double-breasted, brass-buttoned blue blazer, baggy fawn trousers and scuffed suede shoes.

'So nice to see you, dear boy,' Archie Stench boomed, waving a glass of actual whisky. 'Can't move now. Keep the flag flying. I'll be giving you a ring.'

His face clouding slightly, Moray gave a discouraging answering wave. He did not care for Stench, correspondent of the London *Daily Echo*, who also 'on the side' did a weekly social column for the local *Tageblatt* – airy little items, often with a sting in the tail. Several times Moray had been stung.

Fortunately they were near the far end of the big room where, by the wide bay window, a group of their own particular friends had gathered. Here were demure Madame Ludin of the Europa Hof and her delicate husband, standing with Doctor Alpenstück, grave addict of the higher altitudes. Tall, erect, a noted yodeller in his youth, the worthy doctor never missed a Festival. Beyond, beside the ugly Courtet sisters, at a round table from which, short-sightedly, she had cleared all the cocktail biscuits within reach, sat Gallie, the little old Russian Princess Galliatine, who was stone deaf and rarely spoke a word but went everywhere to eat, even to remove food expertly in the large cracked handbag she always carried, bulging from over-use, and containing papers proving her relationship with the famous Prince Yussapov, husband of the Tsar's niece. A pale, limp little creature with a straggle of worn sable on her neck, whatever the past had done to her it had given her a smile of docile sweetness. Not altogether presentable perhaps – still, an authentic princess. A rather different figure occupied the centre of the group, Leonora Schutz-Spengler, and as they drew near Madame von Altishofer murmured humorously:

'We shall hear the full story of Leonora's hunting trip.'

Pausing in the act of narration, Leonora had already acknowledged them with a brilliant smile. She was a vivacious little brunette from the Tessin, with a red laughing mouth, enterprising eyes and pretty teeth, who some years before had nibbled her way into the heart of Herman Schutz, the richest cheese exporter in Switzerland, a large, pallid, heavy man who seemed fashioned from his own product. Yet Leonora was herself worthy of affection, if only for her splendid and amusing parties, junketings which took place at her hilltop villa above the town, in a candle-lit, red wood outbuilding, the walls bristling with contorted

20

mammalian horns, amongst which scores of budgerigars flew, fluttered, perched and twittered while Leonora, wearing a paper hat, prodigally dispensed bortsch, melon soup, goulash, caviar, cheese blintzes, Pekin duck, truffles in port wine, and other exotic foods; before initiating wild and improbable games, all produced out of her own head.

Moray seldom gave much heed to Leonora's excited ramblings, and his thoughts wandered as, speaking in French, she went on describing the trip from which she and her husband had just returned. Vaguely Moray had heard that Schutz, who late in life had developed ambitions as a *jäger*, was renting a shoot, somewhere in Hungary he believed.

Nevertheless, as Leonora irrepressibly continued, his ear was caught by certain phrases, and with a sharp tightening of his nerves, he began to listen with attention. She was not speaking of Hungary but describing a stretch of Highland countryside in terms which suddenly seemed to him familiar. Impossible: he must be mistaken. Yet as she proceeded, his strained suspicion grew. Now she was speaking of the road uphill from the estuary, of the view of the moor from the summit, the river rushing between the high walls of the corrie into the loch, the mountain dominating all. Suddenly he felt himself tremble, his heart turned over and began to beat rapidly. God, could he ever have imagined this turning up again, so unexpectedly. For she had named the mountain, and the river, and the loch, she named lastly the moor her husband had rented, and these utterly unforeseen words sent a painful shock of shame and apprehension through all his body.

Someone was asking her:

'How did you reach this outlandish place?'

'We went by the most fantastic railway – one narrow line, three trains a day – to an adorable little station with such a pretty name. They call it . . .'

He couldn't bear to hear that name, yet he did hear it, and it brought back, though unspoken, the last unavoidable name of all. He turned, muttering some excuse, and moved off, only to discover Stench good-naturedly at his elbow.

'Not going already, dear boy? Or can't you stand the weirdies any longer?'

Somehow he brushed him aside. In the foyer a draught of cool air revived him, brought some order to his confused mind. He mustn't rush off like this, leaving Madame von Altishofer to return alone. He must wait, find a less crowded place – over there, beside that pillar, near the door. He hoped she would not stay long. Indeed, even as he moved to take up his new position she was beside him.

'My dear friend, you are ill.' She spoke with concern. 'I saw you turn quite pale.'

'I did feel rather queer.' With an effort he forced a smile. 'It's fearfully warm in there.'

'Then we shall go at once,' she said decisively.

He made as if to protest, then dropped it. Outside, Arturo stood talking with a group of chauffeurs. They drove off. She wished to take him directly to his villa but, less from politeness than from a desperate need to be alone, he insisted on leaving her at the Seeburg.

'Come in for a drink,' she suggested, as they arrived. 'A real one.' And when he refused, saying that he should rest, she added solicitously: 'Do take care, my friend. If I may, I will telephone you tomorrow.'

At the villa he lay down for an hour, trying to reason with himself. He must not allow a chance word, a mere coincidence, to wreck the serenity he had so carefully built up. Yet it was no chance word, it was a word that had lain hauntingly, tormentingly in the depths of memory for many years. He must fight it, beat it down again into the darkness of the subconscious. He could not do it, could not seal his mind against the buffeting of his thoughts. At dinner he made only a pretence of eating; his depression filled the house, affecting even the servants, who saw in this unusual mood something reflecting upon themselves.

After the meal he went into the drawing-room, stood by the window opening on the terrace. He saw that a storm was about to break, one of those swift, dazzling exhibitions when, shouting to Arturo to put on a Berlioz record, he would watch and listen with a sense of sheer exhilaration. Now, however, he stood moodily viewing the great mass of umbered cloud which had been gathering, unperceived, drifting above the Riesenberg. The air was deadly still, sultry with silence, the light unnatural; a brooding ochre. And now there came a sighing, faint, as from a distance. The leaves trembled and on the flat surface of the lake a ripple passed. Slowly the sky darkened to dull impenetrable lead, masking the mountain, and all at once from the unseen a fork of blue flashed out, followed by the first crashing detonation. Then came the wind, sudden, searing, a circular wind that cut like a whiplash. Under it, with a shudder, the trees bent and grovelled, scattering leaves like chaff. At the garden end the tall twin poplars scourged the earth. The lake, churned into spume, writhed like a mad thing, waves lashed the little pier, the yellow flag swung up. Lightning now played incessantly, the thunder echoing and re-echoing amongst the hidden peaks. And then the rain, large, solitary, speculative drops, not soothing rain, but rain warning, ominous of what at last struck from above, straight sheets of hissing water, a flooding from the sky – the eventual deluge.

Abruptly he turned from the window and went upstairs to his bedroom, more agitated than ever. In the medicine cupboard in his bathroom he found the bottle of phenobarbitone. He had imagined he would never need it again. He took four tablets. Even so he knew he would not sleep. When he had undressed, he threw himself upon the bed and closed his eyes. Outside the rain still lashed the terrace, the waves still broke upon the shore, but it was her name that kept sounding, sounding in his ears ... Mary ... Mary Douglas ... Mary ... Douglas ... bringing him back through the years, to Craigdoran and the days of his youth.

PART TWO

CHAPTER I

IF BRYCE'S ANCIENT motor-cycle had not broken down they would never have met. But as though fated, on that dusty April Saturday afternoon, when he swung back from a spin round the Doran Hills, the driving belt of the near-derelict machine disintegrated, a flying fragment whipping sharp across his right knee. He skidded to a stop, got off stiffly and inspected the damage to his leg, which was less than he had feared, then looked about him. No promise of assistance in the surrounding unpopulated, bracken-covered hills, the wild rush of the river Doran, the wide stretch of moorland threaded by this lonely road and the narrow single-track railway. Even the small station known as Craigdoran Halt, which he had just passed, seemed deserted.

'Damn,' he exclaimed – it couldn't have been more awkward. Ardfillan, the nearest town, must be at least seven miles away; he would have to try the Halt.

Turning, he pushed and limped uphill to the solitary platform, drew the heavy bike back on its stand. The little station was embellished with a border of whitewashed stones, its proud sign 'Gateway to the West Highlands' showered with trailing honeysuckle, a hawthorn hedge shedding blossoms on the track, but he was in no mood to admire. Not a soul in sight, the waiting-room locked, the booking-office closed as for eternity. He was on the point of giving up when in the frosted glass ornamental window stencilled with the words 'Refreshment Room' he caught signs of life: on the inner window-sill a black cat was contentedly washing its face. He pushed on the door, it opened, and he went in.

Unlike the usual station buffet, this was unexpectedly well-ordered and arranged. Four round marble-topped tables occupied the scrubbed boards, there were coloured views of the Highlands upon the walls and, at the far end, a polished mahogany counter behind which hung an oval mirror advertising Brown and Polson's self-raising flour. Before the mirror a young woman was standing with her back towards him, surprised in the act of

27

putting on her hat. Mutually arrested, immobile as waxwork figures, they gazed at each other in the glass.

'When is the next train for Winton?' He broke the silence, addressing her reflection in a tone which failed to conceal his annoyance.

'The last train's gone. There's nothing now till the Sunday-breaker.' She turned and faced him, adding mildly: 'Two o'clock tomorrow afternoon.'

'Where's the porter then?'

'Oh, Dougal's away home this good half hour. Did you not meet him on the road?'

'No . . . I didn't . . .'. He suddenly felt stupidly faint and leaned sideways to support himself against a table, a movement which brought his injured leg into view.

'You've hurt yourself!' she exclaimed, coming forward quickly. 'Here now, sit down and let me see it.'

'It's nothing,' he said, rather dizzily, finding his way to a chair. 'Superficial laceration of the popliteal area. The motor-cycle . . .'

'I thought I heard a bit of a bang. It's a nasty gash, too. Why didn't you speak up at once?'

She was hurrying to get hot water, and presently, kneeling, she had bathed and cleaned the wound and bound it neatly with strips of torn-up napkin.

'There!' On a note of accomplishment she rose. 'If only I had a needle and thread I could stitch up your trouser leg. Never mind, you'll get it done when you're home. What you could do with now is a good cup of tea.'

'No . . . really . . .', he protested. 'I've been a complete nuisance. . . . You've done more than enough for me.'

But she was already busy with the taps of the metal urn on the counter. He had undoubtedly had a shake, and the hot strong tea made him feel better. Watching him with interested curiosity she sat down. Immediately the cat jumped into her lap and began to purr. She stroked it gently.

'Lucky Darkie and me weren't away. There's few enough folks around Craigdoran this early in the year.'

'Or at any other time?' He half smiled.

'No,' she corrected him seriously. 'When the fishing and shooting are on we have a wheen of fine customers. That's why my father keeps this place on. Our bakery is in Ardfillan. If you like we could give you a lift there. He always fetches me at the week-

28

end.' She paused thoughtfully. 'Of course, there's your bike. Is it badly smashed?'

'Not too badly. But I'll have to leave it here. If they'd put it on the Winton train it would be a big help. You see, it's not mine. It belongs to a fellow at the hospital.'

'I don't see why Dougal couldn't slip it in the guard's van as a favour. I'll speak to him first thing Monday. But if your friend's in the hospital he'll not be needing it for a while.'

Amused at her conclusion he explained:

'He's not a patient. A final year medical student, like me.'

'So that's it.' She laughed outright. 'If I'd known I wouldn't have been so gleg at the bandaging.'

Her laughter was infectious, natural, altogether delightful. There was something warm about it, and about her, due not only to her colouring – she had reddish brown hair with gold lights in it and soft brown eyes, dark as peat, set in a fair, slightly freckled skin – but to something sympathetic and outgiving in her nature. She was perhaps four years younger than himself, not more than nineteen, he guessed, and while she was not tall, her sturdy little figure was trim and well proportioned. She wore a tartan skirt, belted with patent leather at the waist, a home-knitted grey spencer, smart well-worn brown brogues, and a little grey hat with a curlew's feather in the brim.

A sudden awareness of her kindness swept over Moray, for him a rare emotion. Yes, she had been decent – that was the word – damned decent to him. And, forgetting the nagging discomfort of his knee and the greater calamity of the damage to his only suit, he smiled at her, this time his own frank, winning smile, that smile which had so often served him through hard and difficult years. Although he had a good brow, regular features, and a fresh skin, with fine light brown naturally wavy hair, he was not particularly good-looking in the accepted sense of the word; the lower part of his face lacked strength. Yet the smile redeemed all his defects, lit up his face, invited comradeship, was filled with promise, expressed interest, understanding and concern at will, and above all radiated sincerity.

'I suppose you realise,' he explained, 'how grateful I am for your extreme kindness. As you've practically saved my life, may I hope that we'll be friends? My name is Moray – David Moray.'

'And I'm Mary Douglas.'

A touch of colour had come into her cheeks but she was not

29

displeased by this frank introduction. She took the hand he held out to her in a firm clasp.

'Well now,' she said briskly, 'if you like to wheel your bike in here I'll take Darkie and lock up. Father'll be here any minute.'

Indeed, they had barely reached the road outside when a pony and trap appeared over the brow of the hill. Mary's father, to whom Moray was introduced, with the full circumstances of his mishap, was a slight little man with a pale, perky face, hands and nails permanently ingrained with flour, and the bad teeth of his trade. A wisp of hair standing up from his forehead and small, very bright brown eyes gave him an odd, bird-like air.

After turning the pony with practised clickings of his tongue, and studying Moray with shrewd, sidelong glances, he summed up Mary's recital.

'I've no use for these machines myself, as ye may observe. I keep Sammy, the pony, for odd jobs, and I've a good steady Clydesdale to draw my bread van. But it might have been worse. We'll see ye safe on the eight o'clock train from Ardfillan. In the meantime, ye maun just come back and have a bite with us.'

'I couldn't possibly impose on you any more.'

'Don't be ridiculous,' Mary said. 'You've got to meet the rest of the Douglases – and Walter, my fiancé. I'm sure he'll be delighted to get acquainted with you. That's to say,' as a thought occurred to her, 'if your folks won't be anxious about you.'

Moray smiled and shook his head.

'No need to worry. I'm quite on my own.'

'On your own?' Douglas inquired.

'I lost both my parents when I was very young.'

'But ye've got relations, surely?'

'None that I have any need of, or that ever wanted me.' The baker's look of sheer incredulity deepened Moray's smile, caused him to offer a frank explanation. 'I've been alone since I was sixteen. But I've managed to put myself through college one way and another, and by being lucky enough to win an odd bursary or so.'

'Dear me,' reflected the little baker, quietly but with real admiration. 'That's a maist commendable achievement.'

He seemed to ponder the matter as they jogged along. Then, straightening himself, he began with increased cordiality to point out and describe the features of the countryside, many of which, he asserted, were associated with the events of 1314 that preceded the battle of Bannockburn.

'Father's a great reader of Scots history,' Mary confided to Moray in apology. 'There's few quirky things he can't tell you about Bruce, or Wallace, or the rest of them.'

They were now approaching Ardfillan and Douglas drew on the shoe brake to ease the pony as they came down the hill towards the old town lying beneath on the shore of the Firth, shimmering in the hazy sunset. Avoiding the Esplanade, they entered a network of quiet back streets and pulled up before a single-fronted shop with the sign in faded gilt: *James Douglas, Baker and Confectioner*; and beneath, in smaller letters: *Marriages Purveyed*; and again, smaller still: *Established 1880*. The place indeed wore an old-fashioned air, and one that seemed scarcely prosperous, since the window displayed no more than a many-tiered model of a wedding cake, flanked by a pair of glass urns containing sugar biscuits.

Meanwhile the baker had sheathed his whip. He shouted:

'Willie!'

A bright young boy in an oversized apron that reached from heel to chin ran out of the shop.

'Tell your aunt we're back, son; then skep round and give me a hand with Sammy.'

With considerable skill Douglas backed the pony through the adjacent narrow pend into a cobbled stable yard.

'Here we are then,' he announced cheerfully. 'Take your invalid upstairs, Mary. I'll be with ye the now.'

They went up by a shallow curving flight of outside stone steps to the house above the shop, where a narrow lobby gave entrance to the front parlour, furnished in worn red plush with tasselled curtains of the same material. In the centre of the room a heavy mahogany table was already set for high tea, and a coal fire glowed comfortably in the grate, before which a black sheepskin rug spread a cosy, tangled pelt. Darkie, released from Mary's arms, immediately took possession of it. She had taken off her spencer, now seemed at home in her neat white blouse.

'Sit down and rest your leg. I'll run down for a wee minute and see to things. We close at six this evening.' She added, with a touch of pride: 'Father doesn't go in for the Saturday night trade.'

When she had gone Moray eased himself into a chair, acutely

aware of the strangeness of this dim, warm, alien room. A coal dropped quietly to the hearth. From a dark corner came the measured tick-tock of a grandfather clock, unseen but for the glint of firelight on its old brass dial. The blue willow-pattern cups on the table caught the light too. Why on earth was he here, rather than bent strainingly over Osler and Cunningham in the cramped attic that was his lodging? He had taken a spin to clear his head – his one practical concession to leisure – before settling down to a long weekend grind. But with his final examination only five weeks away it was lunacy to waste time here, in this unprofitable manner. And yet, these people were so hospitable, and the food on the table looked so damned inviting. With his money running out it was weeks since he had eaten a proper square meal.

The door opened suddenly and Mary was back, carrying a tea tray and accompanied by a stout, dropsical-looking woman and a tall, thin man of about twenty-six or seven, very correct in a dark blue suit and high stiff collar.

'Here's some more of us,' Mary laughed. 'Aunt Minnie and,' she blushed slightly, 'my intended, Mr Walter Stoddart.'

As she spoke her father appeared with the boy, Willie, and after the baker had muttered a quick grace, they all sat down at table.

'I am led to believe,' Stoddart, who, while Mary poured the tea, had been served first with cold ham and great deference by Aunt Minnie, now addressed himself to Moray with a polite smile, 'that you have had a somewhat trying experience. I myself had a somewhat similar adventure on the Luss road when a boy. When was it now, let me see, ah, yes, in nineteen oh nine, that hot summer we had. I was just thirteen years of age and growing fast. A push bicycle, naturally, in that era, and a punctured tyre. Fortunately I sustained nothing more serious than an abrasion of the left elbow, though it might well have been a tragedy. May I trouble you for another sugar, Mary. You know, I think, that my preference is for three lumps.'

'Oh, I'm sorry, Walter dear.'

Stoddart, evidently, was regarded, not only by himself, but by the family, as a person of definite importance. And presently Aunt Minnie, who seemed his chief admirer, conveyed to Moray in a whispered, wheezy aside that Walter was the Town Clerk's son, with a splendid position in the accounts department of the

Gas Department – a real catch for Mary, she supplemented with a meaning, satisfied nod.

The situation intrigued Moray, provoked his sense of humour. Walter's excruciating mannerisms, his condescension towards the Douglases exercised with all the stiff assertiveness of the small-town bureaucrat, even the ostrich-like convulsion of his long thin neck when he drank his tea – all these gave promise of entertainment. While doing full justice to the good things on the table, it amused him to cultivate Stoddart, playing a little on his vanity, and at the same time defining his own position, as co-equal, by relating, in a racy style, some of the more interesting aspects of his work in the out-patient's department of the Infirmary. It was not long before he was rewarded by indications of Walter's growing esteem. Indeed as the meal drew to its close, Stoddart took out his gold watch and clicked it open – this was another and frequent mannerism – meanwhile favouring Moray with a toothy smile.

'It's a great pity I am obliged to leave you so soon. I'm escorting Mary to the Band of Hope Social. Otherwise I should have been delighted to have more of your company. However, I have a suggestion. I am of the opinion that it would be highly irregular for you to convey your motor-cycle to Winton without a ticket, sub rosa, as the saying is, in the manner indicated to me by Mary. It might expose you to all sorts of pains and penalties. After all, the North British Railway does not frame its code of by-laws for fun! Huh, huh! Now what I propose,' he smiled hospitably around the table, 'is that our friend Moray secure the spare part in Winton, travel down next weekend, fit the part, and drive the machine back. This, naturally, will afford us the opportunity of meeting with him again.'

'What a good idea,' Mary glowed. 'Why on earth didn't we think of it.'

'*We*, Mary?' queried Walter, repocketing the watch with dignity. 'I fancy that I . . .'.

'Ay, ye're a knowledgeable chap, Walter. I don't know what we'd do without ye,' interposed the little baker, glancing towards Moray with an ironic twinkle, which indicated that he did not altogether subscribe to the prevailing view of Stoddart's accomplishments. 'Come by all means, lad. Ye'll be verra welcome.'

It was settled, then, and when Mary rose to put on her hat and coat and, accepting the invitation of Walter's crooked arm, was led off by him to the Church Social, she smiled at Moray over her shoulder.

'We'll see you next Saturday, so I won't say goodbye.'

'Nor will I.' Walter bowed. 'I hope to have the pleasure of your further acquaintance.'

Half an hour later Moray left for the station. Willie, who had listened with bright eyes to his stories of the hospital, insisted on accompanying him.

CHAPTER II

MORAY'S LODGING was a small room at the top of a back-to-back tenement near the Blairlaw Docks. The neighbourhood, shut in by a disused city dump known locally as the Tipps, was undoubtedly one of the poorest in Winton. Ragged, rickety children played on the broken, chalk-marked pavements while the women stood gossiping, in shawl and cap, outside the 'close-mouths'. On every street there was a pub or a fish-and-chip shop, while, through the Clydeside fog, the three brass balls of the pawnbroker beckoned irresistibly. Tugs hooted from the river and incessant hammering came from the repair yards. The district was certainly not a pleasure resort, but by cutting over Blairhill into Eldongrove it was within reasonable walking distance of the University and the Western Infirmary. Above all, it was cheap.

The brief though striking account Moray had given Baker Douglas of himself was thus, in some respects, though not in all, the truth. The first twelve years of his life, as an only child of indulgent middle-class parents, had been normal; never affluent, but easy and comfortable. Then his father, local agent of the Caledonia Insurance Company in Overton, had come down with i fluenza, contracted, it was thought, during his door-to-door collections. For a week his wife nursed him while he grew worse. A specialist was called in, and abruptly the diagnosis was altered to typhoid fever, but not before she, too, had contracted the disease. Within the month David found himself thrown upon a distant relative, the widowed half-sister of his mother, a burden accepted unwillingly, an unwanted child. For four years young Moray had undoubtedly suffered neglect, eaten the bitter bread of dependence, but at the age of sixteen an educational policy, prudently taken out by his father, had come into force. It was not much, sufficient only for fees, and a bare subsistence, but it was enough and, helped by a sympathetic schoolmaster who recognised unusual possibilities in his pupil, he had entered for the medical curriculum of Winton University.

But this providential provision was something which Moray, from motives of expediency, or a natural tendency to dramatise his own efforts, sometimes conveniently forgot. With his diffident charm that made most people take to him on sight, it was agreeable, and often helpful, to hint at the tight corners he had been in, the shifts and evasions he had been forced into, the indignities he had endured – shaking the fleas from his trouser ends, using the public convenience on the stair-head, washing his own shirt, eating chips from a greasy newspaper, sustained only by a heroic determination to raise himself out of the ruck and attain the heights.

Admittedly there had been diversions, occasional meals at the home of his friend Bryce, or, through the kindness of one of the Infirmary staff, a free theatre or concert ticket would come his way; and once, in the summer vacation, he had spent an exceptional week at the seaside house of his biology professor. Certainly he had made the most of his opportunities, not only by the profusion of his gratitude when anything was done for him but by a particular earnestness of manner, quite touching, that inspired confidence and affection. 'So good of you to give me a leg-up, sir,' or, 'Jolly decent of you, old chap.' With that modest, self-disparaging expression and those clear, frank eyes, who could help liking him? He was so absolutely sincere. The truth is that, when he was in the mood, he believed everything he said.

But entertainments are never a conspicuous feature of Scottish universities and in recent months they had been few. For this reason alone his encounter with the Douglas family held the attraction of the unusual. During the week, while he attended the Infirmary by day and studied late at night, it remained agreeably at the back of his mind. He found himself looking forward to his visit on the following Saturday.

The morning came grey but fine. After attending out-patients in the forenoon, he took the one o'clock 'workman's special' from Winton Central. This was a low-fare train – the price of the ticket, unbelievably, was fourpence – which ran down the Clyde estuary, serving the shipyard workers en route. He had the new belt with him – Bryce, anticipating trouble, had actually bought it as a spare some weeks before, and had willingly turned it over to him in his easy-going style. At Levenford Junction he changed to the single line, and just after half-past two, as the sun was

36

breaking through the clouds, drew into Craigdoran.

The little white station with its flowering hawthorn and tangle of climbing honeysuckle now wore a familiar aspect. The scent of the honeysuckle filled the air and he heard the hum of an early bee. Two youths, dressed for climbing, with packs on their backs, got out of the train before him. They went into the refreshment room where, peering through the ground-glass window, he saw Mary wrap in waxed paper the sandwiches they bought. Then the youths came out and Mary, following them to the door, looked searchingly along the platform.

'It's you.' She smiled. 'I was beginning to be afraid you'd not come. Is your knee better?'

She beckoned him in, made him sit down. The cat approached and rubbed against his leg.

'I'm sure you've not had your lunch. I'll fetch you some sandwiches and a glass of milk.'

'Please don't,' he said. 'I've had a snack . . . in the . . . the buffet at Levenford Junction.'

'Dear me,' she said quizzically, rather like her father, raising her brows. 'That's extraordinar' peculiar. There never has been a buffet at the Junction.' From the glass bell on the counter she took a plate of sandwiches, then poured a frothing glass of milk. 'There'll be scarcely another soul in here over the weekend and I can't see good food go to waste. You'll just have to oblige me, this once.'

A moment later she seated herself opposite him, struggling, it seemed, against some inner effervescence which grew suddenly beyond control.

'I have news for you,' she exclaimed. 'You've made a most tremendous hit.'

'What!' He drew back, misunderstanding her.

'Walter,' her lips twitched, 'has taken the greatest notion of you. Ever since you left he's done nothing but sing your praises. You're such a nice young fellow.' She fought down laughter. 'He's quite cut up at missing you tonight – he's attending a meeting of the Municipal Officials' Guild in Winton – and I'm to give you his best regrets.' She went on before he could speak. 'He's fixed up a rare jaunt for us tomorrow. We're to sail round the Kyles of Bute, stop for lunch at Gairsay, then back home.'

He stared at her with a blank frown.

'But I can't possibly come down again tomorrow.'

'No need to,' she said calmly. 'Father says you're to stay over with us. You can sleep with our Willie.'

Still he frowned at her; then, gradually, his brow cleared. Never had he met such simple, open-hearted people. He had no out-patients at the Infirmary tomorrow, and surely would not lose much by missing just one day's work. Besides, Sunday in Winton was an unspeakable day which he had always loathed.

'You'll come?' she queried.

'With pleasure. And now I must mend the bike.'

'It's in the left luggage. Dougal put it there out of the way.'

For the next hour he worked, fitting the new belt, which had to be cut and riveted. She came in occasionally to watch, not saying anything, just watching companionably. When he had finished he wheeled out the machine and started it up.

'How about a spin?'

She looked at him doubtfully, a hand on her ear against the frantic blast of the exhaust.

'It's quite safe,' he reassured her. 'You just sit on the carrier and hold tight.'

'I can't get away till the four-thirty comes in. But afterwards, maybe you could take me home. I could ring up Father from the booking office and spare him coming out.'

'That's settled then,' he said gaily.

An unusual mood of lightheartedness took possession of him. Whether due to his escape from work, or the fresh green country-side, he felt lifted up, as though breathing a rarer, brighter air. Until she should be free, and to test the machine, he took a fast run over the hill to Tulliehewan. When he returned, she was all ready to leave. Since Darkie must stay behind she had set out a saucer of milk for his supper.

'So this is where I get on,' she said, perching side-saddle on the carrier.

'You can't sit like that. You'll fall off. You must sit astride.'

She hesitated, then swung one leg across, modestly, yet so inexpertly that before he averted his eyes a sweet prospect was momentarily revealed to him. Blushing, she said:

'I'm not quite up to it yet.'

'You're doing famously.'

Quickly he got into the saddle and set off. At first he went slowly, carefully avoiding the bumps, then, as he felt her gain confidence, he opened the throttle. They tore along, over the moors, the wind whistling past their ears. Her arms were clasped round his waist, her head, turned sideways, was pressed against his shoulder.

'Are you all right?' he shouted.

'Fine,' she called back.

'Enjoying it?'

'It's . . . it's glorious. I've never gone so fast in all my life.'

They were doing at least thirty miles an hour.

When he pulled up at the shop in Ardfillan her cheeks were glowing, her hair blown and burnished by the breeze.

'What a treat.' She laughed into his eyes, swaying a trifle unsteadily, still drunk with speed. 'Come on up. I must run and tidy. I'm sure I'm a perfect sight.'

His welcome by the baker was cordial, and by Willie even more enthusiastic than before. The aunt, however, seemed to accept him with fresh reservations, her eye speculative, at times tending coldly towards suspicion – though he softened her later by listening attentively to her symptoms and suggesting a cordial that might help her shortness of breath. The meal she set before them was macaroni cheese, a wholesome repast though lacking, inevitably, in those refinements that had been produced for Walter. Thereafter the evening passed quietly. Moray played draughts with the baker and was handsomely beaten three times in a row, while Mary, on a low stool by the fireside, worked on a piece of crochet which was clearly intended for her trousseau. Watching it develop, he could not help wondering if it was an edging for a nightdress – a warm, indulgent thought, not lewd. From time to time she would look at the clock and remark, with sedate concern, wholly unlike the girl full of humour and high spirits who had whirled gaily through space with him only an hour ago: 'Walter will be at his meeting now.' And again: 'Surely he'll get a chance to give his speech. He wrote it all out so careful, and was so set on making it.' And finally: 'He should be on his way to the train by this time. I hope he remembered his overshoes, he's such a martyr to cold feet.'

They all retired early. In Willie's back room, which over-looked the yard, Moray had his first real talk with the boy, whose shyness had hitherto kept him silent. It appeared that as a school prize he had recently received an exciting book on David Livingstone, and soon they were in the wilds of Africa together, discovering Lake Nyanza, deploring the ravages of beri-beri and the tsetse fly. Moray had to answer a spate of eager questions, but at last he turned out the light and presently they were asleep.

CHAPTER III

NEXT MORNING WALTER arrived punctually at half-past nine, greeting Moray like an old friend, full of his success on the previous evening. Although a number of ill-bred bounders had left the hall before the conclusion of his address, he had spoken extremely well, and for a good three-quarters of an hour. Having fully earned this day of relaxation he was in the mood to enjoy it. Nothing had pleased him more, he added, than to organise the expedition.

This bumptious effusiveness puzzled Moray. Was there a streak of the woman in Walter or did he, as a man consistently rebuffed by his fellows, so lack male companionship that he fastened on to the first newcomer who came along? Perhaps the prestige of a future doctor attracted him, for he was patently a snob. Or it might be that through vanity he was simply bent on demonstrating his own importance to someone new to the town. With a shrug, Moray gave up.

Mary and her brother had been ready for some time and now they set out, Walter leading the party along the Esplanade towards the pier, obviously determined to do things in style. At the steamer booking office he demanded first-class return tickets, adding casually:

'Three and a half: the boy is under age.'

The booking clerk turned a practised eye on Willie.

'Four full fares,' he said.

'I believe I asked for three and a half.'

'Four,' said the clerk in a tired voice.

An argument then ensued, brief yet fierce on Walter's side, ending when Willie, interrogated by the clerk, truthfully gave his age, thus disqualifying himself from the reduced rate. Not a good start, thought Moray, ironically observing Walter slap down the extra coins with an injured air.

The little red-funnelled paddle-boat came spanking down river and alongside the pier. She was the *Lucy Ashton*. Walter, some-

41

what recovered, explained to Moray that all the North British boats were named after characters in Scott's novels, but he seemed disappointed that they were not to have the *Queen Alexandra*, the new two-funnelled Caledonian turbine; its absence seemed a slight impairment of his prestige.

The gangway was skilfully run out, they went on board, and, looking around, he selected seats in the stern. Then the paddles churned and they were off, across the sparkling estuary and out towards the open firth.

'Delightful, is it not?' Walter murmured, settling back. Things were going better now.

But it was fresh upon the water and before long it became apparent that the situation he had chosen was exposed.

'Don't you think it's a little breezy on this side, dear?' Mary ventured, after several minutes. Head inclined to the wind, she was holding on to her hat.

'Not a bit of it,' Walter answered curtly. 'I want to show Dr Moray all our local points of interest. This gives us an uninterrupted view.'

The view – undoubtedly unimpaired, since most of the other passengers were in the lee of the cabin – was quite lovely, perhaps the most beautiful in all the Western Highlands. But Walter, though complacently owning its charm with all the proprietorship of a cicerone, was more concerned with the commercial import of the towns which fringed the shore.

'That's Scourie over there.' He pointed. 'A thriving community. They put in a new gasholder last year. Twenty thousand cubic feet capacity. There's progress for you. And they have a new sewage disposal project up before the town council. My father knows the Provost. And across on the other side is Port Doran. Can you make out the municipal buildings behind that steeple . . .?'

They were all steadily getting colder. Even Willie had turned blue, and had departed, muttering that he was going to look at the engines. But Walter went remorselessly on. What a goddam bore, thought Moray, with his legs stretched out and hands in his pockets. Scarcely listening now, he was watching Mary who, though very silent, occasionally put in a dutiful word of support. He saw that her entire nature changed in the presence of her fiancé. Her sparkle died, all the fun went out of her, she became reserved, sealed up, conscientiously obedient, like a good pupil

42

in the presence of her teacher. She'll have a hell of a life with that fellow when they're married, he reflected absently – the wind and Walter's monologue were making him drowsy.

At last they threaded the Kyles, swung into Gairsay Bay, and manoeuvred to the pier. Willie, after a search, was retrieved from the warmth of the engine-room and they went ashore.

'This is nice,' breathed Mary, with relief.

The town, a popular resort, had an attractive and prosperous air: a circle of good shops on the front, the hotels mounting up on the wooded hill behind, moorland and mountain beyond.

'And now for lunch,' Walter exclaimed, in the manner of one who has something up his sleeve.

'Oh, yes,' Mary said cheerfully. 'Let's go to Lang's. There it is, quite handy.' She indicated a modest but promising-looking restaurant across the road.

'My dear,' Walter said, 'I wouldn't dream of taking Dr Moray to Lang's. Or you either, for that matter.'

'We always go there when we come with Father,' Willie remarked dourly. 'They have rare hot mutton pies. And Comrie's lemonade.'

'Yes, let's, Walter dear.'

He stilled her with a raised, gloved hand and calmly produced his *pièce de résistance* of the day.

'We are going to lunch at the Grand.'

'Oh, no, Walter. Not the Grand. It's so . . . so snobby . . . and expens . . .'.

Walter threw an intimate, confidential smile at Moray, as though to say, These women!

'It's the best,' he murmured. 'I have reserved a table in advance from my father's office.'

They began to climb the hill towards the Grand, which towered majestically, high above them. The footpath was long, through woods carpeted with bluebells, and steep, in parts excessively so. Occasionally between the trees they caught sight of expensive cars flashing upwards on the main driveway. Moray perceived that the ascent, which Stoddart led like a deerstalker, was tiring Mary. To allow her to rest he stopped and picked a little bunch of bluebells which he tied with a twist of dried grass. and handed to her.

'Exactly the colour of your dress.' He smiled.

At last they reached the summit and Walter, sweating, breath-

43

ing heavily, brought them on to the broad terrace of the hotel where a number of guests were seated in the sunshine. An immediate silence fell as the little party appeared, some curious stares were turned towards it, and someone laughed. The main entrance was on the opposite side of the hotel and Walter had some difficulty in finding the terrace door. But finally, after some wandering, they were in the rich, marble-pillared foyer and Stoddart, having asked directions from an imposing figure in a gold-braided uniform, led the way to the restaurant, a huge, overpowering affair done in white and gold with enormous crystal chandeliers and a rich red pile carpet.

It was absurdly early, only just gone twelve o'clock, and although the waiters were on duty, gathered in a group round the head waiter's desk talking amongst themselves, no one else was in the room.

'Yes, sir?'

The head waiter, a stout, red-faced man in striped trousers, white waistcoat and cutaway, detached himself and came dubiously forward.

'Lunch for three, and a boy,' Stoddart said.

'This way, please.'

His hooded eye had taken them in at a glance: he appeared to lead them off to a distant alcove in the rear, when Walter said pompously:

'I want a table by the window. I have a reservation in the name of the town clerk of Ardfillan.'

The major domo hesitated: he smells a tip, thought Moray satirically, and how wrong he is!

'By the window did you say, sir?'

'That table over there.'

'Sorry, sir. That table is specially reserved for Major Lindsay of Lochshiel and his party of young English gentlemen.'

'The one next it then.'

'That is Mr Menzies' table, sir. A resident. Still, as he rarely comes in before one fifteen, and you'll doubtless have finished by then. . . . If you care to have it . . . ?'

They were seated at Mr Menzies' table. The menu was handed to Walter. It was in Anglicised French.

'Potage à la Reine Alexandra,' he began, reading it through to them, slowly, remarking complacently, in conclusion:

'Nothing like French cooking. And five courses too.'

44

While they sat in solitary state the meal was served, rapidly, and with veiled insolence. It was atrocious, a typical Grand Hotel luncheon, but below the usual standard. First came a thick yellowish soup composed apparently of flour and tepid water; next, a bony fragment of fish which had probably travelled from Aberdeen to Gairsay by the long way through Billingsgate, a fact only partially concealed by a coating of glutinous pink sauce.

'It's not fresh, Mary,' Willie whispered, leaning towards her.

'Hush, dear,' she murmured, struggling with the bones, sitting very straight, her eyes on her plate. Moray saw that under her apparent calm she was suffering acutely. For himself, he did not, in his own phrase, care a tinker's curse – he was not personally involved – but strangely it worried him to see her hurt. He tried to think of something light and gay that would cheer her but it would not come to him. Across the table Walter was now chewing his way through the next course, a slab of stringy mutton served with tinned peas and potatoes which cut and tasted like soap.

The sweet was a chalky blancmange accompanied by tough prunes. The savoury, which followed swiftly, for now they were really being rushed, took the shape of a stiff, spectral sardine, emitting a kind of bluish radiance, and impaled on a strip of desiccated toast. Then, though it was not yet one o'clock and no other guests had as yet appeared, the bill was brought.

If Stoddart had paid this immediately and they had departed forthwith all would have been well. But by this time Walter, through his unfeeling hide, had become conscious of a sense of slight, scarcely to be tolerated by the son of the Ardfillan town clerk. Besides, he had an actuarial mind. He withdrew one of the pencils with which his waistcoat was invariably armed, and began to make calculations on the bill. As he did so a tall, rakish-looking, weatherbeaten man, grey-haired, with a clipped moustache, wearing a faded Black Watch kilt, strolled in from the bar. He was followed by three young men in rough tweeds who had all, Moray immediately perceived, had more than a few drinks. As they took possession of the adjoining table they were noisily discussing how they had fished a beat on the River Gair – apparently the property of the man in the kilt. One of the three, a flashy-looking article, with blond hair and a slack mouth, was rather less than sober, and as he sat down his eye fell on Mary.

Turning, he lolled over the back of his chair, began ogling her while the waiter served their first course, then, with a nudge and a wink, diverted the attention of his companions.

'There's a nice little Scotch trout, Lindsay. Better than anything you landed this morning.'

There was a general laugh as the other two turned to stare at Mary.

'Come now, get on with your soup,' said Lindsay.

'Oh, hang the soup. Let's have the little lady over to our table. She doesn't seem too happy with her Scotch uncle. What do you say, chaps? Shall I do the needful?'

He looked at the others for confirmation and encouragement.

'You'll never chance it, Harris,' grinned one of his friends.

'What do you bet?' He pushed back his chair and got up.

Walter, disturbed at his mathematics, had been nervously aware of them from the moment they entered the room. Now, extremely grey about the gills, he averted his head.

'Take no notice,' he muttered. 'They won't let him come over.'

But Harris was already advancing and with an exaggerated bow he leant over Mary, took possession of her hand.

'Pardon me, my dear. May we have the pleasure of your company?'

Moray saw her shrink back. She had at first blushed deeply but now all the colour had drained from her face. Her lips were colourless and quivering. She looked pleadingly at Walter. Willie too was staring at Stoddart with wide, frightened, yet indignant eyes.

'Sir,' Walter stammered, swallowing with difficulty, 'are you aware you are addressing my fiancée? This is an imposition. I shall be obliged to summon the manager.'

'Quiet, Uncle. We're not interested in you. Come along, dearie.' He tried to draw her to her feet. 'We'll give you a ripping time.'

'Please go,' Mary said in a small, pained voice.

Something in the tone struck home. He hesitated, then with a grimace released her hand.

'No accounting for tastes.' He shrugged. 'Well, if I can't have you, I'll take a lee-itle souvenir.' He picked up Mary's flowers and, pressing them affectedly to his lips, wavered back to his place.

There was a hollow silence. Everyone seemed to be looking at Walter. In particular the man in the weather-stained kilt was observing him with a cruelly satiric twist of his lip. Walter, indeed, was pitifully agitated. Forgetting his intention to query the bill, he fumbled in his pocket-book, hurriedly threw down some notes, and rose like a ruffled hen.

'We are leaving now, Mary.'

Moray got up. There was nothing heroic in his nature, he had no strong leanings towards mortal combat, but he was angry – most of all perhaps at his own wasted day. And a sudden nervous impulse, almost predestined, sent him over to the other table, down at Harris, who did not seem greatly to relish his appearance.

'Weren't you told to get on with your soup? It's a little late now. But let me help you.'

Taking him by the back of the neck, Moray pushed him forward, ground his face hard once, twice, three times into the plate of soup. It was the thick soup, the Potage â la Reine Alexandra, which in the interim had nicely set, so that Harris came up for breath dripping with yellowish glue. Dead silence from the others while, with a swimming motion, he groped for his napkin. Moray picked up the bunch of bluebells, gave them back to Mary, waited a minute with a fast beating heart, then as nothing seemed to happen, except that now the man in the kilt was smiling, he followed the others from the restaurant. Outside, on the steps, Willie was waiting for him. The boy wrung his hand fervently, again and again.

'Well done, Davie. Oh, man, I like ye fine.'

'There was no need for you to interfere,' Walter broke out, as they started down through the woods. 'We were completely within our rights. As if decent people couldn't have a meal in peace. I know about that Lindsay – a kailyard laird – not a fish or a bird on his property, he'll rent to the lowest cockneys from London, but I'll . . . I'll report the matter . . . to the authorities. I won't let it pass, it's a public scandal.' He continued in this strain until they reached the pier, dwelling largely on the rights of the individual and the dignity of man, and concluding with a final vindictive burst. 'I shall certainly put the entire affair before my father.'

'And what will he do?' Willie said. 'Turn off your gas?'

The return journey was sad and silent. It had started to drizzle and they sat in the saloon. Nursing his injuries, Walter had at last ceased his monologue, while Mary, who gazed fixedly ahead, uttered scarcely a word. Willie had taken Moray away to show him the engines.

At Ardfillan, Walter, with a forgiving air, offered his arm to Mary. They walked to the bakery and into the yard, where Moray started up his bike.

'Well,' Walter moodily extended his hand, 'I don't suppose we'll meet again . . . '.

'Come again soon,' Willie cut in quickly. 'Be sure and come.'

'Goodbye, Mary,' Moray said.

For the first time since they left the hotel she looked at him, breathing quickly and with moist eyes. She remained silent, quite silent. But in that steady glance there was something lingering and intense. He saw too that she was no longer holding the little bunch of bluebells: she had pinned them to her blouse and was wearing them upon her breast.

CHAPTER IV

AT THE END of the following week Moray had a real stroke of luck. By special favour of the registrar he was moved from the out-patients' department of the Infirmary and given a month's appointment as house assistant in Professor Drummond's wards, which meant, of course, that he could leave his wretched lodging and live in hospital until his final examination. It was Professor Drummond who, after listening to Moray interrogate a patient, had once remarked, though somewhat dryly: 'You'll get on, my boy. You've the best bedside manner of any student I've ever known.' Moreover, Drummond was one of the examiners in clinical medicine, a significant fact that did not escape Moray and which he intended to make the most of during the next four weeks. He would be alert and assiduous, available at all hours, a demon for work, a regular fixture in the ward. For an eager and willing young man there seemed little hardship in this prospect. Yet in one sense it caused Moray an unaccountable vexation: he would be unable to take sufficient time off to make the journey to Ardfillan.

Ever since that moment of departure after the return from Gairsay, strange forces had been at work in his absorbed and ambitious soul. Mary's final glance, so quiet and intense, had struck him like a wounding arrow. He could not escape the vision of her strained little face, nor – and this was most ominous – did he wish to do so. Despite all his precautions, at odd moments of the day, in the ward or the test room, he would discover himself gazing absently into space. It was she whom he saw, in all her sweetness and simplicity, and he would then be seized by a longing to be with her, the wish to win a smile from her, to be acknowledged as her friend – he did not so far permit himself to frame a stronger and more compromising word.

He had hoped there might be news from her, or from her father, perhaps another invitation which, though he could not accept it, would give him the opportunity to get in touch with the family again. Why did he not hear from them? Since all the attentions had come from their side he had no wish to impose himself further without some hint that he would be welcome. Yet surely he must do something . . . something to clear up this . . . well, this uncertainty. At last, after ten days, when he had brought himself to a state of considerable tension, a postcard, showing a view of Ardfillan, arrived for him at the hospital. Its message was brief.

Dear David,
    I hope you are well. I have been reading more about Africa. There's been some ructions here. When are you coming to see us? I've been missing you.
                                            Yours ever,
                                                Willie.

That same day, immediately the evening round was over, he went into the side room and telephoned Ardfillan. After some delay he was put through to the Douglas shop. Aunt Minnie's voice came to him over the humming line.

'This is David Moray,' he said. 'I had such a nice card from Willie, I thought I'd ring up and see how you were all getting on.'

There was a slight, though definitive pause.

'We are quite well, thank you.'

The coldness of her tone took him aback. He hesitated, then said:

'I have a new job here which keeps me on the go. Otherwise I'd have been in touch with you before.'

She did not answer. He persisted.

'Is Willie there? I'd like to thank him for his card.'

'Willie is at his lessons. I'm afraid I can't disturb him.'

'Mary, then?' He plunged on, almost desperately. 'I would like a word with her.'

'Mary is out at present. With her young man. She has been a trifle poorly lately, but now she has quite recovered. I don't expect her back till late.'

Now he was silent. After a moment, he said, very awkwardly:

'Well, I wish you'd tell her I rang up . . . and give her my best regards.'

He could hear her sharp intake of breath. Her words came with a rush, as though she found them difficult, but felt constrained to get them out.

'I cannot undertake to give any such message, and I hope you won't attempt to repeat it. Furthermore, Mr Moray, although I've no wish to hurt your feelings, it will be best for everyone, including yourself, if you refrain in the future from forcing yourself upon us.'

The receiver at the other end went down with a click. He hung up slowly and turned away, blinking, as if he'd been hit in the face. What was wrong? Forcing himself upon them! What had he done to deserve such an unexpected and stinging rebuff? Back in the resident's office at the end of the corridor he sat down at the desk and tried to find the answer.

The aunt had never been too favourably disposed towards him, and because of her frequent headaches – due, he suspected, to a chronic nephritis – her temper was often, and understandably, short. Yet surely the cause lay deeper – probably in her devotion to Stoddart, coupled with the sudden dislike which Walter had apparently developed towards him. Reasoning in this fashion, though rather dejectedly, Moray still could not believe that Mary was a party to his abrupt dismissal, and on an impulse he took a sheet of prescription paper from the drawer and wrote her a short letter, asking if there might not be some opportunity of meeting her. As he was on emergency duty that night he could not leave the hospital even for a moment, but he got one of the probationers to go out and post the letter.

During the next few days, he awaited an answer with increasing impatience and anxiety. He had almost given up when, towards the end of the week, it arrived.

Dear David,

I shall be coming to Winton with my aunt to do some shopping on Thursday the 9th. If you can manage to be at the clock in the Caledonian Station about six o'clock I believe I could meet you there, but only for half an hour, since I must take the half-past six train home. I do trust that you are well and not working too hard.

Mary.

PS. Willie hopes you received his postcard.

The letter was as lifeless as a railway timetable, yet beneath

51

its dullness ran an undercurrent which stirred Moray deeply. The absence of that animation which she had displayed, which indeed marked everything she had ever done in his company, was painfully evident to him. But he would see her on Thursday next. This at least had been gained.

When the day came his plans were already made. He had arranged with Kerr, another houseman, to take over for two hours in the evening. Professor Drummond never made his evening visit until eight o'clock, so with luck he would be safe. The afternoon had turned wet and a fog was settling on the city as he left the hospital and boarded a yellow tram at Eldongrove. He feared he might be late, but well before the appointed time he was in the Caledonian Station, standing beneath the big central clock. The rush hour was in progress and under the high glass dome, impenetrably coated with the grime of years, crowds were streaming towards the local trains. The place reeked of steam, fog and sulphur fumes, echoed with the shrill blast of departing engines. From the underground platforms of the 'low level' a poisonous smoke welled up in snakey coils as from the inferno.

The clock struck six. Searching amongst all those unknown faces, Moray at last caught sight of her. His heart throbbed as she came towards him, carrying a number of parcels, looking unusually small and unprotected in that thrusting mob. She was wearing a dark brown costume with a short jacket, a thin necklet of fur and small brown hat. Nothing could have better suited her. He had never seen her so formally dressed. It gave her an unsuspected distinction and suddenly he coveted her.

'Mary!' He relieved her of her parcels, untwisting the string from her small gloved fingers. She smiled at him, a trifle wanly, for she seemed tired. The fog had smeared her cheek and marked faint shadows under her eyes.

'So you managed to get away?'

'Yes,' he said, looking at her. There was silence between them, then he added: 'You've been shopping?'

'There were some things I had to get. Aunt Minnie's had a regular field day.' She was making an effort to speak lightly. 'Now she's gone to see a friend . . . or I couldn't have got away.'

'Can't you stay longer?'

She shook her head, with lowered gaze.

'They'll be meeting me at Ardfillan.'

Was there a hint of surveillance in her answer? Whether or

not, her apparent fatigue troubled him, as did her listless tone, the manner in which she hesitated to meet his eye.

'You look as though you needed your tea. Shall we go in there?'

He pointed with some misgivings to the buffet which, flaring with light and packed to the doors, bore slight resemblance to the quiet refreshment room at Craigdoran. But she had already shaken her head.

'I had tea with my aunt at Fraser's.'

He knew this as the big household furnishing emporium. He felt the blood rush to his head.

'Then let's not stand here in this confounded rush. We'll take a walk outside.'

They went out of the main exit and took the back street that led to Argyle Place and the lower end of the station. The fog had thickened. It swirled about them, blurring the street lamps and deadening the sound of the traffic. They seemed to move in a world of their own, but he could not reach her, did not dare to take her arm. Even their words were stilted, formal, utterly meaningless.

'How is the study going?' she asked him.

'All right . . . I hope. And how have things been with you? All well at home?'

'Quite well, thank you.'

'And Walter?'

She did not immediately reply. Then, as though resolved to reveal and explain beyond all question of doubt:

'He's been upset, but he's better now. You see . . . he wanted to fix the date of our wedding. I felt it was a little early . . . I thought we ought to wait a bit. But now it's all settled . . . for the first of June.'

A long pause followed. The first of June, he repeated dully to himself – it was only three weeks away.

'And you're happy about it?' he asked.

'Yes,' she reasoned, in a tone of practical common sense, and with words that seemed to him to have been instilled in her. 'It's the right thing for people to settle down early and get used to each other's ways. Walter's a good man and he'll make a good husband. Besides . . .'. She faltered slightly but went on, '. . . his connections in the town will help our business. Father's not been doing near so well these last few years.'

53

A few large drops fell upon them and in a moment it was raining heavily. They sheltered in the entrance to a shuttered shop.

'I'm sure I wish you the best of luck, Mary.'

'And I do you, David.'

It was completely dark in the narrow passageway. He could not see her but with all his senses he felt her near him. He heard her breathing, quietly yet quickly, and the scent of her wet fur came to him. A frightful weakness came over him, his mouth was dry, and his joints so loosened they barely supported him.

'I mustn't miss my train,' she said, almost in a whisper.

They went back to the station. There was only a minute to spare. Her train was at the platform. He found her a corner seat in a third-class compartment. While he stood on the footboard she lowered the window. The whistle shrilled, the engine emitted a hiss of steam. She leaned out of the window. She was fearfully pale. The rain had streaked the smut on her cheek and draggled her little necklet. The pupils of her eyes were wide and dark. A little vein in her neck was pulsing frantically.

'Goodbye then, David.' Her voice trembled.

'Goodbye . . . Mary.' The hurt in his side was unendurable. She was leaving him for good, he would never see her again.

Then as the train began to move, together, with an instinctive irresponsible, predestined movement, each reached out towards the other. They clung together, closely, blindly, passionately, and their lips met in a wild, delirious, exquisite kiss. Drunkenly, at the end of the platform, the train now moving fast, he jumped from the footboard, staggered and almost fell. Still leaning from the window she was borne into the darkness of the tunnel. His heart was beating like mad with delight, tears had formed under his eyelids and, to his consternation, were running down his cheeks.

CHAPTER V

SUDDENLY, AS FROM a great distance, he remembered that his chief was due at eight o'clock to perform a lumbar puncture – a case which had come into the ward that afternoon. He must rush to the hospital to relieve Kerr. Dashing out of the station into the fog he was fortunate in finding an Eldongrove tram which, though its progress was laborious, took him back in time. Yet how he got through the next two hours he never fully understood. Speech and movements were automatic, he was barely conscious of his own presence in the ward. Once or twice he felt Drummond glancing at him oddly, but he made no comment, and at last, towards ten o'clock, Moray was able to go to his own room and give way to his feelings.

He was in love and, with the ecstasy of her kiss still lingering he knew that she loved him. It was an eventuality which, even remotely, had never entered his mind. All his thoughts, his energy and endeavours, had been concentrated exclusively on one objective, his career: to lift himself out of the swamp of poverty and make a dazzling success of his life. Well, he reasoned, with an upsurge of emotion, if he could achieve this alone, could he not do so with her, encouraged and fortified by one who, despite her modest social status, possessed all the qualities of the perfect helpmate? He could not lose her – the mere idea made him wince, like the prospect of sudden death.

He knitted his brows: what was to be done? The situation in which she was placed, with the date of her wedding fixed, and no more than three weeks off, demanded immediate action. Suppose by some fearful mischance he could not stop it. The thought of Walter, painstakingly precise, exacting the full resources of his connubial rights to their most intimate extent came to him with horrifying vividness. It was enough to drive him frantic. He must write to Mary, write at once, and send the letter to her express.

Suddenly, as he reached towards his desk for paper, the

emergency phone rang. With an exclamation of annoyance he took up the receiver. Macdonald, the switchboard night operator, was speaking.

'Mr Moray . . . '.

'Damn it, Mac – what is it? Another false run?'

'It's a personal call for you. I'll put you through.'

There was a whirring on the line. Then:

'David . . .'

He caught his breath sharply.

'Mary, is it really you?'

Her voice came to him, guarded yet intense.

'I've come down to the shop. . . . The others are asleep and I'm all in the dark. . . . But I simply had to speak to you. . . . Dearest David, I'm so happy.'

He had a swift, sweet vision of her in her nightdress and slippers in the darkness of the little shop.

'I am too, dearest Mary.'

'Ever since that first minute at Craigdoran, when I saw you in the mirror . . . I *knew*, David. And when I thought you didn't care, it fair broke my heart.'

'But you know I do. I'm just wild about you.'

He could hear her long, softly indrawn breath, more thrilling than any answer.

'I can't stop, dearest David. I only wanted you to know that I'll never marry Walter. Never – never. I didn't ever want to, I just let myself be talked into it. And then, when I thought you didn't want me. . . . But now I'll tell him, first thing tomorrow.'

He could not let her face this alone.

'I'll come with you, Mary. I'll ask Drummond for time off.'

'No, David,' she said firmly. 'You have your exam. That's the important thing, for you to get through. After that, come straight away. I'll be waiting for you.' She hesitated. 'And . . . and if you've a wee minute you can write to me in the meantime.'

'I will, Mary. I've already begun a letter.'

'I can't wait till I get it. Now I must go. Goodnight, Davie dear.'

The receiver was replaced. Now she would be creeping upstairs in the silent house to the room beside Willie's. Seizing pen and paper he dashed off a long and fervent letter; then, undressing in a kind of trance, he flung himself into bed.

Next morning, like one inspired, he redoubled his work for the finals. In the intensity of this last spurt time flew. When the day of the examination arrived he entered the Eldon Hall, tense but confident, and took his place at one of the desks. The first papers were distributed. He saw, after a rapid run through, that the questions suited him. He began to write, never once looking up, covering the pages with a flowing legible script. During the next three days, coming and going between the hospital and the University, he took his place at the same desk, set himself to do his utmost, not only for his own sake but for hers.

Then the clinical examination began. In medicine he spotted his case at once: a bronchiectasis with secondary cerebral abscess. He believed he was doing well. On the last day of the examination he went in for his oral. Drummond, sitting with old Murdo Macleish, Regius Professor of Midwifery, known as the Heiland Stot, and Purvis, the external examiner, gave him a friendly nod, remarking to his colleagues:

'This is the fellow with the bedside manner.'

'He's got rather more than that,' said Purvis, glancing through Moray's case-report.

They began to question him, and Moray – fluent, ready to agree, to smile respectfully, and always, always deferential – felt he was giving of his best. Yet the Stot worried him. This formidable character, both a terror and support to generations of Highland students, was already legendary for his brutal frankness and bawdy humour. At his opening lecture of the session it was his habit to summon some shrinking youth to the floor before the entire class, throw him an end of chalk and, pointing to the blackboard with a grim smile, indicate in the coarsest terms his wish to have a pictoral representation of the female private parts. At present he was not saying much but watching Moray intently, with a suspicious look in his small red eye. However, the interview was soon over and Purvis said with a smile: 'I don't think we need keep you.'

When Moray had gone and the door closed behind him he added: 'Nice young fellow.'

The Stot shook himself irritably.

'Smart enough,' he grunted. 'But a bluidy young humbug.'

The other two laughed. At his age, no one took old Murdo seriously.

The results were to be posted on Saturday morning. As Moray walked up the long hill to the University, all his assurance left

57

him. He had been mistaken, he had not done well, he had failed. He scarcely dared approach the notice-board beside the main archway. Bracketed with two others, his name was at the head of the list. He had passed with honours.

He felt faint. After all his years of striving and self-denial the triumph of that moment was beyond belief. It was all the greater because of the sweet knowledge that he would soon share it with her. Barely waiting to receive the congratulations of the others gathered round the board, he went directly to the branch post office at the foot of Gilmore Hill and sent off a telegram.

Arriving Ardfillan 5.30 p.m. train today.

He hoped she would have returned from Craigdoran at that hour, and indeed, when he arrived, she was at the station to meet him. Quickly, quickly, her eyes shining, looking pale yet prettier than ever before, she advanced and, breathlessly unheeding of the others on the platform, offered him her lips. If, in these last hectic days, he had forgotten the warm freshness of her kiss, now it was renewed. As they went out of the station and started towards her home he still held her hand. Overcome, neither had so far spoken a single intelligible word. He saw that she dared not ask the question uppermost in her mind, and though he had planned a long and suspenseful recital of his success he merely said, humbly, not looking at her:

'I've passed, Mary . . . at the top, with honours.'

A sudden nervous tightening of her fingers on his; then, in a voice stifled by feeling, 'I knew you'd do it, Davie dear. But, oh, I'm so glad, so terribly glad you have. Now we can face up to things together.'

He bent towards her in concern.

'It's been difficult for you here?'

'Not exactly easy.' She softened the words by a tender upward glance. 'When I went to tell Walter, at first he thought I was joking. He couldn't believe his ears, that any woman would turn him down. When he found I was in earnest . . . he wasn't . . . nice. Then his parents came to see Father. That was bad too.' She smiled wryly. 'I was called a few fancy names.'

'Oh God,' he groaned, 'to think of you having to suffer that and me not there. I'd like to break that damn fellow's neck.'

'No,' she said seriously. 'I suppose I was to blame. But I can only thank Heaven for being spared the awfulness of getting into that family and,' she pressed close to him, 'for finding you.

I love you, Davie.'

'And I you, Mary.'

'That's everything,' she sighed. 'Nothing else matters.'

'But didn't your own family stand up for you?'

'In a way,' she said. 'But except for Willie they're not too pleased with me for all that. However, here we are, and first we'd better see my father.'

Through an entrance in the near side of the yard she took him into the bakery. It was low and dark, hot from the glow of two draw-plate ovens, and honey-sweet with the smell of a batch of new bread. Douglas, with his foreman, John Donaldson, was shelving the heavy board on which the double Scotch loaves, black crust upwards, were ranged in rows. The baker was in his shirt sleeves, wearing a floury apron, and old white canvas shoes. Over his shoulder he saw Moray enter, yet he finished the shelving, then slowly divested himself of the apron before coming forward.

'It's yourself, then,' he said, unsmiling, offering his hand.

'Father,' Mary burst out, 'David has passed his examination with honours, and come out top of the list.'

'So you're a doctor now. Well, that's something gained.'

He led the way out of the bakery and upstairs to the front parlour, where Willie was at the cleared table doing his lessons and Aunt Minnie seated knitting by the window. The boy gave Moray a swift welcoming smile but the aunt, frowning at her flashing needles, did not once look up.

'Sit down, man, sit down,' said the little baker. 'We've had our tea earlier nor usual today. But . . . well, maybe afterwards, if ye're hungry, Mary'll get you a bite.'

David took a stiff chair by the table. Mary drew another over and sat down by his side.

'Leave the room, Willie,' the aunt said, finally forking her needles into the knitting and favouring Moray with a chilly scrutiny. 'Did you hear me, Willie!'

Willie went out.

'Now, David,' the baker began, 'yet must understand that this has been a bit of a shock to us . . .'

'And to everybody else,' Aunt Minnie cut in, her head shaking with indignation. 'The whole town is ringing with it. It's a positive scandal and disgrace.'

'Ay,' Douglas resumed. 'It has placed us in a most unfortunate position. My daughter had given her plighted word to a worthy man, well connected and highly respected in the borough. Not only was she engaged to be married, the wedding day had been set; when suddenly, without rhyme or reason, she breaks the whole thing off in favour of a total stranger.'

'There was a very good reason, sir. Mary and I fell in love.'

'Love!' exclaimed the aunt in an indescribable tone. 'Before you appeared on that blessed bike of yours, like some – some half-baked Lochinvar, she was in love with Walter.'

'Not at all.' Moray felt Mary's hand steal towards his under the table. 'She never was. And I'm convinced she would never have been happy with him. You've called Stoddart a worthy man. I think he's a pompous, conceited, unfeeling ass.'

'That'll do now,' Douglas interposed sharply. 'Walter may have his peculiarities, but we know he's sound enough underneath.'

'Which is more than we know of you!' threw out the aunt.

'I'm sorry you have such a poor opinion of me.' Moray glanced deprecatingly towards Minnie. 'I hope later on you may change your mind. This isn't the first time an engagement has been broken. Better late than never.'

'It's true,' Mary murmured. 'I never wanted Walter.'

'Then why didn't you say so before, you wicked besom? Now you've put the Stoddarts against us. They'll hate us for ever. And you know what that means to your father.'

'Ay, it's not a pretty prospect. But the least said on that score the better.'

'But I will speak, James.' The aunt bent forward towards Moray. 'You may think everything is easy osey with us here. But it's not. Far from it. What with the big combines and their machine-made bread and their motor delivery trucks rampaging the whole countryside, to say nothing of the alterations we're supposed to make under the new Factory Act, my brother-in-law's had a hard fight this many a year, and him not in the best of health forbye. And Walter, through his father, had definitely promised . . .'.

'That's enough, Minnie.' Douglas raised his hand. 'Least said soonest mended. I've aye managed to stand on my own two legs in the past, and with the help of Providence I hope I'll keep on them in the future.'

A silence followed; then Moray, pressing Mary's hand,

addressed himself to the baker. He had never shown to better advantage, his fresh, clever young face alight with feeling and sincerity.

'I realise that I've caused you a lot of trouble, sir, and pain. I'm truly sorry. But some things just can't be helped. Like lightning . . . they strike you. That's the way it happened with Mary and me. You mayn't think too much of me now,' he half turned towards Aunt Minnie, 'but I'll show you. You'll not regret having me as a son-in-law. I have my degree, and it's a good one. I'll get a job in no time, and it won't be so very long before I've a first-class practice. All I want is to have Mary with me, and I'm sure that's what she wants, too.' He smiled, from one to the other, his diffident, taking, heart-warming smile.

There was a pause. Despite his determination to be firm, the baker could not restrain his nod of approval.

'That's well said, David. And now ye've spoken out I'll allow that from the first . . . like my daughter here . . .' he smiled at Mary, 'I was real taken with ye . . . and wi' all ye have done. Since what maun be maun be, I'll agree ye can be engaged. As for the marriage, there maun be a decent interval, ay, a decent interval to prevent scandal in the town. Take a job for three or four months, then we'll see. What do you say to that, Minnie?'

'Well . . .' the aunt temporised. 'There's no use crying over spilt milk.' Even she had softened, impressed by the tone of Moray's moving little speech. 'Maybe you're right. We mustn't be too hard on them.'

'Oh, thank you, Father . . . thank you, Aunt Minnie.' Mary jumped up a little wildly and kissed them both. Her cheeks were flushed, a lock of hair hung loose across her forehead. She tossed it back triumphantly. 'I knew you'd make everything all right. And now will I get Davie something to eat, Auntie?'

'Fetch him in biscuits and cheese. And some of the new batch of cherry cakes. I ken ye likes them.' She shot a wry glance at Moray. 'He ate six of them the last time he was here.'

'Just one thing more, Father,' Mary pleaded, angelically. 'Can Davie stay the night? Please. I've seen so little of him lately.'

'Well, just for tonight. Tomorrow he'll have to be off seeking that job.' A thought struck the little baker. He added severely: 'And if you're thinking of walking out tonight, Willie'll have to go with you.'

61

Hurrying between the kitchen and the parlour she put a choice little meal before him, but in the wonder of this magic day, food had become a sordid thing; he had little appetite. When he had finished, she put on her hat and coat. Every movement that she made seemed to him special and significant, precious, unique, adorably feminine. Then they went out and, arm in arm in the darkness, walked along the Esplanade with Willie at their side. The boy, excited by the turn of events, was in a talkative mood, putting all sorts of questions to Moray, who had not the heart to tell him he was in the way. Mary, on fire with an equal longing, was more resourceful.

'Willie dear,' she said sweetly, as they reached the end of the promenade, 'I've just remembered I forgot to get Auntie's black striped balls for tomorrow. Here's a threepenny bit. Run back to McKellar's for twopence-worth and get a Fry's chocolate bar for yourself. There's a good boy. Davie and I'll be sitting here when you get back.'

When Willie had scudded off they went into the wooden shelter. It was empty. Seated in the corner, protected from the wind, they clung to each other, the beat of the tide lost in the beating of their hearts. The waves rolled in, a star flashed unseen through the sky. Her lips were dry and warm; the innocence of her kiss, in its ardour and passion, moved him as never before.

'Oh, Davie darling,' she whispered, her cheek against his. 'I'm so happy I could die. I love you so much it's like as if my breast would break.'

CHAPTER VI

THE GRADUATION CEREMONY took place a few days later. Immediately he had turned in his hired cap and gown, Moray set about finding a suitable job. At least two house appointments were his for the asking in the Infirmary. But here, not only was the salary a pittance, he had long ago wisely decided against the long toiling road of academic promotion. Again, several, assistantships were available, mainly from country practitioners, but these he dismissed on sight. These rural G.P.s, he well knew, were not looking for honours graduates; they wanted husky youngsters who would eat anything and, unencumbered by a wife, get out of bed for a midwifery call at any hour of the night. No, he would be lost in such a situation, nor would he accept any stopgap offer: locums, dispensary work, temporary employment with one of the shipping companies, all were rejected. For his own sake and Mary's he must find something better. Intently he scanned the columns of the *Lancet* and the *Medical Journal*, pored over the advertisements of the local newspapers in the reading-room of the Carnegie Public Library. He found nothing that would do. He was worried stiff when at last he came on an unobtrusive panel in the appointments column of the *Winton Herald*.

Wanted for Glenburn Hospital, Cranstown. Resident Phsyician. Salary £500 per annum and unfurnished cottage. Engagement to commence January 1st. Apply the Secretary to the Board Wintonshire Public Health Department.

He drew a long, deep breath. It was right, exactly right, except perhaps for the date of the appointment – but that, balanced against the other advantages, was a detail, immaterial. He knew the hospital and had often admired it on his weekend excursions from the city. Situated in pleasant rolling country, within a long tram ride of Winton, it was known locally as the 'Fever Hospital', having at one time been devoted exclusively

63

to infectious diseases. Now, however, it was mainly given over to the treatment of tubercular children. It was small, of course, no more than four isolated pavilions, holding about sixty beds, with a central office and laboratory, nurses' quarters, and a neat, red-tiled gate lodge. Nothing could be better: the salary was generous, a house was available, obviously they wanted a married man, and the laboratory would afford him facilities for research. A gem of a place, he kept repeating to himself. He knew, of course, that competition would be severe, cut-throat in fact, and as he got up from the reading-room bench he had the look of one going into battle.

The campaign which he forthwith conducted was indeed, in its resourcefulness, subtlety and consummate adroitness, fit to be honoured and recorded as the classic example of job-getting. From his University professors he got testimonials and letters of recommendation, from Drummond a personal introduction to the Wintonshire Medical Officer of Health, and through Bryce's father, who was a baillie of the city, a complete list of the members of the board. He called first on the Medical Officer, whose attitude, though noncommittal, was pleasant, then on the Secretary, who, as a friend and brother Mason of the senior Bryce, was distinctly cordial. Next, he began discreetly, in the evenings, to canvas all the board members at their homes. Here he did well, was even introduced to the sonsie wives of several of these substantial citizens in whom, by judicious shyness, he started warm springs of maternal sympathy. Finally, he cadged a ride in a delivery van to the vicinity of the hospital, made friends with the retiring doctor who was going into practice, shook hands with the head sister and, after a really hard beginning, completely won over the stubby little martinet of a matron. She invited him to tea. The difficulties of his student days, his romantic meeting with Mary, his honours degree, all had by this time been composed into a modest, yet free-flowing tale. In her own cosy sitting-room, over the teacups – it was, he noted, first-rate tea and a delicious homemade sponge – she listened with growing sympathy.

'We'll have to see what can be done,' she finally declared, throwing out her well-starched bust until it crackled. 'And if anyone has influence with that wrong-headed committee, it's yours truly.'

He murmured thanks.

'Now I'll be off, Matron. I've taken far too much of your precious time.'

'Not at all. How are you getting back?'

'As I came,' he said, offhandedly playing an inspired lead. 'On Shanks's mare.'

'Ye *walked* out from Winton! All that way?'

'Well, to be perfectly honest, Matron,' he smiled confusedly, winningly, looking into her eyes, 'I just didn't have the tram fare. So I'll walk back too.'

'You'll do nothing of the sort, doctor. Our driver will take ye in.' She rang the bell. 'Nurse, slip down to the gate lodge and fetch Leckie.'

He rode into the city on the front seat of the old Argyle ambulance. When Leckie returned and reported to the matron, he remarked: 'I hope we get Dr Moray. He's such a nice likeable lad. And keen, forbye. If only I get appointed, says he to me, I'll work my fingers to the bone.'

No opposition could stand against such a virtuoso, pulling out all the emotional stops. A week later his name appeared on the 'short list' of ten candidates and, at the meeting of the board on August 21st, he was unanimously appointed.

Beyond indicating non-committally that he had a possibility in view, Moray had said nothing at Ardfillan of the marvellous prospects offered by Glenburn. Because he had lived so much alone, it was his nature to keep things to himself. Besides, he had been horribly afraid of missing the job. Now however, with the thrill of anticipation, he prepared for the joys of triumphant revelation.

He made his plans with characteristic thoroughness. He went, in the first place, to Gilhouse, the University Bookseller at the foot of Fenner Hill, and sold all his text-books, also his microscope. Since he had spotted a fine oil-immersion Zeiss in the lab. at Glenburn, he would no longer need his own second-hand Wright and Dobson. With a tidy sum in his pocket he crossed Eldongrove Park to a less salubrious neighbourhood and entered the pawnshop at the corner of Blairhill Street where, over the past five years, he had occasionally been an unwilling client. Now the position was reversed. Taking his time, and wisely rejecting the dubious diamond pressed upon him, he selected from the unredeemed pledges a thin gold ring mounted with a nice little aquamarine. Set in velvet in a red leather case it looked extremely handsome, and it was genuine. With this in his pocket he borrowed Bryce's bike and set off for Craigdoran. He arrived at eleven in the forenoon.

'Mary,' he exclaimed, walking straight into the refreshment room and putting his arm round her waist. 'Shut up shop. Now. At once.'

'But, Davie, I still have two more trains . . .'.

'Hang the trains, and the passengers in them, and the entire North British Railway Company. You're coming with me, this very minute. And while you're about it, put a few buns and sandwiches in a bag.'

She gazed at him, half doubtful, half smiling, yet conscious of something compelling behind the lightness of his tone.

'Well,' she conceded finally, 'I don't suppose it'll ruin the company, or Father, this once.'

Ten minutes later they were off together on the bike. He took the Stirling road, turned east at Reston, and about one o'clock, swinging round the outskirts of Cranstoun, came to rest a quarter of a mile along the Glenburn lane.

'This is where we take a stroll, Mary.'

She was confused, vaguely disturbed, did not understand why they should be here, but she accompanied him obediently down the lane. Presently they reached the sweep of ornamental railings which enclosed the hospital. He halted, wise enough to know that at this stage they must penetrate no further. They both peered through the neat, painted railings. The sun was shining on the enclosure, some children in red jackets were seated with a nurse on a bench beside the green stretch of lawn, a blackbird sang in a nearby forsythia bush.

'What a dear wee place,' Mary exclaimed.

'You think so?'

'Who wouldn't, Davie? It's like a picture.'

'Then listen, Mary,' he said, drawing a deep breath. 'This is Glenburn Hospital. These four buildings among the trees are the wards. That's the administrative block in front of them. And over there, with the garden at the back, is the medical superintendent's residence. Not a bad house, is it?'

'It's a sweet wee house,' she answered wonderingly. 'And such a nice garden. Do you know someone there?'

Ignoring her question he went on, pale now and breathing rather fast. 'The medical superintendent has sole and complete charge of the hospital. He has full facilities for research in the hospital laboratory. His salary is £500 per annum, plus the produce of the garden and a free house, that house over there, Mary, in which he is lawfully entitled to keep his own lawful wife.' His voice was cracking with excitement. 'Mary . . . as from the 1st of January they've appointed a new medical superintendent. You're . . . you're looking at him now.'

CHAPTER VII

HE TOOK THE return journey slowly, making a wide detour at Overton that would bring them through the Carse of Louden, along the south shore of Loch Lomond, and up across the moors of Glen Fruin. This was a noted route, one of the prettiest in the West, but Mary saw nothing of it . . . nothing . . . nothing . . . not even the majestic crest of Ben Lomond, towering above the shimmering loch. Dumb with happiness, still stricken by all the thrilling wonder of the miracle he had worked for her, she closed her eyes and hugged him to her with all the grateful love of her overflowing heart.

And he was happy too – how could it be otherwise? – excited by the effect he had so carefully planned and so successfully produced. Yet to his credit, he had regained calm, he did not seek praise, his natural air of modesty remained unchanged. He was in love and had wished to impress less from a sense of self-importance than from the desire to make her suddenly rejoice. Unlike Walter, who, exacting the utmost in adulation, pressed the last drop of juice from every favourable situation, he disliked being fussed over – it offended his fastidious sense and made him uncomfortable. Besides, had he not still another surprise in store for her?

As they topped the long hill which led from the loch to Glen Fruin, he checked the machine and turned off the road into one of the grassy sheep tracks which criss-crossed the moor. Following the path for about a quarter of a mile he drew up at the river beside a bank, deep in heather and bracken, sheltered by a clump of silver birches. Beneath them the moor fell away in a great sweep of purple and gold. Now she could see the mountain and the loch, a shimmering landscape that seemed to her of heaven and which she interpreted in her own fashion.

'What a braw spot, Davie.'

'Braw enough for us to eat our grub.' He teased her. 'All this chasing around should have given you an appetite.'

'I'm too carried away to eat.'

But when they seated themselves and spread out their lunch upon the checked tablecloth she had brought, he made her eat her share, the more so since, amplifying his instructions, she had packed a substantial lunch. Besides buns and sandwiches there were hard-boiled eggs, Clydeside tomatoes and a sausage roll, with a big bottle of that famous local 'mineral', Barr's Iron Brew, to quench their thirst. She had even remembered to bring the wooden plug that knocked down the glass marble in the bottle-neck.

'Oh, Davie,' she murmured, between bites. 'That bonnie wee house . . . I can't get it out my head. Just wait till ye see how I'll look after you there.'

'We have to furnish it,' he warned. 'But we have time before January. Now we're all settled I'll take a locum or something over the next four months, which should give us enough cash for a start, anyway.'

'Dearest Davie. You think, of everything.'

'There's one thing I nearly forgot.' Offhandedly, he dived into his jacket pocket. 'Here it is, lass. Better late than never.'

Watching her as she opened the little red box, he had never been so deeply moved. Completely still she looked at the ring which, like her, was simple yet beautiful. She did not praise the ring, she did not thank him for it, but, turning, she looked into his eyes just as she had done after that day at Gairsay, and in a trembling voice, that he was to remember all his life, she whispered: 'Put it on for me, dear.' Then with a little sigh she reached out her arms towards him.

They lay together on the soft bracken under the hot afternoon sun. Bees were droning faintly amongst the heather flowers, a lark sang its way into the blue, the scent of thyme and the wild orchids filled the air. From far off came the whirr of a risen grouse, then again stillness, but for the quiet ripple of the stream. Her skirt had risen as she lay back and his hand fell upon her knee. Caressingly, he stroked it. Her lips were parted, slightly swollen from the sun, and almost purple against the soft pallor of her face. Her eyelids, masking her doe-soft eyes, had a fainter, bluish tinge. Warm in his arms, she trembled as his fingers, moving upwards, came to rest on the soft bare skin above her long stocking.

His heart was thudding against his side so hard, the sound of it made a rushing in his ears. Another gentle movement, and his hand would find what it sought. He longed for her, but was afraid. Then, close to him, she breathed:

'If you want . . . take me, dear.'

The sun passed behind a cloud, the bees ceased their hum, a circling curlew uttered its mournful cry. They lay still, until at last he whispered humbly:

'Did I hurt you, Mary?'

'Dearest Davie.' She burrowed her head into him. 'It was the sweetest pain of all my life.'

When at last they stirred and gathered up the picnic things, he drove off slowly, a trifle sad and sorry, touched by a rueful sense of regret. Had he not been premature, crushing so much joy into so short a time, snatching so early at the first fruits of happiness? She was so young, so innocent. A fresh surge of tenderness swept over him: should he not have shown restraint and waited? Indeed, from the beginning, had he not rushed on too fast and heedlessly? No, a thousand times no: he banished the thought and lifted a hand from the controls to press once again the softness of her thigh.

'I'm all yours now, Davie.'

She snuggled against him, laughing softly in his ear. No mournful, injured wistfulness for her! She was renewed, confident, more than ever alive. Half turning, he saw that her eyes were fresh and dewy; he had never known her so radiant. She seemed to sense instinctively his vague depression, and gaily, tenderly, possessive as a mother, she lifted him up.

They had reached the summit above Ardfillan when suddenly the heavy cloud that obscured the sun broke upon them in a drenching shower. Hurriedly he slipped the gear lever into neutral and coasted rapidly down hill. He was at the shop in no time, but not before he was unpleasantly damp. Mary, behind him, had escaped the worst of the rain.

Upstairs she insisted that he change into a suit of her father's, but he passed the matter off. He was not really wet he said, there was a good fire in the room, he would soon dry off. In the end they compromised: he put on the baker's carpet slippers and an old tweed jacket Mary found in a cupboard.

Presently the shop was shut and Aunt Minnie appeared, followed a few minutes later by Douglas. The four sat down to the evening meal. Willie, it appeared, was away, spending the weekend at the Boys' Brigade Camp at Whistlefield. At the outset, as the teacups were passed in silence, Moray was painfully embarrassed, asking himself if some intangible evidence of guilt, a lingering aura of those delirious moments of consummation on the moor, was not observable in Mary and himself. Mary's cheeks were flushed, his own, he felt, were pale, and Aunt Minnie was directing oddly suspicious glances from one to the other. The baker, too, seemed unusually reserved and more than usually observant.

But when Mary ended the silence the general tension relaxed. Moray had promised to let her break the news of his appointment in her own way, and she did so with a brio and a sense of drama which far surpassed his own effort of the morning.

First she displayed her ring, which was admired – though grudgingly by the aunt, who remarked, aside: 'I hope it's paid for.'

'I don't think we need worry about *that*, Auntie dear,' Mary answered kindly, with just a hint of patronage. She began forthwith to describe the hospital at Glenburn, painting it in colours rather more glowing than reality, and working without haste towards the climax, which was tremendous.

A long pause followed, then Douglas said, deeply pleased: 'Five hundred pounds and a house . . . and the bit garden for your vegetables. . . . It's fine, man, it's downright handsome.'

'Not to mention the laboratory and the chances of research,' Mary put in quickly.

'This,' the aunt drew in her lips with a hiss of satisfaction, 'will be gall and vinegar to the Stoddarts.'

'Hush, Minnie.' The baker offered his hand to Moray. 'I congratulate you, David. If ever I had a doubt about you and this whole affair, it's gone now, and I can only ask your pardon. Ye're a fine lad. I'm proper glad my daughter is marrying you, and proud to have you as my son-in-law. Now, Minnie, don't you think this calls for a celebration?'

'Without a doubt!' Minnie was won at last.

'Run down then, Mary, to the wee back press – ye'll find the key in the top drawer – and bring up a bottle of my old Glenlivet.'

The bottle was brought and the baker, using sugar and lemon, and with due regard to the varying dilutions of the aged spirit, mixed for each of them a glass of good hot toddy. It was a comforting drink but it came too late for Moray. All evening he had

71

felt his shirt clinging damply to his chest. The toddy made his head hot but his feet were leaden cold. He was relieved when they persuaded him to stay overnight, but when he went to bed he was shivering. He took his temperature, 101°, and knew he had caught a chill.

CHAPTER VIII

MORAY SPENT A restless, fevered night, and when he awoke from the snatch of sleep into which he had fallen, towards morning, he had no difficulty in diagnosing his own case; he was in for a bout of acute bronchitis. His breathing was tight and painful, even without a stethoscope he could hear the râles in his chest, and his temperature had risen to 103°. He waited with commendable self-control until nearly seven o'clock, then knocked on the wall which separated him from Mary's room. He heard her stir, and a few minutes later she came into his room.

'Oh, dear, you're ill,' she exclaimed at once in dismay. 'Half the night I was worrying you'd caught cold.'

'It's nothing much. But I'll be laid up for a bit and I can't make a nuisance of myself here. You'd better ring the hospital.'

'I'll do no such thing.' She had taken his hand, which felt so hot to the touch that her heart contracted with concern. 'You'll stop with us in this very room. And I'll look after you. Who else, indeed!'

'Are you sure, Mary?' Suddenly he wanted her to care for him. And what a bore it would be getting the ambulance, trundling back to the Infirmary as a patient. 'I'll only be a few days. If it's not too much trouble, I'd far rather stay.'

'And so you shall,' she said firmly. 'Now, should I send for the doctor?'

'No, no, of course not. I'll prescribe for myself.'

He raised himself on his elbow and wrote a couple of prescriptions. The effort made him cough.

'That's all I need, Mary. And occasional hot fluids. . . .' He forced a smile. 'And you.'

He was worse than he made out. For ten days he was quite ill, with a high fever and a racking cough. She nursed him devotedly and, for one untrained, with surprising talent. With Aunt Minnie, she poulticed him, brewed him nourishing beef tea, fed him calf's foot jelly with a spoon, made up his bed, exerted to the full her practical mind and housewifely skill to ease his distress. At the crisis of the attack, when he was obliged to have a steam kettle, she sat up half the night tending him. The dislocation of the household was, of course, acute. Meals were upset; sleep lost; service in the shop disturbed; Willie, back from the camp, had to be farmed out with Donaldson, the foreman. When, at the end of the second week, he was able to be up, and to sit in a long chair by the window, he apologised shamefacedly to Douglas for the trouble he had given them all.

'Not another word, Davie,' the little baker interrupted him. 'Ye're one of the family now.' He smiled. 'As good as, anyhow.'

When her father had gone out of the room Mary came over and knelt beside his chair. She gripped his knee tightly.

'Don't ever say you were a bother, Davie. What do you think would have happened to me if I hadn't got you well?'

His eyes filled with tears, he was still rather weak.

'What a perfect wife you'll make me, Mary. Don't think I haven't noticed every single thing you've done.'

Presently he was out, walking with her on the Esplanade, slowly at first, then at a faster pace. Finally he pronounced himself recovered, and ready to look out for a locum tenens that would carry him through the next few months. He still had a stitch in his side that worried him, but he did not speak of it. To complain now would be a poor way to reward their united efforts on his behalf. However, on the following Monday when he travelled by train to Winton to leave his name at the Medical Employment Agency, he had a sharp bout of pain, and decided it might be wise to look in at his old ward and have his chest gone over by Drummond.

It was unexpectedly late when he arrived back at Ardfillan, and Mary, who was serving a woman customer in the shop, read at once the dejection in his expression. The moment she was free, she came towards him, looking up into his face.

'No luck, Davie?'

He tried to smile, but the attempt was scarcely a success.

'As a matter of fact I didn't manage to get to the agency.'

'What went wrong, dear?' she said quickly. She saw that he had something on his mind.

At that moment the shop door pinged and a child came in to buy sweetie biscuits. He broke off, relieved by the interruption.

What a cursed nuisance it all was, and what a damned sickly nuisance of a fellow they would all think him.

'Now, Davie?' She turned to him.

'It's hard to explain, Mary,' he said feebly. 'I'll tell you upstairs.'

It was just on closing time. Hurriedly, she drew the blinds and turned off the lights, then followed him to the upper room. Her father and Aunt Minnie were there with him. He did not know how to begin. There was nothing for it, he had to reveal the reason for his visit to the hospital. Bending forward with elbows on his knees he kept looking at the floor.

'So when I got there Professor Drummond screened me – X-ray that is – and apparently I have a patch of pleurisy on my left lung.'

'Pleurisy!'

'It's very localised,' he said, refraining from mentioning Drummond's insistence that neglect would induce tuberculosis. Striving to keep the despondency from his voice, he added: 'But apparently it knocks out any possibility of a locum.'

'What's to be done then?' Douglas said, looking rather blue, while Mary sat silent, her hands pressed together.

'Well, I could go into the country . . . somewhere not too far away . . .'.

'No, Davie,' Mary intervened nervously. 'You're not to leave us. We'll look after you here.'

He gazed at her dismally.

'Impose myself on you for another two months? Impossible, Mary. How can I hang around here, bone idle, just being a confounded nuisance, on top of all the fearful bother I've given you? I'll . . . I'll get a job on a farm.'

'No farmer in his right mind is going to employ a sick man,' said Douglas. 'Surely the doctor . . . the professor ordered something definite for ye?'

There was a pause. Moray raised his head.

'If you must know, Drummond did say that I need a sea voyage – as a ship's doctor of course. In fact, he insisted on ringing up the Kinnaird Line. . . . He knows someone there . . .'

Now there was a prolonged silence. Finally the baker said:

'That sounds like sense at last. And if it's a question of your health, lad, that's all important. We would keep you here gladly. But would you get better, with the winter coming on? No, no.

Your professor's advice is sound. Did he manage to find ye something?'

Moray nodded, unwillingly.

'There's a boat, the *Pindari*, leaving next week from the Tail of the Bank – for Calcutta – a seven weeks' round trip.'

Another pause followed, then Douglas reflected:

'A voyage to India. Ye'd get sunshine there.'

'Do you want to go?' the aunt asked.

'Good God, no. . . . Sorry, Aunt Minnie. It's the last thing I want. Except that if I must go the pay is good, ninety pounds in all. We could furnish our house with it, Mary.'

All that evening the matter was threshed out and at last was definitely settled. Despite the divergence of opinion, all, even Mary, yielded in the end to the baker's simple argument: health came before all other considerations.

'What good will ye be to anyone – to Mary, yourself, or to Glenburn – if ye don't get yourself well? Ye maun go, lad, that's all about it.'

On the following Tuesday he crossed to Greenock with Mary. It was a wet, stormy afternoon. He looked and felt ill, and the misery of the coming separation lay upon him. And upon her too, yet she was brave, resolved not to give way. Under her windblown tweed hat, raincoat buttoned to her chin, her face was set in a mould of resolute cheerfulness. The *Pindari*, which had arrived overnight from Liverpool to take on a cargo of woollens and mill machinery, lay in the estuary veiled by a driving mist. The wind swept in staggering gusts across the docks, but she insisted on coming to the pier end to see him off, her hand beside his, under the handle of his old leather suitcase, sharing its weight. As the tender plunged and bumped in the strong tide beneath, they held each other closely, passionately, under the grey and dismal sky. Rain, like tears, ran down her cold cheeks, but her lips and breath were warm. Sick at heart, he could not bear to part from her.

'I'll take a chance and stay, Mary. God knows I don't want to go.'

'But you must, dear, for both our sakes. I'll write to you, and count every minute till you're back to me.' Just before she broke away and ran back along the jetty, she took a small package from her raincoat pocket and pressed it into his hand. 'Just so you'll mind me, Davie.'

In the cabin of the heaving tender, on the way out to the ship, he undid the wrappings and looked at what she had given him, It was an old thin gold locket, smaller than a florin piece, that had belonged to her mother. Inside she had placed a little snapshot of herself and in the back, carefully pressed, a single flower of the bluebells he had picked for her at Gairsay.

CHAPTER IX

HE CLAMBERED UP the swaying gangway and came aboard. The merchandise from Winton had already been loaded; he had barely time to report to the captain before the tugs were alongside and they began to nose cautiously down the Firth. He stood on deck, striving to penetrate the mist that shrouded the vague line of the shore where Mary would be standing, watching the departure of this spectral ship. His heart was filled with sadness and love. There were few people on deck – he knew they were returning to Tilbury to pick up the main body of passengers – and the damp emptiness and dripping stanchions increased his melancholy. The deep, despondent sounding of the fog-horn gave him a strange sense of foreboding. As the mist closed down, obliterating the shore, he turned and went below to find his quarters.

His cabin was aft, on the starboard side, next to the chief engineer's, furnished in polished teak wood with red curtains to the ports, a fitted locker and book rack, and a red-shaded bunk lamp, all particularly snug. A washstand with a metal basin that tipped up to let the water away stood in the corner, and above, on a guarded bracket, an electric fan. His consulting room and dispensary, conveniently situated across the alleyway, were both equally well equiped. Although the *Pindari* was an old ship, originally the *Isolde* of the Hamburg-Atlantic Line taken over after the war, she had been reconditioned from stem to stern and was now roomy, comfortable and notably seaworthy, capable of a modest seventeen knots, making a slow, sure run to India with cargo and passengers, touching en route at various ports.

When Moray had unpacked his suitcase, containing his own few things, all washed and ironed by Mary, and the two stock uniforms provided by the company's head office in Winton, he felt completely done; his side was hurting too. A rough Irish Sea and a bad passage up the Channel did not help him. He had difficulty in carrying out his first duty, a medical examination of the native crew, and at nights his cough was so troublesome he got little sleep. Concerned not only for himself but for his engineer neighbour, an elderly Scot named Macrae, whom he must have disturbed, he dosed himself with codeine. However, at Tilbury, where they spent two days at the docks, a letter from Mary put fresh heart in him, and when they cleared the Nore and were actually on their way, he began to feel more himself. The ship had life in her now, the screws thrust forward with a stronger throb, voices and laughter echoed along the companionways.

In the dining saloon each officer took his place at the head of his own table. Moray, at his, was allotted only five passengers, all somewhat elderly and, he had to admit, dull: two well-seasoned Scotch tea planters, Henderson and Macrimmon, returning to Assam, a Mr S. A. G. Mahratta, the Hindu manager of a cotton mill in Cawnpore, and an I.C.S. official and his jaundiced, severe-looking wife, Mr and Mrs Hunt-hunter. Except for the planters, who, particularly after a session in the bar, were inclined to jocularity, and Mahratta, a fussy, hypochondriacal little man with a bad stomach, who was sometimes unintentionally funny, the general tone of the conversation was restrained and promised to be difficult.

But now they were through the grey turbulence of the Bay, sunshine suddenly blazed, sky and sea were blue as they passed through the Straits and cruised up the south-east coast of Spain towards Marseilles, where more cargo was to be taken aboard. Deck games were being set out and Moray was advised by the first officer, a long, lean, goodnatured Irishman named O'Neil, that part of the doctor's duty was to organise them. So Moray, taking paper and pencil, approached the task of rounding up the passengers, at first with a sense of his unfitness for large-scale social intercourse, yet, after some preliminary self-consciousness, with success. His official position made things easier than he had imagined. He need not seek, he was sought after – a ship's surgeon was apparently a position of some consequence. When they arrived at Marseilles, lists of competitors for deck quoits, shuffleboard and table tennis had been drawn up and Moray, with a grimace, began to overhear himself referred to as 'our nice young doctor'.

At Marseilles a long, five-page letter from Mary awaited him. In his cabin he read it eagerly, smiling at her little bits of news, touched by the simple record of all she had been doing, through which there breathed a constant solicitude for his health. She hoped that his pain was gone, his cough less, that he was taking good care of himself. She sent him all her love. Dear Mary, how he missed her. In the surgery, squaring up to his desk, he wrote his reply, telling of all his activities, and was able to catch the outgoing mail before the sack was closed. The *Pindari* was no more than twelve hours in port. Loading completed, the hatches were battened down; then, almost at the last moment – the night train from Paris was late – three new passengers came on board. Since most of the tables in the saloon were fully occupied they were seated with the doctor, and their names added to the passenger list: Mr and Mrs Arnold Holbrook, Miss Doris Holbrook. Surreptitiously, Moray examined them, as they sat down to lunch.

Holbrook was a man of about sixty, not tall, but so heavily thickset as to be short of breath, with a red, porous, mottled face partly covered by a short grizzled beard, and small, bloodshot, genially knowing eyes. He was badly dressed in a greenish ready-made suit, grey flannel shirt and a stringy maroon tie. His wife a little homely woman with small features and a gentle expression, was, in contrast, wearing heavy, fashionable clothes and an elaborate black-sequined toque. Yet she carried them without ease, as though they encumbered her and she would have preferred much simpler attire – instinctively Moray thought of her in an old loose print wrapper, busy with her household duties in a well-stocked kitchen. She wore also so much jewellery that he erroneously assumed it to be paste. The daughter appeared to be not more than twenty. She was tallish, of a pale, dull complexion, with a good figure, dark hair and slate-grey eyes which, sitting erect and silent, she kept lowered sulkily during most of the meal.

Not so Holbrook. In the accents of Manchester, genially, expansively, with an air of experience, he broke the introductory ice, tactfully set conversation going, jollied the Tamil table boy until he had him grinning, started Mahratta off on a diverting account of his recent gastronomic difficulties in London that brought a smile even to the meagre lips of Mrs Hunt-hunter. When he had awakened the table to life, he casually revealed that his son was in Calcutta opening a branch of his business, that Dorrie – he looked towards his daughter, who ignored the affectionate glance – had just left Miss Wainwright's Finishing

80

School in Blackpool, and that their voyage to India was pleasure and business combined. It was only when he proposed ordering champagne all round that a reproving glance from his wife drew him up.

'Ah, well, Mother,' he deferred humorously, 'we'll have it at dinner tonight. That suit you, Dorrie?'

Doris gave him a pettish glance.

'You stop it, Dad. The story of your life will keep.'

'That's my girl.' He laughed indulgently, with a note of pride. 'I like to have you keep me right.'

'And about time.'

'Now, Doris,' her mother warned gently: then, looking round the table, she added, as though in extenuation: 'Our daughter hasn't been too well lately. And the night journey was real tiring for her.'

That same afternoon, as Moray came along the companionway towards his surgery, he found Holbrook standing before the notice board with his hands in his pockets, studying the sports lists.

'It looks as though you've got everyone pretty well booked up, doctor.'

'I've gone through the passenger list fairly thoroughly, sir.'

'Our Dorrie likes a game,' said the other in a reflective tone. 'And she's a dab at most of them. Surely you could find her a partner, doctor.' He paused. 'How about yourself? You're an active young fellow.'

Moray hesitated.

'I'll be glad to, sir,' he said, adding quickly: 'If it's permitted. I'll . . . I'll speak to the first officer.'

'Do that, lad. I'd appreciate it.'

Moray's impressions of Holbrook's daughter had not been favourable; he had no wish to be let in for this job. Besides, as a ship's officer, he doubted if he could participate in the competitions. However, when he had finished his consultations he found O'Neil on the bridge and explained the situation; the big Irishman had already been friendly and helpful, casually tipping him off on his more important duties.

'Sure ye can play, doc,' said O'Neil, in a Belfast accent you could cut with a knife. 'Ye're expected to be nice to the women. Besides, I saw this little bit come aboard. She looks as if she has something.' O'Neil's blue eyes twinkled. 'With luck ye might get a tickle.'

'I wouldn't be interested,' Moray said flatly. His pure-minded feeling for Mary made the suggestion, however goodnatured, unutterably distasteful to him.

'Well, anyhow, be civil – it'll do ye no harm and may do ye some good. The old boy's rolling. Holbrook's Pharmaceuticals. Began in a back street chemist's shop in Bootle. Made a fortune out of pills.' He grinned. 'Moving the bowels of humanity. The answer was in the purgative. Say, that reminds me. Did you ever hear this one?' O'Neil, a brave and gallant soul who had been torpedoed in the war, swimming for five hours in the Atlantic Ocean before being picked up, had a positive mania for telling off-colour stories. Submitting, Moray prepared his smile as the other went on: 'A Yank was coming tearing along the street in Chicago when another Yank standing on the sidewalk stopped him. "Can you direct me to a good chemist?" says he. "Brother," says the other, in a raging hurry, "if ye want God's own chemist just . . ." At the unprintable punch line O'Neil topped his cap to a more rakish angle and lay back on the binnacle, roaring with laughter.

Moray remained on the bridge for another half hour, pacing up and down with the first officer, watching the French coastline slip away, his cheeks whipped by the invigorating wind, which was always keener up top. Drummond had been right; there was health in the tang of the open sea. How much better he was feeling now, and how agreeable life was on board. He had forgotten his promise to Holbrook but when he went below it came to mind, and, with a shrug, he entered Miss Holbrook's name and his own in the doubles events.

CHAPTER X

THE WEATHER CONTINUED fine, the sea calm, the sky brilliant by day, shading through violet sunsets into velvet and luminous nights through which the *Pindari* traced its phosphorescent wake. This was the sea of Jason and Ulysses; at dawn the ship seemed suspended between sky and water, timeless and unreal, except that there, on the starboard bow, was Sardinia, the healthy fragrance of the island borne on a soft and fitful breeze.

Drawing deep, free breaths of this aromatic air without pain or hindrance, Moray knew that his pleurisy had gone. No need now to put his stethoscope on his chest. His skin was tanned, he had never felt better. After those years of prolonged grind, the present conditions of his life seemed altogether too good to be true. Awakened at seven by his cabin 'boy', who, padding barefoot from the galley, brought his *chota hazri* of tea and fresh fruit, he got up half an hour later, took a plunge in the sports deck swimming-pool, then dressed. Breakfast was at nine, after which he made his round of visits or, once a week, accompanied Captain Torrance on the official inspection of the ship. From ten-thirty till noon he was in his surgery. Lunch came at one, and thereafter, except for a nominal surgery at five o'clock, he was free for the rest of the day, expected only to make himself agreeable and obliging to the passengers. At seven-thirty the melodious dinner gong boomed up and down the alleyways – always a welcome sound, since the meals were rich, spicy and plentiful, the native curries especially delicious.

On the following Monday the tournaments began, and just before eight bells, recollecting his engagement, Moray closed the surgery and went up to the sports deck for the first round of the deck-tennis doubles. His partner was already there, wearing a short white skirt and a singlet, standing beside her parents who rather to his embarrassment, had taken deck chairs close to the court so that they might miss nothing of the game. As he apologised for keeping her waiting, although actually he was not late, she did not speak, and barely glanced at him. He scarcely knew whether she was nervous or, as he had suspected at table, merely perverse.

Their opponents arrived, a newly married Ditch couple, the Hendricks, who were on their way out to Chittagong, and the match began. At first Doris was carelessly erratic but, although he had never played the game before, he had a quick eye and managed to cover her mistakes, which he made light of, with his usual good humour. At this, she began to try, and to play brilliantly. She had a straight yet well-developed figure – round, very pretty breasts and hips, and long, well-shaped legs, revealed in motion by her short skirt. The Hendricks, a plump and heavy-footed pair, were no match for them. They won handsomely by six games to two. As he congratulated her, saying, 'Your father told me you were good at games, and you are,' she gave him one of her rare direct looks, fleeting and unsmiling.

'Yes,' she said. 'I've been taught a few tricks, and picked up some on my own. But aren't you going to buy me a drink? Let's have it up here.'

When the deck steward brought two tall lemon squashes, filled with ice, she lay back in her deck chair, with half-closed eyes, sipping her drink through the straw. He glanced at her awkwardly, at a loss as to what to say, a strange predicament for one who could invariably find the right word in the right place. The heat of the game had brought a faint colour into her pale complexion, and caused her singlet to adhere to her breasts, so that the pink of her nipples showed through the thin damp cotton. She's an attractive girl, thought Moray, almost angrily, but what the devil is the matter with her? Had she lost her tongue? Apparently not, for suddenly she spoke.

'I'm glad we won. I wanted to knock out that sickening pair of Dutch love-birds. Can you imagine them in bed together. "Excuse my fat, dear." I'd like to win all the tournaments. If only to spite our delightful passengers. What a crowd they are. I hate them all, don't you?'

'No, I can't say I do.'

'You can't mean it. They're an appalling lot, especially our table. Mrs Hunt-hunter – what a horse-faced hag. Makes me sick. She's common as mud, really. And the ship's lousy too. I never wanted to come on this damn trip. My devoted parents dragged me on board by the hair. My cabin is supposed to be one of the best on A deck. Dad paid through the nose for it. You should see it. A dog kennel, with a bath like the kitchen sink. That's the worst, for, if anything, I like to wash. And can you imagine, natives serving one's food. Why can't they have white stewards?'

'Our table boy seems a very decent jolly sort.'

'Haven't you noticed how he smells? It would kill you. I'm very sensitive about smells, it's something to do with the olfactory nerves the doctor told Mother. Phooey to him – smarmy windbag. The point is, I like people to smell clean.'

'Do I?' he couldn't help asking, ironically.

She laughed, stretching her long legs widely apart.

'Wouldn't you like to know? Frankly, you're the one faint gleam on the horizon. Didn't you notice me taking you in that first day at lunch? I either take to a person or I don't. I can tell at a glance. To be quite frank, I asked Father to get you as my partner. He's not a bad old bird though he is a bit of a soak. And Mother is passable, if only she'd stop clucking over me. But I have to keep them in order, quite often I absolutely *freeze* them, to get them to do what I want. I'm talking an awful lot. Sometimes I talk all the time, sometimes I say nothing, absolutely nothing. I like to treat people that way. I'm proud. I used to drive old Wainwright out of her mind. When she'd start lecturing me I'd simply look at her and throw myself into a coma.'

'She's your headmistress?'

'Was,' she said idly. 'She threw me out.'

'What on earth for?'

She gave him her slow smile.

'That may be revealed in a later instalment.'

On the following afternoon Doris and the doctor successfully played two rounds at bull board and one at deck quoits, and Doris's parents were again spectators. Moray quite enjoyed the games. He'd never met anyone like her before, so amusingly prejudiced and intolerant, so sure of her own privileged position, and yet with a streak underneath of commonness, of vulgarity almost, that redeemed her absurd pretensions. The fact that she liked him was flattering. It was now apparent that the Holbrooks doted upon their daughter, unresponsive though she might be, and he was less surprised than he might have been when they rose and came towards him, quite unusually pleased by the triple victory. Mrs Holbrook gave him a noticeably kind smile.

'You brought our Dorrie out, doctor,' she remarked. 'And did very well yourself, too.'

Doris herself, who was on the point of leaving, said nothing, but meeting his eye she gave him her peculiar half-smile. He talked to her parents for a bit; then as he left to go down to his surgery he observed them put their heads together, Mrs Holbrook apparently urging her husband to action. Indeed, some minutes later, Holbrook rolled into the dispensary, lush, genial and garrulous.

'Nothing the matter with me, doc. Nothing at all. Just felt like a sup of bishmuth. Nothing like bishmuth to ease the stomach. Where do you keep it? I'll help myself.'

Moray indicated the bottle of bismuth, wondering, as he watched the other nudge a generous helping into his palm, if he ought not to alert Holbrook to the state of his liver, which was palpably cirrhotic. Most days with Henderson and Macrimmon, the two tea planters, the old boy, except for his ventures to the sports deck and his chat with the captain on the bridge, was practically a fixture in the bar.

'That's the stuff,' Holbrook exclaimed, licking up the heap of white powder with prehensile thrusts of his furred tongue. 'And here's your fee, doctor.'

'Good heavens, sir, I couldn't take all that. It's . . . it's far too much.'

'Doctor,' said Holbrook, slowly fixing Moray with his small, knowing, injected eye. 'If you want the advice of a man who's seen a lot of this wicked world, when you get the chance of a good thing, take it!'

With warm generosity he pressed a five-pound note into the doctor's hand.

Thoughtfully replacing the bottle on the shelf when Holbrook had gone, Moray, who had been infected by O'Neil's vocabulary, caught himself smiling: 'We'd bloody well better win all the tournaments now.'

This, however, was no more than a pose. The girl had begun to interest him, as a study. At times she seemed far more mature than her years, at others almost backward. One day she would be moodily taciturn, the next full of amusing and provocative talk. What he rather admired in her was her complete indifference to what people thought of her. She never sought popularity and, unlike those who were already first-naming each other in tight little groups, seemed actually to enjoy being an outsider. She had a particular gift for taking off people and could be offensively rude to anyone who tried to flatter or make up to her. Her careless attitude extended even to her personal belongings, of which she had an endless variety. She was always leaving a bag, scarf or sweater on deck, mislaying and losing valuable things without turning a hair. These complexities in her character aroused his curiosity. When at lunch and dinner she would look towards him with her concealed and puzzling smile, he was more at a loss than ever. Oddly enough he was inclined to feel sorry for her.

All this gave an added spice of interest to what the mother had so inaptly phrased as 'bringing Dorrie out' in the tournaments. There was not, in fact, much competition in the games, since many of the passengers were elderly. Only one pair seemed to offer serious opposition, the Kindersleys, a couple with two young children who were returning to Kadur in Mysore after three months' leave. He was about thirty-five, excessively hearty and downright, manager of a small coffee estate that had been hit quite badly by the slump caused by excess production in Brazil. His wife, reputedly a fine lawn tennis player, was a pleasant little woman with a frank, rather serious expression. They sat at the first officer's table. As the *Pindari* drew near to the Suez Canal, Moray and his partner, playing well together, were in all three semi-finals. So also were the Kindersleys.

On the eve of their arrival at Port Said Mrs Holbrook, reclining on the promenade deck, beckoned the doctor, indicating the vacant chair beside her. On several occasions he had been honoured by this invitation and, in response to her gentle questioning, had disclosed enough of his early 'struggles' – comparable in some degree to her own – to win her sympathy and approval. Now, after a comment on the admirable weather and a query as to when the ship would dock, she leaned towards him.

'We're going ashore tomorrow to see the sights, and do some shopping. We expect you to come with us.'

He shook his head.

'I'm terribly sorry, Mrs Holbrook. I have to stay on board. I've all the health papers to attend to with the port M.O.H. And a sick man in the crew who may have to go to hospital.'

'What a pity,' she said, upset. 'Couldn't Mr Holbrook have a word with Captain Torrance?'

'Oh, no,' he interposed hurriedly. 'That's out of the question. The bill of health's most important. The ship can't sail without it.'

'Well,' she said at length, 'we were counting on you. Dorrie will be proper disappointed.'

A short pause followed, then in an intimate manner she began to speak about her daughter. Dorrie was such a dear girl, just the apple of her father's eye, but she had been – well, sometimes a bit of a worry to them. It wasn't as though they hadn't given her the best – yes, the very best education that money could buy; Miss Wainwright's was one of the most select schools in the North of England. She spoke French and could play the piano beautifully, really classical pieces. She'd had all sorts of private lessons in tennis and such-like, elocution and deportment. Father wanted her to have all the advantages. But she was such a highly strung girl, not exactly difficult, but, well, kind of moody and, though, mind you, she could be very lively and outspoken at times, inclined occasionally to get depressed – quite the opposite of her brother Bert who day in and day out was the jolliest chap in the world. Mrs Holbrook paused, her eyes lighting up at the thought of her son. Well, she concluded, she would say no more except that she was really and truly grateful, and Father was too, for the way he had taken an interest in Dorrie, and done her so much good – really, as one might say, wakened her up.

Moray was touched. He liked this homely little woman who, weighted by the expensive trinkets and unbecoming clothes heaped on her by her husband, made no bones about her origin, and was, despite Holbrook's wealth, entirely devoid of social pretensions, yet was so eagerly and, indeed, anxiously solicitous for her daughter. But he hardly knew what to say, and was compelled to fall back on mere politeness.

'Doris is a fine girl. And I'm sure she'll grow out of her little difficulties. Just look how she's doing in the tournaments. And of course, if there's anything I can do to help . . .'.

'You are good, doctor.' She pressed his hand maternally. 'I needn't tell you we've all real taken to you.'

CHAPTER XI

ON THE FOLLOWING day at ten o'clock they were off Port Said, passed the breakwater with the great de Lesseps statue and, after an hour's wait in midstream till the yellow quarantine flag came down, drew into the dock and began to take on oil and water. All the passengers who intended going ashore had left the ship by noon. The Holbrooks waved to Moray as they went down the gangway and he regretted not being with them. Viewed from the boat deck, the town had an enticing and mysterious air. Beyond the huddle of dock sheds it lay yellow and white against a flat horizon made hazy by the heat. Bright tiled roofs and balconies gleamed in the sun. The pencil shapes of twin minarets rose delicately above the narrow crowded streets filled with colour, sound and movement. A pity he could not have accepted Mrs Holbrook's invitation.

However, he had much to occupy him. The Lascar in sick bay was a suspect case of osteomyelitis, and when the port medical officer confirmed the diagnosis there were papers to be signed and irritating delays to be overcome before the man could be moved into the ambulance and transferred to hospital. Then the drinking-water tanks must be checked, after which the captain sent for him, and so it went on. The ship was full of hucksters, policemen, stevedores, Egyptian visitors, and company agents. Four bells struck before he was temporarily free, and as the outgoing post closed in half an hour he scarcely had time to finish and bring up to date the letter to Mary he had been writing at odd moments during the past few days. He felt guilty about this, the more so since, when the agent came aboard at six o'clock, three letters were in the mail sack from her, with one, he judged by the handwriting, from Willie. Rather than skim through these now, when he was so pressed for time, he decided to leave them on his locker and enjoy them at leisure after he turned in tonight. He still had to make out duplicate medical supply sheets for the extra emetine which, since an epidemic of amoebic dysentery was reported in the town, he had obtained from the port M.O. as a precautionary measure. When he had completed the company forms, he took them to the purser's office. Only then did he remember that he was due in the smoke-room, where the Holbrooks had asked him to meet them for a drink before dinner. Aware that he was late he hurried off along the promenade deck, meeting passengers, many in a state of hilarity, wearing fezes and laden with purchases from the bazaars: boxes of Turkish delight and Egyptian cigarettes – made, according to O'Neil, from camels' dung – terracotta models of the Sphinx, brassware covered with hieroglyphics: for the most part junk. Macrimmon, drunkenly draped in a white burnous, had bought a foetus in a glass bottle.

The Holbrooks had returned earlier and were there, all three, when he pushed through the glass swing doors, father, mother and Doris, surrounded by a score of packages. Holbrook, in high good humour, ordered the drinks: double Scotch for himself, champagne cocktails for the others; Mrs Holbrook, who rarely 'indulged' and usually tried to restrain her husband, allowed herself to be persuaded on the plea of a special occasion. Then they began to speak animatedly of their expedition. It had been a great success: they had taken a car and driven out along the shore of Lake Manzala, visited the great Mohammedan mosque, watched the performance of a snake charmer, inspected a collection of scarabs in the museum, lunched in the garden of the Pera Palace Hotel, where they had been given a wonderful fish curry served with sunflower seeds and green chillies, and finally, on the way back to the ship they had discovered a marvellous store.

'Not a trashy place like the bazaars,' said Mrs Holbrook. 'It's owned by a man called Simon Artz. We had a proper time, shopping with him.'

'Artz is a man of parts,' Doris laughed. 'He keeps everything from everywhere.' Holding up the mirror from her bag, she was putting on lipstick. Either from the sun or from excitement her cheeks were faintly flushed, making her eyes brighter. She had never looked more alive.

'So we bought ever so many things for our friends,' Mrs Holbrook resumed. 'And we didn't forget you, doctor. Working hard for us here while we were off enjoying ourselves.' With an affectionate smile she handed him a small oblong package.

Reddening, he took it awkwardly, not knowing whether or not to open it.

'Go on, have a look,' Holbrook urged slyly. 'It won't bite.'

He opened the case, expecting to find some trivial souvenir. Instead it was a red gold wristlet watch, with a delicately plaited gold strap, a Patek Phillippe too, the best and most expensive hand-made Swiss movement. It must have cost the earth. He was speechless.

'You are quite the kindest and most generous people,' he stammered, at last. 'It's the very thing I want and need . . .'.

'Say no more about it, lad,' Holbrook broke in. 'Our Dorrie happened to notice you didn't wear one. 'Twas her that chose it for you.'

Looking suddenly towards her, Moray caught her gaze fixed directly upon him, that challenging, intimate look which somehow bound them together in a kind of conspiracy.

'Don't make a song about it, Dad. Let it pass. Or I'll tell how you asked about the belly dancers.'

Holbrook laughed, drained his glass, and stood up.

'I'm famished. Let's have the steward move this stuff to the cabin and we'll all go right down to dinner.'

When the ship was in port dinner became an elastic meal served at almost any hour, and they were the first to arrive at their table. The sense of intimacy begun in the smoke-room was thus maintained and they made a lively party, of which Doris was the liveliest. Her attitude towards her parents, that of a spoiled only daughter, always superior, and varying between sulky and tolerant contempt, was replaced by a sort of bantering raillery, directed mainly towards her father, who responded in the same style. At first Moray assumed, unkindly enough, that Holbrook had bought her something particularly nice ashore. But no, now he was teasing her for having refused all his offers. Some of her remarks, though perhaps too pointed, were very amusing, especially when she began to take off their absent table companions in malicious little impersonations. This, however, drew from her mother a restraining, 'Now, Dorrie dear, remember . . . not too much.'

At this Doris did give up with a side glance at Moray, which made him party to the entertainment. Meanwhile the engines had started to vibrate and the ship was now clear of the dock. As it began the slow passage through the canal, Mrs Holbrook, obviously pleased by the resurgence of family harmony, suggested that they take their coffee on the upper deck and watch the sunset over the desert. A word from Holbrook to the head steward was enough to overcome every difficulty, and presently, sheltered by an awning on the starboard side, they were sipping hot coffee at a round table set out with a dessert of fresh fruit, chow-chow, and preserved ginger. As the great molten disc slid into that vast waste of sand, palm trees were outlined in the limitless light, a string of camels slowly plodding, Bedouin tents, a nomad tribe. Then in the indigo sky a moon was revealed, brightening as the night advanced. In the main lounge beneath them the ship's orchestra began softly to play a medley of the popular tunes of the day. Moray, who was sitting next to Doris, heard her take a restless breath. Lying back in the deck chair with her arms behind her head, she moved about as though unable to find a relaxed position.

'Aren't you comfortable?' he said. 'Let me get you a cushion.'

'A cushion! Pardon me if I smile. I'll be all right – just a bit worked up tonight.'

'Who wouldn't be? You can feel we're in the East. What a sky.'

'And with music.' She hummed a few bars of 'My Heart Stood Still', stopped, hummed again, then exclaimed: 'If this goes on I'll go half-cocked.'

He laughed.

'Before you do, let me thank you for choosing such a beautiful watch.'

'I know what I like. I liked the watch and quite frankly I like you. D'you mind?'

'Not at all. I'm pleased, and grateful.'

Neither spoke for a minute; then she broke out again.

'Doesn't it do something to you up here? Like bathing in warm milk. Not that I ever have, though it's an idea. The milky way. But you'd keep losing the soap. I wish we were going swimming. Not in the sickening little pool. On a deserted beach, where we'd have it to ourselves, no need to bother about bathing suits.' She laughed again. 'Don't look so shocked, you fool. Don't you ever feel that you're all wound up and excited, right on top of the world?' Tapping her shoe on the deck, she sang: ' "I'm sitting on top of the world, singing a song, rolling along . . .". Such a marvellous sensa . . . shun. When I

get it I'm ready for anything. I have it tonight, if you're interested.'
She stretched at full length, hummed again, then sat up. 'I can't
get that damned tune out of my head. What a slouch you are!
Surely you want to dance. Come on and take a turn.'

There was an awkward pause, then he said:

'I'm afraid I wouldn't be much good to you.'

'Why not?'

'It will probably surprise you. I don't dance.'

'What! Tell me another. You're having me on.'

'No.' He had to smile at her expression. 'I was too busy
shoving myself through college to learn any parlour tricks.'

'Well, now's your big chance. It's dead easy if you have a good
teacher. And that's just what I am.'

'No, really. I'll only walk all over your feet and make a complete ass of myself.'

'Who is there to see you up here? The old man's gone to the
bar and Mother's dozed off. We've got the music, and the moon.
It's a perfect opportunity. And all free, gratis, and for nothing.'
She stood up and held out her hand. 'Come on, I'll put you in
the mood.'

He rose and, rather gingerly, placed his arm round her waist.
They started off.

'It's a foxtrot,' she told him. 'Just keep time. Short steps.
Now turn. Swing round. Hold me closer, I won't break. Closer,
I said. That's better. Strange as it may seem, we're supposed to
do this together.'

It was surprisingly easy. The tune was so catchy, she was such
a good dancer, so responsive, with such an easy laxness of posture,
that he found himself instinctively following the beat of the
rhythm, improvising steps, letting himself go. When the band
below came to the end of the number she gave him a meaning,
condescending nod.

'Didn't I tell you?'

'It's tremendous,' he admitted. 'I'd no idea. And good exercise
too.'

She gave a short odd laugh.

'That's one way to look at it.'

'Of course, you're an expert – wonderful, in fact.'

'It's one of the things I'm really gone on. In my last year at
school I used to sneak out with another girl on Saturday nights
and go to the local Palais. We'd pretend we were pros, you know,

sixpence-a-timers. We had some larks, I can tell you, kidding and carrying on – until one night there was a regular shindy . . .'.

'Was that why you had to leave school?'

Unexpectedly she tossed her head back with an injured air.

'That's a very personal question. I don't like it brought up just like that. It was no blame of mine. Actually, if you want to know, I've danced mostly with Bert, my own brother. And he's respectable enough.' Suddenly she laughed. 'Or is he? Well, never mind, I forgive you. Now get me a cigarette, and bring the lighter. They're in my bag beside the chairs.'

She leaned against him while he flicked her gold lighter.

'You don't use these?' He shook his head when she offered a cigarette. 'What a lot of things you seem to have done without.'

'I'll get them all one day.'

'Don't put it off too long. I always go straight for what I want.'

They stood with their backs to the taffrail until the band struck up again, then she threw away her half-smoked cigarette and turned to him.

'We're off again. Put some feeling into it. Imagine you've just picked me up on the prom at Blackpool and we've really clicked.'

'Good Lord,' he grinned. 'That's not my line at all.'

'That's why you're so nice,' she murmured, pressing a little closer to him. 'But try all the same.'

They danced the next three dances and with each he could feel his improvement. This was a new experience, and exciting that he could pick the steps up so quickly. But with an eye to the proprieties he felt that it must not be overdone. As they approached her mother he drew up.

'Thank you so much, Doris. It's been simply grand, and now,' he looked at his new watch, 'I must say goodnight.'

'Goodnight nothing, it's quite early and we're only beginning to have fun.'

'No, really, Doris, I have to go below.'

She stared at him, her slate-blue eyes clouding with anger and disappointment.

'How stupid can you be? Wasting everything, with this moon and when we're just getting in the mood. We'll sit out for a bit if you're tired.'

'I'm not tired. But I do think it's time we both turned in.'

Mrs Holbrook, who, awakening from her nap, had been watching them indulgently, seemed to think so too. She rose and came towards them.

'Time for bed,' she announced. 'We've all had a busy day.'

'You've certainly made mine a pleasant one,' Moray said gracefully.

'You'll be sorry you let me down like this,' Doris said in his ear, not moving her lips, as he passed her. 'You just wait!'

She's joking, he thought – can't really mean it. Goodnights were exchanged, Doris's a violently sulky one; she looked really put out. Then, with the last bars of 'Desirée' still ringing in his ears, he went below to his cabin, switched on the light, and there, on his locker, confronting him like a reproach, were the letters from home.

Instantly his mood changed. Shocked at his own forgetfulness, he undressed quickly, climbed into his bunk and, swept by compunction, settled himself to read. There were in all half a dozen sheets to Mary's letters filled with her large round careful handwriting. She began by acknowledging his letter from Marseilles, expressing her joy at his improved health. Yet she begged him to be careful still, especially of the night air, and she hoped that his duties were not proving too severe. As for herself, she was well, though missing him badly, marking off the days on her calendar until he would be back. But she was keeping herself busy, with lots of sewing and crochet work. She had bought material for curtains for their house, and also some remnants with which she had begun a patchwork quilt. There was the chance of a nice second-hand parlour suite, very good value, at Grant's just off the Esplanade. She only wished that he might see it, but he would soon, they had promised to reserve it. Unfortunately her father had been somewhat poorly lately, but she had been able to help by doing a bit with Donaldson, the foreman, in the bakery. She signed herself simply: your own Mary.

He finished reading with a worried frown and an odd constriction of his heart. Did he not detect a note of anxiety, an undercurrent of despondency even, in her words? She wrote naïvely, always from an open heart, yet it might be that she had not told all. Hastily, he turned to Willie's letter.

Dear Davie,
    I hope you are well and having a good voyage. I wish I was

95

with you. I would like to see all these foreign countries, especially Africa. Things have not been doing too well here since you left. The weather has been cold and wet and Father had a bad turn with his heart, it was after a man came to see him one day. I think he is bothered about the business. I heard Aunt Millie say that the Stoddarts have fairly got their knife in us. Mary is doing the scones now in the bakehouse. I am sure she is missing you an awful lot. I am too. So tell the captain to get a move on and hurry back.

Affectionately yours,

Willie.

He put down the letter in concern, recognising from the brief and boyish phrases that Mary was having her troubles at home, and missing him too, so badly. His heart melted anew with love and longing, and with contrition, too, when he thought of the comfort, yes, the luxury, of his own pleasant life here. He wished suddenly that he had never taken this voyage. If only he could be beside her now to console and caress her. He must do something . . . something. The need of swift response, of immediate action, grew upon him. He thought for a few moments with knitted brow, then took up the officers' intercommunication phone. He asked for the wireless room. Saving though he was for their future, he must mortgage a little of his pay to reach Mary at once.

'Sparks, I want to send this radiogram.' He gave the address. *'Letters just received Port Said. Don't worry. Everything all right when I return. All my love David.'*

When Sparks had repeated this, word by word, he thanked him and hung up, smiling faintly. How thrilled and delighted she would be to get his message soaring to her across the ocean, and how comforted too! His mind now more at ease, filled with loving thoughts, he switched off the light and settled himself to sleep.

CHAPTER XII

THEY WERE IN the narrows of the Gulf of Suez, the peaks of Sinai shimmering above in a humid haze. For three days it had been hot, a harsh, insufferable heat. In the Red Sea the sun blazed down upon the *Pindari*; the rocks of Aden, grilled to a torrid ochre, cracked and fissured by the heat, were truly barren, and the port itself looked so uninviting that few passengers went ashore. The Holbrooks were amongst those who remained on board. Doris, indeed, since the night of the expedition at Suez, had not appeared on deck, being confined to her cabin with a slight indisposition, Mrs Holbrook explained to Moray. He was on the point of offering his services when a certain reserve in her manner, perhaps a hint that this was a delicate subject, deterred him. He decided it must be some mild monthly upset, a conclusion strengthened when Mrs Holbrook murmured intimately: 'Dorrie occasionally gets these turns, doctor.' So he merely sent his regards adding that the inhuman heat was enough to knock out anyone.

The weather had suddenly made him extremely busy. Apart from a rush of surgery patients suffering from the usual complaints of dhobie itch, prickly heat and over-zealous endeavours to acquire a tan, he had several quite serious cases. He was particularly worried over the two Kindersley children, who had both gone down with acute colitis. Following on the Suez scare of amoebic dysentery, Mrs Kindersley was in a state of near panic, and as the twins were at one point critically ill he had himself begun to fear the worst. But after being in almost constant attendance for forty-eight hours, there was a sharp improvement just before dawn on the third day, and with an inward sigh of relief he was able to relieve the distracted mother. Red-eyed from weariness, collar undone, hair dishevelled, he straightened stiffly, read his clinical thermometer at the light.

'They'll be up and around . . . making a nuisance of themselves

. . .' he smiled and put his arm round her shoulders, 'the beginning of next week.'

She broke down. She was a reserved, self-contained woman but, like Moray, she had barely slept for two nights.

'You've been so completely wonderful, doctor. How can I ever thank you?'

'By turning in and getting some rest. You've got to get fit for our tournament finals.'

'Yes.' She dried her eyes, trying to answer his smile. 'I should like that nice tea-service for our bungalow. But isn't your partner ill?'

'Oh, nothing much, I imagine.'

She had come with him to the cabin door. Now she hesitated, looking at him intently, then she made up her mind.

'Bill and I think a lot of you, doctor – especially after this. . . . We've often wondered if you were, well, beginning to get – mixed up with Miss Holbrook.'

'Mixed up?' he repeated blankly, then with a sudden flush, realising her meaning: 'Of course not.'

'I'm glad.' She pressed his hand. 'She's attractive, and she's obviously completely gone on you. But there's something odd about that girl, something I could never like – Bill says she's a split personality, she gives him the creeps. Now you do forgive me for having spoken?'

'Quite all right.' He tried to speak easily, although he was both embarrassed and offended. 'Now take that triple bromide I gave you and off you go to your bunk.'

Uncomfortably, he went back to his cabin, shaved and showered, drank two cups of coffee, and set out on his round of visits. He had begun to realise that Doris was not popular on the ship. She was often rude, kept a great deal to herself, and doubtless, since she wore an expensive new dress every other night, provoked feminine envy with her nice clothes. Moreover, it seemed to him that their continued success in all the competitions was arousing unfavourable comment. Was this the reason of Mrs Kindersley's dislike? He could scarcely believe it. Her intervention was well-meaning. Even so, he resented it. What right had she to interfere in his affairs, especially since he had been blameless in the matter? And what the devil did Kindersley mean, with his cheap sneer? He was no paragon – a beery, social type that probably hung around the club at Kadur all day; no wonder his wife was so surprised. All morning Moray brooded, and his train of thought, rather than turning him against Doris, swung him in her favour. Admittedly she was not an ordinary, run-of-the-mill type, but was she any the worse for that? There was something to her. Instinctively he rose to her defence. Still, he decided it might be wiser to cut down their efforts in the tournaments.

At the end of the week it suddenly turned cooler, his work and the weather became less hectic. He had time to write a long, loving letter to Mary, with an enclosure specially for Willie. And that same afternoon he was given a further lift when O'Neil took him aside to say:

'I thought you'd like to know, Doc, the skipper had a good word for you on the bridge this morning. In fact, when he heard about the Kindersley kids, he said you were doing a hell of a nice job. The only sawbones we've had yet that didn't get corns on his behind.' The big Irishman paused, took a long look at Moray's new watch, and grinned. 'Present from a grateful patient? Go to it, my boy. You'll soon reach pay-dirt or I'm not from County Down.'

'Haven't I told you I'm not interested,' Moray said, irritably. 'I'm only rather sorry for her because she's such a little outsider.'

'Then why aren't you a little insider?' said O'Neil, and roared with laughter. 'Ah, now, don't be so backward in coming forward, my boy. We're all looking for a bit of skirt on this bloody tub – otherwise it would bore the arse off us. Say, did you ever hear this one . . .'

Moray had to laugh. What a decent sort O'Neil was. There wasn't a bit of harm in his remark, he didn't really mean it – like his profane limericks, it was just fun. Why couldn't the Kindersleys see it that way?

On the following day, when it was even cooler, Doris appeared on deck. He came on her reclining in a sheltered spot, her hair bound with a silk scarf, a light cashmere rug over her knees, looking dull and with dark lines beneath her eyes. She did not move, merely flickered her lashes towards him.

'Hello, stranger, where have you been hiding?' He took the chair beside her. 'Feeling better?'

Injured by his brightness, she did not reply.

'Quite a few people have been laid out by the heat,' he continued. 'But now it's really lovely.'

They were in the Indian Ocean where the soft monsoon made songs in the rigging and a school of young whales, disporting gaily, blew temperate fountains about the ship.

'You've seen our escort,' he went on. 'I thought whales were only found in the Arctic, but O'Neil tells me they're a regular feature of this run.'

She took no notice of the remark, making it sound fatuous. Head pillowed sideways on the chair, she watched him with flat eyes as if she were drugged.

'You're a nice one,' she said.

'Why, Doris, what's the matter?'

'Don't pretend, after what you did. It was an insult. I haven't forgiven you yet. Who have you been dancing with while I was away?'

'No one. I've been waiting on my own special teacher.'

Her expression lightened faintly. She gave him a languid smile.

'Why didn't you come to see me? Oh, well, there wasn't any need. And I can't bear anyone when I have these turns. I don't get them often, mind you, not more than once in six months.'

He looked at her curiously; it wasn't what he had imagined. She went on:

'But they're not exactly fun. Even when the headache goes, they leave me so blasted low.'

'That's not you, Dorrie.'

'Don't give me that, like Mother. When I'm this way I keep thinking what's the good of anything, why go on, what's the use. I feel I'm a terrible person, different from other girls, all so full of sweet ideas. You know what I mean. Clapcows!' She laughed suddenly. 'Where did I get that word?'

'Well, it's good to be a little different from the ordinary.'

'Glad you think so. I used to try to work it all out, that time I was off school for a bit, wanting to be respected, to have everything just right. But I couldn't do anything about it. So now I just do as I feel, you know – what I feel like doing. I can't fight it. Don't you agree? You kill everything that's in you if you don't give way to your feelings.'

'Well . . .' He stared at her perplexedly. Why was she going on like this? He didn't follow her at all.

'You know the motto, be yourself. It's a challenge. I'm glad

I'm feminine, made for love, so I just want to be myself. Did you miss me? But you wouldn't, you beastly rotter, you make friends so easily and get on with everybody. I've never made any real friends, I just don't seem to get on with people, except you.' She paused, said in a low voice: 'Can't you see I've a frightful crush on you?'

He was touched by the admission. Her apathetic voice and unusual depression went to his heart. And of course he was flattered, too.

'Come now, Dorrie, you mustn't give way.' He reached out and pressed her hand. 'If you want to know, I did miss you.'

Inclining her head a little more to one side, she looked at him intently; then, retaining his hand as he made to withdraw, she tucked it beneath the cashmere rug.

'That's cosy. I missed *you* so much.'

Moray was fearfully embarrassed, not only by the unexpectedness of her action but because, undoubtedly without her knowing it, she had pressed his fingers against the warm softness of her thigh.

'Now, Doris,' he tried to speak lightly, 'you can't do that there here – not to the ship's surgeon.'

'But I need a little petting. Mind you, I don't let anybody into my life. Oh, I've been around with boys, some of them high, wide, and handsome, but you're different. I've such an unselfish feeling towards you.'

'Please . . . someone is sure to come along.'

'You can say you're feeling my pulse.' She gave him a malicious caressing look. 'Or else I'll tell them it's what the doctor ordered. Oh, you're doing me so much good. I feel less of a washout already.'

At last with a laugh she released him, but not before a wave of heat brought the blood to his cheeks. Quickly he countered it, forcing a reproving smile.

'You mustn't try these sort of tricks, my girl, or you'll come to a sticky end. In the first place you're too damned attractive, and in the second you might pick the wrong man.'

'But I've picked you.'

'Now listen, and be serious.' He turned the conversation determinedly. 'There's something I've been thinking. It's this. As you're not quite up to the mark, I feel we ought to scratch from the tournaments.'

'What!' she exclaimed, losing her air of indolence. 'Pack up. After we've gone all the way to the finals and are practically sure to win?'

'If we do, and scoop in all the prizes, we're sure to be blamed for pot-hunting.'

'I don't care about the prizes – that plated tea-service and cheap Woolworth china I frankly wouldn't touch with a barge pole. But if I start something I have to finish it, convince people I amount to something – especially that prissy Kindersley bitch. I got my self-respect to think of. I want to show that we're the best in the ship.'

'Well, we may be, but why rub it in?'

'Because I want to rub it in. And when I want a thing I usually get it. I may be a bit down now but I pick up quick. I'll be on top of my form in no time.'

'All right then,' reluctantly he pacified her. 'Have it your way. But we must play Saturday at the latest. It's the captain's dinner that night and the presentation comes before the concert.' He rose. 'Now I must get on with my round. See you anon.'

Saturday came, they did play – in the afternoon – and, as Moray had anticipated, won all three events. Mrs Kindersley and her husband fought hard in the deck-tennis match, but as Doris, quite herself again, played a fast aggressive game they were scarcely good enough. The climax came in the final set when Kindersley, reaching too far, missed his footing, skidded, then upended himself on the deck with a fearful thud.

'Oh, do be careful.' Doris leaned over the net with mock solicitude. 'You're rocking the boat.'

Not many spectators attended the event and a hollow silence greeted the remark. Indeed, when the match ended the applause that greeted the victors was less unenthusiastic than perfunctory. Moray was annoyed although Doris, who was again in high spirits, did not appear to notice any lack of warmth. Nor did her parents who, inevitably, were present. When Moray came off the court Holbrook took his arm and drew him into the smoke-room.

'I thought you and me ought to have a chat, doctor,' he remarked, with an approving smile, when they had found two armchairs in a quiet corner. 'And the better the opportunity the better the deed. Will you have a spot of something? No?

You'll not refuse a lime-juice then. And I'll just take a chota peg of Scotch and soda.'

When the drinks were brought he raised his glass.

'Good health! You know, lad, you remind me of my own young days. I was ambitious too – a chemist's assistant in Bootle, making up prescriptions for ignorant G.P.s who didn't know an acid from an alkali. Many's the time I had to ring up and say: "Doctor, you've prescribed soda bicarb, and hydrochloric acid in the same stomach mixture. If I make it up it'll blow the bottle to bits." Maybe 'twas that sort of thing first gave me the idea that there was money in pharmaceuticals that actually worked. When I'd saved a bit and married the wife and opened my own bit of a shop in Parkin Street, I started off with a few of my own prescriptions: Holbrook's Headache Powders, Holbrook's Senna Paste, Holbrook's Anti-Sprain Liniment. I remember that liniment, it cost me three farthings a bottle, and I sold it for one-and-six. Damn good stuff too, all the Rugby League teams used it, it's still one of our lines today. Well, that was the beginning, lad.'

He took a slow swallow of his drink, then resumed, explaining the growth and expansion of his business, not boastfully, but with the quiet North Country assurance of a man who has built up an immensely successful enterprise and amassed a fortune from it. Holbrook's were now one of the biggest manufacturers of chemists' supplies in the United Kingdom, but the bulk of their profits came from the marketing of a large number of highly profitable proprietary medicines ranging from cough cures to anti-bilious pills.

'And don't you despise them, doctor, they're all first-rate prescriptions, I can show you testimonials by the thousands. I've kept a personal file of grateful letters that would warm your heart.' Holbrook nodded confidingly and warmed his own cockles with another swallow. 'So as we stand now we have the main factory in Bootle, a secondary unit in Cardiff, and big distributing warehouses in London, Liverpool, Glasgow and Belfast. We do a tremendous export trade with the East, and that's why my son Bert is out opening up new offices and larger stockrooms in Calcutta. But that's not all, lad,' Holbrook continued, knowingly prodding Moray with a forefinger. 'We have plans, big plans, for extending to America. Once Bert gets through with Calcutta I'm sending him to New York. He's already spied out a good factory site there. Mind you, it'll be a different kind of trade in the States. Times are changing and we'll go in for high class stuff, vitamins and such-like. We might even have a go at some of the new barbiturates. But believe me, whatever we do we'll make a slap-up success of it.'

He sat back, pulled out a cigar and lit up, wheezed a little, then, his twinkling eyes still holding Moray, he smiled.

'These are my prospects, young fellow me lad. Now what about yours?'

'Well, sir,' Moray had coloured slightly at the directness of the question, 'when I get back from this trip I have a hospital job waiting on me. A good one too, with opportunity for research work and . . . a salary of five hundred a year.'

'Ay, that's a job, lad, right enough and, saving your presence, a pretty ordinary one. I asked about your prospects.'

'Naturally, I'm hoping for advancement . . .'.

'What kind of advancement? A move to a bigger hospital? I'm pretty familiar with that line of country. It'll take years. Once you're in the hospital service you're bogged down in it for life. And for a smart young fellow like you, with brains and personality, that would be a crime.'

'I don't regard it as such,' Moray said stiffly.

'Well, I do. And I wouldn't tell you so if the missus and I didn't think the world of ye. Now look here,' he tipped the ash off his cigar end, 'I'm not a man to beat about the bush. We could use a young medico like you in our business, especially in the American plant. You could advise us on technique, work out new prescriptions, lay out our advertising and, since ye speak of research, get busy in our new laboratory. There would be plenty of opportunity for you. And from our point of view it would help us to have a professional man on the board. As to salary,' he paused, riveting Moray with a friendly, bloodshot eye, 'I would start you at fifteen hundred quid a year, with a possible bonus, and annual increases. Furthermore, I'll go so far as to say that, in time, if things went well between us, there might even be a partnership in store for ye.'

Thoroughly taken aback, stunned, in fact, Moray averted his gaze. The nature of this startling offer, while it had a sound basis of commercial logic, was in reality as transparent as the port-hole through which he now viewed with embarrassment the slowly heaving sky. And Holbrook meant it to be transparent.

104

How to refuse gracefully, without hurting the old boy's feelings, without indeed alienating the entire family, that was the problem At last he said:

'It's extremely generous of you, Mr Holbrook, and I feel deeply honoured by your good opinion of me. But I've accepted the hospital appointment, given my word. I couldn't break it.'

'They'll get somebody else,' Holbrook countered easily. 'Ay, without the slightest trouble. There'll be a regular hard-up rush.'

Moray was silent. He knew that he had only to mention his approaching marriage to kill the offer dead. But for some obscure reason, perhaps an over-sensitivity, an exaggerated delicacy of feeling, he hesitated. He stood so well with this worthy family that he did not relish the thought of shattering – as he undoubtedly would – a very pleasant and satisfactory relationship. Besides, the question of his engagement had never once come up during the voyage. It was not his fault if he had been mistaken for an unattached young man; he had simply not had the opportunity to introduce the subject. How painfully odd it would seem if he were forced to do so now. He'd look an absolute idiot, or worse, as though he had almost been ashamed to speak of Mary. No, with the end of the trip almost in sight, he could not place himself in so invidious a position. It wasn't worth it. In a few more days the Holbrooks would be gone, he would never see them again. And on the voyage home he would take good care to declare his position early so that this kind of contretemps could not possibly recur. In the meantime his best course would be to temporise.

'I needn't say how much I appreciate your interest in me, sir. But naturally, with such an important decision to be made, I'd have to think it over.'

'Do that, lad,' said Holbrook with an encouraging nod. 'The more ye think on it the better you'll like it. And don't forget my bit of advice. When a good thing comes your way, take it.'

Moray went below to his cabin, and shut himself in. He wanted to be alone – not to consider this extraordinary offer, for he had not the slightest intention of accepting it, but, simply for his own satisfaction, to reason in detail how the thing had come about. In the first place, there was no doubt but that Dorrie's parents had taken to him from the start. Mrs Holbrook especially had shown great partiality and had lately become almost maternal in her attitude. Old Holbrook was a tougher article, but he too had been won over, either through his wife's persuasion, or through an actual liking for Moray. In the second place, so far as could be gathered, there would be a definite advantage to Holbrook and his son Bert in the acquisition of an active and clever young doctor for this new American venture. So far so good, thought Moray; but the answer was not yet conclusive. A third decisive motive must have operated to bring the two other factors together.

Moray shook his head unconsciously, in self-disparagement, in immediate renunciation of all conceit, yet there was no escaping the fact that Doris herself must have had an important part in the development of this wholly unexpected situation. Even if he had not the evidence of Mrs Kindersley's recent remarks, there was proof enough in Dorrie's own behaviour. She was not the love-sick type, she would not sigh and moon around, but that look in her eye had a specific meaning that only a fool would misconstrue. Add to this the influence which, as a spoiled only daughter, she exercised over parents who were accustomed to yielding to her wishes, and in this instance willing to see her settled in a suitable marriage, and the answer was complete.

During these reflections Moray had been frowning. Now, looking at himself in the glass, he gave a short, troubled laugh. Doris had really gone in off the deep end – head over heels. No, no, it wasn't funny, not a bit of it. On the contrary – adjusting his expression – he felt put out and embarrassed, although no doubt it was flattering to be sought after and to have a rich, attractive girl so 'completely gone on him' – Mrs Kindersley's absurd phrase came to him again, making him smile – particularly when those moments on the upper deck, and others, came to mind, as they did now, with a sudden disturbing rush.

He checked himself, looked at his watch – that fine Patek Philippe – which showed five minutes to six. Good Lord! He'd forgotten about his surgery hour. He'd have to rush. Life was really exciting these days.

But before he left the cabin he went to his bedside chest and took out the locket Mary had given him. Gazing at her dear sweet face in the little snapshot, a rush of tenderness overwhelmed him. He murmured emotionally:

'As if I'd give you up, my own darling girl.'

Yes, her image would protect him. In future he would be calm and composed, pleasant and agreeable of course, but inflexible to any of *that* nonsense. Only ten days remained before they would be in Calcutta. He swore by all he held dear that he would maintain this attitude of discretion until the danger was past, and the voyage over.

CHAPTER XIII

THE TEN DAYS had passed, they were now in the delta of the Hoogly, and Moray, alone in his surgery, viewing that period in retrospect, found every reason to be satisfied with himself. Yes, he had kept his word. At the captain's dinner, a hilarious affair of paper streamers, toy trumpets, and false noses, he had been a model of discretion. Indeed, he had done better. Resolved not to allow Doris to make an exhibition of herself, and him, before the entire ship, when O'Neil read out the sports prize winners he stood up, diffidently yet calmly, and with an unexpectedness that took everyone by surprise.

'Captain Torrance, Mr O'Neil, ladies and gentlemen, with your kind permission may I say that Miss Holbrook and I fully understood from the start that as one of the ship's officers I was not really eligible to compete in these events. We only went in for the fun of the thing and although we were lucky enough to win, we've both completely agreed we couldn't possibly accept the prizes, which should go in all the events to the runners-up.'

When he sat down, instead of the few desultory handclaps that might have broken out, there was a sudden and sustained eruption of genuine applause. The Holbrooks were delighted, for even they had at last begun to sense the general feeling; Mrs Kindersley went up, smiling, for her tea service; and afterwards the captain actually gave him a word of approval. Only Doris reacted unfavourably with a very dirty look.

'Why the devil did you do that?'

'Just for a change I thought you might like to be popular.'

'Popular my tits. I wanted them to boo us.'

He danced only two dances with her, drank no more than a single glass of champagne, then, on the plea of having letters to write, excused himself and retired to his cabin.

After that, while never easy, it was less difficult. He avoided the boat deck where she usually sat, and when they did meet adopted a tone that was light and jocular. Beyond that, he kept himself strictly busy – the approaching landfall made his plea of extra work a plausible excuse. What Doris thought he did not know: following the dinner she had developed a habit of looking at him with narrowed, almost mocking eyes. Occasionally she smiled, and once or twice, when he made a simple remark, burst out laughing. Certainly her parents suspected nothing; they were more marked in their attentions to him than ever.

He sighed suddenly – it had really been quite a strain – then, rising, he locked up the surgery and went on deck. On the starboard side a group of passengers had gathered, viewing the river bank with an interest made greater by long days at sea. Tall coconut palms rose above the muddy shore lit by a flash of tropical birds, natives knee deep in the yellow water were throwing and drawing their circular nets, catamarans heeled and rippled past, the ship was barely moving, almost stationary, awaiting the river pilot. Amongst the others were the Holbrooks, and finding safety in numbers, Moray joined them. Immediately Mrs Holbrook excitedly took his arm.

'We're so hoping that our Bert will be coming aboard with the pilot . . . not that it's easy . . .'.

As she spoke a motor launch shot from the sandy, palm-lined shore and bobbed alongside the ship, and another figure was observed, looking upwards and waving, beside the uniformed pilot.

'It *is* our Bert,' joyfully exclaimed Mrs Holbrook, and she added proudly to her husband: 'Trust Bert to have managed it.'

He was on board and hugging all three of them within a few minutes, a fair, fattish, pink-faced, jolly fellow of about thirty-one or two, wearing a sportily cut, tight-waisted tussore silk suit, solar topee at an angle, fine two-tone buckskin shoes and a startling club tie. Bert, indeed, though inclined to flesh and, as now appeared when he removed his topee, rather thin on the top, seemed something of a dandy, exhibiting gold in his teeth and, on his person, certain articles of unessential jewellery. His eyes, alight with good-fellowship, were agreeably blue though they protruded slightly and had a faintly glassy sheen. His ready laugh, full of bonhomie and sportsmanship, a real back-slapping laugh, echoed across the deck. Too much thyroid, but a good sort, thought Moray, who had been standing some paces away, as

Bert came forward to be introduced to him.

Their meeting was cordial – anyone, Moray surmised, might be an old friend of Bert's within a couple of hours – but he could see that as yet Dorrie's brother had no inkling of his close friendship with the family, so he soon took off tactfully for his cabin. At lunch, however, when Bert and his father came down from the bar, Moray, already seated at table, discovered a fraternal arm around his shoulders while a well-primed voice exhaled into his ear:

'Didn't rumble you were *with* us, doc. Couldn't be more delighted if I'd won the Calcutta Sweep. We'll have a regular old chinwag later.'

The slow progress up-river gave them, as Bert put it, plenty of time to get together, and it was not long before Moray realised that while Bert might be a sport, a dasher and a josher, just a little flashy perhaps, and with a strong tendency towards pink gins at any hour of the day, he had, like his father, a good heart and a strong sense of family feeling. Moreover, it became equally apparent that for all his gush and gusto Bert had, as his mother put it, a head on his shoulders. He soon revealed himself as a thoroughly knowledgeable fellow, and when it came to business would certainly be a very cool customer with a capacity for getting things done. He had travelled extensively for the firm, had recently spent three months in the United States, and was full of the opportunities and excitements of New York. He talked well, with a man-of-the-world air, a kind of easy intimate verve that exuded cheerfulness and good-fellowship.

In his company Moray found the river passage all too short. He felt an actual disappointment when they reached Calcutta and the *Pindari*, churning the muddy water, began manoeuvring into Victoria Dock while the usual pandemonium of debarkation descended upon the ship. Amidst the uproar Bert remained cool and collected, everything was arranged and under control, speed and efficiency were the order of the day. As they came into the dock his long open Chrysler car and a truck were drawn up, waiting alongside. With his parents and Doris he came down the baggage gangway, first off the ship. Three stewards followed with the luggage. In the customs shed, while other passengers hung about interminably, a nod from Bert to the chief babu saw the Holbrooks through without formality. Then off they rolled in the big car to their reservations at the North Eastern Hotel.

All this happened so fast it left Moray somewhat dashed. There had been goodbyes of course, but hurried ones, given with such preoccupation as to leave him with the unsatisfactory and slightly painful impression of having been rather summarily discarded. Naturally, he was not at liberty to accompany them, yet he felt there might have been definite mention of a future meeting. However, as the *Pindari* would be two weeks in harbour, loading teak, tea, rubber and cotton goods, he told himself that he would have an opportunity to be with them later on. In any event, was it not best that they should have gone, leaving him free of all conflict, his mind undisturbed, at peace? He began to busy himself with his official duties. He was occupied most of the forenoon and when the last passenger had finally quitted the ship his first reaction was one of mild relief. The pressures exerted on him had been exacting: it would be good to relax.

By that evening a sudden inexplicable depression descended upon him, nor did it lift during the days that followed. The captain had taken up his usual quarters on shore and O'Neil, departing gaily for a trip along the coast to Kendrapara, had left Jones, the second mate, an elderly uncommunicative Welshman, to supervise the routine operations. Jones, a frustrated man, stuck with a master's ticket in a subordinate position, had never had much time for Moray, and now he more or less ignored him. He spent much of his day bent over paperback thrillers in the dock canteen, reading and picking his nose, leaving the work in hand to the quartermaster. In the evening he shut himself in his quarters and played his accordion with mournful unction. He never went ashore except to buy ivory elephants to take home to his wife. Already, he assured Moray, he had a glass-cabinetful in his semi-detached house in Porthcawl.

The empty ship, moored to the filthy, mosquito-infested dock, exposed to the racket of unloading, the endless high chatter of the native stevedores, the scream of winches and the rattle of cranes, was unrecognisable as the noble vessel which had so buoyantly breasted the blue water. It made a miserable lodging. The heat was sweltering, mosquitoes swarmed into his cabin, kept him awake at night with their shrill menacing ping, obliged him to take precautionary measures against malaria. Fifteen grains of quinine a day lowered his spirits further. To make matters worse, the agent had issued an advice that the mail boat had been delayed by a strike at Tilbury and would not arrive until the following week. Moray felt himself even more deserted through the absence of letters, and more and more his melancholy thoughts turned towards his departed friends.

Why on earth did he not hear from the Holbrooks? Why . . . why . . . why? First with irritation, then with anxiety, and finally with all the heart-sinking of hope deferred, he kept asking himself that question. It seemed inconceivable that they should have forgotten him, cast him off as a reject, someone they had used on the voyage but had now decided they did not want. Yet this mortifying thought grew within him. He pictured them in their de luxe hotel, every moment of their day delightfully filled with entertainment and sight-seeing, new faces and new friends around them. Amidst such distractions it might after all be easy to forget. And Doris: no doubt she had quickly found another interest, she who had been crazy about him. He winced jealously, between apprehension and anger. This was the most tormenting thought of all. Only his pride and the dread of a rebuff kept him from ringing her at the North Eastern.

In an effort to occupy himself he essayed a tentative expedition ashore. But the docks were miles from the city proper, he could not find a gharry, and after losing himself amongst a huddle of ramshackle huts where squatting natives squirted scarlet betel juice into the pervading dust, he finally acknowledged defeat, and plodded back to the ship, with the wretched sensation that he had reverted to the drab and dismal days of his youth.

It was then that he began really desperately to miss the Holbrooks, and all that he had enjoyed in their society. What a wonderful family they were – how hospitable, generous, and – now he made no bones about it – so rich! He'd never have the luck to meet such people again. Mrs Holbrook was sweet, so kind and motherly. Bert was such a good sort; they had taken to each other on sight. And the offer the old man had made him, admitting that he couldn't accept it, was fantastically favourable, the chance of a lifetime. Never would such a golden opportunity recur. Never. By comparison his future at the little Glenburn Hospital was dimmed to drab insignificance. And he had called himself ambitious.

And Dorrie, did he not regret her most of all? What a damned attractive girl she was – even her variable moods were somehow fascinating. One could never be bored by her. On the contrary, just to be with her was an excitement. At night, sleepless in his stifling cabin, which lay close against the high dock wall, he tossed about in his bunk, thinking of their dances together, of how, looking into his eyes with that intent and silent invitation, she had pressed against him, of that afternoon on the boat deck when all sorts of possibilities had opened to him. A wave of hot longing swept over him. What a fool he had been to reject that seductive offering. How O'Neil would laugh, if he ever came to hear of it. What a clot she must have thought him. Could she be blamed for having written him off altogether? He buried his face in the pillow in an access of misery and self-contempt.

CHAPTER XIV

AT THE END of that week, on a sweltering, gritty forenoon, as Moray leaned idly over the deck rail, his spirits at their lowest ebb, he saw, as in a mirage, the big shining Chrysler enter the dock and roll alongside the ship. Stunned, he raised his hand to his eyes. It couldn't be real, the sun and his imagination had produced a visual hallucination. But no, there, gracefully reclining in the rear, one arm negligently along the upholstered seat back, plump legs nonchalantly crossed, Burma cheroot poised airily between ringed fingers, topee at a rakish tilt, was Bert.

'Do my aged eyes deceive me, or do I perceive the medical officer of the good ship *Pindari*?' Bert called up with a grin: then, in a different voice, 'Bring out your gear, old boy. You're coming to us.'

Moray's heart leaped. They had not forgotten him. Pale with excitement and relief he rushed down to his cabin. What an idiot he had been – of course they wanted him, it couldn't have been otherwise. In less than five minutes he had changed out of his uniform and was in the car with his suitcase, which the native chauffeur bestowed in the boot. As they purred off towards the city, Bert explained the reason for the delay in calling for him – a hitch in the warehouse lease that had taken several days to straighten out. But now the agreement was signed and they were free to let themselves go in a proper good time.

'This is a lively old burg once you savez your way around,' he confided easily. 'Some geezer called it the City of Dreadful Night, but I've found the nights full of something better than dread. There's a couple of little Eurasian nurses – hot stuff and pretty as you find them.' He blew an explanatory kiss into the air. 'I speak with the voice of experience, m'boy. But there, I know you're only interested in our Doris. And believe me, though she's my sister, Dorrie's a pretty good number herself.'

Clear of the outer straggle of dilapidated shacks, they entered

114

the city proper by the wide, crowded stretch of Chowringhe Road, swept past the broad maidan, green with ficus trees and studded with lamentable equestrian statues, then drew up under the tall portico of the North Eastern Hotel. They were bowed in, through the high marble pillared hall, whirling with ceiling fans, and Bert led the way upstairs to the room he had reserved for Moray adjoining their own apartments on the first floor.

'I'll leave you to get straight for half an hour,' he said, looking at his watch. 'Ma and Dad are out, but we'll all meet at tiffin, meaning lunch, Dave.'

When he had gone Moray looked round the room. It was most luxurious – large and cool, tastefully tiled, with latticed jalousies and fresh, draped mosquito curtains shading the large high bed which had been turned down to expose fine spotless linen. The furniture was painted a pale shade of green, and a bowl of roses stood on the dressing table. Beyond was the bathroom, white and gleaming, lush with towels, soap, bath salts and a soft white bath robe. He smiled delightedly. What a difference from his small, stuffy, mosquito-ridden cabin: this was the real thing. He unpacked his few things, had a wash, and was brushing his hair when the door opened and Doris came in.

'Hello,' she said briefly.

He swung round.

'Dorrie . . . how are you?'

'Still breathing, if it interests you.'

They gazed at each other in silence, he with admiring ardour, she with an almost expressionless face. She was wearing a smart new clinging frock in soft petunia colours, fine beige silk stockings and high-heeled suède shoes. She had on a lipstick that matched the predominant pink in her frock, and her hair had been freshly set. She looked different, smarter even than on the ship, older, more attractively sophisticated, and, alas, less attainable. Her scent came towards him.

'You look . . . stunning,' he said huskily.

'Yes,' she said coolly, reading his eyes. 'I believe you're slightly glad to see me.'

'More than slightly. The question is . . . what about you?'

She gave him a long direct stare, then barely smiled.

'You're here, aren't you? That seems to be the answer.'

'Good of you to have me,' he murmured, submissively. 'It was rather miserable down at the docks.'

'I thought it might be,' she said with cold knowledge. 'I wanted to punish you.'

He looked at her blankly.

'What on earth for?'

'I just wanted to,' she answered noncommittally. 'I like to be cruel sometimes.'

'What a little sadist,' he said, trying to catch the facetious note he had once used towards her. Yet as he spoke he had the odd sensation that the balance of their relationship had altered, passed to her. He felt suddenly, dismally, her wish to establish that on shore he had ceased to be the dashing, sought-after young ship's surgeon in his natty company uniform, and was no more than an ordinary young fellow in a worn hand-me-down suit that did not fit and was quite unsuitable for the climate. However, although aware of the effect she had created, she had dropped the subject as though it no longer interested her.

'You like my new dress?'

'It's a dream,' he said, still striving for lightness. 'Did you get it here?'

'We bought the silk in the bazaar yesterday. They have lovely native material there. It was made up in twenty-four hours.'

'Fast work,' he commented.

'And about time,' she said coolly. 'I can't stand waiting, or being put off. To be quite frank, I've had about enough of that in the last two weeks, the way you've been giving me the air. And incidentally, because I've told you off, don't imagine we're all straightened out. I haven't forgiven you yet by a long chop. I'll want a word with you later,' As she turned to go she seemed to relent. Her expression cleared slightly. 'I hope you like your room. I put the roses in myself. I'm just across the corridor –' she flashed him a sly glance, 'if you need anything.'

When she had gone he remained staring at the panels of the closed door. She was offended, and no wonder, after the way he had cold-shouldered her. How stupid and unmannerly he had been to hurt her feelings. He hoped she would come round in the end.

Below, in the great marbled lounge, his welcome by the Holbrook parents was altogether different, almost that of a returned son. Indeed, Mrs Holbrook kissed him on the cheek. Luncheon was more than a reunion, almost a festival. They had a table by the window, overlooking the gardens, four native servants in white tunics with red sashes and turbans stood behind their chairs, the food, chosen by Bert, was rich, spicy and exotic. This was the first time Moray had been in an hotel since that eventful day at the Gairsay Grand, but if a recollection of that other, so different, lunch crossed his mind it was swiftly gone, swept away by Bert's explosive laughter. Exuberantly bent on showing them the town, he was, while juicily disposing of a succulent mango, outlining his programme for the coming week. This afternoon he proposed to take them to the Jain Temple and the Gardens of Manicklola, to see the famous fish in the ornamental lake.

'They're quite remarkable,' he concluded. 'They come to the surface and swim over to you when you call them.'

'Now, now, Bert,' Mrs Holbrook smiled in fond protest.

'Seriously, Mater. I'm not joking. They'll eat out of your hand if you want to feed them.'

'Imagine that! What do fish like best?'

'Chips,' Doris said in a bored voice, then went into fits of laughter.

After a siesta, when the sun had begun to decline, they set off, driving through thronged bazaars where the sacred cattle, garlanded with marigolds, wandered amongst the stalls, butting through the crowds, browsing at will on the fruits displayed. Strange sounds, high-pitched and remote, struck the ear above the high keening of native tongues, a distant temple bell, the booming of a gong, a sudden shrill cry, that lingered, vibrating on the nerves. The air was charged with aromatic scents, heady and provocative, that stung the nostrils and drugged the senses. Moray felt as though he were lifted up, absorbed to a state of extreme excitement and beatitude. His individuality had been extinguished, he was not himself, but had become an altogether different man, entering upon a new and thrilling adventure.

Arrived at the temple, they removed their shoes and entered the incense-misted dusk where the great gold Buddha wore eternally that impassive and ironic smile. They wandered in the gardens of the court jeweller, a network of ornamental filigree, called and fed the huge obedient carp. Moray's intoxication increased. Doris, wearing her new petunia frock and a little plaited straw hat with a double ribbon that fell over the brim in two tantalising little tags, had taken on the special glamour of the afternoon. Seated beside her on the way home, he turned towards her with a surge of gratitude.

'It's all been so wonderful, Dorrie . . . and to see it with you . . .'.

She had sensed the change in him, and while her manner since lunch had been increasingly possessive, whenever he advanced she had chosen to retreat. Now she gave him a grudging little nod, as though prepared at last to relent.

'So you've decided I make a difference.'

'All the difference,' he murmured fervently, then added disconsolately: 'Only you've been so cold. I don't seem to make much difference for you.'

'Don't you?'

Her eyes seemed to cloud. Then, unobserved by the others, she suddenly lifted his hand and set her teeth in his forefinger, a sharp painful bite that went through the skin.

'That ought to show you if I'm cold,' she said. Then, at the sight of his face as instinctively he nursed the hurt, she began to giggle. 'Serve you right, for insulting me these last two weeks.'

Next day Bert took them to the races. He had tickets for the paddock and the club enclosure, also a stable tip for the big race. Nothing could go wrong, nothing, nothing. The horse, Maiden Palm, which Moray backed on his advice, romped home, a winner by three lengths. This was living, this was life! And Doris was being nicer, much nicer, to him. It was as though, having suitably punished him for his past defections, she had finally made up her mind to forget them.

On the day after, they visited the famous Zoological Gardens, crossed to Howrah, and viewed, at a discreet distance, the burning ghats by the Hoogly, drove out to the Royal Calcutta Golf Club for tea, finished with a trip down-river to Sutanati. Money opened the door everywhere. Bert on holiday was a spender, a lavish tipper; Moray saw hundred-rupee notes materialise inexhaustively from Bert's wallet, pass expertly to expectant palms. How wonderful not to pinch and scrape, to count every miserable coin in a penury he had known all his days, but instead to have money, real money, more than enough to enjoy all the good things of life.

Time flew past as one exhilarating event followed another in swift succession. Moray simply let himself go, inhibiting every warning thought, blocking out the past and the future, living only in the present. Yet always the date of the *Pindari's* departure drew near. When it was announced that she would sail on the following Tuesday, the fever in his blood was at its peak. Everything he had longed for all his life was here, ready to his hand, if only he would reach out and take it. Holbrook, suave and amiable, had not again pressed his offer: this had been made and still stood, the solid offer of a man of substance, awaiting Moray's reply. Mrs Holbrook, through increasing hints and promptings, strongly wished and hoped that he would accept. Bert, however, had no doubts whatsoever on the subject. On Friday afternoon when he came in from the Bengal Club, where he had a guest membership, he found Moray in the hotel lounge and drew up a chair beside him.

'I've got a spot of good news, Dave.' They had almost from the beginning been on terms of first-name intimacy. 'I've been trying to find someone who might sub for you on the return voyage. Well, just now at the club I ran into an I.M.S. doctor going home on leave, fellow by the name of Collins. He jumped at the chance of a free trip with pay. He's our man.'

As though stung by a wasp, Moray sat up in his chair. Bert's unexpected announcement, and the assumption of accomplished fact with which he made it, had finally brought the matter to a head. A sudden wave of weakness went over him and, yielding limply, he felt he must at long last unburden himself. After all, to whom could he better disclose and explain his predicament than to a good fellow like Bert?

'Look here, Bert,' he said, haltingly. 'You know I'd naturally ... very much like to accept your father's offer ... and especially to work with you. But ... I wonder if I ought ...'.

'Good Lord, why not? Dorrie apart, we need a medico in the business. We like you. You like us. I hate to stress it, old boy, but for you it's an absolute snip. You know how dear old Wagglespear put it – "There is a tide in the affairs of men." '

'But, Bert ...' he went on abjectly, then broke off. Yet he had to say it, though every word was dragged up from the pit of his stomach. 'There's someone ... a girl ... waiting for me at home.'

Bert stared at him for a long moment, then went into fits of laughter.

'You'll kill me, Dave. Why, I've got girls waiting for me all over Europe – and pretty soon my little Eurasian fancy will be waiting for me in Calcutta.'

'But you don't understand. I've promised to ... to marry her.'

Bert laughed again, briefly, rather sympathetically and under-standingly, then he shook his head.

'You're young for your age, Dave, and still a bit green behind the ears – that's partly why we've all taken to you, I suppose. Why, if you knew girls as I do . . . You think they'll pine away and die if you give them the soldier's farewell? Not on your sweet mucking life – excuse my Hindustani. I'll lay you a level fiver your little friend will get over her disappointment and forget all about you in six months. As for your own feelings in that direc-tion, which haven't struck me as too full of cayenne, remember what Plato or some other old Roman geezer said: "All women are alike in the dark." Seriously, though, I've talked it over with Ma and the old man. We all think you're just the fellow for Dorrie. You'll steady her down. She needs a bit of ballast, for off and on she's,' he hesitated, 'she's had a spot of trouble with her nerves. And she'll give you a bit of tiddley-high which in my humble opinion will knock some of the wool off you and do you a power of good. She's had fellows before, mind you, she's no angel, but you're the one she's gone right overboard on, she damn well means to have you. And let's face it, old man, you've gone so far with us as a family, it would be a crime if you backed out now. So why don't you pass the word and we'll start ringing those old wedding bells? And now we'll have a couple of chota pegs and drink to the future. Boy – boy!' Leaning back in his chair, he shouted for the khidmutgar.

CHAPTER XV

ALTHOUGH TEMPORARILY lulled by this jovial dismissal of his scruples, Moray did not find Bert's arguments altogether convincing or conclusive. He spent a troubled night and, awakening next morning still tense with indecision, decided he must at least go down to the ship and have a talk with Captain Torrance. It was only proper for him to enquire if Dr Collins might be an acceptable substitute, in the event . . . well, in the event that he was unable to make the return trip. The skipper was a sensible man whose advice was worth having; and besides, no one need know of his intention, the moment was favourable. Since Dorrie's mother had pleaded fatigue, nothing definite had been arranged in the way of sightseeing, and he had no engagement with the Holbrooks until the evening, when he was to meet them for the gala dinner and dance which was a regular Saturday night feature at the North Eastern. He got up, shaved and dressed and took a taxi to Victoria Dock.

The sight of the *Pindari*, now almost clear of dunnage, solid and familiar, struck a note of reality that was reassuring, even comforting, suggestive that once on board he might be safe, even from himself. He hastened up the gangplank. But when he reached the chart-room deck both cabins were locked, the quartermaster on duty told him that neither the captain nor Mr O'Neil was aboard. Going below, he could find only the assistant purser, who explained that none of the senior officers would be back from leave until Sunday evening.

'The second mate's on the dock if you want to see him.'

Moray shook his head, turned slowly away.

'By the by,' said the other, 'there's some mail for you.'

He went to his desk and fingered through a bundle of letters from which he handed over two. Moray, with a sudden constriction of his heart, recognised that one, rather thin, was from Willie, the other, thick and bulky, from Mary. He could not bring himself to open them. Later, he told himself. As he stepped off the ship to the dock, where the taxi still awaited him, he stuffed them into his inside pocket.

All that day Moray tried to summon up sufficient will, yet he could not bring himself to read the letters; the reproach of their pure and loving contents was more than he could face. And because he did not open them, because he feared them, he was no longer touched and contrite. Instead there crystallised in his mind an exasperation, almost a resentment, that they should have reached him at this crisis in his life. The letters, still sealed, swung him subconsciously towards Doris and all that the Holbrooks could offer him. Defensively, under the twin urges of money and sex, he set out to construct from his earliest beginnings a logical argument in his own favour: the loss of his parents, the unwanted child, the miseries of impoverished dependence, the superhuman efforts to get his medical degree. Surely he was due a rich reward, and now it was within his grasp. Could he be expected to throw it away, as though it were worthless?

True, there was Mary – he forced himself at least to think the name. But hadn't he been rushed into that affair, carried away by his impulsive nature, inexperience, and the romantic background in which he had discovered her. She too, no doubt, had been swept off her feet by those same untrustworthy and transient influences. He didn't want to hurt her or to leave her in the lurch, but he did owe something to himself. And who knew but what, later on, he might be able . . . well, to do something for her, to make up for his defection. He didn't quite know what, but it was a comforting possibility. Young men made mistakes, repented of them, and made amends – were forgiven. Must he be the exception?

This was his frame of mind when, still uncertain and undecided, he went down somewhat broodingly at eight o'clock to join the Holbrooks in the restaurant. Clearly his mood was not keyed to enjoyment, yet it was amazing and in the circumstances doubtless commendable how, not to put a damper on the party, he cast aside his personal problems and reacted to the lively welcome of his friends. Bert especially was in tremendous form, and the moment he set eyes on Doris he knew that she was in one of her sultry, over-charged moods. She had prepared herself with thoroughness and was wearing a short, sleeveless white dress, cut low in the neckline and embroidered with little crystal beads. It looked what it was, a most expensive piece of flimsiness. It did a great deal for her, and she knew it.

The dinner, which was luscious and prolonged, proved a further reviving influence, and when, after the dessert – a delectable compote of pineapple and persimmons served with chapattis – coffee and cognac were brought, Moray saw what an idiot he had been to mope and worry all day. Now he hadn't a care in the world. Presently they went into the ballroom where the old man had, as usual, done things in style. Champagne stood in an ice-pail beside their orchid-strewn table on the edge of the dance floor, facing the palm-fringed platform occupied by the scarlet-coated band.

'We like to see the young folks enjoying themselves, don't we, Mother?' As they took their places Holbrook made the remark in a sentimental tone induced by several double brandies. 'Couldn't you have found yourself a nice partner too, Bert?'

'I would have, Dad, only I'm sorry I can't stay long,' said Bert, with a wink to Moray. 'Got to see a dog about a man.'

'Have a drop of bubbly before you go.'

The cork popped. They all had a glass of champagne. Then the lights were dimmed, the band struck up a waltz. Bert got to his feet with a theatrically formal bow to Dorrie that exposed and bisected his tight plump buttocks into two full moons.

'May I claim family privilege, and have the honour, Miss Holbrook?'

They danced this first dance in brother-and-sister fashion, then, after downing a second glass of champagne, Bert breezily consulted his watch.

'Good Lord, I must push off or that little poodle will be barking up the wrong tree. Be sure you all have a good time. Cheerio, chin-chin!'

'Don't be too late, Bert dear,' remonstrated Mrs Holbrook. 'You were last night.'

'Certainly not, Mater.' He bent and kissed her. 'Only let's face it, ducky, Bert's a big boy now. See you bright and early in the morning.'

He's off to the little Eurasian, thought Moray. The band struck up a snappy one-step. Mrs Holbrook glanced at Moray, then at Doris, not smiling this time but with serious meaning, as though to say: You two now, and while you're about it make up your minds. Moray could not take the floor with confidence. Besides, he had sampled the cognac thoroughly after dinner, and it seemed

123

to be going well with the champagne.

'If I may say so, my dears,' Mrs Holbrook commented, when they returned, 'you make a very handsome couple.'

Holbrook, smiling indulgently, just a trifle fuzzy, poured them both another glass of champagne. Then they danced again. They danced every dance together, and it seemed as though each time his arm encircled her she drew closer to him, so that every movement of her body provoked an answering movement of his, until they moved as one in a corresponding rhythm that throbbed along his nerves. He could feel that she was wearing very few clothes. At first he had made pretence at a few remarks, commenting on the other dancers and on the band, which was first rate, but she silenced him with a pressure of her arm.

'Don't spoil it.'

Yet if she maintained silence, there was in her wide bright greedy eyes, which she kept fixed unremittingly upon his, something communicative, not an inquiry now, a message rather, impossible to misunderstand, both possessive and intense. Only once did she speak again when, with an impatient glance towards her parents, she murmured restively:

'I wish they'd go.'

They did not, in fact, stay late. At half past ten Mrs Holbrook touched her husband, who was half asleep, on the shoulder.

'Time we old folks were in bed.' Then, with a restraining smile: 'You two can stay just a little while. But don't wait up too long.'

'We won't,' Doris said briefly.

For the next number the lights were lowered, and as they swung round behind the band she said, a trifle unsteadily:

'Let's take a turn outside.'

It was warm and still in the garden and dark under the high screen of greenery. She leaned back against the smooth bole of a great catalpa tree, still looking up at him. Trembling all over, he placed his arm behind her neck and kissed her. In response she pushed her pointed tongue between his lips. Then, as he pressed closer, the button on his cuff caught the string of seed pearls round her throat. The clasp gave way and pearls dropped into the low front of her dress.

'Now you've done it,' she said, with a queer strained laugh, passing her hand across her throat. 'You'll have to find them for me.'

His head was whirling, his heart pounding like mad. He began to search for the necklace, first in the yoke of her dress, then moving between her firmly nippled breasts, further down over the smooth flatness beyond.

'I'll tear your dress.'

'Never mind the dress,' she said, in that same choked voice.

Then he discovered that she was wearing nothing beneath her frock and, since all the time she had the broken necklace in her hand, what he found was not the pearls. He forgot everything; all the suppressed desire of the past weeks went through him in a blinding rush.

'Not here, you fool.' She broke away quickly. 'In your room . . . in five minutes.'

He went straight upstairs, tore off his clothes, switched off the light and flung himself into the bed. A shaft of moonlight pierced the darkness as she came in, closing the door behind her. She took off her dressing gown, stood stark naked, then parted the mosquito curtains. Her body had an almost sultry warmth as she wound her arms tightly round his neck and drew him towards her, fastening her mouth on his so that her teeth edged into his lower lip. She was breathing quickly and under her crushed breast he could hear the hot pulsing of her heart.

'Quick,' she breathed. 'Can't you see I'm dying for you?'

If he had not at once realised that she was not a virgin, now he would have known it by the nature of her response. When at last she lay back, though not releasing him, she gave a long-drawn-out sigh, then pulled his head down beside her on the pillow again.

'You were good, darling. Was I?'

'Yes,' he said in a low voice, and meant it.

'What a lot of time we've wasted. Couldn't you see I wanted you, wanted you like mad, right from the start? But it's going to be perfect from now on. We'll tell them in the morning. Then we'll both be off with Bert to New York. Oh, God, couldn't you have seen how gone I am on you? I'll never have enough of you – you'll see.' With her tongue she touched, played with his lips, stroked his body with her finger tips. A sudden rigor passed over her. 'Again,' she whispered, 'only longer this time . . . and the next. It's so lovely, make it last.'

She remained with him till the first grey light of dawn.

That morning, after hilarious congratulations at breakfast, he took a walk to clear his head. He felt a trifle listless, but she was really the goods, he could scarcely wait until tonight, and of course there was the job, the money, and the future all secure. Damn it all, a fellow had to look after himself. In the dulled state of his mind, it was less difficult to shut out the past and think only of the future. Passing across the Howrah Bridge he leaned suddenly over the parapet and without looking, taking his hand from his inside pocket, dropped the two letters, still unopened, into the filthy, corpse-polluted waters of the sacred Ganges.

PART THREE

CHAPTER I

DAWN COMES EARLY in the Swiss Oberland. Its hurtful brightness and the clanging of the cowbells awoke him. As he had feared, the pheno-barbitone had failed to act, and in those hours of wakefulness he had relived every moment of those fatal, youthful months until, tortured, at three in the morning he had fumbled for a capsule of sodium anytal, which had given him a brief respite of total blackout. Now, with throbbing temples, deadened by the drug, he faced the situation dully yet with almost desperate resolution, aware that, at long last, he must take the decisive step.

Wilenski had told him so, at that last consultation in New York, smiling down encouragingly, as he always did, with one arm across the headrest of the couch and lapsing into that caressing Southern accent which he used to untie the inner tangles of his patients.

'You may have to go back one day, just to break that little old guilt-complex for keeps. Actually, you want to go back, partly because you've got a suppressed nostalgia for home, but of course mainly to see your – your friend and straighten things out with her. Well, why not? Better late than never. If things haven't gone too well for her, you're in a position to help. Why,' his smile took on a genial slyness, 'now you're a gay widower, if you find her still attractive, you could clear the whole thing up by marrying her – provided, of course, she's free.'

'She will never have married.' He had no doubts whatsoever on that score, though he hoped she might have found happiness.

'Keep what I'm telling you in mind, then. And if you feel you're getting into trouble again, take my advice and go back.'

Yes, he would do it, and at once. Relief came to him with the reaffirmation of his decision. He pressed the bell and, after consulting the Swissair schedule, told Arturo to ring Zurich and reserve a seat on the two o'clock plane for Prestwick. He got up, shaved, dressed, breakfasted downstairs. Afterwards, while Arturo packed his valise, he smoked a pensive cigarette. He was taking only a few things, returning quietly, humbly, without the slightest fuss or ostentation, no Rolls, no signs of wealth, nothing. The thought, arousing sombre anticipation, injected his melancholy with a transitory gleam. As for the villa, in his absence, with a household so well organised, staffed by such trustworthy servants – he had hinted to them of an urgent business appointment – it was simplicity itself to leave, even at a moment's notice.

The phone rang: he rose and went to the instrument. As he had expected, it was Frida von Altishofer.

'Good morning. Am I disturbing you?'

'Not at all.'

'Then tell me quickly. Are you well . . . better?'

His frightful night made him long for a word of sympathy, but he knew this to be unwise.

'Definitely better.'

'I am so glad – and relieved, my friend. Shall we go walking this morning?'

'I wish we could. However . . .' he cleared his throat and delivered the polite fiction he had prepared: yesterday there had been a telegram, purely a matter of business, but upsetting, as she had observed, which he ought to put right by a visit to his British lawyer. He must leave this morning.

There was a sharp silence in which he sensed surprise, disappointment, perhaps even a hint of dismay, but quickly she recovered herself.

'Of course you must go – such a man of affairs. But do not tire yourself. And come back soon, before I leave for Baden. You know how much you will be missed.'

Arturo drove him to the airport in the Humber utility car, thus setting the tone of moderation for the entire journey. In Zurich it was his custom to lunch at the Baur-au-Lac, but today he passed by that admirable hotel, telling Arturo, who expressed concern, that he would probably get some sort of snack on the plane. They were early at the airport but fortunately the plane was on time, and at two o'clock precisely it took off. As the D.C.7 soared through low cloud into the blue his fixed expression did not relax, yet a strange elation took possession of him. He was going back, at last, back after thirty years to the country of his birth. Why in God's name had he delayed so long? – for there

130

alone could he find peace of mind, a final liberation from that remorse which from time to time had fallen upon him like a dark oppressive cloud. A word came to mind, edifying and full of promise. He was not a religious man, but there it was: Redemption! He repeated it to himself, slowly, earnestly.

Suddenly, elevated though they were, his thoughts were interrupted. The pretty stewardess was smiling down at him in her smart blue uniform, serving the snack he had deprecated and which now appeared as an excellent meal appetisingly arranged on a tray: smoked salmon, a wing of chicken with braised celery, peach melba, and a glass of excellent champagne. After this, despite his wretched night, he felt more himself, and drowsed over the Irish Sea, but always with an eye for the landfall of the Scottish coast. Prestwick was sighted at half past six, in the indigo haze of an early twilight through which pin-point lights had begun to sparkle. Their landing was smoothly perfect and, only a few moments after, he was hearing with quickened pulse the almost forgotten burr of his native tongue. Bareheaded, on the tarmac, he drew deep breaths of the soft lowland air.

Home, at last . . . home. Unconsciously he murmured the famous words of Rob Roy Macgregor: 'My foot is on my native heath.' Emotion flooded him.

Outside the customs shed the coach was waiting, and presently it set off, running smoothly through the Ayrshire farmland. Eagerly he kept rubbing the moisture from his window in the effort to snatch glimpses of the darkened landscape, scarcely realising the passage of time until the noise of traffic alerted him: they were at the air terminal in Winton.

He took a taxi to the Central Hotel where he secured a room on the quiet side, away from the station platforms and the noise of trains. Now it was late and he was tired. He ordered milk and sandwiches brought to him; then, after a hot bath in which for fifteen minutes he soaked, relaxing his tense nerves, he went to bed. He slept immediately.

CHAPTER II

NEXT MORNING, AWAKENING early to the thrilling awareness
that he was actually in Winton, physically present, in the city
of his youth, scene of his homeric strivings as a student, he had
to damp down a great sweep of sentiment. He must be calm and
judicious in his approach to this great turning point of his life.
Yet as he rose quickly, dressed, and went down to breakfast
in the warm, red-carpeted coffee-room, where for the first time
in thirty years he tasted with relish real Scottish porridge and
cream, followed, to the accompaniment of tea and toast, by an
authentic finnon haddock, he was increasingly alert to the
momentous prospects of the day.

Immediately he had finished his third cup of excellent tea
he went to the lounge, took up the *Winton Herald* and, running
through the advertisements, obtained the name of a motor hire
agency. A small car, while inconspicuous, would facilitate his
journey to Ardfillan and any subsequent movements which might
be necessary. A curious inhibition withheld him from the
obvious course of asking the head porter to arrange the hire, and
instead he telephoned the agency personally. Could he have
explained this vaguely irrational act? He was not known at the
hotel, it seemed altogether unlikely that he would be recognised,
yet all his instincts impelled him to concealment. At any rate,
after requesting that the car, a small standard model, be delivered
at the Central at the earliest possible moment, he was promised
it, after some pressing, for one o'clock.

Restlessly, he looked at his watch: it was now just past eleven.
With two hours to spare he went out, surrendering to the impulse
to make a brief pilgrimage to the familiar places of his youth.
The city, grey, cold, and soot-encrusted as ever, still with its
overcast of smoke, showed few alterations from the days when he
walked its drab and bustling pavements. At the corner of Grant
and Alexandra Streets he boarded the yellow tram that would
take him to Eldongrove Park. Outside the Park gates he got off,

walked slowly through the gardens and, with increasing melancholy, up the hill to the University. But here, wandering through the shadows of the old cloisters, recollections of his student days were so painful and acute that, after a brief survey, he hastened from the precincts, passing at the lower gates the Gilhouse shop where he had sold his microscope to buy the ring with the little blue stone for Mary. His eye moistened. What a pitiful gift, compared to all that he could shower upon her now. Yet it had taken every penny he possessed. No one could have accused him of meanness or of the least foreknowledge of all that was to follow.

From Eldongrove it was not far to the Blairhill tenement and, driven by his mood, he took the road over the hill down to the docks. Yes, his old lodging still stood, a disreputable barrack, grimier, even more sordid, than before. Gazing upwards he saw himself, as a youth, bent over his books behind that narrow garret window. How he had battled and endured, fitting himself for a great and wonderful career.

And what, in God's name, had he made of his life? After noble beginnings, what had been the result? As he stood there, gazing upwards with an air of vacancy, a shaft of sincere compunction pierced him and he experienced not only genuine and bitter regret, but also an overwhelming sense of the futility of all that he had done since he left that attic room.

He had made a fortune, a large fortune, but how? Not as a brilliant surgeon, a specialist of the first order, esteemed and revered in his profession, but as a wretched pill-maker, a time-serving purveyor of popular remedies, of slight clinical significance, advertisements for which debased the landscape, and all sold at such profit over cost as to constitute a further imposition on the public. No, he must not be too hard on himself; some of his work – the group of analgesics he had developed from the phenothiazines, for instance – had been of value. Yet on the whole, what a burlesque of the career he had planned. Why, under heaven, had he done it? Why, above all, had he been such a fool as to marry Doris Holbrook?

Surely, on that fateful voyage, he might have foreseen her psychotic tendencies, realised that the moods he found so entertaining on board would be insufferable later on, that the physical excitements she offered him would quickly pall. His mind went back to the neat little Cos Cob house her father had set them up in, convenient to the new Connecticut offices in Stamford. She had adored it – for six months – then suddenly hated it. Their move to nearby Darien, at first an immense success, was soon an equal failure. She seemed incapable of settling down or of adapting herself to a new environment, and his refusal to move again had started her off on daily trips to New York, almost a commuter on the morning and evening trains. Then came her futile art and sculpture classes, her style of dress increasingly extreme, her new, ever-changing, dubious acquaintances with whom he soon suspected she was deceiving him. When he remonstrated there were recriminations, estrangements, shouts through locked doors, hysteric reconciliations. She wanted to go back to Blackpool – could one believe it! More incredible still was the fact that now she actually seemed to hate him. When, after a long interval, he had smilingly attempted to resume marital relations, she had picked up her ivory hairbrush and practically brained him!

But he was getting on fast. Divorce might mean a break with the Holbrooks; he managed to put up with her. After five years in Darien an act of appeasement by old Holbrook had given them Fourways, a handsome property in the Quaker Ridge district of Greenwich. Quieter, conservative people here, the garden club – he persuaded her to join – their modest entertaining; he had hopes that she might settle down. All an illusion. Gradually, through increasingly erratic and intractable moods, fits of violence and periods of amnesia, she passed into depressive delusions. Finally the moment when Wilenski, called in consultation, put a consoling hand on his shoulder.

'Paranoid schizophrenia. She will have to be certified.'

And then, for fifteen years, he had been the man with a wife in a mental clinic, awaiting the results of the insulin and electro-shock treatments, the slight improvements and deeper relapses, enduring the whole hopeless muddle, until the unmentionable relief of that terminal hypostatic pneumonia.

Was it surprising, in these tragic circumstances, that – himself walking the tightrope of nerve tension – he had needed, had thrown himself into, his work with Bert. There was nothing wrong with Bert, good, decent, genial Bert, who had always stood by him fair and square, helped him repeatedly in dealing with Doris, even admitted liability in the matter for having glossed over her adolescent attacks, and who, after old Mr Holbrook's death, had given him outright an equal partnership in the rich and expanding American firm.

And work apart, as a man sorely victimised, had he not been justified in devoting himself *to himself*: to set out to cultivate his personality, to study the arts, acquire languages, French, German and Italian to be precise, to dress with taste – in short, to develop himself into a finely mannered man, consciously dated in his style – in his reading he favoured the gracious Edwardians – a veritable 'man of distinction' who with his natural charm and ability to please could command, even in this appalling age when all sense of values had gone by the board, immediate interest, attention and respect. And of course, in his position, he had a physical obligation to himself, which as a well-read man he could sanction – if this were necessary – by quoting Balzac's pointed letter on the subject to Madame de Hanska. He too had no intention of allowing himself to degenerate into impotence and imbecility! Naturally he recoiled from promiscuous adultery, from those brief and unreliable encounters that took place after cocktail parties in cars parked in the country club shrubbery. Chance threw him in the way of a quiet little woman – he had always preferred the small-boned type – a widow in her early thirties, blonde and of Polish extraction, her name Rena, who worked, humbly enough, as a binder in a Stamford commercial publishing house. His tactful approach produced surprisingly agreeable results. He found her both soothing and satisfying, neat, clean in her person, undemanding, and absurdly grateful for his help. Soon a discreet and regular arrangement was reached between them. He even grew quite fond of her, in her own way, and though she was fearfully broken up when he left America, he had done the right thing with a generous settlement.

Yes, there had been good reason for the pattern of his life, yet though self-exoneration brought some relief his thoughts were still painful as he turned away and, descending Blairhill, made his way back to the Central. Here he could not even think of lunch. But, feeling the need of something in preparation for his journey, he took a glass of dry sherry and an Abernethy biscuit in the bar, after which he felt better.

The car arrived at the specified hour and when he had signed the necessary papers and paid the deposit he drove off. No need to ask the way. Free of the busy streets, he took the main western road, past the Botanic Gardens and the Westland playing fields, then on to the highway leading from the city outskirts to the lower reaches of the Firth. This, since his time, had been widened and improved, yet while now it bypassed the shipyards and steel works of the riverside industrial towns it still was the road that had taken him to Mary. He drove slowly, prolonging his sensations, though almost overcome by them as, one after another, known sounds and scenes broke upon him. That steady rat-a-tat from the yards, the hoot of the Erskine ferry boat, a long-drawn rusty wail from an outgoing tramp – these blended to a haunting dissonance that fairly ravaged him, as did the fleeting vistas of green woods and gleaming water, of distant purple mountain crests that sudden outward, upward sweeps of the way revealed to him. All, all brought before him, in sweet anguish, the image of the one woman he had truly loved.

Some thirty miles from Winton he reached the village of Reston and, turning off the main route, took the winding, narrow road that followed the widening estuary towards Ardfillan. His heart was beating like those shipyard hammers as he entered the little town, all so unchanged, as though he had left it only the day before. Still the same narrow strip of esplanade lapped by quiet waves, the iron bandstand, the tiny pier, the curve of low grey houses, the square church towers. So blurred was his vision, he had to stop the car momentarily. Oh, God, he had stopped exactly opposite that same wooden shelter where, when Willie was sent on the errand, he had taken Mary in his arms. He was in a turmoil, confused thoughts poured through his mind: would he find her greatly altered, would she recognise, let alone forgive him, was it even possible that she might refuse to see him?

At last he took himself in hand, drove further along the front and parked the car. Then, with lowered head, he walked up the lane giving access to the Douglas shop. He reached the familiar back street, lifted his head, then suddenly drew up. The shop was no longer there. Instead, a high brick frontage from which a whirring of machinery emerged, confronted him. He had built with such irrational confidence on finding everything as he had left it that he was less disappointed than stupefied. After a few blank moments he moved further along the narrow cobbled way, and saw that a wide new cross street had been cut at right angles to the old, giving access to a large double-fronted glittering establishment with a neon sign: *Town and Country Bakeries Ltd.*

Motionless, he stood gazing at the trays of starkly coloured cakes which filled the windows, then he crossed the street and went into the shop. Two pert-looking young girls in mauve dresses with white collars and cuffs were behind the counter.

'Excuse me,' he said, 'I am seeking a family who once owned a shop in this vicinity. The name is Douglas.'

They were of the age that construes the unusual as the absurd, and seemed prepared to giggle. But something, perhaps the excellence of his clothes, restrained them. One glanced at the other.

'I never heard tell of any Douglas, did you, Jenny?'

'Me neither,' Jenny said, with a shake of her head.

There was a pause, then the first girl said:

'Maybe old Mr Donaldson could help you. He's been here a long time.' Now she did giggle. 'A lot longer than us.'

'Donaldson?' The name touched a chord of memory.

'Our caretaker. If you go through the van entrance on the left you'll find his wee house opposite the bakery.'

He thanked her and, following her directions, found himself in what had once been the Douglas yard, greatly enlarged now, with the big machine bakehouse on the left, a garage for motor vans facing him, and on the right the old stable converted to a small one-storey apartment. He rang the bell and after an interval slow steps were heard within. The door opened, revealing the stooping, steel-spectacled figure of a man of seventy in a cloth cap, worn back to front, a black alpaca apron and carpet slippers. When Moray questioned him, he remained silent for a moment, soberly reflective.

'Know of James Douglas?' he answered finally. 'I think I should. I was his foreman for more nor twenty years.'

'Then I hope you can give me news of him, and his family.'

'Come in a minute,' Donaldson said. 'It's nippy by the door, this time of year.'

Moray followed him into a small dark kitchen with a faint blink of fire in the grate, the stuffy, untidy room of an old man living alone. Donaldson pointed to a chair, then, still wearing his cap, shuffled to his own corner and sat down below the wooden pipe rack.

'You're a friend of the Douglases?' he inquired, with caution.

'Of long ago,' Moray said hurriedly. 'And now almost a complete stranger here.'

'Well . . .', the other said slowly, 'the story of the Douglases

137

is not a very cheery one. James, poor man, is dead and in his grave, lang syne, and Minnie, the sister-in-law, too. Ye may as well know that for a start. Ye see, James failed in his business and was made a bankrupt – there was queer work behind it, to do with condemning the property and making the new street, all by order of the town council. Anyhow, the disgrace just fair killed James, for he was an upright man and as honest as the day. Minnie, who was aye an ailing sort of body, soon followed him up the road to the cemetery. So that was that, and in place of James's shop we got these grand premises, and pastries that would rot your bowels – not that I have anything against the company, mind ye, they kept me on and gave me this bit of a job.'

He broke off, lost momentarily in the past. Intently Moray pressed forward.

'There was a daughter, was there not?'

'Ay,' the other nodded. 'Mary . . . and she had her troubles too. When she was a lass she got engaged to some fly-by-night that away and left her. A sore, sore heart she had for many a day. When I cam' out the auld bakehouse I used to see her greetin' by her window. But in time she come to, got verra religious in fact, and some years later when the new young minister, Urquhart by name, came to the Longend church, and a fine man he was, she had the luck to marry him. And 'deed, a nice bairn she gave him a year or so after.'

Stunned, Moray sat rigid in his chair. She had married, forgotten him, or at least betrayed what he had believed to be a unique and lifelong love: more painful still, had borne another man a child. In his present state of mind it seemed a desecration. And yet, for all his chill dismay, reason had not entirely left him. Who was he to deny her the right to happiness, if indeed she had found it?

At last, in a strained voice, he said:

'She is here, then, in the town, with her husband?'

'No. She left Ardfillan with her daughter not long after the husband died.'

'Died?' he exclaimed.

The old man nodded.

'He wasna' one of the strongest, ye ken, and when we had the big Spanish 'flu epidemic in thirty-four he was taken to his eternal reward.'

Unconsciously, Moray relaxed slightly, drew an easier breath.

The situation was suddenly and to some degree ameliorated. Dreadful, of course, to have lost a young husband whom he, on his part, would never have wished the slightest harm. Still, the unfortunate fellow had apparently been weakly from the start; the motive on Mary's side might well have been pity rather than love. Partially restored, and with renewed feeling, he put his final question.

'Where did they go, Mary and her daughter?'

'A village in the Lothians. Markinch they call it. The daughter wanted to train for a nurse and they sought a place that was near to Edinburgh. But what's come of them since I cannot tell ye. They werena' in the best of circumstances, and they've never looked near Ardfillan since the day they left.'

A long silence followed while Moray, with bent head, tried to reassemble his thoughts. Then, still visibly affected, he stood up and with a word of thanks pressed a note into Donaldson's hand. The old man, after feigning reluctance to accept it, was peering at his visitor across his spectacles with growing curiosity.

'My sight isna' what it was,' he remarked, as he accompanied Moray to the door. 'But I have an odd notion that I've seen you before. I'd like fine to ken who ye are?'

'Just think of me as someone who means to do well for Mary Douglas and her daughter.'

He made the statement firmly, with the consciousness of a new honesty of purpose and, turning, made his way back to the car. Now he perceived how illusory his hopes had been, how all his imaginings had been falsely based on a romantic re-creation of the past. Had he actually expected, after thirty years, to find Mary as on the day he had abandoned her, sweet with the freshness of youth, tenderly passionate, still virginal? God knows he would have wished it so. But the miracle had not occurred and now, having heard the history of a woman who wept for him late and long, who married, though not for love, then lost an invalid husband, who suffered hardships, ill-fortune, perhaps even poverty, yet sacrificed herself to bring up her daughter to a worthy profession – knowing all this, he had returned to reality, to the calm awareness that the Mary he would find at Markinch would be a middle-aged woman, with work-worn hands and tired, gentle eyes, bruised and beaten by the battle of life, but because of that the more willing, perhaps, to forgive and accept his generous attentions.

His heart warmed to these thoughts as he drove back to Winton through the fascination of the deepening river dusk. Then, all at once, it occurred to him that he had forgotten to ask Donaldson about Willie. Inexcusable omission! What, he now wondered, had happened to that bright little boy, the eager inquirer of their evening hours? Well, he would find out soon enough, and from Mary herself.

Seven o'clock was striking when he reached the hotel, and having eaten little all day he was thoroughly sharp set. After a quick wash and brush-up he descended to the grill room, ordered a double rump steak, onions, baked Arran Chief potato, and a pint of the local Macfarlane's ale – all with such aplomb that he might never have been away. Afterwards he proposed to yield to the rich seductions of golden syrup tart. How good these native dishes were. He attacked them hungrily, secure in the knowledge that he would leave for Edinburgh and Markinch first thing tomorrow.

CHAPTER III

ALTHOUGH THE CAR was not running particularly well, misfiring occasionally on one cylinder, he decided to retain it rather than face a chafing delay at the agency, and at eleven o'clock on the following morning, having settled his bill at the Central, he set out for Edinburgh. According to his road map, Markinch lay some five miles inland from Dalhaven on the east coast, a small village apparently – at least he had not heard of it – and its limited population would undoubtedly facilitate his search.

The day was grey and breezy, with woolpack clouds tumbling about the sky, but in the early afternoon, when he reached Edinburgh, a low sun broke through, sending shafts of brilliance from the Castle ramparts across the gardens of Princes Street. A good omen, he thought, setting his course along the eastern road to Portobello. Here the traffic was held up for a few minutes at the Cross to let the Portobello Girls' Pipe Band go through, on their way, he fancied, to some local gathering. It did him good to see the bonnie Scots lassies swing past to the strains of 'Cock o' the North', their kilts swishing about their hurdies, Glengarry ribbons streaming in the blast of the chanters. Scotland's natural resources, he told himself, with a smile, his discriminating eye singling out several most promising little pipers. But the hooting of cars behind recalled him and he drove on, through Musselburgh and Newbigging. He struck the coast beyond Gosford Bay and, drawing up beside a deserted beach, ate the sandwiches they had packed for him at the Central. Then he was off again. The sea had a sparkle, and a keen wind blew across the cropped links and the yellow dunes fringed with sharp-edged, bleached grass and tangled aromatic wrack. Offshore on his left the Bass Rock came in sight, and far ahead, on the landward side, the green cap of Berwick Law. Gulls were wheeling and calling above the blowing sands. He could taste the salt in the spray-filled, gritty air; the tang of it against his teeth was the very feel of home.

He had fixed on Dalhaven in advance, as a convenient centre, but when he arrived and circled the town seeking an inn, he could find nothing that looked suitable. The low, windswept houses, built of red sandstone, cowered about the fishing harbour with an inhospitable air, while the inhabitants, confronted with a stranger, proved dourly uncommunicative. Eventually, however, he found a friendly native and was directed with strong recommendations to the Marine Hotel, which stood above the golf course two miles beyond the town. This he discovered to be altogether superior, an establishment of the first class, where he was quietly welcomed by the manageress and shown to an excellent front room.

When he had washed he made inquiry as to the exact route, and after a short drive inland through winding country roads lined with hawthorn trees came to the village of Markinch, which as from an inner voice, he knew suddenly to be his true and final objective.

This conviction calmed his nerves, as he drove slowly down the single deserted street. Whitewashed cottages stood on either side, climbing nasturtiums still flowering against their walls. Not a soul in sight, only an old collie half asleep, one eye open, by the kerb. There was a general store and post office combined, then came a smithy, an oldfashioned shop with bottle-glass window panes and the sign: *Millinery* above, then across the way what looked like a small dispensary with the notice outside: *Welfare Centre*. In which of these should he make his inquiry? Perhaps the store and post office, although this would, unfortunately, bring notice of his arrival into the public domain. At the end of the street he was about to turn when some distance ahead he saw the village church and the adjoining manse. A thought struck him, induced by the recollection of a remark of Donaldson's, and by the desire also for privacy and discretion. He continued towards the church, which was of Scots baronial design with a square tower instead of a steeple, parked the car opposite, then advanced towards the manse, a small but decent greystone dwelling, and pulled the brass handle of the bell.

After a considerable interval the door was opened, and by the minister himself, a small sallow man with extremely short legs and an oversized head topped by a bush of grey hair. His old black suit and the frayed edge of his clerical collar gave him a disheartened appearance, confirmed by the cast of his features. A pen in one hand and a heavily corrected manuscript in the

142

other suggested that he had been disturbed in the preparation of his sermon, but his manner was civil enough.

'What can I do for you, sir?'

'If I may trouble you, I am seeking a lady by the name of Urquhart.' Now the new name came more easily to Moray; at first it had wounded him to think of her as other than Mary Douglas. 'I understand she lives in your parish.'

'Ah, you must mean our excellent district nurse.' The little man's expression cleared, showed willingness to assist. 'She lives above the welfare centre you've just gone by. She is a very busy young person but if she's not at home you will find her in the dispensary from five until six.'

'I'm much obliged to you,' Moray said, well satisfied. 'You are obviously speaking of my friend's daughter. I presume that her mother lives with her?'

'Her mother?' The minister paused, studying the other. 'You are a stranger in these parts?'

'I've been away for many years.'

'Then you'd no idea how ill she had been.'

'Ill?'

The minister made a gesture of affirmation.

'I fear I must prepare you for sad news. I buried Kathy's mother in our churchyard just nine months ago.'

The words, spoken with professional condolence, were reinforced by the church bell which now, like a passing knell, struck the hour with a harsh cracked note. There could be, there was, no mistake . . . it was the finish of his seeking, the end. Not disappointment alone but actual shock must have shown in Moray's face, painful shock, that drove the blood from his heart and forced him to lean against the lintel of the door.

'My dear sir . . . come in and sit down for a minute. Here in the lobby.' Taking Moray's arm he led him to a chair in the hall. 'I see it has affected you deeply.'

'I had hoped so much to see her,' Moray muttered. 'A very dear friend.'

'And a truly worthy woman, my dear sir, among the chosen of my flock. Don't grieve, you will meet her in the hereafter.'

The afflicted man had not much confidence at that moment in the promise of the hereafter. She was gone, carrying with her to the grave the memory of his unfaithfulness. To the end, he had remained for her despicable, a festering wound in her

143

memory. And now he could never redeem himself, never break the hateful complex which perpetually threatened his peace of mind, must continue to bear the burden of his guilt. Bowed with sorrow, disappointment, and a welling self-pity, he heard the parson run on, extolling the dead woman.

'Her daughter, too,' the other continued, 'has the same high standards, a most devoted girl. But now, if you're more composed, perhaps my wife could offer you a cup of tea.'

Moray straightened and, though still not master of himself, had the wisdom to decline.

'Thank you, no.'

'Then I feel sure you would like me to show you where she lies.'

They went to the graveyard behind the church. The grave, marked by a simple Celtic cross, was indicated, and the minister, lingering a moment, between sympathy and curiosity, said:

'You are of our persuasion, I trust. If so I hope we may see you at divine service on Sunday. The Word is a great healer. Are you residing in the neighbourhood?'

'At the Marine,' Moray mumbled.

'Ah, an excellent hotel – Miss Carmichael, the manageress, is a good friend of ours.' The credentials of the stranger thus established, he introduced himself with an almost pathetic eagerness to be of service. 'My name is Fotheringay – Matthew Knox Fotheringay, B.A. of Edinburgh, at your disposal, sir, should you require me further.'

With a bow, he moved discreetly away.

Alone, Moray still gazed down upon the green sward of which a long rectangle, the turf annealed yet still slightly elevated, presented a sad, significant outline. There lay that sweet body which in youth he had caressed. And in the form of sweet youth he now visualised her – as on that day upon the moor, while the lark sang above the heather, and the stream rippled over its fretted, pebbled bed. Clearly he saw her, fresh and glowing, with her trim figure, her red-brown hair and peat-dark eyes, with youth, youth pulsing through her, alive. Overcome, he supported himself against the granite monument and closed his smarting eyes.

How long he remained bent and motionless he never knew. A slight sound, a footstep on the gravel path, disturbed him. He turned, raised his head, then almost collapsed. There, risen from the grave, Mary Douglas stood before him, Mary, exactly as

144

he knew her, as he had dreamed of her a moment ago, the fearful, ghostly illusion heightened by the spray of white flowers clasped to her breast. He tried to cry out, but he could make no sound. Dizzily, with swimming head, he realised that it was Mary's daughter, the mortal image of her mother.

'I must have startled you.' She came towards him, concerned. 'Are you all right?'

'Yes,' he said, confusedly. 'But thoroughly ashamed of myself . . . behaving so stupidly.' And seeking an excuse, he added: 'I – was quite unprepared . . . You see . . .'.

She look at him understandingly.

'I met our minister, on the way in. You were a friend of my dear mother's.'

He inclined his head, indicating respectful sadness.

'And of all your family. They were very good to me when I was a poor . . . and homeless student.'

Her face expressed sympathy and kindness. It was evident that his grief at the grave had strongly predisposed her in his favour.

'Then you knew James, my grandfather?'

'A wonderful man . . . I could see that, though I was a heedless young fellow then.'

'And Uncle Willie?' she asked, with a warmer sympathy.

'Willie and I were the best of friends,' he said, with a half sigh of recollection. A sudden inspiration led him to validate their association. 'We often bunked together. Long talks we had at night. He was a fine boy.'

'Yes,' she said, 'I can believe that.'

There was a pause, during which he could not bring himself to look at her. His mind was not yet clear, not fully adjusted to this extraordinary turn of the wheel. He still regretted the mother and all that her loss entailed, yet it had begun to dawn on him that in the daughter he might still find the opportunity he sought. Perhaps, after all, it wasn't the end of his journey; at least, in sudden anxiety, so he fervently hoped. With an effort he maintained an air of calm.

'I must introduce myself. My name is Moray – David Moray.'

Her expression did not change. As she took the hand he held out to her, he could barely suppress a sharp breath of relief. She did not know of him, nor of his unedifying history. Why had he doubted? Mary would never have told her, the secret was still locked up in that poor broken heart, now stilled for ever, down there, six feet under his expensive hand-made shoes.

'You have my name,' she was saying shyly, while he still held her hand. 'Kathy Urquhart.'

He gave her, though still with quiet sadness, his most winning smile.

'Then, if I may, as an old friend of your dear mother, and of all your family, I shall call you Kathy.' He said it kindly, almost humbly, anxious to put her at ease, to make her feel at home with him. Then, standing aside in subdued fashion, with a sense of compunction and responsibility, conscious of his defects and deficiencies, of all his misdeeds of the past, he watched her as she placed her few chrysanthemums in a green enamelled vase before the Celtic cross and began, with a few touches, to move some fallen beech leaves from the sward.

She was bareheaded, wearing a dark blue, noticeably shabby coat over her denim nurse's uniform of lighter blue, and one of her shoes, he observed with a pang, was patched, a neat patch to be sure, yet an actual cobbler's patch. These little economies, so apparent to his expert examining eye, moved him. We will change all that, he told himself, with a sudden burst of feeling. Yes, his opportunity *was* here, certain and predestined, he felt it in his bones.

'There!' she exclaimed, straightening herself with a confiding smile. 'We're all tidy for the Sabbath. And now,' she hesitated shyly, scarcely daring, yet venturing to say it, '. . . would you like to come away home with me for a nice cup of tea?'

They walked down the pathway of the graveyard together.

CHAPTER IV

SEATED BY THE window in the room above the dispensary while she went into the kitchenette to infuse the tea, he glanced about him, surprised by the want of comfort, the bareness of all that met his eye. Not even a rug on the scrubbed and polished wooden floorboards, the furnishings scanty, little more than a square deal table and some horsehair covered chairs, the fireplace blackleaded yet lacking coal, the walls white-distempered, relieved by only one picture and that a religious subject, a reproduction from the *Christian Herald* of a bad copy of Valdez Leal's *Transfiguration*. There were a few books, mainly nursing manuals and a Bible, on a shelf. A hart's-tongue fern in an earthenware pot stood on a blue saucer on the window-sill beside a work basket holding a piece of knitting, ready to be picked up. But while admitting its spartan neatness, and the touch of brightness which a vase of wild asters on the mantelpiece, caught in the yellow light of sunset, gave to it, he saw in the room, as in the little alcove bedroom, the door of which on entering she had quickly closed, disturbing evidence of straitened circumstances. On the tray, too, which hospitably she now brought in, the china was of poor quality and the single plate held nothing more than buttered slices of cottage loaf. He could not altogether understand it, yet with a sudden lift of mood he reasoned that the more help she needed the more would he be able to give her.

'If only I'd known you were coming,' a little flustered, pouring the tea, she reproached herself as she handed him his cup, 'I'd have had something nice. When I'm busy I don't bother about shopping till the Saturday. But never mind me, tell me about yourself. . . . You've been abroad.'

'Yes, for many years. You may imagine what it's meant to me, coming home.' He sighed, then smiled. 'Now that I am here I mean to make an extended stay.'

'Where were you?'

'Mostly in America.'

'I almost hoped you'd say Africa.' She half smiled to him, though her gaze, passing beyond, was remote. 'Uncle Willie is out there – at Kwibu, on the border of northern Angola.'

Although he gave no sign, he nevertheless experienced a strong sensation of relief. Willie would certainly have known him; any premature meeting might well have induced a most undesirable crisis.

'You don't surprise me a bit,' he said pleasantly, with a light note of interest. 'Even as a boy Willie was wild about Africa. Why, he and I walked practically every mile of the way with Livingstone, to Lake Victoria. And when Stanley found him you should have heard us cheer. But Angola, isn't that rather primitive country?'

'It's all that. Since Uncle went out he's had some terrible rough years. But things are going better now. I've all sorts of interesting snaps I can show you. They give a good idea of the conditions out there.'

At this stage he thought it wise not to enlarge on the question of Willie's pioneer activities – whether mining or engineering he could not guess – so he refrained from pressing the matter.

'When you've time I'll enjoy seeing the photographs. But what I really want to hear about is your own work here.'

She made involuntarily a shy, disclaiming gesture.

'Oh, it's nothing much. Just the usual run of district nursing, health visiting, and the like. I go round the countryside on my bicycle, sometimes on foot. Then there's the Welfare Centre for pre- and post-natal care, with a clinic – we call it the milk bar – for the babies. And odd times I do a turn at the Cottage Hospital in Dalhaven.'

'All that sounds as if they work you much too hard.' He had already noticed that her hands were rough and badly chapped.

'It's nice to be busy,' she said cheerfully. 'And they're very decent. I have Thursday afternoons off and three weeks' holiday in the year – I still have two weeks of it to go, in fact.'

'Then you like your job?'

She simply nodded, with a reserve more convincing than any outburst of enthusiasm. 'At the same time, there isn't quite enough scope here. But – well, I have something much better in view.'

At this remark, and the reserve with which she made it, a disconcerting thought crossed his mind. Although he knew it to be bad taste, he had to say it.

'You mean to get married?'

She laughed outright, showing even white teeth against healthy pink gums, a wonderful laugh that fell sweetly, re-assuringly on his ears.

'Good gracious, no,' she exclaimed, composing herself at last. 'Who would I find round here but a few farm laddies that think of nothing but their Saturday night dances and the movies in Dalhaven? Besides,' she continued, slowly and very seriously, 'I'm – well, so set on my work, I scarcely think I could ever give it up for anything – or anyone.'

All this was exactly as he would have wished it. Quite alone and without encumbrances, sensibly though not permanently attached to a worthy but dull and unrewarding profession, she could not have been a more perfect subject for his affectionate and philanthropic attention. His thoughts flashed ahead. Un-acquainted with the law, he wondered if she might be made his ward: adoption seemed to him unfeasible, reminiscent of orphan-ages and partaking of frustrated parenthood. Be that as it may, his heart swelled with genuine feeling. He was, always had been, a most generous man, no one could deny him that slight virtue. What couldn't he do for her! He mustn't force things unduly least he alarm her, since it was apparent that she had taken him for a man of moderate means. Yet this was an aspect of the situa-tion which struck him as being rich, in the double sense of that word, with the most delightful possibilities of revelation and fulfilment.

In the silence that had fallen between them, he considered her as, with lowered gaze, she put together the used tea things on the tray. She was, after all, not quite the living replica of her mother he had fancied in that first emotional shock. She had the same fresh complexion, dark brown eyes and short slightly thickened nose, the same soft chestnut hair clustering naturally on her neck. Yet her expression was different, reflective, almost reserved, the mouth wider, fuller, more sensitively curved, and in the set of the lips he saw evidence of a nature less given to gaiety. There was a certain aloofness about her that he liked – a sense of detachment. She smiled rarely, yet when she did it was the sweetest thing he had ever seen. But what struck him most was her touching look of youthfulness. Mary had been a sturdy lass with rounded breasts and well marked hips. This girl was slender, almost undeveloped – an immaturity contrasting with her serious air that strongly aroused his most protective instincts. He meant no injury to the dead when he concluded that this sweet child, equal in looks, had more depth, perhaps even greater capacity for feeling. . . . He came to himself. A hint of emabrrassment, something in her manner which she was unwilling to express, made him suddenly recollect that Fotheringay, the minister, had told him her dispensary began at five. Glancing at his watch, he discovered it to be ten minutes past the hour. He rose precipitously.

'My dear Kathy, I've stayed much too long,' he apologised. 'I'm keeping you from your patients.'

'They'll not mind waiting a few minutes. It's not every day I have visitors.'

'Then just let me say quickly what a joy it's been for me to . . . to discover you. I hope this fortunate meeting will be the first of many, for you must understand that I've much to repay for the kindness of your family.'

When she had seen him to the door he walked to his car, and drove back to the hotel meditating emotionally on the events of this extraordinary, this memorable afternoon. Sadness mingled with a kind of exhilaration. Here he had come, from the highest motives, and instead of an ageing woman who might have met him with reproaches, even rancour, remaining unresponsive to his offers of amendment and assistance, he had found a poor, hard-working girl who stood in need of, and must benefit by, his help. He deplored the loss of the mother, it had been a blow, yes, had cut him to the heart. But there was compensation in this dear child, who might, but for unavoidable circumstances, have been his own daughter, and on her, in reparation for the past, he would bring to bear, readily and freely, a benign influence, wise, helpful, paternal. The ways of Providence were indeed wise and inscrutable, beyond the mind of man.

CHAPTER V

THAT EVENING AFTER dinner he arranged with the manageress of the hotel to have a sitting-room. Fortunately there was one adjoining his bedroom, a large comfortable apartment with a good fireplace which Miss Carmichael confidently assured him 'drew well'. This settled, he put through a trunk call to his villa, in Switzerland.

When Arturo answered, almost comically delighted to hear his voice, Moray instructed him to dispatch golf clubs and additional clothing by air freight from Zurich. As to mail, he should use his discretion and forward those letters which seemed important. Was there any news? Everything was going well, Arturo replied, the weather kept fine, they had picked the damsons and the plums, Elena had made ten kilos of jam, one of the pier-master's children had been sick but was well again, and Madame von Altishofer had telephoned twice asking for his address: should he give it? Although gratified by her solicitude Moray, after considering for a moment, indicated that he would be writing to Madame himself.

But later, as he prepared for bed, his mood changed unexpectedly. Reviewing this eventful day he was struck, suddenly, by a chilly wave of self-condemnation. How quick he had been to find consolation in the prospect of exercising his charity on Kathy. How wrong to forget his own dear Mary, to accept the daughter and forget the mother, with no more than momentary sorrow. *An ageing woman who might have received him with rancour* – had he actually thought of her in such terms a bare hour after viewing her lonely grave? Never, never, would she have met him with anything but forgiveness and love. Standing in his long silk monogrammed sleeping-jacket, one of the individual coats specially tailored for him by Gruenmann in Vienna, he raised his eyes to the ceiling and swore he would make reparation openly, tomorrow. The thought comforted him.

Next day, true to his vow of the previous evening, he obtained from Miss Carmichael the name of Edinburgh's premier florist and telephoned his order. Presently there arrived by special delivery a great gorgeous wreath of arum lilies. This he took personally to the cemetery and placed reverently beneath the Celtic cross. Then, setting forth freely, swinging his stick, he turned towards the sea and walked upon the links, taking deep breaths of the bracing air. Resisting all inclination, he did not go near Markinch, wisely reflecting that whatever Kathy might be to him he was to her still more or less a stranger. However, on the day after, which was Sunday, he dressed in a dark suit and sombre tie, ascertained the time of morning service from the invaluable Miss Carmichael, and set out for the village kirk.

He had not been to church for more years than he could readily remember. On Sundays in America he had played golf with Bert Holbrook, gone through the routine of the usual exurbia weekend at the local Country Club, where the course bore the surprising name of Wee Pinkie Burn. The members, for the most part New York executives who bedecked themselves in remarkable sporting attire, ranging from chartreuse shorts to scarlet tam-o'-shanters, were a friendly and congenial group. But he had never felt quite at home there. He was not the type who could readily be at ease in the exuberant bon-homie of mass masculine society; and besides, he felt that they all knew of his unfortunate domestic situation and must therefore pity him. Still, it was a good course and he enjoyed the golf, at which he excelled. When the Sunday was too wet for play he usually went to the laboratory at the works. On one rainy and fortunate Sunday he had come up with the formula for, of all things, a new perfume, which Bert, with his unerring instinct for a selling name, had immediately christened *Church Parade*, and which, marketed as a sideline, had made a small fortune for the firm. It must, he estimated, be a matter of fifteen years since, on that Friday when Doris was finally certified and taken away to Wilenski's clinic at Appletree Farm, he had sneaked into the back seat of St. Thomas's Church on Fifth Avenue. On his way to the University Club almost next door his eye had fallen on the sign: 'Open all day for prayer and meditation.' He was feeling so abject, almost psycho himself, that he had thought it might help him to go in. But it hadn't: although he had crouched in a back seat, gazing furtively towards the dim altar, and had even shed a few miserable tears – for he could weep on appropriate occasions – he emerged without the faintest sense of benefit or improvement, obliged to fall back on his original intention: a Turkish bath at the Club.

Now, however, his state of mind was altogether more propitious. He approached the little country church, to which a sparse congregation was being summoned by the discordant pealing of a cracked bell, in a mood of keen anticipation. And immediately, as he entered, he had the satisfaction of Kathy's swiftly lowered glance of recognition. When the service began with a hymn, sung rather uncertainly, and later, during Fotheringay's sermon, which was long and dull, a truly laboured effort, he had the privilege of observing her, though always discreetly, as she sat with the village children. He was struck by the competence with which she controlled her restless charges and by the patience she brought, sitting very erect, to the tedious discourse. Her profile had a purity of outline that reminded him of an Italian primitive – Uccello, perhaps, No, no – her sweetness of expression suggested a much later canvas – Chardin's *The Young Teacher*, he decided finally, pleased to have hit it exactly, but wincing at an increasing volume of disharmony from the choir.

His reward came afterwards when, outside the church doors, he waited for her. She came out with Mrs Fotheringay. The minister's wife was a short, stout woman with a downright manner and a broad, plain, honest face, her lined but keen blue eyes set behind highly coloured cheekbones – a Raeburn face, Moray thought instinctively. She wore her 'Sunday best,' an antique black feathered hat and a dark grey costume that had seen much service and was now too tight for her. Moray was introduced and presently, after a few moments' conversation, they were joined by Fotheringay. Immediately, Moray congratulated the minister on his sermon.

'Most edifying,' he said. 'Listening to you, sir, I was reminded of a spiritual experience I had in the church of St. Thomas's in New York.'

At the implied comparison with the great city Fotheringay reddened with pleasure.

'It was good of you to come to our country service. We are a small congregation and our poor old bell does not attract many people from the outside world.'

153

'I did notice,' Moray raised his brows deprecatingly, 'that the tone was not particularly clear.'

'Nor loud,' the other said, glancing upwards towards the church tower with sudden irritation. 'The bell fell last year from a rotted cross-beam. It will take near to eighty pounds to recast it. And where is a poor parish to find that siller?'

'At least there is nothing wrong with your voice,' Moray said diplomatically. 'I found you most eloquent. And now,' he went on agreeably, 'I'm going to take the liberty of inviting all three of you to Sunday dinner. I've made arrangements at the hotel. I hope you are free to come.'

A brief, rather blank pause ensued: such invitations were not current in the district. But almost at once Fotheringay's expression cleared.

'You're very kind, sir. I must confess that when I come out of the pulpit I always seem to be sharp set.' He glanced almost jocularly at his wife. 'What do you say, my dear? Our little roast will do tomorrow, and you won't have to wash up today.'

From the start, with the blunt look of a woman who must be convinced rather than persuaded, she had been openly taking stock of this newcomer who had arrived so dramatically from the unknown. But her first impressions seemed not unfavourable and the prospect of emancipation from those menial duties imposed by the meagreness of her husband's stipend was a mollifying one. She gave Moray a dry sort of smile.

'It'll be a treat for me. If Matthew gets his appetite in the pulpit, I lose mine by the kitchen stove.'

Kathy looked pleased, less perhaps at the prospect of her own visit to the Marine than at this hospitable treatment of her old friends. After Moray had settled them in the car, the minister and Kathy behind, Mrs Fotheringay beside him in front, he drove off. From the outset he had realised that the Fotheringays must be won over, if necessary propitiated, and everything seemed to be going well.

At the hotel they were welcomed by Miss Carmichael. As the season was virtually over – only a few visitors remained in the hotel – half of the main restaurant was closed and she had given them a table by the fire in the cosy breakfast room, a privacy especially pleasing. The food, simple and unpretentious, was of the first quality: a Scotch broth, saddle of Lothian lamb with roast potatoes and garden beans, home-made trifle laced with sherry and topped with double country cream, then a native Dunlop cheese and hot oatcakes. Moray had hoped the parson and his spouse would enjoy this repast and they did, especially Mrs Fotheringay, who ate with hearty and honest appreciation of the good things. The more he saw of this plain, outspoken woman, the more he liked her. But what gave him most satisfaction was the fine blood that the nourishing meal – so different from the meagre fare which, he was convinced, awaited her at home – gradually brought to Kathy's cheeks, making her eyes brighter, her smile warmer. Thank heaven, he thought, she isn't all spirit, and pressing her to another helping of trifle, he set out to ensure that the flesh was not neglected. Indeed, with that flexibility which enabled him to attune himself to any society, he was the perfect host. Kindly and serious rather than gay, he charmed them all. Keeping the conversation moving with discretion, he spoke briefly of his business in America, of his early retirement and return to Europe, finally of the home he had made for himself above the Schwansee; and, since Kathy was listening with attentive interest, he took pains and, with feeling, described the lake, the village, the surrounding landscape.

'You should see it under snow, as it will be soon.' He concluded on a high note. 'A mantle of the purest white.'

'It sounds a braw spot,' Mrs Fotheringay said. Assured that her first doubts had been unjustified, she had long since thawed towards him, revealing an unsuspected archness. 'You're a lucky chiel to live amongst such beauty.'

'Lucky, yes.' He smiled. 'But lonely, too.'

'Then you're not married?'

'I have been a widower for some years.'

'Oh, dear,' she exclaimed, concerned. 'But you have children?'

'None.' He raised his eyes, looked at her gravely. 'My marriage . . . was not a particularly joyful one.'

The painful words, so obviously the understatement of a perfect gentleman, produced a sudden silence. But before this became prolonged he rallied them.

'That's all past. And now I'm happy to be back in my own country and in this present company.' He smiled. 'Shall we go into the lounge for coffee?'

Regretfully the minister looked at his watch.

'I'm afraid we must decline. Kathy has her Sunday School class at three. And it's after half-past two.'

'Good gracious,' said Mrs Fotheringay. 'How time has flown. And so very agreeably too. We're most indebted to our new friend. Come, dear, we'll leave the men for a wee minute.' She rose and took Kathy's arm, adding with her usual directness, 'Miss Carmichael will show us where to tidy up.'

Left alone with the parson, who had also risen and was standing by the window viewing the sea, Moray seized the opportunity to take his cheque book from his inside pocket. A few strokes of his ballpoint pen and he got to his feet.

'As a token of friendship and good will, permit me to offer you this so that your congregation may be summoned fittingly.'

Fotheringay turned sharply. A dejected little stick of a man, with more bile than blood in his veins, he was now completely overcome. Staring at the cheque, all taken aback, he stammered:

'My dear sir . . . this is more than generous . . . it's . . . it's *munificent.*'

'Not at all. It's a pleasure. One I can well afford.' Moray placed a finger on his lips. 'And please – not a word to the others.'

As he spoke the two ladies returned and Mrs Fotheringay, struck by her husband's attitude, cried out:

'Matthew! What on earth's the matter?'

He took a deep breath, swallowed the dry lump in his throat.

'I cannot help it. I must speak. Mr Moray has just given me the eighty pounds to recast our bell!'

There was a sharp silence. A deeper colour had rushed into his wife's cheeks, already flushed by the substantial meal.

'Well, I never,' she said in a low voice. 'That is most extraordinar' handsome.' She came slowly towards Moray and took his hand tightly in both of hers. 'That wretched bell has had my poor old man worried near out of his wits. I just cannot thank you enough. But there, I hadn't been five minutes in your company before I kenned ye were *one of the best.*'

He was not often at a loss but now the genuine feeling in her voice unexpectedly embarrassed him.

'Nothing . . . nothing,' he said awkwardly. 'If I'm to get you back in time we ought to be on our way.'

Ignoring their protests he insisted on taking them back in the little car. This time the Fotheringays were in the rear seat, Kathy beside him. During the short run she did not speak, but as he said goodbye outside the manse she remained behind the others to thank him – quickly, shyly, but with unmistakable sincerity.

CHAPTER VI

ON MONDAY AFTERNOON his golf clubs and two valises arrived by special delivery van from Prestwick Airport: he had known that the good Arturo would not fail him. The sight of his beautiful leather bag and shining true-temper clubs stimulated him, and although it was late in the day he went to the clubhouse, introduced himself to the secretary, and arranged for a temporary membership. Then he got hold of the professional and had just time to play twelve holes with him. The open, rolling course suited Moray, he was in excellent form, and when fading light forced them to stop he was actually one up on his opponent, a dour and stocky Scot, who had started with all the expert's disdain of the amateur, but rapidly and rather comically changed his views.

'Ye hit a verra sweet ball, sir,' he conceded, as they walked back to the clubhouse for a drink. 'It's not often I come up against a visitor that can beat me. Would ye care for a return tomorrow?'

Moray accepted.

'Ten o'clock sharp,' he said, slipping a pound note to the other. 'And perhaps we'll go out again in the afternoon.'

Firmly, he was controlling his persistent wish to go to Markinch. Not only was discretion imperative, lest his motives be misconstrued; he well knew the wisdom of delay, the advantage of an interlude in which expectation could develop and recollection could have its way.

He took no action until noon on Wednesday, when he wrote a note, which he dispatched by the hotel boots, a lad of seventeen.

My dear Kathy,

I have to go to Edinburgh to do some shopping tomorrow. As I believe you are off duty that afternoon, if you have nothing better to do would you care to come with me? Unless I hear

158

to the contrary I will call for you at two o'clock.

Most sincerely yours,
David Moray.

His fear that she might not be free was quickly removed; a verbal message of acceptance was brought back by the boy, and on the following afternoon when he drew up at the dispensary she was waiting for him outside, dressed in a clean white blouse, a speckled grey Harris tweed skirt which, at a glance, he decided she had made herself, and, as the breeze was keen, the rather shabby coat in which he had first seen her. Though her fresh young face redeemed everything, exhaling an innocent smell of brown soap, it was an unbecoming outfit, little better than that of a country maidservant on her day out. Nevertheless it pleased him, especially the worn coat, since it might present the opportunity he sought. She would be difficult to convince, but he meant to try.

How delightful it was to find her beside him after those three days of self-enforced abstinence. Not only had she been glad to see him, her mood was lighter than before, she seemed full of expectation for their expedition. He sensed that she was becoming less shy of him. After they had driven for some time in silence, she said:

'This is much nicer than the bus. It was good of you to ask me. And convenient, too. It so happens I have an errand in Edinburgh.'

'Then we'll do it whenever we arrive,' he said heartily. 'Just tell me where you want to go.'

'Number 10a George Street,' she told him. 'The offices of the Central African Missionary Society.'

He glanced at her quickly. Their eyes met for only an instant before he returned his gaze to the road ahead, yet she had caught the blankness of his expression, and with a smile she said:

'Did you not know? Uncle Willie is out there for the Society? It's my fault for not showing you the photographs, but I thought you surely understood. He's been working for years in the foreign missionary field.'

It took him a few moments to overcome his surprise.

'No . . . I didn't quite realise . . .'.

'Well, he is. And doing wonderfully under the most difficult conditions. You've no idea of what he's been through.'

In spite of himself, and his lack of sympathy for Willie's spiritual objectives, he was impressed by her glowing and ingenuous tone. A sentimental recollection of the bright-eyed little boy in Ardfillan thirty years ago came over him.

'Well, well. Come to think of it, it's just the thing I would have expected of Willie. I honour him for it.'

'I knew you would,' she said in a low voice.

'I must admit . . .'. They were now in the outskirts of Edinburgh and a momentary difficulty in negotiating the traffic caused him to pause, before resuming. 'Yes, I admit I was puzzled at your asking me to take you to the – to George Street. But I see it now. I suppose they keep you in touch with Willie's movements.'

'Indeed they do. And besides, the least I can do is to send him regular parcels. I arrange it through the Society. They know what he needs and are able to buy the right things at reasonable prices.'

'You go in and leave the money?'

'Why not?' she answered light-heartedly. 'It's little enough. Uncle Willie's worth more than that. Besides, he's the only relative I've got.'

He saw then the reason for her cheap clothes, poor lodging and indifferent food, saw the purpose of her sparing way of life. This devotion touched him, yet his main sensation was one of indignation that she should be denied the things that were due her, and he had a sudden impulse to speak of the resources at his command, of all that he could, and would, do for her. But his instinct warned him – no, no, he thought, not yet; above all he must avoid too sudden, too startling an advance.

They were now approaching the centre of the city and, following the directions she gave him, he turned off Princes Street at the Scott monument, drove for some distance along Craig Terrace, then, after crossing a wide square, arrived at a grey stone building marked by a well-polished brass plate bearing the name of the Society. It had the look of an old dwelling house, Victorian in character, which, he surmised, had been donated by some deceased benefactor, possibly the pious widow of a city merchant. In the windows several posters were displayed showing representations of what appeared to be, at this distance, distressing groups of emaciated native children.

'Miss Arbuthnot will be expecting me,' she told him as she

stepped briskly from the car. 'I won't be more than a few minutes.'

She was as good as her word. There was just time to smoke a Sobranie cigarette – he had been careful to bring a plentiful supply of his special brand from Switzerland – before she reappeared. The dashboard clock, which was actually going, showed only half-past three. But glancing at it she apologised, rather breathlessly.

'Och, I have kept you waiting.'

'Not a bit of it. Was everything all right?'

'Oh, fine, thank you.'

'Now then, Kathy,' he said, decisively engaging gear, 'you've done your good deed for the day and you're in my hands for the rest of the afternoon. Let's forget Central Africa for a bit and think a little about ourselves. First of all we'll park the car, then we'll go shopping together.'

He found a garage nearby and presently, taking her arm, he guided her back to Princes Street. The sun was shining as they walked along. In the gardens opposite roses were still blooming and a cool breeze fluttered the leaves of the plane trees. Above, the battlements of the Castle were as though cut clean by a knife against a wide swathe of luminous sky. He still held her arm protectively, steering her along the crowded pavement.

'Isn't Princes Street nice?' she remarked. 'They say it's the bonniest street in Europe.'

'It *is* a bonnie street, Kathy,' he answered gaily, 'and full of bonnie shops – all with lovely things in them.'

'Ay,' she nodded soberly, 'and all dreadful expensive.'

He burst out laughing. A wonderful mood was descending upon him. The scene, the sun, the brisk invigorating air, all exhilarated him.

'Kathy, Kathy,' he exclaimed, pressing her elbow. 'You'll be the death of me. When you know me better you'll realise that the one thing I really enjoy is spending money.'

She had to smile in sympathy, though a little doubtfully.

'Well,' she said practically, 'so long as you don't waste it.'

'My dear, you're the very one who ought to know that what's spent on others is never wasted.'

'Oh, you're so right,' she agreed, her expression clearing. 'That was the most splendid and generous thing you did, giving the bell to Mr Fotheringay.'

'Yes, the old boy's got his bell. But we mustn't forget poor

Mrs F., who got nothing – and I think she's had plenty of that all her life. So we must find something pretty for her. But first of all,' he had stopped opposite Ferguson's, the confectioners, 'I want to send some Edinburgh rock to two little friends of mine in Switzerland.'

He went in with her and ordered a large box of the famous sweet to be mailed to the children of the pier-master in Schwansee. Next he sought her advice and, in a neighbouring shop, purchased a fine capacious black lizard-skin handbag for the minister's wife.

'It's a beauty.' Kathy stroked the shining leather admiringly. 'And I know it's the very thing she's wanting.'

'Then you'll have the pleasure of giving it to her.'

Emerging, he conveyed her further along the street towards an establishment which, as he drove in, he had observed to be of special merit.

'Now,' he announced in great good humour and with a rather mischievous air, 'I'm going in here to do some real shopping.'

He took a step forward, but as he prepared to lead the way in she stopped him hurriedly.

'Don't you see – this isn't a man's shop.'

'No,' he replied, looking down at her seriously. 'It isn't. But I'm going in – to buy you a new coat – and a few other things which I'm sure you need. Now, not a word. I'm an old family friend, you must learn to accept me as . . . well, someone like Uncle Willie. Or better still, as an older brother. And as such, I simply can't have you sending all your money to Angola and doing without absolute necessities – a pretty girl like you.'

A warm colour had risen to her brow. She tried to speak but could not. Her eyes fell.

'I never bother what I have on – not much, anyway.' Then, to his relief, she looked at him again and, unable to resist, after a faint tremor of her lips, she smiled. 'I mustn't pretend. I suppose I like to be as nice as the rest.'

'And you shall be, only nicer.'

They went into the shop which, as he had surmised, was of the first order. Aided by a discreet, mature saleswoman who rustled towards them, and ignoring all Kathy's whispered protests, he selected a coat of fine Shetland material, warm yet light, new gloves and shoes, a hand-blocked silk scarf, and finally a restrained yet tasteful dark green lovat suit. He wished to do more,

162

infinitely more: nothing would have given him greater joy than to have swathed her in those rich furs past which, with a speculative glance, the saleswoman had tentatively led him. But he dared not – not yet. While Kathy retired to the fitting room upstairs he took an armchair in the elegant red-carpeted salon, stretched out his legs, and lit a cigarette, perfectly at home. Presently she came down, and, with lowered gaze, stood before him. He could not believe his eyes, so startling was the change. She looked ravishing.

'Madame is rather different in the lovat, sir.' The saleswoman, with an air of achievement, was studying him covertly.

Under that experienced gaze he restrained himself.

'A great success,' he said coolly. 'It seems to fit.'

'Naturally, sir. The young lady is a perfect thirty-four.'

He insisted that she wear the suit and the new coat: the other articles, elegantly wrapped, were easily portable, the old discarded coat could be sent to Markinch with her Harris skirt. When the bill was presented, though he was careful not to expose the total, she kept murmuring remorsefully in his ear, but as she left the shop in her new possessions he did not fail to notice the sparkle of pleasure in her eyes. He had done well, he reflected with an inward thrill, and this was only the beginning.

She remained silent as they walked back together along the street, where the low sun behind a bank of clouds cast a golden gleam, then looking straight ahead she said:

'I think you are the kindest person, Mr Moray. I only hope you have not ruined yourself.'

He shook his head.

'I told you I had something to repay. But it is you who are repaying me.'

She half turned, looking at him steadily.

'That's just about the nicest thing that's ever been said to me.'

'Then you will do a nice thing for me? Mr Moray is so stiff, won't you please call me David?'

'Oh, I will,' she said shyly.

Before the silence became awkward he exclaimed lightly:

'Good gracious! Past five o'clock. Time for tea. I've been running the show so far, but now I'm going to let you take over. Which place do you recommend?'

She named a café unhesitatingly as being not only the best but moderate in price. It was not far off and presently they were seated upstairs in a bright, warm room filled with the cheerful sound of voices and overlooking the gardens across the way. The table, in Scottish fashion, was already laden with tempting scones and buns, and with a many tiered-central stand bearing every variety of that native confection made of sponge, icing and marzipan, known as a 'French' cake. He handed her the menu which was safely anchored in a little metal ball.

'What do you suggest?'

'Are you hungry?' she asked.

'Starving.'

'So am I.' She gave him a modest, playful smile. 'You haven't forgotten what a good Scots high tea is?'

'Indeed I haven't. And the best I had were in your old home at Ardfillan.'

'Well, there's a dish they have here, fried fillet of fish with parsley sauce; it doesn't sound much but it would just melt in your mouth.'

He looked at her quizzically.

'Is it expensive?'

She laughed outright, freely and spontaneously, such a happy laugh it evoked responsive smiles from dour Edinburgh citizens at the adjoining tables.

'It'll cost a good half crown. And after the perfect ransom you've spent today I think I'd better pay.'

When the waitress approached he let Kathy give the order. The fish, as she had promised, was delicious, fresh from the sea, the toast hot buttered, the tea strong and scalding. The excitement of the expedition and the consciousness that she was looking her best had released her from shyness, giving her an animation that made her companionship the more delightful, since already he had detected an introspective strain in her nature, even a tendency to sadness, and it was good to be able to lift her to a lighter frame of mind. And how attractive she was in her new smart outfit, so transformed as to draw towards her many admiring glances, which he clearly saw but of which she remained unaware. Yes, he thought, watching her indulgently, she's worth all that I mean to do for her, she'll do me credit.

When they had finished they sat for some time in a communicative silence, then she gave a contented sigh.

'It's a shame this wonderful day has to end. But I must be back to relieve Nurse Ingram at seven o'clock.'

'Must you really?' he exclaimed with a note of disappointment.

'I'm afraid I must.'

'And I was hoping we could stay and go on to a theatre. Wouldn't you have liked that?'

She lowered her eyes, but after a moment raised them and looked at him frankly.

'It will probably amaze you, Mr Moray – I mean, David – I have never been to the theatre in my life. When Mother was alive we went every year to the Orpheus Choir's performance of "The Messiah". And I've been to concerts at the Usher Hall.'

'But the regular theatre – good plays, the opera, and suchlike?'

She shook her head with such a look it touched him to the heart.

'But Kathy dear, I can't bear to think what you've missed. Didn't you ever want to go?'

'No – not really.'

'But why?'

She paused, as if to consider his question. In the end she said, simply:

'Mother didn't care for me to go. Besides, I suppose I've been too busy . . . and had other things on my mind.'

'What a serious little person you are.'

'Don't you think we're living at a pretty serious time.'

'Yes,' he had to admit, 'I suppose we are.'

Her capacity to astound him seemed unlimited. And how withdrawing she could be at times, when that contained expression came into her eyes. Yet how wonderful, in this age of debased morality, to find such fresh unspoiled innocence.

'Come then, my dear,' he said gently. 'I'll take you home.'

He drove back slowly through the little towns on the firth where lights were already springing up against the encroaching night, and as the car purred softly he meditated on the future. Virgin soil, he repeated to himself, worthy of any effort on his part. Time was on his side of course but there was much to be done. Despite her sweetness and native wit he was obliged to acknowledge, as a man of the world, that she was a simple and untutored girl, knowing nothing of music, art, or literature. That one picture in her room – terrrible: those few text-books and the Bible, edifying no doubt, but scarcely comprehensive. Poor child, she was probably too hard-worked, too tired at night to read. That must be changed, she must be educated, taught several languages, attend a good university, Geneva or Lausanne would be suitable, take a course in, say, social science. All this, and mixing with cultured and civilised people would give her poise, smooth out her little gaucheries, bring her to perfection. Her upbringing must in a sense be held responsible – pure and spartan though it had been, it had undoubtedly been . . . well . . . narrow. And this obsession with Willie, splendidly unselfish though it might be, was a nuisance and must be watered down. But the most pressing need was to remove her from her present work. Indeed, she had hinted that she was preparing to leave it, and with an idea of encouraging this, he said:

'I've been wondering if you'd take me on your round one day. I'd be most interested. Could it be this week?'

'Of course,' she said readily. 'Not tomorrow, for I have to see the County Medical Officer at Dalhaven, but the day after if you like.'

'Good. I'll call for you at nine o'clock.'

When they reached Markinch he collected her parcels, escorted her to her door, stilled her renewed thanks, said goodnight kindly yet briefly. The day he had so carefully planned would speak for itself. A bond had been created between them; he would not risk breaking it by doorstep sentiment.

CHAPTER VII

MORAY TURNED IN early that night with an unusual sense of serenity, conscious that everything had passed off well, had indeed been perfect. And what a refreshing little companion she had proved, how supremely restful! Properly educated she could be a source of interest to him, a new objective in his life, besides affording him the long-sought satisfaction of an exercise in virtue. He fell asleep as soon as he had settled his head comfortably on the pillow.

Next morning when his early tea was brought the weather, unfortunately, had changed. Heavy rain beating on the window gave no inducement to rise in haste. Having swallowed his tea and the thin bread and butter that accompanied it, he lay back and closed his eyes, but failing to get off again rang for the morning paper. The boots, who brought it up, handed him a packet of mail forwarded by Arturo from Schwansee: a few business communications from his New York brokers, a couple of bills, several dividends, an illustrated catalogue of a sale of Daumier drawings to be held in Bern, and finally a letter from Madame von Altishofer. He opened it.

> Gasthof Lindenhof
> Baden-Baden.
> Thursday, the 15th.

My dear friend,

I hear from my correspondents in Schwansee that you are not yet returned to your villa and I begin to fear that some mischance is responsible for your prolonged absence, especially since I have no single word from you since your unexpected departure. Has your business proved more tiresome than you foretold? Or can it be that you are ill? I trust sincerely that both of these suspicions, which have lately troubled me, are not well founded. But please, you must take time to send me news of yourself. I am sure you acknowledge that nothing could exceed my deep interest in all concerning you.

The weather has been pleasant here and I am much the better of my residence. But I am dull – dull – in fact I am becoming increasingly aware of being alone. I do not freely make new friends, and saving an old acquaintance, an invalid lady I met at the spa, I speak rarely to anyone. And how quietly I exist. I rise early, drink the waters, then take my coffee and zwieback at a little nearby café. Afterwards I walk into the hills – you know how much I love to walk – then come back to this modest pension, where they are so very good to me, and eat my simple mittagessen on the terrace under the linden tree. I then rest for an hour or so. The afternoon I sit in the gardens, still green and blooming, having selected carefully a chair not too near the orchestra which since my arrival has already fourteen times dispensed Strauss's Wiener-Walzer. Here, I pass the time partly in dreaming, partly in studying the faces of those who pass. Are they happy, I ask myself? So often I doubt it. At least I find them altogether different from the people one met and knew when first I came here with my parents in my early youth. This reflection depresses me and I hasten to the pavilion where I have my cup of tea – not, alas, so good as your delicious Twinings – and a slice of the English plum cake. In the evening I do not venture to the casino, the sight of all those greedy eyes repels me. Instead I take my nice book – now I am reading again 'Anna Karenina' – and retire to the ever open window of my room. The light of my lamp attracts an occasional moth, fireflies gleam beneath the linden tree, I begin to feel sleepy and so, in the words of your Mr Pepys, to bed.

That, dear friend, is my day. Is it not simple and a little sad? Yes, sad because I miss you, and your charming kameradschaft. I also need your advice, since a man from Basle – someone in chemicals – asks to buy the Seeburg. I do not wish to part with that beloved house which I know you also admire, but circumstances are now most difficult. So write me soon and let me know when you will be home. As there is nothing to take me back to Schwansee until you are there, I shall remain in Baden until I hear from you.

Forgive me for revealing my regard for you,

Sincerely,
Frida von Altishofer.

He put down the letter slowly. A nice letter he told himself, despite its rather stilted style, the letter of a well born and distinguished woman who was utterly devoted to him. Normally he would have been touched by it, but now, perhaps because of his mood, the aftermath of yesterday, it found him unresponsive. He was glad, naturally, to hear from her, flattered that she should miss him, yet at the moment he could not generate his usual interest in her activities. And was she not slightly exaggerating her solitude? She was a woman who invited and enjoyed society. That frugal lunch, too, struck an incongruous note. He well knew that she was not averse to the pleasures of the table, and on her last visit to Baden had brought back a marvellous recipe for chestnut soup. In any case, he was not in the mood to answer today. He would advise her about the Seeburg, but later; at present he had other things upon his mind.

It was almost noon when he got up and began idly to dress. After lunch the rain continued. He hung about the hotel trying to occupy himself with some ancient magazines, devoted mainly to Scottish sport and agriculture. Then an impulse took hold of him to get out the car and drive to Markinch, but he reflected that she would not be there. She had told him that she must go to Dalhaven. Still, he would have the satisfaction of passing her window. . . . At this absurdity he drew himself up with a sudden selfconscious flush. He would see her tomorrow and must wait. Gazing in bored fashion out of the blurred windows of the lounge he hoped the weather would turn fine.

But when the next day came it was still raining, the sky remained heavily overcast. Nevertheless he was in a mood of cheerful expectation as he backed the car out of the hotel garage and drove between the sodden hedgerows towards Markinch.

She had already finished the forenoon clinic when he arrived. She locked the dispensary door and, carrying her black bag, got in beside him.

'Good morning.' He greeted her, feeling how good it was to see her again. 'Or rather, what a morning! I'm glad to be driving you today. Not having you cycle around in the rain.'

'I don't mind cycling,' she said. 'Or the rain either.'

The tone of the remark mildly surprised him but he made no comment except to say:

'Anyhow, I'm entirely at your disposal. Where do we go?'

'Towards Finden. I can't promise you beautiful country. It's all poor clay land. And Finden is a poor village, built round a brickworks that's just been re-started after a long shut-down.'

'Well, it's not a day for viewing the scenery,' he said amiably, and after asking and receiving directions he set off through the village.

As they proceeded, she remained unnaturally silent, and he began to fancy a certain reserve in her manner. Not exactly a coldness. But she had lost that uplifted and responsive spirit that marked their day in Edinburgh, when he had felt the beginnings of a sympathetic understanding throb between them. After glancing sideways towards her several times, he said: 'You look tired.' And indeed she had not her usual air of well-being. 'You've been working too hard.'

'I enjoy hard work.' She spoke in that same odd, rather constrained tone. 'And I've quite a number of serious cases on hand.'

'That proves you've been doing too much. You're quite pale.' He paused. 'Surely it's time you took the remainder of your vacation?'

'In this weather?'

'All the more reason for you to get away from it.'

She did not answer. And why did she not look at him? He waited a few moments then said:

'What is wrong, Kathy? Have I offended you in any way?'

She blushed deeply, vividly, all over her fresh young face.

'No, no,' she said hastily. 'Please don't think that. Nothing could be further from the truth. It's just that . . . probably I am a little out of sorts.'

It was true enough, though very far from the full explanation. Yet how could she tell him of the mood which had followed their day in Edinburgh, or of the intensity of her reaction to it? On awakening yesterday morning she had experienced, in warm and sleepy recollection, an afterglow of happiness, but this had been succeeded, almost immediately, by a sharp pang of troubled conscience. The gay and spendthrift adventure of the day before, far exceeding all her previous experience, now took on the colours of an act of self-indulgence, almost of wrong-doing. With what silly vanity she had preened herself in her new clothes. They were beautiful, of course, but they were not for the likes of her. Be not solicitous what you put on – had she forgotten that? She felt guilty . . . guilty, untrue to herself and all that she had been

170

brought up to believe. Remembrance of the smart saleswoman, seeing her undressed in her cheap rayon slip and darned navy blue woollen knickers, patting and patronising her in the fitting room, made her flush painfully. What would her dear mother have thought had she seen her then!

It was not Mr Moray, or rather – true to her promise she corrected herself – David, who was to blame. No one could have been kinder or more generous, he had meant well, acted from the most disinterested motives. He was so nice, too, so interesting and companionable, and had such a tactful and pleasing way with him that it would have seemed most ungracious to refuse his gifts. Yet an inner sense told her that she should have done so. Yes, the fault had been entirely hers, and she must see that it was not repeated.

She had risen quickly, washed in cold water and put on her uniform. But as she did so, trying to fix her mind on the work awaiting her at Dalhaven Hospital and the difficult interview with the M.O.H., when she must tell him of her intention to leave the Welfare Service, the prospect looked so flat and dull she could scarcely face it. Worst of all, longing came over her for a repetition of the previous unique day, not necessarily a return to the city, but something of a similar nature, under the same kindly guidance and patronage.

Abruptly, with all the firmness of a mind habituated to self-discipline, she had put the thought away, yet even now she had not altogether forgiven herself. However, as they drew near the first cottage she was due to visit she willed herself to throw off her constraint. Turning to him she asked if he would like to come inside with her.

'That's why I'm here,' he exclaimed. 'I want to see everything.'

The cottage was tenanted by a farm-worker whose leg had been caught in a threshing machine at the last harvest. He lay in the usual alcove bed in the dark little kitchen, where also were his wife, a defeated-looking woman in a torn wrapper, and three half-dressed unwashed young children, one of whom was crawling on the floor with naked buttocks, slavering over a slice of bread and jam. The room was in a state of disorder, used pots piled in the sink, greasy dishes on the table which was covered by an old soiled newspaper. Into this mess and muddle, which left him appalled, Kathy walked with an air of unconcern, said good morning to the woman and the children, calling each by name, then turned to the bed.

'Well, John, man, how are you today?'

'Oh, not so bad, nurse.' His face had cleared at the sight of her. 'It's just that, like the wife there, I never seem to get out the bit.'

'Tuts, man, don't give up. You'll be getting about in a week or so. Now let's have a look at you.' As she opened her bag, she added casually: 'This gentleman is a friend who has come along to say hello to you.'

It was a severe and extensive injury. Viewing it across her shoulder Moray could see that only by the barest margin had the femoral artery escaped. Several of the tendons had been severed, and as healing had not taken place by first intention, some of the sutures had gone septic. He watched as, having noted pulse and temperature, she cleansed the wound, renewed the dressing and rebandaged the leg, meanwhile maintaining a flow of encouraging remarks. Finally, straightening, she said:

'John here doesn't know how lucky he's been. Another inch and the thresher would have been through the big blood vessel of the leg.' In an undertone to Moray, modestly displaying her knowledge, she added: 'It's called the femoral artery.'

He restrained a smile, accepted the information with an appreciative glance, meanwhile continuing to observe her as she closed her bag and moved from the bed exclaiming:

'That's enough for you, John. Now let's give your lass a hand.' She turned to his wife. 'Come away now, Jeannie Lang, and get a move on. If you redd up the dishes, I'll see to the bairns.'

It was amazing: in fifteen minutes she had washed and dressed the children, swept and straightened up the room, dried the dishes as they were handed dripping from the sink. Then, almost in the same breath, she had rolled down her sleeves and was on her way out, calling over her shoulder:

'Don't forget now, send to the Centre for the children's milk this evening.'

Moray made no comment until they were back in the car and he had restarted the motor, then he said:

'That was well done, Kathy.'

'Oh, I'm used to it,' she said lightly. 'It's just a matter of method.'

'No, it was much more than that. You seemed to put new heart in them.'

She shook her head.

'The Lord knows, they need it, poor things.'

It continued dismally wet and windy, the tangle of country by-roads which served her district were smeared in liquid mud, the labourers' and brick-workers' rows of cottages, small, poor homesteads, all were dripping and bedraggled in the rain. Yet this wretchedness seemed never to depress her. The troubled mood of the morning was gone. As she stepped from the car with her black nurse's bag, splashing her way towards damp kitchens and attic bedrooms, there was about her an alacrity beyond professional pretence, an unforced willingness he couldn't understand. Although she wanted him to stay in the shelter of the car, he insisted on accompanying her: something unknown compelled him to do so. All that day he watched her at work; tending nursing mothers and fractious children; a schoolgirl with a painfully scalded arm, the dressing so adherent it must be removed with time-consuming care; the wife of a brick-worker propped up in bed, struggling with asthma; then the old people, some bedridden, full of their tedious complaints, one old man, helpless and incontinent, who must be washed, the sheets changed, his bedsores cleaned with spirit.

And beyond all this were the extra duties she imposed upon herself: the dusty rooms, smelling of lamp oil, to be aired and tidied, soiled linen to be rinsed, dishes washed, milk to be heated, soup put to simmer on the kitchen range; all under conditions which would have reduced him to the lowest ebb of melancholia, and all accomplished not with quiet competence alone, but with a sympathy, a sense of spirited enterprise that left him baffled.

He might, at times, have obtruded with a remark arising from his own knowledge, for this renewed contact with sickness and disease, although so long deferred, induced a strange evocation of the days when he had walked the wards of Winton Infirmary. Yet he refrained, mainly because, in an effort to interest him, she had continued to make simple little medical comments on the condition of her patients. He did not wish to wound her.

In the late afternoon, on one of her last visits, when she had been to a case in a row of cottages, a woman called her in from a neighbouring doorway. Angus, her youngest, had 'a bit of a rash,' she thought that nurse ought to have a look at him. The

173

boy, looking fevered and uncomfortable, was lying down under a plaid shawl on two chairs placed end to end. His mother said that he complained of headache and had refused the dinner. Then she had seen his spots, some of them like little blisters.

Kathy talked with him for a minute, then, having gained his confidence, turned back the shawl and undid his shirt. At the sight of the rash Moray could see her face change. After sending the mother into the scullery on a pretext she turned to him.

'Poor boy,' she whispered. 'It's the smallpox. They've had two cases down in Berwick and I'm terribly afraid this is another. I'll have to notify the M.O.H. at once.'

He hesitated; then, for her own sake, felt obliged to intervene. In a tone which lightly parodied the professional manner, he said:

'Take another look, nurse.'

She stared at him, disconcerted at his use of that word, above all to find him smiling at her.

'What do you mean?'

'Only that you needn't worry, Kathy.' He bent forward, pointing to illustrate his remarks. 'Just look at the distribution of these vesicles. They're centripetal, none at all on the hands, feet, or face. Also they're not multilocular and show no signs of umbilication. Finally these papules are at different stages of development – unlike smallpox where the lesions appear simultaneously. Taken with the mildness of the prodromal symptoms there isn't the slightest doubt about the diagnosis. Chickenpox. Tell his mother to give him a dose of castor oil, some baking soda for the itching, and he'll be over it in a week.'

Her expression of surprise had gradually deepened until now she seemed almost petrified.

'Are you sure?'

'I am absolutely and positively certain.' He read the unspoken question in her eyes. 'Yes, I'm a doctor, Kathy.' He spoke with a kind of mild frankness, half in apology. 'Does that shock you?'

She could scarcely speak.

'It fair takes my breath away. Why did you not tell me?'

'Well, you see . . . I've never been in practice.'

'Never practised! It's beyond belief. Why in all the world not?'

'It's a long story, Kathy. And one I've wanted to tell you ever

174

since we met. Will you hear it . . . when you've finished your round?'

After a brief but intense silence, during which she still gazed at him wide-eyed, she nodded uncertainly, then, as Angus's mother returned, she reassured her, gave her Moray's instructions, and they went out. In another half hour she had finished for the day and, without further ado, he pressed hard on the accelerator and drove fast to the hotel. As the deserted lounge was cold and draughty he took her up directly to his sitting-room, where a bright driftwood fire blazed, pressed the bell and ordered hot consommé and buttered toast to be brought immediately. Her look of fatigue, which had worried him that morning, had suddenly intensified – and no wonder, he thought bitterly, after those long hours of chill and sodden slavery. He did not say a word until she was refreshed and warmed, then he drew his chair up to hers.

'I've so many things to tell you I scarcely know how to begin, and the last thing I want to do is to bore you.'

'Oh, you won't. I must hear why you never practised.'

He shrugged slightly.

'A poor student just through college, with an honours degree. A sudden exceptional offer to work in the laboratory of a large commercial enterprise. It's as simple as that, my dear.'

She studied him earnestly for a full minute.

'But what a waste – what a dreadful waste!'

'I was doing scientific work,' he reasoned mildly, translating his adventures with the pills and perfumes into more acceptable terms.

'Oh, I daresay,' she said, with vigour. 'That's very well for some. But a man like you, with such personality . . .'. She coloured, but went on bravely: 'Yes, such gifts, to throw away the chance of helping people, the sick and the suffering, the real purpose of the doctor. It seems a crying shame.' A thought arrested her. 'Have you never thought to take it up again?'

'At this late hour!' Hurriedly, to correct any false impression the unfortunate phrase might have given her, he added with pardonable subtraction: 'I'm not far off the middle forties.'

'What of it! You're fit, healthy, in the prime of life: yes, a young-looking man. Why don't you go back to your real work? Remember the parable of the buried talents.'

'I should have to brush some of the dust off mine.'

At her gratifying reference to his youthful appearance he had smiled so engagingly she was forced to smile in sympathy.

'At least you put me right on my smallpox scare. And me trying to tell you about the femoral artery. What a cheek!'

There was a brief silence. How sweet she was with the firelight playing upon her earnest young face against the darkness stealing into the room. A wave of protective tenderness, almost, but not quite, paternal, swept over him. He half rose.

'Let me get you another cup of that soup.'

'No, no, it was really good, made me much better, but I want, I would like to . . . go on with our talk.'

'You feel strongly on that subject?' His brows were raised humorously.

'I do, oh, I do. It's my idea of what life should be – helping people. It's what we're here for, to do our best for one another. And the greatest of all is charity – that's what I was brought up to believe. That's why I trained as a nurse.'

The spiritual content of her words was mildly discouraging but he accepted them kindly. Then, with firmness, he said:

'Kathy, you're a wonderful nurse – haven't I seen you in action? I admire and respect you for the work you're doing, though frankly I don't think you strong enough for it, but we'll let that pass. What I do feel, however, is that you could exercise *your* talents on a different, let's say a higher level, with much broader and rewarding results. Now, now, wait a minute.' Gently, he stilled her interruption and resumed. 'Ever since we met there's something which I've hidden from you, deliberately, because I wanted you to take to me, to like me on my own merits, if I have any.' He smiled. 'And I hope you do like me?'

'I do, very much,' she answered, with impetuous sincerity. 'I've never met anyone who's made such . . . such an impression on me.'

'Thank you, Kathy dear. So now I'm free to tell you, with all the humility in the world, that I am rather well off. I'm sorry I can't put it less crudely, for in fact, I'm lamentably and outrageously rich – for which I was never more grateful than at this moment, because of what it'll enable me to do for you. No, please,' he raised his hand again, 'you must let me finish.' Then after a pause, in a graver manner, he went on. 'I'm a lonely man, Kathy. My marriage was unhappy . . . well, let's face it, a tragedy. My poor wife was for years confined to a mental institution, and she died there. I have no children, no one like you to occupy me. All my life I've worked hard. Now, at an early age, I've retired, with ample leisure and more material possessions than I need, or deserve.' He paused again. 'I've already told you that I owe a great debt to your family – don't ask me what it is, or you'll remind me of my graceless and ungrateful youth. All I need to say is that I must repay that debt, and I want to do so by interesting myself in you, by taking you out of this drab environment, giving you a fitting background, and all the things that you deserve. A full, rich, and rewarding life, and not of course an idle one, for as you have humanitarian ideals you may fulfil them with my co-operation, and with the resources I can put at your disposal.'

While he was speaking she had been looking at him with growing agitation, and now that he had finished she lowered her eyes and for an appreciable moment remained silent. At last she said:

'You are very kind. But it is impossible.'

'Impossible?'

She inclined her head.

'Why?' he asked, persuasively.

Again there was a silence.

'You have probably forgotten . . . but that first day I told you I was giving up the district work for something better. At the end of next month I'm going out to Angola . . . to work with Uncle Willie at the Mission.'

'Oh, no,' he exclaimed in a loud, startled voice.

'But I am.' Smiling faintly, she looked up and met his eyes. 'Uncle Willie is coming home to fetch me on the 7th of next month. We'll fly back together on the 28th.'

Almost stupidly he asked:

'And how long do you mean to stay there?'

'For good,' she answered simply. 'I gave my notice to the M.O.H. yesterday.'

A prolonged stillness descended on the room. She was leaving – he calculated quickly – in five weeks' time. The news devastated him – his hopes blasted, plans fatally ruined – no, he could not, would not accept it. The projects, so well considered, which he entertained, had reached possessive force, not only for her sake, but for his own. She was to be *his* mission in life. Nothing so inane as this wild desire for self-immolation in the wilds of a tropical jungle must interfere. Never, never. But his wits were coming back to him, he saw the danger of opposing her outright and risking an immediate break. He must work for time and opportunity to change her mind. When he spoke his voice was calm, with the right note of regret.

'This is a severe disappointment, Kathy, a blow in fact. But I can see how intensely, how close this lies to your heart.'

She had been prepared for opposition. At this quiet acceptance her eyes brimmed with grateful sympathy.

'You understand so well.'

'And I'll help, too.' The thought seemed to revive him. 'Willie will have a donation for the Mission – and a handsome one – by the next mail. You've only to let me have his address.'

'Oh, I will, I will. How can I thank you!'

'But that is only the beginning, my dear. Didn't I tell you how much I want to do for you? And the future will prove it. As for the present – let me think. When did you say Willie would return?'

'In about a fortnight's time. We leave three weeks after.'

He was silent, his brows contracted in thought.

'I believe I have it,' he said at length. 'As you're to disappear so unexpectedly and so soon I think you might reasonably give me a little of your remaining time. Furthermore, I'm worried about your health. You're quite run down and if you're to stand up to hard work in tropical heat you owe yourself a holiday, or at least a rest. So I suggest, with all reserve, that you take the two weeks' vacation still owing to you and spend it at my home among the mountains. Willie, on his return, will join us there, and even though neither of you can stay long, we'll have the happiest reunion in the world!'

For five fatal seconds he thought she would refuse. Surprise and doubt clouded her open expression, but this, merging through indecision, was followed by a hesitant smile. He saw that his inclusion of Willie in the invitation had been sheer inspiration. But was it enough? Doubt had returned to her eyes.

'It would be nice,' she said slowly. 'But wouldn't it be too much trouble for you?'

'Trouble! I don't know the meaning of the word.'

'The mountain air would be good for Uncle Willie,' she reflected, 'coming beck from Kwibu.'

'And for you, going out there.' With an effort he maintained

178

a matter-of-fact tone. 'So you'll come?'

'I want to,' she said in a low voice, looking small and un-protected in the deep armchair. 'But there are difficulties. My work, for instance. Then as I've given notice I might not be allowed my vacation. I'd have to see Matron or the M.O.H. about it.' She took a long breath. 'I'm on duty at the hospital for the rest of this week. Will you please let me think it over till then?'

At that moment he saw there was nothing he could do but agree.

CHAPTER VIII

HE DROVE HER back to Markinch for the evening clinic. When they arrived, afraid of saying something injudicious in his present state of mind, he confined himself to a few words of good-bye and a restrained though speaking glance. Then he started back slowly towards the hotel.

The rain had ceased, and, with that perversity of Scottish weather which occasionally at the end of a drenching day affords an illusory promise of better things, a bar of clear light appeared on the horizon. But this transient brightness did little to raise his spirits, and presently he drew into the side of the road to think things over and switched off the ignition.

Yes, it was a nasty set-back, made worse since it was the last thing he'd expected. Who could have foreseen it? A sweet young girl bent on throwing herself away on a pack of primitive, painted savages who could no more appreciate her than – well, than they could the lovely little Bonnard that hung in his study at Schwansee. His hand shook with vexation as he thumbed at his gold lighter and drew deeply at a cigarette. Of course, he could not deny that he had heard or read of such extraordinary cases. Hadn't some rich young society woman renounced her fortune recently and gone to live on bananas with some eccentric doctor in the Brazilian jungle? Then again, nuns went out as nursing sisters, but that was part of their vocation. And he supposed that the wives of missionaries, if they felt it their duty, might accompany their husbands. Yet in this instance there was no need for renunciation, no moral or matrimonial obligation; in all its aspects the project appeared to him preposterous and futile.

What could he do about it? – that was the question. Lighting one cigarette after another, an excess completely foreign to his moderate habit, he applied himself to the problem with a concentration made possible by the force of his indignation. The simplest solution, of course, would be to abandon his plans, to give up, spare himself all further trouble, and go home. No, no, that he could never do: he rejected the thought outright. Apart from his tacit obligation to her and to himself, he had in the short time become fond, yes, extremely fond of little Kathy. The mere idea of never seeing her again was too defeatist, too dismal to be entertained.

The more he reflected, the more he became convinced that his best chance of winning her from her obsession lay in showing her, even briefly, the fullness and richness of the life he could give her. Brought up so strictly, isolated, one might say, from the world, she hadn't the faintest idea of what he could do for her. If only he might take her to Europe, demonstrate the charm and elegance of the great Continental cities he knew so intimately: Paris, Rome, Vienna, with their art galleries, historic buildings, famous monuments and churches, their choice restaurants and fine hotels, and introduce her thereafter to the comfort and resources of his home, she must surely swing to reason and be convinced. His invitation, then, made on the spur of the moment, had been a brilliant stroke, which now after serious deliberation he could not improve upon. All that remained was to ensure that she accept. But how? Casting around for assistance and support, it was not long before the obvious person came to mind.

At this, he stubbed out his cigarette, pushed hard on the starter button, then swung round and drove back through Markinch to the manse. Within five minutes he was there. As he parked the car and entered the drive he made out a rough scaffolding on the upper part of the tower and heard Fotheringay's voice raised commandingly within, all of which seemed to indicate that the bell was in process of being removed. But he had no wish to meet the minister, to be embarrassed by further expressions of gratitude; and with relief, as he passed through the overgrown laurel shrubbery, he saw Mrs Fotheringay in the vegetable garden at the side of the house. He went straight towards her. She wore a man's battered felt hat, an old stained mackintosh and heavy tackety boots, and in her hand she held a pair of garden shears.

'You have really caught me in my braws,' she exclaimed, with a wry though welcoming smile, as he approached. 'I've been slaughtering slugs. After the rain they fairly go for my cauliflowers. But I seem to have done for most of them. Come away ben the house.'

'If you don't mind,' he hesitated, 'might I speak to you here?' She studied his expression frankly, then without a word led the way to a green-painted trellis summer-house that stood at the foot of the garden. Seating herself on the wooden bench, she indicated a place beside her, then, after a further scrutiny, she said:

'So Kathy has finally told you?'

Her penetration surprised him, but it was helpful, giving him a lead.

'I heard only an hour ago.'

'And ye don't approve?'

'Who would?' he said in a suppressed voice. 'The very idea, a young girl burying herself for life in that wilderness. I'm . . . I'm inexpressibly distressed.'

'Ay, I thought you might be upset.' She spoke slowly, wrinkling up her broad weatherbeaten brow. 'And ye're not the only one. My guid man is against it, though as the minister it's hard for him to speak out. But I'm just the minister's wife and I say that it's an awfu' pity.'

'It would be bad enough at any time. But now especially, when trouble seems to be stirring in Africa . . .'

She nodded soberly, restrainingly, but he was not to be held back.

'She's not fit for it. After her work today she was quite done up. Why is she going? What's the reason of it all? Is it this uncle of hers that's responsible?'

'Ay, in a way, I suppose she's going for Willie's sake. But for her own too.'

'You mean from religious motives?'

'Well, maybe . . . though not entirely.'

'But she is religious?'

'She's good, in the best sense of the word.' She spoke with feeling, lapsing more and more into the doric. 'She helps us in the church, teaches the bairns, but – she's not the kind that aye has a Bible under her oxter and the whites of her eyes turned up. No, to understand her reasons for going, ye must understand Kathy. I don't have to tell ye that she's unusual in this shameless day and age, different as chaff from good Lothian corn from the horse-tailed, empty-headed sexy little besoms ye see gaddin' around, wi' their jazz and their rock and roll, out for nothing but a good time, or a bad one I might say. She's a serious, sensitive lass, quiet mind ye, but high strung, with a mind and ideals of her own. Her upbringing – for her mother was unco' strict – has had a deal to do with it. And living away out here in the country has kept her very much to herself. Then, since Willie went out to Angola, where apparently there's baith sickness and starvation, she seems, as was only nat'ral, to have become more and more taken up with this idea of helping him. Help where it's maist needed – service, that's her word for't. It's become the one thing, ay, the mainspring of her life.'

He was silent, biting his lip in protest.

'But she can be of service without burying herself.'

'Hav'na I told her that, again and again.'

'Why doesn't Willie tell her? He must realise that the whole thing is utterly impractical.'

'Willie is not practical.' She seemed about to say more but merely added: 'He doesna' really live in this world.'

'Well, I do,' he exclaimed, with nervous feeling. 'I'm interested in Kathy. You must have seen that. I want to *do* things – for her own good. Give her all that she needs and deserves.'

She made no reply but continued to look at him with question-ing eyes, in which also there was such open sympathy that he was seized by the sudden emotional necessity to unburden him-self, to justify his motives and win her completely to his side by a full admission of the past. The impulse was irrestible. Yielding, he took an agitated breath; then rapidly, at times almost inar-ticulately, and sparing himself considerably in the narration, he told her all that had brought him to Markinch.

'So, you see, I've every reason, every right, to make up for the past. Why, if I hadn't taken that unlucky voyage, Kathy,' his voice almost broke, 'might well have been my own daughter.'

In the pause that followed he kept his eyes lowered. When he raised them her smile was kinder than before.

'I guessed as much from the start. Kathy's mother was a reserved woman, but once she was showing me an old album, and there, on a page, was a spray of pressed flowers. In my usual style I made a bit joke about them. She looked away and sighed, and said just enough to let me know there was someone she had cared for dearly before her marriage.'

He flinched slightly at this too vivid evocation of his desertion, but recovered himself quickly.

'Then you'll help me! I've asked her to come to Switzerland to meet Willie in my home. If I can get them both there, Kathy especially, in a fresh environment, I believe I can make them see reason. And she does need a holiday, poor child. Will you persuade her to come? She's sure to ask your advice.'

She did not immediately answer, but continued to consider him with a reflective, womanly air. Then, as though giving expression to her thoughts:

'It's a strange thing. I've hoped, ay, and prayed, that something would turn up to save Kathy from this step in the dark. It's not just the danger, which is bad enough, for Willie, the crazy loon, has near been killed half a dozen times, it's the fact that she's so intense, she'll wear herself out in a twelvemonth in that ungodly climate. And she's such a dear sweet lass, made for different things. Well, it seemed hopeless, and then at the very last, when I've given up and she's on the point of going, you come along like a second father, since ye've put it that way, and it's plain to me why ye've been sent.' She paused, reached over and put her large roughened hand on his. 'We all do heedless things when we're young. It's no matter that ye made a mistake then. I believe you're an upstanding, generous-hearted man. There's not many I would trust with Kathy, but I trust *you*. If only you can take her out of this rut, get her to travel a bit, mix with people, and, best of all, find her a braw steady young husband who'll give her a good home and children to look after, someone who'll look after *her*, then you'll have more than made up for things.' She pressed his hand firmly. 'I believe in the intervention of Providence. Although you may not know it, I've a sound notion you're the answer to what I've been seeking, and I'll help you all I can.'

His eyes were still moist as he left the manse. He felt restored, purified by his confession and, aware of the worth of that good woman's promise, sufficiently reassured to wait patiently for word from Kathy. She had warned him that she would be fully occupied at the Dalhaven hospital until the end of the week. He must not, he told himself, expect an answer till then. Yet when the first day merged into the second, and the second into the third, a restless uncertainty began to torment him, his concern returned and his mood grew less hopeful. There was nothing else to engage his attention or to relieve the monotony of waiting. The weather had turned cold and windy, the sea raged, spume and blown sand whirled across the dunes and links. Even if he had been in the mood, golf was out of the question. Finlay, the professional, had shut up his shop and gone back to club-making in Dalhaven. The hotel, too, had suddenly contracted, more rooms were closed with windows shuttered, the last of the autumn guests had taken their departure, and only two permanent residents, both elderly ladies, remained with Moray to share the rigours of the north-eastern gales. Since he could no longer offer the excuse of a vacation, people both here and abroad were beginning to wonder at his prolonged stay. Miss Carmichael had twice asked him if he could give her some idea of his plans, while in Schwansee his admirable servants were becoming uneasy about him. Yet all this was as nothing compared with his increasing anxiety, the realisation that time was going on, shrinking the limited period at his disposal.

On Saturday, in an effort to distract his mind, he decided to spend some hours away from the hotel and to make inquiry in Edinburgh regarding the possibility of plane reservations. He passed the forenoon in the city; then, as the sky had brightened, rather than return early he set off idly in the car to explore the northern countryside. He lost his way, not unpleasantly, a couple of times in rural surroundings, stopped to ask directions and drink a glass of milk at a small farm-steading, started off again to get his bearings, and in the end must have wandered further than he knew, for suddenly, as he began to think of turning back, he found himself in a strangely familiar landscape. Looking about him with a tightening of his nerves, he marked one feature after another. There could be no mistake. Perhaps it was not chance but some strange subconscious prompting that had brought him here. He was in the Fruin valley, on the deserted side road that led up from the loch, through that same stretch of lovely heath-land where, on the day they came back from the hospital at Glenburn, all those years ago, Mary had given herself to him.

A strange weakness took hold of him, made him want to turn back, but he resisted it. With a set expression he drove on for a few miles, then, pressing hard on the foot brake, skidded to a stop. Yes, it was the very spot. Undecided, he sat for some moments, a rigid figure, then he got out of the car and walked across the grassy verge to the moor which, as he advanced, presently fell away into that sheltered, unforgettable dingle where the stream ran clear and strong over its pebbled bed. My God, he thought, it's exactly the same, everything so unchanged it might all have happened yesterday.

Standing there, with a hollow stomach and a fast-beating heart, the past re-created itself before him. The arrival on the bike, the picnic in the warm sunshine, the laughter and tender glances, the hum of the honey bees, and then under the blue sky, while the curlews circled and called unheeded, the joy and fear of those ecstatic moments when, irresistibly drawn, they clung together He saw it all, felt it all, lingered over it, in a bath of sentimental recollection, until with a start of panic, an actual physical shock, he pressed his hand across his eyes.

The girl in his arms was not his long-lost love. Every sensation, every burning detail of that passionate scene, he had relived not with the mother but with the daughter. It was Kathy he had held so closely in his arms, whose soft warm lips had pressed on his, who had yielded in sweet abandon. He cried out to the deserted heath. Utterly unnerved, struck by a sudden shame, he broke away, stumbled uncertainly up the slope and through the tufted heather, back to the car. Like a man possessed he drove away. Why had he not realised it before? He was in love – not with the old, but with the new. His thought of Kathy as his daughter, a ward whom he might protect, had been no more than self-deception, a protective camouflage, of his subconscious desire. From the first moment of their meeting, his original love, long cherished as the one love of his life, had been re-created, reinforced and transposed to her. Not only was the image there, fresh, young, even more beautiful, but a living, flesh-and-blood reality as well. Staring fixedly ahead, steering automatically, he tried to stem this tide of sensation. The situation was a delicate one, quite proper of course, nothing dishonourable about it, yet somehow arousing scruples, calling for second thoughts or at least restraint, otherwise the evil-minded might discover a bad odour where none existed. But how could they? His motives were of the highest, his feelings, natural, honest, and normal, could never be construed as incestuous, he had no cause for compunction, no reason to recoil. Who could blame him? How could it have been otherwise? The thought gave him release, filled him with a sudden pulsing joy, and the future, which hitherto had never exactly taken shape, now fell into place precisely, took on colours that were enchantingly sensuous and vivid. And, God, how young he felt, rejuvenated in fact, by this exciting double passion so enticingly made one.

Now, more than ever, must there be no hesitation, no more delay. Discretion always, of course – no ill-advised or premature revelation of his feelings. But he would telephone her at Dalhaven immediately he got back. Down went the accelerator, the car flew, as on wings. Arrived at the hotel he leaped out, made directly for the telephone booth in the hall, was about to enter when the porter signalled to him from the desk.

'There's a message for you, sir. Mrs Fotheringay called when you were out. She brought you this note with her best regards.'

The man handed him a plain sealed envelope with his name written on it. He dared not open it here. Hurrying upstairs to his room he tore it open and with unsteady fingers drew out the cheap sheet of notepaper within. A glance told him it was from Kathy.

> Dear David,
>
> We have been so busy at the hospital I have scarcely had any time to myself, but yesterday afternoon I was off duty and had a long talk with Mrs Fotheringay. Afterwards I spoke to Matron who has agreed to release me and let me have my remaining two weeks' holiday beginning Monday next. So I shall be free then to accept your kind offer to take me to Switzerland, and I have written to Uncle Willie telling him of your invitation to join us there.
>
> Sincerely yours,
>
> Kathy.
>
> I am very happy to be going with you.

No need to telephone, of her own free will she would come with him. He sat down in a convenient soft armchair, suffused by a glow of triumph. And on the way to Schwansee, mindful of his original intention, why shouldn't they stop off at his favourite city, at Vienna, just for a few days, to give her a taste of Continental life? He re-read the letter: so she had written to Willie. A cable would be quicker, better too. Tomorrow he would send one, a long, frank, personal message that would explain things to Willie and so ease their eventual meeting. Once again he read the postscript: *I am very happy to be going with you.* There was only one thing possible for a man of such taste and feeling, a man of his particular refinement, untouched by the crudity and vulgarities of this barbarous age. He raised the shabby little scrap of paper and pressed it to his lips.

CHAPTER IX

FROM AN ALTITUDE of twenty thousand feet the Caravelle began gradually to edge down from the starry night sky into the darker plateau of cloud below. Moray glanced at his watch: half past nine. He turned to his companion.

'Not long now. You must be tired.'

Their journey had been protracted, with delays at London and Paris, but he, at least, would not have missed a minute of it. To sit beside her, so closely, in the intimacy of the de luxe class cabin, observing with amused yet tender solicitude her reactions to her first flight, anticipating what he judged to be her wishes, though she expressed none – this, and her companionship, had afforded him a rare and precious pleasure. Since it was all so strange to her, she had not said much, and because of these silences which seemed to indicate some slight degree of tension, he now struck a note of encouragement.

'I do hope you're going to enjoy yourself, dear Kathy. Forget about slogging through the mud at Markinch and have a real holiday. Let yourself go a bit.' He laughed. 'Let's both relax and be – well – human.'

'Oh, I'm only too human,' she smiled responsively. 'You'll maybe think I'm a regular nuisance before long.'

The voice of the stewardess on the inter-communication system broke in upon them.

'We are now arriving at Vienna Airport. Please fasten your safety belts and extinguish all cigarettes.'

She was still inexpert, and helpfully he guided her fingers to make the adjustment of her belt. As he touched her small trim waist and felt the warmth of her body, a sudden joy took possession of him.

The lights of the airport, now visible below, tilted sharply as the plane banked, then with a final turn and a perfect approach they were on the runway, manoeuvring towards the wooden customs shed.

'It's a poor little airport,' he told her as they descended, 'not built up since the war. But we'll soon get you through.'

With practised efficiency, he was as good as his word. In less than seven minutes they came out to the main driveway and there, as his cable had commanded, was the Rolls, gleaming under the neon lights, with Arturo, in his best uniform, all bows and smiles, in attendance. Of this he had said nothing, meaning to surprise her, and he succeeded. When greetings had been exchanged with Arturo and they purred off into the night, enclosed by a fur rug and the soft grey upholstery, she murmured, in a small voice, 'What a lovely car.'

'I've never appreciated it more than now.' He patted her hand reassuringly under the rug. 'It'll help in showing you around.'

The road to Vienna from the Flughaven was, he knew, a bad introduction to gaiety, being flanked by a long succession of cemeteries and, as though this were not enough, by mournful establishments for the manufacture and display of tombstones. But now the kindly darkness masked these grim intimations of mortality. Within half an hour the cheerful illuminated city welcomed them. They drew up at the Prinz Ambassador. It was not a large hotel but it was luxurious and he preferred it to the others as the most Viennese in character, with a delightful old-world situation overlooking the Donner fountain and the Kapuziner Kirche. Here, too, he was known and appreciated, quickly shown to a double suite on the upper floor, the sitting-room a period piece in brocade and red velvet with a dazzling central chandelier, crystal wall lights and a baroque gesso table where already the direction had set out a great vase of bronze chrysanthemums and a basket of choice fruits.

'Now, Kathy,' he said decisively, when he had approved her bedroom and adjoining modern bathroom, both done in a delightful pale yellow with dove grey hangings, 'you're quite exhausted, in spite of your protests, so I shall say goodnight. I'm going to order something nice sent up to you on a tray, then you'll take your bath and go straight to bed.'

How wise he was, how gentle and courteous. He could tell from her eyes that he had divined exactly what she wanted. Not a word more was needed, only the simple, graceful exit. He raised her wrist lightly, brushed it with his lips, nodded briskly, then with a cheerful: 'We'll meet at breakfast in the morning,' he was gone.

He rang for the floor waiter, ordered breast of chicken sandwiches and hot chocolate to be sent up, then descended to the restaurant. Before going in he lit a Sobranie, and took, bareheaded, a short stroll along the Ringstrasse. How good to be in Vienna again, to hear laughter in the streets and waltz music coming from the cafés, even to see the naughty little *dirnen* starting out on their evening promenade. Scotland was very well, if one accepted the weather, excellent for golf and fishing, but this was better, more *gemütlich*, more his style altogether. And once she found her feet, how Kathy would adore it.

Next morning came clear and fine, a crisp autumnal day, and at nine o'clock, when breakfast was wheeled in, he went through the sitting-room, tapped discreetly on her door. She was up, already dressed, occupying herself with some knitting while waiting to be summoned. They sat down together. He poured the coffee, hot, fragrant and delicious, the very best coffee; it frothed into the fine Meissen porcelain cups, white as the snowy tablecloth and decorated with a gold crown. The butter, on ice, had the colour of cream, the honey in its silver pot was a rich golden yellow. The rolls, crisp and sweet smelling, were still warm from the bakehouse.

'Try one of those,' he said informatively. 'They're Kaisersemmeln – fit for an emperor. They've been going for almost a century. So you had a good night? Well, I'm delighted. Now you'll be ready for a good day's sightseeing.'

'I'm looking forward to it.' She glanced up inquiringly. 'Shall we need to go by car?'

He saw instantly that she was shy of using the Rolls. What a dear unspoiled child she was, and so sweet this morning, all dewy fresh from sleep. He said sympathetically.

'We must drive this morning, we are going some little distance. But another time we'll use Shank's mare.'

The phrase must have pleased her. She smiled.

'That will be nice, David. Don't you think, when you walk, you see more? And more of the people, too.'

'You're going to see everything, my dear.'

Arturo was already waiting outside and could be seen from the window pacing up and down, maintaining vigil against the press of an admiring and inquisitive crowd. When at last they descended he whipped off his cap, bowed respectfully, and presented Kathy with a single rosebud and – delighted gesture – a brass-headed pin.

'You see,' Moray murmured in her ear, 'how much my good

Italian approves . . .'.

She had blushed deeply but, when they were seated in the car, submitted while he pinned the rose to the lapel of her lovat suit. Then they were off, bound for the Kahlenberg.

It was a dazzling drive, winding upwards through clean bright little suburbs to the high pine-clad greensward of the Wiener Wald. The sun shone, the air, electric with the hint of frost, was crystal clear, so that, when they breasted the ultimate slope, suddenly, far below, the whole panorama of Vienna lay revealed with breath-taking brilliance. Leaving the car, they wandered about the summit while he pointed out the landmarks of the city: the Belvedere Palace, St Stephen's Kirche, the Hofburg, the Opera House, and, just opposite, the famous Sacher's, where he proposed to take her for lunch.

'Is it a very grand place?'

'One of the best in Europe.'

At this, she hesitated, then diffidently placed her hand upon his arm.

'David, couldn't we just have something here?' With her glance she indicated the little café just across the way. 'It looks such a nice simple place. And up here it's so lovely.'

'Well,' he queried doubtfully, 'simple is the word. And the menu will be simpler still.'

'Probably good plain wholesome food.'

When she looked at him like that, her cheeks glowing in the keen air, he had to yield.

'Come along then. We'll risk it together.'

He could refuse her nothing, though his forebodings were more than justified. A bare trestle table, cheap cutlery, and the inevitable Wiener Schnitzel, tough and rather tasteless, with which, of all things, they drank apfelsaft. Yet she did not seem to mind, appeared actually to enjoy it, and so, in the end, he became good-humouredly reconciled. Afterwards they sat for some time – she was still fascinated by the view – then, towards two o'clock, returned to the car and set out for Schonbrunn.

This was the special treat he had promised himself, for, as one set inflexibly against the architectural horrors of the modern age, he had a romantic affection for the stately eighteenth century summer palace of Maria Theresa and the lovely gardens, designed in the old French manner, which surrounded it. Besides, the role of cicerone was dear to him. From the moment they passed through the massive iron gateway he laid himself out to be interesting and, since he knew his subject, he was handsomely successful. Wandering through the great baroque apartments he re-created the Imperial Court in all its luxury and splendour. Vividly he sketched the life of Maria Theresa: from the quaint demure little maiden – he paused before her portrait at the age of six – in her long gown of blue and gold brocade, reproducing the dress of a fashionable Viennese lady, who seeing her father in state array called out, to the diversion of the entire court: 'Oh, what a fine papa! Come here, papa, and let me admire you' – from that sweet child to the woman of strong and noble individuality, central figure in the politics of Europe, patron of the arts, mother of five sons and eleven daughters who, asked on her death bed if she suffered greatly, as indeed she did, answered calmly – her last words:

'I am sufficiently at ease to die.'

Time passed unnoticed. Never had he let himself go with such dramatic fervour. They were both surprised to discover that it was almost six and beginning to get dark when they came out again to the cobbled entrance court.

'Good heavens,' he exclaimed, in apology, 'I've walked and talked you to a shadow. And, what's worse, made you miss your tea. That's inexcusable in Austria where the kuchen are so marvellous.'

'I wouldn't have missed *this* for anything,' she said quickly. 'You know so much and make everything so real.'

Apparently he had given her something to think about, for on the way back to the hotel, after a reflective silence, she remarked:

'The privileged classes certainly did well for themselves in those days. But what was life like for ordinary people?'

'Not quite so attractive.' He laughed. 'It's said that in Vienna more than thirty thousand families had each no more accommodation than a single room. And if the room happened to be fairly large, two families lived in it – divided by a clothes-line!'

'How dreadful!' she said, in a pained voice.

'Yes,' he agreed, comfortably. 'It's wasn't a good age in which to be poor.'

'And even now,' she went on, 'I've seen signs of poverty here. As we came out, children barefoot, begging in the streets . . .'.

'There always have been, always will be beggars in Vienna. But it's a city of love, laughter, and song. They're quite happy.'

'I wonder,' she said slowly. 'Can people be happy when they're hungry? I was talking to the woman who came to do my room this morning – she speaks very good English. She's a widow with four young children, her husband was killed in some trouble during the occupation, and I can tell you she's had a fearful struggle, with the high cost of everything, just to keep her family *alive*.'

'Doesn't that sound like the usual hard-luck story?'

'No, David, she's a decent wee body and completely genuine.'

'Then you must give her something from your pocket money.'

'Oh, I have!'

The pleased exclamation made him glance at her sideways. After they left the airport, so that she should have something to spend, he had pressed a bunch of notes into her purse – probably some 1500 Austrian schillings, the equivalent of twenty pounds sterling.

'How much did you give her?'

She looked up at him rather timidly.

'All.'

'Oh, no, Kathy.' Then he burst out laughing. 'What a little do-gooder you are. Parting with your entire fortune at one go.'

'I'm sure she'll put it to good use.'

'Well, if it pleases you, it pleases me,' he said, still amused. 'And one has to be liberal and a little crazy in Vienna. I love this city, Kathy – so much that it hurts me to see how quickly it is changing. You must take it all in now, my dear, for only too soon, like so many of the beautiful places of the world, it will be completely ruined. Just look at that horror on your right.' They were passing a tall new working-class apartment building. 'That faceless nightmare of steel and concrete full of hundreds of little rooms like dog kennels has replaced a lovely old baroque house, a petit palais that was bulldozed down twelve months ago so they could stick up this – this penitentiary.'

'You don't like it?'

'Who could?'

'But, David,' she took a full thoughtful breath, 'the people who live in it will like it. They'll have a sound roof over their heads and comfort too, heating, hot water, proper sanitary arrangements, and privacy. Isn't that better than pigging it across a clothes-line?'

He frowned at her quizzically.

'Won't they pig it in any case? But that's not the point. What one resents is the destruction of beauty that's going on all over the world. Tractors and trucks tearing about, gouging and rooting at the lovely monuments of the past, acres of jerry buildings springing up, all identical and all so drearily ugly. England is now swallowed up by dreary suburbs. Italy is full of factories. Why, even in Switzerland they're crowding scores of tenements on to their loveliest lakeside sites – though not near me, thank God.'

'Yes, it's a new world we have to live in,' she agreed, after a moment. 'But that's all the more reason to make the best of it. And to do our best to make it better.'

She looked at him inquiringly, as though anxious to know how he would answer her remark. But by this time they had reached the Ringstrasse, where lights were springing out and people beginning to leave their offices, congregating at the pavement cafés, talking, laughing, bringing a note of anticipation to the air. It was a fascinating hour and here, at least, there was nothing to offend his eye. As they slid easily through the evening traffic he drew near to her and, in the gathering dusk, passed his arm through hers.

'I've worn you out with lectures and arguments. You must rest in your room for an hour. Then we'll go out to dinner.'

He had sensed that she was shy of going to Sacher's, yet for her own sake decided he would take her there. With a little encouragement she would soon overcome her constraint: besides, at Sacher's one need not dress. As eight o'clock struck on the clock of St Stephen's he escorted her downstairs and out of the hotel. As the night was fine, they walked the short distance along Kärntnerstrasse. The glassed-in terrace of the restaurant was crowded but he had taken the precaution of making a discreet reservation in the little side room known as the Red Bar. He could see that his choice of table gave her confidence and, glancing across the menu, which he had been studying, his expression became reminiscent.

'I hope we'll get something as nice as the fish you chose in Edinburgh. Our first meal together. I'll never forget it. Tell me, do you like foie gras?'

'I don't know.' She shook her head. 'But I suppose I might.'

'Well, then, we'll have it. With some Garnierter Rehrücken and Salzburger Nockerln to follow.' He gave the order, adding: 'As we're in Austria we must honour the country and drink a little Durnsteiner Katzensprung. It comes from the lovely Danube valley about fifty miles from here.'

The foie gras was brought, tenderly pink; he sniffed it delicately, assuring himself it was the real Strasbourg, adequately truffled, then ordered it served with raspberry sauce. When the wine was shown, sampled, approved and poured, he raised his glass.

'Let's drink a little toast to ourselves.' Then, mildly, as she hesitated: 'Remember, you promised to be human. I want to get you out of that dear little Scottish shell of yours.'

Obediently, though a trifle tremulously, she raised the long-stemmed glass, put her lips to the fragrant, amber liquid.

'It tastes like honey.'

'And is just as harmless. I think you know me by this time, Kathy.'

'Oh, I do, David. You're so very nice.'

The venison was all he had expected, served with a savoury radish and apple sauce. He ate slowly, as was his custom, and with feeling, giving to each mouthful the respectful attention it deserved. In the adjoining alcove someone had begun to play softly on the piano, a Strauss waltz of course, but in this setting how right – charming, haunting, melodious.

'Isn't this agreeable,' he murmured across the table. He loved to see the colour come and go in her fresh young cheeks. What a darling she was, arousing the best in his nature, bringing out all that was good in him.

The sweet, as he had hoped, proved to be a triumph. Reading her expression, at which he was not expert, he explained:

'It's made almost entirely from fresh eggs and cream.'

'How many eggs?' she wondered.

He turned to the waiter.

'Herr Ober, how many eggs in Salzburger Nockerln?'

The man shrugged, but with politeness.

'So many, sir, you forget the number. If Madame wishes to make good Nockerln she must not count the eggs.'

Moray raised his eyebrows at Kathy across the table.

'We'll have to start a poultry farm.'

She broke into a peal of laughter, like a schoolgirl.

'Oh, the poor hens, trying to keep up with *that*.'

Delighted with her unusual high spirits, he did not fail to notice that she offered no objection to his hint of their future association.

Presently the bill arrived and, after a casual survey, he paid it with a note of high denomination, and tipped so lavishly as to produce a succession of bows, almost a royal progress.

As they came out of the restaurant they were met on the pavement by the usual outstretched hands – the match and paper flower sellers, the cripples, fake and genuine, the ragged old man with the wheezy accordion, the old women who now had nothing to sell but flattery. With the change from the bill he gave freely, indiscriminately, just to be rid of them; then, escaping towards the hotel, he was unexpectedly rewarded. She took his arm and of her own accord came close to him as they walked towards the Neuer Markt.

'I'm so glad you did that. I'd have felt ashamed after that delicious, expensive meal if you hadn't. But then that's just you, David, to be so unsparingly kind and generous. And what a day you've given me. Everything so new and exciting. I can scarcely believe it all. When I think that only a few days ago I was washing dishes in Jeannie Lang's back kitchen, it's . . . it's like a dream.'

It was so good to see her relaxed, free of her inhibitions, actually gay. Listening in indulgent silence, he let her run on, aware that her one glass of honey-tasting Durnsteiner could not alone have induced this mood but that he was in the main responsible for it. And in a sudden flashback he remembered that with Mary he had shown the same talent, one might even say the power, of lifting her from her serious preoccupation to a new lightheartedness. It was an auspicious omen.

Only too soon they were at the hotel. Outside her room she turned to him to day goodnight.

'Thank you for a most wonderful time, David. If you won't forget our day in Edinburgh, I can tell you I'll never forget this one here.'

He lingered a moment, unwilling to let her go.

'Did you really enjoy it, Kathy?'

'Terribly.'

'Sure?'

'Cross my heart.'

'Then tell me, what did you like most of all?'

She paused in the act of closing her door, became suddenly serious, seemed to examine her thoughts. With averted head, not looking at him, she said very simply:

'Being with you.' Then she was gone.

CHAPTER X

DURING THE NEXT three days the weather, though colder, remained brilliantly fine. Conditions could not have been more perfect for the pleasures and excitements of continued sightseeing. Varying his programme with commendable skill, Moray escorted her to the Hofburg and Hofgarten, to the Imperial Museum of Fine Arts, the Rathaus, the Belvedere, the Parliament. They took tea in Demel's, made the tour of the fashionable shops in the Graben, attended a performance at the Spanish Riding School – which, however, proved rather a disappointment since, although reserving comment, she had obviously disliked seeing the lovely white horses strained into unnatural circus attitudes. He had also accompanied her on a visit to Anna the chambermaid's four children, all lined up in a row and dressed in new warm clothes with strong winter boots, and this had been perhaps the most successful expedition of all. These were, Moray told himself, the happiest days he had ever known. She had brought joy and sweetness into his life, renewed his buoyant youth. The more he saw of her, the more he realised he could not do without her.

And yet at times she puzzled him, even caused him an odd concern. Was she truly entertained by all that he so engagingly displayed? Impossible to doubt; he had seen her eyes light up a score of times, fill with interest and animation. Nevertheless there had been occasions when, while willingly attentive, she seemed troubled, nervously disturbed. At one moment she drew near, very near to him, and the next suddenly drew back. She had a strange capacity for receding into herself and could surprise him by her constancy to her own point of view.

When in the Graben he had vainly used all the subtlety he possessed to induce her to accept a gift – a necklace, simple in design but set with emeralds – which, unthinkingly and with slight knowledge of the price, she had admired.

'It's beautiful,' she had answered, with a shake of her head, 'but it is not for me.'

And nothing would move her. Nevertheless, though as yet she remained unaware, he meant to have his way.

His greatest surprise lay in the realisation that his money counted for so little with her. She had not responded to the luxury of the hotel, rich and elaborate meals were becoming merely an embarrassment to her, and he sensed that she had preferred the little hired car to the silent comfort of his Rolls. Once, indeed, when he dropped a hint on the subject she had unexpectedly replied:

'But, David, money can't buy any of the things that really matter.'

Disappointed and somewhat chagrined by this lack of appreciation, he was nevertheless comforted by the thought that he would be loved or, as he now dared to hope, was being loved for himself alone. And since the simplicities of life so obviously pleased her, he decided to divert her attention towards Switzerland and the restful quiet she would find there. Vienna had not been a mistake; not only had he got to know her better, he had made progress, great progress, in these last few days. Intimacy had been positively established, a current of vibrations now passed between them. Though she herself might still be unaware, he knew from her sudden changes of colour, the touch of her hand, the brightening of her eye when he appeared, that she was passing the point of no return. Every instinct told him so. And to see and feel this shy, intense young girl gradually expanding under the novel compulsions of love was the most delicious experience of his life.

On Saturday morning, when they had finished breakfast, he remarked lightly, but with an undertone of consideration:

'It begins to look as though we've had enough of the city for the time being. Would you like to leave tomorrow for Schwansee? If this cold continues we'll undoubtedly have snow in the Oberland and that's something you shouldn't miss.'

The warmth of her response gave immediate confirmation of his intuition.

'I'd like it better than anything – that is, if it suits you to go. I do so love the country. Not,' she added quickly, 'that I am not happy to be here.'

'Then that's settled! We'll take the Sunday afternoon plane. I'll send Arturo on ahead today – the journey by road across the Arlberg would be much too trying for you at this time of year. But before we leave,' he paused and smiled, 'there is just one more hurdle for you to clear, I think you'll find it a pleasure and not a penance.'

'Yes?' she queried rather uncertainly.

'There is a gala at the Opera House tonight – *Madame Butterfly* . . . but a quite exceptional performance, since Tebaldi is singing. And the décor is by Benois. It's been practically impossible to get tickets but I've succeeded by a stroke of luck. As I'm sure you'll enjoy this particular opera, will you come?'

'Yes, David,' she answered with only a scarcely perceptible hesitation. 'But I'm worried at the way you keep putting yourself about for me.'

'Don't give it a thought.' He did not tell her that only by the payment of an enormous premium, effected through the concierge, had he been able at this late date to secure a loge. 'By the way, we'll take it easy today so that you'll be fresh for tonight.'

Both were glad of the rest, especially since the sky had become overcast and a keen wind blowing down from Semmering made passage through the streets a chilly business. However, after giving Arturo his instructions to leave for home he was out and about in the afternoon, on some affair of his own. At his suggestion they had an early dinner in the sitting-room: no more than a cup of strong turtle soup, omelette fines herbes with pommes pont neuf, pêche melba and coffee: by design a light meal, but good.

When they had finished he stood up.

'It's a nuisance, my dear little Puritan, but we have to dress up a bit for this affair. Luckily I knew your size, so you'll find something in your room. I had your nice Anna lay it out for you.' He put a comradely arm about her shoulder, bent forward close to her in his most winning manner. 'Please wear it – for my sake.'

Humming a snatch of the love duet from *Butterfly* under his breath, he changed in leisurely manner: first the electric razor until the smoothness of his cheek satisfied him, then a hot bath followed by a tepid shower, a good rub down, and a dust of plain talcum. The hotel valet had already put out his evening clothes, with the onyx and diamond links and studs in the fresh frilled starched shirt, the black silk socks half folded over, the patent shoes, trees removed and tongues turned back, set nearly by the armchair. Arturo could not have done better, he must remember to tip the man. At last he was ready. A touch of Eau de Muget and a brisk drill with his monogrammed ivory-backed, military brushes – thank God he had kept his hair – completed the picture. He studied himself in the glass. He had always looked well in white tie and tails – no one could touch Caraceni, in the Boncompagni, for perfection of cut – and tonight, in all modesty, he knew unquestionably that he made a handsome, distinguished, and amazingly youthful figure. In a spirit of some anticipation he switched off the light – the habit persisted from his youth – and went into the sitting-room.

She did not keep him waiting. Presently the door opened and slowly she came out wearing the green dress he had chosen for her and, to his delight, the thin necklet of emeralds that so exactly matched it. Literally, he held his breath as, still slowly, with lowered eyes and cheeks faintly flushed, she advanced and stood before him. If he had thought her ravishing in the lovat suit, now there was no word to fit the case.

'Kathy,' he said in a low voice, 'you will not like me to say this, but I must. You look enchantingly and unutterably lovely.'

He had never in his life spoken such absolute truth. So young, so fresh, and with that warm complexion and reddish gold hair, green undoubtedly was her colour. What he would make of her when he took her to Dior or Balenciaga! But was she trembling? She moistened her lips.

'It is the most beautiful dress,' she said haltingly. 'And, after all, you bought me the necklace.'

'Just to go with your frock,' he said gaily, determined to lighten her mood. 'A few green beads.'

'No. Anna was admiring them. She says they are cabochon emeralds.'

'Ah, well! I only hope your escort looks good enough to go with them.'

She looked at him, then looked away.

'I never knew there could be anyone like you.' He saw that she was seeking a phrase; it came with unusual awkwardness. 'You're . . . you're just out of this world.'

'I hope I won't be for some time.' He laughed. 'And now let's be off. It will delight your democratic spirit – since Arturo is away, we must take a taxi.'

'Am I to wear these gloves?' she asked nervously, on the way down. 'They seem so long.'

'Wear them or carry them, as you please, dearest Kathy, it makes no difference. You can't improve upon perfection.'

The concierge, though shocked that in such splendour they

should be denied their usual conveyance, bowed them into a respectable cab. In a few minutes they arrived at the Opera House, passed through the crowded foyer and were shown to the loge he had secured in the second circle. Here, in the privacy of the snug, red-carpeted little box, which was all their own, he felt her relax. Free of her nervousness, she gazed out upon the brilliant scene with increasing interest and excitement while he, seated close behind, looking over her shoulder through his opera glasses, had the delightful consciousness of reproducing that incomparable Renoir on the same theme, not, alas, his own, but one he had always admired.

'This is new, of course, rebuilt since the war,' he explained. 'A little too white and glittering perhaps – the Viennese tend to overdo their crystal – but still quite charming.'

'Oh, it is,' she agreed unreservedly.

'And as you see, everyone in their best bib and tucker for Tebaldi. Incidentally, as she'll be singing in Italian I ought to give you an idea of what it's all about. It opens at Nagasaki in Japan where Pinkerton, an officer in the United States navy, has arranged through a broker to marry a sweet little Japanese girl, Cho-Cho-San . . . '. Concisely he ran through the main points of the story, concluding: 'It's very sentimental, as you see, one of Puccini's lighter offerings, far from being grand opera, but nevertheless delightfully moving and poignant.'

He had no sooner concluded than a burst of applause announced the appearance of the conductor, Karajan. The lights dimmed, the overture began, then slowly the curtain went up, revealing a Japanese interior of exquisite delicacy.

Moray had already seen this opera twice at the Metropolitan in New York, where he had been for years a season-ticket holder, and where, in fact, he had several times heard Tebaldi sing. Once he had assured himself that the great diva was in voice, he was able to devote himself to the reactions of his companion, and unobserved, with a strange and secret expectation, he watched the changing expressions that lit then shadowed her intent young face.

At first she seemed confused by the novelty of the experience and the oriental strangeness of the scene. But gradually she became absorbed. The handsome Pinkerton, whom he had always found insufferable, obviously repelled her. He could sense her rising sympathy for Cho-Cho-San and a worried precognition of impending disaster. When the curtain fell at the end of the first act she was quite carried away.

'Oh, what a despicable man,' she exclaimed, turning to him with flushed cheeks. 'One knows from the beginning that he is worthless.'

'Vain and self-indulgent, perhaps,' he agreed. 'But why do you dislike him so much?'

She lowered her eyes as though reflecting, then said:

'To me, it's the worst thing – never to think of others, but only of oneself.'

The second act, opening on a note of tender sadness, sustained by an undertone of hope deferred, would, he knew, affect her more acutely than the first. As it proceeded, he did not look at her, feeling it an intrusion to observe such unaffected swelling of the heart. But towards the end of the scene, as the lights dimmed upon the stage and Cho-Cho-San lit her lantern by the doorway to begin her nightly vigil, while the haunting melody of the aria 'Un bel dì' swelled then faded from the darkening room, he took one swift glance at his companion. Tears were streaming down her cheeks.

'Dearest Kathy.' He bent towards her. 'If it is upsetting you, we will leave.'

'No, no,' she protested chokingly. 'It's sad but it's wonderful. And I must see what happens. Just lend me your handkerchief, mine is useless now. Thank you, dear, dear David – you are so kind. Oh, that poor, sweet girl. That any man could be so inhuman, so – so beastly.' Her voice failed, yet she willed herself to be composed.

Indeed, during the third act, rising through unbearable pathos to the final shattering tragedy, she retained control. When the curtain fell and he dared look towards her she was not weeping, but her head had fallen forward on her breast, as though she could endure no more.

They left the theatre. Still overcome, she did not speak until they were in their taxi; then, secure from observation, she said, in a muffled voice:

'I shall never forget this evening . . . never . . .'

He chose his words carefully.

'I knew you had feeling, a great capacity for emotion. I hoped you would be moved.'

'Oh, I was, I was. . . . And the best thing of all, dear David, was seeing it with you.'

202

No more than that, but enough for him to sense through her still quivering nerves a melting softness towards him. Silently, gently questing in the closed intimacy of the cab, he took her small hand in his.

She did not withdraw it. What had happened to her? Nothing, ever, like this, before. Oh, she had naturally had attentions paid her. While attending her nursing classes, a student at the University, working for his M.A. degree, had been strongly attracted to her. She had not responded. At the hospital during the previous Christmas festivities, the young asistant doctor had tried to kiss her under the mistletoe, succeeding only in clumsily reaching her left ear. She had passed off the attempt with indifference, and refused, later, when he asked her to go to the New Year's dance. She knew herself to be a serious-minded person, not interested in young men, sharing indeed her mother's view, so often forced upon her until it had become her own, that they were brash, inconsiderate and undependable.

But David was none of these things, instead his qualities were exactly opposite. And his maturity, oddly reassuring, had from the first appealed to her. He was still holding her hand, quietly and soothingly, as they reached the hotel. Nor did he relinquish it then. The night concierge was half asleep at his desk as they entered and took the lift to their floor. In the corridor he paused, opened the door of their sitting-room, conscious of a quick thread of pulse in her imprisoned fingers, his own heart beating fast.

'I ordered hot chocolate to be left for us. It would restore you, dearest Kathy.'

'No.' Half turned away from him, she shook her head. 'Nothing . . . please.'

'You're still upset. I can scarcely bear to let you go.'

He led her, unresisting, into the room where, as he had said, a Thermos jug, with fruit and sandwiches covered by a napkin, had been placed upon the table. The room was faintly lit by a single shaded light that cast a soft glow on the carpet while the walls remained in shadow, and they too were in shadow as they faced each other.

'Dearest Kathy,' he said again. 'What can I say? What can I do for you?'

Still not looking at him, she answered in a stifled voice.

'I'll be all right in the morning.'

'It's almost morning now,' he reasoned gently, despite his pounding blood, 'and you're not all right. What really is the matter?'

'Nothing, nothing . . . I don't know. I feel lost somehow. I've never been like this before – sad and happy at the same time.'

'But how can you be lost when you're with me?'

'Oh, I know, I know,' she admitted, then hurried inarticulately on. 'That wretched man has made me see how different – but that's just the trouble. You're so . . . '. She broke off, tears coursing afresh down her cheeks.

Her head was bowed, but placing his fingers beneath her chin he raised her tear-stained face so that they looked into each other's eyes.

'Kathy darling,' he murmured in a tone of ultimate tenderness, 'I'm in love with you. And I believe that you love me.'

Bending, he kissed her upturned fresh young lips, innocent of make-up – which he abominated – and deliciously salt from her tears. The next instant, with a gulping sob, she was closely in his arms, her wet flushed cheek pressed hard against his breast.

'David – dearest David.'

But it was only for a moment. With a cry she broke away.

'It's no use – no use at all. I should have known it from the beginning.'

'But why, Kathy? We love each other.'

'How can we love each other three thousand miles away? You know I'm going away. We'd only break our hearts. Mine is breaking now.'

'You could stay, Kathy?'

'Never – it's impossible.'

He had caught her wrist to keep her from flying to her room. Still straining away from him like a captive bird, she went on wildly.

'I must go. All my life I've been preparing for that one thing – training as a nurse, getting experience at Dalhaven. I've thought of nothing else. I'm needed out there. . . . Uncle Willie expects it. . . . Most of all, I promised Mother before she died that I would go, and I would never fail her, never.'

'Don't, Kathy,' he cut in, fearfully. 'For God's sake – you mustn't do it.'

'I must do it for God's sake . . . for both our sakes.'

She freed herself and, half running towards her room, was gone.

He stared painfully at the closed door. Resisting an impulse to follow her, he began to pace the soft piled carpet in a state of acute agitation. Yet, with the imprint of her soft lips still lingering on his, gradually his distress passed and his main feeling became one of joy. She loved him, utterly, unmistakably, with all her heart. Nothing else mattered. There were difficulties in the way, but they could be overcome. He must, and would, persuade her. Anything else was unthinkable. At all costs he would have her.

Suddenly he felt strong, filled with vigour, and an immense potentiality for love. Hungry, too, As his eye fell upon the good things on the table, he became conscious of the hours that had elapsed since dinner – and the meal had not been notably substantial. Seating himself, he poured the chocolate, still steaming hot, folded back the napkin and began the sandwiches. Ah! Caviar, and the real Beluga, too. Absently, yet with relish, he scoffed the lot.

CHAPTER XI

HE HAD FORECAST snow in Switzerland and, as though confirming his infallibility, snow had greeted them – an early, light covering that had frozen hard and now lay glittering under cobalt skies. For almost a week they had been in Schwansee, rigidly conforming to the covenant of restraint which, as a condition of her coming, she had obliged him to accept. Throughout this horrid stalemate of emotion, in a frantic effort to sway her, he had made simplicity and calm the order of the day. Their too theatrical welcome by Arturo and Elena had been quickly suppressed, staidness imposed, and plain meals commanded, served with an absence of formality. Straining to demonstrate the desirability of his picturesque landscape, he took her walking every afternoon in the crisp, tingling air: excursions, conducted mainly in silence, which brought them into the white foothills of the Alps, seen above as soaring pinnacles made rosy by the rising and setting of the sun. In the evenings, seated in the library on either side of the crackling log fire, tired less from their long outings than from persistent strain, he gave her a programme of his records – selecting mainly Handel, Bach, Mozart – which, rising from time to time, he played upon the stereophonic radiogram, its varnished mahogany skilfully concealed in his lacquer Coromandel cabinet. No one knew of his return, there were no intrusive visitors, no distractions, just themselves alone.

How idyllic under normal circumstances such an existence would have been. But, alas, beneath that superficial control a bowstring tension quivered insufferably with, for him, a rankling sensation of frustration and defeat. With all his charm and subtlety he had tried to dissuade her from her intention to desert him, and he had failed. Persuasion and argument alike had proved futile. And time was flying – indeed, had flown. She must leave when Willie arrived in three days' time.

This inflexibility in one so young, untried and inexperienced, remained for him a perpetual source, not of anguish alone, but of

206

stupefaction. It was not as though she did not love him. Every hour of the day presented him with evidence of her suffering through the constant suppression of her natural desires. Now when he accidentally touched her hand, as in passing a dish at table, the tremor that ran through her was physically perceptible. And how often, when she thought herself unobserved, had he surprised her glance bent upon him, charged with longing, with all the sad hunger of the heart.

One morning, although visitors were proscribed, he had felt he must introduce her to his two little friends, the children of the pier-master. So Hans and Suzy were summoned, introduced, and given 'elevenses' of cherry cake and orangeade. Afterwards all four had gone into the garden to make a snow-man from a drift blown against the thick bole of the Judas tree. This snow, beneath its hard crust, was soft and malleable, and he tied back the swing he had put up for them last summer, so they could get at it. What fun the children had, what shouts of glee, what rosy cheeks and sparkling eyes! Watching them, he had said to her, almost curtly:

'Wouldn't you like to have children like these?'

She had flushed, then paled as from a sudden hurt.

'They are sweet.' She avoided his question. 'So completely natural and unspoiled.'

Why – why – why should she refuse his love, the children he could give her, and all the immense advantages of his wealth and position? Above all, what could the alternative offer? That same afternoon, when they took their favourite walk along the high ridge of the Riesenthal, he kept asking himself these questions with a kind of brooding, desperate despondency induced for the first time by a gleam, a breaking through so to speak, a compelled recognition that there *must* be something in her point of view. And although a truce had been declared between them, as they strode along the high path between the silver-dusted pine trees he could hold back no longer.

'Dearest Kathy, I've no wish to reopen our wounds, but it would help to – to soothe mine, if only I could get a fuller understanding of your motives. Are you leaving me mainly because you have plédged your word?'

'Partly for that reason,' she answered, walking with lowered head. 'But also for another.'

'What other?'

'As I told you, because of what I believe is demanded of all of us. We're living at a terrible time, David. We just seem to be drifting towards self-destruction, moral and physical. Beneath the surface we're all terrified. Yet the world keeps moving away from God. We'll never get through unless everyone, every single person, does something about it, each his own part, no matter how small. Oh, I'm not clever, but it's so obvious, what Uncle Willie says – that we must prove love is stronger than hatred – show that courage, self-denial, and above all charity, can defeat brutality, selfishness and fear.'

Mentally he had made the state of the world taboo, except to reflect that *it would see him out*. But in spite of this he was impressed – who wouldn't have been by such ingenuous fervour?

'So because of your ideas of – of duty and service, you condemn yourself to a life of hardship and misery.'

'Misery?' Quickly she raised her head in protest. 'You can't imagine the personal rewards of such a life.'

'A life of self-sacrifice.'

'It's the only way life can be lived. Nowadays especially.'

'You can't be serious.'

'I was never more in earnest. Wait till you see Uncle Willie. He's had what you might think of as a miserable time, and a great deal of illness, but he's the happiest person in the world.'

He was silent. This hitherto had been beyond him, something outside his conception of life. Could one really be happy out there, *doing good*, in that confounded wilderness? He asked himself the question with a sense of growing agitation.

'And there's more than happiness,' she went on, with difficulty, still striving to express herself. 'There's contentment and peace of mind and a sense of accomplishment. One can never get these by enjoying oneself, by running after pleasure all the time, shutting one's eyes to the agony of others. And they certainly can't be bought. But if one does a really fine job, something to benefit other people – people in need . . . Oh, I'm no good at explaining things, but surely you understand what I mean . . . '. She broke off. 'If you had practised as a doctor you would know . . . and I think – please forgive me, David – I'm sure you would have been a much happier man.'

Again he kept silence, biting his lip, and switching with his steel-pointed stick at the iced lumps of snow turned back by the passage of farm wagons. She was enunciating, naïvely, a humanitarian cliché. And yet, wasn't there more than a grain of truth in what she said? In the pursuit of the rewards of this world, had he found anything but heartache, ennui, recurrent dissatisfactions and regrets, and a bunch of neurotic complexes which had more than once brought him to the verge of a breakdown?

'Dear Kathy!' With sudden self-pity and a rush of sentiment. 'I've always wanted to be good, and to do good, but circumstances have been too much for me.'

'You are good,' she said earnestly. 'It's – it's looking out of your face. You only need the opportunity to prove it to yourself.'

'Do you honestly believe that?'

'With all my heart.'

'My God, Kathy – if you knew what my life had been, what I've endured until . . . well, virtually, until I met you.' Emotionally, he went on: 'As a young man, in India, trapped – yes, literally trapped – into a disastrous marriage and then, for years, the American treadmill, trying to get on . . . on . . . on, finding some refuge in the arts, but only a temporary respite, make-believe, really never achieving true satisfaction though deluding myself that I had. It all springs from my poor unwanted childhood. The whole tree of my life, roots, stem, and branch, was formed then. I've been told,' he refrained from mentioning Wilenski, 'I know it too, all my present being comes from those early years when I had nobody but myself.'

'All that you've said only convinces me that you still can do great things.'

He was too moved to reply and they continued in constrained silence. But her words vibrated in his mind and he felt that she was right – the potential for high achievement still lay within him. What was that line? 'Do noble deeds, not dream them all day long.' He remembered suddenly the last advice Wilenski had given him on leaving New York: 'When you get over there, for heaven's sake find yourself something worthwhile to do, something to do with other people, that'll take your mind off yourself.' Why had he ignored, forgotten this? It had taken Kathy to remind him. Her sweetness and goodness, the purity of her being – he did not shrink from the phrase – had worked on him unconsciously, affected him without his knowing it. How could it have been otherwise?

He was about to speak when, looking up, he saw they had reached the mountain hut where on a previous occasion they had stopped for coffee. It was a poor brew made from some inferior powder, but it was hot, Kathy had appeared to like it, and the peasant woman, skirt kilted over her striped petticoat, was already welcoming them. They sat down on the wooden terrace, in the cold sunshine, both conscious of something momentous and unavoidable developing between them. Nervously, he began drumming on the table, took a quick incautious sip of coffee, spilling it slightly, for his hand shook, then said suddenly:

'I do admit, Kathy, that everyone ought to have some worthy objective in life. I had hoped to find it in devoting myself to you here. But now – it begins to seem as though something more is being demanded of me.'

'What, David?' Her lips were trembling.

'Can't you guess? You're the one who's made me feel it, not only by speaking out now, but simply by your presence. Kathy,' he murmured, in a low, reaching-out voice, 'all other considerations apart, do *you* really need me?'

She looked at him, drawn beyond endurance.

'How can you ask that?' Then with a sudden weakening of control, pitifully avoiding his eyes: 'I need you so much . . . I want you to come with me.'

It was out at last, she had been forced to say it, the unspoken longing that until now she had kept locked up within her breast. He gazed at her in a shaken silence of revelation, realising that he had wanted and waited for that plea through all these recent days of strain.

'You mean,' he said slowly, demanding more, at least a repetition, 'to take the trip out with you?'

'No, no . . . to stay.' She spoke almost feverishly. 'As a doctor, there's the greatest need for you. Uncle Willie is planning a little hospital adjoining the orphanage. You would find there the very work you are fitted for, which in your heart you are seeking. And we would be together, working together, happy.'

'To be with you, Kathy,' he conceded feelingly, 'I'd give my right arm. But think of the changes it would mean, in my – my way of living for one thing. Then again, it's some time since I took my medical degree.'

'You could brush up quickly – you're so clever. And you'd get used to the life.'

'Yes, dear Kathy, but there are other difficulties.' The inordinate desire to be pressed further made him go on. 'Financial affairs that require constant attention, responsibilities; then as regards the mission, you know I'm not a religious man. While agreeing with what you've just said, I doubt if I could surrender my mind to your spiritual convictions.'

'The work you'd do is the best kind of religion. In time, David, you would know the meaning of grace. Oh, I can't speak of such things, I never could, in words they become stiff and wooden, I can only feel them in my heart. And you would too ... if you'd only come.'

Their hands glided together. Hers, from inner strain, was cold, a marble hand; he held it tightly until the blood began to throb. Never had he felt closer to her. All her soul seemed to flow into him.

The arrival of the peasant woman cut into this splendid moment. While he looked up at her, unseeingly, she pointed to the northern sky and said, practically:

'Es wird Schnee kommen. Schau'n sie, diese Wolken. Es ist besser Sie gehen zurück nach Schwansee.'

'She's advising us to get back home.' Returning to earth, he answered Kathy's inquiring glance. 'Snow is forecast and it's already clouding over.'

He paid the score, leaving generous *trinkgeld*, and they set off back along the ridge, now in total silence, for he was deep in thought. The air had turned grey, cold and very still and the sun was dropping fast behind the mountains like a great blood-orange. Within the hour they had descended to the flatlands and, worried for her in the chill twilight, he looked forward to reaching the villa quickly. But as they were about to cross the short stretch of main road that intersected the path to Schwansee, a red sports M.G. flew past, hesitated, screeched to a stop, and noisily reversed towards them.

'Hello, hello, hello,' came the effusive greeting in high-pitched tones. 'I felt sure it was you, dear boy.'

Jarred out of his meditation, Moray recognised with misgiving the brass-buttoned blazer of Archie Stench. Leaning airily out of the window from the driver's seat, smiling with all his teeth, Stench extended a gloved hand which Moray accepted with the forced affability of extreme annoyance. The solemn pattern of the afternoon was shattered.

'This is Miss Urquhart, daughter of an old friend,' he said quickly, bent on extinguishing the suggestive gleam already

211

glittering slyly in Stench's eye. 'Her uncle, a missionary in Central Africa, is joining her in two days' time.'

'But how inter-esting.' Archie split and stressed the word. 'Coming here?'

'For a brief visit,' Moray nodded coldly.

'I should like to meet him. Africa is in the news, and *how*. The wind of change. Ha, ha. Dear old Mac. It's quite a breeze now in the Congo. Are you enjoying your stay, Miss Urquhart? You are staying with Moray, I presume?'

'Yes,' Kathy replied to both questions. 'But I shall be leaving soon.'

'Not for wildest Africa?' Ogling, Stench threw out the question facetiously.

'Yes.'

'Good Lord!' Stench thrilled. 'You're really serious? Sounds like quite a story. You mean you're in the missionary racket – sorry, I mean business – yourself?'

Kathy half smiled, to Moray's annoyance, as though taking no exception to Stench's persistence.

'I am a nurse,' she explained, 'and I'm going out to help my uncle – he's opening a hospital at Kwibu, on the Angola border.'

'Good work!' Stench glowed. 'While everyone's running away from that windy area you're rushing in. The nation ought to hear about it. We British have to keep the flag flying. I'll drop over when your uncle arrives. You'll give me a drink, dear boy. just for old lang syne? Well, got to be off. I'm all in. Been down at the Pestalozzi Village doing a conjuring show for the kids. Sixty kilometres each way. Dam' bore. But decent little brats. Cheerio, Miss Urquhart; chin-chin, dear boy. Wonderful to have you back!'

As he drove off Archie called out, ensuring his prospective visit:

'Don't forget, I'll be giving you a ring.'

'He seems nice,' Kathy remarked conversationally, when they had crossed the road. 'Good of him to entertain those children.'

'Yes, he's always up to something like that. But – well, a bit of a bounder I'm afraid,' Moray answered in the tone of one unwillingly forced to condemn, adding, as though this accounted for everything, 'Correspondent for the *Daily Echo*.'

The unfortunate meeting at this particular moment, when vital soul-subduing issues surged in his mind, had thoroughly put him out. Stench was a menace. Confound it, he thought, brought back to the mundane, in half an hour news of his return with Kathy would be all over the canton.

Indeed, no sooner had they got back and taken tea than the phone rang.

'Put it through to the study,' he told Arturo briefly. 'Excuse me for a few minutes, dear Kathy. Friend Stench has been at work.'

Upstairs, he unhooked the receiver, pressed the red button with an irritable premonition immediately confirmed by Madame von Altishofer's contralto overtones.

'Welcome home, dear friend! I heard only this moment that you were returned. Why did you not let me know? It has been so long. You have been missed greatly; everyone is talking about your mysterious absence. Now, how soon may I come to see you, and your exciting young visitor who has designs on darkest Africa?'

It was amazing how disagreeable he found this intrusion – not only what she said, but her manner, her inverted English, even her modulated well-bred voice. He cleared his throat, launched into a perfunctory explanation, the essence of which was simply that the demands of old family friends had detained him much longer than he had anticipated.

'Relatives?' she queried politely.

'In a way,' he said evasively. 'When my other guest arrives I hope you'll come over and meet them both.'

'But before, you must come to me for a drink.'

'I wish I could. But I have so many things to attend to, after being away.' Looking out of the window he saw that the first frail snowflakes were beginning to drift down. He seized upon the topic. 'Good gracious! It's actually snowing. I'm afraid we're in for an early winter.'

'No doubt,' she said, with a little laugh. 'But are we reduced to speaking of the weather?'

'Of course not. We'll get together soon.'

Frowning, he hung up, terminating the conversation, annoyed at her interference – no, that was totally unjust; despite her Germanic strong-mindedness she was a thoroughly nice woman and he had perhaps over-encouraged her. He was very much on edge. Again he had a strange feeling that time was closing in upon him. Downstairs he was disappointed to find that Kathy had gone to her room. She did not appear again until dinner, and then he saw that, to please him, she had put on the green dress. Touched to the heart, he knew that there was only one woman in the world for him. He wanted her with a need so extreme he had to turn away without his usual compliment, without a word. All evening, despite his efforts to entertain, he was not himself – preoccupied, obsessed rather, with the need of achieving some decision, in the ever-dwindling hours at his disposal. After he had played a few records she must have seen that he wished to be alone, for on the plea of fatigue she went early to bed, leaving him in the library.

CHAPTER XII

WHEN SHE HAD gone he stood for several minutes listening to her light movements in the room above. Then, automatically, he began to slip the long-playing discs into their polythene covers and to replace them in the cabinet. He half opened one of the three tall windows and peered across the terrace into the night. The snow, beginning with light flurries, had fallen steadily all through the late afternoon, gentle, silent, clouding the air with great drifting flakes. Now the garden was blanketed, nothing visible beyond, life seemed extinguished. No sounds disturbed the unnatural stillness but the abandoned wail of a paddle boat groping its way across the shrouded lake, and the faint whine of the *bise* springing up, imperceptible at first, but gaining in force. He well knew that wind, spiralling down from the mountains with immediate violence, and recognised through all his senses the portents of a storm. Within five minutes, as he had foreseen, the wind was howling round the house, creaking the shutters and tearing at the roof tiles. The air, turned colder, edged the whirling flakes with ice. They fell sharper, mixed with a heavy spattering hail and clots of driven snow. The trees, unseen but plainly audible, had begun that familiar mad fandango which, mingling Berlioz with the blast, he had so often dramatised for his own entertainment.

But his mood was too disturbed to permit of Berlioz. Wagner would have been more appropriate, he reflected grimly, something like the Ride of the Valkyries, but he had no heart for anything, could think only of the fateful decision he must make, and of her. He shut the window and pulled the tasselled cord that drew the pale pink quilted curtains, wondering if she were asleep, or if, as seemed probable, the storm had disturbed her. The thought of her lying there, alone, listening wide-eyed to the harsh discords of the night! If only he might go to her. But of course he could not. God, how restless he was, he must compose himself, try to clear his mind. Taking a book from the shelves, a new biography of Lord Curzon, he threw himself into a chair. But he could not settle to read, not even of Curzon, a man he deeply admired, had in fact unconsciously adopted as an exemplar. His attention wavered, the words ran together into a meaningless blur. He got up, looked at the Tompion longcase clock: only half past ten: too early for bed, he'd never sleep. Never. In the drawing-room he began to pace up and down, head bowed, without a glance towards his paintings, so often a consolation in the past. He felt unendurably hot, suppressed an inordinate impulse to go out on to the snow-bound terrace, went instead to the pantry and turned down the thermostat. No sounds came from the kitchen; Arturo and Elena had retired to their own quarters. Even they had shown signs of disquiet lately, as though waiting, uneasily, for an announcement. Returning to the drawing-room, he was about to resume his pacing when forcibly he drew up short, facing at last the core of his problem.

Once it had been established, finally, that she would not stay, only one possible course of action remained open to him. Though he had stubbornly evaded the issue, he saw that from the beginning, when he set eyes on her in Markinch churchyard, the end had been inevitable, part of his destiny. It was the pressing need to amend his life that in the first instance had brought him back to his native land. Now she offered the very opportunity he sought, and with it all the wonder of her love. How could he refuse? She had become an absolute necessity to him. If he should lose her through vacillation or stupidity, life would be impossible. Hadn't he learned that lesson from his sad youthful mistake? He must accompany her to Kwibu, give himself up completely to the work ordained for him. And why not? It was splendid work. He truly wanted to be the new person she would make of him. And he would be. It was not too late. It was not impossible. Others had found that saving spark, and in comparable manner. He had read of them, tortured men in spiritual travail, who discovered themselves in strange suspenseful backgrounds, habitually tropical, and at the last gasp.

'I'll go,' he said out loud. 'It's the only way.'

When he had spoken these thrilling words, he experienced an immediate singing sensation of release. He felt lighter suddenly, freed, as if a load had been lifted from his shoulders. What a liberation – almost a transfiguration! Was it what they called a *conversion*? She had spoken of grace, and now he seemed not alone to sense its meaning, but actually to feel it flowing into and through him. A sweet ichor, a fountain of light – the words came to him as, with head thrown back, he looked upwards, deeply and genuinely moved, experiencing fully this moment of beatitude, even feeling himself, though distantly, in touch with Heaven. He could not yet ascend to the heights, he had been earthbound too long, and so he did not attempt a prayer, but that – later perhaps – might come.

Slowly, he relaxed. It was done, the die heroically cast. Gladness overwhelmed him. And how easy it had been, simply an acceptance of the truth and an offering of himself. Why had he hesitated so long, keeping her waiting in an agony of protracted uncertainty? For she had suffered, poor little thing, perhaps more acutely than he. If only he could tell her now, spare her these extra hours of suspense. Yet would it be quite proper? Right and reason were on his side. But no, he felt it might scarcely be correct. Well, at least he would rest with a mind at peace.

After standing motionless for several minutes he switched off the lights and went slowly upstairs to his room. Still inspired, warm with salvation, he took a tepid bath and his usual dust with talcum, put on his sleeping coat, morocco slippers and dressing gown, sat down on the edge of his bed. He must really turn in. Yet the excitement of his decision kept mounting within him. His good news simply would not keep, physically he could not contain it. Was she asleep? If not, it would be only Christian charity to deliver the good tidings now, in person. He got up, hesitated, speculatively opened his door, and gazed across the long upper landing. Then, holding his breath, he tiptoed cautiously, without a single creak, over the thick Wilton carpet towards her room.

The wind, still roaring outside, intensified the inner stillness of the darkened landing as he paused outside her door. He almost turned back. Then, his pulse sounding in his ears, he tapped upon the panel, gently turned the handle.

'Kathy,' he whispered, 'are you awake?'

An immediate stirring in the darkness answered him, even before her startled voice came back.

'David!'

'Don't be alarmed, dear Kathy. I thought the storm might

217

have kept you awake. And as you are . . . I have something important to tell you.'

Feeling his way forward, he came to the bed and knelt down beside it. Faintly, he could see the outline of her head upon the pillow, of a bare arm resting upon the counterpane. He touched it lightly, reassuringly.

'Kathy, dearest Kathy. My mind is made up. I had to let you know at once. I am coming with you.'

'David!' she said again, in a soft thrilling whisper. He could feel the sudden joy that took possession of her, every nerve in her seemed alive. 'Oh, thank you – thank you, from my heart.'

'You're not angry with me . . . for disturbing you?'

'Angry! Oh, my dear, I've been lying here, longing and longing to hear what you have just told me.'

'I couldn't bear the thought of you waiting, through what might have been a sleepless night.' He paused. 'Now I am here, may I stay a little while and talk?'

'Yes, stay, stay. I am wide awake now. Shall I switch on the lamp?'

'No, dearest. I can see you clearly now.'

'And I can see you.' She gave a low joyful sigh. 'Oh, I'm so happy. Do you know what I was half dreaming, just before you came in?'

'Tell me, dear.'

'That we were out in Kwibu together and that Uncle Willie . . .' she hesitated, then opened her heart, 'that Uncle Willie was marrying us in the Mission church.'

'And so he will, dear Kathy.'

They remained looking at each other. His heart, swelling in his side, was a pain and a delight. With gentle fingers he began gently to stroke her arm.

'I am still thinking of our future,' she went on in a lulled, dreamy voice. 'All settled. You and I together.'

Outside rain and hail kept drumming on the window, then came a flash and a crack of thunder. He shivered slightly.

'Dear David, you are cold. Please get a rug to cover yourself.'

'It is chilly.' A lump rose in his throat, yet he spoke reasonably, with calm moderation. 'If you could share the counterpane, we could bundle – like they do in the Islands at home. There's so much we have to say to one another.'

A moment later he lay beside her, but in the semi-darkness, fumbling to lift the counterpane, almost inadvertently, he had raised also the blanket and linen sheet that covered her. Her face was close to his on the pillow. At first she had turned rigid, lying so still he thought she had ceased to breathe, then he felt that she was trembling. Quickly he reassured her.

'Dearest, you know I don't mean to distress you.'

'But David . . .'.

'I respect and cherish you more than anything in the world.'

Gradually, very slowly, she relaxed. The warmth of her young body came to him through her cotton nightdress. The rain hissed down the gutters and thunder rolled and echoed amongst the mountains. Half turning, he pressed his lips against her hair.

'David, this is wrong,' she said at last, in a breaking voice. 'Please don't let us do a wrong thing.'

'Darling,' he said, with deep conviction, 'how could it be wrong? We are already one in the sight of Heaven.'

'Yes, David, but please let us wait, dear.'

'Don't you love me enough?'

'Oh, I do – I do – so much that it hurts. But we'd be so sorry, after.'

'No, dear Kathy, love like ours is itself a forgiveness.'

'But David . . .'.

'And surely my – our mutual pledge makes this moment a sacred one.' He could feel the struggle within her. He murmured earnestly: 'It cannot be wrong, dear, when in only a few days, almost a matter of hours, Willie will marry us.'

He took her in his arms, inhaling the scent of her fresh young skin. How thin and slight she was, how young, and how violently her little heart was beating against his breast, like a bird just captured and fluttering in its cage.

'No, David, dearest.'

Then, nature overcame, released her from conscience. Sighing, she put both her hands behind his neck and kissed him fiercely. 'I cannot help it. I love you so much it's. . . like dying.'

A consciousness of rectitude welled up in him. Whispering, he sought to still her trembling. Pure unprofane sex was no sin, a sanctification rather, almost an act of worship – that had been said recently, ecclesiastically, had it not? – in a court of law. Tenderly enclosing her, he readjusted his embrace, but with prayerful gentleness. How sweet at last to taste the slow pleasure, the mounting rapture, all in the odour of sanctity. Later, as he felt her tears on his cheek, he sighed, appeased, though still exalted.

'You are crying. But why, dear child?'

'I'm afraid for what we've done, David.'

'Was it not sweet for you too, my love?'

'Yes, it was sweet,' her voice stifled in the pillow. 'But it was a sin, David, and God will punish us.'

'No, dearest. He knows. He will understand. And if you think it was just a little wrong, you know we will make up for it.'

She is different from her mother, he thought dreamily, as of a shadow passing before him. Mary had no regrets. Yet she too had turned religious, in the end.

'Don't, dear,' he said soothingly, wiping her hot sad face with the cool entangled sheet. 'Think of our work – of the happiness that lies ahead of us.'

'Yes, David.' Striving obediently to check her tears, she clung to him. 'I am trying . . . thinking of you and me, David, in the little Mission church.'

CHAPTER XIII

At zurich airport, striding to and fro between the flower stall and the newspaper kiosk that flanked the exit of the *douane*, Moray expanded his chest with a long deep breath, suffused by a new sense of the joy of living. The sensation was so strong he smiled involuntarily, and it was a proud smile. Often he had experienced a delightful consciousness of himself, but never before with such intensity as now. He had seen the Super-Constellation land, it could be no more than a matter of minutes before Willie appeared. Admittedly he was nervous, and for that reason, among others, had managed to persuade Kathy not to accompany him, explaining that for her so emotional a reunion was best conducted in private. In any event, she was still rather agitated, not yet quite herself. When he looked into her room before leaving for the airport, he had been concerned to find her kneeling in contrite prayer. But while he respected these tender scruples, they would pass. If he himself felt a twinge of compunction, he was sustained by the inner consciousness that he was at last on the way he had sought so long, loved for the vital decision he had taken, a man with a mission in life, soon to savour the joy of energetic action, the thrill of enthusiasm, the sacred peace of duty accomplished. Rising early, he had squared his shoulders against the task ahead. Already the latest medical textbooks had been ordered by telephone, inquiries sent out as to tropical equipment, consideration given to the adjustment and settlement of his affairs. Looking back he now regarded the emptiness, the falsity, of his previous life with shamed and scornful self-contempt. But the future prospect exonerated him, filled him with the double anticipation of spiritual regeneration and the sweetness of continued love.

He paused abruptly in his promenading. Customs examination was over, the passengers of the big Trans-World plane from Luanda via Lisbon were filing through the glass doors, and there, at the end of the line, came a tall, emaciated-looking man with sloping shoulders, carrying a small blue airlines zipper bag, dressed in an open-necked drab shirt and a thin khaki service suit, the blouse with flat pockets suggestive of the war-time pattern. He wore no hat and his streaky sun-bleached hair had the same colour as his face which, lined and sunken, was of a withered yellow. But his eyes, though hollow in their orbits, were still youthful, almost unnaturally bright, and, meeting them across the crowd, Moray knew that, unmistakably, this was Willie.

They shook hands. Then to Moray's relief – for despite his newfound faith in himself he had experienced a sudden wilting inrush of near-panic – Willie smiled.

'You knew me,' he said. 'And I knew you, too.'

'Wonderful to see you again. Kathy is expecting you at the house. Was it a good flight? Have you had lunch?' In his excitement Moray almost babbled, there was so much he wanted to say, to explain, all in one breath.

Willie did not want lunch but said he would be glad of a cup of coffee.

'You feel the cold, coming back,' he added mildly.

And no wonder, thought Moray. No overcoat and such an outfit. Aloud he said:

'We'll go immediately your luggage is brought out.'

'This is it.' Willie indicated the zipper bag. 'All I need. Some shirts and a pack of coloured slides. You know I can't stay long.'

In the café below the restaurant the waitress brought two steaming cups. As Willie applied himself to his, Moray took a painful yet purposeful inspiration.

'I want to explain everything to you, Willie . . . in the hope of your forgiveness. It's a long tragic story, but perhaps you'll listen, for it has a – I fully believe – a good ending. You see, when I . . . '.

'Don't,' said Willie, fixing the other with tired, brilliant eyes. 'That's all in the past and forgotten. Human beings should not judge one another. I had your cable and Kathy's letter. So not another word.'

An immense wave of gratitude flowed over Moray, so warm and overwhelming it left him speechless. In total silence he sat watching Willie nursing the hot cup, drinking in little gulps. If there seemed no flesh on his body, there was less on his hands; the fingers holding the cup were skeletal. He noticed also that Willie

had a marked tic which periodically caused his head to jerk laterally, exposing a scar that ran from one side of the neck to the larynx.'

'I see you've spotted my beauty scratch.' Willie had caught his eye. "One of my old scoundrels was a prize spear-thrower in the early days. Now he's my chief catechist. It doesn't trouble me much, though once in a while I lose my voice. It was worth it."

All this was said in such a natural lighthearted manner as to impress Moray even more. He'd have given a lot, there and then, to announce the intention that burned inside him. But no, Kathy had claimed the privilage of imparting this sensation, linked to the news of their marriage, so with all his newfound self-denial he refrained, saying instead:

"If you're ready we may as well be off."

In the station wagon Moray turned the heating full on, but they hadn't gone far before he observed that Willie was shivering. He wanted to stop and offer his overcoat, but this, although St Francis of Assisi had set the precedent, struck him as officious in the present case. Yet his heart glowed towards Willie. Dressed as he was, with that explosive tic and his strange shivering remoteness, Willie looked odd, extremely odd, but there was something real about him, he was undoubtedly a man. Already Moray had identified himself with him and, half turning, while still keeping one eye on the road, he said:

'If I had some idea of your plans, it would enable me to make the best possible arrangements for your stay.'

'I'm due in Edinburgh on the eleventh. Let's see,' Willie reflected, 'that's three days from now. I've some serious matters to put before my committee. And a lecture to deliver in the Usher Hall. Kathy,' he added, 'had better come along to help me and collect her gear.'

'Must you both go so soon?' Moray exclaimed in a disappointed tone. 'I'd banked on keeping you for some time.'

'It's all very pressing. We shall not stay long in Edinburgh but work down to London, lecturing on the way. I'm needed at the Mission. So I've arranged to fly back to Kwibu on the twenty-first.'

'Good heavens, that's sooner than we expected – less than two weeks from today. And I did want to do something for you here.'

Already, at the back of his mind, Moray had felt the need of a definite act to mark his departure from Schwansee. He meant to go off with a bang. No hole-and-corner business, no slinking off, he'd march out with head high and flags flying. And now, under the stress of urgency, this idea took definite form: he'd have a farewell party, introduce Willie to a gathering of his friends, there would be a frank declaration by himself, an appropriate speech by Willie – ah, that suggested an added attraction.

'You say you're to deliver some lectures?'

'They call it a lecture.' Willie smiled. 'Just a little descriptive talk about the Mission, chiefly our beginnings there, illustrated by coloured slides. I only do it to raise funds.'

'Then,' said Moray warmly, 'why don't you raise some here? Give the lecture in my house tomorrow. I can promise you a substantial response.'

'I wouldn't mind,' Willie said, after a moment's thought. 'I'm not much of a speaker. At least I could run through some of it.'

'Good, then that's settled.'

They were now beyond Lachen, on the last stretch of their journey, yet the dazzling view of the mountains which presented itself brought no comment from Willie. Instead Moray became increasingly aware that his companion, drawn up in the corner of the seat and despite the fact that the station wagon had become excessively warm, was enduring a sharp return of his earlier shivering fit. Momentarily neglecting the road, Moray turned full round to find the other's over-bright gaze bent apologetically upon him.

'Don't mind me,' Willie said. 'I felt this coming on in the plane. Just a little snatch of fever.'

Reverting to eyes front, Moray groped along the seat and found Willie's bony fingers. They were dry and hot.

'Good heavens, man, you're obviously getting a temperature. You must go to bed immediately when we get back.'

Selecting an interlude between the rigors, Willie smiled.

'If I lay down every time I had a temperature I'd never be up.'

'What is it?' Moray asked, after a pause. 'Malaria?'

'It could be. But then I've so many interesting bugs inside me – amoebae, cocci, trypanosomes, and whatnot – one never knows.'

'Surely not trypanosomes?'

224

'Oh, yes, I've had a go of sleeping sickness. Then I did have to be flat on my back.'

'We'll stop at the chemist's and at least get you some quinine.'

'Thank you, David, you're a goodhearted chap. However, I've had a staple diet of quinine so long it's stopped doing any good. I stoke up with atabrine and paludrin occasionally, though actually it's better to let the bugs fight it out amongst themselves. If you leave them alone the different strains go into battle and knock each other out.'

Good God, thought Moray, staring straight ahead and frowning, this man is a hero or a saint – or else he's a little bit dotty.

But now they were in Schwansee and, turning up the hill from the lake, into the winding avenue lined with acacia trees, Moray drew up at his house. Immediately Kathy rushed from the porch – she had been waiting more than an hour for the sound of the car.

Watching the reunion of uncle and niece, Moray suffered a twinge of jealousy that it should be so affectionate. But, manfully, he dismissed the unworthy sentiment – Kathy, he well knew, was all his own. He smiled at her meaningly.

'Show Willie to his room, my dear. I'm sure you have lots to say to him.'

When he had washed and restored himself with a quick glass of amontillado he went into the library to wait for her. She was a long time in coming down, and although he occupied himself by drawing up a list of the people he meant to invite to the lecture party – Arturo would telephone them later in the day – he had begun to feel anxious at the delay when the door swung open and she appeared. Her cheeks were flushed, she flew like a homing dove straight into his arms.

'I've explained everything. Uncle Willie is coming down to have a talk with you, so I won't stay. I think it's all right. I'm sure he likes you . . . And, oh, dearest David, I'm happy again.'

When she had gone, he waited with a touch of apprehension, aware of the many points on which he might be interrogated. But when Willie arrived his expression, with its mixture of patience and kindness, was far from intimidating. Standing there, with his sloping shoulders and thin, dangling hands, his bones seemed loosely strung together under the thin, parchment-dry skin. He looked at Moray from under his brows with those bright, luminous eyes, in an embarrassed manner, made evident by an exacerbation of his tic.

'Kathy has told me,' he said. 'I could be glad for all our sakes. She wants you. I want you. But . . . ' he hesitated, 'do you really want to come? I think you should consider that question carefully before you proceed.'

Moray, who had hoped for warm acceptance, perhaps even for congratulations, stared at Willie, disappointed and at a loss.

'I have considered it. And I do want to come. Of course . . . ' his eyes fell, 'I suppose you've good reason to distrust me.'

'No, no, it's not that, David. I only feel that you must be strongly attached to your own way of life. Perhaps that life may call you back in spite of yourself. You may not succeed in breaking away from it.'

'You misjudge me,' Moray protested seriously, with unmistakable sincerity. 'My life, my old life, has become obnoxious to me. For a long time, even before I set eyes on Kathy, I had felt how empty and trivial it was – a useless existence. Now I know that I needn't be a slave to the past, that it's possible for me to make what I will of myself. I'm determined to build a new – a happy life.'

'A happy life,' Willie repeated, as though reflecting on the words. 'When you say that, are you not thinking only of yourself? That kind of life has no part in our work. Happiness should never be regarded as an end in itself – it is found only in a total absence of concern about oneself. If you come with us you'll be called on to do many things which are neither pleasant nor enjoyable.'

'I recognise that,' Moray said, in a hurt voice, not without dignity. 'But with Kathy at my side, and your help, I believe I can acquit myself creditably. At least I will try.'

There was a stillness during which Willie gazed intently at Moray. His eyes were guileless but held something searching in their depths. Then he smiled and held out his hand.

'I believe you will,' he said, with sudden cheerfulness. 'And if you do, you will be rewarded in a manner far beyond your present expectation. I believe, David, that anyone who has been accorded talents such as yours must devote them to the service of his fellow men. If he does he'll achieve the ultimate purpose of every man's being. If he does not he will be consumed by unhappiness and sooner or later suffer an atrocious punishment.

So for your sake as well as my own I rejoice in your decision. It's all settled then. And I may now tell you how much your help will mean to me – you and Kathy, doctor and nurse, a team of husband and wife working together, it's a gift straight from the Lord.'

CHAPTER XIV

MORAY'S SENSE OF the dramatic had been a feature of his character even in those early days when he had so carefully built up that thrilling surprise for Mary in demonstrating the wonders of Glenburn Hospital and the little house which, alas, they were never to occupy. As a different man, and in a different cause, yet with unchanged enthusiasm, he had resolved to make his farewell party for Willie's lecture an occasion that would be remembered in Schwansee long after he had gone. His preparations had been elaborate, and now the day, the hour, and the moment had arrived. They were here, all his friends, seated expectantly in a neat semicircle in the drawing-room where, against the closed double doors, a white screen had been unrolled. A projector, hired for the occasion, stood on a Pembroke table at the other end, already connected to an electric point.

From the beginning, when Leonora Schutz arrived in a new hat with Dr Alpenstuck, quickly followed by little Gallie and Archie Stench, who had given her a lift, then by Madame Ludin and her husband, and finally, after an anxious interval, by Frida von Altishofer, the party had gone well, progressively enlivened by his excellent buffet and superlative champagne. Leonora was in a gay mood, her laugh ascending with an extra trill; Stench, wandering around, glass in hand, kept repeating, 'Lavish, dear boy. Indubitably lavish,' while little Gallie, handbag at the ready, kept smiling to herself that secret, self-contained smile of the very deaf. One did not expect an equal response from the placid Ludins but even they had responded to the current of anticipation in the air. Moray was pleased – perhaps Archie had been active, dropping hints in his usual fashion, but not enough, he hoped, to spoil his final surprise. Once or twice, glancing at Madame von Altishofer, who partook sparingly of the good things, he wondered how much she guessed of his decision, and a queer conviction came over him that already though by what means he could not decide, she *knew*. Yet her manner, pleasantly amiable, so especially nice towards Kathy, altogether so completely at ease – occasionally he had even caught her eyes resting upon him quizzically – gave no indicaton of the disappointment he might have expected of her. He could only commend her breeding and hope, charitably, that memories of their friendship would survive unimpaired.

What did particularly gratify him was the success, deserved though unexpected, of his two house guests, Kathy especially, though he might have wished her a little less nervous, more socially at ease. Still, Madame Ludin and the vivacious Leonora made much of her, while the ubiquitous Archie hovered unsteadily around, full of giggling compliments. Willie, too, though at first, because of his unclerical appearance, rather oddly regarded, had soon proved a centre of sympathetic interest. Observing them both, Moray was filled with a warm sense of comradeship. He had never felt happier. He was like a schoolboy breaking up at the end of term, going off for the holidays. How satisfying, how charged with anticipation these last three days had been, days of cosy intimacy during which they had held long talks, discussed plans, grown together into a close-knit partnership. The sweetness of Kathy's presence, the joy of knowing that she loves him, had been intensified by Willie's presence. To be with Willie was to realise the value of the work that he, himself, would do. Yes, amazing, in this short time, the effect Willie had produced upon him, by his practical, human cheerfulness, even by his silences. Inspired, Moray told himself repeatedly how glad he was to have linked his life with a character so transparently simple yet strong – and, with it all, so good. Somehow you felt that Willie loved the whole human race.

And now it was time for him to give his lecture. Moray stepped forward and, taking him by the arm, led him towards the circle of chairs. As he did so, he was swept again by a deep, sincere wave of feeling, of affection, and more, for this thin, sickly string of a man in the faded khaki suit. He rapped with his knuckles on the occasional table, causing a cessation of chatter and a polite craning of necks.

'Ladies and gentlemen, or rather good friends all, my dear friend the Rev. Willie Douglas will now deliver his address. Afterwards I may have just a few words to say to you.'

Facing his audience, who had come mainly from curiosity, in the secret expectation of an entertainment such as might be given by some eccentric performer, like a conjurer producing rabbits out of a hat, Willie stood awkwardly, a lanky and ungainly figure, his arms hanging loosely from his sloping shoulders, his neck twitching faster than usual. But he was smiling, a gentle and remote smile that humanized all his oddity.

'Don't be alarmed,' he told them mildly, 'I'm not going to preach at you, or lecture you either, for that matter. Instead, I think it might interest you to hear how, with God's help, a little Christian colony was built from nothing in the remote wilderness of Central Africa. And please don't hesitate to interrupt if you have any questions to ask, or if I'm not making things clear.'

Moving over to the projector he cleared his throat and, in an informal conversational manner, went on:

'First of all, how did we get there? It wasn't so easy, twenty years ago. Usually missionaries go out from our headquarters in Melopo two or three together, but that wasn't possible in this instance. All that could be spared me was a native catechist, but he was a fine man, baptised Daniel – I'll show you his photograph presently. Well, off we started, bound for the Kwibu district in the extreme north-east, one of the wildest parts of the borderland between Angola and the Congo. Since we wanted to take cattle with us and as the country was so rough and rocky, we had decided to use an old ox-waggon for transport instead of a truck. It was a blessing we did so, otherwise we should never have got there. I had made a few short trips around Melopo while gathering experience and learning the dialects, but this beat anything I'd ever seen. Let me give you some idea of the country we went through. It's not the sort of country you associate with the tropics, swamps and steaming jungles and such-like, but it had a few problems of its own. Of course these photographs, and many of the others, were taken at a later date.'

In succession he showed a number of slides on the screen: deep, dried-up river beds choked with boulders, precipitous slopes of sharp-edged black rocks in tangles of yellow scrub, thickets of thornbush so dense as to evoke a murmur from his audience.

'How on earth did you get through those, dear boy?' Archie voiced the general feeling. 'Didn't they tear you to shreds?'

'We lost a little skin.' Willie smiled. 'But we averaged at least fifty yards an hour. Yet that wasn't the worst. Just after we got through that last bit I showed you, because of my stupidity we

230

lost our compass and wandered off the high northern tableland into the Cazar desert. It was a bad mistake – sand, deep sand, everywhere, and low scrubby bush, a waterless waste land. In the heat and blinding dust storms we ran out of water and would have fared rather badly if we hadn't come on three Bushmen who led us to a sucking hole – a muddy pit they had dug in the sand.'

'Aren't the Bushmen dreadful little aboriginals, with hair all over their faces?' asked Leonora, intelligently.

'These were not large, only four feet in height,' Willie answered gently. 'But they were certainly not dreadful, for if they had not humanely shared their scanty supply of water, neither my companion nor I would have survived. In fact we very nearly didn't, for presently my good catechist went down with dysentery, three of the oxen sickened and died, and I – well, by this time we were both covered with sores from tick and mosquito bites, so I got a touch of malaria. As if this wasn't enough, the waggon chains broke and it was really a miracle that we did at last reach our destination, Kwibu, the chief village of the district and tribal headquarters of the Abatu. I have an old photograph which I took shortly after arrival.' He projected another slide on the screen. 'As you see, it's just a scattered collection of conical mud hovels roofed with palm thatch, no cultivation whatsoever, and in the background you can make out a few skeleton cattle, poor starved creatures, always covered with flies, wandering miserably around on the parched ground.

'Well, we had arrived, and were feeling pleased with ourselves, when we received a nasty shock. The chief of the Abatu wouldn't let me enter the village. Here he is, all painted up for the occasion, and I think you'll agree that I was not wise to press him too hard.'

'Oh dear,' Leonora thrilled with sympathy. 'What a fearful old sinner.'

'Sometimes the biggest of sinners make the best of saints,' Willie smiled. 'And old Tshosa hasn't done so badly, as you'll see. However, at that time he wasn't too full of brotherly love, so we were obliged to up stakes and move off some distance, to higher ground above the village where there was a small clump of tacula trees and a spring. Here, first of all, we set to and built a little hut. It was hot work. I wasn't used yet to the sweltering temperature, and the tacula wood was so tough it blunted my

231

axe. We didn't have any roofing material, and by now we were running very short of food supplies.'

'I was going to ask you that,' interposed Madame Ludin. 'How did you live? Catering is my business and I'd be interested to know.'

'Our only food was a kind of porridge. I would boil my kettle and pour the boiling water into a bowl containing a handful of oatmeal. It sounds little enough, but it's good solid Scotch fare and stood by us well.'

'It wouldn't me,' exclaimed Archie. 'I'm all for the liquid Scotch.'

'Anyway,' said Willie, joining in the laugh, 'we had already started to make a garden and to dig ditches to carry the spring to irrigate the land. Properly watered, the grass grew amazingly quickly, we raised mealies, potatoes and Indian corn, and our remaining oxen began to thrive. All this time none of the tribe came near me; our only visitors were lions, cheetahs and an occasional rhinoceros.'

'Oh dear. Did you shoot them?' said Leonora. She was fascinated by Willie, his oddness, his tic, that marvellous sweet expression. A thought flashed through her giddy brain: if there was game, why not take Herman on safari, drop in on the Mission, like a Hemingway heroine? But he was answering her question.

'No,' he said thoughtfully. 'We've never had a gun. They came close too, but I scared them away by throwing pebbles at them.'

'Good heavens, weren't you afraid?'

He shook his head.

'I think we didn't fear them because we were both terribly weak and our spirits were at a low ebb, especially when the rainy season began, continuous thunderstorms followed by a plague of white ants. Daniel and I were both ill with fever. He was so weak he had to be fed with a spoon. I didn't seem to be doing any good; it looked as though our Heavenly Father had no use for us at all. But just when I felt ready to give up, Tshosa, the chief, suddenly appeared, at the head of a long line of his best warriors, all carrying spears. It was an alarming sight and I was very frightened, for of course I thought it was all up with us. But no, he had come bearing an offering.' Willie paused with a faint smile. 'Would you like to guess what it was?'

No one seemed able to advance a suggestion but they were all listening intently.

'Well,' Willie said, 'it was a bowl of blood and milk, the Abatu token of friendship. So I drank this awful brew, though it was a struggle, and communications were established between us. It appeared that they had been closely watching my gardening efforts, and now they wanted me to show them how to cultivate their dried-up land. Well, we began to work their fields for them and presently, in return, got some of the tribe – mostly women, for they did all the hard labour, poor things – to build a little church of sun-dried mud bricks. This is it.' A poor little shanty with a palmetto roof and sacking over the window and door appeared on the screen. 'Here I began my first services, trying to plant the seeds of the gospel in the minds of those poor savages. Then I went often to the cattle posts to try to explain Christian principles to the men, and especially to teach the children. It wasn't easy, we had to face primitive ignorance and ingrained superstition. And there was always the danger of a sudden mass uprising incited by those who feared the word of God because it might undermine their prestige and destroy the pagan fetishism that's the basis of many tribal customs. For instance, I had some little trouble with this fellow.' Another slide came on the screen.

'Oh, what a horrible old man,' exclaimed Leonora. 'He's worse than the chief.'

'That's the witch doctor and rain maker. When the droughts came, and they were frequent, his job was to dispel them with magic. And when his mumbo-jumbo didn't work he blamed it on the bad medicine of the new religion. During my second year we had a dry spell so prolonged and serious that things looked very bad for us. I don't think I ever prayed so hard for rain – I almost cracked the heavens.'

'And the rains came,' Leonora murmured in a dreamy voice. She already felt herself a little in love with Willie.

'No, not a drop,' Willie said calmly, and paused. 'But I had a sudden idea, an inspiration if you like – that my spring, which disappeared high on the hill, might be running down the slope *underground*. I'd never done a stroke of water divining in my life but I cut myself a mangana twig, which was the nearest I could find to hazel, asked the good Lord to help me if He didn't want to see His servant without a head, and started walking down the hill towards the village. By the time I got there the whole

233

tribe were round me, watching, including our friend there on the screen. Suddenly, just outside the chief's hut, the twig gave a twitch. I thought it might only be my shaky nerves, but I took a chance and told them to dig. Twenty feet down we came on a rushing subterranean stream that went right through the centre of the village. I couldn't describe to you the wild scene that followed, for I was on my knees reciting the fourteenth Psalm, but since that moment we have never lacked water and it was then that I made my first converts.'

There was a ripple of interest and appreciation, a spontaneous reaction that fell warmly on Moray's ears. Now a full partner in this splendid enterprise, he exchanged a quick communicative glance with Kathy.

Meanwhile Willie had resumed, describing the further progress of the Mission, the slow and painful emergence from darkness to light of a savage, isolated tribe. There had been setbacks of course, and some bad disasters. His original church had been burned down and when, having gained a mastery of the language, he tried to change the tribal initiation rites, in which youths and young girls were subjected to indescribable indignities, he'd had a difficult time. But for the intervention of Tshosa the entire Mission would have been wiped out. As it was, three of his converts were killed and several attempts made on his life. The following year a Swedish missionary, his nearest neighbour, ninety miles away, and his wife and two little daughters were murdered – all beheaded. It was so difficult to change the hearts of men inured to brutality and bloodshed that he had determined to concentrate on the children; by early teaching he could obtain positive results, and for this reason he had built the school and, later, the orphanage. He showed several slides of these little ones grouped around Daniel the catechist, now an old man, touching photographs which caused Leonora to exclaim: 'Oh dear, aren't the whites of their eyes so divinely pathetic.'

'Their eyes are pathetic because so many of them have trachoma. And as you see, some of the faces are pitted with smallpox scars.'

'Then it's not a healthy district?' someone asked.

'Unfortunately not. Malaria is still endemic, sleeping sickness too, and we get a lot of hookworm and filariasis, even an odd case of leprosy.'

So the main necessity was now a hospital, and – with a half

smile towards Moray – he hoped to have this soon. Proper medical treatment would prove of immense benefit. Still, after nearly twenty years of continuous labour he was not ashamed of the results: the fine stone church, the school and orphanage, the proper mission house – he displayed them on the screen – all were rather different from that first mud shed. And he now had over three hundred practising church members, besides four catechists and several out-stations in the bush which he visited in rotation every month in his jeep. Needless to say, they still had their troubles. He was worried over the situation that might develop in the neighbouring province of Kasai. If the civil authority failed there, now that the Belgians were going out, there might be some disorders. And they were very near, in fact two of his new out-stations were actually across the border. Nothing had happened so far, at least nothing to speak of, but because of the possibility of trouble he must get back to the Mission quickly, to be on hand if needed.

'And now,' Willie said, with an apologetic smile, looking at the clock, 'that's about all. I only hope I haven't bored you and that you'll forgive me for having taken so much of your time.'

When he concluded there was a cordial round of applause, a tribute only faintly tempered by the slight note of misgiving on which the talk had ended. Encouraged by the general approbation which, through his inclusion in the scheme of medical reform, must apply in some measure to himself, Moray seized the appropriate moment and stood up. He was normally a confident speaker but now he was restrained, almost humble. Still, the words came to him.

'I think I speak for all of us, in offering warmest thanks to our good friend for his stimulating and moving discourse. His has been a supremely brave and unselfish accomplishment – an epic humanitarian achievement. Incidentally,' he added, striving for humorous parenthesis, 'if you should wish to express your appreciation in more tangible form, a salver has been placed for that purpose in the hall. And now,' he followed on quickly, 'if I may impose upon you for a moment, I should like to add a personal postscript to what has already been said.' He paused, almost overcome by a rush of feeling. 'The truth is . . . I've come to a decision that may surprise you . . . but which I hope you will hear with understanding.'

A stir passed over the audience, a decided stir.

'You might imagine it to be a sudden decision. It is not. Although I've been happy here I've been conscious of a prompting, an urge, one might say, towards a more active, a more useful existence, in which my medical knowledge might be utilised, not for reward but for good. And in how remarkable a manner that intention has been given effect. Early last month it so happened that I felt myself recalled to my native country. Here I made contact with a family I had known and loved in my youth, a family, in short, of which Kathy and Willie are members. Kathy I had not known, the joy of finding her was therefore all the greater. Willie I already knew. He and I, in those early days, had been friends, he as a little lad, I as a thoughtless though striving youth, and often, during our long conversations, he had thrilled me with his boyish enthusiasm for the missionary life. And now the wheel has turned full circle.' He paused, so affected he could scarcely go on. 'My friends, I don't want to weary you with the story of a soul's regeneration. I will say simply that I am going out with Willie to the Mission, as a doctor, and Kathy, my dear Kathy,' he moved over to where she stood beside the projector and placed his arm about her shoulders, 'will be there with us, as my wife.'

Now, indeed, there was a marked reaction which took the form of an immediate silence, followed by a sudden outburst. In a hurry, everyone got up and began to speak at once. Congratulations were showered on Moray, his hand was shaken, the ladies pressed round Kathy.

'More champagne,' Stench shouted. 'A toast to the bride and groom.'

Champagne was available, the toast was drunk, it seemed as though the party would begin all over again. Most encouraging of all was Madame von Altishofer's composed acceptance of the accomplished fact. He had feared trouble, some marring exhibition of pique or displeasure, but no, her behaviour had been perfect, a smile of congratulation, gently tinged with sadness perhaps, yet a definite smile for him, and for Kathy a kiss upon the cheek.

Indeed, when half an hour later the others had begun to leave and, standing in the hall, he was speeding them on their way, she stopped briefly for a final word.

'Dear friend, I rejoice in your happiness. Such a sweet child. All that – and heaven too, with this splendid new work.'

'You are most kind, Frida.'

'Ah, I had a premonition that we should lose you, even when I was at Baden and you did not write.'

'I always knew you were intuitive,' he said guardedly.

'Unfortunately, yes. But all that is past. Now is the time to be practical, to show the value of a true friend who also is, as you say, matter-of-fact. Your *déménagement* in so short a time will be most difficult. You will need help, and if you wish I can give it. Your little one tells me she leaves with her splendid Willie tomorrow. I would wish to come then, but as you may be at the airport . . . yes ? . . . very well, shall I come the day after ?'

'You're most thoughtful,' he said, realising after a moment's reflection that nothing could be more acceptable. She was so capable, and already he had begun to worry about the complexity of the arrangements that must be made. 'I shall expect you. And thank you.'

She smiled, and passed through the door.

Immediately he hurried back to rejoin Kathy and Willie in the salon. He took the salver from the hall table with him.

'Well, was it a success ?' he asked gaily.

'It went ever so well,' Kathy said, looking flushed and happy. 'Did you think so too, Willie ?'

He nodded. He was sitting down, looking tired.

'They were all very kind.'

'Let's just see how kind,' Moray said slyly. He was in tremendous spirits. With the air of a conspirator he handed the salver to Kathy and, while she held it, began to count the money. There was a respectable heap of fifty- and hundred-franc bills and one coin – a two-franc piece.

'I bet that's from little Gallie,' Moray laughed.

'Then it means a lot,' Willie said, unexpectedly.

'Oh, yes,' Kathy agreed warmly. 'I liked her much the best.'

There was a pause, then Kathy said again:

'Haven't you forgotten that bit of paper at the bottom ?'

'Have I ? Good lord, don't tell me someone's chipped in with a bad cheque. Take a look, Kathy.'

She gazed at the cheque, quite speechless, then she handed it to Willie. Still silent, she looked at Moray, then suddenly put her arms around his neck and kissed him.

CHAPTER XV

NEXT DAY, AT two in the afternoon, Moray arrived back from Zurich, still rather cast down by the departure of Kathy and Willie for Edinburgh on the noon plane, yet charged with vigorous purpose. Only eleven days remained before he would join them at London Airport, and much must be accomplished in that brief span; the need for immediate action was imperative. As he let himself into the house – following the departure of his guests he had given Arturo and Elena the afternoon off – he felt glad of Madame von Altishofer's promise of assistance and hoped she would not fail to turn up next morning.

However, he had only begun to go through his mail in the study when, to his surprise, he heard the beat of her litle Dauphine in the drive. Leaving unopened the *Journal of Tropical Medicine*, to which he had just subscribed, and a parcel of lightweight nylon camping equipment that promised to be interesting, he went to meet her.

'Am I too prompt?' She spoke briskly, looking extremely workmanlike in a grey linen skirt and knitted grey cardigan. 'I happened to see you pass in the Humber and thought not to waste the afternoon.'

'You're quite right,' he agreed heartily, leading the way into the library. 'There's so much to do, the sooner we start the better.'

'Tell me then, what, roughly, are your plans?' She sat, not in the chair, but on the arm, indicating instant obédient readiness.

'The villa, of course, will be put on the market. Arturo and Elena will move into the chalet and act as *gardiens* of the property until it is sold.'

'And your things?'

'My pictures and silver must go provisionally to the bank. Their ultimate disposition will be in my lawyer's hands – Stieger is a most reliable man. My furniture and books can remain here temporarily – quite safe if the house is shuttered.'

'These lovely books,' she exclaimed, looking at the long double rows of fine Sangorski bindings. 'You cannot leave them so, in a shut-up house, or they will become altogether foxed. Every one must be separately wrapped, and that is something I can do for you.'

'Arturo . . . ' he began.

'No.' She got up smilingly. 'He will have enough on his hands. And he is so overthrown by your going, he is not fit for anything extra. Besides, I love books; my father had a famous library at Kellenstein. So off to your own work and leave this to me.' As he moved towards the door, she added, tactfully, but with a glance both ironic and approving: 'By the way, I suppose you have read Mr Stench's article in the *Tageblatt*.'

'I haven't seen today's papers. What article?'

'It is a piece about your party for the Mission, but there is much in it about you, and of your courage in going out there, in spite of this tribal affair. It is most flattering.'

He reddened, chiefly from pleasure, thinking of his friends in Melsburg and so many others in the canton who would read of him.

'Archie is rather a nuisance,' he said. 'Though basically good at heart. I hope he didn't overdo it. And what's this tribal affair?'

'Apparently an outbreak of some sort, probably no more than the general unrest your friend referred to in his lecture. Now tell me, where may I find lots of wrapping paper?'

'In the pantry. Elena has stacks of it in a cupboard.'

When she went off he stirred himself and set about his first important task, to make the inventory of his antiques. This was something after his own heart and as he toured the house with paper and pen, noting down this piece and that – the Charles II red lacquer cabinet bought at the Antique Fair in London, the exquisitely mellowed Queen Anne bureau listed in Macquoid's classic *The Age of Walnut*, the Louis XVI fauteuils he had bid for successfully at the Parke-Bernet Galleries – waves of recollection, of bitter-sweet nostalgia, flowed over him. It was hard to part with these costly trifles, yet never had he felt so spiritually elevated, so convinced of the merit of his renunciation. Archie Stench was right. He *was* doing a worth-while thing.

The tabulation was not quite complete when, at five o'clock, Madame von Altishofer found him brooding over his Elizabethan buffet in the dining-room.

'Time for tea,' she announced.

He looked up.

'Have you finished?'

'Not nearly. The books alone will take at least another half day. But workers of the world require refreshment. And I have presumed to make a few *amaretti*.'

The break was in fact most welcome.

'What good biscuits,' he remarked. 'I never associated you with the domestic virtues.'

'One learns from necessity – and disappointments, of which I've had many. Please take another.'

'I shouldn't.' He smiled deprecatingly. 'The impression I've received lately is that I'm rather over-addicted to the pleasures of the table.'

'What nonsense,' she said spiritedly. 'Now especially, to build your strength, you should be eating well. Goodness alone knows what wretched fare you will get out there.'

'I'll be all the better for it. I supped plenty of porridge in my youth.'

'In your youth, yes, dear friend.' She smiled tolerantly. 'But now?'

A brief silence followed this remark, during which she gazed round the, as yet, undenuded room, her eyes coming to rest on the lovely pastel of Madame Melo and her child.

'Do you remember the afternoon you showed me the Vuillard? It seems only yesterday, yet so much has happened in that short time. Promise me to keep your paintings on the walls until the last possible moment. You often told me you could not live without them, and certainly that you would never sell them.' A thought seemed to strike her. She hesitated, glanced away, then towards him, finally exclaimed impulsively: 'Must you really sell your home? Couldn't you keep it, well, as a kind of rest house which you could fall back on in case of need? Dear friend, I worry about you, and the last thing I wish is that you should get one of those tropical diseases that have broken up poor Willie. And what a catalogue he recited, malaria, sleeping sickness, leprosy and the rest; the poor man looks ill enough to have half of them himself. . . . But as I was saying, if you should contract something serious, at least you would have a safe place in a proper climate to recover and recuperate.'

He looked at her, at first frowning, as in doubt, then thoughtfully. The idea had never occurred to him and, at first sight, it appeared to have considerable merit. Why should he sell out in a blind rush; he had not the slightest financial need. Besides, if he took time, with mounting property values he would undoubtedly secure a far better price. But no, no, that would be merely temporising, playing around with half-measures, a dangerous procedure at all times. He was going for good, and would not return. He shook his head decisively.

'No. I prefer to make a clean, sharp cut.'

'Yes, I suppose you are right. Always you see things so clearly, never thinking of yourself. I did wrong to make such a weak proposal, but it is because I think only of you. God knows I shall never for one moment have peace once you are out there.'

'But why, Frida? It's not so dreadful at the Mission.'

'Oh, my friend, because you are brave and strong, don't pretend in order to make this easier for me. You understand, better than I, the dangers that will surround you. Last night, for thinking of that poor Swedish family whose heads were hacked off, I could not sleep. If such a cruel death occurs for a man after many years of service, what might not occur to you, a newcomer.'

He glanced at her irritably, with a touch of asperity.

'For goodness' sake, Frida, don't exaggerate.'

'Exaggerate, because I tell you of the thoughts of one small bad night. If that were all I feared for you, I should be happy. But besides the fevers, are there not beasts of the jungle, scorching sun and torrential rains, and, worst of all, this trouble in the Congo. Mr Stench says it is beginning and must spread. And you are so near. But why am I so foolish to talk of what you already fully understand?' She stood up abruptly. 'Work – work, that's what we must do, in order not to think for a moment of the future. There are some books on the high shelves of the library that I cannot reach. When I have put away the tea trolley you must hand them down to me. After that, it is time for me to rush back to Seeburg.'

He moved slowly into the library, frowning, vaguely displeased, not with her, for no one could have his interests more at heart, but rather with the manner of her presentation of the obvious. As if he did not realise what he was getting into. Absurd. The books to which she referred were mainly special full folio editions of the Paragon art series, but although his eye was cast towards them they left no conscious imprint on his retina. Finally, however, with a slight start, he came to himself, decided against fetching the step-ladder from the basement and instead brought forward the long needlepoint stool that had its place before the fireplace. Mounting, he reached up and, one at a time, began to transfer the heavy, richly clasped and padded volumes to a lower and more accessible shelf. He had almost finished when she appeared and stood watching him.

Only three books now remained at the end of the top shelf. Hurrying, he stretched up and sideways, took hold of all three. But in the effort of lifting he lost his balance and, still clutching the books above his head, was obliged to make a quick backward step off the stool that brought him safely though jarringly to the floor.

'Well done,' she complimented him. 'You saved yourself most cleverly.'

'Yes . . . ' he spoke through compressed lips, 'but I rather think I've wrenched my back.'

'You did come down sharply. You must sit down and rest.'

He seated himself cautiously on the end of the stool and, with his hand pressed against the affected part, watched while she wrapped up the Paragon edition.

'Now, you are better?' she inquired, when she had finished.

'Not altogether. But it's nothing, it'll pass.'

'If not, you must see to it. For tonight take aspirin and get Arturo to rub you. Have you some antidolor liniment?'

'I think there's some in the medicine cabinet.'

She continued to study him sympathetically, head on one side.

'I wish I did not have to leave you, but there. . . . Now do not forget, antidolor and aspirin, after your bath. No, don't get up. I will let myself out. And for tomorrow, shall we say ten o'clock?'

He nodded agreement, with as little movement as possible, and, when she had gone, remained seated for several further minutes, prodding his back with a speculative finger. Then, as everything seemed intact, he got up and began, though awkwardly, to move about. The inventory was complete, he must now arrange a meeting with his lawyer. He went to the telephone, dialled Stieger's number. It was the girl, his secretary, who answered, with that sing-song cadence which the local Swiss imparted to their school-taught English.

'I am sorree, Mr Moree, Herr Stieger is in Munich.'

'When will he be back?'

'Saturday morneeng. But if eet is important I will telephone heem.'

He reflected quickly.

'Saturday will be all right. Make an appointment for eleven a.m.'

'Very well, Mr Moree. I will myself inform Herr Stieger.'

He swung away from the phone, an injudicious movement that made him wince. Annoying that Stieger was away; he wanted everything done quickly; yes, at once. His earlier mood of vigorous confidence, a state verging on exaltation, had lapsed, he felt a longing for Kathy: the touch of her lips, her sweet glance of encouragement. For one who had always enjoyed his own society it was strange how he now disliked being alone. If only Madame von Altishofer had not been obliged to dash away – what a help she was, in his present emergency. The idea of a solitary dinner did not appeal to him, moreover he felt he owed it to himself to turn in early. He rang for Arturo, told him to prepare a tray and take it up to the study, explained the necessity of massage later on, then, passing between the piles of wrapped books, he tuned in the radio to the evening broadcast of the B.B.C. Lately he had been so preoccupied with his own affairs he had not listened to the news. But he was too late, immediately a voice said:

'That is the end of the news.'

With an exclamation he switched off and went upstairs, reminding himself to take his vitamin tablets.

CHAPTER XVI

PUNCTUALLY AT TEN o'clock next morning the door bell rang and Arturo, with an expression more enigmatic than usual, showed Madame von Altishofer to the drawing-room where Moray, seated on the sofa before the open Dutch cabinet, was pensively contemplating his collection of Chinese porcelain.

When he had greeted her and asked to be excused from rising he waved an expressive hand.

'The futile tyranny of possessions. All this will have to be packed. When I bought it with such joy, and every piece is authentic K'hang Hsi, little did I think it would be such a nuisance in the end.'

'I will pack it.' She spoke quietly. 'So it will be no nuisance. But first, how is your back?'

'No worse, I hope, though I slept badly. But I seem to have developed a queer sort of limp.'

'A limp?'

'In my right leg, when I walk.'

'Then you must see to it at once.'

'No.' He shook away the suggestion. 'It can't be serious. At least I'll give it another day.'

Turning from the cabinet he found her gaze bent upon him in a fashion so oddly concerned it gave him quite a start.

'Is anything wrong, Frida?'

'No, no,' she said quickly, forcing a smile. 'I was thinking only of your injury. I hope you will be able to go to the party this afternoon.'

'What party?'

'Why, naturally, Leonora's.'

'I know nothing of it.'

'But surely you are invited. We are all going, all our circle. It must be a mistake that you are overlooked. So you will come with me, yes?'

He bit his lip, vexed that he should have been left out, at this

244

last hour, already regarded by the others as a dead letter.

'I'm much too busy to go. Anyhow, the lecture party was my swan song. I'm no longer interested in Leonora's frivolous nonsense.'

'I am sorry, my friend. I know that all is finished for you here and that you must seek society where you are going, if indeed it is possible to find it among these – these uncivilised people.'

'I shall have Willie and my dear wife,' he said sharply. 'And my work will be to civilise the people.'

'But of course, you will be very happy,' she agreed in a conciliatory tone. 'Still, three together is a limited group after the interesting society to which you have been accustomed. But now, no more, you have enough to worry you. I must go to finish the books. Another time, perhaps tomorrow, I will see to the porcelain.'

What's the matter with her, he asked himself, when she had departed for the library. Yesterday she had been bright and brisk, today a subdued melancholy clouded her yellow eyes. He found the change in her mood and manner quite inexplicable.

As the forenoon wore on, he took time off from his desk, where he was busy with the settlement of all outstanding accounts, to look in at the library – ostensibly to inspect her progress but actua'ly to determine if her mood had changed. It had not, was indeed keyed to a lower pitch.

'Something is on your mind, Frida,' he said, on his second visit.

On one knee beside the bottom shelf, she straightened, but without looking at him.

'There is nothing, nothing.'

The evasion in her tone was only too apparent. At lunch – she had consented solely as an economy of time to remain for a light meal – he made an effort to dispel the gloom.

'You're eating nothing. May I give you some of this salad?'

'Thank you, no.'

'Another slice of galantine.'

'Nothing more, please. I have little appetite today.'

'Then if you've finished, let's take a rest on the terrace. The sun is quite strong now.'

Outside it was distinctly warm, and Wilhelm had swept away the snow and put out garden chairs. They sat down facing the marvellous skyline of the Alps.

'You have the finest view in Switzerland,' she murmured. 'At least for a few more days.'

A silence followed, then thinking to please, perhaps to placate her, he said: 'I hope you understand, Frida, that I will always have the highest regard for you.'

'Will you?'

'Always. Moreover, Frida, I don't take your help for granted. I'd like you to choose something for yourself from my collection as a souvenir.'

'You are generous, my friend, but I do not care for souvenirs. Always they invoke sadness.'

'But you must. I insist.'

'Then if I am to be sad, I shall be deeply so. You shall give me the small photograph standing on the right side of your desk.'

'You mean the little snapshot of you and me on the Riesen-berg.'

'Exactly. That I will keep for remembrance.'

'My dear Frida.' He smiled chidingly. 'You sound like an obituary notice.'

She gave him a long sombre look.

'That is not surprising.' Then, her reserve breaking down: 'Mein Gott, how I am sad for you. I meant not to show you this, but soon enough you must know.'

She opened her handbag, took out a newspaper clipping, handed it to him. He saw that it had been cut from that morning's *Daily Echo*, a paper she did not usually take, and was headed:

Five Hundred Die in Congo Massacre.

Quickly, he read the dispatch:

Last night in Kasai Province, where for the past few weeks there have been signs of trouble brewing beneath the surface, tribal war at last broke loose. A savage and unprovoked attack was made on the village of Tochilenge by dissident Balubas. The village, which changed hands in fierce fighting twice, was set on fire and is now a shell. An estimated five hundred lie dead beneath the scorched palm and banana trees.

'Now,' she said, 'you know where you are going.'

He looked up, meeting her gaze which had remained fixed upon him. He was not in the least discomposed, confirmed rather, hardened and fortified.

'Frida,' he said coldly, 'I'm perfectly aware that for the past two days you have been trying to dissuade me from going – no doubt with the best intentions. But I don't think you quite understand how deeply I'm in love. I fully realise that conditions are bad out there. But I *am* going. I would follow Kathy to the ends of the earth.'

She compressed her lips.

'Yes, my friend,' she sighed. 'Is it not always like that when an elderly man is possessed by a young girl? And always the end is so tragic. How well I remember that great German film, *The Blue Angel*.'

He coloured with indignation.

'The circumstances are in no way comparable.'

'No,' she agreed, in an extinguished voice. 'The old professor went only to the circus. You are going . . . '. She turned her head, shielding her face with one hand to hide emotion. 'Yes, I feel it in my heart . . . you are going to . . . '. Even then she could not say it, merely adding in a low voice: 'To something much worse.'

An angry retort had risen to his lips but, respecting her distress, he stifled it. She had always been one to conceal her feelings, tears were not her medium of expression, yet she was clearly upset. Upright in his chair, he stared straight ahead at the distant snow-capped peaks. A prolonged silence descended upon them. Finally, in a subdued manner, but still with averted head, she rose.

'My friend, I can do no more for you today. Tomorrow I will come.'

'I'm sorry,' he muttered, put out by this unexpected departure. 'Must you really go?'

'Yes, until tomorrow. If I am to visit with Madame Schutz and our friends, first I must compose myself.'

He did not protest further, saw her to her car, waited till the beat of the Dauphine died away. Then he closed the gate and limped back to the house. Deliberately, word for word, he read the newspaper clipping again, then decisively tore it up.

During that afternoon he continued his preparations, but always with an eye on the clock. At five he was to telephone Kathy at Markinch, where she was staying at the manse: the arrangement had been made before she left. After the trials and problems of the last two days, how he looked forward to it!

After a quick cup of tea, he went to the telephone, dialled long distance and gave the Fotheringays' number. There was little traffic on the lines and within ten minutes he was put through. To his delight it was Kathy herself who answered: but of course she would be seated at the phone, waiting for his call.

'Kathy, it's you! How are you, my dear?'

'Quite well, David. And most terribly busy. It's so lucky you caught me. I was just rushing off to Edinburgh this very minute.'

Chilled slightly, he said: 'What have you been doing?'

'Oh, everything. . . . Getting ready to go .. . . Like you, I suppose.'

'Yes, I've been busy too. It's very near now.'

'Oh, it is. And I'm so happy and excited. I'll be sending you all particulars of where we are to meet in London whenever I find a minute to write.'

'I was rather expecting a letter from you, dear.'

'Were you, David? I thought, as we were to be together so soon. . . . And I've worried about Uncle Willie. He's been running quite a high temperature since we came here, and he's due to give his talk this evening.'

'I'm sorry,' he said rather perfunctorily, thinking of his own troubles. 'Give him my best wishes.'

'Oh, I will, David. And I'll write you tonight, whenever we get back from Edinburgh.'

'I don't wish to force you to write, Kathy.'

'But, David dear . . . '. She broke off. 'Are you cross?'

'No, dear. Still, I will say I've felt rather lonely. I've been hard at it here. I've hurt my back. And through it all I've been longing to hear from you, just a word to say that you're missing me.'

'Oh, I have missed you, dear . . . '. The catch in her voice made her words indistinct, ' . . . just so busy, and Uncle Willie ill . . . I didn't think . . . '.

'All right, my dear,' he said, mollified by her distress. 'But if Willie is so ill, will he be able to leave on the twenty-first?'

'He will go, David,' she said confidently. 'Even if he has to be carried on the plane on a stretcher.'

Much good he'll be in that condition, he thought rather acidly, then regretted it, for he was devoted to Willie.

'I suppose you've seen that fighting has started in Kasai.'

'Yes, and it may be serious. But of course we've been expecting it. Now, dear, I really must go. I think I hear the bus. Uncle Willie is outside calling for me to come.'

'Wait, Kathy . . . '.

'If I don't go, dear, we'll miss the bus and Uncle Willie will be late for his lecture. Goodbye for just now, dear David. We'll be together soon.'

She had gone, or at least had been obliged to go, leaving him disappointed and with a chilling impression of neglect. What an unsatisfactory talk it had been, making so much of Willie, so little of himself. No, no, he mustn't think like that – quickly he banished his unworthy jealousy. Kathy loved him, the poor child had simply been rushed and harassed, and telephone conversations were never satisfactory. He found these excuses for her, but illogically the sense of slight persisted, remained with him all evening.

At bedtime, still upset, he decided to take a sleeping pill, a thing he had not done for weeks. Fifteen centigrammes of soneryl, followed by a glass of hot milk, sent him into a deep sleep which should have lasted for at least six hours. Unfortunately this was marred, broken in fact, by a frightful yet ridiculous dream.

He was lying on a camp bed in an unknown place behind high black rocks. The air, filled with the hum of insects, was insufferably hot – the humid heat of a tropical night. Darkness was everywhere, yet he could see faintly, and gradually became aware of the tall shadowy form of a man standing some paces away, gazing ahead. The man wore a khaki shirt and trousers and short gum-boots. Although the face remained invisible, he knew the man to be Willie. He tried to call to him, but although his lips formed the words no sounds emerged. Suddenly, to his horror, he saw three enormous beasts advancing from beyond. They were lions, at least they had the size and shape of lions, but to their appearance something preternatural had been added which gave to them a ferocity that paralysed him. Behind these beasts a line of Abatu tribesmen, armed with spears, stood outlined against the further darkness. He attempted vainly to rise. He wanted to get away – anything to escape this double danger. The futile effort made the sweat pour from him. Then, as he gave himself up for lost, the man who was Willie began to laugh and, picking up some pebbles, flipped them casually at the lions, like a boy taking random shots at an alley cat. Immediately the beasts stopped, hesitated for a moment, then came on again with a terrifying rush.

'The Lord is our shepherd,' Willie said. 'A silver collection will be taken later.'

Immediately the charge ceased. The lions faced about and sat up on their haunches in a begging attitude, whereupon the black soldiers began to mark time and clap their hands. Then, with disharmony resembling that of the Markinch choir, they boomed out the hymn 'Onward, Christian Soldiers.'

The grotesque and ridiculous vision was too sudden a release. Moray tried to laugh, to howl with laughter, and finally let out a shout that woke him up.

Exhausted, yet relieved by the reality of his own bedroom, he lay for a long time gloomily pondering the reasons for this absurd and painful fantasy. What rankled most of all was his own behaviour. Was he as weak as that? God, no – he would not admit it. He set his teeth and shook the thing off. Obviously, he decided, a subconscious conflict between his admiration for Willie's heroic and self-sacrificing life and his own past indifference towards religion. With that he got up. The luminous dial of his Gubelin bedside-clock showed three o'clock. Feeling around, he stripped off his wet pyjama jacket and, having rubbed himself down, put on a fresh one and returned to bed. After turning uneasily for more than an hour he got off to sleep.

CHAPTER XVII

NEXT MORNING WHEN he awoke, only half rested, he was bitterly annoyed with himself. He rose hurriedly, prompted by a sense of shame, welcoming as a corrective the discomfort of his strained back which now seemed definitely worse. Ranging about the house, restlessly awaiting Madame von Altishofer's arrival, he checked and rechecked his preparations: the inventory was complete, all his papers were in order, the bank had been notified, his appointment with Stieger definitely arranged for the following day. All that remained, then, was to finish off his packing. Impatiently, his ears alert for the sound of the Dauphine, he looked at his watch: past ten o'clock. Why on earth did she not come? Punctuality had always been outstanding amongst her many virtues. He was on the point of telephoning when, with a disproportionate sense of relief, he heard her step on the gravel drive. The door bell rang. He answered it himself.

'You didn't drive. I wondered why you were late. Come along in. I'll take your coat.'

'Thank you, no. I will not come in. Or at least only to the hall.'

He stared at her, blankly, as she took a bare step forward across the threshold. She was not wearing her usual grey working outfit, but the faded russet costume and the *bersagliere* hat in which she went walking. Yet it was her expression, calm yet firm, that astonished him most of all, and caused him, fearing some disaster, to exclaim: 'What's wrong, Frida?'

She did not immediately answer; then, gazing at him almost pityingly with those remarkable yellow eyes, she said: 'My friend, despite my great wish to help you, I have decided I must not see you now, or ever again.'

'What!' In his confusion he brought out the word with difficulty. 'But why? You promised. I'm relying on you to do the porcelain.'

'The porcelain,' she echoed with scornful emphasis. 'What does

251

that matter? You have no use for it now. You will never see it again.'

'But I – I need your help for other things.'

'Then I must not give it.' Still with her gaze fixed upon him, she shook her head slowly from side to side. 'It is altogether too painful for me. Better, in your own words, the sharp, clean cut.'

A moment of complete silence followed, during which he could find nothing to say except 'why', and he had said that before. Then she went on, with that same solemnity, almost sounding a note of doom.

'My friend, my dear friend, my feeling for you, and it is deep beyond your knowledge, has misled me. I am a woman, and weakly I have given in, to help you. But yesterday, at the party, meeting all your friends, I see that I have been wrong, greatly wrong. For all are in dismay, all have the same opinion of you.'

'I'm obliged for their concern,' he muttered, nettled that they should have discussed him in his absence. 'But I don't see how I merit it.'

'*They* see it!' Her voice stung him. 'They were, every one, speaking of you, a man who has worked all his life to make a great success, and become rich, who has good friends, and a beautiful home. And who, no longer young, throws all, all away, for a sudden idea, so extreme that even your Mr Stench was saying, in his nasty smiling way, you had bitten more than you could chew.'

'I'm obliged to Stench, and the others,' he said bitterly. 'Nevertheless, I believe I know what I'm doing.'

'But *do* you? Now you are so busy, so obsessed, you never read or even listen to the news. Yesterday Mr Stench was telling us – it had just come in – that in another town, Kalinda, which is so near your Willie's place, hordes of these tribesmen came with flaming arrows and cutlasses, broke into the Belgian mission and massacred all who were inside. Not killed alone, first mutilated them, cutting off their hands. Mein Gott, when I think of *your* hands, so fine and sensitive, which I have always admired, and some beastly savage hacking them off, do you wonder that I, and others too, are heartbroken for you?'

He bit his lip, frowning, uneasiness and anger striving for mastery in him. Anger predominated.

"You seem to forget that Willie warned me there might be danger. I've fully considered the risks to run."

"I don't believe it."

"Do you accuse me of lying?"

"I accuse you of deliberate self-deception."

"If so, it's from the highest motives."

"So you want to be a holy martyr, perhaps be shot with arrows, for a change, like Sebastian, and win a harp and a halo after." Her eyes narrowed scornfully. "I am speaking in your true interest when I tell you . . ."

'It's no use,' he interrupted her sharply. 'You won't dissuade me.'

They faced each other during a long and, on her part, a calculated silence.

'So you are going,' she said at last, in a hard voice.

'Yes.'

'Then go. You are totally blind and devoid of sense, in fact quite out of your mind.'

'Thank you.'

They were quarrelling, creating a scene – the realisation caused him an acute distress.

'You say you do this because of a great ideal, to amend your life. You do not. It is all done for the sake of going to bed with a silly young woman, a religious killjoy, who has infatuated you, who has no maturity, no meeting of minds, a common nurse who does not know a Bonnard from a bedpan.'

Pale to the lips under these insults, delivered with a fatal, telling force, he ran true to form in his indignant reply: 'You are speaking of the young lady who will be my wife.'

'And as such, what do you delude yourself she can give you? Not passion, for it is not in her. These religious women are without sex.' He winced. 'For passion such as you demand, you need a strong, vital body. An answering force which she does not possess. She is feeble. And she is already bound to her Willie, you are for her only a father figure. Besides, you have too strong a competitor. She cannot love both you and the Lord.'

'I'm afraid I must ask you to leave.'

She was breathing with a deep, though controlled violence, a Wagnerian prima donna, splendid in figure, with fire in her eyes. Then all at once she was calm, cold as ice.

'Yes, I am leaving. But do not forget that I have warned you. And remember one important thing: if you should return to reason, I am still at the Seeburg, still your friend.'

He barely waited until she had passed the drive before shutting the door with a bang. He was furiously angry, hurt, outraged, and above all inflexibly confirmed in his intention. How dared she take such scandalous liberties with Kathy and himself! This, and the maddening fact that his friends had made him the object of their malicious gossip at the party, was in itself enough to fuse and forge his resolution into solid steel. What stung most of all, quickened by a flashback thought to that night of docile surrender, was the shameful allegation against the pudendum of his future bride. A father figure indeed, competing for affection against Willie and the Lord – could any allegation be more unjust, more unutterably shameful – blasphemous, in fact? Yet that poisoned barb, worst of all, had pierced deep and still quivered in his flesh. To make matters worse, in slamming the heavy door he had aggravated his strained back and now, blaming her all the more since the casualty was basically her fault, he found that his limp had become more pronounced.

Altogether he was so worked up, he could not bring himself to remain passive in the house. What then? It was essential that he get his back put right at once and, as he had additionally some final purchases to make, he decided to take the train for Zurich and consult his good friend Dr Muller. Having cancelled lunch, he was driven by the mystified Arturo to Schwansee station in time to take the 11.45 *schnellzug*.

Settling himself in the comfortable window seat – no other trains, in his opinion, could match the Swiss – he opened the *Gazette Suisse* which, almost instinctively, he had picked up at the bookstall. Naturally, Madame von Altishofer had exaggerated in order to alarm him; nevertheless it was true, as she suggested, that he had lately been too preoccupied to heed external events. He rarely did heed them, preferring to banish from his exclusive life the shocks and discords of a disordered world. Now, however, he felt it would repay him to sift the news. He had no need to sift. There, on the front page, were the headlines. *MASSACRE ATROCE A LA MISSION KALINDA.*

Still keyed to a high intensity, he read the graphic report. More than a hundred persons, men, women and children, who had sought refuge in the mission, had been butchered with inhuman ferocity. In this blood-bath the missionaries themselves, two Franciscan priests, had been singled out for special treatment, first mutilated, then beheaded, and their bodies hacked to bits.

It was a gruesome story, yet it had the ring of truth and following on the earlier slaughter at Tochilenge, was undoubtedly part of the general pattern of frenzied outrage that had broken loose.

Frida had spoken the truth: what an end for a sensitive, civilised man. A quiver of nausea constricted his stomach as he lowered the paper and gazed out at the placid Swiss landscape, the belled, brown cows grazing peacefully in the green pastures amongst the pear and cherry trees. Perhaps, after all, in making his heroic decision he had not fully weighed the obligations and dangers imposed by it. But he killed the thought before it entered his mind. Even if he had not wanted to go, he wanted Kathy. He would never turn back.

The train drew into Zurich station and he got out, finding the step down so awkward he wished he had brought a stick. His noticeable limp drew sympathetic glances as he traversed the Bahnhofstrasse, but making an effort he managed his shopping at Grieder's which, unlike so many of the other establishments, did not close between twelve and two. Then, with scarcely a thought of the Baur-au-Lac, he lunched sparingly at Sprungli's on minced veal and noodles followed by compote and a café crême. He was, indeed, too upset, too depressed to eat, and in this chastened mood he took a taxi to Dr Muller's office in Gloria-strasse, being fortunate to get hold of the good doctor before his consultations had begun. Muller, moreover – and this seemed even more important – was unaware of his visitor's imminent departure for the Dark Continent. At this moment either con-gratulations or reproaches would have been equally unbearable to Moray, who came immediately to the point, enumerated his symptoms, and concluded: 'I'm almost sure I've slipped a disc.'

Muller, a ruddy, jovial little man in an over-size starched white coat, who looked as though he enjoyed good living, had listened to the recital in the hunched attitude he assumed at his desk, darting occasional good-humoured glances at Moray. Now he got up, made an examination which to Moray seemed brief, almost cursory.

'A slight sprain of your latissimas dorsi. Get your man to rub you with a good liniment.'

'I have, and it's no better.'

'Naturally, it will take a few days.'

'But this limp I have developed, surely that is rather a matter for concern.'

'Purely psychosomatic. A protective transference of your worry about your back – though why that should worry you I can't imagine. I suppose there's nothing else on your mind, no more pressing anxiety?'

Frowning, Moray chose to ignore the question.

'Then you don't think I should have a spinal X-ray?'

'Mein Gott,' Muller laughed the idea away, 'here we do not X-ray for a simple strain.'

Moray left the doctor's office in worse case than when he entered, trying not to limp, an effort that exaggerated the condition and made him stiffen and drag his leg.

'Confound the fellow,' he muttered to himself. 'He has this psychosomatic nonsense on the brain.'

He was tempted to seek another opinion, but the fear of making himself ridiculous restrained him. Instead, in the hope that exercise might help, he walked down the hill to the Belvedere, then wandered along the front of the Zürichsee. A pale sun, glinting on the still water through a nacreous haze, had made the afternoon tranquil and luminous. Yet this strange light flooded him with confused misgiving – a doubt of the truth of his own reality, a desolate consciousness of his own insecurity in a hostile world. What was he doing here, limping aimlessly, his mind clouded by a host of conflicting thoughts that struck at him like a swarm of hornets? The direction his life was taking suddenly seemed preposterous. He felt a loss of support, an impression of falling into an abyss. Why had Frida made that violent and upsetting attack on him this morning? It was unpardonable and yet, seeking her motive, he found much to excuse and even to forgive. She was in love with him, jealous of Kathy, broken by the thought of his departure, fearful for his safety and health. Deeply, he regretted the rupture between them. He had always liked and admired her and had been to blame, perhaps, in encouraging her hopes of a closer relationship. Yet in the circumstances it was best that their friendship should be severed.

With an effort he pulled himself together, hailed a taxi and was driven to the station. The evening paper, which he read on the return journey, amply confirmed the bad news of the morning – an official statement had been issued from the United Nations deploring the outrage against innocent civilians. There was also a report that smallpox and bubonic plague had broken out; appeals for medical assistance had been broadcast. When he got

256

home an hour later he found nothing to alleviate his despondency: no telephone message from Kathy, not even a letter, and the house now in such a state of upheaval – stacked books on the library floor, his silver in tissue paper, curtains dismantled in the salon – that all sense of comfort and security was gone. When he was enduring all this, abandoning everything for her sake, Kathy owed him at least a few words of encouragement and support. He must speak with her at once.

He went to the library telephone and put through a call to the Fotheringay manse in Markinch. The delay on this occasion was interminable, yet he would not leave the instrument. At last, following a muddle of Scottish accents at the local exchanges, a lamentable connection was established. It was Mrs Fotheringay who spoke; he could scarcely hear her voice over the persistent hum, and once intelligible contact was made, all proved fruitless. Willie and Kathy had left on the previous day, were now on their way through England, probably in Manchester, though at what address she did not know. She could, however, give him the number of the mission centre in Edinburgh, where they might be able to help him.

Cutting short the conversation, which she would have prolonged indefinitely, he rang the Edinburgh number, and was more successful in getting through. But here also he drew blank. Mr Douglas had delivered his lecture in Edinburgh and departed for London with his niece. They had no knowledge of his present address.

He ate a poor dinner and afterwards moved to the study, the only sitting-room which still remained habitable. Almost an hour later, while he sat brooding, suddenly the telephone rang.

His pulse missed a beat. He knew that it was Kathy, compelled by love and an instinctive awareness of his present need. He was at the phone in a second.

But, no – his heart sank sickeningly – it was not the sweet expected voice that came from the void, but the glottal accents of Stieger, his lawyer, who, detained in Munich, asked for a postponement of their appointment until Monday.

'Naturally, if the matter is urgent, I will fly back tomorrow morning and return to Munich in the evening.'

'No,' Moray said, struggling to recover himself. 'There's no immediate need. Don't put yourself out. Monday will suit equally well.'

'Then we will meet in three days' time.'

Three days, Moray reflected, as he hung up the phone; no harm could come of this brief postponement. At least it would afford him a breathing spell to recover and consolidate his forces. He was conscious of a vague feeling of relief.

CHAPTER XVIII

A WEEK HAD passed. Was it a week? Waiting like this, ready to go off, everything settled, it was difficult to keep track of the days. But of course, today was Sunday, and a wet one, drenching rain turning the snow into muddy slush, the mountains invisible behind swollen, dropsical clouds. God, what a horrible day, so damnably depressing to anyone, like himself, susceptible to weather. He turned from the window and for perhaps the twentieth time took Kathy's letter from his pocket, her solitary letter posted on the morning after she had been to Edinburgh. She must have written and mailed it immediately she got back to Markinch.

Dear David,

It was wonderful to hear your voice on the phone, and truly I have not had time to write you before. As I told you, Uncle Willie has had a real bad attack of fever. But he won't give up the lecture tour and we'll be leaving soon for our journey through England. When we get to London we'll be staying with Mr and Mrs Robertson, Scottish friends of Mrs Fotheringay's. Their address, if you are writing is, 3 Hillside Drive, Ealing, N.W.11. It is handy for London Airport. Everything is now arranged. Uncle Willie has got all three tickets and made the reservations. The flight number is AF 4329. The plane leaves on Tuesday the 21st at eleven p.m., so we shall meet you in the assembly hall one hour before the time of departure. We will be there from nine o'clock onwards so that there will be no mistake, and there must not be, for Uncle Willie is desperately anxious to leave. Things have been going from bad to worse at Kwibu and if we are to save the mission outstations in Kasai we must get back at once. I am so much looking forward to working with you out there, and to the rewards it will bring us. Dear David, this is the first time I have written you and it is difficult to say all that I mean. But you know my hopes are centred on you and that I will soon be your own true wife.

Kathy.

PS. Uncle Willie says be sure and be in time.

With a renewed sense of disappointment, Moray put down the letter which, when it arrived, he had opened so eagerly. Surely he might have expected something better than these few brief, restrained lines. Instead of the bare schedule of their departure, couldn't she have dwelt more freelingly on her love, said that she was missing him, that she longed to be once again in his arms? In all her vocabulary was there no stronger word than 'dear'? He admitted that she was shy, poor child, troubled by the conscious-ness of their intimacy – so he construed the phrase 'I will soon be your own true wife' – and limited by the small size of the note-paper. Yet she had found space to devote to Willie – his lectures, his fever, his anxieties and arrangements, his request not to be late. Not a word, not a single inquiry as to his own state of mind and body, or the distress and difficulties he might be experiencing, away from her. Really, it was too bad. He loved her, he wanted her, and all she could do was to throw Willie at his head.

This strange feeling that he had been deserted was intensified by the isolation of his present existence. His normal routine was broken, he had said goodbye to his friends in Schwansee, no one came to see him, they had all written him off as a departed member of their group. And Frida – for more than a week he had not set eyes upon her, although on several occasions, in the hope of meeting her, he had essayed a halting walk in the rain round the lake shore towards her domain. He missed the companion-ship she had so freely given and which, now above all, when certainty and uncertainty chased each other across his mind, he so sorely needed. Bitterly he regretted the rift between them, the result of a few outspoken words on her part which, realising their purpose, he had already condoned. Surely he could not leave her without attempting to resolve their differences. Time was getting so short, so very short; in two days he would be off. He ought to go up the hill to visit her. Yet something, pride perhaps, a restraining gleam of caution, had hitherto intervened.

The summons to lunch recalled him. He ate in abstracted silence, without appetite; then, as was his Sunday habit, took a short nap. Awakening about three he saw that the rain poured down more mercilessly than ever. He got up, moved about the house, checked his packed suitcases, smoked a cigarette, tried to kill time, but gradually his spirits sank, reached their lowest ebb and, after resisting during the hours of daylight, as the miserable grey afternoon turned to sodden evening, he succumbed to the craving for one word of human comfort. Frida would give it. She was, had always been, his friend. They would not argue, would discuss nothing involving controversy, would simply spend in sympathy one last quiet restorative hour of human intercourse.

Hurriedly, before he could change his mind, he put on his Aquascutum, took an old golf umbrella from the stand and, letting himself unobtrusively out of the house, hobbled off. The ferry took him across the lake, but for a lame man it was a long walk and a stiff climb up the steep, winding path to the schloss. Yet he was there at last, trembling at the knees like a horse after a stiff pull. God, he thought, what a wreck I've become.

Almost lost in the low clouds, the tall Seeburg towered above him. Built of rough mountain granite in the seventeenth century Swiss style, with a machicolated roof and twin pepperpot towers, it had, in the swollen darkness, a spectral, haunted air, an impression heightened by the harsh croaking of drenched ravens sheltering beneath the overhang of the eaves. Advancing on the mossy terrace outside the narrow double windows that gave on to her sitting-room, he drew up with a catch of breath. Yes, there she sat, alone on the sofa, beside the antique tiled stove, working at her needlepoint under a single shaded light that barely illuminated the large and lofty apartment, sparsely furnished with heavy high-backed walnut chairs and a great Bavarian armoire. Her favourite little weimaraner, Peterkin, lay on the rug at her feet with his nose between his paws.

The sombre domesticity of the scene touched Moray. With an agitated hand he tapped on the pane. Immediately she raised her head, turned towards the outer darkness; then, putting down her work, she came slowly forward and opened the tall window. For a long moment she looked at him fixedly, then in a calm, firm voice, totally devoid of solicitude, she said:

'My poor friend, how ill you look. Come! I will help you. So.' Taking his arm she guided him towards the sofa. 'Here you must sit and rest.'

'Thank you,' he muttered, breathing with difficulty. 'As you see, I'm rather under the weather. You may remember I hurt my back. It hasn't quite cleared up.'

'Yes,' she said, standing over him. 'Three times I have seen you by the lake, attempting to take your walk. I said to myself, unfortunate man, soon he will come to me.'

No note, no sign of triumph was evident in her tone or manner, but a kind of calm protectiveness, as though she were dealing with a favoured yet refractory pupil.

'I felt I must come,' he defended himself hurriedly. 'I couldn't bear to leave the breach between us permanently unhealed. I . . I am due to go the day after tomorrow.'

She did not answer but sat down beside him on the sofa and took his hand, holding it with strong, compelling fingers. For several moments there was absolute silence; then, gazing at him intently and speaking with the calm conviction of accomplished fact:

'My poor friend, you are not quite yourself. And now it is for a woman who knows and understands you, who has for you the best and strongest feelings, yes, it is now time for her to save you from yourself.'

'From myself?' he repeated, confused and startled.

'You have been led foolishly into a bad situation. Because you are an honourable man and, although ill, would wish to be a brave one, you want to go through with it. Even when it is plain you will not survive.' She paused quietly. 'But for that I will not stand aside.'

In the ensuing silence, compelled by a strange mixture of attraction and revulsion, he forced himself to raise his head and look at her.

'I must admit,' he said, trying to assert himself, 'with this lameness, I'm . . . almost in doubt. I mean, it has crossed my mind as to whether I'll be *able* to go as arranged, or whether I should follow later.'

'You are no longer in doubt, my friend. I do not intend to let you go.'

A complex shock passed through him, a combination of opposites, positive and negative charges of electricity perhaps, anyhow a decided shock.

'But I'm committed . . . in every way,' he protested.

'Yes, you have been wrong.' She lifted a forefinger in admonition. 'And stupid also. But listen. When you are walking in the mountains and discover yourself upon the wrong road, do you continue and fall into a crevasse? No. When you have asked directions of someone who knows better you turn and go back. That is what you will do.'

'No, no. I couldn't. What would Kathy and Willie think of me? Even the people here, after all the talk, my speech at the party, the publicity in the *Tageblatt*. I'd be the laughing-stock of the canton when they still saw me around.'

'They will not still see you around,' she answered, almost casually. 'For you must go away for a long holiday . . . with me.'

Again he started visibly, but she held him silent with a faint calm smile, went on in the same even, conversational tone.

'First we go to Montecatini, where there are wonderful baths for your back, and also, once you are better, a fine golf course where I will walk with you and admire your play. After, we take a cruise on that nice select little ship the *Stella Polaris*. Only then, in the Spring, do we return here, by which time all the silly business is finished and long forgotten.'

Immobilised by those hypnotic eyes he stared at her as though in a trance, yet perceiving, for the first time, that her hair had been freshly rinsed and set, that – as if she had expected him – she wore a new mauve silk dress, high in the waist, full and pleated in the skirt, a dress at once classic and correct, which enhanced her natural distinction. Certainly a fine figure of a woman and still beautiful – at a distance. Yet from close range his dilated pupils mirrored the commencing stigmata of middle-age; the faint reticulated network beneath the orbits, the slight sag of the muscular neckline, the speckled discoloration of the strong even teeth. How could this be compared with that other sweet face, that frail, fresh young body? An inward sigh shook him. And yet – in his present lamentable state – wasn't she a haven, an anchorage, a lady too, cultured, distinguished, and, in the ultimate analysis, not unbedworthy? He drew a sharp breath, was about to speak when, with a gleam of ridicule, she forestalled him.

'Yes, I am a reasonable bargain. And I will be the proper wife for you – by day and by night. Have I not also had strong longings during the years I have lived alone? We shall fulfil together. And what an interest for us both to restore and redecorate the Seeburg, to fill it with your beautiful things! We shall have a salon more famous than was Coppée in the days of Mme. de Stael.'

He still mumbled a protest.

'I'm terribly fond of you, dear Frida. But . . . '.

'But, yes, my poor man, and I of you. For once and all, I will not let you go out there to destroy yourself.'

A silence. What more could he say, or do? He felt over-powered, dominated, possessed, yet filled with a slow, creeping tide of comfort. The plan she presented was so sane, so agreeable in all respects – vastly different from that dark future which, during these last few days, he had come to dread. Acceptance would be like sliding into a warm bath after a long exhausting journey. He closed his eyes and slid. The relief was indescribable. He lay back on the sofa.

'Oh, my God, Frida . . . I feel I want to tell you everything . . . from the very beginning.'

And he did, at length, with feeling.

'Ah, yes,' she murmured, sympathetically if ambiguously, when he concluded. 'I see it all.'

'You're the only woman who has ever understood me.'

As he spoke the dog stirred from sleep, looked up and, with a bark of recognition, jumped on to his knees.

'You see,' she nodded, 'Peterkin accepts you also. Now you are tired. Rest while I bring something to restore you.' She was soon back, glass in hand. 'This is from your own country, very old and special. I have kept it for you for a long time. Now, to please me, you must drink all.'

The one spirit he detested was whisky – it always disagreed with him, soured his stomach, upset his liver. But he did need a stimulant, and he wanted to please her; besides, he hadn't the will to resist.

'Well done,' she commended him, resuming her place beside him. 'Now we will sit quiet as two mice in church until you feel better.'

As he had expected, the whisky went straight to his head. His face became flushed and in no time at all he felt, not better, but stupid and inflamed. Presently, observing him, she said thought-fully: 'I have been considering the best way to arrange our marriage. It must be done not only most quietly, but also quickly, if we are to get away before all the fuss, which you fear so much, becomes known. Yes?'

'The sooner we clear out the better.'

'Then it is best that we go to Basle, leaving early tomorrow. It will take altogether three days, for there are several formalities. But we can be back here on Wednesday evening.'

'And then, dear Frida?'

'Off on our long holiday next morning.'

Hazily he saw her smiling down at him. Damn it, she wasn't a bad-looking gammer, with those wonderful eyes and that solid, Wagnerian body which gave promise of well sprung resilience. What was she saying?

'You were sweet a moment ago. You called me dear Frida.'

'You are rather a dear, you know.' Unexpectedly, he sniggered. 'A regular Brunnhilde.'

'It is for you to know – in the future. You have never seen the upstairs of the Seeburg. My room, that will be our room, is nice. That we shall not look at this evening. But after? So? You will not find me cold. Some people do not need the love of the body, but with us it will be natural and frequent. Yes? And necessary also, for it puts one at ease. Now let us talk about our so pleasant future.'

An hour later, the Dauphine bore him triumphantly to the villa. In the close darkness of the little car she patted his cheek and gave a meaning little laugh.

'Now, like me, you will have happy dreams. Goodnight, mein lieber Mann, tomorrow I will come to you early. We must start for Basle before nine o'clock.'

Dead beat, but dulled and comforted, he stumbled into the house, thankful for the fact that he was so extinguished he must instantly fall asleep.

'I'm going straight to bed,' he told Arturo, in a voice he made an effort to keep normal. 'See that you lock up before you turn in. And I'll want breakfast at eight sharp.'

'Yes, sir,' said Arturo, somewhat blankly. 'And tonight, will you have your hot milk and sandwiches upstairs?'

No, he thought, not after the whisky, he was still not quite sober.

'Nothing tonight.' He paused, confronted by the necessity of conveying the change in his plans. Well, with Arturo it would not be so difficult; he had been quite broken up at the prospect of his departure.

'By the way,' he sought for the words, 'something quite unexpected has come up. I shall not after all be obliged to leave for good, but only for a matter of perhaps three months.'

Several shades of expression passed over the other's face before radiance shone from it.

'Oh, sir, I am so happy, so filled with joy, so thankful to the good God and Santa Philomena to whom I pray for you to stay. Only wait till I tell Elena.'

Arturo's extravagant delight was an added solace. Such loyalty, such affectionate devotion he thought, on his way up the stairs, and from Elena too, both so deeply attached to him. And now for bed.

Gazing upwards with a queer expression, Arturo watched him enter his bedroom, then he turned and went back to the pantry. Elena looked at him expectantly. He responded with an affirmative gesture and a significant grimace.

'You were right. The German has hooked him. Got him by the short hairs.'

'Madre d' Dio.' She let out the exclamation and broke into broad Neapolitan. 'Lu viecchio 'nzannaluto.'

'He's that, all right.' Arturo shrugged in agreement. 'And how he will suffer.'

'But so also will we,' said Elena despondently. 'That squaldrina will watch the money like a Swiss tax collector. Goodbye to our little ribasso from the market when she gets her claws on the bills.'

'Still, it's better than having him go. We can still milk him.'

'Llecca 'o culo a chillu viecchio 'nzannaluto?'

'That's it, lay on the butter thick.' He went to the cupboard, took out a bottle and drew the cork. 'He's the softest touch I ever handled.'

'Watch out though, with her around.'

'I know what I'm doing. Besides, we have to make the most of him while he's got it. Before she finishes, that *culo* will take everything off him.'

'Chella fetente va a ferni c' 'o mette 'nterra,' said Elena, with meaning.

At this prediction of complete emasculation for their employer they looked at each other and burst into fits of laughter.

CHAPTER XIX

THREE DAYS LATER, at the hour of twilight on Wednesday afternoon, the Humber utility car, mud-bespattered as from a journey, slid unobtrusively through the village of Schwansee, swung discreetly into the familiar acacia drive and drew up at Moray's villa.

'Well, here we are, Frida.' Pulling off his driving gloves he stated the obvious with a congratulatory smile, adding, with a glance at the dashboard clock, 'and dead on time.'

The successful secrecy with which they had invested their wedding gave him a distinct glow of achievement; it had all gone exactly according to plan. He squeezed out of the driving seat and, hurrying round the car, helped her with uxorious solicitude to alight. At the same moment the door of the villa swung open and Arturo appeared, advanced with a determined smile of welcome.

'Everything all right?' Moray asked aside, as the man removed the suitcases from the boot.

'Quite all right, sir. We have the salon in order again with the china all arranged. But the library and the other rooms will take more time.'

'You'll have time. We shall be off tomorrow for quite a long spell.' He seemed to hesitate. 'There were no messages of any kind?'

'None, sir.'

Impossible to repress that involuntary breath of relief. He had feared the possibility of a last-minute telephone call, a distressing message awaiting his return. But no, they had gone off, without a word, exactly as Frida had predicted, off to the Mission, to their work – not his, it had never been his – yes, their life's work, which, by its very complexities, its difficulties and dangers, would absorb them, make Kathy speedily forget. How misguided he had been ever to imagine that he could beneficially link his future to that dear dedicated girl, yet how wise, in her interests and his own, to realise his mistake before it was too late. And now there would be no more idealistic nonsense, no more reaching after spiritual moonbeams: safely married to a mature and distinguished woman he experienced a warm feeling of security, a sense of having at last reached journey's end.

'Bring tea quickly, Arturo,' he said, following Frida into the drawing-room. Seating himself beside her on the Chesterfield settee, he glanced round appreciatively. Yes, everything was in order, exactly as *before* – the word had now a definite historic import, like A.D. or B.C., denoting the demarcation between his pre- and post-redemption periods. His pictures bloomed more attractively than ever – God, to think he could ever have existed without them – his silver shone, his porcelain, freshly washed and arranged, gleamed in the light of a heart-warming fire of crackling cedar logs.

'Isn't this *gemütlich*?' He gave her an intimate smile. 'To be back, together, and to have managed it all so cleverly.'

'But of course, David. You will find I manage things always well.' She gave him a short pleasant nod. 'You will see later, when we are established at the Seeburg.'

He was about to answer – a compliment was on his tongue – when Arturo came in, wheeling the tea trolley, so instead, rubbing his hands, he said: 'Ah, tea. Will you pour, darling?'

Meanwhile Arturo, having adjusted the trolley, was offering him the salver from the hall.

'Your mail, sir.'

'What a lot of letters,' she exclaimed, lifting the silver teapot – George I, 1702. 'It appears that you are an important man.'

'Mostly business.' He shrugged, running them through. But one, apparently, was not. With a shrinking of his nerves he recognised Kathy's round, even writing. But, glancing covertly at the date stamps on the envelope, he was immediately reassured. The latter had been posted on the 17th, four days before her departure, and received at Schwansee on Monday the 20th, the day he left for Basle with Frida. As such, thank heaven, it could contain neither reproaches nor regrets. With a cautious side glance at Frida, who was still pouring tea, he slid it unobserved into his side pocket – he would read it later, when he was alone.

'Since we speak of business,' she added sugar and lemon and handed him his cup, 'you must one day soon tell me of your affairs – perhaps when we are at Montecatini, yes? I have a very good head for these things. The actions of the German chemicals, for example, these are strong at this moment.'

'They are,' he agreed, tolerantly, as he leaned forward to cut the cake. 'And we're comfortably supplied with them.'

'That is nice. And German bonds. These also are affording a high rate of interest.'

'I see you're going to be a great help, dear. Now try this. It's Elena's special recipe and she's baked it in your honour.' He watched while she sampled the slice of cherry cake he handed her. 'Good, isn't it?'

'Yes, it is good – quite good. But it can be better, much better. For one thing there is too much vanilla and too little fruit. Afterwards I will show her properly.'

'You'll have to be tactful, dear. Elena is terribly touchy.'

'Oh, my poor David, you make me smile. As if I was without great experience! Why, at Kellenstein we had a staff, in and out, of fifteen persons, all requiring to be overseen. Here, I am sure, you have been ill served and also well cheated. No doubt your good Elena has many private arrangements, besides taking out fresh butter and eggs, while your wonderful Arturo – don't I know these Neapolitans – is all smiling in front and all stealing behind.'

A momentary misgiving troubled him, gone when she patted his hand with a protective smile.

'Another cup of your nice Twinings. That, at least, I shall not change.'

How gracefully she managed the tea things – to the manner born, neither nervous like Kathy nor clumsy like Doris, who in those distant almost forgotten days had always upset things during her attacks. Yes, after all his troubled years he had been right in this, his ultimate decision. He had always aspired to a well-bred woman, not only for the social advantages she would bring him, but also for that extra refinement with which, from her breeding, she would enrich their conjugal intimacies. Ah, yes, Frida would remake his life. And how restful was the immediate prospect: Montecatini, the *Polaris* cruise – she had already made their cabin reservations at the American Express in Basle – and then all the interest of restoring the Seeburg. Comfortable though his villa was, it would never be more than a bourgeois little house, really unfitted to hold his treasures which would now adorn and transform the big schloss above the lake.

Yet, through his complacency, as he sipped his tea in the warm comfortable room, he could not restrain his thoughts from reverting, not exactly self-accusingly, but with a kind of pricking discomfort, to that plane, which even now, after its overnight stop at Lisbon, must be winging towards Luanda. Surely by now she must have got over the worst of it. She was young, she would recover, sorrow did not last forever, time was the great healer. . . He consoled himself with these and other profundities.

'I believe you are asleep.' A half-chiding, half-amused voice recalled him.

'No – no – not really. But on that subject, Frida, must you really spend the night at Seeburg? Why not stay here? After all, we *are* married.'

'Yes, we are nice married people, and for that reason must be sensible.'

'But why, dear Frida? It's been quite, well, difficult for me, away with you two nights . . . and separate rooms.'

She laughed, well pleased.

'I am glad you have the same feeling as I. But for newly-weddeds it is better to make the honeymoon away. For me there is more novelty. And for you, especially, it is better to be free of recent associations that might trouble you.'

'Yes,' he agreed, unwillingly. 'I suppose there's something in that. Still . . . '.

Assuagingly, she pressed against him imprinting the edge of her corsets upon his short ribs, then, before he could encircle her, withdrew.

'So . . . our need will grow if held back. I promise I will be nice for you at Montecatini. The Freiherr, my late husband, was a strong man in the bed, yet never did I fail to answer him with equal vigour. Since we are married, I can openly speak of these things. And now I will go upstairs. After that long drive I have much need to wash.'

When she left the room he sat half-dozing before the hot fire, as though drugged by the scent of the burning cedar. At times his mind became an absolute blank; then, recovering, he enjoyed a moment of calm relaxation. Five, ten, fifteen minutes passed. What was she doing upstairs? Taking a bath? He had not liked that reference to the late lamented baron, but at least it showed she wasn't frigid. He thought drowsily of her ample dugs, those extensile mountaineering thighs. Then absently, through his euphoria, he remembered the belated letter. Whatever his reluctance, he owed it to Kathy to read and cherish it as a last sweet message. Feeling in his pocket he withdrew it and after considering the envelope again, and confirming the date stamps, he manfully opened it.

As he did so he became conscious of the ringing of a bell. The front door? Yes. He sat up suddenly, hoping to high heaven that it was not a caller. If one of their friends, Stench particularly, burst in upon them at this precise moment, it would be a fatal embarrassment, would in fact ruin all their plans for a discreet departure. He should have warned Arturo to say he was not at home. Too late now, the fellow was answering the door.

He got up, parted the curtains of the side window and peered out at the dark driveway. No car – it couldn't be a caller, must be a tradesman or a travelling pedlar; he had no need to worry. Yet the conversation at the door appeared to be prolonged. Straining his ears he heard Arturo say, almost entreatingly: 'Please, if you will wait here, I will see.'

'But there's no need,' a thin voice answered, with a strained note of urgency. 'I'm expected. I'll go straight in.'

Moray's heart contracted. My God, he thought, it can't be. I'm dreaming, or out of my mind. Instinctively he took a few steps backwards. Futile retreat. There came the sound of hurried footsteps in the hall and the next instant Kathy was before him.

'David!' she cried, in sheer relief. 'I thought from Arturo you weren't here.' All her body seemed to incline towards him: then, running forward, she put her arms round him and laid her head against his breast.

He had turned deathly white, his face blank with horror and amazement. It was a nightmare, unreal, couldn't be true. He stood frozen into paralysed stillness.

'Oh, David, dear David,' she kept murmuring. 'Just to be with you again.'

He could not speak, the skin around his mouth had suddenly become tight. But at last he gasped: 'Kathy . . . what . . . why are you here?'

'Because I need you now . . . so much more . . . '. Still close to him, she looked up as though uncomprehending. 'You know that Uncle Willie sent me?'

'Willie?' he echoed, like a parrot.

'Didn't you get my letter?'

'No – yes – at least . . . I've been away.'

'Then you don't know. Oh, David, it's too terrible. The entire Mission is destroyed, burned to the ground. There's been a fearful outbreak by armed terrorists. They're fighting all around, and almost all of our people are dead. All Uncle Willie's work, the labour of twenty years, destroyed.' Tears were beginning to flow down her cheeks. 'Uncle Willie has gone out to see the worst, if they'll allow him to get there, but he knows it's finished. He wouldn't let me go with him. He's broken-hearted. I think he'll have to give up. And for me, there's nothing out there now . . . I have . . . only you, dear David. Oh, I thank God for that. But for you, I think I would have lost my mind.'

Silence. A cold sweat of panic beaded his forehead; his heart kept banging irregularly in his side. He broke away slightly, hand pressed against his brow, still struggling for speech.

'This . . . dreadful, Kathy. A great shock. If I had only known . . .'

She looked at him with faithful, uncomprehending eyes.

'But, David, when you didn't come to the airport I felt sure you had my letter telling you everything.'

'Yes, precisely . . . it's just . . . so difficult . . . having been away.' What he was saying he scarcely knew, and she had begun to look at him strangely, nervously too, with a sudden anxiety in her tired, thin little face.

'David, is anything wrong?'

'Nothing, except . . . it's all so unfortunate . . . so unforeseen.'

Now all the joy that was in her died. She showed real alarm, seemed to shrink into herself.

'David, please, for pity's sake.'

Oh God, he thought, this can't go on, I must, I'll have to tell her. He tried to pull himself together.

'Kathy . . . '. He braced himself. 'Dear Kathy . . . '.

He could not go on, could not to save his life have spoken the words. There followed a moment of complete and frightful silence. His mouth filled with bitter water, and through it all he kept thinking, I could have had her here, on my own terms, if only I had waited. It was agony. And as he stood rigid with clenched hands, unable to meet her frightened eyes, the door opened and Frida came into the room. Arrested by the scene, with one comprehensive glance she took it in; then, without change of expression, came quietly forward.

272

'Kathy, you are here,' she said, and kissed her on the cheek. At the same time she made towards Moray a brusque gesture of dismissal which said decisively, go, this you must leave to me.

Still rooted, he seemed unable to set himself in motion, but somehow, stumbling forward, he got himself out of the room. Kathy was very pale, but had stopped crying. Bewilderment and alarm had dried her tears.

'What is wrong with David? Is he ill?'

'I think he is unwell slightly, at this moment. The shock, you see. But come, dear child, we must sit down and be composed and have a little talk together.' Persuasively, an arm round Kathy's shoulder, she led her to the settee. 'Now first, my dear, how did you arrive here?'

'By plane to Zurich, train to Melsburg, then the little steamboat to Schwansee.'

'What a tiring journey. Wouldn't you like to rest or have some refreshment?'

'No, thank you, no.' Kathy was shivering slightly, her teeth pressed together to prevent them chattering.

'At least a cup of tea. It can be brought so quickly.'

'Oh, nothing, please. I only want to know about David.'

'Yes, of course, we must speak of David, for he is, like that nice book says, the heart of the matter. But we must speak plainly of him, for even if it gives pain we must establish the truth.' She paused and took Kathy's hand in hers. 'You see, dear child, this David whom you love is a very nice man, so full always with good intentions, yet, alas, not always with the strength to perform them, which is often sad for him and for others. Have you not an English proverb, the pavement of hell is made of good intentions? Did you never ask yourself, dear little Kathy, for what real reason he came back to discover your family in Scotland? You thought, to repay a youthful kindness. That was not so. It pains me to tell you, and it will pain you to hear. It was because as a young man this David was the lover of your mother, really her lover if you understand me, had promised marriage, then cruelly left her, for a rich man's only daughter.'

'No – no.' She took a sharp anguished breath, her pupils wide with shock. 'It's impossible. You're making this up.'

'How do I make it up when I have heard it all from David himself? Yes, he is the kind of man who seeks to discharge his guilt by an emotional confession. And succeeds. With weeping too, for, like other great men, he weeps easily – like a woman.'

'I won't . . . I won't listen to you.'

'But you must, dear Kathy, for your own sake. So our David came back full of the best intentions to make his wrong completely right. And when your mother was unfortunately not available, you became the object of his kind attentions. And it was all good in the beginning, yes, beautifully good and proper, but then things changed a little, he wished very nobly to do even more for you, and so – for those soft charming men have so much a way with women – on the promise to marry and go to your mission he became your lover, as with your mother.'

'Stop!' Distractedly she covered her ears. 'I can't – I'll not hear any more. It's too horrible.'

'Certainly it is not a nice thought, to seduce first the mother, then the daughter, and all with the highest intentions. Yet I assure you he is not altogether bad, compared with others, for I know men, dear child, and some are by far more horrible, as you say, than David, who is only selfish and weak, avoiding trouble and difficulty for himself at all costs. No, do not run away.' Detainingly, as Kathy tried to rise, she held her arm. 'Can't you see I speak for your own good. I must show you your mistake. If you had married this famous David he would have tired of you and in six months broken your heart. You are altogether different, not of the same kind. You would never convert him to religion, or even to work again as a doctor. Nor could he have made you like his stupid antiques or his famous pictures, all a mode created by the dealers. Your marriage would have been a fatal disaster.'

Kathy sat quite still, her expression blurred, as though the structure of her face had given way. There was something terrifying in her immobility. She felt feverishly sick, stripped of all that she had prized, degraded and unclean. She wanted to get away but there was no strength in her, only weakness and self-disgust.

'So, is it not evident? The wife this David needs is not a sweet, gentle girl such as you, but a woman strong enough to master him, one who will make him obey, and do always, always what is needed.'

Kathy's eyes widened suddenly, great pools of darkness in her small white face.

'You,' she gasped.

'Yes. Today we were married in Basle.'

Silence again. Kathy's brows, knit in pain, gave her a twisted look. What thoughts raced through her tortured mind! Her head drooped, could not contain or combat them – the meeting at her mother's grave, that charming, serious smile, a friend of your family, the day in Edinburgh, so gay and generous, the round of visits, what a wonderful nurse, but quite worn out, a cup of soup, my dear, so tenderly, and then Vienna, strange and whirling confusion of lights, sounds, music, Pinkerton, dear David, you could never be like that, Switzerland next, a mantle of purity, yes, I will come with you, the little mission church, one in the sight of heaven, and then, like her dear dead mother. . . . Oh God, she could not bear it. She jumped up, wildly, frantically, bent only on escape.

But Frida had risen quickly and stood at the door, blocking the way.

'Wait, Kathy, you must be sensible. Believe me, I mean well by you. There is much we can do for you.'

'Let me go. All I want is to go away . . . to go home.'

'Kathy, the car will take you to the hotel.'

'No, no . . . I'll take the boat . . . I only want to go home.'

The doorway was still blocked. She looked feverishly round, ran to the french window, flung it open.

'Stop, Kathy.'

But she had already dashed across the terrace and the lawn to the narrow garden path that led to the village. Down the steep path she ran, into the darkness, mindless of the unseen steps, falling to her knees in her desperate haste, rising again, straining through the vicious shadows, seeking only to escape. Dark shapes of bushes whipped against her like things alive, stinging her with all the malice of mankind. Shocked out of sorrow, she was no longer herself, not altogether living, moving in a confused and tragic dream. In the dim world in which she ran, everything within her drifted away but pain, all was gone. She was lost.

Frida could not follow. Standing silent and distressed at the open french window, which threw out a following beam, she watched, watched until the stumbling, wavering little figure was lost as the brutal night took possession of it. Then, turning slowly, she shook her head, closed the window and, advancing into the hall, called upstairs. He came down slowly, nervously, with watery eyes and a veal-white face. He had been seated on the upper landing, trying to steady himself with one of his monogrammed Sobranies.

'It is all settled,' she told him calmly. 'She has gone.'

'But where . . . and how ' His voice shook.

'I offered the car but she prefers to return as she came, by boat. She goes home at once. All she wishes is to go home.'

'But Frida . . . ' he faltered. 'She has given up her job. She can't go to Willie. Where is her home?'

'You have put the question. You had better answer it.'

A pause.

'Was she – much hurt?'

'Yes.'

'In – in what way?'

'Cannot you guess?'

'What did you tell her?'

'The truth. For her sake and ours it was necessary to perform a surgical operation. And I did so.'

'You told everything?'

'Yes.'

'But you – explained that I had meant well.'

'All was explained.'

'And yet – she was hurt – badly?'

'Yes.' With increasing sharpness: 'Have I not already said it.'

'Surely she understood I couldn't go out there.'

'She did not come here for you to go.'

He threw up his hands.

'But how in God's name was I to know the Mission would burn down.'

'In the present circumstances it was more than a possibility. They are making bonfires of all the missions.'

'My God, Frida, I feel horribly upset. I worry about her getting back.' He looked at the clock. 'She may have missed the boat – and it's the last to Melsburg. I should go after her . . . if she's still on the pier.'

'Then go.'

She said it cuttingly. The look in her yellow eyes, with their narrow slits of pupils, made him flush and wilt.

'No,' he said. 'You're quite right. It wouldn't be wise.'

Silence again. Then firmly she put her hand on his shoulder.

'For the sake of pity, pull yourself into something like a man. She is young and, like her mother, will get over it. You can afford to make a settlement to her, and a large one. Later you must send it in proper legal form.'

'Yes.' His face lifted slightly. 'I can do that, thank God, and I will. Make her comfortable for life. But, Frida ... '. He hesitated, then, after a longish pause, said pleadingly, 'I don't want to be alone tonight.'

She seemed to study him, with almost a clinical curiosity, seemed about to refuse, then relented.

'Well, then, though you should be punished, I shall stay. You must go upstairs and take your bath. Then to bed, for you are tired. I will speak with the servants and have a tray brought to you. Afterwards I will come.'

He looked at her abjectly.

'Bless you, Frida.'

She waited until he had climbed the stairs; then, passing through the drawing-room, she went out upon the terrace. The moon, behind ragged clouds, shone faintly. It was thawing, the snow on the lawn had turned a dirty yellow, a damp sensual smell of leaves filled the air. She gazed out across the lake. Yes, there was the steamer, a little fountain of light, cosy and bright, already on its way, quite far on its way, to Melsburg. A faint thrum of the engines came back to her. Kathy must just have managed to get on board. Turning, she looked down at the little pier. Yes. All quiet and deserted. The single yellow lamp that was kept alight all night shone upon the solitary wooden bench. No one was seated there.

CHAPTER XX

STARTING PAINFULLY FROM a restless snatch of sleep Moray awoke to the muddled consciousness of unfamiliar darkness. Where was he? And why alone? Then, through the oppression clamped on his forehead, the first dulled glint of consciousness brought the humiliating answer.

God, it had been frightful, his inability to find consolation in Frida's arms! She had tried to help him, at first with desire, then with encouragement, and finally in a state of weary patience. All useless – he could not succeed. And then, sorely tried by his futile fumblings, she had said, in a tone which concealed contempt but not bitterness and frustration: 'We both need some rest if we're to be off tomorrow morning. Would it not be wise if you moved to another room?'

And so he was here, in the guest room – a guest, almost, in his own house. Why, he agonised, had his normal virility deserted him? Had the sudden shock of Kathy's reappearance induced a depressive impotence? It might well be so – the oversized female in his antique bed, her musky odours and muscular anatomy, had brought paralysing images of the slender young form he had once possessed: Kathy, whom he could easily have had, and instead had hopelessly lost.

Kathy . . . Stretched out on his back, he groaned. If only he had not failed her, everything would have turned out as he had wished. Oh God, what a fool he had been, in his weakness, his craving for sympathy, to marry Frida. She had caught him: he had swallowed the bait, hook, line and sinker, and was now landed, gasping, on the bank. And how skilfully she had angled for him: first that resigned acceptance of his departure, congratulations, sweet offers of assistance; then the gradual dissemination of doubt, working up to a frontal assault upon his fears; and finally, when he had been sufficiently reduced, that determined stand, a command virtually, to take her. Miserably

278

he acknowledged her strength. She would possess him body and soul.

God, what a horrible situation! Weak rage flooded him, followed by a spasm of self-disgust. Tears came burning to his eyes at the thought of his disloyalty to Kathy. Yet it had not been a deliberate betrayal, he told himself, simply a moment of aberration, a lapse for which he had already been punished, and for which he would eventually make amends.

Amends – yes, that was still the key, the imperative word. At all costs he must not lose contact with Kathy. No matter what had happened she was still his responsibility, his charge, as essential to him as he to her. He must, yes, he must get in touch with her at once. A letter, explanatory, contrite yet constructive, was the immediate necessity, not only to outline his plans to make provision for her, but also to express the hope that when sorrow had been tempered by compassion they might meet again. He would pour out his heart in it, and since he must leave early with Frida tomorrow it was essential for him to write it now. A faint and wavering gleam dawned in the grisly prospect of his future. There was always hope – one need never give up; with his money especially there were many ways and means. Perhaps in due course everything might be straightened out. He began even to envisage, though dimly, an amicably arranged divorce that would set him free. Surely he could rely on his dear child's forgiveness.

Stirring himself with an effort, he got up, switched on the light and, while struggling into his dressing gown, looked at his wrist watch. Twenty minutes to twelve – he couldn't have been asleep for much more than an hour. Guardedly, he felt his way across the landing. Rhythmic unmelodious crescendos, percolating from his room, now hers, made him wince. He hastened past. Downstairs in the library, he sat at the bureau by the window, switched on the shaded lamp, and took notepaper from the central inlaid drawer. Then, pen in hand, he stared into the outer darkness, anxiously seeking the most appropriately touching form of address. Should it be 'Dear Kathy,' 'My Dearest Kathy,' or even 'Darling Kathy,' or simply the restrained, sombre, but oh, so significant, 'My Dear'?

After some thought he had decided on the last when, through his abstraction, he became conscious of a glow, shining distantly through the opacity of the night. The moon is rising, he thought, seeing a hopeful omen in this sudden brightness; he was indeed in a mood receptive to signs and portents. Yet it could scarcely be the moon, for the sky still remained darkly unbroken and the light itself seemed less a radiance than a strange coruscation, a shifting sparkle of pin-point lights dancing like wildfire against the unseen waters of the lake below. What on earth was it? Accustomed to the wildest elements unleashed amongst these unpredictable peaks, he was unlikely to be startled by any terrestrial phenomenon. Yet so overwrought and unstable was his present state of mind, he could not repress a faint shiver of distrust. He got to his feet, opened the french window and, despite the lightness of his attire – he had always had a tendency to catch cold – went out on the terrace.

The night, as he had suspected, was pitch and unexpectedly chill. Clutching his thin dressing gown about him he peered down towards the lights. They were near, mysteriously and disconcertingly near. But suddenly he understood, and in a reflex of absurd relief could have smiled, though he did not, at his own foolishness. It was the little fishing fleet, half a dozen boats bouncing gaily on the waves, the men casting their nets, night fishing with naphtha flares. The felchen must be running, and in shoals, to have brought them out so late.

He was about to turn back into the comfort of the house when a thought arrested him. Surely the felchen didn't run in winter and never, to his knowledge, in this part of the lake? They always swarmed at the mouth of the river where it flowed in through the Reisenberg gorge. And shading his eyes – though this was unnecessary – for a more particular scrutiny, he saw with amazement that a number of people were gathered on the pier. At this hour of the night! He hesitated. He wanted to leave it, leave the matter as it stood, but something impelled him to run into the house for his field glasses, the splendid Zeiss binoculars he had bought in Heidelberg.

At first he could not find them, but after rummaging untidily through several drawers, they came to hand. Back on the terrace, he focussed them hurriedly. Then, just as he saw that all the flares were now congregated round the pier, one by one all of them went out and a curtain of darkness, barely relieved by the feeble pier lamp, cut off his view.

He lowered the glasses uncertainly. He had a splitting headache and for some extraordinary reason his heart was fluttering against his ribs. He ought to go in, he had the letter to write, the letter beginning simply and movingly, 'My Dear.' And he would have gone in, but the sound of approaching footsteps detained him. He swung round. Two men, at first dimly seen, then gradually taking recognisable shape, were coming up the path from below. The pier-master and Herr Sacht from the village Polizeiwache.

It had always been for him a source of mild entertainment that the cantonal police, in entire outward look – their stiff helmet, blue uniform and capacious boots – bore so close a resemblance to the London bobbies: perhaps a delicate compliment, he had surmised, contrived in earlier days to make the visiting English milords feel safe and more at home. But now Moray was not entertained, nor did he feel safe and reassured as Herr Sacht and his companion advanced towards him. He felt instead a sinking of his heart that was the sickening premonition of unknown yet inevitable disaster.

'Grüss Gott, mein Herr.' Respectfully, apologetically almost, the pier-master made himself spokesman – Sacht, a slow and stolid man, was at all times sparing of words. 'We have some trouble down below, and have come for your advice – though not wishing to disturb you. A young woman . . . '.

'No . . . no . . . ' said Moray, barely breathing.

'Alas, yes. We have just found her.'

'But how . . . ?' He could say nothing more. Pale and rigid, he had ceased to breathe.

'After the night boat I heard a splash – like a springing fish. Of it, I thought nothing. But when I made my last round of the pier, there was a handbag, fallen down, and in the water, floating, a lady's small brown hat. I thought it wise to alarm the Polizei.' He glanced at Sacht, who nodded in heavy confirmation. 'We got the boats out and after dragging, just two hours, we found the young person – of course completely dead.' He paused in respectful sympathy. 'I fear it is – may be a friend to you. . . . The young Englische girl, she who came this afternoon on the five o'clock boat.'

He drew back, staring at them, horrified. Then, all at once he was crying hysterically.

'Oh, my God, it can't be. But yes, a young lady . . . she did come . . . Kathy . . . Kathy Urquhart . . . a friend, as you say, daughter of an old, very dear friend. . . . She left us, running,

281

running to catch the last boat . . . '.

'Ach, so?' Sacht said, with a slow comprehending nod. 'She was running, in the darkness. Perhaps – or surely, then, this has been an accident.'

Moonfaced, Moray looked from one to the other, grasping towards the chance of exoneration, dizzily seeking a way out of the impact of this atrocious disaster.

'But what else could it be?' Struggling, he forced himself to bring out explanatory words. 'She was on her way home, looked in to visit me again . . . briefly . . . to say goodbye. She was a nurse, you understand . . . fully trained . . . a fully trained nurse . . . meaning to work with her uncle in Africa . . . a missionary. I wanted to send her back by car . . . but she had her ticket and liked the boat. She must have slipped, missed her footing . . . it had been raining, the melting snow is very treacherous. . . . And now . . . '. He covered his face with his hand.

'It is sad for you, Herr Moray,' said the pier-master, 'and we do not wish to cause you inconvenience. But you could help. Herr Sacht says, if only you will come to identify the body, he can then complete his report.'

'Yes, of course. . . . Yes, I will come.' His tone was expressive of assistance, complete willingness to co-operate.

'First you must put on warmer clothes, so you do not get chilled. We will wait here until you are ready.'

He had not realised his state of undress. In the hall cupboard he found a coat, cap and scarf, a pair of felt-lined snow boots. Hastily rejoining the other two, he went down the path. Still in a state of shock, he was instinctively, protectively, acting a part, but as they approached the little pier, where a silent group stood gathered outside the low wooden shed that served as waiting-room, he could not repress a shudder of numbed and silent dread.

The group parted, still in silence, as they drew near. They went into the bare waiting-room, where they had laid her on the pitch-pine table under a single hanging electric globe. There was no sheet; she lay half covered by a fisherman's jacket which Sacht now discreetly withdrew. At first Moray could not look. Frozen. Too much to demand of him. A physical impossibility. He stared woodenly at the near end of the table, seeing only the worn sole of one small brown shoe, hearing a slow steady drop of water from the upper edge of the table. The room smelled of the drifted fume of the paraffin flares and of stale cigarette smoke. Wandering away to safety, his gaze caught an ashtray, stamped Melsburg Bier, on the floor. It was filled with stubs and had been removed. But the pier-master was speaking to him; he must look or they would begin to think something was seriously out of order. Slowly and with great effort he raised and twisted his head, still protecting himself, not looking at the face, not yet, making only a swift and limited survey.

Her total stillness was astounding, and her extraordinary immaturity. God knew he had reason to know that she was small and slight – but never had he dreamed her to be so – so young as this. The sodden clothes moulded her thin body, cupped the tender breasts, bisected the slender limbs, nakedly revealing the delicate swell between, the mons veneris – the phrase came – he was a doctor – and all, all with the stark indecency of death. One of her stockings had come down, wrinkling about the ankle, a button on the blouse was undone; one hand, the palm upturned receptively, the soaked skin already blanched, hung over the table edge.

A faint convulsion went through him as, knowing it must be done, he forced himself to look towards her face. Once he had looked, he could not look away. Upturned to the light, the face was shrunken and of a greenish colour, the blue lips flattened and fallen away, the drenched hair plastered back from the brow, hanging in dank switches about the thin white neck, still exuding the trickle that kept drip, dripping to the floor. Almost unrecognisable in its dead ugliness, the face was wrapped in a strange unbearable enigma. Most mysterious, most unbearable, were the eyes, still open, expressionless, gazing directly at him. Within their unfathomable depths, suddenly, in a moment of truth, he saw himself, exactly as he was, without illusion, naked under the watchful sky.

'Ach so? It is the young English lady?' It was spoken in a low voice of sympathy.

Moray turned, made a slow, melancholy gesture of assent. Revelation might have shattered him, but habit, the style and form of years, persisted.

'Alas – yes,' he said, with careful articulation. 'It is too painful for words. Cut off so suddenly – and so young. Only an accident could account for it. Did you observe the shoe, the sole – worn smooth? On the wet planks of the pier – the slippery edge . . . '.

'Yes, it is always bad in such weather.' The pier-master spoke defensively. 'But not possible for me to dry it.'

'Oh, I only pray God she did not suffer.'

'Ach, no,' Sacht said, crudely, yet trying to be kind. 'The cold of the water would kill quickly.' He had taken out his notebook.

'Well, you will want particulars,' Moray said, and standing erect, he gave them calmly, name, age, nationality, while Sacht indited in the dog-eared book with a moistened stub of pencil.

When it was all done, the pier-master, presuming in his sympathy, pressed Moray's arm.

'You do not look well, Herr Moray. Come to my house for a cup of coffee.'

'You are most kind. But, thank you, no.' He turned to Sacht. 'You are finished with me now? I suppose you have no further need of me.'

'For the present, no. But of course we will require you at the *Leichenschau.*'

'Ah, the inquest . . . '. Moray said, in an extinguished voice. 'You consider it will be necessary?'

'It is for you only a formality, Herr Moray, but officially required, for the records of the Stadt.'

'I see.' He drew himself up. 'You understand, of course, that it will be my privilege to defray all expenses of the interment.'

Was there anything more to say? Apparently not. He shook hands with both men and, not looking again, went out.

Though he went slowly, sparing himself with many enforced stops, his breath suffocated him as he went up the hill. He was sweating too, despite the cold, an abject sweat that ran from his armpits and the back of his knees, sweating from the ghastly futility of his effort at self-deception. All part of the usual sham, the impressive front, the grand façade. He knew the truth now, the truth about himself. And soon they would all know. Yes, it would all come out, all, all, the party for Willie, his engagement to Kathy, the heroic announcement of his departure for Africa. And now, within a few days, he was still here, married to Frida, and Kathy dead. God, what would they think of him? The gossip, the scandal, the odium that would fall upon him. And he couldn't escape it, not this time, couldn't leave with Frida in the morning, couldn't slide away and conveniently forget. He must stay for the *Leichenschau,* stay till it all came out, and afterwards stay bound hatefully to Frida, who would never let him go, but would grind him down remorselessly to an ultimate subjection. And all this when he might have had Kathy, when even at this moment she might have been alive, warm and loving, in his arms.

In a spasm of sweltering despair he clenched his teeth and hung on to the railings for support. It was a bad dream, a nightmare, impossible to grasp how it had come about. He had meant well, tried to do the right thing, oh God yes, he had tried so hard, he had wanted to do well for everyone. It simply wasn't in him to hurt even a fly. He couldn't be blamed if, with the best intentions, he had over-estimated his strength, broken down and been obliged to withdraw. It had not been a deliberate betrayal, simply a moment of . . . no, he'd said that before, it was no use any more. Simply wouldn't work. The instant of illumination when he stared into those dead eyes had shattered his self-constructed image. The hollow shell had broken, there was nothing left, nothing. In destroying her, he had destroyed himself.

Amongst the ruins, the clearness with which he viewed the stale imposture of his life was amazing, stereoscopic, four dimensional. All that had happened was his own doing, springing not from accident, but from something within, always his propensity for taking the way he thought most advantageous for himself. A genius at dodging responsibility, trouble, unpleasant issues, he saw with a sudden access of reason that he had developed to his logical conclusion. And yet, such a nice man, a charmer, cultured too, patron of the arts. How often had he heard, and merited, these compliments. Pity it was all gone – or would shortly go: reputation, position, freedom, happiness, hope in the future, and, naturally, his belief in himself. A queer logic had begun to take hold of him, comforting almost. He nodded twice in complete agreement. Imprisoned, walled in, every outlet sealed.

He reached the top of the hill and paused, exhausted but, strangely, more reasonable than ever. What a view! And a lovely night! A faint air stirring, the moon, alive again, drifting from the clouds, a soft mist rising from the lake, a nocturnal barge, unseen, chugged distantly. His thoughts strayed. A man had once told him that chugging note was his earliest childhood memory. Who? He had forgotten. It would have been interesting to ask him what he meant by it. Elusive shapes, records of his own past, swelled and faded in his mind. Say what they liked, he'd had an interesting life. An owl hooted in the orchard.

Suddenly he caught sight of a hedgehog, a small brown ball, moving into its own shadow across the lawn with painful lack of speed. Of all things, a hedgehog; amused, he almost smiled, recollecting how Wilhelm had reviled the little creature for its shallow rootings. He lost contact momentarily, then suddenly became aware of where he stood.

'*Cercis siliquastrium* . . . ' he murmured. 'The leaves are used for salads in the East.'

Yes, a lovely tree in summer, dangling its purple drops that fell staining the lawn. A winepress. He had always been poetic.

He ceased to mediate and, under the moving branches of the tree, raised his head in a sudden, upward glance. The swing, with its long ropes, was oscillating gently in the breeze. Seductive, the motion – it fascinated him. Following the gentle movements across the face of the moon, he simply couldn't take his eyes away. The faint rhythmic creak of the metal cleats began to beat a little tune inside his brain. Reality had left off, illusion was brightening his eys. He was beginning to understand everything in a peculiar and interesting way. This extraordinary calm was the most marvellous sensation he had ever experienced. And now he was talking to himself, in a quiet, confidential manner, carefully forming the words: restitution, complete vindication, the court of last appeal – absolving all guilt, restoring his ideal self. He stood there for a long time smiling to himself, enjoying his triumphant acquittal in advance, before he decided it was time for him to produce the evidence.

Next morning, just after seven o'clock, directed by the new Madame, Arturo went to the guest room, knocked on the door and brought in the breakfast tray: fresh orange juice, toast and boiled eggs, mountain honey, delicious Toscanini coffee in the silver Thermos. Arturo was in an unhappy frame of mind, almost convinced now that he would not keep his situation, but he said good morning, put the tray down on the oval occasional table by the window. Then he drew the lined silk curtains and flung the shutters back into their automatic catches.

The morning was cold, grey with mist, the raw air made his eyes water, and the wine he had drunk last night had left him with a thick head. He was about to close the window when he straightened suddenly, wondering if he were still not quite himself. He peered into the mist, not seeing clearly, yet held by an extraordinary mirage. Turning his head, slowly, he saw that there was no one in the bed. He caught his breath, slewed round again, more slowly, then convulsively stepped back, knocking over the tray with a crash. A breeze from the lake had stirred and thinned the luminous haze. Now he saw quite clearly what was hanging in the tree.

NEL BESTSELLERS

Crime

T013 332	CLOUDS OF WITNESS	*Dorothy L. Sayers*	40p
W003 011	GAUDY NIGHT	*Dorothy L. Sayers*	40p
T012 484	FIVE RED HERRINGS	*Dorothy L. Sayers*	40p

Fiction

W002 775	HATTER'S CASTLE	*A. J. Cronin*	60p
W002 777	THE STARS LOOK DOWN	*A. J. Cronin*	60p
T012 271	THE WARSAW DOCUMENT	*Adam Hall*	40p
T011 305	THE STRIKER PORTFOLIO	*Adam Hall*	40p
T009 084	SIR, YOU BASTARD	*G. F. Newman*	30p
T012 522	THURSDAY, MY LOVE	*Robert H. Rimmer*	40p
T013 820	THE DREAM MERCHANTS	*Harold Robbins*	75p
W002 783	79 PARK AVENUE	*Harold Robbins*	50p
T012 255	THE CARPETBAGGERS	*Harold Robbins*	80p
T011 801	WHERE LOVE HAS GONE	*Harold Robbins*	70p
T013 707	THE ADVENTURERS	*Harold Robbins*	80p
T006 743	THE INHERITORS	*Harold Robbins*	60p
T009 467	STILETTO	*Harold Robbins*	30p
T010 406	NEVER LEAVE ME	*Harold Robbins*	30p
T011 771	NEVER LOVE A STRANGER	*Harold Robbins*	70p
T011 798	A STONE FOR DANNY FISHER	*Harold Robbins*	60p
T011 461	THE BETSY	*Harold Robbins*	75p
T010 201	RICH MAN, POOR MAN	*Irwin Shaw*	80p
W002 761	THE SEVEN MINUTES	*Irving Wallace*	75p

Historical

T009 750	THE WARWICK HEIRESS	*Margaret Abbey*	30p
T011 607	THE SON OF YORK	*Margaret Abbey*	30p
T011 585	THE ROSE IN SPRING	*Eleanor Fairburn*	30p
T011 593	HARRY THE KING	*Brenda Honeyman*	35p
T009 742	THE ROSE BOTH RED AND WHITE	*Betty King*	30p
W003 010	THE VIXENS	*Frank Yerby*	40p
T006 921	JARRETT'S JADE	*Frank Yerby*	40p
T010 988	BRIDE OF LIBERTY	*Frank Yerby*	30p

Science Fiction

W002 839	SPACE FAMILY STONE	*Robert Heinlein*	30p
W002 844	STRANGER IN A STRANGE LAND	*Robert Heinlein*	60p
T011 844	DUNE	*Frank Herbert*	75p
T012 298	DUNE MESSIAH	*Frank Herbert*	40p
W003 001	DRAGON IN THE SEA	*Frank Herbert*	30p

War

W002 484	THE FLEET THAT HAD TO DIE	*Richard Hough*	25p
W002 805	HUNTING OF FORCE Z	*Richard Hough*	30p
T011 755	TRAWLERS GO TO WAR	*Lund and Ludlam*	40p
W002 831	NIGHT	*Francis Pollini*	40p
T010 074	THE GREEN BERET	*Hilary St. George Saunders*	40p
T010 066	THE RED BERET	*Hilary St. George Saunders*	40p

Western

T010 619	EDGE – THE LONER	*George Gilman*	25p
T010 600	EDGE – TEN THOUSAND DOLLARS AMERICAN	*George Gilman*	25p
T010 929	EDGE – APACHE DEATH	*George Gilman*	25p

General

T011 763	SEX MANNERS FOR MEN	*Robert Chartham*	30p
W002 531	SEX MANNERS FOR ADVANCED LOVERS	*Robert Chartham*	25p
P002 367	AN ABZ OF LOVE	*Inge and Sten Hegeler*	60p

NFL P.O. BOX 11, FALMOUTH, CORNWALL

Please send cheque or postal order. Allow 6p per book to cover postage and packing.

Name..

Address...

....

Title ....
(SEPTEMBER)